ALEX RIDER: the missions

Anthony is a popular children's writer, whose books now sell in more than a dozen countries around the world. They include *Stormbreaker* (shortlisted for the 2000 Children's Book Award) and its sequels, *Point Blanc* (shortlisted for the 2001 Children's Book Award), *Skeleton Key* (shortlisted for the Blue Peter Book Award as "The Book I Couldn't Put Down"), and the No.1 bestseller *Eagle Strike*; *Groosham Grange* and its sequel *Return to Groosham Grange*; *Granny* (shortlisted for the 1994 Children's Book Award); and the Diamond Brothers Trilogy – *The Falcon's Malteser* (which has been filmed with the title *Just Ask for Diamond*) and two sequels, *South by South East* (which was dramatized in six parts on TV) and *Public Enemy Number Two* – to which three short novels have been added: *I Know What You Did Last Wednesday*, *The French Confection* and *The Blurred Man*. Anthony also writes extensively for TV and cinema with credits including *Foyle's War*, *Murder in Mind*, *Midsomer Murders* and the horror film, *The Gathering*. Married to the television producer, Jill Green, Anthony lives in north London with his two children, Nicholas and Cassian, and their dog, Plucky.

Also by Anthony Horowitz:

Diamond Brothers books

The Falcon's Malteser
South by South East
Public Enemy Number Two
The Blurred Man
The French Confection
I Know What You Did Last Wednesday

Other books by the same author

The Devil and His Boy
Granny
Groosham Grange
Return to Groosham Grange
The Switch

ALEX RIDER
the missions

ANTHONY HOROWITZ

WALKER BOOKS
AND SUBSIDIARIES
LONDON • BOSTON • SYDNEY • AUCKLAND

This is a work of fiction. Names, characters, places and incidents are either the product of the author's imagination or, if real, are used fictitiously.

First published individually as *Stormbreaker* (2000), *Point Blanc* (2001), *Skeleton Key* (2002) and *Eagle Strike* (2003) by Walker Books Ltd, 87 Vauxhall Walk, London SE11 5HJ

This edition published 2003

2 4 6 8 10 9 7 5 3 1

This book has been typeset in Officina Sans Book

Printed and bound in Great Britain by Creative Print and Design (Wales), Ebbw Vale

British Library Cataloguing in Publication Data:
a catalogue record for this book
is available from the British Library

ISBN 0-7445-8396-9

www.walkerbooks.co.uk

STORMBREAKER

POINT BLANC

SKELETON KEY

EAGLE STRIKE

STORMBREAKER

FUNERAL VOICES

When the doorbell rings at three in the morning, it's never good news.

Alex Rider was woken by the first chime. His eyes flickered open but for a moment he stayed completely still in his bed, lying on his back with his head resting on the pillow. He heard a bedroom door open and a creak of wood as somebody went downstairs. The bell rang a second time and he looked at the alarm clock glowing beside him. 3.02 a.m. There was a rattle as someone slid the security chain off the front door.

He rolled out of bed and walked over to the open window, his bare feet pressing down the carpet pile. The moonlight spilled on to his chest and shoulders. Alex was fourteen, already well-built, with the body of an athlete. His hair, cut short apart from two thick strands hanging over his forehead, was fair. His eyes were brown and serious. For a moment he stood silently, half hidden in the shadow, looking out. There was a police car parked outside. From his second-floor window Alex could see the black ID number on the roof and the caps of the two men who were standing in front of the door. The porch light went on and, at the same time, the door opened.

"Mrs Rider?"

"No. I'm the housekeeper. What is it? What's happened?"

"This is the home of Mr Ian Rider?"

"Yes."

"I wonder if we could come in..."

And Alex already knew. He knew from the way the police stood there, awkward and unhappy. But he also knew from the tone of their voices. Funeral voices ... that was how he would describe them later. The sort of voices people use when they come to tell you that someone close to you has died.

He went to his door and opened it. He could hear the two policemen talking down in the hall, but only some of the words reached him.

"...a car accident ... called the ambulance ... intensive care ... nothing anyone could do ... so sorry."

It was only hours later, sitting in the kitchen, watching as the grey light of morning bled slowly through the west London streets, that Alex could try to make sense of what had happened. His uncle – Ian Rider – was dead. Driving home, his car had been hit by a lorry at Old Street roundabout and he had been killed almost instantly. He hadn't been wearing a seat belt, the police said. Otherwise, he might have had a chance.

Alex thought of the man who had been his only relation for as long as he could remember. He had never known his own parents. They had died in an accident, that one a plane crash, a few weeks after he had been born. He had been brought up by his father's brother (never "uncle" – Ian Rider had hated that word) and had spent most of his fourteen years in the same terraced house in Chelsea, London, between the King's Road and the river. But it was only now Alex realized just how little he knew about the man.

A banker. People said Alex looked quite like him. Ian Rider was always travelling. A quiet, private man who liked good wine, classical music and books. Who didn't seem to have any girlfriends ... in fact he didn't have any friends at all. He had kept himself fit, had never smoked and had dressed expensively. But that wasn't enough. That wasn't a picture of a life. It was only a thumbnail sketch.

"Are you all right, Alex?" A young woman had come into the room. She was in her late twenties, with a sprawl of red hair and a round, boyish face. Jack Starbright was American. She had come to London as a student seven years ago, rented a room in the house – in return for light housework and baby-sitting duties – and had stayed on to become housekeeper and one of Alex's closest friends. Sometimes he wondered what the Jack was short for. Jackie? Jacqueline? Neither of them suited her and, although he had once asked, she had never said.

Alex nodded. "What do you think will happen?" he asked.

"What do you mean?"

"To the house. To me. To you."

"I don't know." She shrugged. "I guess Ian will have made a will. He'll have left instructions."

"Maybe we should look in his office."

"Yes. But not today, Alex. Let's take it one step at a time."

Ian's office was a room running the full length of the house, high up at the top. It was the only room that was always locked – Alex had only been in there three or four times, never on his own. When he was younger, he had fantasized that there might be something strange up there; a time machine or a UFO. But it was only an office with a desk, a couple of filing cabinets, shelves full of papers and books. Bank stuff – that's what Ian said. Even so, Alex wanted to go up there now. Because it had never been allowed.

"The police said he wasn't wearing his seat belt." Alex turned to look at Jack.

She nodded. "Yes. That's what they said."

"Doesn't that seem strange to you? You know how careful he was. He always wore his seat belt. He wouldn't even drive me round the corner without making me put mine on."

Jack thought for a moment, then shrugged. "Yeah, it's strange," she said. "But that must have been the way it was. Why would the police have lied?"

The day dragged on. Alex hadn't gone to school even though, secretly, he had wanted to. He would have preferred to escape back into normal life – the clang of the bell, the crowds of familiar faces – instead of sitting there, trapped inside the house. But he had to be there for the visitors who came throughout the morning and the rest of the afternoon.

There were five of them. A solicitor who knew nothing about a will, but seemed to have been charged with organizing the funeral. A funeral director who had been recommended by the solicitor. A vicar – tall, elderly – who seemed disappointed that Alex didn't look more upset. A neighbour from across the road – how did she even know that anyone had died? And finally a man from the bank.

"All of us at the Royal & General are deeply shocked," he said. He was in his thirties, wearing a polyester suit with a Marks & Spencer tie. He had the sort of face you forgot even while you were looking at it, and had introduced himself as Crawley, from Personnel. "But if there's anything we can do..."

"What will happen?" Alex asked for the second time that day.

"You don't have to worry," Crawley said. "The bank will take care of everything. That's my job. You leave everything to me."

The day passed. Alex killed a couple of hours in the evening playing his Nintendo 64 – and then felt vaguely guilty when Jack caught him at it. But what else was he to do? Later on she took him to a Burger King. He was glad to get out of the house, but the two of them barely spoke. Alex assumed Jack would have to go back to America. She certainly couldn't stay in London for ever. So who would look after him? By law, he was still too young to look after himself. His whole future looked so uncertain that he preferred not to talk about it. He preferred not to talk at all.

And then the day of the funeral arrived and Alex found himself dressed in a dark jacket, preparing to leave in a black car that had come from nowhere, surrounded by people he had never met. Ian Rider was buried in the Brompton Cemetery on the Fulham Road, just in the shadow of Chelsea football ground, and Alex knew where he would have preferred to be on that Wednesday afternoon. About thirty people had turned up but he hardly recognized any of them. A grave had been dug close to the lane that ran the length of the cemetery and, as the service began, a black Rolls-Royce drew up, the back door opened and a man got out. Alex watched him as he walked forward and stopped. Overhead, a plane coming in to land at Heathrow momentarily blotted out the sun. Alex shivered. There was something about the new arrival that made his skin crawl.

And yet the man was ordinary to look at. Grey suit, grey hair, grey lips and grey eyes. His face was expressionless, the eyes behind the square, gun-metal spectacles completely empty. Perhaps that was what disturbed Alex. Whoever this man was, he seemed to have less life than anyone in the cemetery. Above or below ground.

Someone tapped Alex on the shoulder and he turned round to see Mr Crawley leaning over him. "That's Mr Blunt," the personnel manager whispered. "He's the chairman of the bank."

Alex's eyes travelled past Blunt and over to the Rolls-Royce. Two more men had come with him, one of them the driver. They were wearing identical suits and, although it wasn't a particularly bright day, sunglasses. Both of them were watching the funeral with the same grim faces. Alex looked from them to Blunt and then to the other people who had come to the cemetery. Had they really known Ian Rider? Why had he never met any of them before? And why did he find it so difficult to believe that any of them really worked for a bank?

"...a good man, a patriotic man. He will be missed."

The vicar had finished his grave-side address. His choice of words struck Alex as odd. Patriotic? That meant he loved his country. But as far as Alex knew, Ian Rider had barely spent any time in it. Certainly he had never been one for waving the Union Jack. He looked round, hoping to find Jack, but saw instead that Blunt was making his way towards him, stepping carefully round the grave.

"You must be Alex." The chairman was only a little taller than him. Close to, his skin was strangely unreal. It could have been made of plastic. "My name is Alan Blunt," he said. "Your uncle often spoke about you."

"That's funny," Alex said. "He never mentioned you."

The grey lips twitched briefly. "We'll miss him. He was a good man."

"What was he good at?" Alex asked. "He never talked about his work."

Suddenly Crawley was there. "Your uncle was Overseas Finance Manager, Alex," he said. "He was responsible for our foreign branches. You must have known that."

"I know he travelled a lot," Alex said. "And I know he was very careful. About things like seat belts."

"Well, sadly he wasn't careful enough." Blunt's eyes, magnified by the thick lenses of his spectacles, lasered into his own and for a moment Alex felt himself pinned down, like an insect under a microscope. "I hope we'll meet again," Blunt went on. He tapped the side of his face with a single grey finger. "Yes..." Then he turned and went back to his car.

It was as he was getting into the Rolls-Royce that it happened. The driver leaned across to open the back door and his jacket fell open, revealing the shirt underneath. And not just the shirt. The man was wearing a leather holster with an automatic pistol strapped inside. Alex saw it even as the man, realizing what had happened, quickly straightened up and pulled the jacket across his chest. Blunt had seen it too. He turned back and looked again at Alex. Something very close to an emotion slithered over his face. Then he got into the car, the door closed and he was gone.

A gun at a funeral. Why? Why would bank managers carry guns?

"Let's get out of here." Suddenly Jack was at his side. "Cemeteries give me the creeps."

"Yes. And quite a few creeps have turned up," Alex muttered.

They slipped away quietly and went home. The car that had taken them to the funeral was still waiting, but they preferred the open air. The walk took them fifteen minutes. As they turned the corner into their street, Alex noticed a removals van parked in front of the house, the words STRYKER & SON painted on its side.

"What's that doing...?" he began.

At the same moment, the van shot off, its wheels skidding over the surface of the road.

Alex said nothing as Jack unlocked the door and let them in

but, while she went into the kitchen to make some tea, he looked quickly round the house. A letter that had been on the hall table now lay on the carpet. A door that had been half open was now closed. Tiny details, but Alex's eyes missed nothing. Somebody had been in the house. He was almost sure of it.

But he wasn't certain until he got to the top floor. The door to the office which had always, always been locked, was unlocked now. Alex opened it and went in. The room was empty. Ian Rider had gone and so had everything else. The desk drawers, the cupboards, the shelves ... anything that might have told him about the dead man's work had been taken.

"Alex...!" Jack was calling to him from downstairs.

Alex took one last look around the forbidden room, wondering again about the man who had once worked there. Then he closed the door and went back down.

HEAVEN FOR CARS

With Hammersmith Bridge just ahead of him, Alex left the river and swung his bike through the lights and down the hill towards Brookland School. The bike was a Condor Junior Roadracer, custom-built for him on his twelfth birthday. It was a teenager's bike with a cut-down Reynolds 531 frame, but the wheels were full-sized so he could ride at speed with hardly any rolling resistance. He spun past a Mini and cut through the school gates. He would be sorry when he grew out of the bike. For two years now it had almost been part of him.

He double-locked it in the shed and went into the yard. Brookland was a new comprehensive, red brick and glass, modern and ugly. Alex could have gone to any of the smart private schools around Chelsea, but Ian Rider had decided to send him here. He had said it would be more of a challenge.

The first lesson of the day was maths. When Alex came into the classroom, the teacher, Mr Donovan, was already chalking up a complicated equation on the board. It was hot in the room, the sunlight streaming in through the floor-to-ceiling windows put in by architects who should have known better. As Alex took his place near the back, he wondered how he was going to get through the lesson. How could he possibly think about algebra when there were so many other questions churning through his mind?

The gun at the funeral. The way Blunt had looked at him. The van with STRYKER & SON written on the side. The empty office. And the biggest question of all, the one detail that refused to go away. The seat belt. Ian Rider hadn't been wearing a seat belt.

But of course he had.

Ian Rider had never been one to give lectures. He had always said Alex should make up his own mind about things. But he'd had this thing about seat belts. The more Alex thought about it, the less he believed it. A collision at a roundabout. Suddenly he wished he could see the car. At least the wreckage would tell him that the accident had really happened, that Ian Rider really had died that way.

"Alex?"

Alex looked up and realized that everyone was staring at him. Mr Donovan had just asked him something. He quickly scanned the blackboard, taking in the figures. "Yes, sir," he said, "x equals seven and y is fifteen."

The maths teacher sighed. "Yes, Alex. You're absolutely right. But actually I was just asking you to open the window."

Somehow he managed to get through the rest of the day, but by the time the final bell rang, his mind was made up. While everyone else streamed out, he made his way to the secretary's office and borrowed a copy of Yellow Pages.

"What are you looking for?" the secretary asked. Jane

Bedfordshire was a young woman in her twenties, and she'd always had a soft spot for Alex.

"Breakers' yards..." Alex flicked through the pages. "If a car got smashed up near Old Street, they'd take it somewhere near by, wouldn't they?"

"I suppose so."

"Here..." Alex had found the yards listed under "Car Dismantlers". But there were dozens of them fighting for attention over four pages.

"Is this for a school project?" the secretary asked. She knew Alex had lost a relative, but not how.

"Sort of..." Alex was reading the addresses, but they told him nothing.

"This one's quite near Old Street." Miss Bedfordshire pointed at the corner of the page.

"Wait!" Alex tugged the book towards him and looked at the entry underneath the one the secretary had chosen:

J.B. STRYKER
Heaven for cars...
J.B. Stryker, Auto Breakers
Lambeth Walk, LONDON
Tel: 020 7123 5392
...call us today!

"That's in Vauxhall," Miss Bedfordshire said. "Not too far from here."

"I know." But Alex had recognized the name. J.B. Stryker. He thought back to the van he had seen outside his house on the day of the funeral. STRYKER & SON. Of course it might just be a coincidence, but it was still somewhere to start. He closed the book. "I'll see you, Miss Bedfordshire."

"Be careful how you go." The secretary watched Alex leave,

wondering why she had said that. Maybe it was his eyes. Dark and serious, there was something dangerous there. Then the telephone rang and she forgot him as she went back to work.

J.B. Stryker's was a square of wasteland behind the railway tracks running out of Waterloo Station. The area was enclosed by a high brick wall topped with broken glass and razor wire. Two wooden gates hung open, and from the other side of the road Alex could see a shed with a security window and beyond it the tottering piles of dead and broken cars. Everything of any value had been stripped away and only the rusting carcasses remained, heaped one on top of the other, waiting to be fed into the crusher.

There was a guard sitting in the shed, reading the *Sun*. In the distance, a crane coughed into life, then roared down on a battered Ford Mondeo, its metal claw smashing through the window to scoop up the vehicle and carry it away. A telephone rang somewhere in the shed and the guard turned round to answer it. That was enough for Alex. Holding his bike and wheeling it along beside him, he sprinted through the gates.

He found himself surrounded by dirt and debris. The smell of diesel was thick in the air and the roar of the engines was deafening. Alex watched as the crane swooped down on another of the cars, seized it in a metallic grip and dropped it into a crusher. For a moment the car rested on a pair of shelves. Then the shelves lifted up, toppling the car over and down into a trough. The operator – sitting in a glass cabin at one end of the crusher – pressed a button and there was a great belch of black smoke. The shelves closed in on the car like a monster insect folding in its wings. There was a grinding sound as the car was crushed until it was no bigger than a rolled-up carpet. Then the operator threw a gear and the car was squeezed out, metallic toothpaste being chopped up by a hidden blade. The slices tumbled on to the ground.

Leaving his bike propped against the wall, Alex ran further into the yard, crouching down behind the wrecks. With the din from the machines, there was no chance that anyone would hear him, but he was still afraid of being seen. He stopped to catch his breath, drawing a grimy hand across his face. His eyes were watering from the diesel fumes. The air was as filthy as the ground beneath him.

He was beginning to regret coming – but then he saw it. His uncle's BMW was parked a few metres away, separated from the other cars. At first glance it looked absolutely fine, the metallic silver bodywork not even scratched. Certainly there was no way this car could have been involved in a fatal collision with a lorry or anything else. But it was his uncle's car. Alex recognized the number plate. He hurried closer, and it was then he saw that the car was damaged after all. The windscreen had been smashed, along with all the windows on one side. Alex made his way round the bonnet. He reached the other side. And froze.

Ian Rider hadn't died in any accident. What had killed him was plain to see – even to someone who had never seen such a thing before. A spray of bullets had caught the car full on the driver's side, shattering the front tyre, then smashing the windscreen and side windows and punching into the side panels. Alex ran his fingers over the holes. The metal felt cold against his flesh. He opened the door and looked inside. The front seats, pale grey leather, were strewn with fragments of broken glass and stained with patches of dark brown. He didn't need to ask what the stains were. He could see everything. The flash of the machine gun, the bullets ripping into the car, Ian Rider jerking in the driver's seat...

But why? Why kill a bank manager? And why had the murder been covered up? It was the police who had brought the news, so they must be part of it. Had they deliberately lied? None of it made sense.

"You should have got rid of it two days ago. Do it now."

The machines must have stopped for a moment. If there hadn't been a sudden lull, Alex would never have heard the men coming. Quickly he looked across the steering wheel and out the other side. There were two of them, both dressed in loose-fitting overalls. Alex had a feeling he'd seen them before. At the funeral. One of them was the driver, the man he had seen with the gun. He was sure of it.

Whoever they were, they were only a few paces away from the car, talking in low voices. Another few steps and they would be there. Without thinking, Alex threw himself into the only hiding place available, inside the car itself. Using his foot, he hooked the door and closed it. At the same time, he became aware that the machines had started again and he could no longer hear the men. He didn't dare look up. A shadow fell across the window as the two men passed. But then they were gone. He was safe.

And then something hit the BMW with such force that Alex cried out, his whole body caught in a massive shock wave that tore him away from the steering wheel and threw him helplessly into the back. At the same time, the roof buckled and three huge metal fingers tore through the skin of the car like a fork through an eggshell, trailing dust and sunlight. One of the fingers grazed the side of his head – any closer and it would have cracked his skull. Alex yelled as blood trickled over his eye. He tried to move, then was jerked back a second time as the car was yanked off the ground and tilted high up in the air.

He couldn't see. He couldn't move. But his stomach lurched as the car swung in an arc, the metal grinding and the light spinning. It had been picked up by the crane. It was going to be put inside the crusher. With him inside.

He tried to raise himself up, to punch through the windows. But the claw of the crane had already flattened the roof, pinning his left leg, perhaps even breaking it. He could feel nothing. He lifted a hand and managed to pound on the back window, but he couldn't break the glass, and even if the workmen were staring at the BMW, they would never see anything moving inside.

His short flight across the breaker's yard ended with a bone-shattering crash as the crane deposited the car on the iron shelves of the crusher. Alex tried to fight back his sickness and despair and think of what to do. He had seen a car being processed only a few minutes before. Any moment now, the operator would send the car tipping into the coffin-shaped trough. The machine was a Lefort Shear, a slow-motion guillotine. At the press of a button, the two wings would close on the car with a joint pressure of five hundred tonnes. The car, with Alex inside it, would be crushed beyond recognition. And the broken metal – and flesh – would then be chopped into sections. Nobody would ever know what had happened.

He tried with all his strength to free himself. But the roof was too low. His leg and part of his back were trapped. Then his whole world tilted and he felt himself falling into darkness. The shelves had lifted. The BMW slid to one side and fell the few metres into the trough. Alex felt the metalwork collapsing all around him. The back window exploded and glass showered around his head, dust and diesel fumes punching into his nose and eyes. There was hardly any daylight now, but looking out of the back he could see the huge steel head of the piston that would push what was left of the car through the exit hole on the other side.

The engine tone of the Lefort Shear changed as it prepared for the final act. The metal wings shuddered. In a few seconds' time, the two of them would meet, crumpling the BMW like a paper bag.

Alex pulled with all his strength and was astonished when his leg came free. It took him perhaps a second – one precious second – to work out what had happened. When the car had fallen into the trough, it had landed on its side. The roof had buckled again ... enough to free him. His hand scrabbled for the door – but of course that was useless. The doors were too bent. They would never open. The back window! With the glass gone, he could crawl through the frame, but only if he moved fast...

The wings began to move. The BMW screamed as two walls of solid steel relentlessly crushed it. Glass shattered. One of the wheel axles snapped with the sound of a thunderbolt. The darkness closed in. Alex grabbed hold of what was left of the back seat. Ahead of him he could see a single triangle of light, shrinking faster and faster. With all his strength, he surged forward, finding some sort of purchase on the gear column. He could feel the weight of the two walls pressing down on him. Behind him the car was no longer a car, but the fist of some hideous monster snatching at the insect that he had become.

His shoulders passed through the triangle, out into the light. But his legs were still inside. If his foot snagged on something he would be squeezed into two pieces. Alex yelled out loud and jerked his knee forward. His legs came clear, then his feet, but at the last moment his shoe caught on the closing triangle and disappeared back into the car. Alex imagined he heard the sound of the leather being squashed, but that was impossible. Clinging to the black, oily surface of the observation platform at the back of the crusher, he dragged himself clear and managed to stand up.

He found himself face to face with a man so fat that he could barely fit into the small cabin of the crusher. The man's stomach was pressed against the glass, his shoulders squeezed into the corners. A cigarette dangled on his lower lip as his mouth fell open and his eyes stared. In front of him was a boy in the rags of what had once been a school uniform. A whole sleeve had been torn off and his arm, streaked with blood and oil, hung limply by his side. By the time the operator had taken all this in, come to his senses and turned the machine off, Alex had gone.

He clambered down the side of the crusher, landing on the one foot that still had a shoe. He was aware now of pieces of jagged metal lying everywhere. If he wasn't careful, he would cut the other foot open. His bicycle was where he had left it, leaning against the wall, and gingerly, half-hopping, he made for it. Behind him he heard the cabin of the crusher open and a man's voice call out, raising the alarm. At the same time, a second man ran forward, stopping between Alex and his bike. It was the driver, the man he had seen at the funeral. His face, twisted into a hostile frown, was curiously ugly; greasy hair, watery eyes, pale, lifeless skin.

"What do you think...!" he began. His hand slid into his jacket. Alex remembered the gun and instantly, without even thinking, swung into action.

He had started learning karate when he was six years old. One afternoon, with no explanation, Ian Rider had taken him to a local club for his first lesson and he had been going there, once a week, ever since. Over the years he had passed through the various *Kyu* – student – grades. But it was only the year before that he had become a first grade *Dan*, a black belt. When he had arrived at Brookland School, his looks and accent had quickly brought him to the attention of the school bullies; three hulking sixteen-year-olds. They had cornered him once behind the bike shed. The encounter had lasted less than a minute, and after it one of the bullies had left Brookland and the other two had never troubled anyone again.

Now Alex brought up one leg, twisted his body round and lashed out. The back-kick – *Ushiro-geri* – is said to be the most lethal in karate. His foot powered into the man's abdomen with such force that he didn't even have time to cry out. His eyes bulged and his mouth half-opened in surprise. Then, with his hand still halfway into his jacket, he crumpled to the ground.

Alex jumped over him, snatched up his bike and swung himself on to it. In the distance, a third man was running towards him. He heard the single word "Stop!" called out. Then there was a crack and a bullet whipped past. Alex gripped the handlebars and pedalled as hard as he could. The bike shot forward, over the rubble and out through the gates. He took one look over his shoulder. Nobody had followed him.

With one shoe on and one shoe off, his clothes in rags and his body streaked with blood and oil, Alex knew he must look a strange sight. But then he thought back to his last seconds inside the crusher and sighed with relief. He could have been looking a lot worse.

ROYAL & GENERAL

The bank rang the following day.

"This is John Crawley. Do you remember me? Personnel Manager at the Royal & General. We were wondering if you could come in."

"Come in?" Alex was half dressed, already late for school.

"This afternoon. We found some papers of your uncle's. We need to talk to you ... about your own position."

Was there something faintly threatening in the man's voice? "What time this afternoon?" Alex asked.

"Could you manage half past four? We're on Liverpool Street. We can send a cab—"

"I'll be there," Alex said. "And I'll take the tube."

He hung up.

"Who was that?" Jack called out from the kitchen. She was cooking breakfast for the two of them, although how long she could remain with Alex was a growing worry. Her wages hadn't been paid. She had only her own money to buy food and pay for the running of the house. Worse still, her visa was about to expire. Soon she wouldn't even be allowed to stay in the country.

"That was the bank." Alex came into the room, wearing his spare uniform. He hadn't told her what had happened at the breaker's yard. He hadn't even told her about the empty office. Jack had enough on her mind. "I'm going there this afternoon," he said.

"Do you want me to come?"

"No. I'll be fine."

He came out of Liverpool Street tube station just after four-fifteen that afternoon, still wearing his school uniform: dark blue jacket, grey trousers, striped tie. He found the bank easily enough. The Royal & General occupied a tall, antique-looking building with a Union Jack fluttering from a pole about fifteen floors up. There was a brass name-plate next to the main door and a security camera swivelling slowly over the pavement.

Alex stopped in front of it. For a moment he wondered if he was making a mistake going in. If the bank had been responsible in some way for Ian Rider's death, maybe they had asked him here to arrange his own. No. The bank wouldn't kill him. He didn't even have an account there. He went in.

In an office on the seventeenth floor, the image on the security monitor flickered and changed as Street Camera #1 smoothly cut across to Reception Cameras #2 and #3 and Alex passed from the brightness outside to the cool shadows of the interior. A man sitting behind a desk reached out and pressed a button and the camera zoomed in until Alex's face filled the screen.

"So he came," the chairman of the bank muttered.

"That's the boy?" The speaker was a middle-aged woman. She had a strange, potato-shaped head and her black hair looked as if it had been cut using a pair of blunt scissors and an upturned bowl. Her eyes were almost black too. She was dressed in a severe grey suit and she was sucking a peppermint. "Are you sure about this, Alan?" she asked.

Alan Blunt nodded. "Oh yes. Quite sure. You know what to do?"

This last question was addressed to his driver, who was standing uncomfortably, slightly hunched over. His face was a chalky white. He had been like that ever since he had tried to stop Alex in the breaker's yard. "Yes, sir," he said.

"Then do it," Blunt said. His eyes never left the screen.

In Reception, Alex had asked for John Crawley and was sitting on a leather sofa, vaguely wondering why so few people were going in or out. The reception area was wide and airy, with a brown marble floor, three elevators to one side and, above the desk, a row of clocks showing the time in every major world city. But it could have been the entrance to anywhere. A hospital. A concert hall. Even a cruise liner. The place had no identity of its own.

One of the lifts pinged open and Crawley appeared in his usual suit, but with a different tie. "I'm sorry to have kept you waiting, Alex," he said. "Have you come straight from school?"

Alex stood up but said nothing, allowing his uniform to answer the man's question.

"Let's go up to my office," Crawley said. He gestured. "We'll take the lift."

Alex didn't notice the fourth camera inside the lift, but then it was concealed on the other side of the two-way mirror that covered the back wall. Nor did he see the thermal intensifier next to the camera. But this second machine both looked at him and through him as he stood there, turning him into a pulsating mass of different colours, none of which translated into the cold steel of a hidden gun or knife. In less than the time it took Alex to blink, the machine had passed its information down to a computer which had instantly evaluated it and then sent its own signal back to the circuits that controlled the elevator. *It's OK. He's unarmed. Continue to the fifteenth floor.*

"Here we are!" Crawley smiled and ushered Alex out into a long corridor with an uncarpeted, wooden floor and modern lighting. A series of doors was punctuated by framed paintings, brightly coloured abstracts. "My office is just along here." Crawley pointed the way.

They had passed three doors when Alex stopped. Each door had a name-plate and this one he recognized – 1504: Ian Rider. White letters on black plastic.

Crawley nodded sadly. "Yes. This was where your uncle worked. He'll be much missed."

"Can I go inside?" Alex asked.

Crawley seemed surprised. "Why do you want to do that?"

"I'd be interested to see where he worked."

"I'm sorry." Crawley sighed. "The door will have been locked and I don't have the key. Another time perhaps." He gestured again. He used his hands like a magician, as if he was about to produce a fan of cards. "I have the office next door. Just here."

They went into 1505. It was a large, square room with three windows looking out over the station. There was a flutter of red and blue outside and Alex remembered the flag he had seen. The flagpole was right next to Crawley's office. Inside there was a desk and chair, a couple of sofas, in the corner a fridge, on the wall a couple of prints. A boring executive office. Perfect for a boring executive.

"Please, Alex. Sit down," Crawley said. He went over to the fridge. "Can I get you a drink?"

"Do you have Coke?"

"Yes." Crawley opened a can and filled a glass, then handed it to Alex. "Ice?"

"No thanks." Alex took a sip. It wasn't Coke. It wasn't even Pepsi. He recognized the over sweet, slightly cloying taste of supermarket cola and wished he'd asked for water. "So what do you want to talk to me about?"

"Your uncle's will—"

The telephone rang and with another hand-sign, this one for "excuse me", Crawley answered it. He spoke for a few moments then hung up again. "I'm very sorry, Alex. I have to go back down to Reception. Do you mind?"

"Go ahead." Alex settled himself on the sofa.

"I'll be about five minutes." With a final nod of apology, Crawley left.

Alex waited a few seconds. Then he poured the cola into a potted plant and stood up. He went over to the door and back into the corridor. At the far end, a woman carrying a pile of papers appeared and then disappeared through a door. There was no sign of Crawley. Quickly, Alex moved back to the door of 1504 and tried the handle. But Crawley had been telling the truth. It was locked.

Alex went back into Crawley's office. He would have given anything to spend a few minutes alone in Ian Rider's office. Somebody thought the dead man's work was important enough to keep hidden from him. They had broken into his house and cleaned out everything they'd found in the office there. Perhaps the next-door room might tell him why. What exactly had Ian Rider been involved in? And was it the reason why he had been killed?

The flag fluttered again and, seeing it, Alex went over to the window. The pole jutted out of the building exactly halfway between rooms 1504 and 1505. If he could somehow reach it, he should be able to jump on to the ledge that ran along the side of the building outside room 1504. Of course, he was fifteen floors up. If he jumped and missed there would be about seventy metres to fall. It was a stupid idea. It wasn't even worth thinking about.

Alex opened the window and climbed out. It was better not to think about it at all. He would just do it. After all, if this had been the ground floor, or a climbing-frame in the school yard, it would have been child's play. It was only the sheer brick wall stretching down to the pavement, the cars and buses moving like toys so far below and the blast of the wind against his face that made it terrifying. Don't think about it. Do it.

Alex lowered himself on to the ledge outside Crawley's office. His hands were behind him, clutching on to the windowsill. He took a deep breath. And jumped.

A camera located in an office across the road caught Alex as he launched himself into space. Two floors above, Alan Blunt was still sitting in front of the screen. He chuckled. It was a humourless sound. "I told you," he said. "The boy's extraordinary."

"The boy's quite mad," the woman retorted.

"Well, maybe that's what we need."

"You're just going to sit here and watch him kill himself?"

"I'm going to sit here and hope he survives."

Alex had miscalculated the jump. He had missed the flagpole by a centimetre and would have plunged down to the pavement if his hands hadn't caught hold of the Union Jack itself. He was hanging now with his feet in mid-air. Slowly, with huge effort, he pulled himself up, his fingers hooking into the material. Somehow he managed to climb back up on to the pole. He still didn't look down. He just hoped that no passer-by would look up.

It was easier after that. He squatted on the pole, then threw himself across to the ledge outside Ian Rider's office. He had to be careful. Too far to the left and he would crash into the side of the building, but too far the other way and he would fall. In fact he landed perfectly, grabbing hold of the ledge with both hands and then pulling himself up until he was level with the window. It was only then that he wondered if the window would be locked. If so, he'd just have to go back.

It wasn't. Alex slid the window open and hoisted himself into the second office, which was in many ways a carbon copy of the first. It had the same furniture, the same carpet, even a similar print on the wall. He went over to the desk and sat down. The first thing he saw was a photograph of himself, taken the summer before on the Caribbean island of Guadeloupe, where he had gone diving. There was a second picture tucked into the corner of the frame. Alex aged five or six. He was surprised by the photographs. He had never thought of Ian Rider as a sentimental man.

Alex glanced at his watch. About three minutes had passed since Crawley had left the office, and he had said he would be back in five. If he was going to find anything here, he had to find it quickly. He pulled open a drawer of the desk. It contained five or six thick files. Alex took them and opened them. He saw at once that they had nothing to do with banking.

The first was marked: NERVE POISONS – NEW METHODS OF CONCEALMENT AND DISSEMINATION. Alex put it aside and looked at the second. ASSASSINATIONS – FOUR CASE STUDIES. Growing ever more puzzled, he quickly flicked through the rest of the files, which covered counter-terrorism, the movement of uranium across Europe and interrogation techniques. The last file was simply labelled: STORMBREAKER.

Alex was about to read it when the door suddenly opened and two men walked in. One of them was Crawley. The other was the driver from the breaker's yard. Alex knew there was no point trying to explain what he was doing. He was sitting behind the desk with the

Stormbreaker file open in his hands. But at the same time he realized that the two men weren't surprised to see him there. From the way they had come into the room, they had expected to find him.

"This isn't a bank," Alex said. "Who are you? Was my uncle working for you? Did you kill him?"

"So many questions," Crawley muttered. "But I'm afraid we're not authorized to give you the answers."

The other man lifted his hand and Alex saw that he was holding a gun. He stood up behind the desk, holding the file as if to protect himself. "No—" he began.

The man fired. There was no explosion. The gun spat at Alex and he felt something slam into his heart. His hand opened and the file tumbled to the ground. Then his legs buckled, the room twisted and he fell back into nothing.

"SO WHAT DO YOU SAY?"

Alex opened his eyes. So he was still alive! That was a nice surprise.

He was lying on a bed in a large, comfortable room. The bed was modern but the room was old, with beams running across the ceiling, a stone fireplace and narrow windows in ornate wooden frames. He had seen rooms like this in books when he was studying Shakespeare. He would have said the building was Elizabethan. It had to be somewhere in the country. There was no sound of traffic. Outside he could see trees.

Someone had undressed him. His school uniform was gone. Instead he was wearing loose pyjamas, silk from the feel of them. From the light outside he would have guessed it was early evening. He found his watch lying on the table beside the bed and he reached out for it. The time was twelve o'clock. It had been half past four when he was shot with what must have been a drugged dart. He had lost a whole night and half a day.

There was a bathroom leading off the bedroom; bright white tiles and a huge shower behind a cylinder of glass and chrome. Alex stripped off the pyjamas and stood for five minutes under a jet of steaming water. He felt better after that.

He went back into the bedroom and opened the cupboard. Someone had been to his house in Chelsea. All his clothes were here, neatly hung up. He wondered what Crawley had told Jack. Presumably he would have made up some story to explain his sudden disappearance. He took out a pair of Gap combat trousers, a Nike sweatshirt and trainers, got dressed, then sat on the bed and waited.

About fifteen minutes later there was a knock and the door opened. A young Asian woman in a nurse's uniform came in, beaming.

"Oh, you're awake. And dressed. How are you feeling? Not too groggy, I hope. Please come this way. Mr Blunt is expecting you for lunch."

Alex hadn't spoken a word to her. He followed her out of the room, along a corridor and down a flight of stairs. The house was indeed Elizabethan, with wooden panels along the corridors, ornate chandeliers and oil paintings of old, bearded men in tunics and ruffs. The stairs led down into a tall, galleried room with a rug spread out over flagstones and a fireplace big enough to park a car in. A long, polished wooden table had been laid for three. Alan Blunt and a dark, rather masculine woman unwrapping a sweet were already sitting down. Mrs Blunt?

"Alex." Blunt smiled briefly, as if it was something he didn't enjoy doing. "It's good of you to join us."

Alex sat down. "You didn't give me a lot of choice."

"Yes. I don't quite know what Crawley was thinking of, shooting you like that, but I suppose it was the easiest way. May I introduce my colleague, Mrs Jones."

The woman nodded at Alex. Her eyes seemed to examine him minutely, but she said nothing.

"Who are you?" Alex asked. "What do you want with me?"

"I'm sure you have a great many questions. But first, let's eat." Blunt must have pressed a hidden button, or else he was being overheard, for at that precise moment a door opened and a waiter – in white jacket and black trousers – appeared carrying three plates. "I hope you eat meat," Blunt continued. "Today it's *carré d'agneau*."

"You mean roast lamb."

"The chef is French."

Alex waited until the food had been served. Blunt and Mrs Jones drank red wine. He stuck to water. Finally, Blunt began.

"As I'm sure you've gathered," he said, "the Royal & General is not a bank. In fact it doesn't exist ... it's nothing more than a cover. And it follows, of course, that your uncle had nothing to do with banking. He worked for me. My name, as I told you at the funeral, is Blunt. I am chief executive of the Special Operations division of MI6. And your uncle was, for want of a better word, a spy."

Alex couldn't help smiling. "You mean ... like James Bond?"

"Similar, although we don't go in for numbers. Double O and all the rest of it. He was a field agent, highly trained and very courageous. He successfully completed assignments in Iran, Washington, Hong Kong and Cairo – to name but a few. I imagine this must come as a bit of a shock to you."

Alex thought about the dead man, what he had known of him. His privacy. His long absences abroad. And the times he had come home injured. A bandaged arm one time. A bruised face another.

Little accidents, Alex had been told. But now it all made sense. "I'm not shocked," he said.

Blunt cut a neat slice of meat. "Ian Rider's luck ran out on his last mission," he went on. "He had been working undercover here in England, in Cornwall, and was driving back to London to make a report when he was killed. You saw his car at the yard."

"Stryker & Son," Alex muttered. "Who are they?"

"Just people we use. We have budget restraints. We have to contract some of our work out. Mrs Jones here is our head of Special Operations. She gave your uncle his last assignment."

"We're very sorry to have lost him, Alex." The woman spoke for the first time. She didn't sound very sorry at all.

"Do you know who killed him?"

"Yes."

"Are you going to tell me?"

"No. Not now."

"Why not?"

"Because you don't need to know. Not at this stage."

"All right." Alex put down his knife and fork. He hadn't actually eaten anything. "My uncle was a spy. Thanks to you he's dead. I found out too much, so you knocked me out and brought me here. Where am I, by the way?"

"This is one of our training centres," Mrs Jones said.

"You've brought me here because you don't want me to tell anyone what I know. Is that what this is all about? Because if it is, I'll sign the Official Secrets Act or whatever it is you want me to do, but then I'd like to go home. This is all crazy anyway. And I've had enough. I'm out of here."

Blunt coughed quietly. "It's not quite as easy as that," he said.

"Why not?"

"It's certainly true that you did draw attention to yourself both at the breaker's yard and then at our offices on Liverpool Street. And it's also true that what you know and what I'm about to tell you must go no further. But the fact of the matter is, Alex, we need your help."

"My help?"

"Yes." He paused. "Have you heard of a man called Herod Sayle?"

Alex thought for a moment. "I've seen his name in the newspapers. He's something to do with computers. And he owns racehorses. Doesn't he come from somewhere in Egypt?"

"No. From the Lebanon." Blunt took a sip of wine. "Let me tell you his story, Alex. I'm sure you'll find it of interest.

"Herod Sayle was born in complete poverty in the back streets of Beirut. His father was a failed hairdresser. His mother took in washing. He had nine brothers and four sisters, all living together in three small rooms along with the family goat. Young Herod never went to school and he should have ended up unemployed, unable to read or write, like the rest of his family.

"But when he was seven, something occurred that changed his life. He was walking down Olive Street, in the middle of Beirut, when he happened to see an upright piano fall out of a fourteenth-storey window. Apparently it was being moved and it somehow overturned. Anyway, there were a couple of American tourists walking along the pavement below and they would both have been crushed – no doubt about it – except that at the last minute Herod threw himself at them and pushed them out of the way. The piano missed them by a millimetre.

"Of course, they were enormously grateful to the young waif, and it now turned out that they were very rich. They made enquiries about him and discovered how poor he was ... the very clothes he was wearing had been passed down by all nine of his brothers. And so, out of gratitude, they more or less adopted him. Flew him out of Beirut and put him into a school over here, where he made astonishing progress. He got nine O-levels and – here's an amazing coincidence – at the age of fifteen he actually found himself sitting next to a boy who would grow up to become prime minister of Great Britain. Our present prime minister, in fact. The two of them were at school together.

"I'll move quickly forward. After school, Sayle went to Cambridge, where he got a first in Economics. He then set out on a career that went from success to success. His own radio station, record label, computer software ... and, yes, he even found time to buy a string of racehorses, although for some reason they always seem to come last. But what drew him to our attention was his most recent invention. A quite revolutionary computer which he calls the Stormbreaker."

Stormbreaker. Alex remembered the file he had found in Ian Rider's office. Things were beginning to come together.

"The Stormbreaker is being manufactured by Sayle Enterprises," Mrs Jones said. "There's been a lot of talk about the design. It has a black keyboard and black casing—"

"With a lightning bolt going down the side," Alex said. He had seen a picture of it in *PC Review*.

"It doesn't only look different," Blunt cut in. "It's based on a completely new technology. It uses something called the round processor. I don't suppose that will mean anything to you."

"It's an integrated circuit on a sphere of silicon about one millimetre in diameter," Alex said. "It's ninety per cent cheaper to produce than an ordinary chip because the whole thing is sealed in, so you don't need clean rooms for production."

"Oh. Yes..." Blunt coughed. "Well, the point is, later today, Sayle Enterprises are going to make a quite remarkable announcement.

They are planning to give away tens of thousands of these computers. In fact, it is their intention to ensure that every secondary school in Britain gets its own Stormbreaker. It's an unparalleled act of generosity, Sayle's way of thanking the country that gave him a home."

"So the man's a hero."

"So it would seem. He wrote to Downing Street a few months ago:

"My Dear Prime Minister

You may remember me from our schooldays together. For almost forty years I have lived in England and I wish to make a gesture, something that will never be forgotten, to express my true feelings towards your country.

"The letter went on to describe the gift and was signed *Yours humbly*, by the man himself. Of course, the whole government was cock-a-hoop.

"The computers are being assembled at the Sayle plant down in Port Tallon, Cornwall. They'll be shipped across the country at the end of this month and on April first there's to be a special ceremony at the Science Museum in London. The prime minister is going to press the button that will bring all the computers on-line ... the whole lot of them. And – this is top secret by the way – Mr Sayle is to be rewarded with British citizenship, which is apparently something he has always wanted."

"Well, I'm very happy for him," Alex said. "But you still haven't told me what this has got to do with me."

Blunt glanced at Mrs Jones, who had finished her meal while he was talking. She unwrapped another peppermint and took over.

"For some time now, our department – Special Operations – has been concerned about Mr Sayle. The fact of the matter is, we've been wondering if he isn't too good to be true. I won't go into all the details, Alex, but we've been looking at his business dealings ... he has contacts in China and the former Soviet Union; countries that have never been our friends. The government may think he's a saint, but there's a ruthless side to him too. And the security arrangements down at Port Tallon worry us. He's more or less got his own private army. He's acting as if he's got something to hide."

"Not that anyone will listen," Blunt muttered.

"Exactly. The government's too keen to get their hands on these computers to listen to us. That was why we decided to send our own man down to the plant. Supposedly to check on security. But in fact his job was to keep an eye on Herod Sayle."

"You're talking about my uncle," Alex said. Ian Rider had told him that he was going to an insurance convention. Another lie in a life that had been nothing but lies.

"Yes. He was there for three weeks and, like us, he didn't exactly take to Mr Sayle. In his first reports, he described him as short-tempered and unpleasant. But at the same time, he had to admit that everything seemed to be fine. Production was on schedule. The Stormbreakers were coming off the line. And everyone seemed to be happy.

"But then we got a message. Rider couldn't say very much because it was an open line, but he told us that something had happened. He said he'd discovered something. That the Stormbreakers mustn't leave the plant and that he was coming up to London at once. He left Port Tallon at four o'clock. He never even got to the motorway. He was ambushed in a quiet country lane. The local police found the car. We arranged for it to be brought up here."

Alex sat in silence. He could imagine it. A twisting lane with the trees just in blossom. The silver BMW gleaming as it raced past. And, round a corner, a second car waiting... "Why are you telling me all this?" he asked.

"It proves what we were saying," Blunt replied. "We have our doubts about Sayle, so we send a man down. Our best man. He finds out something and he ends up dead. Maybe Rider discovered the truth—"

"But I don't understand!" Alex interrupted. "Sayle is giving away the computers. He's not making any money out of them. In return he's getting British citizenship. Fine! What's he got to hide?"

"We don't know," Blunt said. "We just don't know. But we want to find out. And soon. Before these computers leave the plant."

"They're being shipped out on the thirty-first of March," Mrs Jones added. "Only about two weeks from now." She glanced at Blunt. He nodded. "That's why it's essential for us to send someone else to Port Tallon. Someone to continue where your uncle left off."

Alex smiled queasily. "I hope you're not looking at me."

"We can't just send in another agent," Mrs Jones said. "The enemy has shown his hand. He's killed Rider. He'll be expecting a replacement. Somehow we have to trick him."

"We have to send in someone who won't be noticed," Blunt continued. "Someone who can look around and report back without being seen themselves. We were considering sending down a woman. She might be able to slip in as a secretary or receptionist. But then I had a better idea.

"A few months ago, one of these computer magazines ran a competition. *Be the first boy or girl to use the Stormbreaker. Travel to Port Tallon and meet Herod Sayle himself.* That was the first prize – and it was won by some young chap who's apparently a bit of a whizz kid when it comes to computers. Name of Felix Lester. Fourteen years old. The same age as you. He looks a bit like you too. He's expected down at Port Tallon less than two weeks from now."

"Wait a minute—"

"You've already shown yourself to be extraordinarily brave and resourceful," Blunt said. "First of all at the breaker's yard ... that was a karate kick, wasn't it? How long have you been learning karate?" Alex didn't answer, so he went on. "And then there was that little test we arranged for you at the bank. Any boy who would climb out of a fifteenth-floor window just to satisfy his own curiosity has to be rather special, and it seems to me that you are very special indeed."

"What we're suggesting is that you come and work for us," Mrs Jones said. "We have enough time to give you some basic training – not that you'll need it, probably – and we can equip you with a few items that may help you with what we have in mind. Then we'll arrange for you to take the place of this other boy. You'll go to Sayle Enterprises on the twenty-ninth of March. That's when this Lester boy is expected. You'll stay there until the first of April, which is the day of the ceremony. The timing couldn't be better. You'll be able to meet Herod Sayle, keep an eye on him and tell us what you think. Perhaps you'll also find out what it was that your uncle discovered and why he had to die. You shouldn't be in any danger. After all, who would suspect a fourteen-year-old boy of being a spy?"

"All we're asking you to do is report back to us," Blunt said. "That's all we want. Two weeks of your time. A chance to make sure these computers are everything they're cracked up to be. A chance to serve your country."

Blunt had finished his dinner. His plate was completely clean, as if there had never been any food on it at all. He put down his knife and fork, laying them precisely side by side. "All right, Alex," he said. "So what do you say?"

There was a long pause.

Blunt was watching him with polite interest. Mrs Jones was unwrapping yet another peppermint, her black eyes seemingly fixed on the twist of paper in her hands.

"No," Alex said.

"I'm sorry?"

"It's a dumb idea. I don't want to be a spy. I want to be a footballer. Anyway, I have a life of my own." He found it difficult to choose the right words. The whole thing was so preposterous he almost wanted to laugh. "Why don't you ask this Felix Lester to snoop around for you?"

"We don't believe he'd be as resourceful as you," Blunt said.

"He's probably better at computer games." Alex shook his head. "I'm sorry. I'm just not interested. I don't want to get involved."

"That's a pity," Blunt said. His tone of voice hadn't changed but there was a heavy, dead quality to the words. And there was something different, too, about him. Throughout the meal he had been polite; not friendly, but at least human. In an instant, that had disappeared. Alex thought of a toilet chain being pulled. The human part of him had just been flushed away.

"Then we'd better move on to discuss your future," he continued. "Like it or not, Alex, the Royal & General is now your legal guardian."

"I thought you said the Royal & General didn't exist."

Blunt ignored him. "Ian Rider has, of course, left the house and all his money to you. However, he left it in trust until you are twenty-one. And we control that trust. So there will, I'm afraid, have to be some changes. The American girl who lives with you."

"Jack?"

"Miss Starbright. Her visa has expired. She'll be returned to America. We propose to put the house on the market. Unfortunately, you have no relatives to look after you, so I'm afraid that also means you'll have to leave Brookland. You'll be sent to an institution. There's one I know just outside Birmingham. The Saint Elizabeth in Sourbridge. Not a very pleasant place, but I'm afraid there's no alternative."

"You're blackmailing me!" Alex exclaimed.

"Not at all."

"But if I agree to do what you ask...?"

Blunt glanced at Mrs Jones. "Help us and we'll help you," she said.

Alex considered, but not for very long. He had no choice and he knew it. Not when these people controlled his money, his present life, his entire future. "You talked about training," he said.

Mrs Jones nodded. "That's why we brought you here, Alex. This is a training centre. If you agree to what we want, we can start at once."

"Start at once." Alex spoke the three words without liking the sound of them. Blunt and Mrs Jones were waiting for his answer. He sighed. "Yeah. All right. It doesn't look like I've got very much choice."

He glanced at the slices of cold lamb on his plate. Dead meat. Suddenly he knew how it felt.

DOUBLE O NOTHING

For the hundredth time, Alex cursed Alan Blunt using language he hadn't even realized he knew. It was almost five o'clock in the evening, although it could have been five o'clock in the morning: the sky had barely changed at all throughout the day. It was grey, cold, unforgiving. The rain was still falling, a thin drizzle that travelled horizontally in the wind, soaking through his supposedly waterproof clothing, mixing with his sweat and his dirt, chilling him to the bone.

He unfolded his map and checked his position once again. He had to be close to the last RV of the day – the last rendezvous point – but he could see nothing. He was standing on a narrow track made up of loose grey shingle that crunched under his combat boots when he walked. The track snaked round the side of a mountain with a sheer drop to the right. He was somewhere in the Brecon Beacons and there should have been a view, but it had been wiped out by the rain and the fading light. A few trees twisted out of the side of the hill, with leaves as hard as thorns. Behind him, below him, ahead of him, it was all the same. Nowhere Land.

Alex hurt. The ten-kilogram Bergen rucksack he had been forced to wear cut into his shoulders and had rubbed blisters on his back. His right knee, where he had fallen earlier in the day, was no longer bleeding but still stung. His shoulder was bruised and there was a gash along the side of his neck. His camouflage outfit – he had swapped his Gap combat trousers for the real thing – fitted him badly, cutting his legs and under his arms but hanging loose everywhere else. He was close to exhaustion, he knew, almost too tired to feel how much pain he was in. But for the glucose and caffeine tablets in his survival pack, he would have ground to a halt hours ago. He knew that if he didn't find the RV soon, he would be physically unable to continue. Then he would be thrown off the course. "Binned" as they called it. They would like that. Swallowing down the taste of defeat, Alex folded the map and forced himself on.

It was his ninth – or maybe his tenth – day of training. Time had begun to dissolve into itself, as shapeless as the rain. After his lunch with Alan Blunt and Mrs Jones, he had been moved out of the manor-house and into a crude wooden hut in the training camp a few miles away. There were nine huts in total, each equipped with four metal beds and four metal lockers. A fifth had been squeezed into one of them to accommodate Alex. Two more huts, painted a different colour, stood side by side. One of these was a kitchen and mess hall. The other contained toilets, sinks and showers – with not a single hot tap in sight.

On his first day there, Alex had been introduced to his training officer, an incredibly fit black sergeant. He was the sort of man who thought he'd seen everything. Until he saw Alex. And he had examined the new arrival for a long minute before he had spoken.

"It's not my job to ask questions," he had said. "But if it was, I'd want to know what they're thinking of, sending me children. Do you have any idea where you are, boy? This isn't Butlins. This isn't the Club Méditerranée." He cut the word into its five syllables and spat them out. "I have you for eleven days and they expect me to give you the sort of training that should take fourteen weeks. That's not just mad. That's suicidal."

"I didn't ask to be here," Alex had said.

Suddenly the sergeant was furious. "You don't speak to me unless I give you permission," he shouted. "And when you speak to me, you address me as 'sir'. Do you understand?"

"Yes, sir." Alex had already decided that the man was even worse than his geography teacher.

"There are five units operational here at the moment," the officer went on. "You'll join K Unit. We don't use names. I have no name. You have no name. If anyone asks you what you're doing, you tell them nothing. Some of the men may be hard on you. Some of them may resent you being here. That's too bad. You'll just have to live with it. And there's something else you need to know. I can make allowances for you. You're a boy, not a man. But if you complain, you'll be binned. If you cry, you'll be binned. If you can't keep up, you'll be binned. Between you and me, boy, this is a mistake and I want to bin you."

After that, Alex joined K Unit. As the sergeant had predicted, they weren't exactly overjoyed to see him.

There were four of them. As Alex was soon to discover, the Special Operations division of MI6 sent its agents to the same training centre used by the Special Air Service – the SAS. Much of the training was based on SAS methods and this included the numbers and make-up of each team. So there were four men, each with their own special skills. And one boy, seemingly with none.

They were all in their mid-twenties, spread out over the bunks in companionable silence. Two of them smoking. One dismantling and reassembling his gun – a 9mm Browning High Power pistol. Each of them had been given a code-name: Wolf, Fox, Eagle and Snake. From now on, Alex would be known as Cub. The leader, Wolf, was the one with the gun. He was short and muscular with square shoulders and black, close-cropped hair. He had a handsome face, made slightly uneven by his nose, which had been broken at some time in the past.

He was the first to speak. Putting the gun down, he examined Alex with cold, dark grey eyes. "So who the hell do you think you are?" he demanded.

"Cub," Alex replied.

"A bloody schoolboy!" Wolf spoke with a strange, slightly foreign accent. "I don't believe it. Are you with Special Operations?"

"I'm not allowed to tell you that." Alex went over to his bunk and sat down. The mattress felt as solid as the frame. Despite the cold, there was only one blanket.

Wolf shook his head and smiled humourlessly. "Look what they've sent us," he muttered. "Double O Seven? Double O Nothing more like."

After that, the name stuck. Double O Nothing was what they called him.

In the days that followed, Alex shadowed the group, not quite part of it but never far away. Almost everything they did, he did. He learned map-reading, radio communication and first aid. He took part in an unarmed combat class and was knocked to the ground so often that it took all his nerve to persuade himself to get up again.

And then there was the assault course. Five times he was shouted and bullied across the nightmare of nets and ladders, tunnels and ditches, swinging tightropes and towering walls, that stretched for almost half a kilometre through, and over, the woodland beside the huts. Alex thought of it as the adventure playground from hell. The first time he tried it, he fell off a rope and into a pit that seemed to have been filled on purpose with freezing slime. Half drowned and filthy, he had been sent back to the start by the sergeant. Alex thought he would never get to the end, but the second time he finished it in twenty-five minutes – which he cut to seventeen minutes by the end of the week. Bruised and exhausted though he was, he was quietly pleased with himself. Even Wolf only managed it in twelve.

Wolf remained actively hostile towards Alex. The other three men simply ignored him, but Wolf did everything he could to taunt or humiliate him. It was as if Alex had somehow insulted him by being placed in the group. Once, crawling under the nets, Wolf lashed out with his foot, missing Alex's face by a centimetre. Of course, he would have said it was an accident if the boot had connected. Another time he was more successful, tripping Alex up in the mess hall and sending him flying, along with his tray, cutlery and steaming plate of stew. And every time he spoke to Alex, he used the same sneering tone of voice.

"Goodnight, Double O Nothing. Don't wet the bed."

Alex bit his lip and said nothing. But he was glad when the four men were sent off for a day's jungle survival course – this wasn't part of his own training – even though the sergeant worked him twice as hard once they were gone. He preferred to be on his own.

But on the eighth day, Wolf did come close to finishing him altogether. It happened in the Killing House.

The Killing House was a fake; a mock-up of an embassy used to train the SAS in the art of hostage release. Alex had twice watched K Unit go into the house, the first time swinging down from the roof, and had followed their progress on closed-circuit TV. All four men were armed. Alex himself didn't take part because someone somewhere had decided he shouldn't carry a gun. Inside the Killing House, mannequins had been arranged as terrorists and hostages. Smashing down the doors and using stun grenades to clear the rooms with deafening, multiple blasts, Wolf, Fox, Eagle and Snake had successfully completed their mission both times.

This time Alex had joined them. The Killing House had been booby-trapped. They weren't told how. All five of them were unarmed. Their job was simply to get from one end of the house to the other without being "killed".

They almost made it. In the first room, made up to look like a huge dining-room, they found the pressure pads under the carpet and the infrared beams across the doors. For Alex it was an eerie experience, tiptoeing behind the other four men, watching as they dismantled the two devices, using cigarette smoke to expose the otherwise invisible beams. It was strange to be afraid of everything and yet see nothing. In the hallway there was a motion detector which would have activated a machine gun (Alex assumed it was loaded with blanks) behind a Japanese screen. The third room was empty. The fourth was a living-room with the exit – a set of french windows – on the other side. There was a tripwire, barely thicker than a human hair, running the entire width of the room, and the french windows were alarmed. While Snake dealt with the alarm, Fox and Eagle prepared to neutralize the tripwire, unclipping an electronic circuit board and a variety of tools from their belts.

Wolf stopped them. "Leave it. We're out of here." At the same moment, Snake signalled. He had deactivated the alarm. The french windows were open.

Snake was the first out. Then Fox and Eagle. Alex would have been the last to leave the room, but just as he reached the exit he found Wolf blocking his way.

"Tough luck, Double O Nothing," Wolf said. His voice was soft, almost kind.

The next thing Alex knew, the heel of Wolf's palm had rammed into his chest, pushing him back with astonishing force. Taken by surprise, he lost his balance and fell, remembered the tripwire and tried to twist his body to avoid it. But it was hopeless. His flailing left hand caught the wire. He actually felt it against his wrist. He hit the floor, pulling the wire with him. And then...

The HRT stun grenade has been used frequently by the SAS. It's a small device filled with a mixture of magnesium powder and mercury fulminate. When the tripwire activated the grenade, the mercury exploded at once, not just deafening Alex but shuddering through him as if it could rip out his heart. At the same time, the magnesium ignited and burned for a full ten seconds. The light was so blinding that even closing his eyes made no difference. Alex lay there with his face against the hard wooden floor, his hands scrabbling against his head, unable to move, waiting for it to end.

But even then it wasn't over. When the magnesium finally burned out, it was as if all the light had burned out with it. Alex stumbled to his feet, unable to see or hear, not even sure any more where he was. He felt sick to his stomach. The room swayed around him. The heavy smell of chemicals hung in the air.

Ten minutes later he staggered out into the open. Wolf was waiting for him with the others, his face blank, and Alex realized he must have slipped out before he'd hit the ground. An angry sergeant walked over to him. Alex hadn't expected to see a shred of concern in the man's face and he wasn't disappointed.

"Do you want to tell me what happened in there, Cub?" he demanded. When Alex didn't answer, he went on. "You ruined the exercise. You fouled up. You could get the whole unit binned. So you'd better start telling me what went wrong."

Alex glanced at Wolf. Wolf looked the other way. What should he say? Should he even try to tell the truth?

"Well?" The sergeant was waiting.

"Nothing happened, sir," Alex said. "I just wasn't looking where I was going. I stepped on something and there was an explosion."

"If that was real life, you'd be dead," the sergeant said. "What did I tell you? Sending me a child was a mistake. And a stupid, clumsy child who doesn't look where he's going ... that's even worse!"

Alex stood where he was, just taking it. Out of the corner of his eye, he could see Wolf half smiling.

The sergeant had seen it too. "You think it's so funny, Wolf? You can go clean up in there. And tonight you'd better get some rest. All of you. Because tomorrow you've got a forty kilometre hike. Survival rations. No fire. This is a survival course. And if you do survive, then maybe you'll have a reason to smile."

Alex remembered the words now, exactly twenty-four hours later. He had spent the last eleven of them on his feet, following the trail the sergeant had set out for him on the map. The exercise had begun at six o'clock in the morning after a grey-lit breakfast of sausages and beans. Wolf and the others had disappeared into the distance ahead of him a long time ago, even though they had been given 25-kilogram rucksacks to carry. They had also been given only eight hours to complete the course. Allowing for his age, Alex had been given twelve.

He rounded a corner, his feet scrunching on the gravel. There was someone standing ahead of him. It was the sergeant. He had just lit a cigarette and Alex watched him slide the matches back into his pocket. Seeing him there brought back the shame and the anger of the day before and at the same time sapped the last of his strength. Suddenly Alex had had enough of Blunt, Mrs Jones, Wolf ... the whole stupid thing. With a final effort he stumbled the last hundred metres and came to a halt. Rain and sweat trickled down the side of his face. His hair, now dark with grime, was glued across his forehead.

The sergeant looked at his watch. "Eleven hours, five minutes. That's not bad, Cub. But the others were here three hours ago."

Bully for them, Alex thought. He didn't say anything.

"Anyway, you should just make it to the last RV," the sergeant went on. "It's up there."

He pointed to a wall. Not a sloping wall. A sheer one. Solid rock rising fifty metres up without a handhold or a foothold in sight. Even looking at it, Alex felt his stomach shrink. Ian Rider had taken him climbing – in Scotland, in France, all over Europe. But he had never attempted anything as difficult as this. Not on his own. Not when he was so tired.

"I can't," he said. In the end the two words came out easily.

"I didn't hear that," the sergeant said.

"I said, I can't do it, sir."

"Can't isn't a word we use around here."

"I don't care. I've had enough. I've just had..." Alex's voice cracked. He didn't trust himself to go on. He stood there, cold and empty, waiting for the axe to fall.

But it didn't. The sergeant gazed at him for a long minute. He nodded his head slowly. "Listen to me, Cub," he said. "I know what happened in the Killing House."

Alex glanced up.

"Wolf forgot about the closed-circuit TV. We've got it all on film."

"Then why—?" Alex began.

"Did you make a complaint against him, Cub?"

"No, sir."

"Do you want to make a complaint against him, Cub?"

A pause. Then, "No, sir."

"Good." The sergeant pointed at the rock face, suggesting a path up with his finger. "It's not as difficult as it looks," he said. "And they're waiting for you just over the top. You've got a nice cold dinner. Survival rations. You don't want to miss that."

Alex drew a deep breath and started forward. As he passed the sergeant, he stumbled and put out a hand to steady himself, brushing against him. "Sorry, sir," he said.

It took him twenty minutes to reach the top and, sure enough, K Unit was already there, crouching around three small tents that they must have pitched earlier in the afternoon. Two for two men sharing. One, the smallest, for Alex.

Snake, a thin, fair-haired man who spoke with a Scottish accent, looked up at Alex. He had a tin of cold stew in one hand, a teaspoon in the other.

"I didn't think you'd make it," he said. Alex couldn't help but notice a certain warmth in the man's voice. And for the first time he hadn't called him Double O Nothing.

"Nor did I," Alex said.

Wolf was squatting over what he hoped would become a campfire, trying to get it started with two flints while Fox and Eagle watched. He was getting nowhere. The stones only produced the smallest of sparks, and the scraps of newspaper and leaves that he had collected were already far too wet. Wolf struck at the stones again and again. The others watched, their faces glum.

Alex held out the box of matches that he had pick-pocketed from the sergeant when he had pretended to stumble at the foot of the rock face.

"These might help," he said.

He threw the matches down, then went into his tent.

TOYS AREN'T US

In the London office, Mrs Jones sat waiting while Alan Blunt read the report. The sun was shining. A pigeon was strutting back and forth along the ledge outside as if keeping guard.

"He's doing very well," Blunt said at last. "Remarkably well, in fact." He turned a page. "I see he missed target practice."

"Were you planning to give him a gun?" Mrs Jones asked.

"No. I don't think that would be a good idea."

"Then why does he need target practice?"

Blunt raised an eyebrow. "We can't give a teenager a gun," he said. "On the other hand, I don't think we can send him to Port Tallon empty-handed. You'd better have a word with Smithers."

"I already have. He's working on it now."

Mrs Jones stood up as if to leave. But at the door she hesitated. "I wonder if it's occurred to you that Rider may have been preparing him for this all along," she said.

"What do you mean?"

"Preparing Alex to replace him. Ever since the boy was old enough to walk, he's been in training for intelligence work ... but without knowing it. I mean, he's lived abroad, so he now speaks French, German and Spanish. He's been mountain-climbing, diving and skiing. He's learned karate. Physically he's in perfect shape." She shrugged. "I think Rider wanted Alex to become a spy."

"But not so soon," Blunt said.

"I agree. You know as well as I do, Alan – he's not ready yet. If we send him into Sayle Enterprises, he's going to get himself killed."

"Perhaps." The single word was cold, matter-of-fact.

"He's fourteen years old! We can't do it."

"We have to." Blunt stood up and opened the window, letting in the air and the sound of the traffic. The pigeon hurled itself off the ledge, afraid of him. "This whole business worries me," he said. "The prime minister sees the Stormbreakers as a major coup, for himself and for his government. But there's still something about Herod Sayle that I don't like. Did you tell the boy about Yassen Gregorovich?"

"No." Mrs Jones shook her head.

"Then it's time you did. It was Yassen who killed his uncle. I'm sure of it. And if Yassen was working for Sayle—"

"What will you do if Yassen kills Alex Rider?"

"That's not our problem, Mrs Jones. If the boy gets himself killed, it will be the final proof that there is something wrong. At the very least it'll allow me to postpone the Stormbreaker project and take a good hard look at what's going on at Port Tallon. In a way, it would almost help us if he *was* killed."

"The boy's not ready yet. He'll make mistakes. It won't take them long to find out who he is." Mrs Jones sighed. "I don't think

Alex has got much chance at all."

"I agree." Blunt turned back from the window. The sun slanted over his shoulder. A single shadow fell across his face. "But it's too late to worry about that now," he said. "We have no more time. Stop the training. Send him in."

Alex sat hunched up in the back of the low-flying C-130 military aircraft, his stomach churning behind his knees. There were twelve men sitting in two lines around him – his own unit and two others. For an hour now, the plane had been flying at just one hundred metres, following the Welsh valleys, dipping and swerving to avoid the mountain peaks. A single bulb glowed red behind a wire mesh, adding to the heat in the cramped cabin. Alex could feel the engines vibrating through him. It was like travelling in a spin-drier and microwave oven combined.

The thought of jumping out of a plane with an oversized silk umbrella would have made Alex sick with fear – but only that morning he'd been told that he wouldn't in fact be jumping himself. A signal from London. They couldn't risk him breaking a leg, it said, and Alex guessed that the end of his training was near. Even so, he'd been taught how to pack a parachute, how to control it, how to exit a plane and how to land, and at the end of the day the sergeant had instructed him to join the flight – just for the experience. Now, close to the drop zone, Alex felt almost disappointed. He'd watch everyone else jump and then he'd be left alone.

"T minus five..."

The voice of the pilot came over the speaker system, distant and metallic. Alex gritted his teeth. Five minutes until the jump. He looked at the other men, shuffling into position, checking the cords that connected them to the static line. He was sitting next to Wolf. To his surprise, the man was completely quiet, unmoving.

It was hard to tell in the half-darkness, but the look on his face could almost have been fear.

There was a loud buzz and the red light turned green. The assistant pilot had climbed through from the cockpit. He reached for a handle and pulled open a door set in the back of the aircraft, allowing the cold air to rush in. Alex could see a single square of night. It was raining. The rain howled past.

The green light began to flash. The assistant pilot tapped the first pair on their shoulders and Alex watched them shuffle over to the side and then throw themselves out. For a moment they were there, frozen in the doorway. Then they were gone, like a photograph crumpled and spun away by the wind. Two more men followed. Then another two, until only the final pair had still to jump.

Alex glanced at Wolf, who seemed to be struggling with a piece of equipment. His partner was moving to the door without him, but still Wolf didn't look up.

The other man jumped. Suddenly Alex was aware that only he and Wolf were left.

"Move it!" the assistant pilot shouted above the roar of the engines.

Wolf picked himself up. His eyes briefly met Alex's and in that moment Alex knew. Wolf was a popular leader. He was tough and he was fast, completing a forty-kilometre hike as if it was just a stroll in the park. But he had a weak spot. Somehow he'd allowed this parachute jump to get to him and he was too scared to move. It was hard to believe, but there he was, frozen in the doorway, his arms rigid, staring out. Alex glanced back. The assistant pilot was looking the other way. He hadn't seen what was happening. And when he did? If Wolf failed to make the jump, it would be the end of his training and maybe even the end of his career. Even hesitating would be bad enough. He'd be binned.

Alex thought for a moment. Wolf hadn't moved. Alex could see his shoulders rising and falling as he tried to summon up the courage to go. Ten seconds had passed. Maybe more. The assistant pilot was leaning down, stowing away a piece of equipment. Alex stood up. "Wolf," he said.

Wolf didn't even hear him.

Alex took one last quick look at the assistant pilot, then kicked out with all his strength. His foot slammed into Wolf's backside. He'd put all his strength behind it. Wolf was caught by surprise, his hands coming free as he plunged into the swirling night air.

The assistant pilot turned round and saw Alex. "What are you doing?" he shouted.

"Just stretching my legs," Alex shouted back.

The plane curved in the air and began the journey home.

Mrs Jones was waiting for him when he walked into the hangar. She was sitting at a table, wearing a grey silk jacket and trousers with a black handkerchief flowing out of her top pocket. For a moment she didn't recognize him. Alex was dressed in a flying suit. His hair was damp from the rain. His face was pinched with tiredness and he seemed to have grown older very fast. None of the men had arrived back yet. A truck had been sent to collect them from a field about three kilometres away.

"Alex?" she said.

Alex looked at her but said nothing.

"It was my decision to stop you jumping," she said. "I hope you're not disappointed. I just thought it was too much of a risk. Please. Sit down."

Alex sat down opposite her.

"I have something that might cheer you up," she went on. "I've brought you some toys."

"I'm too old for toys," Alex said.

"Not these toys."

She signalled and a man appeared, walking out of the shadows, carrying a tray of equipment, which he set down on the table. The man was enormously fat. When he sat down, the metal chair disappeared beneath the spread of his buttocks and Alex was surprised it could even take his weight. He was bald, with a black moustache and several chins, each one melting into the next and finally into his neck and shoulders. He wore a pinstriped suit which must have used enough material to make a tent.

"Smithers," he said, nodding at Alex. "Very nice to meet you, old chap."

"What have you got for him?" Mrs Jones demanded.

"I'm afraid we haven't had a great deal of time, Mrs J," Smithers replied. "The challenge was to think what a fourteen-year-old might carry with him – and adapt it." He picked the first object off the tray. A yo-yo. It was slightly larger than normal, made of black plastic. "Let's start with this," Smithers said.

Alex shook his head. He couldn't believe any of this. "Don't tell me!" he exclaimed. "It's some sort of secret weapon..."

"Not exactly. I was told you weren't to have weapons. You're too young."

"So it's not really a hand grenade? Pull the string and run like hell?"

"Certainly not. It's a yo-yo." Smithers pulled out the string, holding it between a podgy finger and thumb. "However, the string *is* a special sort of nylon. Very advanced. There are thirty metres of it and it can lift weights of up to one hundred kilograms. The actual yo-yo is motorized and clips on to your belt. Very useful for climbing."

"Amazing." Alex was unimpressed.

"And then there's this." Smithers produced a small tube. Alex read the side: ZIT-CLEAN, FOR HEALTHIER SKIN. "Nothing personal," Smithers went on apologetically, "but we thought it was something a boy of your age might use. And it is rather remarkable." He opened the tube and squeezed some of the cream on to his finger. "Completely harmless when you touch it. But bring it into contact with metal and it's quite another story." He wiped his finger, smearing the cream on to the surface of the table. For a moment nothing happened. Then a wisp of acrid smoke twisted upwards in the air, the metal sizzled and a jagged hole appeared. "It'll do that to just about any metal," Smithers explained. "Very useful if you need to break through a lock." He took out a handkerchief and wiped his finger clean.

"Anything else?" Mrs Jones asked.

"Oh yes, Mrs J. You could say this is our pièce de résistance." He picked up a brightly coloured box that Alex recognized at once as a Nintendo Game Boy Color. "What teenager would be complete without one of these?" he asked. "This one comes with four games. And the beauty of it is, each game turns the computer into something quite different."

He showed Alex the first game. "If you insert Nemesis, the computer becomes a fax/photocopier which gives you direct contact with us and vice versa." A second game. "Exocet turns the computer into an X-ray device. It has an audio function too. The headphones are useful for eavesdropping. It's not as powerful as I'd like, but we're working on it. Speed Wars is a bug finder. I suggest you use it the moment you're shown to your room. And finally ... Bomber Boy."

"Do I get to play that one?" Alex asked.

"You can play all four of them. But as the name might suggest, this is actually a smoke bomb. You leave the game cartridge somewhere in a room and press START three times on the console and it will go off. Useful camouflage if you need to escape in a hurry."

"Thank you, Smithers," Mrs Jones said.

"My pleasure, Mrs J." Smithers stood up, his legs straining to take the huge weight. "I'll hope to see you again, Alex. I've never had to equip a boy before. I'm sure I'll be able to think up a whole host of quite delightful ideas."

He waddled off and disappeared through a door which clanged shut behind him.

Mrs Jones turned to Alex. "You leave tomorrow for Port Tallon," she said. "You'll be going under the name of Felix Lester." She handed him a folder. "We've sent the real Felix Lester on holiday in Scotland. You'll find everything you need to know about him in here."

"I'll read it in bed."

"Good." Suddenly she was serious and Alex found himself wondering if she was herself a mother. If so, she could well have a son of his age. She took out a black and white photograph and laid it on the table. It showed a man in a white T-shirt and jeans. He was in his late twenties with blond, close-cropped hair, a smooth face, the body of a dancer. The photograph was slightly blurred. It had been taken from a distance, as if with a hidden camera. "I want you to look at this," she said.

"I'm looking."

"His name is Yassen Gregorovich. He was born in Russia but he now works for many countries. Iraq has employed him. Also Serbia, Libya and China."

"What does he do?" Alex asked, though looking at the cold face with its blank, hooded eyes, he could almost guess.

"He's a contract killer, Alex. We believe he killed Ian Rider."

There was a long pause. Alex stared at the photograph, trying to print it on his mind.

"This photograph was taken six months ago, in Cuba. It may have been a coincidence but Herod Sayle was there at the same time. The two of them might have met. And there is something else." She paused. "Rider used a code in the last message he sent. A single letter. Y."

"Y for Yassen."

"He must have seen Yassen somewhere in Port Tallon. He wanted us to know—"

"Why are you telling me this now?" Alex asked.

"Because if you see him – if Yassen is anywhere near Sayle Enterprises – I want you to contact us at once."

"And then?"

"We'll pull you out. If Yassen finds out you're working for us, he'll kill you too."

Alex smiled. "I'm too young to interest him," he said.

"No." Mrs Jones took the photograph back. "Just remember, Alex Rider, you're never too young to die."

Alex stood up.

"You'll leave tomorrow morning at eight o'clock," Mrs Jones said. "Be careful, Alex. And good luck."

Alex walked across the hangar, his footsteps echoing. Behind him, Mrs Jones unwrapped a peppermint and slipped it into her mouth. Her breath always smelt faintly of mint. As head of Special Operations, how many men had she sent to their deaths? Ian Rider and maybe dozens more. Perhaps it was easier for her if her breath was sweet.

There was a movement ahead of him and he saw that the parachutists had got back from their jump. They were walking towards him out of the darkness, with Wolf and the other men from K Unit right at the front. Alex tried to step round them but he found Wolf blocking his way.

"You're leaving," Wolf said. Somehow he must have heard that Alex's training was over.

"Yes."

There was a long pause. "What happened on the plane..." he began.

"Forget it, Wolf," Alex said. "Nothing happened. You jumped and I didn't, that's all."

Wolf held out a hand. "I want you to know ... I was wrong about you. I'm sorry I gave you such a hard time. But you're all right. And maybe ... one day it would be good to work with you."

"You never know," Alex said.

They shook.

"Good luck, Cub."

"Goodbye, Wolf."

Alex walked out into the night.

PHYSALIA PHYSALIS

The silver-grey Mercedes SL600 cruised down the motorway, travelling south. Alex was sitting in the front passenger seat, with so much soft leather around him that he could barely hear the 389-horsepower, 6-litre engine that was carrying him towards the Sayle complex near Port Tallon, Cornwall. But at eighty miles per hour, the engine was only idling. Alex could feel the power of the car. One hundred thousand pounds' worth of German engineering. One touch from the thin, unsmiling chauffeur and the Mercedes would leap forward. This was a car that sneered at speed limits.

Alex had been collected that morning from a converted church in Hampstead, north London. This was where Felix Lester lived. When the driver had arrived, Alex had been waiting with his luggage and there'd even been a woman – an MI6 operative – kissing him, telling him to clean his teeth, waving goodbye. As far as the driver was concerned, Alex was Felix. That morning Alex had read through the file and knew that Lester went to a school called St Anthony's, had two sisters and a pet Labrador. His father was an architect. His mother designed jewellery. A happy family – *his* family if anybody asked.

"How far is it to Port Tallon?" he asked.

So far the driver had barely spoken a word. He answered Alex without looking at him. "A few hours. You want some music?"

"Got any John Lennon?" That wasn't his choice. According to the file, Felix Lester liked John Lennon.

"No."

"Forget it. I'll get some sleep."

He needed the sleep. He was still exhausted from the training and wondered how he would explain all the half-healed cuts and bruises if anyone saw under his shirt. Maybe he'd tell them he got bullied at school. He closed his eyes and allowed the leather to suck him into sleep.

It was the feeling of the car slowing down that woke him. He opened his eyes and saw a fishing village, the blue sea beyond, a swathe of rolling green hills and a cloudless sky. It was a picture off a jigsaw puzzle, or perhaps a holiday brochure advertising a forgotten England. Seagulls swooped and cried overhead. An old tug – tangled nets, smoke and flaking paint – pulled into the quay. A few locals, fishermen and their wives, stood around, watching. It was about five o'clock in the afternoon and the village was caught in the silvery, fragile light that comes at the end of a perfect spring day.

"Port Tallon," the driver said. He must have noticed Alex opening his eyes.

"It's pretty."

"Not if you're a fish."

They drove round the edge of the village and back inland, down a lane that twisted between strangely bumpy fields. Alex saw the ruins of buildings, half-crumbling chimneys and rusting metal wheels, and knew that he was looking at an old tin mine. They'd mined tin in Cornwall for three thousand years until one day the tin had run out. Now all that was left were the holes.

A couple of kilometres down the lane a linked metal fence sprang up. It was brand new, ten metres high, topped with razor wire. Arc lamps on scaffolding towers stood at regular intervals and there were huge signs, red on white. You could have read them from the next county.

"Trespassers will be shot," Alex muttered to himself. He remembered what Mrs Jones had told him. *He's more or less got his own private army. He's acting as if he's got something to hide.* Well, that was certainly his own first impression. The whole complex was somehow shocking, alien to the sloping hills and fields.

The car reached the main gate, where there was a security cabin and an electronic barrier. A guard in a blue and grey uniform with **SE** printed on his jacket waved them through. The barrier lifted automatically. And then they were following a long, straight road over a stretch of land that had somehow been hammered flat, with an airstrip on one side and a cluster of four hi-tech buildings on the other. The buildings were large, smoked glass and steel, each one joined to the next by a covered walkway. There were two aircraft next to the landing-strip. A helicopter and a small cargo plane. Alex was impressed. The whole complex must have been about five kilometres square. It was quite an operation.

The Mercedes came to a roundabout with a fountain at the centre, swept round it and continued up towards a fantastic, sprawling house. It was Victorian, red brick topped with copper domes and spires that had long ago turned green. There must have been at least sixty windows on the five floors facing the drive. It was a house that just didn't know when to stop.

The Mercedes pulled up at the main entrance and the driver got out. "Follow me."

"What about my luggage?" Alex asked.

"It'll be brought."

Alex and the driver went through the front door and into a hall dominated by a huge canvas – Judgement Day, the end of the world, painted four centuries ago as a swirling mass of doomed souls and demons. There were works of art everywhere. Watercolours and oils, prints, drawings, sculptures in stone and bronze, all crowded together with nowhere for the eye to rest. Alex followed the driver along a carpet so thick that he almost bounced. He was beginning to feel claustrophobic and was relieved when they passed through a door and into a vast room that was practically bare.

"Mr Sayle will be here shortly," the driver said, and left.

Alex looked around him. This was a modern room with a curving steel desk near the centre, carefully positioned halogen lights and a spiral staircase leading down from a perfect circle cut in the ceiling high above. One entire wall consisted of a single sheet of glass and, walking over to it, Alex realized that he was looking at a gigantic aquarium. The sheer size of the thing drew him towards it. It was hard to imagine how many thousands of litres of water the glass held back, but he was surprised to see that the tank was empty. There were no fish, although it was big enough to hold a shark.

And then something moved in the turquoise shadows and Alex gasped with a mixture of horror and wonderment as the biggest jellyfish he had ever seen drifted into view. The main body of the creature was a shimmering, pulsating mass of white and mauve, shaped roughly like a cone. Beneath it, a mass of tentacles covered with circular stingers twisted in the water, at least ten metres long. As the jellyfish moved, or drifted in an artificial current, its tentacles writhed against the glass so that it looked almost as if it was trying to break out. It was the single most awesome and repulsive thing Alex had ever seen.

"*Physalia physalis*." The voice came from behind him and Alex twisted round to see a man coming down the last of the stairs.

Herod Sayle was short. He was so short that Alex's first impression was that he was looking at a reflection that had somehow been distorted. In his immaculate and expensive black suit, with gold signet ring and brightly polished black shoes, he looked like a scaled-down model of a multimillionaire businessman. His skin was very dark, so that his teeth flashed when he smiled. He had a round, bald head and very horrible eyes. The grey irises were too small, completely surrounded by white. Alex was reminded of tadpoles before they hatch. When Sayle stood next to him, the eyes were almost at the same level as his and held less warmth than the jellyfish.

"The Portuguese man-o'-war," Sayle continued. He had a heavy accent brought with him from the Beirut marketplace. "It's beautiful, don't you think?"

"I wouldn't keep one as a pet," Alex said.

"I came upon this one when I was diving in the South China Sea." Sayle gestured at a glass display case and Alex noticed three harpoon guns and a collection of knives resting in velvet slots. "I love to kill fish," Sayle went on. "But when I saw this specimen of

Physalia physalis, I knew I had to capture it and keep it. You see, it reminds me of myself."

"It's ninety-nine per cent water. It has no brain, no guts and no anus." Alex had dredged up the facts from somewhere and spoken them before he knew what he was doing.

Sayle glanced at him, then turned back to the creature hovering over him in its tank. "It's an outsider," he said. "It drifts on its own, ignored by the other fish. It is silent and yet it demands respect. You see the nematocysts, Mr Lester? The stinging cells? If you were to find yourself wrapped in those, it would be an exquisite death."

"Call me Alex," Alex said.

He'd meant to say Felix, but somehow it had slipped out. It was the most stupid, the most amateurish mistake he could have made. But he had been thrown by the way Sayle had appeared and by the slow, hypnotic dance of the jellyfish.

The grey eyes squirmed. "I thought your name was Felix."

"My friends call me Alex."

"Why?"

"After Alex Ferguson. I'm a big fan of Manchester United." It was the first thing Alex could think of. But he'd seen a football poster in Felix Lester's bedroom and knew that at least he'd chosen the right team.

Sayle smiled. "That's most amusing. Alex it shall be. And I hope we will be friends, Alex. You are a very lucky boy. You won the competition and you are going to be the first teenager to try out my Stormbreaker. But this is also lucky, I think, for me. I want to know what you think of it. I want you to tell me what you like ... what you don't." The eyes dipped away and suddenly he was businesslike. "We have only three days until the launch," he said. "We'd better get a *bliddy* move on, as my father used to say. I'll have my man take you to your room and tomorrow morning, first thing, you must get to work. There's a maths program you should try ... also languages. All the software was developed here at Sayle Enterprises. Of course, we've talked to children. We've gone to teachers, to education experts. But you, my dear ... Alex. You will be worth more to me than all of them put together."

As he had talked, Sayle had become more and more animated, carried away by his own enthusiasm. He had become a completely different man. Alex had to admit that he'd taken an immediate dislike to Herod Sayle. No wonder Blunt and the people at MI6 mistrusted him! But now he was forced to think again. He was standing opposite one of the richest men in England, a man who had decided, out of the goodness of his heart, to give a huge gift to British schools. Just because he was small and slimy, that didn't necessarily make him an enemy. Perhaps Blunt was wrong after all.

"Ah! Here's my man now," Sayle said. "And about *bliddy* time!"

The door had opened and a man had come in, dressed in the black suit and tails of an old-fashioned butler. He was as tall and thin as his master was short and round, with a thatch of ginger hair above a face so pale it was almost paper-white. From a distance it had looked as if he was smiling, but as he drew closer Alex gasped. The man had two horrendous scars, one on each side of his mouth, twisting up all the way to his ears. It was as if someone had attempted to cut his face in half. The scars were a gruesome shade of mauve. There were smaller, fainter scars where his cheeks had once been stitched.

"This is Mr Grin," Sayle said. "He changed his name after his accident."

"Accident?" Alex found it hard not to stare at the terrible wounds.

"Mr Grin used to work in a circus. It was a novelty knife-throwing act. For the climax he used to catch a spinning knife between his teeth, but then one night his elderly mother came to see the show. She waved to him from the front row and he got his timing wrong. He's worked for me for a dozen years now and, although his appearance may be displeasing, he is loyal and efficient. Don't try to talk with him, by the way. He has no tongue."

"Eeeurgh!" Mr Grin said.

"Nice to meet you," Alex muttered.

"Take him to the blue room," Sayle commanded. He turned to Alex. "You're fortunate that one of our nicest rooms has come up free – here, in the house. We had a security man staying there. But he left us quite suddenly."

"Oh? Why was that?" Alex asked casually.

"I have no idea. One moment he was here, the next he was gone." Sayle smiled again. "I hope you won't do the same, Alex."

"Ri ... wurgh!" Mr Grin gestured at the door and, leaving Herod Sayle standing in front of his huge captive, Alex left the room.

He was led along a passage past more works of art, up a staircase and then along a wide corridor with thick wood-panelled doors and chandeliers. Alex assumed that the main house was used for entertaining. Sayle himself must live here. But the computers would be constructed in the modern buildings he had seen opposite the airstrip. Presumably he would be taken there tomorrow.

His room was at the far end. It was a large room with a four-poster bed and a window looking out on to the fountain. Darkness had fallen and the water, cascading ten metres through the air over a semi-naked statue that looked remarkably like Herod Sayle, was eerily illuminated by a dozen concealed lights. Next to the window was a table with an evening meal already laid out for him:

ham, cheese, salad. His bag was lying on the bed.

He went over to it – a Nike sports bag – and examined it. When he had closed it up, he had inserted three hairs into the zip, trapping them in the metal teeth. They were no longer there. Alex opened the bag and went through it. Everything was exactly as it had been when he had packed, but he was certain that the sports bag had been expertly and methodically searched.

He took out the Game Boy Color, inserted the Speed Wars cartridge and pressed the START button three times. At once the screen lit up with a green rectangle, the same shape as the room. He lifted the Game Boy up and swung it around him, following the line of the walls. A red flashing dot suddenly appeared on the screen. He walked forward, holding the Game Boy in front of him. The dot flashed faster, more intensely. He had reached a picture, hanging next to the bathroom, a squiggle of colours that looked suspiciously like a Picasso. He put the Game Boy down and carefully lifted the canvas off the wall. The bug was taped behind it, a black disc about the size of a ten pence piece. Alex looked at it for a minute, wondering why it was there. Security? Or was Sayle such a control freak that he had to know what his guests were doing every minute of the day and night?

Alex put the picture back. There was only one bug in the room. The bathroom was clean.

He ate his dinner, showered and got ready for bed. As he passed the window, he noticed activity in the grounds near the fountain. There were lights shining out of the modern buildings. Three men, all dressed in white overalls, were driving towards the house in an open-top Jeep. Two more men walked past. These were security guards, dressed in the same uniform as the man at the gate. They were both carrying semi-automatic machine guns. Not just a private army, but a well-armed one.

He got into bed. The last person who had slept here had been his uncle, Ian Rider. Had he seen something, looking out of the window? Had he heard something? What could have happened that meant he had to die?

Sleep took a long time coming to the dead man's bed.

LOOKING FOR TROUBLE

Alex saw it the moment he opened his eyes. It would have been obvious to anyone who slept in the bed, but of course nobody had slept there since Ian Rider had been killed. It was a triangle of white slipped into a fold in the canopy above the four-poster bed. You had to be lying on your back to see it – like Alex was now.

It was out of his reach. He had to balance a chair on the mattress and then stand on the chair to reach it. Wobbling, almost falling, he finally managed to trap it between his fingers and pull it out.

In fact it was a square of paper, folded twice. Someone had drawn on it, a strange design with what looked like a reference number beneath it.

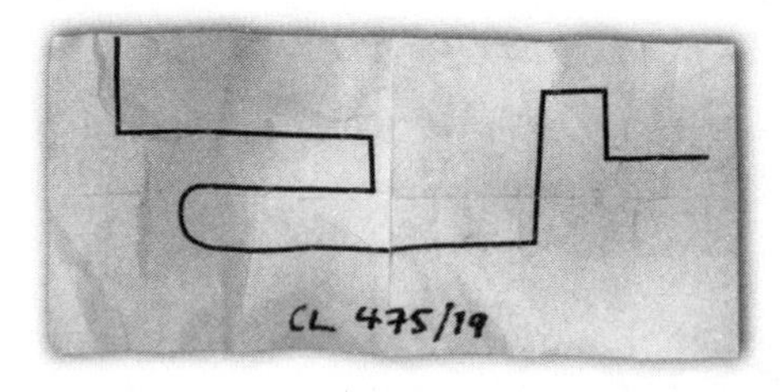

There wasn't very much of it, but Alex recognized Ian Rider's handwriting. But what did it mean? He pulled on some clothes, went over to the table and took out a sheet of plain paper. Quickly, he wrote a brief message in block capitals.

FOUND THIS IN IAN RIDER'S
ROOM. CAN YOU MAKE
ANY SENSE OF IT?

Then he found his Game Boy, inserted the Nemesis cartridge into the back, turned it on and passed the screen over the two sheets of paper, scanning first his message and then the design. Instantaneously, he knew, a machine would click on in Mrs Jones's office in London and a copy of the two pages would scroll out of the back. Maybe she could work it out. She was, after all, meant to work for Intelligence.

Finally, Alex turned off the Game Boy then removed the back and hid the folded paper in the battery compartment. The diagram had to be important. Ian Rider had hidden it. Maybe it was what had cost him his life.

There was a knock at the door. Alex went over and opened it. Mr Grin was standing outside, still wearing his butler's uniform.

"Good morning," Alex said.

"Geurgh!" Mr Grin gestured and Alex followed him back down the corridor and out of the house. He felt relieved to be out in the air, away from all the artwork. As they paused in front of the fountain there was a sudden roar and a propeller-driven cargo plane dipped down over the roof of the house and landed on the runway.

"If gring gly," Mr Grin explained.

"Just as I thought," Alex said.

They reached the first of the modern buildings and Mr Grin pressed his hand against a glass plate next to the door. There was a green glow as his fingerprints were read, and a moment later the door slid soundlessly open.

Everything was different on the other side of the door. From the art and elegance of the main house, Alex could have stepped into the next century. Long white corridors with metallic floors. Halogen lights. The unnatural chill of air-conditioning. Another world.

A woman was waiting for them, broad-shouldered and severe, her blonde hair twisted into the tightest of buns. She had a strangely blank, moon-shaped face, wire-framed spectacles and no make-up apart from a smear of yellow lipstick. She wore a white coat with a name tag pinned to the top pocket. It read: VOLE.

"You must be Felix," she said. "Or is it now, I understand, Alex? Yes! Allow me to introduce myself. I am Fräulein Vole." She had a thick German accent. "You may call me Nadia." She glanced at Mr Grin. "I will take him from here."

Mr Grin nodded and left the building.

"This way." Vole began to walk. "We have four blocks here. Block A, where we are now, is Administration and Recreation. Block B is Software Development. Block C is Research and Storage. Block D is where the main Stormbreaker assembly line is found."

"Where's breakfast?" Alex asked.

"You have not eaten? I will send you a sandwich. Herr Sayle is very keen for you to begin at once with the experience."

She walked like a soldier – back straight, her feet, in black leather shoes, rapping against the floor. Alex followed her through a door and into a bare, square room with a chair and a desk and, on the desk, the first actual Stormbreaker he had ever seen.

It was a beautiful machine. The iMac might have been the first computer with a real sense of design, but the Stormbreaker had far surpassed it. It was black apart from the white lightning bolt down one side – and the screen could have been a porthole into outer space. Alex sat behind the desk and turned it on. The computer booted itself instantly. A fork of animated lightning sliced across the screen, there was a swirl of clouds, and then in burning red the letters **SE**, the logo of Sayle Enterprises, formed itself. Seconds later, the desktop appeared, with icons for maths, science, French – every subject – ready to be accessed. Even in those brief seconds, Alex could feel the speed and the power of the computer. And Herod Sayle was going to put one in every school in the country! He had to admire the man. It was an incredible gift.

"I leave you here," Fräulein Vole said. "It is better for you, I think, to explore the Stormbreaker on your own. Tonight you will have dinner with Herr Sayle and you will tell him your feeling."

"Yeah – I'll tell him my feeling."

"I will have the sandwich sent in to you. But I must ask you to please not leave the room. There is, you understand, the security."

"Whatever you say, Mrs Vole," Alex said.

The woman left. Alex opened one of the programs and for the next three hours lost himself in the state-of-the-art software of the Stormbreaker. Even when his sandwich arrived, he ignored it, letting it curl on the plate. He would never have said that schoolwork was fun, but he had to admit that the computer made it lively. The history program brought the battle of Port Stanley to life with music and video clips. How to extract oxygen from water? The science program did it in front of his eyes. The Stormbreaker even managed to make geometry almost bearable, which was more than Mr Donovan at Brookland had ever done.

The next time Alex looked at his watch it was one o'clock. He had been in the room for over four hours. He stretched and stood up. Nadia Vole had told him not to leave, but if there were any secrets to be found at Sayle Enterprises, he wasn't going to find them here. He walked over to the door and was surprised to find that it opened as he approached. He went out into the corridor. There was nobody in sight. Time to move.

Block A was Administration and Recreation. Alex passed a number of offices, then a blank, white-tiled cafeteria. There were about forty men and women, all in white coats and identity tags, sitting and talking animatedly over their lunches. He had chosen a good time. Nobody passed him as he continued through a Plexiglas walkway into Block B. There were computer screens everywhere, glowing in cramped offices piled high with papers and printouts. Software Development. Through to Block C – Research – past a library with endless shelves of books and CD-ROMs. Alex ducked in behind a shelf as two technicians walked past, talking together. He was out of bounds, on his own, snooping around without any idea of what he was looking for. Trouble, probably. What else could there be to find?

He walked softly, casually, down the corridor, heading for the last block. A murmur of voices reached him and he quickly stepped into an alcove, squatting down beside a drinking fountain as two men and a woman walked past, all wearing white coats, arguing about web servers. Overhead, he noticed a security camera swivelling towards him. In another five seconds it would be on him, but he still had to wait until the three technicians had gone before he could sprint forward, just ahead of the wide-angle lens.

Had it seen him? Alex couldn't be sure. But he did know one thing: he was running out of time. Maybe the Vole woman would have checked up on him already. Maybe someone would have brought lunch to the empty room. If he was going to find anything, it would have to be soon.

He started along the glass passage that joined Blocks C and D, and here at last there was something different. The corridor was split in half, with a metal staircase leading down into what must have been some sort of basement. And although every building and every door he had seen so far had been labelled, this staircase was blank. The light stopped about halfway down. It was almost as if the stairs were trying not to get themselves noticed.

The clang of feet on metal. Alex shrank back and a moment later Mr Grin appeared, rising out of the floor like a vampire on a bad day. As the sun hit his dead, white face, his scars twitched and he blinked several times before walking off into Block D.

What had he been doing? Where did the stairs go? Alex hurried down them. It was like stepping into a morgue. The air-conditioning was so strong that he could feel it on his forehead and on the palms of his hands, fast-freezing his sweat.

He stopped at the bottom of the stairs. He was in another long passageway, stretching back under the complex, the way he had come. It led to a single metal door. But there was something very strange. The walls of the passage were unfinished; dark brown rock with streaks of what looked like zinc or some other metal. The floor was also rough, and the way was lit by old-fashioned bulbs hanging on wires. It all reminded him of something ... something he had seen very recently. But he couldn't remember what.

Somehow Alex knew that the door at the end of the passage would be locked. It looked as if it had been locked for ever. Like the stairs, it was not labelled. And somehow it seemed too small to be important. But Mr Grin had just come up the stairs. There was only one place he could have come from and that was the other side. The door had to lead somewhere!

He reached it and tried the handle. It wouldn't move. He pressed his ear against the metal and listened. Nothing, unless ... was he imagining it? ... a sort of throbbing. A pump or something like it. Alex would have given anything to see through the metal – and suddenly he realized that he could. The Game Boy was in his pocket. He took it out, inserted the Exocet cartridge, turned it on and held it flat against the door.

The screen flickered into life; a tiny window through the metal door. Alex was looking into a large room. There was something tall and barrel-shaped in the middle of it. And there were people. Ghostlike, mere smudges on the screen, they were moving back and forth. Some of them were carrying objects – flat and rectangular. Trays of some sort? There seemed to be a desk to one side, piled with apparatus that he couldn't make out. Alex pressed the brightness control, trying to zoom in. But the room was too big. Everything was too far away.

He fumbled in his pocket and took out the earphones. Still holding the Game Boy against the door, he pressed the wire into the socket and slipped the earphones over his head. If he couldn't see, at least he might be able to hear – and sure enough the voices came through, faint and disconnected, but audible through the powerful speaker system built into the machine.

"...in place. We have twenty-four hours."

"It's not enough."

"It's all we have. They come in tonight. At 0200."

Alex didn't recognize any of the voices. Amplified by the tiny machine, they sounded like a telephone call from abroad on a very bad line.

"...Grin ... overseeing the delivery."

"It's still not enough time."

And then they were gone. Alex tried to piece together what he had heard. Something was being delivered. Two hours after midnight. Mr Grin was arranging the delivery.

But what? Why?

He had just turned off the Game Boy and put it back into his pocket when he heard behind him the squeak of a shoe that told him he was no longer alone. He turned round and found himself facing Nadia Vole. Alex realized that she had tried to sneak up on him. She had known he was down here.

"What are you doing, Alex?" she asked. Her voice was poisoned honey.

"Nothing," Alex said.

"I asked you to stay in the computer room."

"Yes. But I'd been there all morning. I needed a break."

"And you came down here?"

"I saw the stairs. I thought they might lead to the toilet."

There was a long silence. Behind him, Alex could still hear – or feel – the throbbing from the secret room. Then the woman nodded as if she had decided to accept his story. "There is nothing down here," she said. "This door leads only to the generator room. Please..." She gestured. "I will take you back to the main house, yes? And later you must prepare for the dinner with Herr Sayle. He wishes to know your first impressions of the Stormbreaker."

Alex walked past her and back towards the stairs. He was certain of two things. The first was that Nadia Vole was lying. This was no generator room. She was hiding something. And she hadn't believed him either. One of the cameras must have spotted him and she had been sent to find him. So she knew that he was lying to her.

Not a good start.

Alex reached the staircase and climbed up into the light, feeling the woman's eyes, like daggers, stabbing into his back.

NIGHT VISITORS

Herod Sayle was playing snooker when Alex was shown back into the room with the jellyfish. It was hard to say quite where the heavy wooden snooker table had come from, and Alex couldn't avoid thinking that the little man looked slightly ridiculous, almost lost at the far end of the green baize. Mr Grin was with him, carrying a footstool which Sayle stood on for each shot. Otherwise he would barely have been able to reach over the edge.

"Ah ... good evening, Felix. Or, of course, I mean Alex!" Sayle exclaimed. "Do you play snooker?"

"Occasionally."

"How would you like to play against me? There are only two reds left – then the colours. But I'm willing to bet that you don't manage to score a single point."

"How much?"

"Ha ha!" Sayle laughed. "Suppose I was to bet you ten pounds a point?"

"As much as that?" Alex looked surprised.

"To a man like myself, ten pounds is nothing. Nothing! Why, I could quite happily bet you a hundred pounds a point!"

"Then why don't you?" The words were softly spoken but they were still a direct challenge. Sayle gazed thoughtfully at Alex. "Very well," he said. "A hundred pounds a point. Why not? I like a gamble. My father was a gambling man."

"I thought he was a hairdresser."

"Who told you that?"

Silently, Alex cursed himself. Why was he never more careful when he was with this man? "I read it in a paper," he said. "My dad got me some stuff to read about you when I won the competition."

"A hundred pounds a point, then. But don't expect to get rich." Sayle hit the white, sending one of the reds straight into the middle pocket. The jellyfish floated past as if watching the game from its tank. Mr Grin picked up the footstool and moved it round the table. Sayle laughed briefly and followed the butler round, already sizing up the next shot, a fairly tricky black into the corner. "So what does your father do?" he asked.

"He's an architect," Alex said.

"Oh yes? What has he designed?" The question was casual, but Alex wondered if he was being tested.

"He's been working on an office in Soho," Alex said. "Before that he did an art gallery in Aberdeen."

"Yes." Sayle climbed on to the footstool and aimed. The black missed the corner pocket by a fraction of a millimetre, spinning back into the centre. Sayle frowned. "That was your *bliddy* fault," he snapped at Mr Grin.

"Warg?"

"Your shadow was on the table. Never mind, never mind!" He turned to Alex. "You've been unlucky. None of the balls will go in. You won't make any money this time."

Alex pulled a cue out of the rack and glanced at the table. Sayle was right. The last red was too close to the cushion. But in snooker there are other ways to win points, as Alex knew only too well. It was one of the many games he had played with Ian Rider. The two of them had even belonged to a club in Chelsea and Alex had represented the junior team. This was something he hadn't mentioned to Sayle. He carefully aimed at the red, then hit. Perfect.

"Nowhere near!" Sayle was back at the table before the balls had even stopped rolling. But he had spoken too soon. He stared as the white ball hit the cushion and rolled behind the pink. He'd been snookered. For about twenty seconds he measured up the angles, breathing through his nose. "You've had a bit of *bliddy* luck!" he said. "You seem to have accidentally snookered me. Now, let me see..." He concentrated, then hit the white, trying to curve it round the pink. But once again he was out by about a millimetre. There was an audible click as it touched the pink.

"Foul shot," Alex said. "Six points to me. Does that mean I get six hundred pounds?"

"What?"

"The foul is worth six points to me. At a hundred pounds a point—"

"Yes, yes, yes!" Saliva flecked Sayle's lips. He was staring at the table as if he couldn't believe what had happened.

His shot had exposed the red ball. It was an easy shot into the top corner and Alex took it without hesitating. "And another hundred makes seven hundred," he said. He moved down the table, brushing past Mr Grin. Quickly he judged the angles. Yes...

He got a perfect kiss on the black, sending it into the corner with the white spinning back for a good angle on the yellow. One thousand four hundred pounds plus another two hundred when he dropped the yellow immediately afterwards. Sayle could only watch in disbelief as Alex pocketed the green, the brown, the blue and the pink in that order and then, down the full length of the table, the black.

"I make that four thousand, one hundred pounds," Alex said. He put down the cue. "Thank you very much."

Sayle's face had gone the colour of the last ball. "Four thousand...! I wouldn't have gambled if I'd known you were this *bliddy* good," he said. He went over to the wall and pressed a button. Part of the floor slid back and the entire billiard-table disappeared into it, carried down by a hydraulic lift. When the floor slid back, there was no sign that it had ever been there. It was a neat trick. The toy of a man with money to burn.

But Sayle was no longer in the mood for games. He threw his billiard-cue over to Mr Grin, hurling it almost like a javelin. The butler's hand flicked out and caught it. "Let's eat," Sayle said.

The two of them sat at opposite ends of a long glass table in the room next door while Mr Grin served smoked salmon, then some sort of stew. Alex drank water. Sayle, who had cheered up once again, had a glass of vintage red wine.

"You spent some time with the Stormbreaker today?" he asked.

"Yes."

"And...?"

"It's great," Alex said, and meant it. He still found it hard to believe that this ridiculous man could have created anything so sleek and powerful.

"So which programs did you use?"

"History. Science. Maths. It's hard to believe, but I actually enjoyed them!"

"Do you have any criticisms?"

Alex thought for a moment. "I was surprised it didn't have 3D acceleration."

"The Stormbreaker is not intended for games."

"Did you consider a headset and integrated microphone?"

"No." Sayle nodded. "It's a good idea. I'm sorry you've only come here for such a short time, Alex. Tomorrow we'll have to get you on to the Internet. The Stormbreakers are all connected to a master network. That's controlled from here. It means they have free twenty-four-hour access."

"That's cool."

"It's more than cool." Sayle's eyes were far away, the grey irises small, dancing. "Tomorrow we start shipping the computers out," he said. "They'll go by plane, by lorry and by boat. It will take just one day for them to reach every point of the country. And the day after, at twelve o'clock noon exactly, the prime minister will honour me by pressing the START button which will bring every one of my Stormbreakers on-line. At that moment, all the schools will be united. Think of it, Alex! Thousands of schoolchildren – hundreds of thousands – sitting in front of the screens, suddenly together. North, south, east and west. One school. One family. And then they will know me for what I am!"

He picked up his glass and emptied it. "How is the goat?" he asked.

"I'm sorry?"

"The stew. The meat is goat. It was a recipe of my mother's."

"She must have been an unusual woman."

Herod Sayle held out his glass and Mr Grin refilled it. Sayle was gazing at Alex curiously. "You know," he said. "I have a strange feeling that you and I have met before."

"I don't think so—"

"But yes. Your face is familiar to me. Mr Grin? What do you think?"

The butler stood back with the wine. His dead, white head twisted round to look at Alex. "Eeeg Raargh!" he said.

"Yes, of course. You're right!"

"Eeeg Raargh?" Alex asked.

"Ian Rider. The security man I mentioned. You look a lot like him. Quite a coincidence, don't you think?"

"I don't know. I never met him." Alex could feel the danger getting closer. "You told me he left suddenly."

"Yes. He was sent here to keep an eye on things, but if you ask me he was never any *bliddy* good. Spent half his time in the village. In the port, the post office, the library. When he wasn't snooping around here, that is. Of course, that's something else you have in common. I understand Fräulein Vole found you today..." Sayle's pupils crawled to the front of his eyes, trying to get closer to Alex. "You were off limits."

"I got a bit lost." Alex shrugged, trying to make light of it.

"Well, I hope you don't go wandering again tonight. Security is very tight at the moment and, as you may have noticed, my men are all armed."

"I didn't think that was legal in Britain."

"We have a special licence. At any rate, Alex, I would advise you to go straight to your room after dinner. And stay there. I would be inconsolable if you were accidentally shot and killed in the darkness. Although it would, of course, save me four thousand pounds."

"Actually, I think you've forgotten the cheque."

"You'll have it tomorrow. Maybe we can have dinner together. Mr

Grin will be serving up one of my grandmother's recipes."

"More goat?"

"Dog."

"You obviously had a family that loved animals."

"Only the edible ones." Sayle smiled. "And now I must wish you good night."

At one-thirty in the morning, Alex's eyes blinked open and he was instantly awake.

He slipped out of bed and dressed quickly in his darkest clothes, then left the room. He was half surprised that the door was unlocked and the corridors seemed to be unmonitored. But this was, after all, Sayle's private house and any security would have been designed to stop people coming in, not leaving.

Sayle had warned him not to leave the house. But the voices behind the metal door had spoken of something arriving at two o'clock. Alex had to know what it was.

He found his way into the kitchen and tiptoed past a stretch of gleaming silver surfaces and an oversized American fridge. Let sleeping dogs lie, he thought to himself, remembering what was being served for tomorrow's dinner. There was a side door, fortunately with the key still in the lock. Alex turned it and let himself out. As a last-minute precaution he locked the door and kept the key. Now at least he had a way back in.

It was a soft, grey night with a half-moon forming a perfect D in the sky. D for what? Alex wondered. Danger? Discovery? Or disaster? Only time would tell. He took two steps forward, then froze as a searchlight rolled past, centimetres away, directed from a tower he hadn't even seen. At the same time he became aware of voices, and two guards walked slowly across the garden, patrolling the back of the house. They were both armed and Alex remembered what Sayle had said. An accidental shooting would save him four thousand pounds. And given the importance of the Stormbreakers, would anyone care just how accidental the shooting might have been?

He waited until the men had gone, then took the opposite direction, running along the side of the house, ducking under the windows. He reached the corner and looked round. In the distance, the airstrip was lit up and there were figures – more guards and technicians – everywhere. One man he recognized, walking past the fountain towards a waiting truck. He was tall and gangly, silhouetted against the lights, a black cut-out. But Alex would have known Mr Grin anywhere. *They come in tonight. At 0200.* Night visitors. And Mr Grin was on his way to meet them.

The butler had almost reached the truck and Alex knew that if he waited any longer he would be too late. Throwing caution to the wind, he left the cover of the house and ran out into the open, trying to stay low and hoping his dark clothes would keep him invisible. He was only fifty metres from the truck when Mr Grin suddenly stopped and turned round as if he had sensed there was someone there. There was nowhere for Alex to hide. He did the only thing he could, and threw himself flat on the ground, burying his face in the grass. He counted slowly to five, then looked up. Mr Grin was turning once again. A second figure had appeared ... Nadia Vole. It seemed she would be driving. She muttered something as she climbed into the front. Mr Grin grunted and nodded.

By the time Mr Grin had walked round to the passenger door, Alex was once again up and running. He reached the back of the truck just as it began to move. It was similar to trucks he had seen at the SAS camp. It could have been army surplus. The back was tall and square, covered with tarpaulin. Alex clambered on to the moving tailgate and threw himself in. He was only just in time. Even as he hit the floor, a car started up behind him, flooding the back of the truck with its headlamps. If he had waited even a few seconds more, he would have been seen.

In all, a convoy of five vehicles left Sayle Enterprises. The truck Alex was in was the last but one. As well as Mr Grin and Nadia Vole, at least a dozen uniformed guards were making the journey. But to where? Alex didn't dare look out the back, not with a car right behind him. He felt the truck slow down as they reached the main gate and then they were out on the main road, driving rapidly uphill, away from the village.

Alex felt the journey without seeing it. He was thrown across the metal floor as they sped round hairpin bends, and he only knew they had left the main road when he suddenly found himself being bounced up and down. The truck was moving more slowly. He sensed they were going downhill, following a rough track. And now he could hear something, even over the noise of the engine. Waves. They had come down to the sea.

The truck stopped. There was the opening and slamming of car doors, the scrunch of boots on rocks, low voices talking. Alex crouched down, afraid that one of the guards would throw back the tarpaulin and discover him, but the voices faded and he found himself once again alone. Cautiously, he slipped out the back. He was right. The convoy had parked on a deserted beach. Looking back, he could see a track leading down from the road which twisted up over the cliffs. Mr Grin and the others had gathered beside an old stone jetty that stretched out into the black water. He was carrying a torch. Alex saw him swing it in an arc.

Growing ever more curious, Alex crept forward and found a hiding-place behind a cluster of boulders. It seemed they were waiting for a boat. He looked at his watch. It was exactly two o'clock. He almost wanted to laugh. Give the men flintlock pistols and horses and they could have come straight out of a children's book. Smuggling on the Cornish coast. Could that be what this was all about? Cocaine or marijuana coming in from the Continent? Why else would they be here in the middle of the night?

The question was answered a few seconds later. Alex stared, unable to believe quite what he was seeing.

A submarine. It had emerged from the sea with the speed and impossibility of a huge stage illusion. One moment there was nothing and then it was there in front of him, ploughing through the sea towards the jetty, its engine making no sound, water streaking off its silver casing and churning white behind it. The submarine had no markings, but Alex thought he recognized the shape of the diving plane slashing horizontally through the conning tower and the shark's tail rudder at the back. A Chinese Han Class 404 SSN? Nuclear-powered. Armed, also, with nuclear weapons.

But what was it doing here, off the coast of Cornwall? What was going on?

The tower opened and a man climbed out, stretching himself in the cold morning air. Even without the half-moon, Alex would have recognized the sleek, dancer's body and the close-cropped hair of the man whose photograph he had seen only a few days before. It was Yassen Gregorovich. The contract killer. The man who had murdered Ian Rider. He was dressed in grey overalls. He was smiling.

Yassen Gregorovich had supposedly met Sayle in Cuba. Now here he was in Cornwall. So the two of them *were* working together. But why? Why would the Stormbreaker project need a man like him?

Nadia Vole walked to the end of the jetty and Yassen climbed down to join her. They spoke for a few minutes but, even assuming they were speaking in English, there was no chance of their being overheard. Meanwhile, the guards from Sayle Enterprises had formed a line stretching back almost to the point where the vehicles were parked. Yassen gave an order and, as Alex watched from behind the rocks, a large metallic silver box with a vacuum seal appeared, held by unseen hands, at the top of the submarine's tower. Yassen himself passed it down to the first of the guards, who then passed it back up the line. About forty more boxes followed, one after another. It took almost an hour to unload the submarine. The men handled the boxes carefully. They didn't want to break whatever was inside.

By three o'clock they were almost finished. The boxes were now being packed into the back of the truck that Alex had vacated. And that was when it happened.

One of the men standing on the jetty dropped one of the boxes. He managed to catch it again at the last minute, but even so, it banged down heavily on the stone surface. Everyone stopped. Instantly. It was as if a switch had been thrown, and Alex could almost feel the raw fear in the air.

Yassen was the first to recover. He darted forward along the jetty, moving like a cat, his feet making no sound. He reached the box and ran his hands over it, checking the seal, then nodded slowly. The metal wasn't even dented.

With everyone else so still, Alex heard the exchange that followed.

"It's OK. I'm sorry," the guard said. "It's not damaged and I won't do that again."

"No. You won't," Yassen agreed, and shot him.

The bullet spat out of his hand, red in the darkness. It hit the man in the chest, propelling him backwards in an awkward cartwheel. The man fell into the sea. For a few seconds he looked up at the moon as if trying to admire it one last time. Then the black water folded over him.

It took them another twenty minutes to load the truck. Yassen got into the front with Nadia Vole. Mr Grin went in one of the cars.

Alex had to time his return carefully. As the truck picked up speed, rumbling back up towards the road, he left the cover of the rocks, ran forward and pulled himself in. There was hardly any room, but he managed to find a hole and squeeze himself into it. He ran a hand over one of the boxes. It was about the size of a tea chest, unmarked, and cold to touch. He tried to find a way to open it, but it was locked in a way he didn't understand.

He looked back out of the truck. The beach and the jetty were already far below them. The submarine was pulling out to sea. One moment it was there, sleek and silver, gliding through the water. Then it had sunk below the surface, disappearing as quickly as a bad dream.

DEATH IN THE LONG GRASS

Alex was woken up by an indignant Nadia Vole knocking at his door. He had overslept.

"This morning it is your last opportunity to experience the Stormbreaker," she said.

"Right," Alex said.

"This afternoon we begin to send the computers out to the schools. Herr Sayle has suggested that you take the afternoon for leisure. A walk, perhaps, into Port Tallon? There is a footpath that goes through the fields and then by the sea. You will do that, yes?"

"Yes, I'd like that."

"Good. And now I leave you to put on some clothing. I will come back for you in ... *zehn Minuten*."

Alex splashed cold water on his face before getting dressed. It had been four o'clock by the time he had got back to his room and he was still tired. His night expedition hadn't been quite the success he'd hoped. He had seen so much – the submarine, the silver boxes, the death of the guard who had dared to drop one – and yet in the end he still hadn't learnt anything.

Was Yassen Gregorovich working for Herod Sayle? He had no proof that Sayle knew he was here. And what about the boxes? They could have contained packed lunches for the staff of Sayle Enterprises for all he knew. Except that you didn't kill a man for dropping a packed lunch.

Today was 31 March. As Vole had said, the computers were on their way out. There was only one day to go until the ceremony at the Science Museum. But Alex had nothing to report and the one piece of information that he had sent – Ian Rider's diagram – had also drawn a blank. There had been a reply waiting for him on the screen of his Game Boy when he turned it on before going to bed.

UNABLE TO RECOGNIZE DIAGRAM OR LETTERS/NUMBERS. POSSIBLE MAP REFERENCE BUT UNABLE TO SOURCE MAP. PLEASE TRANSMIT FURTHER OBSERVATIONS.

Alex had thought of transmitting the fact that he had actually sighted Yassen Gregorovich. But he had decided against it. If Yassen was there, Mrs Jones had promised to pull him out. And suddenly Alex wanted to see this through to the end. Something was going on at Sayle Enterprises. That much was obvious. And he'd never forgive himself if he didn't find out what it was.

Nadia Vole came back for him as promised and he spent the next three hours toying with the Stormbreaker. This time he enjoyed himself less. And this time, he noticed when he went to the door, a guard had been posted in the corridor outside. It seemed that Sayle Enterprises wasn't taking any more chances where he was concerned.

One o'clock arrived and at last the guard released him from the room and escorted him as far as the main gate. It was a glorious afternoon, the sun shining as he walked out on to the road. He took a last look back. Mr Grin had just come out of one of the buildings and was standing some distance away, talking into a mobile phone. There was something unnerving about the sight. Why should he be making a telephone call now? And who could possibly understand a word he said?

It was only once he'd left the plant that Alex was able to relax. Away from the fences, the armed guards and the strange sense of threat that pervaded Sayle Enterprises, it was as if he was breathing fresh air for the first time in days. The Cornish countryside was beautiful, the rolling hills a lush green, dotted with wild flowers.

Alex found the footpath sign and turned off the road. He had worked out that Port Tallon was a couple of miles away, a walk of less than an hour if the route wasn't too hilly. In fact, the path climbed upwards quite steeply almost at once, and suddenly Alex found himself perched over a clear, blue and sparkling English Channel, following a track that zigzagged precariously along the edge of a cliff. To one side of him fields stretched into the distance, their long grass bending in the breeze. To the other there was a fall of at least fifty metres to the rocks and water below. Port Tallon itself was at the very end of the cliffs, tucked in against the sea. It looked almost too quaint from here, like a model in a black and white Hollywood film.

He came to a break in the path, a second, much rougher track leading away from the sea and across the fields. His instincts would have told him to go straight ahead, but a footpath sign pointed to the right. There was something strange about the sign. Alex hesitated for a moment, wondering what it was. Then he dismissed it. He was walking in the countryside and the sun was shining. What could possibly be wrong? He followed the sign.

The path continued for about another quarter of a mile, then dipped down into a hollow. Here the grass was almost as tall as Alex, rising up all around him, a shimmering green cage. A bird suddenly erupted in front of him, a ball of brown feathers that spun round on itself before taking flight. Something had disturbed it. And that was when Alex heard the sound – an engine getting closer. A tractor? No. It was too high-pitched and moving too fast.

Alex knew he was in danger the same way an animal does. There was no need to ask why or how. Danger was simply there. And even as the dark shape appeared, crashing through the grass, he was throwing himself to one side, knowing – too late now – what it was that had been wrong about the second footpath sign. It had been brand new. The first sign, the one that had led him off the road, had been weather-beaten and old. Someone had deliberately led him away from the correct path and brought him here.

To the killing field.

He hit the ground and rolled into a ditch on one side. The vehicle burst through the grass, its front wheel almost touching his head. Alex caught a glimpse of a squat black thing with four fat tyres, a cross between a miniature tractor and a motorbike. It was being ridden by a hunched-up figure in grey leathers, with helmet and goggles. Then it was gone, thudding down into the grass on the other side of him and disappearing instantly, as if a curtain had been drawn.

Alex scrambled to his feet and began to run. There were two of them. He knew what they were now. He'd ridden similar things himself, on holiday, in the sand-dunes of Death Valley, Nevada. Kawasaki four-by-fours, powered by 400cc engines with automatic transmission. Quad bikes.

They were circling him like wasps. A drone, then a scream, and the second bike was in front of him, roaring towards him, cutting a swathe through the grass. Alex hurled himself out of its path, once again crashing into the ground, almost dislocating his shoulder. Wind and engine fumes whipped across his face.

He had to find somewhere to hide. But he was in the middle of a field and there was nowhere – apart from the grass itself. Desperately, he fought through it, the blades scratching at his face, half-blinding him as he tried to find his way back to the main path. He needed other people. Whoever had sent these machines (and now he remembered Mr Grin talking on his mobile phone), they couldn't kill him if there were witnesses around.

But there was no one, and they were coming for him again ... together this time. Alex could hear the engines, whining in unison, coming up fast behind him. Still running, he glanced over his shoulder and saw them, one on each side, seemingly about to overtake him. It was only the glint of the sun and the sight of the grass slicing itself in half that revealed the horrible truth. The two cyclists had stretched a length of cheesewire between them.

Alex threw himself head-first, landing flat on his stomach. The cheesewire whipped over him. If he had still been standing up, it would have cut him in half.

The quad bikes separated, arcing away from each other. At least that meant they must have dropped the wire. Alex had twisted his knee in the last fall and he knew it was only a matter of time before they cornered him and finished him off. Half limping, he ran forward, searching for somewhere to hide or something to defend himself with. Apart from some money, he had nothing in his pockets, not even a penknife. The engines were distant now, but he knew they would be closing in again at any moment. And what would it be next time? More cheesewire? Or something worse?

It was worse. Much worse. There was the roar of an engine and then a billowing cloud of red fire exploded over the grass, blazing it to a crisp. Alex felt it singe his shoulders, yelled and threw himself to one side. One of the riders was carrying a flame-thrower! He had just aimed a bolt of fire eight metres long, meaning to burn Alex alive. And he had almost succeeded. Alex was saved only by the narrow ditch he'd landed in. He hadn't even seen it until he had thudded to the ground, into the damp soil, the jet of flame licking at the air just above him. It had been close. There was a horrible smell: his own hair. The fire had singed the ends.

Choking, his face streaked with dirt and sweat, he clambered out of the ditch and ran blindly forward. He had no idea where he was going any more. He only knew that in a few seconds the quad would be back. He had taken about ten paces before he realized he had reached the edge of the field. There was a warning sign and an electrified fence stretching as far as he could see. But for the buzzing sound the fence was making, he would have run right into it. The fence was almost invisible, and the quad bikers, moving fast towards him, would be unable to hear the warning sound over their own engines...

He stopped and turned round. About fifty metres away from him, the grass was being flattened by the still invisible quad as it made its next charge. But this time Alex waited. He stood there, balancing on the heels of his feet, like a matador. Twenty metres, ten... Now he was staring straight into the goggles of the rider, saw the man's uneven teeth as he smiled, still gripping the flame-thrower. The quad smashed down the last barrier of grass and leapt onto him ... except that Alex was no longer there. He had dived to one side and, too late, the driver saw the fence and rocketed on, straight into it. The man screamed as the wire caught him around the neck, almost garrotting him. The bike twisted in mid-air, then crashed down. The man fell into the grass and lay still.

He had torn the fence out of the ground. Alex ran over to the man and examined him. For a moment he thought it might be Yassen, but it was a younger man, dark-haired, ugly. Alex had never seen him before. The man was unconscious but still breathing. The flame-thrower lay, extinguished, on the ground beside him. Behind him, he heard the other bike, some distance away but closing. Whoever these people were, they had tried to run him down, cut him in half and incinerate him. He had to find a way out before they got really serious.

He ran over to the abandoned quad, which had come to rest lying on its side. He heaved it up again, jumped onto the seat and pressed the starter. The engine sprang into life. At least there were no gears to worry about. Alex twisted the accelerator and gripped the handlebars as the machine jolted him forward.

And now he was slicing through the grass, which became a green blur as the quad carried him back towards the footpath. He couldn't hear the other bike but hoped that the rider would have no idea what had happened and so wouldn't be following him. His bones rattled as the quad hit a rut and bounced upwards. He had to be careful. Lose his concentration for a second and he would be on his back.

He cut through another green curtain and savagely pulled on the handlebars to bring himself round. He had found the footpath – and also the edge of the cliff. Just three metres more and he would have launched himself into space and down to the rocks below. For a few seconds he sat where he was, the engine idling. That was when the other quad appeared. Somehow the second rider must have guessed what had happened. He had reached the footpath and was facing Alex, about two hundred metres away. Something glinted in his hand, resting on the handlebar. He was carrying a gun.

Alex looked back the way he had walked. It was no good. The path was too narrow. By the time he had turned the quad round, the armed man would have reached him. One shot and it would all be over. Could he go back into the grass? No, for the same reason. He had to move forward, even if that meant heading for a straight-on collision with the other quad.

Why not? Maybe there was no other way.

The man gunned his engine and spurted forward. Alex did the same. Now the two of them were racing towards each other down a narrow path, a bank of earth and rock suddenly rising up to form a barrier on one side and the edge of the cliff on the other. There wasn't enough room for them to pass. They could stop or they could crash ... but if they were going to stop they had to do it in the next ten seconds.

The quads were getting closer and closer, moving faster all the time. The man couldn't shoot him now, not without losing control. Far below, the waves glittered silver, breaking against the rocks. The edge of the cliff flashed by. The noise of the other quad filled Alex's ears. The wind rushed into him, hammering at his chest and face. It was like the old-fashioned game of chicken. One of them had to stop. One of them had to get out of the way.

Three, two, one...

It was the enemy who finally broke. He was less than five metres away, so close that Alex could make out the perspiration on his forehead. Just when it seemed that a crash was inevitable, he twisted his quad and swerved off the path, up on to the embankment. At the same time, he tried to fire his gun. But he was too late. His quad was slanting, tipping over on to just two of its wheels, and the shot went wild. The man yelled out. Firing the gun had caused him to lose what little control he had left. He fought with the quad, trying to bring it back on to four wheels. It hit a rock and bounced upwards, landed briefly on the footpath, then continued over the edge of the cliff.

Alex had felt the machine rush past him, but he had seen little more than a blur. He had shuddered to a halt and turned round just in time to watch the other quad fly into the air. The man, still screaming, had managed to separate himself from the bike on the way down, but the two of them hit the water at the same moment. The quad sank a few seconds before the man.

Who had sent him? It was Nadia Vole who had suggested the walk, but it was Mr Grin who had actually seen him leave. Mr Grin had given the order – he was sure of it.

Alex took the quad all the way to the end of the path. The sun was still shining as he walked down into the little fishing village, but he couldn't enjoy it. He was angry with himself because he knew he'd made too many mistakes.

He should have been dead now, he knew. Only luck and a low-voltage electric fence had managed to keep him alive.

DOZMARY MINE

Alex walked through Port Tallon, past the Fisherman's Arms public house and up the cobbled street towards the library. It was the middle of the afternoon but the village seemed to be asleep; the boats bobbing in the harbour, the streets and pavements empty. A few seagulls wheeled lazily over the rooftops, uttering the usual mournful cries. The air smelled of salt and dead fish.

The library was red-bricked, Victorian, sitting self-importantly at the top of a hill. Alex pushed open the heavy swing-door and went into a room with a tiled, chessboard floor and about fifty shelves fanning out from a central reception area. Six or seven people were sitting at tables, working. A man in a thickly knitted jersey was reading *Fisherman's Week*. Alex went over to the reception desk. There was the inevitable sign – SILENCE PLEASE. Beneath it a smiling, round-faced woman sat reading *Crime and Punishment*.

"Can I help you?" Despite the sign, she had such a loud voice that everyone looked up when she spoke.

"Yes..."

Alex had come here because of a chance remark made by Herod Sayle. He had been talking about Ian Rider. *Spent half his time in the village. In the port, the post office, the library*. Alex had already seen the post office, another old-fashioned building near the port. He didn't think he'd learn anything there. But the library? Maybe Rider had come here looking for information. Maybe the librarian would remember him.

"I had a friend staying in the village," Alex said. "I was wondering if he came here. His name's Ian Rider."

"Rider with an I or a Y? I don't think we have any Riders at all." The woman tapped a few keys on her computer, then shook her head. "No."

"He was staying at Sayle Enterprises," Alex said. "He was about forty, thin, fair hair. He drove a BMW."

"Oh yes." The librarian smiled. "He did come here a couple of times. A nice man. Very polite. I knew he didn't come from around here. He was looking for a book—"

"Do you remember which book?"

"Of course I do. I can't always remember faces, but I never forget a book. He was interested in viruses."

"Viruses?"

"Yes. That's what I said. He wanted some information..."

A computer virus! This might change everything. A computer virus was the perfect act of sabotage: invisible and instantaneous. A single blip written into the software and every single piece of information in the Stormbreaker software could be destroyed at any time. But Herod Sayle couldn't possibly want to damage his own creation. That would make no sense at all. So maybe Alex had been wrong about him from the very start. Maybe Sayle had no idea what was really going on.

"I'm afraid I couldn't help him," the librarian continued. "This is only a small library and our grant's been cut for the third year running." She sighed. "Anyway, he said he'd get some books sent down from London. He told me he had a box at the post office..."

That made sense too. Ian Rider wouldn't have wanted information sent to Sayle Enterprises, where it could be intercepted.

"Was that the last time you saw him?" Alex asked.

"No. He came back about a week later. He must have got what he wanted because this time he wasn't looking for books about viruses. He was interested in local affairs."

"What sort of local affairs?"

"Cornish local history. Shelf CL." She pointed. "He spent an afternoon looking in one of the books and then he left. He hasn't been back since then, which is a shame. I was rather hoping he'd join the library. It would be nice to have a new member."

Local history. That wasn't going to help him. Alex thanked the librarian and made for the door. His hand was just reaching out for the handle when he remembered.

CL 475/19.

He reached into his pocket and took out the square of paper he had found in his bedroom. Sure enough, the letters were the same. CL. They weren't showing a grid reference. CL was the label on a book!

Alex went over to the shelf the librarian had shown him. Books grow old faster when they're not being read and the ones gathered here were long past retirement, leaning tiredly against one another for support. CL 475/19 – the number was printed on the spine – was called *Dozmary: The Story of Cornwall's Oldest Mine.*

He carried it over to a table, opened it and quickly skimmed through it, wondering why a history of Cornish tin should have been of interest to Ian Rider. The story it told was a familiar one.

The mine had been owned by the Dozmary family for eleven generations. In the nineteenth century there had been four hundred mines in Cornwall. By the early 1990s there were only three. Dozmary was still one of them. The price of tin had collapsed and the mine itself was almost exhausted, but there was no other work in the area and the family had continued running it even though the mine was quickly exhausting them. In 1991, Sir Rupert Dozmary, the last owner, had quietly slipped away and blown his brains out. He was buried in the local churchyard in a coffin made, it was said, of tin.

His children had closed down the mine, selling the land above it to Sayle Enterprises. The mine itself was sealed off, with several of the tunnels now underwater.

The book contained a number of old black and white photographs: pit ponies and old-fashioned lanterns. Groups of figures standing with axes and lunch boxes. Now all of them would be under the ground themselves. Flicking through the pages, Alex came to a map showing the layout of the tunnels at the time when the mine was closed.

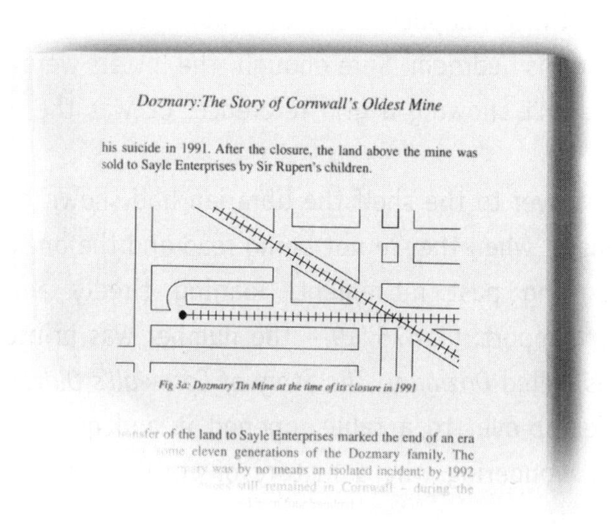

Dozmary: The Story of Cornwall's Oldest Mine

his suicide in 1991. After the closure, the land above the mine was sold to Sayle Enterprises by Sir Rupert's children.

Fig 3a: Dozmary Tin Mine at the time of its closure in 1991

...nsfer of the land to Sayle Enterprises marked the end of an era ... eleven generations of the Dozmary family. The ... was by no means an isolated incident: by 1992 ... still remained in Cornwall – during the

It was hard to be sure of the scale, but there was a labyrinth of shafts, tunnels and railway lines running for miles underground. Go down into the utter blackness of the underground and you'd be lost instantly. Had Ian Rider made his way into Dozmary? If so, what had he found?

Alex remembered the corridor at the foot of the metal staircase. The dark brown, unfinished walls and the light bulbs hanging on their wires had reminded him of something, and suddenly he knew what it was. The corridor must be nothing more than one of the tunnels from the old mine! Suppose Ian Rider had also gone down the staircase. Like Alex, he had been confronted with the locked metal door and had been determined to find his way past it. But he had recognized the corridor for what it was – and that was why he had come back to the library. He had found a book on the Dozmary Mine – this book. The map had shown him a way to the other side of the door.

And he had made a note of it!

Alex took out the diagram that Ian Rider had drawn and laid it on the page, on top of the printed map. Holding the two sheets together, he held them up to the light.

This was what he saw.

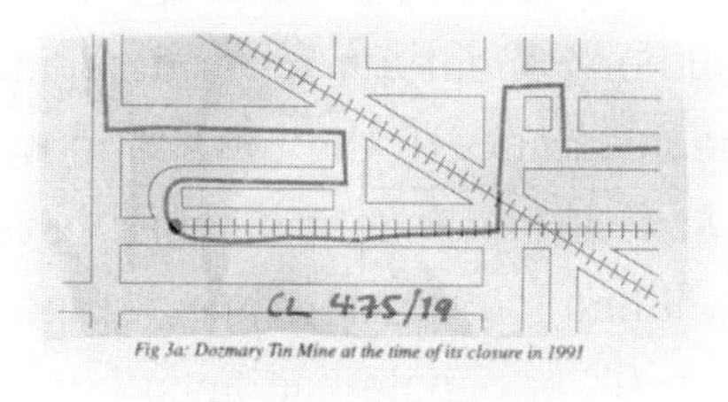

Fig 3a: Dozmary Tin Mine at the time of its closure in 1991

The lines that Rider had drawn on the sheet fitted exactly over the shafts and tunnels of the mine, showing the way through. Alex was certain of it. If he could find the entrance to Dozmary, he could follow the map through to the other side of the metal door.

Ten minutes later he left the library with a photocopy of the page. He went down to the harbour and found one of those maritime stores that seem to sell anything and everything. Here he bought himself a powerful torch, a jersey, a length of rope and a box of chalk.

Then he climbed back into the hills.

Back on the quad, Alex raced across the cliff tops with the sun already sinking in the west. Ahead of him he could see the single chimney and crumbling tower that he hoped would mark the entrance to the Kerneweck Shaft, which took its name from the ancient language of Cornwall. According to the map, this was where he should begin. At least the quad had made his life easier. It would have taken him an hour to reach it on foot.

He was running out of time and he knew it. Already the Stormbreakers would have begun leaving the plant, and in less than twenty-four hours the prime minister would be activating them. If the software really had been bugged with some sort of virus, what would happen? Some sort of humiliation for both Sayle and the British government? Or worse?

And how did a computer bug tie in with what he had seen the night before? Whatever the submarine had been delivering at the jetty, it hadn't been computer software. The silver boxes had been too large. And you don't shoot a man for dropping a diskette.

Alex parked the quad next to the tower and went in through an arched doorway. At first he thought he must have made some sort of mistake. The building looked more like a ruined church than the entrance to a mine. Other people had been here before him. There were a few crumpled beer cans and old crisp packets on the floor and the usual graffiti on the walls. JRH WAS HERE. NICK LOVES CASS. Visitors leaving the worst parts of themselves behind in fluorescent paint.

His foot came down on something that clanged and he saw that he was standing on a metal trapdoor, set into the concrete floor. Grass and weeds were sprouting round the edges, but putting his hand against the crack he could feel a draught of air rising from below. This must be the entrance to the shaft.

The trapdoor was bolted down with a heavy padlock, several centimetres thick. Alex swore under his breath. He had left the zit cream back in his room. The cream would have eaten through the bolt in seconds, but he didn't have the time to go all the way back to Sayle Enterprises to get it. He knelt down and shook the padlock in frustration. To his surprise, it swung open in his hand. Somebody had been here before him. Ian Rider – it had to be. He must have managed to unlock it, and hadn't fully closed it again so that it would be ready when he came back.

Alex pulled the padlock out and grabbed hold of the trapdoor. It took all his strength to pull it up and, as he did so, a blast of cold air hit him in the face. The trapdoor clanged back and he found himself looking into a black hole that stretched further than the daylight could reach. Alex shone his torch into the hole. The beam went about fifty metres, but the shaft went further. He found a pebble and dropped it in. At least ten seconds passed before the pebble rattled against something far below.

A rusty ladder ran down the side of the shaft. Alex checked that the quad was out of sight, then looped the rope over his shoulder and shoved the torch into his belt. He didn't enjoy climbing into the hole. The metal rungs were ice-cold against his hands, and his shoulders had barely sunk beneath the level of the ground before the light was blotted out and he felt himself being sucked into a darkness so total that he couldn't even be sure he had eyes. But he couldn't climb *and* hold on to the torch. He just had to feel his way, a hand then a foot, descending further and ever further until at last his heel struck the ground and he knew he had reached the bottom of the Kerneweck Shaft.

He looked up. He could just make out the entrance he had climbed through – small, round, as distant as the moon. Breathing heavily, trying to fight off the sense of claustrophobia, he pulled out the torch and flicked it on. The beam leapt out of his hand, pointing the way ahead and throwing pure, white light on to his immediate surroundings. Alex was at the start of a long tunnel, the uneven walls and ceiling held back by wooden beams. The floor was already damp and a sheen of salt water hung in the air. It was cold in the mine. He had known it would be and before he moved he pulled on the jersey he had bought, then chalked a large X on the wall. That had been a good idea too. Whatever happened down here, he wanted to be sure he could find the way back.

At last he was ready. He took two steps forward, away from the vertical shaft and into the start of the tunnel, and immediately felt the weight of the solid rock, soil and remaining streaks of tin bearing down on him. It was horrible here. It really was like being buried alive, and it took all his strength to force himself on. After about fifty paces he came to a second tunnel, branching off to the left. He took out the photocopied map and examined it in the torchlight. According to Ian Rider, this was where he had to turn off. He swung the torch round and followed the tunnel, which slanted downwards, taking him deeper and deeper into the earth.

There was absolutely no sound in the mine apart from his own rasping breath, the crunch of his footsteps and the quickening thud of his heart. It was as if the blackness was wiping out sound as well as vision. Alex opened his mouth and called out, just to hear something. But his voice sounded small and only reminded him of the huge weight above his head. This tunnel was in bad repair. Some of the beams had snapped and fallen in and, as he passed, a trickle of gravel hit his neck and shoulders, reminding him that the Dozmary mine had been kept locked for a reason. It was a hellish place. It could collapse at any time.

The path took him ever deeper. He could feel the pressure pounding in his ears and the darkness seemed even thicker and more oppressive. He came to a tangle of iron and wire, some sort of machine long ago buried and forgotten. He climbed over it too quickly, cutting his leg on a piece of jagged metal. He stood still for a few seconds, forcing himself to slow down. He knew he couldn't panic. *If you panic, you'll get lost. Think what you're doing. Be careful. One step at a time.*

"OK. OK..." He whispered the words to reassure himself, then continued forward.

Now he emerged into a sort of wide, circular chamber, formed by the meeting of six different tunnels, all coming together in a star shape. The widest of these slanted in from the left with the remains of a railway track. He swung the torch and picked out a couple of wooden wagons which must have been used to carry equipment down or tin back up to the surface. Checking the maps, he was tempted to follow the railway, which seemed to offer a short cut across the route that Ian Rider had drawn. But he decided against it. His uncle had turned the corner and gone back on himself. There had to be a reason. Alex made another two chalk crosses, one for the tunnel he had left, another for the one he was entering. He went on.

This new tunnel quickly became lower and narrower until Alex couldn't walk unless he crouched. The floor was very wet here, with pools of water reaching his ankles. He remembered how near he was to the sea and that brought another unpleasant thought. What time was high tide? And when the water rose, what would happen inside the mine? Alex suddenly had a vision of himself trapped in blackness with the water rising up his chest, his neck, over his face. He stopped and forced himself to think of something else. Down here, on his own, far beneath the surface of the earth, he couldn't make an enemy of his imagination.

The tunnel curved, then joined a second railway line, this one bent and broken, covered here and there in rubble which must have fallen from above. But the metal tracks made it easier to move forward, picking up and reflecting the torch. Alex followed them all the way to a junction with the main railway. It had taken him thirty minutes and he was almost back where he had started but, shining the torch around him, he saw why Ian Rider had sent him the long way round. There had been a tunnel collapse. About thirty metres up the line, the main railway was blocked.

He crossed the tracks, still following the maps, and stopped. He looked at the paper, then again at the way ahead. It was impossible. And yet there was no mistake.

He had come to a small, round tunnel dipping steeply down. But after ten metres the tunnel simply stopped, with what looked like a sheet of metal barring the way. Alex picked up a stone and threw it. There was a splash. Now he understood. The tunnel was completely submerged in water as black as ink. The water had risen up to the ceiling of the tunnel so that, even assuming he could swim in temperatures that must be close to zero, he would be unable to breathe. After all his hard work, after all the time he had spent underground, there was no way forward.

Alex turned. He was about to leave, but even as he swung the torch round, the beam picked up something lying in a heap on the ground. He went over to it and leant down. It was a diver's dry suit and it looked brand new. Alex walked back to the water's edge and examined it with the torch. This time he saw something else. A rope had been tied to a rock. It slanted diagonally into the water and disappeared. Alex knew what it meant.

Ian Rider had swum through the submerged tunnel. He had worn a dry suit and he had managed to fix a rope to guide him through. Obviously he had planned to come back. That was why he had left the padlock open. It seemed that once again Alex had been helped by the dead man. The question was, did he have the nerve to go on?

He picked up the dry suit. It was too big for him, although it would probably keep out the worst of the chill. But the cold wasn't the only problem. The tunnel might run for ten metres. It might run for a hundred. How could he be sure that Ian Rider hadn't used scuba equipment to swim through? If Alex went down there, into the water, and ran out of breath halfway, he would drown. Pinned underneath the rock in the freezing blackness. He couldn't imagine a worse way to die.

But he had come so far, and according to the map he was nearly there. Alex swore. This was not fun. At that moment he wished he had never heard of Alan Blunt, Sayle Enterprises or the Stormbreaker. But he couldn't go back. If his uncle had done it, so could he. Gritting his teeth, he pulled on the dry suit. It was cold, clammy and uncomfortable. He zipped it up. He hadn't taken off his ordinary clothes and perhaps that helped. The suit was loose in places, but he was sure it would keep the water out.

Moving quickly now, afraid that if he hesitated he would change his mind, Alex approached the water's edge. He reached out and took the rope in one hand. It would be faster swimming with both hands, but he didn't dare risk it. Getting lost in the underwater tunnel would be as bad as running out of air. The result would be exactly the same. He had to keep hold of the rope to allow it to guide him through. Alex took several deep breaths, hyperventilating and oxygenating his blood, knowing it would give him a few precious extra seconds. Then he plunged in.

The cold was ferocious, a hammer blow that nearly forced the air out of his lungs. The water pounded at his head, swirling round his nose and eyes. His fingers were instantly numb. His whole system felt the shock, but the dry suit was holding, sealing in at least some of his body warmth. Clinging to the rope, he kicked forward. He had committed himself. There could be no going back.

Pull, kick. Pull, kick. Alex had been underwater for less than a minute but already his lungs were feeling the strain. The roof of the tunnel was scraping his shoulders and he was afraid that it would tear through the dry suit and gouge his skin as well. But he didn't dare slow down. The freezing cold was sucking the strength out of him. Pull and kick. Pull and kick. How long had he been under? Ninety seconds? A hundred? His eyes were tight shut, but if he opened them there would be no difference. He was in a black, swirling, freezing version of hell. And his breath was running out.

He pulled himself forward along the rope, burning the skin off the palms of his hands. He must have been swimming for almost two minutes. It felt closer to ten. He *had* to open his mouth and breathe, even if it was water that would rush into his throat... A silent scream exploded inside him. Pull, kick. Pull, kick. And then the rope tilted upwards and he felt his shoulders come clear, and his mouth was wrenched open in a great gasp as he breathed air and knew that he had made it, perhaps with only seconds to spare.

But made it to where?

Alex couldn't see anything. He was floating in utter darkness, unable to see even where the water ended. He had left the torch at the other side, but he knew that even if he wanted to he didn't have the strength to go back. He had followed the trail left by a dead man. It was only now that he realized it might lead only to the grave.

BEHIND THE DOOR

Alex swam slowly forward, completely blind, afraid that at any moment he would crack his skull against rock. Despite the dry suit, he was beginning to feel the chill of the water and knew that he had to find his way out soon. His hand brushed against something but his fingers were too numb to tell what it was. He reached out and pulled himself forward. His feet touched the bottom. And it was then that he realized. He could see. Somehow, from somewhere, light was seeping into the area beyond the submerged tunnel.

Slowly, his vision adjusted itself. Waving his hand in front of his face, he could just make out his fingers. He was holding on to a wooden beam, a collapsed roof support. He closed his eyes, then opened them again. The darkness had retreated, showing him a crossroads cut into the rock, the meeting place of three tunnels. The fourth, behind him, was the one that was flooded. As vague as the light was, it gave him strength. Using the beam as a makeshift jetty, he clambered on to the rock. At the same time, he became aware of a soft throbbing sound. He couldn't be sure if it was near or far, but he remembered what he had heard under Block D, in front of the metal door, and he knew that he had arrived.

He stripped off the dry suit. Fortunately, it had kept the water out. The main part of his body was dry, but ice-cold water was still dripping out of his hair, down his neck, and his trainers and socks were sodden. When he moved forward his feet squelched and he had to take his trainers off and shake them out before he could go on. Ian Rider's map was still folded in his pocket, but he no longer had any need of it. All he had to do was follow the light.

He went straight forward to another intersection, then turned right. The light was so bright now that he could actually make out the colour of the rock – dark brown and grey. The throbbing was also getting louder and Alex could feel a rush of warm air streaming down towards him. He moved forward cautiously, wondering what he was about to come to. He turned a corner and suddenly the rock on both sides gave way to new brick, with metal grilles set at intervals just above the level of the floor. The old mine shaft had been converted. It was being used as the outlet for some sort of air-conditioning system. The light that had guided Alex was coming out of the grilles.

He knelt beside the first of these and looked through into a large, white-tiled room, a laboratory with complicated glass and steel equipment laid out over work surfaces. The room was empty. Tentatively, Alex took hold of the grille, but it was firmly secured, bolted into the rock face. The second grille belonged to the same room. It was also screwed on tight. Alex continued up the tunnel to a third grille. This one looked into a storage room filled with the silver boxes that Alex had seen being delivered by the submarine the night before.

He took the grille in both hands and pulled. It came away from the rock easily, and looking closer he understood why. Ian Rider had been here ahead of him. He had cut through the bolts which had held it in place. Alex set the grille down silently. He felt sad. Ian Rider had found his way through the mine, drawn the map, swum through the submerged tunnel and opened the grille all on his own. Alex wouldn't have got nearly as far as this without his help, and he wished now that he had known his uncle a little better and perhaps admired him a little more before he died.

Carefully, he began to squeeze through the rectangular hole and lower himself into the room. At the last minute – lying on his stomach with his feet dangling below – he reached for the grille and set it back in place. Provided nobody looked too closely, they wouldn't see anything wrong. He dropped down to the ground and landed, catlike, on the balls of his feet. The throbbing was louder now, coming from somewhere outside. It would cover any noise he made. He went over to the nearest of the silver boxes and examined it. This time it clicked open in his hands, but when he looked inside it was empty. Whatever had been delivered was already in use.

He checked for cameras, then crossed to the door. It was unlocked. He opened it, one centimetre at a time, and peered out. The door led on to a wide corridor with an automatic sliding door at each end and a silver handrail running its full length.

"Nineteen hundred hours. Red shift to assembly line. Blue shift to decontamination."

The voice rang out over a loudspeaker system, neither male nor female; emotionless, inhuman. Alex glanced at his watch. It was already seven o'clock in the evening. It had taken him longer than he'd thought to get through the mine. He stole forward. It wasn't exactly a passage that he had found. It was more an observation platform. He reached the rail and looked down.

Alex hadn't had any idea what he would find behind the metal door, but what he was seeing now was far beyond anything he could have imagined. It was a huge chamber, the walls – half naked rock, half polished steel – lined with computer equipment, electronic meters, machines that blinked and flickered with a life of their own. It was staffed by forty or fifty people, some in white coats, others in overalls, all wearing armbands of different colours: red, yellow, blue and green. Arc lights beamed down from above. Armed guards stood at each doorway, watching the work with blank faces.

For this was where the Stormbreakers were being assembled. The computers were being slowly carried in a long, continuous line along a conveyor-belt, past the various scientists and technicians. The strange thing was that they already looked finished ... and, of course, they had to be. Sayle had told him. They were actually being shipped out during the course of that afternoon and night. So what last-minute adjustment was being made here in this secret factory? And why was so much of the production line hidden away? What Alex had seen on his tour of Sayle Enterprises had only been the tip of the iceberg. The main body of the factory was here, underground.

He looked more closely. He remembered the Stormbreaker that he had used, and now he noticed something that he hadn't seen then. A strip of plastic had been drawn back in the casing above each of the screens to reveal a small compartment, cylindrical and about five centimetres deep. The computers were passing underneath a bizarre machine – cantilevers, wires and hydraulic arms. Opaque silver test tubes were being fed along a narrow cage, moving forward as if to greet the computers: one tube for each computer. There was a meeting point. With infinite precision, the tubes were lifted out, brought round and then dropped into the exposed compartments. After that, the Stormbreakers were accelerated forward. A second machine closed and heat-sealed the plastic strips. By the time the computers reached the end of the line, where they were packed into red and white Sayle Enterprises boxes, the compartments were completely invisible.

A movement caught his eye and Alex looked beyond the assembly line and through a huge window into the chamber next door. Two men in space suits were walking clumsily together, as if in slow motion. They stopped. An alarm began to sound and suddenly they disappeared in a cloud of white steam. Alex remembered what he had just heard. Were they being decontaminated? But if the Stormbreaker was based on the round processor there couldn't possibly be any need for such an extreme – and anyway, this was like nothing Alex had ever seen before. If the men *were* being decontaminated, what were they being decontaminated from?

"Agent Gregorovich report to the Biocontainment Zone. This is a call for Agent Gregorovich."

A lean, fair-haired figure dressed in black detached himself from the assembly line and walked languidly towards a door that slid open to receive him. For the second time Alex found himself looking at the Russian contract killer, Yassen Gregorovich. What was going on? Alex thought back to the submarine and the vacuum-sealed boxes. Of course. Yassen had brought the test tubes that were even now being inserted into the computers. The test tubes were some sort of weapon that he was using to sabotage them. No. That wasn't possible. Back in Port Tallon, the librarian had told him that Ian Rider had been asking for books about computer viruses...

Viruses.

Decontamination.

The Biocontainment Zone...

Understanding came – and with it, something cold and solid jabbing into the back of his neck. Alex hadn't even heard the door open behind him, but he slowly stiffened as a voice spoke softly into his ear.

"Stand up. Keep your hands by your sides. If you make any sudden moves, I'll shoot you in the head."

He looked slowly round. A single guard stood behind him, a gun in his hand. It was the sort of thing Alex had seen a thousand times in films and on television, and he was shocked by how different the reality was. The gun was a Browning automatic pistol and one twitch of the guard's finger would send a 9mm bullet shattering through his skull and into his brain. The very touch of it made him feel sick.

He stood up. The guard was in his twenties, pale-faced and puzzled. Alex had never seen him before – but more importantly, he had never seen Alex. He hadn't expected to come across a boy. That might help.

"Who are you?" he asked. "What are you doing here?"

"I'm staying with Mr Sayle," Alex said. He stared at the gun. "Why are you pointing that at me? I'm not doing anything wrong."

He sounded pathetic. Little boy lost. But it had the desired effect. The guard hesitated, slightly lowering the gun. At that moment Alex struck. It was another classic karate blow, this time twisting his body round and driving his elbow into the side of the guard's head, just below his ear. He had almost certainly knocked him out with the single punch, but he couldn't take chances and followed it through with a knee to the groin. The guard folded up, his pistol falling to the ground. Quickly, Alex dragged him back, away from the railing. He looked down. Nobody had seen what had happened.

But the guard wouldn't be unconscious long and Alex knew he had to get out of there – not just back up to ground level but out of Sayle Enterprises itself. He had to contact Mrs Jones. He still didn't know how or why, but he knew now that the Stormbreakers had been turned into killing machines. There were less than seventeen hours until the launch at the Science Museum. Somehow Alex had to stop it from happening.

He ran. The door at the end of the passage slid open and he found himself in a curving white corridor with windowless offices built into what must be yet more shafts of the Dozmary Mine. He knew he couldn't go back the way he had come. He was too tired and, even if he could find his way through the mine, he'd never be able to manage the swim a second time. His only chance was the door that had first led him here. It led to the metal staircase that would bring him to Block D. There was a telephone in his room. Failing that, he could use the Game Boy to transmit a message. But MI6 had to know what he had found out.

He reached the end of the corridor, then ducked back as three guards appeared, walking together towards a set of double doors. Fortunately they hadn't seen him. Nobody knew he was there. He was going to be all right.

And then the alarm went off. A klaxon barking electronically along the corridors, leaping out from the corners, echoing everywhere. Overhead, a light began to flash red. The guards wheeled round and saw Alex. Unlike the guard on the observation platform, they didn't hesitate. As Alex dived head-first through the nearest door, they brought up their machine guns and fired. Bullets slammed into the wall beside him and ricocheted along the passageway. Alex landed flat on his stomach and kicked out, slamming the door behind him. He straightened up, found a bolt and rammed it home. A second later there was an explosive hammering on the other side as the guards fired at the door. But it was solid metal. It would hold.

He was standing on a gantry leading down to a tangle of pipes and cylinders, like the boiler room of a ship. The alarm was as loud here as it had been by the main chamber. It seemed to be coming from everywhere. Alex leapt down the staircase three steps at a time and skidded to a halt, searching for a way out. He had a choice of three corridors, but then he heard the rattle of feet and knew that his choice had just become two. He wished now that he had thought to pick up the Browning automatic. He was alone and unarmed. The only duck in the shooting gallery, with guns everywhere and no way out. Was this what MI6 had trained him for? If so, eleven days hadn't been enough.

He ran on, weaving in and out of the pipes, trying every door he came to. A room with more space suits hanging on hooks. A shower room. Another, larger laboratory with a second door leading out and, in the middle, a glass tank shaped like a barrel and filled with green liquid. Tangles of rubber tubing sprouting out of the tank. Trays filled with test tubes all around.

The barrel-shaped tank. The trays. Alex had seen them before – as vague outlines on his Game Boy. He must have been standing on the other side of the second door. He ran over to it. It was locked from the inside, electronically, by the glass identification plate against the wall. He would never be able to open it. He was trapped.

Footsteps approached. Alex just had time to hide himself on the floor, underneath one of the work surfaces, before the first door was thrown open and two more guards ran into the laboratory. They took a quick look around – without seeing him.

"Not here!" one of them said.

"You'd better go up!"

One guard walked out the way he had come. The other went over to the second door and placed his hand on the glass panel. There was a green glow and the door buzzed loudly. The guard threw it open and disappeared. Alex rolled forward as the door swung shut and just managed to get his hand into the crack. He waited a moment, then stood up. He pulled the door open. As he had hoped, he was looking out into the unfinished passageway where he had been surprised by Nadia Vole.

The guard had already gone on ahead. Alex slipped out, closing the door behind him, cutting off the sound of the klaxon. He made his way up the metal stairs and through a swing-door. He was grateful to find himself back in the fresh air. The sun had already set, but across the lawn the airstrip was ablaze, artificially illuminated by the sort of lights Alex had seen on football pitches. There were about a dozen lorries parked next to each other. Men were loading them up with heavy, square, red and white boxes. The cargo plane that Alex had seen when he arrived rumbled down the runway and lurched into the air.

Alex knew that he was looking at the end of the assembly line. The red and white boxes were the same ones he had seen in the underground chamber. The Stormbreakers, complete with their deadly secret, were being loaded up and delivered. By morning they would be all over the country.

Keeping low, he ran past the fountain and across the grass. He thought about making for the main gate, but he knew that was hopeless. The guards would have been alerted. They'd be waiting for him. Nor could he climb the perimeter fence, not with the razor wire stretched out across the top. No. His own room seemed the best answer. The telephone was there. And so were his only weapons: the few gadgets that Smithers had given him four days – or was it four years? – ago.

He entered the house through the kitchen, the same way he had left it the night before. It was only eight o'clock, but the whole place seemed to be deserted. He ran up the staircase and along the corridor to his room on the first floor. Slowly, he opened the door. It seemed his luck was holding out. There was nobody there. Without turning on the light, he went inside and snatched up the telephone. The line was dead. Never mind. He found his Game Boy, all four cartridges, his yo-yo and the zit cream and crammed them into his pockets. He had already decided not to stay there. It was too dangerous. He would find somewhere to hide out. Then he would use the Nemesis cartridge to contact MI6.

He went back to the door and opened it. With a shock he saw Mr Grin standing in the hallway, looking hideous with his white face, his ginger hair and his mauve, twisted smile. Alex reacted quickly, striking out with the heel of his right hand. But Mr Grin was quicker. He seemed to shimmy to one side, then his hand shot out, the side of it driving into Alex's throat. Alex gasped for breath but no breath came. The butler made an inarticulate sound and lashed out a second time. Alex got the impression that behind the livid scars he really was grinning, enjoying himself. He tried to avoid the blow, but Mr Grin's fist hit him square on the jaw. He was spun into the bedroom, falling backwards.

He never even remembered hitting the floor.

THE SCHOOL BULLY

They came for Alex the following morning.

He had spent the night handcuffed to a radiator in a small, dark room with a single barred window. It might once have been a coal cellar. When Alex opened his eyes, the grey, first light of the morning was just creeping in. He closed them and opened them again. His head was thumping and the side of his face was swollen where Mr Grin had hit him. His arms were twisted behind him and the tendons in his shoulders were on fire. But worse than all this was his sense of failure. It was 1 April, the day when the Stormbreakers would be unleashed. And Alex was helpless. He was the April fool.

It was just before nine o'clock when the door opened and two guards came in with Mr Grin behind them. The handcuffs were unlocked and Alex was forced to his feet. Then, with a guard holding him on each side, he was marched out of the room and up a flight of stairs. He was still in Sayle's house. The stairs led to the hall with its huge painting of Judgement Day. Alex looked at the figures, writhing in agony on the canvas. If he was right, the image would soon be repeated all over England. And it would happen in just three hours' time.

The guards half-dragged him through a doorway and into the room with the aquarium. There was a high-backed wooden chair in front of it. Alex was forced to sit down. His hands were cuffed behind him again. The guards left. Mr Grin remained.

He heard the sound of feet on the spiral staircase, saw the leather shoes coming down before he saw the man who wore them. Then Herod Sayle appeared, dressed in an immaculate pale grey silk suit. Blunt and the people at MI6 had been suspicious of the Middle-Eastern multimillionaire from the very start. They'd always thought he had something to hide. But even they had never guessed the truth. He wasn't a friend of Alex's country. He was its worst enemy.

"Three questions," Sayle snapped. His voice was utterly cold. "Who are you? Who sent you here? How much do you know?"

"I don't know what you're talking about," Alex said.

Sayle sighed. If there had been anything comical about him when Alex had first seen him, it had completely evaporated. His face was bored and businesslike. His eyes were ugly, full of menace. "We have very little time," he said. "Mr Grin...?"

Mr Grin went over to one of the display cases and took out a knife, razor-sharp with a serrated edge. He held it up close to his face, his eyes gleaming.

"I've already told you that Mr Grin used to be an expert with knives," Sayle continued. "He still is. Tell me what I want to know, Alex, or he will cause you more pain than you could begin to imagine. And don't try to lie to me, please. Just remember what happens to liars. Particularly to their tongues."

Mr Grin took a step closer. The blade flashed, catching the light.

"My name is Alex Rider," Alex said.

"Rider's son?"

"His nephew."

"Who sent you here?"

"The same people who sent him." There was no point lying. It didn't matter any more. The stakes had become too high.

"MI6?" Sayle laughed without any sign of humour. "They send fourteen-year-old boys to do their dirty work? Not very English, I'd have said. Not cricket, what?" He had adopted an exaggerated English accent. Now he walked forward and sat down behind the desk. "And what of my third question, Alex? How much have you found out?"

Alex shrugged, trying to look casual to hide the fear he was really feeling. "I know enough," he said.

"Go on."

Alex took a breath. Behind him, the jellyfish drifted past like a poisonous cloud. He could see it out of the corner of his eye. He tugged at the handcuffs, wondering if it would be possible to break the chair. There was a sudden flash and the knife that Mr Grin had been holding was suddenly quivering in the back of the chair, a hair's breadth from his head. The edge of the blade had actually nicked the skin of his neck. He felt a trickle of blood slide down over his collar.

"You're keeping us waiting," Herod Sayle said.

"All right. When my uncle was here, he got interested in viruses. He asked about them at the local library. I thought he was talking about computer viruses. That was the natural assumption. But I was wrong. I saw what you were doing last night. I heard them talking on the speaker system. Decontamination and Biocontainment Zones.

They were talking about biological warfare. You've got hold of some sort of real virus. It came here in test tubes, packed into silver boxes, and you've put them into the Stormbreakers. I don't know what happens next. I suppose when the computers are turned on, people die. They're in schools, so it'll be schoolchildren. Which means you're not the saint everyone thinks you are, Mr Sayle. A mass-murderer. A *bliddy* psycho, I suppose you might say."

Herod Sayle clapped his hands softly together. "You've done very well, Alex," he said. "I congratulate you. And I feel you deserve a reward. So I'm going to tell you everything. In a way it's appropriate that MI6 should have sent me a real English schoolboy. Because, you see, there's nothing in the world I hate more. Oh yes..." His face twisted with anger and for a moment Alex could see the madness alive in his eyes. "You *bliddy* snobs with your stuck-up schools and your stinking English superiority! But I'm going to show you. I'm going to show you all!"

He stood up and walked over to Alex. "I came to this country forty years ago," he said. "I had no money. My family had nothing. But for a freak accident, I would probably have lived and died in Beirut. Better for you if I had! So much better!

"I was sent here by an American family, to be educated. They had friends in north London and I stayed with them while I went to the local school. You cannot imagine how I was feeling then. To be in London, which I had always believed to be the heart of civilization. To see such wealth and to know that I was going to be part of it! I was going to be English! To a child born in a Lebanese gutter, it was an impossible dream.

"But I was soon to learn the reality..." Sayle leant forward and yanked the knife out of the chair. He tossed it to Mr Grin, who caught it and spun it in his hand.

"From the moment I arrived at the school, I was mocked and

bullied. Because of my size. Because of the colour of my skin. Because I couldn't speak English well. Because I wasn't one of them. They had names for me. Herod Smell. Goat-boy. The Dwarf. And they played tricks on me. Drawing-pins on my chair. Books stolen and defaced. My trousers ripped off me and hung out on the flagpole, underneath the Union Jack." Sayle shook his head slowly. "I had loved that flag when I first came here," he said. "But in only weeks I came to hate it."

"Lots of people are bullied at school—" Alex began – and stopped as Sayle back-handed him viciously across the face.

"I haven't finished," he said. He was breathing heavily and there was spittle on his lower lip. Alex could see him reliving the past. And once again he was allowing the past to destroy him.

"There were plenty of bullies in that school," he said. "But there was one who was worse than any of them. He was a small, smarmy shrimp of a boy, but his parents were rich and he had a way with the other children. He knew how to talk his way around them ... a politician even then. Oh yes. He could be charming when he wanted to be. When there were teachers around. But the moment their backs were turned, he was on to me. He used to organize the others. *Let's get the Goat-boy. Let's push his head in the toilet.* He had a thousand ideas to make my life miserable and he never stopped thinking up more. All the time he goaded me and taunted me and there was nothing I could do because he was popular and I was a foreigner. And do you know who that boy grew up to be?"

"I think you're going to tell me anyway," Alex said.

"I *am* going to tell you. Yes. He grew up to be the *bliddy* prime minister!"

Sayle took out a white silk handkerchief and wiped his face. His bald head was gleaming with sweat. "All my life I've been treated the same way," he continued. "No matter how successful I've become, how much money I've made, how many people I've employed. I'm still a joke. I'm still Herod Smell, the Goat-boy, the Lebanese tramp. Well, for forty years I've been planning my revenge. And now, at last, my time has come. Mr Grin..."

Mr Grin went over to the wall and pressed a button. Alex half-expected the snooker table to rise out of the floor, but instead a panel slid up on every wall to reveal floor-to-ceiling television screens which immediately flickered into life. On one screen Alex could see the underground laboratory, on another the assembly line, on a third the airstrip with the last of the lorries on its way out. There were closed circuit television cameras everywhere and Sayle could see every corner of his kingdom without even leaving the room. No wonder Alex had been discovered so easily.

"The Stormbreakers are armed and ready. And yes, you're right, Alex. Each one contains what you might call a computer virus. But that, if you like, is my little April fools' joke. Because the virus I'm talking about is a form of smallpox. Of course, Alex, it's been genetically modified to make it faster and stronger ... more lethal. A spoonful of the stuff would destroy a city. And my Stormbreakers hold much, much more than that.

"At the moment it's isolated, quite safe. But this afternoon there's going to be a bit of a party at the Science Museum. Every school in Britain will be joining in, with the schoolchildren gathered round their nice, shiny new computers. And at midday, on the stroke of twelve, my old friend the prime minister will make one of his smug, self-serving speeches and then he'll press a button. He thinks he'll be activating the computers and in a way he's right. Pressing the button will release the virus and by midnight tonight there will be no more schoolchildren in Britain, and the prime minister will weep as he remembers the day he first bullied Herod Sayle!"

"You're mad!" Alex exclaimed. "By midnight tonight you'll be in jail."

Sayle dismissed the thought with a wave of the hand. "I think not. By the time anyone realizes what has happened, I'll be gone. I'm not alone in this, Alex. I have powerful friends who have supported me—"

"Yassen Gregorovich."

"You *have* been busy!" He seemed surprised that Alex knew the name. "Yassen is working for the people who have been helping me. Let's not mention any names or even nationalities. You'd be surprised how many countries there are in the world who loathe the English. Most of Europe, just to begin with. But anyway..." He clapped his hands and went back to his desk. "Now you know the truth. I'm glad I was able to tell you, Alex. You have no idea how much I loathe you. Even when you were playing that stupid game with me, the snooker, I was thinking how much pleasure it would give me to kill you. You're just like the boys I was at school with. Nothing has changed."

"You haven't changed," Alex said. His cheek was still smarting where Sayle had hit him. But he'd heard enough. "I'm sorry you were bullied at school," he said. "But lots of kids get bullied and they don't turn into nutcases. You're really sad, Mr Sayle. And your plan won't work. I've told MI6 everything I know. They'll be waiting for you at the Science Museum. So will the men in white coats."

Sayle giggled. "Forgive me if I don't believe you," he said. His face was suddenly stone. "And perhaps you forget that I warned you about lying to me."

Mr Grin took a step forward, flipping the knife over so that the blade landed in the flat of his hand.

"I'd like to watch you die," Sayle said. "Unfortunately, I have a pressing engagement in London." He turned to Mr Grin. "You can walk with me to the helicopter. Then come back here and kill the boy. Make it slow. Make it painful. We should have kept back some smallpox for him – but I'm sure you'll think of something much more creative."

He walked to the door, then stopped and turned to Alex.

"Goodbye, Alex. It wasn't a pleasure knowing you. But enjoy your death. And remember, you're only going to be the first..."

The door swung shut. Handcuffed to the chair with the jellyfish floating silently behind him, Alex was left alone.

DEEP WATER

Alex gave up trying to break free of the chair. His wrists were bruised and bloody where the chain had cut into him, and the cuffs were too tight. After thirty minutes, when Mr Grin still hadn't come back, he'd tried to reach the zit cream that Smithers had given him. He knew it would burn through the handcuffs in seconds and the worst thing was, he could actually feel it, where he had put it, in the zipped-up outer pocket of his combat trousers. But although his outstretched fingers were only a few centimetres away, try as he might, he couldn't reach it. It was enough to drive him mad.

He had heard the clatter of a helicopter taking off and knew that Herod Sayle must be on his way to London. Alex was still reeling from what he had heard. The multimillionaire was completely insane. What he was planning was beyond belief, a mass-murder that would destroy Britain for generations to come.

Alex tried to imagine what was about to happen. Tens of thousands of schoolchildren would be sitting in their classes, gathered round their new Stormbreakers, waiting for the moment – at midday exactly – when the prime minister would press his button and bring them on-line. But instead there would be a hiss and a small cloud of deadly smallpox vapour would be released into the crowded room. And minutes later, all over the country, the dying would begin. Alex had to close his mind to the thought. It was too horrible. And yet it was going to happen in just a couple of hours' time. He was the only person who could stop it. And here he was, tied down, unable to move.

The door opened. Alex twisted round, expecting to see Mr Grin, but it was Nadia Vole who hurried in, closing the door behind her. Her pale round face seemed flushed and her eyes, behind the glasses, were afraid. She came over to him.

"Alex!"

"What do you want?" Alex recoiled away from her as she leant over him. Then there was a click and, to his astonishment, his hands came free. She had unlocked the handcuffs! He stood up, wondering what was going on.

"Alex, listen to me," Vole said. The words were tumbling quickly and softly out of her yellow-painted lips. "We do not have much time. I am here to help you. I worked with your uncle – Herr Ian Rider." Alex stared at her in surprise. "Yes. I am on the same side as you."

"But nobody told me—"

"It was better for you not to know."

"But..." Alex was confused. "I saw you with the submarine. You knew what Sayle was doing..."

"There was nothing I could do. Not then. It's too hard to explain. We do not have time to argue. You want to stop him – no?"

"I need to find a phone."

"All the phones in the house are coded. You cannot use them. But I have a mobile in my office."

"Then let's go."

Alex was still suspicious. If Nadia Vole had known so much, why hadn't she tried to stop Sayle before? On the other hand, she had released him – and Mr Grin would be back any minute. He had no choice but to trust her. He followed her out of the room, round the corner and up a flight of stairs to a landing with a statue of a naked woman, some Greek goddess, in the corner. Vole paused for a moment, resting her hand against the statue's arm.

"What is it?" Alex asked.

"I feel dizzy. You go on. It's the first door on the left."

Alex went past her, along the landing. Out of the corner of his eye he saw her press down on the statue's arm. The arm moved ... a lever. By the time he knew he had been tricked, it was too late. He yelled out as the floor underneath him swung round on a hidden pivot. He tried to stop himself falling, but there was nothing he could do. He crashed onto his back and slid down, through the floor and into a black plastic tunnel which corkscrewed beneath him. As he went, he heard Nadia Vole laugh triumphantly – and then he was gone, desperately trying to find a purchase on the sides, wondering what would be at the end of his fall.

Five seconds later he found out. The corkscrew spat him out. He fell briefly through the air and splashed into cold water. For a moment he was blinded, fighting for air. Then he rose to the surface and found himself in a huge glass tank filled with water and rocks. That was when he realized, with horror, exactly where he was.

Vole had deposited him in the tank with the giant jellyfish: Herod Sayle's Portuguese man-o'-war. It was a miracle that he hadn't crashed right into it. He could see it in the far corner of the tank, its dreadful tentacles with their hundreds of stinging cells, twisting and spiralling in the water. There was nothing between him and it. Alex fought back the panic, forced himself to keep still. He realized that thrashing about in the water would only create the current that would bring the creature over to him. The jellyfish had no eyes. It didn't know he was there. It wouldn't ... couldn't attack.

But eventually it would reach him. The tank he was in was huge, at least ten metres deep and twenty or thirty metres long. The glass rose above the level of the water, far out of his reach. There was no way he could climb out. Looking down through the water, he could see light. He realized he was looking into the room he had just left, Herod Sayle's private office. There was a movement – everything was vague and distorted through the rippling water – and the door opened. Two figures walked in. Alex could barely make them out, but he knew who they were. Fräulein Vole and Mr Grin. They stood together in front of the tank. Vole was holding what looked like a mobile telephone in her hand.

"I hope you can hear me, Alex." The German woman's voice rang out from a speaker somewhere above his head. "I am sure you will have seen by now that there is no way out of the tank. You can tread water. Maybe for one hour, maybe for two. Others have lasted for longer. What is the record, Mr Grin?"

"Ire naaargh!"

"Five and a half hours. Yes. But soon you will get tired, Alex. You will drown. Or perhaps it will be fast and you will drift into the embrace of our friend. You see him ... no? It is not an embrace to be desired. It will kill you. The pain, I think, will be beyond the imagination of a child. It is a pity, Alex Rider, that MI6 chose to send you here. They will not be seeing you again."

The voice clicked off. Alex kicked in the water, keeping his head above the surface, his eyes fixed on the jellyfish. There was another blurred movement on the other side of the glass. Mr Grin had left the room. But Vole had stayed behind. She wanted to watch him die.

Alex looked up. The tank was lit from above by a series of neon strips, but they were too high to reach. Beneath him he heard a click and a soft, whirring sound. Almost at once he became aware that something had changed. The jellyfish was moving! He could see the translucent cone, with its dark mauve tip, heading towards him. Underneath the creature, the tentacles slowly danced.

He swallowed water and realized he had opened his mouth to cry out. Vole must have turned on the artificial current. That was what was making the jellyfish move. Desperately he kicked out with his feet, moving away from it, surging through the water on his back. One tentacle floated up and draped itself over his foot. If he hadn't been wearing trainers, he would have been stung. Could the stinging cells penetrate his clothes? Almost certainly. His trainers were the only protection he had.

He reached the back corner of the aquarium and paused there, one hand against the glass. He already knew that what Vole had said was true. If the jellyfish didn't get him, tiredness would. He had to fight every second to stay afloat, and sheer terror was sapping his strength.

The glass. He pushed against it, wondering if he could break it. Perhaps there was a way... He checked the distance between himself and the jellyfish, took a deep breath and dived down to the bottom of the pool. He could see Nadia Vole watching. Although she was a blur to him, he would be crystal clear to her. She didn't move, and Alex realized with despair that she had expected him to do just this.

He swam to the rocks and looked for one small enough to bring to the surface. But the rocks were too heavy. He found one about the size of his own head, but it refused to move. Vole hadn't tried to stop him because she knew that all the rocks were set in concrete. Alex was running out of breath. He twisted round and pushed himself up towards the surface, only seeing at the last second that the jellyfish had somehow drifted above him. He screamed, bubbles erupting out of his mouth. The tentacles were right over his head. Alex contorted his body and managed to stay down, flailing madly with his legs to propel himself sideways. His shoulder slammed into the nearest of the rocks and he felt the pain shudder through him. Clutching his arm in his hand, he backed into another corner and rose up, gasping for breath as his head broke through the surface of the water.

He couldn't break the glass. He couldn't climb out. He couldn't avoid the touch of the jellyfish for ever. Although he had brought all the gadgets Smithers had given him, none of them could help him.

And then Alex remembered the cream. He let go of his arm and ran a finger up the side of the aquarium. The tank was a marvel of engineering. Alex had no idea how much pressure the water was exerting on the huge plates of glass, but the whole thing was held together by a framework of iron girders that fitted round the corners on both the inside and outside of the glass, the metal faces held together by rivets.

Treading water, he unzipped his pocket and took out the tube. ZIT-CLEAN, FOR HEALTHIER SKIN. If Nadia Vole could see what he was doing, she would think he had gone mad. The jellyfish was drifting towards the back of the aquarium. Alex waited a few moments, then swam forward and dived for a second time.

There didn't seem to be very much of the cream given the

thickness of the girders and the size of the tank, but Alex remembered the demonstration Smithers had given him, how little he had used. Would the cream even work underwater? There was no point worrying about that now. Alex held the tube against the metal corners at the front of the tank and did his best to squeeze a long line of cream all the way down the length of the metal, using his other hand to rub it in around the rivets.

He kicked his feet, propelling himself across to the other side. He didn't know how long he would have before the cream took effect, and anyway, Nadia Vole was already aware that something was wrong. Alex saw that she had stood up again and was speaking into a phone, perhaps calling for help.

He had used half the tube on one side of the tank. He used the second half on the other. The jellyfish was hovering above him, the tentacles reaching out as if to grab hold of him and stop him. How long had he been underwater? His heart was pounding. And what would happen when the metal broke?

He just had time to come up and take one breath before he found out.

Even underwater, the cream had burned through the rivets on the inside of the tank. The glass had separated from the girders and, with nothing to hold it back, the huge pressure of water had smashed it open like a door caught in the wind. Alex didn't see what happened. He didn't have time to think. The world spun and he was thrown forward as helpless as a cork in a waterfall. The next few seconds were a twisting nightmare of rushing water and exploding glass. Alex didn't dare open his eyes. He felt himself being hurled forward, slammed into something, then sucked back again. He was sure he had broken every bone in his body. Now he was underwater. He struggled to find air. His head broke through the surface but even so, when he finally opened his mouth, he was amazed he could actually breathe.

The front of the tank had blown off and thousands of litres of water had cascaded into Herod Sayle's office. The water had smashed the furniture and blown the windows out. It was still draining away through the floor. Bruised and dazed, Alex stood up, water curling round his ankles.

Where was the jellyfish?

He had been lucky that the two of them hadn't become tangled up in the sudden eruption of water. But it could still be close. There might still be enough water in Sayle's office to allow it to reach him. Alex backed into a corner of the room, his whole body taut. Then he saw it.

Nadia Vole had been less fortunate. She had been standing in front of the glass when the girders broke and she hadn't been able to get out of the way in time. She was lying on her back, her legs limp and broken. The Portuguese man-o'-war was all over her. Part of it was sitting on her face and she seemed to be staring at him through the quivering mass of jelly. Her yellow lips were drawn back in an endless scream. The tentacles were wrapped all around her, hundreds of stinging cells clinging to her arms and legs and chest. Feeling sick, Alex backed away to the door and staggered out into the corridor.

An alarm had gone off. He only heard it now, as sound and vision came back to him. The screaming of the siren shook him out of his dazed state. What time was it? Almost eleven o'clock. At least his watch was still working. But he was in Cornwall, at least a five-hour drive from London, and with the alarms sounding, the armed guards and the razor wire, he'd never make it out of the complex. Find a telephone? No. Vole had probably been telling the truth when she'd said they were blocked. And anyway, how could he get in touch with Alan Blunt or Mrs Jones at this late stage?

They'd already be at the Science Museum.

Just one hour left.

Outside, over the din of the alarm, Alex heard another sound. The splutter and roar of a propeller. He went over to the nearest window and looked out. Sure enough, the cargo plane that had been there when he arrived was preparing to take off.

Alex was soaking wet, battered and almost exhausted. But he knew what he had to do.

He spun round and began to run.

ELEVEN O'CLOCK

Alex burst out of the house and stopped in the open air, taking stock of his surroundings. He was aware of alarms ringing, guards running towards him and two cars, still some distance away, tearing up the main drive, heading for the house. He just hoped that, although it was obvious something was wrong, nobody would yet know what it was. They shouldn't be looking for him – at least, not yet. That might give him the edge.

It looked like he was already too late. Sayle's private helicopter had gone. Only the cargo plane was left. If Alex was going to reach the Science Museum in London in the fifty-nine minutes left to him, he had to be on it. But the cargo plane was already in motion, rolling slowly away from its chocks. In a minute or two it would go through the pre-flight tests. Then it would take off.

Alex looked around and saw an open-top army Jeep parked on the drive near the front door. There was a guard standing next to it, a cigarette dropping out of his hand, looking around to see what was happening – but looking the wrong way. Perfect. Alex sprinted across the gravel. He had brought a weapon from the house. One of Sayle's harpoon guns had floated past him just as he'd left the room and he'd snatched it up, determined to have something he could use to defend himself with at last. It would have been easy enough to shoot the guard right then. A harpoon in the back and the Jeep would be his. But Alex knew he couldn't do it. Whatever Alan Blunt and MI6 wanted to turn him into, he wasn't ready to shoot in cold blood. Not for his country. Not even to save his own life.

The guard looked up as Alex approached, and fumbled for the pistol he was wearing in a holster at his belt. He never made it. Alex used the handle of the harpoon gun, swinging it round and up to hit him, hard, under the chin. The guard crumpled, the pistol falling out of his hand. Alex grabbed it and leapt into the Jeep, grateful to see the keys were in the ignition. He turned them and heard the engine start up. He knew how to drive. That was something else Ian Rider had made sure he'd learnt, as soon as his legs were long enough to reach the pedals. The other cars were closing in on him. They must have seen him attack the guard. The plane had wheeled round and was already taxiing up to the start of the runway.

He wasn't going to reach it in time.

Maybe it was the danger closing in from all sides that had sharpened his senses. Maybe it was his close escape from so many dangers before. But Alex didn't even have to think. He knew what to do as if he had done it a dozen times before. And maybe his training had been more effective than he'd thought.

He reached into his pocket and took out the yo-yo that Smithers had given him. There was a metal stud on the belt he was wearing and he slammed the yo-yo against it, feeling it click into place, as it had been designed to. Then, as quickly as he could, he tied the end of the nylon cord round the bolt of the harpoon. Finally, he tucked the pistol he had taken from the guard into the back of his combats. He was ready.

The plane had completed its pre-flight tests. It was facing down the runway. Its propellers were at full speed.

Alex slammed the gears into first, released the handbrake and gunned the Jeep forward, shooting over the drive and on to the grass, heading for the airstrip. At the same time there was a chatter of machine-gun fire. He yanked down on the steering wheel and twisted away as his wing mirror exploded and a spray of bullets slammed into the windscreen and door. The two cars, speeding towards him, head-on, were getting closer and closer. Each of them had a guard in the back seat, leaning out of the window, firing at him. Alex swerved between them, and for a horrible second there was actually one on each side. He was sandwiched between the two cars, with guards firing at him left and right. But then he was through. The guards missed him and hit each other. He heard one of them yell out and drop his gun. One of the cars lost control and crashed into the front of the house, metalwork crumpling against brick. The other screeched to a halt, reversed, then came after him again.

The plane had begun to move down the runway. Slowly at first, but rapidly picking up speed. Alex hit the tarmac and followed.

His foot was pressed down, the accelerator against the floor. The Jeep was doing about seventy – not fast enough. For just a few seconds Alex was parallel with the cargo plane, only a couple of metres from it. But already it was pulling ahead. At any moment it would be in the air.

And straight ahead of him, the way was blocked. Two more

Jeeps had arrived on the runway. More guards with machine guns balanced themselves, half crouching, on the seats. Alex realized the only reason they weren't firing was that they were afraid of hitting the plane. But the plane had already left the ground. Ahead of him, and just to his left, Alex saw the front wheel separate itself from the runway. He glanced in his mirror. The car that had chased him from the house was right on his tail. He had nowhere left to go.

One car behind him. Two Jeeps ahead of him. The plane now in the air, the back wheels lifting off. Everything happening at once.

Alex let go of the steering wheel, grabbed the harpoon gun and fired. The harpoon flashed through the air. The yo-yo attached to Alex's belt spun, trailing out thirty metres of specially designed advanced nylon. The pointed head of the harpoon buried itself in the underbelly of the plane. Alex felt himself almost being torn in half as he was yanked out of the Jeep on the end of the cord. In seconds he was forty, fifty metres above the runway, dangling underneath the plane. His Jeep swerved, out of control. The other two Jeeps tried to avoid it – and failed. Both of them hit it in a three-way head-on collision. There was an explosion – a ball of flame and a fist of grey smoke that followed Alex up as if trying to snatch him back. A moment later there was another explosion. The second car had tried to avoid the two Jeeps but it had been travelling too fast. It ploughed into the burning wrecks, flipped over and continued, screeching on its back along the runway before it too burst into flames.

Alex saw little of this. He was suspended from the plane by a single thin white cord, twisting round and round as he was carried ever further into the air. The wind was rushing past him, battering into his face and deafening him. He couldn't even hear the propellers, just above his head. The belt was cutting into his waist.

He could hardly breathe. Desperately he scrabbled for the yo-yo and found the control he wanted. A single button ... he pressed it. The tiny, powerful motor inside the yo-yo began to turn. The yo-yo rotated on his belt, pulling in the cord. Very slowly, a centimetre at a time, Alex was drawn up towards the plane.

He had aimed the harpoon carefully. There was a door at the back of the plane and when he turned off the engine mechanism in the yo-yo, he was close enough to reach out for its handle. He wondered who was flying the plane and where he was going. The pilot must have seen the destruction down on the runway but he couldn't have heard the harpoon. He couldn't know he'd picked up an extra passenger.

Opening the door was harder than he'd expected. He was still dangling under the plane and every time he got close to the handle the wind drove him back. He could still hardly see. The wind was tearing into his eyes. Twice his fingers found the metal handle, only to be pulled away before he could turn it. The third time, he managed to get a better grip but it still took all his strength to yank the handle down.

The door swung open and he clambered into the hold. He took one last look back. The runway was already three hundred metres below. There were two fires raging, but at this distance they seemed no more than match-heads. Alex unplugged the yo-yo, freeing himself. Then he reached into the waistband of his combats and took out the gun.

The plane was empty apart from a couple of bundles that Alex vaguely recognized. There was a single pilot at the controls, and something on his instrumentation must have told him the door was open, because he suddenly twisted round. Alex found himself face to face with Mr Grin.

"Warg?" the butler muttered.

Alex raised the gun. He doubted if he would have the courage to use it. But he wasn't going to let Mr Grin know that.

"All right, Mr Grin," he shouted above the noise of the propellers and the howl of the wind. "You may not be able to talk but you'd better listen. I want you to fly this plane to London. We're going to the Science Museum in south Kensington. It can't take us more than half an hour to get there. And if you think about trying to trick me, I'll put a bullet in you. Do you understand?"

Mr Grin said nothing.

Alex fired the gun. The bullet slammed into the floor just beside Mr Grin's foot. Mr Grin stared at Alex, then nodded slowly.

He reached out and pulled the joy-stick. The plane dipped and began to head east.

TWELVE O'CLOCK

London appeared.

Suddenly the clouds rolled back and the midday sun brought the whole city, shining, into view. There was Battersea Power Station, standing proud with its four great chimneys still intact, even though much of its roof had long ago been eaten away. Behind it, Battersea Park appeared as a square of dense green bushes and trees that were making a last stand, fighting back the urban spread. In the far distance, the Millennium Wheel perched like a fabulous silver coin, balancing effortlessly on its rim. And all around it, London crouched; gas towers and apartment blocks, endless rows of shops and houses, roads, railways and bridges stretching away on both sides, separated only by the bright silver crack in the landscape that was the River Thames.

Alex saw all this with a clenched stomach, looking out through the open door of the aircraft. He'd had fifty minutes to think about what he had to do. Fifty minutes while the plane droned over Cornwall and Devon, then Somerset and the Salisbury Plains before reaching the North Downs and flying on towards Windsor and London.

When he had got into the plane, Alex had intended to use its radio to call the police or anyone else who might be listening. But seeing Mr Grin at the controls had changed all that. He remembered how fast the man had been both outside his bedroom and throwing the knife when Alex was handcuffed to the chair. He knew he was safe enough in the cargo area, with Mr Grin strapped into the pilot's seat at the front of the plane. But he didn't dare get any closer. Even with the gun it would be too dangerous.

He had thought of forcing Mr Grin to land the plane at Heathrow. The radio had started squawking the moment they'd entered London airspace and had only stopped when Mr Grin turned it off. But that would never have worked. By the time they'd reached the airport, touched down and coasted to a halt, it would have been far too late.

And then, sitting hunched up in the cargo area, Alex had recognized the two bundles lying on the floor next to him. They had told him exactly what he had to do.

"Eeerg!" Mr Grin said. He twisted round in his seat and for the last time Alex saw the hideous smile that the circus knife had torn through his cheeks.

"Thanks for the ride," Alex said, and jumped out of the open door.

The bundles were parachutes. Alex had checked them out and strapped one on to his back when they were still over Reading. He was glad that he'd spent a day on parachute training with the SAS, although this flight had been even worse than the one he'd endured over the Welsh valleys. This time there was no static line. There was no one to reassure him that his parachute was properly packed. If he could have thought of any other way to reach the Science Museum in the seven minutes he had left, he would have taken it. There was no other way. He knew that. So he had jumped.

Once he was over the threshold, it wasn't so bad. There was a moment of dizzying confusion as the wind hit him once again. He closed his eyes and forced himself to count to three. Pull too early and the parachute might snag on the plane's tail. Even so, his hand was clenched and he had barely muttered the word "three" before he was pulling with all his strength. The parachute blossomed open above him and he was jerked back upwards, the harness cutting into his armpits and sides.

They had been flying at four thousand feet. When Alex opened his eyes, he was surprised by his sense of calm. He was dangling in the air underneath a comforting canopy of white silk. He felt as if he wasn't moving at all. Now that he had left the plane, the city seemed even more distant and unreal. It was just him, the sky and London. He was almost enjoying himself.

And then he heard the plane coming back.

It was already a couple of kilometres away, but even as he watched he saw it bank steeply to the right, making a sharp turn. The engines rose and then it levelled out – it was heading straight towards him. Mr Grin wasn't going to let him get away so easily. As the plane drew closer and closer he could almost see the man's never-ending smile behind the window of the cockpit. Mr Grin intended to steer the plane right into him, to cut him to shreds in mid-air.

But Alex had been expecting it.

He reached down and took out the Game Boy. This time there was no game cartridge in it: but while he had been on the plane he had taken out Bomber Boy and slid it across the floor. That was where it was now. Just behind Mr Grin's seat.

He pressed the START button three times.

Inside the plane, the cartridge exploded, releasing a cloud of acrid yellow smoke. The smoke billowed out through the hold, curling against the windows, trailing out of the open door. Mr Grin vanished, completely surrounded by smoke. The plane wobbled, then plunged down.

Alex watched the plane dive. He could imagine Mr Grin blinded, fighting for control. The plane began to twist, slowly at first, then faster and faster. The engines whined. Now it was heading straight for the ground, howling through the sky. Yellow smoke trailed in its wake. At the last minute, Mr Grin managed to bring the nose up again. But it was much too late. The plane smashed into what looked like a deserted piece of dockland near the river and disappeared in a ball of flame.

Alex looked at his watch. Three minutes to twelve. He was still a thousand feet in the air and unless he landed on the very doorstep of the Science Museum, he wasn't going to make it. Grabbing hold of the cords, using them to steer himself, he tried to work out the fastest way down.

Inside the East Hall of the Science Museum, Herod Sayle was coming to the end of his speech. The entire chamber had been transformed for the great moment when the Stormbreakers would be brought on-line.

The room was caught between old and new, between stone colonnades and stainless steel floors, between the very latest in hi-tech and old curiosities from the Industrial Revolution.

A podium had been set up in the centre for Sayle, the prime minister, the press secretary and the minister of state for education. In front of it were twelve rows of chairs – for journalists, teachers, invited friends. Alan Blunt was in the front row, as emotionless as ever. Mrs Jones, dressed in black with a large brooch on her lapel, was next to him. On either side of the hall, television towers had been constructed, with cameras focusing in as Sayle spoke. The speech was being broadcast live to schools throughout the country and it would also be shown on the evening news. The hall was packed with another two or three hundred people standing on first and second-floor galleries, looking down on the podium from all sides. As Sayle spoke, tape recorders turned and cameras flashed. Never before had a private individual made so generous a gift to the nation. This was an event. History in the making.

"...it is the prime minister, and the prime minister alone, who is responsible for what is about to happen," Sayle was saying. "And I hope that tonight, when he reflects on what has happened today throughout this country, he will remember our days together at school, and everything he did at that time. I think tonight the country will know him for the man he is. One thing is sure. This is a day you will never forget."

He bowed. There was a scatter of applause. The prime minister glanced at his press secretary, puzzled. The press secretary shrugged with barely concealed rudeness. The prime minister took his place in front of the microphone.

"I'm not quite sure how to respond to that," he joked, and all the journalists laughed. The government had such a large majority that they knew it was in their best interests to laugh at the prime minister's jokes. "I'm glad Mr Sayle has such happy memories of our schooldays together and I'm glad that the two of us, together, today, can make such a vital difference to our schools."

Herod Sayle pointed at a table slightly to one side of the podium. On the table was a Stormbreaker computer and next to it, a mouse. "This is the master control," he said. "Click on the mouse and all the computers will come on-line."

"Right." The prime minister lifted his finger and adjusted his position so that the cameras could get his best profile. Somewhere outside the museum, a clock began to strike.

Alex heard the clock from about three hundred feet, with the roof of the Science Museum rushing towards him.

He had seen the building just after the plane had crashed. It hadn't been easy finding it, with the city spread out like a three-dimensional map right underneath him. On the other hand, he had lived his whole life in west London and had visited the museum often enough. First he had seen the Victorian jelly mould that was the Albert Hall. Directly south of that was a tall white tower surmounted by a green dome: Imperial College. As Alex dropped, he seemed to be moving faster. The whole city had become a fantastic jigsaw puzzle and he knew he only had seconds to piece it together. A wide, extravagant building with churchlike towers and windows. That had to be the Natural History Museum. The Natural History Museum was on Cromwell Road. How did you get from there to the Science Museum? Of course, turn left at the lights up Exhibition Road.

And there it was. Alex pulled at the parachute, guiding himself towards it. How small it looked compared to the other landmarks, a rectangular building with a flat grey roof, jutting in from the main road. Part of the roof consisted of a series of arches, the sort of thing you might see on a railway station or perhaps on an enormous conservatory. They were a dull orange in colour, curving one after the other. It looked as if they were made of glass. Alex could land on the flat part. Then all he would have to do was look through the curved windows. He still had the gun he had taken from the guard. He could use it to warn the prime minister. If he had to, he could use it to shoot Herod Sayle.

Somehow he managed to manoeuvre himself over the museum. But it was only as he fell the last two hundred feet, as he heard the clock strike twelve, that he realized two things. He was falling much too fast. And he had missed the flat roof.

In fact the Science Museum has two roofs. The original is Georgian and made of wired glass. But sometime in the recent past it must have leaked, because the curators have constructed a second roof of plastic sheeting over the top. This was the orange roof that Alex had seen.

He crashed into it feet-first. The roof shattered. He continued straight through, into an inner chamber, just missing a network of steel girders and maintenance ladders. He barely had time to register what looked like a brown carpet, stretched out over the curving surface below. Then he hit it and tore through that too. It was no more than a thin cover, designed to keep the light and dust off the glass underneath. With a yell, Alex smashed through the glass. At last his parachute caught on a beam. He jerked to a halt, swinging in mid-air inside the East Hall.

This was what he saw.

Far below him, all around him, three hundred people had stopped and were staring up at him in shock. There were more people sitting on chairs directly underneath him and some of them had been hit. There was blood and broken glass. A bridge made of green glass slats stretched across the hall. There was a futuristic information desk and in front of it, at the very centre of everything, was a makeshift stage. He saw the Stormbreaker first. Then, with a sense of disbelief, he recognized the prime minister standing, slack-jawed, next to Herod Sayle.

Alex hung in the air, dangling at the end of the parachute. As the last pieces of glass fell and disintegrated on the terracotta floor, movement and sound returned to the East Hall in an ever-widening wave.

The security men were the first to react. Anonymous and invisible when they needed to be, they were suddenly everywhere, appearing from behind colonnades, from underneath the television towers, running across the green bridge, guns in hands that had been empty a second before. Alex had also drawn his gun, pulling it out from the waistband of his combats. Maybe he could explain why he was here before Sayle or the prime minister activated the Stormbreakers. But he doubted it. Shoot first and ask questions later was a line from a bad film. But even bad films are sometimes right.

He emptied the gun.

The bullets echoed around the room, surprisingly loud. Now people were screaming, the journalists punching and pushing as they fought for cover. The first bullet went nowhere. The second hit the Prime Minister in the hand, his finger less than a centimetre away from the mouse. The third hit the mouse, blowing it into fragments. The fourth hit an electrical connection, smashing the plug and short-circuiting it. Sayle had dived forward, determined to click on the mouse himself. The fifth and sixth bullets hit him.

As soon as Alex had fired the last bullet, he dropped the gun, letting it clatter to the floor below, and held up the palms of his hands. He felt ridiculous, hanging there from the roof, his arms outstretched. But there were already a dozen guns pointing at him and he had to show them he was no longer armed, that they didn't need to shoot. Even so, he braced himself, waiting for the security men to open fire. He could almost imagine the hail of bullets tearing into him. As far as they were concerned, he was some sort of crazy terrorist who had just parachuted into the Science Museum and taken six shots at the prime minister. It was their job to kill him. It was what they'd been trained for.

But the bullets never came. All the security men were equipped with radio headsets and, in the front row, Mrs Jones had control. The moment she had recognized Alex she had spoken urgently into her brooch. *Don't shoot! Repeat – don't shoot! Await my command!*

On the podium, a plume of grey smoke rose out of the back of the broken, useless Stormbreaker. Two security men had rushed to the prime minister, who was clutching his wrist, blood dripping from his hand. Journalists had begun to shout questions. Photographers' cameras were flashing and the television cameras, too, had been swung round to focus in on the figure swaying high above. More security men were moving to seal off the exits, following orders from Mrs Jones, while Alan Blunt looked on, for once in his life out of his depth.

But there was no sign of Herod Sayle. The head of Sayle Enterprises had been shot twice – but somehow he had disappeared.

YASSEN

"You slightly spoiled things by shooting the prime minister," Alan Blunt said. "But all in all you're to be congratulated, Alex. You not only lived up to our expectations. You far exceeded them."

It was late afternoon the following day, and Alex was sitting in Blunt's office at the Royal & General building on Liverpool Street wondering just why, after everything he had done for them, the head of MI6 had to sound quite so much like a second-rate public school headmaster giving him a good report. Mrs Jones was sitting next to him. Alex had refused her offer of a peppermint, although he was beginning to realize it was all the reward he was going to get.

She spoke now for the first time since he had come into the room. "You might like to know about the clearing-up operation."

"Sure..."

She glanced at Blunt, who nodded.

"First of all, don't expect to read the truth about any of this in the newspapers," she began. "We put a D-notice on it, which means nobody is allowed to report what happened. Of course, the ceremony at the Science Museum was being televised live, but fortunately we were able to cut transmission before the cameras could focus on you. In fact, nobody knows that it was a fourteen-year-old boy who caused all the chaos."

"And we plan to keep it that way," Blunt muttered.

"Why?" Alex didn't like the sound of that.

Mrs Jones dismissed the question. "The newspapers had to print something, of course," she went on. "The story we've put out is that Sayle was attacked by a hitherto unknown terrorist organization and that he's gone into hiding."

"Where is Sayle?" Alex asked.

"We don't know. But we'll find him. There's nowhere on earth he can hide from us."

"OK." Alex sounded doubtful.

"As for the Stormbreakers, we've already announced that there's a dangerous product fault and that anyone turning them on could get electrocuted. It's embarrassing for the government, of course, but they've all been recalled and we're bringing them in now. Fortunately, Sayle was so fanatical that he programmed them so that the smallpox virus could only be released by the prime minister at the Science Museum. You managed to destroy the trigger, so even the few schools that have tried to start up their computers haven't been affected."

"It was very close," Blunt said. "We've analyzed a couple of samples. It's lethal. Worse even than the stuff Iraq was brewing up in the Gulf War."

"Do you know who supplied it?" Alex asked.

Blunt coughed. "No."

"The submarine I saw was Chinese."

"That doesn't necessarily mean anything." It was obvious that Blunt didn't want to talk about it. "You can just be sure that we'll make all the necessary enquiries—"

"What about Yassen Gregorovich?" Alex asked.

Mrs Jones took over. "We've closed down the plant at Port Tallon," she said. "We already have most of the personnel under arrest. Unfortunately we weren't able to talk to either Nadia Vole or the man you knew as Mr Grin."

"He never talked much anyway," Alex said.

"It was lucky that his plane crashed into a building site," Mrs Jones went on. "Nobody else was killed. As for Yassen, I imagine he'll disappear. From what you've told us, it's clear that he wasn't actually working for Sayle. He was working for the people who were sponsoring Sayle ... and I doubt they'll be very pleased with him. Yassen is probably on the other side of the world already. But one day, perhaps, we'll find him. We'll never stop looking."

There was a long silence. It seemed that the two spymasters had said all they wanted. But there was one question that nobody had tackled.

"What happens to me?" Alex asked.

"You go back to school," Blunt replied.

Mrs Jones took out an envelope and handed it to Alex.

"A cheque?" he asked.

"It's a letter from a doctor, explaining that you've been away for three weeks with flu. Very bad flu. And if anyone asks, he's a real doctor. You shouldn't have any trouble."

"You'll continue to live in your uncle's house," Blunt said. "That housekeeper of yours, Jack Whatever, she'll look after you. And that way we'll know where you are if we need you again."

Need you again. The words chilled Alex more than anything that had happened to him in the past three weeks. "You've got to be kidding," he said.

"No." Blunt gazed at him quite coolly. "It's not my habit to make jokes."

"You've done very well, Alex," Mrs Jones said, trying to sound more conciliatory. "The prime minister himself asked us to pass on his thanks to you. And the fact of the matter is that it could be wonderfully useful to have someone as young as you—"

"As talented as you—" Blunt cut in.

"—available to us from time to time." She held up a hand to ward off any argument. "Let's not talk about it now," she said. "But if ever another situation arises, perhaps we can get in touch then."

"Yeah. Sure." Alex looked from one to the other. These weren't people who were going to take no for an answer. In their own way, they were both as charming as Mr Grin. "Can I go?" he asked.

"Of course you can," Mrs Jones said. "Would you like someone to drive you home?"

"No thanks." Alex got up. "I'll find my own way."

He should have been feeling better. As he took the lift down to the ground floor, he reflected that he'd saved thousands of schoolchildren, he'd beaten Herod Sayle and he hadn't been killed or even badly hurt. So what was there to be unhappy about? The answer was simple. Blunt had forced him into this. In the end, the big difference between him and James Bond wasn't a question of age. It was a question of loyalty. In the old days, spies had done what they'd done because they loved their country, because they believed in what they were doing. But he'd never been given a choice. Nowadays, spies weren't employed. They were used.

He came out of the building, meaning to walk up to the tube

station, but just then a cab drove along and he flagged it down. He was too tired for public transport. He glanced at the driver, huddled over the wheel in a horribly knitted, home-made cardigan, and slumped on to the back seat.

"Cheyne Walk, Chelsea," Alex said.

The driver turned round. He was holding a gun. His face was paler than it had been the last time Alex saw it and the pain of two bullet wounds was drawn all over it, but – impossibly – it was Herod Sayle.

"If you move, you *bliddy* child, I will shoot you," Sayle said. His voice was pure venom. "If you try anything, I will shoot you. Sit still. You're coming with me."

The doors clicked shut, locking automatically. Herod Sayle turned round and drove off, down Liverpool Street, heading for the City.

Alex didn't know what to do. He was certain that Sayle planned to shoot him anyway. Why else would he have taken the huge chance of driving up to the very door of MI6 headquarters in London? He thought about trying the window, perhaps trying to get the attention of another car at a traffic light. But it wouldn't work. Sayle would turn round and kill him. The man had nothing left to lose.

They drove for ten minutes. It was a Saturday and the City was closed. The traffic was light. Then Sayle pulled up in front of a modern, glass-fronted skyscraper with an abstract sculpture – two oversized bronze walnuts on a slab of concrete – outside the front door.

"You will get out of the car with me," Sayle commanded. "You and I will walk into the building. If you think about running, remember that this gun is pointing at your spine."

Sayle got out of the car first. His eyes never left Alex. Alex guessed that the two bullets must have hit him in the left arm and shoulder. His left hand was hanging limp. But the gun was in his right hand. It was perfectly steady, aimed at Alex's lower back.

"In..."

The building had swing-doors and they were open. Alex found himself in a marble-clad hall with leather sofas and a curving reception desk. There was nobody here either. Sayle gestured with the gun and Alex walked over to a bank of lifts. One of them was waiting. They got in.

"The twenty-ninth floor," Sayle said.

Alex pressed the button. "Are we going up for the view?" he asked.

Sayle nodded. "You make all the *bliddy* jokes you want," he said. "But I'm going to have the last laugh."

They stood in silence. Alex could feel the pressure in his ears as the lift rose higher and higher. Sayle was staring at him, his damaged arm tucked into his side, supporting himself against the door. Alex thought about attacking him. If he could just get the element of surprise. But no... They were too close. And Sayle was coiled up like a spring.

The lift slowed down and the doors opened. Sayle waved with the gun. "Turn left. You'll come to a door. Open it."

Alex did as he was told. The door was marked HELIPAD. A flight of concrete steps led up. Alex glanced at Sayle. Sayle nodded. "Up."

They climbed the steps and reached another door with a push-bar. Alex pressed it and went through. He was back outside, thirty floors up, on a flat roof with a radio mast and a tall metal fence running round the perimeter. He and Sayle were standing on the edge of a huge cross, painted in red. Looking around, Alex could see right across the City to Canary Wharf. It had seemed a quiet spring day when Alex left the Royal & General offices. But up here the wind streaked past and the clouds boiled.

"You ruined everything!" Sayle howled. "How did you do it? How did you trick me? I'd have beaten you if you'd been a man! But they had to send a boy! A *bliddy* schoolboy! Well, it isn't over yet! I'm leaving England. Do you see...?"

Sayle nodded and Alex turned to see that there was a helicopter hovering in the air behind him. Where had it come from? It was red and yellow, a light, single-engine aircraft with a figure in dark glasses and helmet hunched over the controls. The helicopter was a Colibri EC120B, one of the quietest in the world. It swung round over him, its blades beating at the air.

"That's my ticket out of here!" Sayle continued. "They'll never find me! And one day I'll be back. Next time, nothing will go wrong. And you won't be here to stop me. This is the end for you! This is where you die!"

There was nothing Alex could do. Sayle raised the gun and took aim, his eyes wide, the pupils blacker than they had ever been, mere pinpricks in the bulging whites.

There were two small, explosive cracks.

Alex looked down, expecting to see blood. There was nothing. He couldn't feel anything. Then Sayle staggered and fell on to his back. There were two gaping holes in his chest.

The helicopter landed at the centre of the cross. Yassen Gregorovich got out.

Still holding the gun that had killed Herod Sayle, he walked over and examined the body, prodding it with his shoe. Satisfied, he nodded to himself, tucking the gun away. He had switched off the engine of the helicopter and behind him the blades slowed down and stopped. Alex stepped forward. Yassen seemed to notice him for the first time.

"You're Yassen Gregorovich," Alex said.

The Russian nodded. It was impossible to tell what was going on in his head. His clear blue eyes gave nothing away.

"Why did you kill him?" Alex asked.

"Those were my instructions." There was no trace of an accent in his voice. He spoke softly, reasonably. "He had become an embarrassment. It was better this way."

"Not better for him."

Yassen shrugged.

"What about me?" Alex asked.

The Russian ran his eyes over Alex, as if weighing him up. "I have no instructions concerning you," he said.

"You're not going to shoot me too?"

"Do I have any need to?"

There was a pause. The two of them gazed at each other over the corpse of Herod Sayle.

"You killed Ian Rider," Alex said. "He was my uncle."

Yassen shrugged. "I kill a lot of people."

"One day I'll kill you."

"A lot of people have tried." Yassen smiled. "Believe me," he said, "it would be better if we didn't meet again. Go back to school. Go back to your life. And the next time they ask you, say no. Killing is for grown-ups and you're still a child."

He turned his back on Alex and climbed into the helicopter cabin. The blades started up and a few seconds later the helicopter rose back into the air. For a moment it hovered at the side of the building. Behind the glass, Yassen raised his hand. A gesture of friendship? A salute? Alex raised his hand. The helicopter spun away.

Alex stood where he was, watching it, until it had disappeared in the dying light.

POINT BLANC

GOING DOWN

Michael J. Roscoe was a careful man.

The car that drove him to work at seven-fifteen each morning was a custom-made Mercedes with reinforced-steel doors and bulletproof windows. His driver, a retired FBI agent, carried a Beretta sub-compact semi-automatic pistol and knew how to use it. There were just five steps from the point where the car stopped to the entrance of Roscoe Tower on New York's Fifth Avenue, but closed-circuit television cameras followed him every inch of the way. Once the automatic doors had slid shut behind him, a uniformed receptionist – also armed – watched as he crossed the foyer and entered his own private lift.

The lift had white marble walls, a blue carpet, a silver handrail and no buttons. Roscoe pressed his hand against a small glass panel. A sensor read his fingerprints, verified them and activated the lift. The doors slid shut and the lift rose to the sixtieth floor without stopping. Nobody else ever used it. Nor did it ever stop at any of the other floors in the building. While it was travelling up, the receptionist was on the telephone, letting Mr Roscoe's staff know that he was on his way.

Everyone who worked in Roscoe's private office had been hand-picked and thoroughly vetted. It was impossible to see him without an appointment. Getting an appointment could take three months.

When you're rich, you have to be careful. There are cranks, kidnappers, terrorists – the desperate and the dispossessed. Michael J. Roscoe was the chairman of Roscoe Electronics and the ninth or tenth richest man in the world – and he was very careful indeed. Ever since his face had appeared on the front cover of *Time* magazine ("The Electronics King") he had realized that he had become a visible target. So when in public he walked quickly, with his head bent. The glasses that he wore had been chosen to hide as much as possible of his round, handsome face. His suits were expensive but anonymous. If he went to the theatre or to dinner, he always arrived at the last minute, preferring not to hang around. There were dozens of different security systems in his life and, although they had once annoyed him, he had allowed them to become routine.

But ask any spy or security agent. Routine is the one thing that can get you killed. It tells the enemy where you're going and when you're going to be there. Routine was going to kill Michael J. Roscoe and this was the day death had chosen to come calling.

Of course, Roscoe had no idea of this as he stepped out of the lift directly into his private office – a huge room occupying the corner of the building, with floor-to-ceiling windows giving views in two directions; Fifth Avenue to the north, Central Park to the west. The two remaining walls contained a door, a low bookshelf and, next to the lift, a single oil painting: a vase of flowers by Vincent Van Gogh.

The black glass surface of his desk was equally uncluttered. A computer, a leather notebook, a telephone and a framed photograph of a fourteen-year-old boy. As he took off his jacket and sat down, Roscoe found himself looking at the picture of the boy. Blond hair, blue eyes and freckles. Paul Roscoe looked remarkably like his father forty years ago. Roscoe was now fifty-four, beginning to show his age despite his year-round tan. His son was almost as tall as him. The picture had been taken the summer before, on Long Island. They had spent the day sailing. Then they'd had a barbecue on the beach. It had been one of the few happy days they'd ever had together.

The door opened and his secretary came in. Helen Bosworth was English. She had left her home and her husband to come and work in New York and loved every minute of it. She had been working in this office for eleven years, and in all that time she had never forgotten a detail or made a mistake.

"Good morning, Mr Roscoe," she said.

"Good morning, Helen."

She set down a folder on his desk. "The latest figures from Singapore. Costings on the R-15 Organizer. You have lunch with Senator Andrews at twelve-thirty. I've booked the Ivy—"

"Did you remember to call London?" Roscoe asked.

Helen Bosworth blinked. She never forgot anything, so why had he asked? "I spoke to Alan Blunt's office yesterday afternoon," she said. Afternoon in New York would have been evening in London. "Mr Blunt was not available but I've arranged a person-to-person call for you this afternoon. We can have it patched through to your car."

"Thank you, Helen."

"Shall I have your coffee sent through to you?"

"No thank you, Helen. I won't have coffee today."

Helen Bosworth left the room, seriously alarmed. No coffee? Whatever next? Mr Roscoe had begun his day with a double espresso for as long as she had known him. Could it be that he was ill? He certainly hadn't been himself recently ... not since Paul had got back from that school in the South of France. And this phone call to Alan Blunt in London! Nobody had ever told her who he was but she had seen his name in a file once. He was something to do with British military intelligence. MI6. What was Mr Roscoe doing talking to a spy?

Helen Bosworth returned to her office and soothed her nerves, not with a coffee – she couldn't stand the stuff – but with a refreshing cup of English breakfast tea. Something very strange was going on and she didn't like it. She didn't like it at all.

Meanwhile, sixty floors below, a man had walked into reception wearing grey overalls with an ID badge attached to his chest. The badge identified him as Sam Green, maintenance engineer with X-Press Elevators Inc. He was carrying a briefcase in one hand and a large silver toolbox in the other. He set them both down in front of the reception desk.

Sam Green was not his real name. His hair – black and a little greasy – was fake, as were his glasses, moustache and uneven teeth. He looked fifty years old but was actually nearer thirty. Nobody knew his real name but, in the business he was in, a name was the last thing he could afford. He was known as the Gentleman and he was one of the highest paid and most successful contract killers in the world. He had been given his nickname because he always sent flowers to the families of his victims.

The receptionist glanced at him.

"I'm here for the elevator," he said. He spoke with a Bronx accent even though he had never spent more than a week there in his life.

"What about it?" the receptionist asked. "You people were here last week."

"Yeah. Sure. We found a defective cable on elevator twelve. It had to be replaced but we didn't have the parts. So they sent me back." The Gentleman fished in his pocket and pulled out a crumpled sheet of paper. "You want to call Head Office? I've got my orders here."

If the receptionist had called X-Press Elevators Inc., he would have discovered that they did indeed employ a Sam Green – although he hadn't shown up for work for two days. This was because the real Sam Green was at the bottom of the Hudson River with a knife in his back and a twenty-pound block of concrete attached to his feet. But the receptionist didn't make the call. The Gentleman had guessed he wouldn't bother. After all, the lifts were always breaking down. There were engineers in and out the whole time. What difference would one more make?

The receptionist jerked a thumb. "Go ahead!" he said.

The Gentleman put away the letter, picked up his case and his toolbox, and went over to the lifts. There were a dozen public lifts servicing the skyscraper, plus a thirteenth for Michael J. Roscoe. Lift number twelve was at the end. As he went in, a delivery boy with a parcel tried to follow. "Sorry," the Gentleman said. "Closed for maintenance." The doors slid shut. He was on his own. He pressed the button for the sixty-first floor.

He had been given this job only a week before. He'd had to work fast – killing the real maintenance engineer, taking his identity, learning the layout of Roscoe Tower and getting his hands on the sophisticated piece of equipment he had known he would need. His employers wanted the multimillionaire eliminated as quickly as possible. More importantly, it had to look like an accident. For this, the Gentleman had demanded – and been paid – two hundred thousand American dollars. The money was to be paid into a bank account in Switzerland; half now, half on completion.

The lift door opened. The sixty-first floor was used mainly for maintenance. This was where the water tanks were housed, also the computers that controlled the heat, air-conditioning, security cameras and lifts throughout the building. The Gentleman turned off the lift, using the manual override key that had once belonged to Sam Green, then went over to the computers. He knew exactly where they were. In fact, he could have found them wearing a blindfold. He opened his briefcase. There were two sections to the case. The lower part was a laptop computer. The lid was fitted out with a number of drills and other tools, each of them strapped into place.

It took him fifteen minutes to cut his way into the Roscoe Tower mainframe and connect his laptop to the circuitry inside. Hacking his way past the Roscoe security systems took a little longer, but at last it was done. He tapped a command into his keyboard. On the floor below, Michael J. Roscoe's private lift did something it had never done before. It rose up one extra floor – to level sixty-one. The door, however, remained closed. The Gentleman did not need to get in.

Instead, he picked up the briefcase and the silver toolbox and carried them back into the same lift he had taken from reception. He turned the override key and pressed the button for the fifty-ninth floor. Once again, he deactivated the lift. Then he reached up and pushed. In the top of the lift was a trapdoor that opened outwards. He pushed the briefcase and the silver box ahead of him, then pulled himself up and climbed onto the roof of the lift.

He was now standing inside the main lift shaft of Roscoe Tower. He was surrounded on four sides by girders and pipes blackened with oil and dirt. Thick steel cables hung down, some of them humming as they carried their loads up and down. Looking down, he could see a seemingly endless square tunnel, illuminated only by the chinks of light from the doors that slid open and shut again as the other lifts arrived at various floors. Somehow the breeze had made its way in from the street, spinning dust that stung his eyes. Next to him was a set of lift doors which, had he opened them, would have led him straight into Roscoe's office. Above these, over his head and a few metres to the right, was the underbelly of Roscoe's private lift.

The toolbox was next to him, on the lift roof. Carefully, he opened it. The sides of the case were lined with thick sponge. Inside, in the specially moulded space, was what looked like a complicated film projector, silver and concave with a thick glass lens. He took it out, then glanced at his watch. Eight-thirty-five. It would take him an hour to connect the device to the bottom of Roscoe's lift, and a little more to ensure it was working. He had plenty of time.

Smiling to himself, the Gentleman took out a power screwdriver and began to work.

At twelve o'clock, Helen Bosworth called through on the telephone. "Your car is here, Mr Roscoe."

"Thank you, Helen."

Roscoe hadn't done much that morning. He had been aware that only half his mind was on his work. Once again, he glanced at the photograph on his desk. Paul. How could things have gone so wrong between a father and a son? And what could have happened in the last few months to make them so much worse?

He stood up, put his jacket on and walked across his office, on his way to lunch with Senator Andrews. He often had lunch with politicians. They either wanted his money, his ideas ... or him. Anyone as rich as Roscoe was a powerful friend and politicians need all the friends they can get.

He pressed the lift call button and the doors slid open. He took one step forward.

The last thing Michael J. Roscoe saw in his life was a lift with white marble walls, a blue carpet and a silver handrail. His right foot, wearing one of the black leather shoes that were handmade for him by a small shop in Rome, travelled down to the carpet and kept going ... right through it. The rest of his body followed, tilting into the lift and then through it. And then he was falling sixty floors to his death. He was so surprised by what had happened, so totally unable to understand what had happened, that he didn't even cry out. He simply fell into the blackness of the liftshaft, bounced twice off the walls, then crashed into the solid concrete of the basement, two hundred metres below.

The lift remained where it was. It looked solid but, in fact, it wasn't there at all. What Roscoe had stepped into was a hologram being projected into the empty space of the liftshaft where the real lift should have been. The Gentleman had programmed the door to open when Roscoe pressed the call button, and had quietly watched him step into oblivion. If the billionaire had just looked up for a moment, he would have seen the silver hologram projector beaming the image, a few metres above him. But a man getting into a lift on his way to lunch does not look up. The Gentleman had known this. And he was never wrong.

At twelve-thirty-five, the chauffeur called up to say that Mr Roscoe hadn't arrived at the car. Ten minutes later, Helen Bosworth alerted security, who began to search the foyer of the building.

At one o'clock, they called the restaurant. The senator was there, waiting for his lunch guest. But Roscoe hadn't shown up.

In fact, his body wasn't discovered until the next day, by which time the billionaire's disappearance had become the lead story on American TV news. A bizarre accident – that's what it looked like. Nobody could work out what had happened. Because of course, by that time, the Gentleman had reprogrammed the mainframe, removed the projector and left everything as it should have been before quietly leaving the building.

Two days later, a man who looked nothing like a maintenance engineer walked into JFK International Airport. He was about to board a flight for Switzerland. But first of all he visited a flower shop and ordered a dozen black tulips to be sent to a certain address. The man paid with cash. He didn't leave a name.

BLUE SHADOW

The worst time to feel alone is when you're in a crowd. Alex Rider was walking across the playground, surrounded by hundreds of boys and girls of about his own age. They were all heading in the same direction, all wearing the same blue and grey uniform, all of them probably thinking much the same thoughts. The last lesson of the day had just ended. Homework, tea and television would fill the remaining hours until bed. Another schoolday. So why did he feel so out of it, as if he were watching the last weeks of the term from the other side of a giant glass screen?

Alex jerked his backpack over one shoulder and continued towards the bike shed. The bag was heavy. As usual, it contained double homework – French and history. He had missed two weeks of school and he was having to work hard to catch up. His teachers had not been sympathetic. Nobody had said as much, but when he had finally returned with a doctor's letter (*...a bad dose* *of flu with complications...*) they had nodded and smiled and secretly thought him a little bit pampered and spoiled. On the other hand, they had to make allowances. They all knew that Alex had no parents, that he had been living with an uncle who had died in some sort of car accident. But even so. Two weeks in bed! Even his closest friends had to admit that was a bit much.

And he couldn't tell them the truth. He wasn't allowed to tell anyone what had really happened. That was the hell of it.

Alex looked around him, at the children streaming through the school gates, some dribbling footballs, some on their mobile phones. He looked at the teachers, curling themselves into their second-hand cars. At first, he had thought that the whole school had somehow changed while he was away. But he knew now that what had happened was worse. Everything was the same. It was he who had changed.

Alex was fourteen years old, an ordinary schoolboy in an ordinary west London comprehensive. Or he had been. Only a few weeks ago, he had discovered that his uncle had been a secret agent, working for MI6. The uncle – Ian Rider – had been murdered and MI6 had forced Alex to take his place. They had given him a crash course in SAS survival techniques and sent him on a lunatic mission on the south coast. He had been chased, shot at and almost killed. And at the end of it he had been packed off and sent back to school as if nothing had happened. But first they had made him sign the Official Secrets Act. Alex smiled at the memory of it. He didn't need to sign anything. Who would have believed him anyway?

But it was the secrecy that was getting to him now. Whenever anyone asked him what he had been doing in the weeks he'd been away, he'd been forced to tell them that he'd been in bed, reading, slouching around the house, whatever. Alex didn't want to boast about what he'd done, but he hated having to deceive his friends. It made him angry. MI6 hadn't just put him in danger. They'd locked his whole life in a filing cabinet and thrown away the key.

He had reached the bike shed. Somebody muttered a "goodbye" in his direction and he nodded, then reached up to brush away the single strand of fair hair that had fallen over his eye. Sometimes he wished that the whole business with MI6 had never happened. But at the same time – he had to admit it – part of him wanted it all to happen again. Sometimes he felt that he no longer belonged in the safe, comfortable world of Brookland School. Too much had changed. And at the end of the day, anything was better than double homework.

He lifted his bike out of the shed, unlocked it, pulled the backpack over both his shoulders and prepared to ride away. That was when he saw the beat-up white car. Back again outside the school gates. For the second time that week.

Everyone knew about the man in the white car.

He was in his twenties, bald, and had two broken stumps where his front teeth should have been and five metal studs in his ear. He didn't advertise his name. When people talked about him, they called him Skoda – after the make of his car. But there were some who said that his name was Jake and that he had once been at Brookland. If so, he had come back like an unwelcome ghost; here one minute, vanishing the next – somehow always a few seconds ahead of any passing police car or over-inquisitive teacher.

Skoda sold drugs. He sold soft drugs to the younger kids and harder stuff to any of the sixth-formers stupid enough to buy it. It seemed incredible to Alex that Skoda could get away with it so easily, dealing his little packets in broad daylight. But of course there was a code of honour in the school. No one turned anyone into the police, not even a rat like Skoda. And there was always the fear that if Skoda went down, some of the people he supplied – friends, classmates – might go with him.

Drugs had never been a huge problem at Brookland, but recently that had begun to change. A clutch of seventeen-year-olds had started buying Skoda's goods and, like a stone dropped into a pool, the ripples had rapidly spread. There had been a spate of thefts, as well as one or two bullying incidents – younger children being forced to bring in money for older kids. The stuff Skoda was selling seemed to get more expensive the more you bought of it – and it hadn't been cheap at the start.

Alex watched as a heavy-shouldered boy with dark hair and serious acne lumbered over to the car, paused by the window and then continued on his way. He felt a sudden jolt of anger. The boy's name was Colin and just twelve months ago he had been one of Alex's best friends. In fact, Colin had been popular with everyone. But then everything had changed. He had become moody and withdrawn. His work had gone downhill. Suddenly nobody had wanted to know him – and this was the reason. Alex had never thought much about drugs, apart from knowing that he would never take them himself. But he could see that the man in the white car wasn't just poisoning a handful of dumb kids. He was poisoning the whole school.

A policeman on foot patrol appeared, walking towards the gate. A moment later, the white car was gone, black smut bubbling from a faulty exhaust. Alex was on his bike before he knew what he was doing, pedalling fast out of the playground, swerving round the school secretary, who was also on her way home.

"Not too fast, Alex!" she called out, and sighed when he ignored her. Miss Bedfordshire had always had a soft spot for Alex without knowing quite why. And she alone in the school had wondered if there hadn't been more to his absence than the doctor's note had suggested.

The white Skoda accelerated down the road, turning left, then right, and Alex thought he was going to lose it. But then it twisted through the maze of back streets that led up to the King's Road and hit the inevitable four o'clock traffic jam, coming to a halt about two hundred metres ahead.

The average speed of traffic in London is, at the start of the twenty-first century, lower than it used to be in Victorian times. During normal working hours, any bicycle will beat any car on just about any journey at all. And Alex wasn't riding just any bike. He still had his Condor Junior Roadracer, hand-built for him in the workshop that had been open for business in the same street in Holborn for more than fifty years. He'd recently had it upgraded with an integrated brake and gear-lever system fitted to the handlebar, and he only had to flick his thumb to feel the bike click up a gear, the lightweight titanium sprockets spinning smoothly beneath him.

He caught up with the car just as it turned the corner and joined the rest of the traffic on the King's Road. He would just have to hope that Skoda was going to stay in the city, but some-how Alex didn't think it likely that he would travel too far. The drug dealer hadn't chosen Brookland School as a target simply because he'd been there. It had to be somewhere in his general neighbourhood – not too close to home but not too far either.

The lights changed and the white car jerked forward, heading west. Alex was pedalling slowly, keeping a few cars behind, just in case Skoda happened to glance in his mirror. They reached the corner known as World's End and suddenly the road was clear and Alex had to switch gears again and pedal hard to keep up. The car drove on, through Parson's Green and down towards Putney. Alex twisted from one lane to another, cutting in front of a taxi and receiving the blast of a horn as his reward. It was a warm day and he could feel his French and history homework dragging down his back. How much further were they going? And what would he do when they got there? Alex was beginning to wonder if this had been a good idea when the car turned off and he realized they had arrived.

Skoda had pulled into a rough tarmac area, a temporary carpark next to the River Thames, not far from Putney Bridge. Alex stayed on the bridge, allowing the traffic to roll past, and watched as the drug dealer got out of his car and began to walk. The area was being redeveloped, another block of prestige flats rising up to bruise the London skyline. Right now, the building was no more than an ugly skeleton of steel girders and prefabricated concrete slabs. It was surrounded by a swarm of men in hard hats. There were bulldozers, cement mixers and, towering above them all, a huge canary-yellow crane. A sign read:

Riverview House
ALL VISITORS
REPORT TO
THE SITE OFFICE

Alex wondered if Skoda had some sort of business on the site. He seemed to be heading for the entrance. But then he turned off. Alex watched him, puzzled.

The building site was wedged in between the bridge and a cluster of modern buildings. There was a pub, then what looked like a brand-new conference centre, and finally a police station with a carpark half filled with official cars. But right next to the building site, sticking out into the river, was a wooden jetty with two cabin cruisers and an old iron barge quietly rusting in the murky water. Alex hadn't noticed the jetty at first, but Skoda walked straight onto it, then climbed onto the barge. He opened a door and disappeared inside. Was this where he lived? It was late in the day. Somehow, Alex doubted he was about to set off on a pleasure cruise down the River Thames.

He got back on his bike and cycled slowly to the end of the bridge, and then down towards the carpark. He left the bike and his backpack out of sight and continued on foot, moving more slowly as he approached the jetty. He wasn't afraid of being caught. This was a public place and even if Skoda did reappear, there would be nothing he could do. But he was curious. Just what was the drug dealer doing onboard a barge? It seemed a bizarre place to have stopped. Alex still wasn't sure what he was going to do, but he wanted to have a look inside. Then he would decide.

The wooden jetty creaked under his feet as he stepped onto it. The barge was called *Blue Shadow* but there was little blue left in the flaking paint, the rusty ironwork and the dirty, oil-covered decks. The barge was about ten metres long and very square, with a single cabin in the centre. It was lying low in the water and Alex guessed that most of the living quarters would be underneath. He knelt down on the jetty and pretended to tie his shoelaces, hoping to look through the narrow, slanting windows. But all the curtains were drawn. What now?

The barge was moored on one side of the jetty. The two cruisers were side by side on the other. Skoda wanted privacy – but he must also need light, and there would be no need to draw the curtains on the far side with nothing there apart from the river. The only trouble was, to look in the other windows Alex would have to climb onto the barge itself. He considered briefly. It had to be worth the risk. He was near enough to the building site. Nobody was going to try to hurt him with so many people around.

He placed one foot on the deck, then slowly transferred his weight onto it. He was afraid that moving the barge would give him away. Sure enough, the barge dipped under his weight; but Alex had chosen his moment well. A police launch was sailing past, heading up the river and back into town. The barge bobbed naturally in its wake and by the time it settled Alex was onboard, crouching next to the cabin door.

Now he could hear music coming from inside. The heavy beat of a rock band. He didn't want to do it, but he knew there was only one way to look in. He tried to find an area of the deck that wasn't too covered in oil, then lay flat on his stomach. Clinging onto the handrail, he lowered his head and shoulders over the side of the barge and shifted himself forward so that he was hanging almost upside-down over the water.

He was right. The curtains on this side of the barge were open. Looking through the dirty glass of the window, he could see two men. Skoda was sitting on a bunk, smoking a cigarette. There was a second man, blond-haired and ugly, with twisted lips and three days' stubble, wearing a torn sweatshirt and jeans, making a cup of coffee at a small stove. The music was coming from a ghetto-blaster perched on a shelf. Alex looked around the cabin. Apart from two bunks and the miniature kitchen, the barge offered no living accommodation at all. Instead it had been converted for another purpose. Skoda and his friend had turned it into a floating laboratory.

There were two metal work-surfaces, a sink and a pair of electric scales. Everywhere there were test tubes and Bunsen burners, flasks, glass pipes and measuring spoons. The whole place was filthy – obviously neither of the men cared about hygiene – but

Alex knew that he was looking into the heart of their operation. This was where they prepared the drugs they sold; cut them down, weighed them and packaged them for delivery to local schools. It was an incredible idea – to put a drugs factory on a boat, almost in the middle of London and only a stone's throw away from a police station. But at the same time, it was a clever one. Who would have looked for it here?

The blond man suddenly turned round and Alex hooked his body up and slithered backwards onto the deck. For a moment he was dizzy. Hanging upside-down, the blood had drained into his head. He took a couple of breaths, trying to collect his thoughts. It would be easy enough to walk over to the police station and tell the officer in charge what he had seen. The police could take over from there.

But something inside Alex rejected the idea. Maybe that was what he would have done a few months before. Let someone else take care of it. But he hadn't cycled all this way just to call in the police. He thought back to his first sighting of the white car outside the school gates. He remembered Colin, his friend, shuffling over to it and felt once again a brief blaze of anger. This was something he wanted to do himself.

What could he do? If the barge had been equipped with a plug, Alex would have pulled it out and sunk the entire thing. But of course it wasn't as easy as that. The barge was tied to the jetty by two thick ropes. He could untie them, but that wouldn't help either. The barge would drift away, but this was Putney; there were no whirlpools or waterfalls. Skoda would simply turn the engine on and cruise back again.

Alex looked around him. On the building site, the day's work was coming to an end. Some of the men were already leaving and, as he watched, he saw a trapdoor open about a hundred metres above him and a stocky man begin the long climb down from the top of the crane. Alex closed his eyes. A whole series of images had suddenly flashed into his mind, like different sections of a jigsaw.

The barge. The building site. The police station. The crane with its great hook dangling underneath the jib.

And Blackpool funfair. He'd gone there once with his housekeeper, Jack Starbright, and had watched as she'd won a teddy bear, hooking it out of a glass case with a mechanical claw and carrying it over to a chute.

Could it be done? Alex looked again, working out the angles. Yes. It probably could.

He stood up and crept back across the deck to the door that Skoda had entered. There was a length of wire lying to one side and he picked it up, then wound it several times round the handle of the door. He looped the wire over a hook in the wall and pulled it tight. The door was effectively locked. There was a second door at the back of the boat. Alex secured that one with his own bicycle padlock. As far as he could see, the windows were too narrow to crawl through. There was no other way in or out.

He crept off the barge and back onto the jetty. Then he untied it, leaving the thick rope loosely curled up beside the metal pegs – the stanchions – that had secured it. The river was still. It would be a while before the barge drifted away.

He straightened up. Satisfied with his work so far, he began to run.

HOOKED

The entrance to the building site was crowded with construction workers preparing to go home. Alex was reminded of Brookland an hour earlier. Nothing really changed when you got older – except that maybe you weren't given homework. The men and women drifting out of the site were tired, in a hurry to be away. That was probably why none of them tried to stop Alex as he slipped in among them, walking purposefully as if he knew where he was going, as if he had every right to be there.

But the shift wasn't completely finished yet. Other workers were still carrying tools, stowing away machinery, packing up for the night. They were all wearing protective headgear and, seeing a pile of plastic helmets, Alex snatched one up and put it on. The great sweep of the block of flats that was being built loomed up ahead of him. To pass through it he was forced into a narrow corridor between two scaffolding towers. Suddenly a thickset man in white overalls stepped in front of him, blocking his way.

"Where are you going?" he demanded.

"My dad..." Alex gestured vaguely in the direction of another worker and kept walking. The trick worked. The man didn't challenge him again.

He was heading for the crane. It was standing in the open, the high priest of the construction. Alex hadn't realized how very tall it was until he reached it. The supporting tower was bolted into a massive block of concrete. The tower was very narrow – once he had squeezed through the iron girders he could reach out and touch all four sides. A ladder ran straight up the centre. Without stopping to think – if he thought about it he might change his mind – Alex began to climb.

It's only a ladder, he told himself. You've climbed ladders before. You've got nothing to worry about.

But this was a ladder with three hundred rungs. If Alex let go or slipped, there would be nothing to stop him falling to his death. There were rest platforms at intervals but Alex didn't dare stop to catch his breath. Somebody might look up and see him. And there was always a chance that the barge, loose from its moorings, might begin to drift.

After two hundred and fifty rungs, the tower narrowed. Alex could see the crane's control cabin directly above him. He looked back down. The men on the building site were suddenly very small and far away. He climbed the last stretch of ladder. There was a trapdoor over his head, leading into the cabin. But the trapdoor was locked.

Fortunately, Alex was ready for this. When MI6 had sent him on his first mission, they had given him a number of gadgets – he couldn't exactly call them weapons – to help him out of tight corners. One of these was a tube marked ZIT-CLEAN, FOR HEALTHIER SKIN. But the cream inside the tube did much more than clean up spots.

Although Alex had used most of it, he had managed to hold onto the last remnants and often carried the tube with him, as a sort of souvenir. He had it in his pocket now. Holding onto the ladder with one hand, he took the tube out with the other. There was very little of the cream left but Alex knew that a little was all he would need. He opened the tube, squeezed some of the cream onto the lock and waited. There was a moment's pause, then a hiss and a wisp of smoke. The cream was eating into the metal. The lock sprang open. Alex pushed back the trapdoor and climbed the last few rungs. He was in.

He had to close the trapdoor again to create enough floor space to stand on. He found himself in a square metal box, about the same size as a sit-in arcade game. There was a pilot's chair with two joysticks – one on each arm – and, instead of a screen, a floor-to-ceiling window with a spectacular view of the building site, the river and the whole of west London. A small computer monitor had been built into one corner and, at knee level, there was a radio transmitter.

The joysticks on the arms were surprisingly uncomplicated. Each had just six buttons. There were even helpful diagrams to show what they did. The right hand would lift the hook up and down. The left hand would move it along the jib – closer to or further from the cabin. The left hand also controlled the whole top of the crane, rotating it 360 degrees. It couldn't have been much simpler. Even the start button was clearly labelled. A big button for a big toy. Everything about the crane reminded Alex of an oversized Meccano kit.

He pushed the button and felt power surge into the control cabin. The computer lit up with a graphic of a barking dog as the warm-up program came into life. Alex eased himself into the operator's chair. There were still twenty or thirty men on the site.

Looking down between his knees, he could see them moving silently far below. Nobody had noticed that anything was wrong. But he knew he still had to move fast.

He pressed the green button on the right-hand control – green for go – then touched his fingers against the joystick and pushed. Nothing happened! Alex frowned. Maybe it was going to be more complicated than he'd thought. What had he missed? He rested his hands on the joysticks, looking left and right for another control. His right hand moved slightly and suddenly the hook soared up from the ground. It was working!

Unknown to Alex, when he gripped the handles of the joysticks, heat sensors concealed inside had read his body temperature and activated the crane. All modern cranes have the same security system built into them, in case the operator has a heart attack and falls against the controls. There can be no accidents. Body heat is needed to make the crane work.

Luckily for him, this crane was a Liebherr 154 EC-H, one of the most modern in the world. The Liebherr is incredibly easy to use – and remarkably accurate. Now Alex pushed sideways with his left hand and gasped as the crane swung round. In front of him he could see the jib stretching out, swinging high over the rooftops of London. The more he pushed, the faster the crane went. The movement couldn't have been smoother. The Liebherr 154 has a fluid coupling between the electric motor and the gears so that it never jolts or shudders – it glides. Alex found a white button under his thumb and pressed it. The movement stopped at once.

He was ready. He would need some beginner's luck, but he was sure he could do it – provided nobody looked up and saw the crane moving. He pushed with his left hand again and this time waited as the jib of the crane swung all the way round past Putney Bridge and over the River Thames. When the jib was pointing directly over the barge, he stopped. Now he manoeuvred the cradle with the hook. First he slid it right to the end of the jib. Then, using his other hand, he lowered it; quickly to begin with, more slowly as it drew closer to ground level. The hook was solid metal. If he hit the barge, Skoda might hear it and Alex would have given himself away. Carefully now, one centimetre at a time. Alex licked his lips and, using all his concentration, took careful aim.

The hook crashed into the deck. Alex cursed. Surely Skoda would have heard it and would even now be grappling with the door. Then he remembered the ghetto-blaster. Hopefully, the music would have drowned out the noise. He lifted the hook, at the same time dragging it across the deck towards him. He had seen his target. There was a thick metal stanchion welded into the deck at the near end. If he could just loop the hook around the stanchion he would have caught his fish. Then he could reel it in.

His first attempt missed the stanchion by more than a metre. Alex forced himself not to panic. He had to do this slowly or he would never do it at all. Working with his left and right hands, balancing one movement against the other, he dragged the hook over the deck and then back towards the stanchion. He would just have to hope that the ghetto-blaster was still playing and that the sliding metal wasn't making too much noise. He missed the stanchion a second time. This wasn't going to work!

No. He could do it. It was the same as the funfair ... just bigger. He gritted his teeth and manoeuvred the hook a third time. This time he saw it happen. The hook caught hold of the stanchion. He had it!

He looked down. Nobody had noticed anything wrong. Now ... how did you lift? He pulled with his right hand. The cable became taut. He actually felt the crane take the weight of the barge. The whole tower tilted forward alarmingly and Alex almost slid out of his seat. For the first time he wondered if his plan was actually possible.

Could the crane lift the barge out of the water? What was the maximum load? There was a white placard at the end of the crane arm, printed with a measurement: 3900KG. Surely the boat couldn't weigh that much. He glanced at the computer screen. One set of digits was changing so rapidly he was unable to read them. They were showing the weight that the crane was taking. What would happen if the boat was too heavy? Would the computer initiate an automatic cut-out? Or would the whole thing just fall over?

Alex settled himself in the chair and pulled back, wondering what would happen next.

Inside the boat, Skoda was opening a bottle of gin. He'd had a good day, selling more than a hundred pounds' worth of merchandise to the kids at his old school. And the best thing was, they'd all be back for more. Soon he'd only sell them the stuff if they promised to introduce it to their friends. Then the friends would become customers too. It was the easiest market in the world. He'd got them hooked. They were his to do with as he liked.

The blond-haired man he was working with was called Mike Beckett. The two of them had met in prison and had decided to go into business together when they got out. The boat had been Beckett's idea. There was no proper kitchen, no toilet and it was freezing in winter ... but it worked. It even amused them to be so close to a police station. They enjoyed watching the police cars or boats going past. Of course, the pigs would never think of looking right on their own doorstep.

Suddenly Beckett swore. "What the...?"

"What is it?" Skoda looked up.

"The cup..."

Skoda watched as a cup of coffee, which had been sitting on a shelf, began to move. It slid sideways, then fell off with a clatter, spilling cold coffee on the grey rag they called a carpet. Skoda was confused. The cup seemed to have moved on its own. Nothing had touched it. He giggled. "How did you do that?" he asked.

"I didn't."

"Then..."

Beckett was the first to realize what was happening – but even he couldn't guess the truth. "We're sinking!" he shouted.

He scrabbled for the door. Now Skoda felt it for himself. The floor was tilting. Test tubes and beakers slid into each other then crashed to the floor, glass shattering. He swore and followed Beckett – uphill now. With every second that passed, the rake was becoming steeper. But the strange thing was that the barge didn't seem to be sinking at all. On the contrary, the front of it seemed to be rising out of the water.

"What's going on?" he yelled.

"The door's jammed!" Beckett had managed to open it a crack, but the padlock on the other side was holding it firm.

"There's the other door!"

But the second door was now high above them. Bottles rolled off the table and smashed. In the kitchen, soiled plates and mugs slid into each other, pieces flying. With something between a sob and a snarl, Skoda tried to climb up the mountainside that the inside of the boat had become. But it was already too steep. The door was almost over his head. He lost his balance and fell backwards, shouting as – one second later – the other man was thrown on top of him. The two of them rolled into the corner, tangled up in each other. Plates, cups, knives, forks and dozens of pieces of scientific equipment crashed into them. The walls of the barge were grinding with the pressure. A window shattered. A table turned itself into a battering-ram and hurled itself at them. Skoda felt a bone snap in his arm and screamed out loud.

The barge was completely vertical, hanging above the water at 90 degrees. For a moment it rested where it was. Then it began to rise...

Alex stared at the barge in amazement. The crane was lifting it at half speed – some sort of override had come into action, slowing the operation down – but it wasn't even straining. Alex could feel the power under his palms. Sitting in the cabin with both hands on the joysticks, his feet apart and the jib of the crane jutting out ahead of him, he felt as if he and the crane had become one. He only had to move a centimetre and the boat would be brought to him. He could see it, dangling on the hook, spinning slowly. Water was streaming off the stern. It was already clear of the water, rising up about a metre every five seconds. He wondered what it must be like inside.

The radio beside his knee hissed into life.

"Crane operator! This is base. What the hell do you think you're doing? Over!" A pause, a burst of static. Then the metallic voice was back. "Who is in the crane? Who's up there? Identify yourself!"

There was a microphone snaking towards Alex's chin and he was tempted to say something. But he decided against it. Hearing a teenager's voice would only panic them more.

He looked down. There were about a dozen construction workers closing in on the base of the crane. Others were pointing at the boat, jabbering amongst themselves. No sounds reached the cabin. It was as if Alex was cut off from the real world. He felt very secure. He had no doubt that more workers would have already started climbing the ladder and that it would all be over soon, but for the moment he was untouchable. He concentrated on what he was doing. Getting the barge out of the water had been only half his plan. He still had to finish it.

"Crane operator! Lower the hook! We believe there are people inside the boat and you are endangering their lives. Repeat. Lower the hook!"

The barge was high above the water, dangling on the end of the hook. Alex moved his left hand, turning the crane round so that the boat was swung in an arc along the river and then over dry land. There was a sudden buzz. The jib came to a halt. Alex pushed the joystick. Nothing happened. He glanced at the computer. The screen had gone blank.

Someone at ground level had come to their senses and done the only sensible thing. They had switched off the power. The crane was dead.

Alex sat where he was, watching the barge swaying in the breeze. He hadn't quite succeeded in what he had set out to do. He had planned to lower the boat – along with its contents – safely into the carpark of the police station. It would have made a nice surprise for the authorities, he had thought. Instead, the boat was now hanging over the conference centre that he had seen from Putney Bridge. But at the end of the day, he didn't suppose it made much difference. The end result would be the same.

He stretched his arms and relaxed, waiting for the trapdoor to burst open. This wasn't going to be easy to explain.

And then he heard the tearing sound.

The metal stanchion that protruded from the end of the deck had not been designed to carry the entire weight of the barge. It was a miracle that it had lasted as long as it had. As Alex watched, open-mouthed, from the cabin, the stanchion tore itself free. For a few seconds it clung by one edge to the deck. Then the last metal rivet came loose.

The barge had been sixty metres above the ground. Now it began to fall.

*   *   *

In the Putney Riverside Conference Centre, the chief constable of the Metropolitan Police was addressing a large crowd of journalists, TV cameras, civil servants and government officials. He was a tall, thin man who took himself very seriously. His dark blue uniform was immaculate, every piece of silver – from the studs on his epaulettes to his five medals – was polished until it gleamed. This was his big day. He was sharing the platform with no less a personage than the home secretary himself. The assistant chief constable was there and also seven lower-ranking officers. A slogan was being projected onto the wall behind him.

WINNING THE WAR AGAINST DRUGS

Silver letters on a blue background. The chief constable had chosen the colours himself, knowing that they matched his uniform. He liked the slogan. He knew that it would be in all the major newspapers the next day – and, just as important, a photograph of himself.

"We have overlooked nothing!" he was saying, his voice echoing around the modern room. He could see the journalists scribbling down his every word. The television cameras were all focused on him. "Thanks to my personal involvement and efforts, we have never been more successful. Home Secretary..." He smiled at the senior politician, who smiled toothily back. "But we are not resting on our laurels. Oh no! Any day now we hope to announce another breakthrough."

That was when the barge hit the glass roof of the conference centre. There was an explosion. The chief constable just had time to dive for cover as a vast, dripping object plunged down towards him. The home secretary was thrown backwards, his spectacles flying off his face. His security men froze, helpless. The boat crashed into the space in front of them, between the stage and the audience. The side of the cabin had been torn off and what was left of the laboratory was exposed, with the two dealers sprawled together in one corner, staring dazedly at the hundreds of policemen and officials who now surrounded them. A cloud of white powder mushroomed up and then fell onto the dark blue uniform of the chief constable, covering him from head to toe. The fire alarms had gone off. The lights fused and went out. Then the screaming began.

Meanwhile, the first of the construction workers had made it to the crane cabin and was gazing in astonishment at the fourteen-year-old boy he had found there.

"Do you...?" he stammered. "Do you have any idea what you've just done?"

Alex glanced at the empty hook and at the gaping hole in the roof of the conference centre, at the rising smoke and dust. He shrugged apologetically.

"I was just working on the crime figures," he said. "And I think there's been a drop."

SEARCH AND REPORT

At least they didn't have far to take him.

Two men brought Alex down from the crane, one above him on the ladder and one below. The police were waiting at the bottom. Watched by the incredulous construction workers, he was frog-marched off the building site and into the police station just a few buildings away. As he passed the conference centre, he saw the crowds pouring out. Ambulances had already arrived. The home secretary was being whisked away in a black limousine. For the first time, Alex was seriously worried, wondering if anyone had been killed. He hadn't meant it to end like this.

Once they got to the police station, everything happened in a whirl of slamming doors, blank official faces, whitewashed walls, forms and phone calls. Alex was asked his name, his age, his address. He saw a police sergeant tapping the details into a computer, but what happened next took him by surprise. The sergeant pressed ENTER and visibly froze. He turned and looked at Alex, then hastily left his seat. When Alex had entered the police station he'd been the centre of attention, but suddenly everyone was avoiding his eye. A more senior officer appeared. Words were exchanged. Alex was led down a corridor and put into a cell.

Half an hour later, a female police officer appeared with a tray of food. "Supper," she said.

"What's happening?" Alex asked. The woman smiled nervously, but said nothing. "I left my bike by the bridge," Alex said.

"It's all right, we've got it." She couldn't leave the room fast enough.

Alex ate the food: sausages, toast, a slice of cake. There was a bunk in the room and, behind a screen, a sink and a toilet. He wondered if anyone was going to come in and talk to him, but nobody did. Eventually he fell asleep.

The next thing he knew, it was seven o'clock in the morning. The door was open and a man he knew only too well was standing in the cell, looking down at him.

"Good morning, Alex," he said.

"Mr Crawley."

John Crawley looked like a junior bank manager and when Alex had first met him he had indeed been pretending that he worked for a bank. The cheap suit and striped tie could both have come from a Marks & Spencer "Boring Businessman" range. In fact, Crawley worked for MI6. Alex wondered if the clothes were a cover or a personal choice.

"You can come with me now," Crawley said. "We're leaving."

"Are you taking me home?" Alex asked. He wondered if anyone had been told where he was.

"No. Not yet."

Alex followed Crawley out of the building. This time there were no police officers in sight. A car with a driver stood waiting outside. Crawley got into the back with Alex.

"Where are we going?" Alex asked.

"You'll see." Crawley opened a copy of the *Daily Telegraph* and began to read. He didn't speak again.

They drove east through the City and up towards Liverpool Street. Alex knew at once where he was being taken and, sure enough, the car turned into the entrance of a seventeen-storey building near the station and disappeared down a ramp into an underground carpark. Alex had been here before. The building pretended to be the headquarters of the Royal & General bank. In fact, this was where the Special Operations division of MI6 was based.

The car stopped. Crawley folded his paper away and got out, ushering Alex ahead of him. There was a lift in the basement and the two of them took it to the sixteenth floor.

"This way." Crawley gestured to a door marked 1605. The Gunpowder Plot, Alex thought. It was an absurd thing to flash into his mind, a fragment of the history homework he should have been doing the night before. 1605 – the year Guy Fawkes had tried to blow up the Houses of Parliament. Oh well, it looked as if the homework was going to have to wait.

Alex opened the door and went in. Crawley didn't follow. When Alex looked round, he was already walking away.

"Shut the door, Alex, and come in."

Once again, Alex found himself standing opposite the prim, unsmiling man who headed the Special Operations division of MI6. Grey suit, grey face, grey life ... Alan Blunt seemed to belong to an entirely colourless world. He was sitting behind a wooden desk in a large, square office that could have belonged to any business anywhere in the world. There was nothing personal in the room, not even a picture on the wall or a photograph on the desk. Even the pigeons pecking on the windowsill outside were grey.

Blunt was not alone. Mrs Jones, his senior officer, was with him, sitting on a leather chair, wearing a mud-brown jacket and dress, and – as usual – sucking a peppermint. She looked up at Alex with black, beadlike eyes. She seemed to be more pleased to see him than her boss was. It was she who had spoken. Blunt had barely registered the fact that Alex had come into the room.

Then Blunt looked up. "I hadn't expected to see you again so soon," he said.

"That's just what I was going to say," Alex replied. There was a single empty chair in the office. He sat down.

Blunt slid a sheet of paper across his desk and examined it briefly. "What on earth were you thinking of?" he demanded. "This business with the crane? You've done an enormous amount of damage. You've practically destroyed a two million pound conference centre. It's a miracle nobody was killed."

"The two men in the boat will be in hospital for months," Mrs Jones added.

"You could have killed the home secretary!" Blunt continued. "That would have been the last straw. What *were* you doing?"

"They were drug dealers," Alex said.

"So we've discovered. But the normal procedure would have been to dial 999."

"I couldn't find a phone." Alex sighed. "They turned off the crane," he explained. "I was going to put the boat in the carpark."

Blunt blinked once and waved a hand as if dismissing everything that had happened. "It's just as well that your special status came up on the police computer," he said. "They called us, and we've handled the rest."

"I didn't know I had special status," Alex said.

"Oh yes, Alex. You're nothing if not special." Blunt gazed at him for a moment. "That's why you're here."

"So you're not going to send me home?"

"No. The fact is, Alex, we were thinking of contacting you anyway. We need you again."

"You're probably the only person who can do what we have in mind," Mrs Jones added.

"Wait a minute!" Alex shook his head. "I'm far enough behind at school as it is. Suppose I'm not interested?"

Mrs Jones sighed. "We could, of course, return you to the police," she said. "As I understand it, they were very keen to interview you."

"And how is Miss Starbright?" Blunt asked.

Jack Starbright – the name was short for Jackie or Jacqueline, Alex wasn't sure which – was the housekeeper who had been looking after Alex since his uncle had died. She was a bright, red-haired American girl who had come to London to study law but had never left. Blunt wasn't interested in her health, Alex knew that. The last time they'd met, he'd made his position clear. So long as Alex did as he was told, he could stay living in his uncle's house with Jack. Step out of line and she'd be deported to America and Alex would be taken into care. It was blackmail of course, pure and simple.

"She's fine," Alex said. There was quiet anger in his voice.

Mrs Jones took over. "Come on, Alex," she said. "Why pretend you're an ordinary schoolboy any more?"

She was trying to sound more friendly, more like a mother. But even snakes have mothers, Alex thought.

"You've already proved yourself once," she went on. "We're just giving you a chance to do it again."

"It'll probably come to nothing," Blunt continued. "It's just something that needs looking into. What we call a search and report."

"Why can't Crawley do it?"

"We need a boy."

Alex fell silent. He looked from Blunt to Mrs Jones and back again. He knew that neither of them would hesitate for a second before pulling him out of Brookland and sending him to the grimmest institution they could find. And anyway, wasn't this what he had been asking for only the day before? Another adventure. Another chance to save the world.

"All right," he said. "What is it this time?"

Blunt nodded at Mrs Jones, who unwrapped a sweet and began.

"I wonder if you know anything about a man called Michael J. Roscoe?" she asked.

Alex thought for a moment. "He was that businessman who had an accident in New York." He'd seen the news on TV. "Didn't he fall down a liftshaft or something?"

"Roscoe Electronics is one of the largest companies in America," Mrs Jones said. "In fact it's one of the largest in the world. Computers, videos, DVD players ... everything from mobile phones to washing-machines. Roscoe was very rich, very influential—"

"And very short-sighted," Alex cut in.

"It certainly seems to have been a very strange and even a careless accident," Mrs Jones agreed. "The lift somehow malfunctioned. Roscoe didn't look where he was going. He fell into the liftshaft and died. That's the general opinion. However, we're not so sure."

"Why not?"

"First of all, there are a number of details that don't add up. On the day Roscoe died, a maintenance engineer by the name of Sam Green called at Roscoe Tower on Fifth Avenue. We know it was Green – or someone who looked very much like him – because we've seen him. They have closed-circuit security cameras and he was filmed going in. He said he'd come to look at a defective cable. But according to the company that employed him, there was no defective cable and he certainly wasn't acting under orders from them."

"Why don't you talk to him?"

"We'd like to. But Green has vanished without trace. We think he might have been killed. We think someone might have taken his place and somehow set up the accident that killed Roscoe."

Alex shrugged. "I'm sorry. I'm sorry about Mr Roscoe. But what's it got to do with me?"

"I'm coming to that." Mrs Jones paused. "The strangest thing of all is that, the day before he died, Roscoe telephoned this office. A personal call. He asked to speak to Mr Blunt."

"I met Roscoe at Cambridge University," Blunt said. "That was a long time ago. We became friends."

That surprised Alex. He didn't think of Blunt as the sort of man who had friends. "What did he say?" he asked.

"Unfortunately, I wasn't here to take the call," Blunt replied. "I arranged to speak with him the following day. By that time, it was too late."

"Do you have any idea what he wanted?"

"I spoke to his assistant," Mrs Jones said. "She wasn't able to tell me very much, but she understood that Roscoe was concerned about his son. He has a fourteen-year-old son, Paul Roscoe."

A fourteen-year-old son. Alex was beginning to see the way things were going.

"Paul was his only son," Blunt explained. "I'm afraid the two of them had a very difficult relationship. Roscoe divorced a few years ago and although the boy chose to live with his father, they didn't really get on. There were the usual teenage problems but, of course, when you grow up surrounded by millions of dollars these problems sometimes get amplified. Paul was doing badly at school.

He was playing truant, spending time with some very undesirable friends. There was an incident with the New York police – nothing serious and Roscoe managed to hush it up, but it still upset him. I spoke to Roscoe from time to time. He was worried about Paul and felt the boy was out of control. But there didn't seem to be very much he could do."

"So is that what you want me for?" Alex interrupted. "You want me to meet this boy and talk to him about his father's death?"

"No." Blunt shook his head and handed a file to Mrs Jones.

She opened it. Alex caught a glimpse of a photograph; a dark-skinned man in military uniform. "Remember what we told you about Roscoe," she said. "Because now I want to tell you about another man." She slid the photograph round so that Alex could see it. "This is General Viktor Ivanov. Ex-KGB. Until last December he was head of the Foreign Intelligence Service and probably the second or third most powerful man in Russia after the president. But then something happened to him too. It was a boating accident on the Black Sea. His cruiser exploded ... nobody knows why."

"Was he a friend of Roscoe's?" Alex asked.

"They probably never met. But we have a department here that constantly monitors world news, and their computers have thrown up a very strange coincidence. Ivanov also had a fourteen-year-old son, Dimitry. And one thing is certain. The young Ivanov certainly knew the young Roscoe because they went to the same school."

"Paul and Dimitry..." Alex was puzzled. "What was a Russian boy doing at a school in New York?"

"He wasn't in New York." Blunt took over. "As I told you, Roscoe was having trouble with his boy. Trouble at school, trouble at home. So last year he decided to take action. He sent Paul to Europe, to a place in France, a sort of finishing school.

Do you know what a finishing school is?"

"I thought it was the sort of place where rich people used to send their daughters," Alex said. "To learn table manners."

"That's the general idea. But this school is for boys only, and not just ordinary boys. The fees are ten thousand pounds a term. This is the brochure. You can have a look." He passed a heavy, square booklet to Alex. Written on the cover, gold letters on black, were the two words:

POINT BLANC

"It's right on the French-Swiss border," Blunt explained. "South of Geneva. Just above Grenoble, in the French Alps. It's pronounced *Point Blanc*." He spoke the words with a French accent. "Literally, *white point*. It's a remarkable place. Built as a private home by some lunatic in the nineteenth century. As a matter of fact, that's what it became after he died ... a lunatic asylum. It was taken over by the Germans in the Second World War. They used it as a leisure centre for their senior staff. After that, it fell into disrepair until it was bought by the current owner, a man called Grief. Dr Hugo Grief. He's the principal of the school. What I suppose you'd call the head teacher."

Alex opened the brochure and found himself looking at a colour photograph of Point Blanc. Blunt was right. The school was like nothing he had ever seen; something between a German castle and a French château, straight out of a Grimm's fairy tale. But what drew Alex's breath, more than the building itself, was the setting. The school was perched on the side of a mountain, with nothing but mountains all around; a great pile of brick and stone surrounded by a snow-covered landscape. It seemed to have no business being there, as if it had been snatched out of an ancient city and accidentally dropped there. No roads led to the school. The snow continued all the way to the front gate. But looking again, Alex saw a modern helicopter pad projecting over the battlements. He guessed that was the only way to get there ... and to leave.

He turned the page.

Welcome to the Academy at
POINT BLANC...

the introduction began. It had been printed in the sort of lettering Alex would expect to find on the menu of an expensive restaurant.

> *...a unique school that is much more than a school, created for boys who need more than the ordinary education system can provide. In our time we have been called a school for "problem boys", but we do not believe the term applies.*
>
> *There are problems and there are boys. It is our aim to separate the two.*

"There's no need to read all that stuff," Blunt said. "All you need to know is that the academy takes in boys who have been expelled from all their other schools. There are never very many of them there. Just six or seven at a time. And it's unique in other ways too. For a start, it only takes the sons of the super-rich—"

"At ten thousand pounds a term, I'm not surprised," Alex said.

"You'd be surprised just how many parents have applied to send their sons there," Blunt went on. "But I suppose you've only got to look at the newspapers to see how easy it is to go off the rails when you're born with a silver spoon in your mouth. It doesn't matter if they're politicians or popstars; fame and fortune for the parents often brings problems for the children ... and the more successful the parents are, the more pressure there seems to be.

The academy went into business to sort the young people out, and by all accounts it's been a great success."

"It was established twenty years ago," Mrs Jones said. "In that time it's had a client list you'd find hard to believe. Of course, they've kept the names confidential. But I can tell you that parents who have sent their children there include an American vice-president, a Nobel Prize-winning scientist and a member of our own royal family!"

"As well as Roscoe and this man, Ivanov," Alex said.

"Yes."

Alex shrugged. "So it's a coincidence. Just like you said. Two rich parents with two rich kids at the same school. They're both killed in accidents. Why are you so interested?"

"Because I don't like coincidence," Blunt replied. "In fact, I don't believe in coincidence. Where some people see coincidence, I see conspiracy. That's my job."

And you're welcome to it, Alex thought. He said, "Do you really think the school and this man Grief might have had something to do with the two deaths? Why? Had they forgotten to pay the fees?"

Blunt didn't smile. "Roscoe telephones me because he's worried about his son. The next day he's dead. We've also learnt from Russian intelligence sources that a week before he died, Ivanov had a violent argument with his son. Apparently Ivanov was worried about something. Now do you see the link?"

Alex thought for a moment. "So you want me to go to this school," he said. "How are you going to manage that? I don't have parents and they were never rich anyway."

"We've already arranged that," Mrs Jones said. Alex realized that she must have made her plans before the business with the crane ever happened. Even if he hadn't drawn attention to himself, they would have come for him. "We're going to supply you with a wealthy father. His name is Sir David Friend."

"Friend ... as in Friend's supermarkets?" Alex had seen the name often enough in the newspapers.

"Supermarkets. Department stores. Art galleries. Football teams." Mrs Jones paused. "Friend is certainly a member of the same club as Roscoe. The billionaires' club. He's also heavily involved in government circles, as personal adviser to the prime minister. Very little happens in this country without Sir David being involved in some way."

"We've created a false identity for you," Blunt said. "From this moment on, I want you to start thinking of yourself as Alex Friend, the fourteen-year-old son of Sir David."

"It won't work," Alex said. "People must know that Friend doesn't have a son."

"Not at all." Blunt shook his head. "He's a very private person and we've created the sort of son no father would want to talk about. Expelled from Eton. A criminal record ... shoplifting, vandalism and possession of drugs. That's you, Alex. Sir David and his wife, Caroline, don't know what to do with you. So they've enrolled you in the academy. And you've been accepted."

"And Sir David has agreed to all this?" Alex asked.

Blunt sniffed. "As a matter of fact, he wasn't very happy about it – about using someone as young as you. But I spoke to him at some length and, yes, he agreed to help."

"So when am I going to the academy?"

"Five days from now," Mrs Jones said. "But first you have to immerse yourself in your new life. When you leave here, we've arranged for you to be taken to Sir David's home. He has a house in Lancashire. He lives there with his wife – and he has a daughter. She's one year older than you. You'll spend the rest of the week with the family, which should give you time to learn everything you need to know. It's vital that you have a strong cover. After that, you'll leave for Grenoble."

"And what do I do when I get there?"

"We'll give you a full briefing nearer the time. Essentially, your job is to find out everything you can. It may be that this school is perfectly ordinary and that there was in fact no connection between the deaths. If so, we'll pull you out. But we want to be sure."

"How will I get in touch with you?"

"We'll arrange all that." Mrs Jones ran an eye over Alex, then turned to Blunt. "We'll have to do something about his appearance," she said. "He doesn't exactly look the part."

"See to it," Blunt said.

Alex sighed. It was strange really. He was simply going from one school to another. From a London comprehensive to a finishing school in France. It wasn't quite the adventure he'd been expecting.

He stood up and followed Mrs Jones out of the room. As he left, Blunt was already sifting through documents as if he'd forgotten that Alex had been there or even existed at all.

THE SHOOTING PARTY

The chauffeur-driven Rolls-Royce Corniche cruised along a tree-lined avenue, penetrating ever deeper into the Lancashire countryside, its 6.75 litre light pressure V8 engine barely a whisper in the great green silence all around. Alex sat in the back, trying to be unimpressed by a car that cost as much as a house. Forget the Wilton wool carpets, the wooden panelling and the leather seats, he told himself. It's only a car.

It was the day after his meeting at MI6 and, as Mrs Jones had promised, his appearance had completely changed. He had to look like a rebel – the rich son who wanted to live life by his own rules. So Alex had been dressed in purposefully provocative clothes. He was wearing a hooded sweatshirt, Tommy Hilfiger jeans – frayed at the ankles – and trainers that were falling apart on his feet. Despite his protests, his hair had been cut so short that he almost looked like a skinhead and his right ear had been pierced. He could still feel it throbbing underneath the temporary stud that had been put in to stop the hole closing.

The car had reached a set of wrought-iron gates which opened automatically to receive it. And there was Haverstock Hall, a great mansion with stone figures on the terrace and seven figures in the price. Sir David had bought it a few years ago, Mrs Jones had told him, because he wanted a place in the country. Half the Lancashire countryside seemed to have come with it. The grounds stretched for miles in every direction, with sheep dotted across the hills on one side and three horses watching from an enclosure on the other. The house itself was Georgian: white brick with slender windows and columns. Everything looked very neat. There was a walled garden with evenly spaced beds, a square glass conservatory housing a swimming pool, and a series of ornamental hedges with every leaf perfectly in place.

The car stopped. The horses swung their necks round to watch Alex get out, their tails rhythmically beating at flies. Nothing else moved.

The chauffeur walked round to the boot. "Sir David will be inside," he said. He had disapproved of Alex from the moment he had set eyes on him. Of course, he hadn't said as much, he was too professional. But he showed it with his eyes.

Alex moved away from the car, drawn towards the conservatory on the other side of the drive. It was a warm day, the sun beating down on the glass, and the water on the other side looked suddenly inviting. He passed through a set of doors. It was hot inside the conservatory. The smell of chlorine rose up from the water, stifling him.

He had thought the pool was empty but, as he watched, a figure swam up from the bottom, breaking through the surface just in front of him. It was a girl, dressed in a white bikini. She had long black hair and dark eyes but her skin was pale. Alex guessed she must be about fifteen years old and remembered what Mrs Jones had told him about Sir David Friend. "He has a daughter ... one year older than you." So this must be her. He watched her pull herself out of the water. Her body was well-shaped, closer to the woman she would become than the girl she had been. She was going to be beautiful. That much was certain. The trouble was, she already knew it. When she looked at Alex, arrogance flashed in her eyes.

"Who are you?" she asked. "What are you doing in here?"

"I'm Alex."

"Oh yes." She reached for a towel and wrapped it around her neck. "Daddy said you were coming – but I didn't expect you to just walk in like this." Her voice was very adult and upper-class. It sounded strange, coming out of that fifteen-year-old mouth. "Do you swim?" she asked.

"Yes," Alex said.

"That's a shame. I don't like having to share the pool. Especially with a boy. And a smelly London boy at that." She ran her eyes over Alex, taking in the torn jeans, the shaven hair, the stud in his ear. She shuddered. "I can't think *what* Daddy was doing, agreeing to let you stay," she went on. "And having to pretend you're my brother! What a ghastly idea! If I did have a brother, I can assure you he wouldn't look like you."

Alex was wondering whether to pick the girl up and throw her back into the pool – or out through a window – when there was a movement behind him and he turned to see a tall, rather aristocratic man with curling grey hair and glasses, wearing a sports jacket, an open-necked shirt and cords. He too seemed a little jolted by Alex's appearance, but he recovered quickly, extending a hand. "Alex?" he enquired.

"Yes."

"I'm David Friend."

Alex shook his hand. "How do you do," he said politely.

"I hope you had a good journey. I see you've met my daughter." He smiled at the girl who was now sitting beside the pool drying herself, ignoring them both.

"We haven't actually introduced ourselves," Alex said.

"Her name is Fiona. I'm sure the two of you will get on fine." Sir David didn't sound convinced. He gestured back towards the house. "Why don't we go and talk in my study?"

Alex followed him back across the drive and into the house. The front door opened into a hall that could have come straight out of the pages of an expensive magazine. Everything was perfect, the antique furniture, ornaments and paintings placed exactly so. There wasn't a speck of dust to be seen and even the sunlight streaming in through the windows seemed almost artificial, as if it was only there to bring out the best in everything it touched. It was the house of a man who knows exactly what he wants and has the time and the money to get it.

"Nice place," Alex said.

"Thank you. Please come this way." Sir David opened a heavy, oak-panelled door to reveal a sophisticated, modern office beyond. There was a desk with a chair on either side, a pair of computers, a white leather sofa and a series of metal bookshelves. Sir David showed Alex to a chair and sat down behind the desk.

He was unsure of himself. Alex could see it immediately. Sir David Friend might run a business empire worth millions – even billions – of pounds, but this was a new experience for him. Having Alex there, knowing who and what he was. He wasn't quite sure how to react.

"I've been told very little about you," he began. "Alan Blunt got in touch with me and asked me to put you up here for the rest of the week, to pretend that you're my son. I have to say, you don't look anything like me."

"I don't look anything like myself either," Alex said.

"You're on your way to some school in the French Alps. They want you to investigate it." He paused. "Nobody asked me my opinion," he said, "but I'll give it to you anyway. I don't like the idea of a fourteen-year-old boy being used as a spy. It's dangerous—"

"I can look after myself," Alex cut in.

"I mean, it's dangerous to the government. If you manage to get yourself killed and anyone finds out, it could cause the prime minister a great deal of embarrassment. I advised him against it, but for once he disagreed with me. It seems that the decision had already been made. This school – the academy – has already telephoned me to say that the assistant director will be coming here to pick you up next Saturday. It's a woman. A Mrs Stellenbosch. That's a South African name, I think..."

Sir David had a number of bulky files on his desk. He pushed them forward. "In the meantime, I understand you have to familiarize yourself with details about my family. I've prepared a number of files. You'll also find information here about the school you're meant to have been expelled from, Eton. You can start reading them tonight. If you need to know anything more, just ask. Fiona will be with you the whole time." He glanced down at his fingertips. "I'm sure that in itself will be quite an experience for you."

The door opened and a woman came in. She was slim and dark-haired, very much like her daughter. She was wearing a simple mauve dress with a string of pearls around her neck. "David..." she began, then stopped, seeing Alex.

"This is my wife," Friend said. "Caroline, this is the boy I was telling you about, Alex."

"It's very nice to meet you, Alex." Lady Caroline tried to smile but her lips only managed a faint twitch. "I understand you're going to stay with us for a while."

"Yes, Mother," Alex said.

Lady Caroline blushed.

"He has to pretend to be our son," Sir David reminded her. He turned to Alex. "Fiona doesn't know anything about MI6 and the rest of it. I don't want to alarm her. I've told her that it's connected with my work ... a social experiment, if you like. She's to pretend you're her brother. To give you a week in the country as part of the family. I'd prefer it if you didn't tell her the truth."

"Dinner is in half an hour," Lady Caroline said. "Do you eat venison?" She sniffed. "Perhaps you'd like a wash before you eat? I'll show you to your room."

Sir David passed the files to Alex. "You've got a lot of reading to do. I'm afraid I have to go back to London tomorrow – I have lunch with the president of France – so I won't be able to help you. But, as I say, if there's anything you don't know—"

"Fiona Friend," Alex said.

Alex had been given a small, comfortable room at the back of the house. He took a quick shower, then put his old clothes back on again. He liked to feel clean, but he had to look grimy. It suited the character of the boy he was supposed to be.

He opened the first of the files. Sir David had been thorough. He had given Alex the names and recent histories of just about the entire family, as well as photographs of holidays, details of the house in Mayfair, the flats in New York, Paris and Rome and the villa in Barbados. There were newspaper clippings, magazine articles ... everything he could possibly need.

A gong sounded. It was seven o'clock. Alex went downstairs and into the dining-room. This was a room with six windows and a polished table long enough to seat sixteen. But there were only the three of them there: Sir David, Lady Caroline and Fiona. The food had already been served, presumably by a butler or maid. Sir David gestured to an empty chair. Alex sat down.

"Fiona was just talking about Don Giovanni," Lady Caroline said. There was a pause. "It's an opera. By Mozart."

"I'm sure Alex isn't interested in opera," Fiona said. She was in a bad mood. "In fact, I doubt if we have *anything* in common. Why do I have to pretend he's my brother? The whole thing is completely—"

"Fiona," Sir David muttered in a low voice.

"Well, it's all very well having him here, Daddy, but it *is* meant to be my Easter holiday." Alex realized that Fiona must go to a private school. Her term would have ended earlier than his. "I don't think it's fair."

"Alex is here because of my work," Sir David continued. It was strange, Alex thought, the way they talked about him as if he wasn't actually there. "I know you have a lot of questions, Fiona, but you're just going to have to do as I say. He's only with us until the end of the week. I want you to look after him."

"Is it something to do with the supermarkets?" Fiona asked.

"Fiona!" Sir David didn't want any more argument. "It's what I told you. An experiment. And you will make him feel welcome!"

Fiona picked up her glass and looked directly at Alex for the first time since he had come into the room. "We'll see about that," she said.

* * *

The week seemed endless. After only two days, Alex had decided that if he had really been a son in this frigid, self-important family, he probably *would* have ended up rebelling. Sir David had left at six o'clock the first morning and was still in London, sending messages to his wife and daughter by e-mail. Lady Caroline did her best to avoid Alex. Once or twice she drove into the town near by, but otherwise she seemed to spend a lot of time in bed. And Fiona...

When she wasn't quoting opera, she was boasting about her lifestyle, her wealth, her holidays around the world. At the same time, she made it clear how much she disliked Alex. She'd asked him several times what he was really doing at Haverstock Hall. Alex had shrugged and said nothing – which had made her dislike him all the more.

On the third day, she introduced him to some of her friends.

"I'm going shooting," she told him. "I don't suppose you want to come."

Alex shrugged. He had memorized most of the details in the files and figured he could easily pass as a member of the family. Now he was counting the hours until the woman from the academy arrived to take him away.

"Have you ever been shooting?" Fiona asked.

"No," Alex said.

"I go hunting and shooting," Fiona said. "But of course, you're a city boy. You wouldn't understand."

"What's so great about killing animals?" Alex asked.

"It's part of the country way of life. It's traditional." Fiona looked at him as if he were stupid. It was how she always looked at him. "Anyway, the animals enjoy it."

The shooting party turned out to be young and – apart from Fiona – entirely male. There were five of them waiting on the edge of a wood that was part of the Haverstock estate. Rufus, the leader, was sixteen, well-built with dark curly hair. He seemed to be Fiona's official boyfriend. The others – Henry, Max, Bartholomew and Fred – were about the same age. Alex looked at them with a heavy heart. They had uniform Barbour jackets, tweed trousers, flat caps and Huntsman leather boots. They spoke with uniform public school accents. Each of them carried a shotgun, with the barrel broken over his arm. Two of them were smoking. They gazed at Alex with barely concealed contempt. Fiona must have already told them about him. The London boy.

Quickly, she made the introductions. Rufus stepped forward.

"Nice to have you with us," he drawled. He ran his eyes over Alex. "Up for a bit of shooting, are we?"

"I don't have a gun," Alex said.

"Well, I'm afraid I'm not going to lend you mine." Rufus snapped the barrel back into place and held it up for Alex to see. It was eighty centimetres of gleaming steel stretching out of a dark walnut stock decorated with ornately carved, solid silver sideplates. "It's an over-under shotgun with detachable trigger, handmade by Abbiatico and Salvinelli," he said. "It cost me thirty grand – or my mother, anyway. It was a birthday present."

"It can't have been easy to wrap," Alex said. "Where did she put the ribbon?"

Rufus's smile faded. "You wouldn't know anything about guns," he said. He nodded at one of the other teenagers, who handed Alex a much more ordinary weapon. It was old and a little rusty. "You can use this one," he said. "And if you're very good and don't get in the way, maybe we'll let you have a cartridge."

They all laughed at that. Then the two smokers put out their cigarettes and they set off into the wood.

Thirty minutes later, Alex knew he had made a mistake in coming.

The boys blasted away left and right, aiming at anything that moved. A rabbit spun in a glistening red ball. A wood pigeon tumbled out of the branches and flapped around on the leaves below. Whatever the quality of their weapons, the teenagers weren't good shots. Many of the animals they shot were only wounded, and Alex felt a growing sickness following this trail of blood.

They reached a clearing and paused to reload. Alex turned to Fiona. "I'm going back to the house," he said.

"Why? Can't stand the sight of a little blood?"

Alex glanced at a rabbit about fifty metres away. It was lying on its side with its back legs kicking helplessly. "I'm surprised they let you carry guns," he said. "I thought you had to be seventeen."

Rufus had overheard him. He stepped forward, an ugly look in his eyes. "We don't bother with rules in the countryside," he muttered.

"Maybe Alex wants to call a policeman!" Fiona said.

"The nearest police station is forty miles from here."

"Do you want to borrow my mobile?"

They all laughed again. Alex had had enough. Without saying another word, he turned round and walked off.

It had taken them thirty minutes to reach the clearing, but thirty minutes later he was still stuck in the wood, completely surrounded by trees and wild shrubs. Alex realized he was lost. He was annoyed with himself. He should have watched where he was going when he was following Fiona and the others. The wood was enormous. Walk in the wrong direction and he might blunder onto the moors ... and it could be days before he was found. At the same time, the spring foliage was so thick that he could barely see ten metres in any direction. How could he possibly find his way? And should he try to retrace his steps or continue forward in the hope of stumbling on the right path?

Alex sensed danger before the first shot was fired. Perhaps it was the snapping of a twig or the click of a metal bolt being slipped into place. He froze – and that was what saved him. There was an explosion – loud, close – and a tree one step ahead of him shattered, splinters of wood dancing in the air.

Alex turned round, searching for whoever had fired the shot. "What are you doing?" he shouted. "You nearly hit me!"

Almost immediately there was a second shot and, just behind it, a whoop of excited laughter. And then Alex realized. They hadn't mistaken him for an animal. They were aiming at him for fun!

He dived forward and began to run. The trunks of the trees seemed to press in on him from all sides, threatening to bar his way. The ground beneath him was soft from recent rain and dragged at his feet, trying to glue them into place. There was a third explosion. He ducked, feeling the gunshot spray above his head, shredding the foliage.

Anywhere else in the world, this would have been madness. But this was the middle of the English countryside and these were rich, bored teenagers who were used to having things their own way. Alex had insulted them. Perhaps it had been the jibe about the wrapping paper. Perhaps it was his refusal to tell Fiona who he really was. But they had decided to teach him a lesson and they would worry about the consequences later. Did they mean to kill him? "We don't bother with rules in the countryside," Rufus had said. If Alex was badly wounded – or even killed – they would somehow get away with it. A dreadful accident. He wasn't looking where he was going and stepped into the line of fire.

No. That was impossible.

They were trying to scare him, that was all.

Two more shots. A pheasant erupted out of the ground, a ball of spinning feathers, and screamed up into the sky. Alex ran on, his breath rasping in his throat. A thick briar reached out across his chest and tore at his clothes. He still had the gun he had been given and he used it to beat a way through. A tangle of roots almost sent him sprawling.

"Alex? Where *are* you?" The voice belonged to Rufus. It was high-pitched and mocking, coming from the other side of a barrier of leaves. There was another shot, but this one went high over his head. They couldn't see him. Had he got away?

Alex came to a stumbling, sweating halt. He had broken out of the wood but he was still hopelessly lost. Worse – he was trapped. He had come to the edge of a wide, filthy lake. The water was a scummy brown and looked almost solid. No ducks or wild birds were anywhere near the surface. The evening sun beat down on it and the smell of decay drifted up.

"He went that way!"

"No ... through here!"

"Let's try the lake..."

Alex heard the voices and knew that he couldn't let them find him here. He had a sudden image of his body, weighed down with stones, at the bottom of the lake. But that gave him an idea. He had to hide.

He stepped into the water. He would need something to breathe through. He had seen people do this in films. They would lie in the water and breathe through a hollow reed. But there were no reeds here. Apart from grass and thick, slimy algae, nothing was growing at all.

One minute later, Rufus appeared at the edge of the lake, his gun hooked over his arm. He stopped and looked around with eyes that knew the forest well. Nothing moved.

"He must have doubled back," he said.

The other hunters had gathered behind him. There was a tension between them now, a guilty silence. They knew the game had gone too far.

"Let's forget him," one of them said.

"Yeah."

"We've taught him a lesson."

They were in a hurry to get home. The group disappeared back the way they had come. Rufus was left on his own, still clutching his gun, searching for Alex. He took one last look across the water, then turned to follow them.

That was when Alex struck. He had been lying under the water, watching the vague shapes of the teenagers as if through a sheet of thick brown glass. The barrel of the shotgun was in his mouth. The rest of the gun was just above the surface of the lake. He was using the hollow tubes to breathe through. Now he rose up – a nightmare creature oozing mud and water, with fury in his eyes. Rufus heard him, but he was too late. Alex swung the shotgun, catching Rufus in the small of the back. Rufus grunted and fell to his knees, his own gun falling out of his hands. Alex picked it up. There were two cartridges in the breach. He snapped the gun shut.

Rufus looked at him and suddenly all the arrogance had gone and he was just a stupid, frightened teenager, struggling to get to his knees.

"Alex!" The single word came out as a whimper. It was as if he was seeing Alex for the first time. "I'm sorry!" he snivelled. "We weren't really going to hurt you. It was a joke. Fiona put us up to it. We just wanted to scare you. Please!"

Alex paused, breathing heavily. "How do I get out of here?" he asked.

"Just follow the lake round," Rufus said. "There's a path..."

Rufus was still on his knees. There were tears in his eyes. Alex realized that he was pointing the silver-plated shotgun in his direction. He turned it away, disgusted with himself. This boy wasn't the enemy. He was nothing.

"Don't follow me," Alex said, and began to walk.

"Please...!" Rufus called after him. "Can I have my gun back? My mother would kill me if I lost it."

Alex stopped. He weighed the weapon in his hands, then threw it with all his strength. The hand-crafted Italian shotgun spun twice in the dying light then disappeared with a splash into the middle of the lake. "You're too young to play with guns," he said.

He walked away, letting the forest swallow him up.

THE TUNNEL

The man sitting in the gold, antique chair turned his head slowly and gazed out of the window at the snow-covered slopes of Point Blanc. Dr Hugo Grief was almost sixty years old with short white hair and a face that was almost colourless too. His skin was white, his lips vague shadows. Even his tongue was no more than grey. And yet, against this blank background, he wore circular wire spectacles with dark red lenses. The effect was startling. And, for him, the entire world would be the colour of blood. He had long fingers, the nails beautifully manicured. He was dressed in a dark suit buttoned up to his neck. If there were such a thing as a vampire, it would look very much like Hugo Grief.

"I have decided to move the Gemini Project into its last phase," he said. He spoke with a South African accent, biting into each word before it left his mouth. "There can be no further delay."

"I understand, Dr Grief."

There was a woman sitting opposite Dr Grief, dressed in tight-fitting Lycra with a sweat band round her head. This was Eva Stellenbosch. She had just finished her morning work-out – two hours of weightlifting and aerobic exercise – and she was still breathing heavily, her huge muscles rising and falling. Mrs Stellenbosch had a facial structure that wasn't quite human, with lips curving out far in front of her nose and wisps of bright ginger hair hanging over a high-domed forehead. She was holding a glass filled with some milky green liquid. Her fingers were thick and stubby. She had to be careful not to break the glass.

She sipped her drink, then frowned. "Are you sure we're ready?" she asked.

"We have no choice in the matter. We have had two unsatisfactory results in the last few months. First Ivanov. Then Roscoe in New York. Quite apart from the expense of arranging the terminations, it's possible that someone may have connected the two deaths."

"Possible, but unlikely," Mrs Stellenbosch said.

"The intelligence services are idle and inefficient, it is true. The CIA in America. MI6 in England. Even the KGB! They're all shadows of what they used to be. But even so, there's always the chance that one of them might have accidentally stumbled onto something. The sooner we end this phase of the operation, the more chance we have of remaining ... unnoticed." Dr Grief brought his hands together and rested his chin on his fingertips. "When is the final boy arriving?" he asked.

"Alex?" Mrs Stellenbosch emptied her glass and set it down. She opened her handbag and took out a handkerchief which she used to wipe her lips. "I am travelling to England tomorrow," she said.

"Excellent. You'll take the boy to Paris on the way here?"

"Of course, Doctor. If that is what you wish."

"It is very much what I wish, Mrs Stellenbosch. We can do all the preliminary work there. It will save time. What about the Sprintz boy?"

"I'm afraid we still need another few days."

"That means that he and Alex will be here at the same time."

"Yes."

Dr Grief considered. He had to balance the risk of the two boys meeting against the dangers of moving too fast. It was fortunate that he had a scientific mind. His calculations were never wrong. "Very well," he said. "The Sprintz boy can stay with us for another few days."

Mrs Stellenbosch nodded.

"Alex Friend is an excellent catch for us," Dr Grief said

"Supermarkets?" The woman sounded unconvinced.

"His father has the prime minister's ear. He is an impressive man. His son, I am sure, will meet all our expectations." Dr Grief smiled. His eyes glowed red. "Very soon, we'll have Alex here at the academy. And then, at last, the Gemini Project will be complete."

"You're sitting all wrong," Fiona said. "Your back isn't straight. Your hands should be lower. And your feet are pointing the wrong way."

"What does it matter, so long as you're enjoying yourself?" Alex asked, speaking through gritted teeth.

It was the fourth day of his stay at Haverstock Hall and Fiona had taken him out riding. Alex wasn't enjoying himself at all. Before the ride, he'd had to endure the inevitable lecture – although he had barely listened. The horses were Iberian or Hungarian. They'd won a bucketful of gold medals. Alex didn't care. All he knew was that his horse was big and black and attracted flies. And that he was riding it with all the style of a sack of potatoes on a trampoline.

The two of them had barely mentioned the business in the forest. When Alex had limped back to the house, soaked and freezing, Fiona had politely fetched him a towel and offered him a cup of tea.

"You tried to kill me!" Alex said.

"Don't be silly!" Fiona looked at Alex with something like pity in her eyes. "We would never do that. Rufus is a very nice boy."

"What...?"

"It was just a game, Alex. Just a bit of fun."

And that was it. Fiona had smiled as if everything had been explained and then gone to have a swim. Alex had spent the rest of the evening with the files. He was trying to take in a fake history that lasted fourteen years. There were uncles and aunts, friends at Eton, a whole crowd of people he had to know without ever having met any of them. More than that, he was trying to get the feel of this luxurious lifestyle. That was why he was here now, out riding with Fiona – she upright in her riding jacket and breeches, he bumping along behind.

They had ridden for about an hour and a half when they came to the tunnel. Fiona had tried to teach Alex a bit of technique – the difference, for example, between walking, trotting and cantering. But this was one sport he had already decided he would never take up. Every bone in his body had been rattled out of place and his bottom was so bruised he wondered if he would ever be able to sit down again. Fiona was enjoying his torment. He even wondered if she had chosen a particularly bumpy route to add to his bruises. Or maybe it was just a particularly bumpy horse.

There was a single railway line ahead of them, with an automatic level-crossing equipped with a bell and flashing lights to warn motorists of any approaching train. Fiona steered her horse – a smaller grey – towards it. Alex's horse automatically followed. He assumed they were going to cross the line, but when she reached the barrier, Fiona stopped.

"There's a short-cut we can take if you want to get home," she said.

"A short-cut would be great," Alex admitted.

"It's that way." Fiona pointed up the line, and there was the tunnel, a gaping black hole in the side of a hill, surrounded by dark red Victorian brick. Alex looked at her to see if she was joking. She was obviously quite serious. He turned back to the tunnel. It was like the barrel of a gun, pointing at him, warning him to keep away. He could almost imagine the giant finger on the trigger, somewhere behind the hill. How long was it? Looking more carefully, he could see a pin-prick of light at the other end. Perhaps up to a kilometre away.

"You're not being serious," he said.

"Actually, Alex, I don't usually tell jokes. When I say something, I mean it. I'm just like my father."

"Your father isn't barking mad," Alex muttered.

Fiona pretended not to hear him. "The tunnel is exactly one kilometre long," she explained. "There's a bridge on the other side, then another level-crossing. If we go that way, we can be home in thirty minutes. Otherwise it's an hour and a half back the way we came."

"Then let's go the way we came."

"Oh Alex, don't be such a scaredy-cat!" Fiona pouted at him. "There's only one train an hour on this line and the next one isn't due for" – she looked at her watch – "twenty minutes. I've been through the tunnel a hundred times and it never takes more than five minutes. Less if you canter."

"It's still crazy to ride on a railway line."

"Well, you'll have to find your own way home if you turn back." She kicked with her heels and her horse jerked forward, past the barrier and onto the line. "I'll see you later."

But Alex followed her. He would never have been able to ride back to the house on his own. He didn't know the way and he could barely control the horse. Even now it was following Fiona with no prompting from him. Would the two animals really enter the darkness of the tunnel? It seemed incredible, but Fiona had said they'd done it before and sure enough the horse walked into the side of the hill without even hesitating.

Alex shivered as the light was suddenly cut off behind him. It was cold and clammy inside. The air smelled of soot and diesel. The tunnel was a natural echo-chamber. The horses' hooves rattled all around them as they struck against the gravel between the sleepers. What if his horse stumbled? Alex put the thought out of his mind. The leather saddles creaked. Slowly his eyes got used to the dark. A certain amount of sunshine was filtering in from behind. More comfortingly, the way out was visible straight ahead, the circle of light widening with every step as they drew nearer. He tried to relax. Perhaps this wasn't going to be so bad after all.

And then Fiona spoke. She had slowed down, allowing his horse to catch up with hers. "Are you still worried about the train, Alex?" she said. "Perhaps you'd like to go faster..."

He heard the riding crop whistle through the air and felt his horse jerk as Fiona whipped it hard on the rear. The horse whinnied and leapt forward. Alex was thrown backwards, almost off the saddle. Digging in with his legs he just managed to cling on, but the top half of his body was at a crazy angle, the reins tearing into the horse's mouth. Fiona laughed. Alex was aware only of the wind rushing past him, the thick blackness spinning round his face and the horse's hooves striking heavily at the gravel as the animal careered forward. Dust blew into his eyes, blinding him. He thought he was going to fall.

But then, miraculously, they had burst out into the light. Alex fought for his balance and brought the horse back under control, pulling back with the reins and squeezing the horse's flanks with his knees. He took a deep breath, spat out an oath and waited for Fiona to appear.

His horse had come to rest on the bridge that she had mentioned. The bridge was fashioned out of thick iron girders and spanned a river. There had been a lot of rain that month and, about fifteen metres below him, the water was racing past, dark green and deep. Carefully, he turned round to face the tunnel. If he lost control here it would be easy to fall over the edge. The sides of the bridge couldn't have been more than a metre high.

He could hear Fiona approaching. She had been cantering after him, probably laughing the entire way. He gazed into the tunnel – and that was when the grey burst out, raced past him and disappeared through the level-crossing on the other side of the bridge.

But Fiona wasn't on it.

The horse had come out alone.

It took Alex a few seconds to work it out. His head was reeling. She must have fallen off. Perhaps her horse had stumbled. She could be lying inside the tunnel. On the track. How long was there until the next train? Twenty minutes, she had said. But at least five of those minutes had gone, and she might have been exaggerating to begin with. What should he do? He had only three choices.

Go back in on foot.

Go back in on the horse.

Go home and forget about her.

No. He had only two choices. He knew that. He swore for a second time, then seized hold of the reins. Somehow he would get this horse to obey him. He had to get the girl out and he had to do it fast.

Perhaps his desperation managed to communicate itself to the horse's brain. The animal wheeled round and tried to back away, but when Alex kicked with his heels it stumbled forward and reluctantly entered the darkness of the tunnel for a second time. Alex kicked again. He didn't want to hurt it but he could think of no other way to make it obey him.

The horse trotted on. Alex searched ahead. "Fiona!" he called out. There was no reply. He had hoped that she would be walking towards him, but he couldn't hear any footsteps. If only there was more light!

The horse stopped and there she was, right in front of him, lying on the ground, her arms and chest actually on the line. If a train came now, it would cut her in half. It was too dark to see her face, but when she spoke he heard the pain in her voice.

"Alex," she said. "I think I've broken my ankle."

"What happened?"

"There was a cobweb or something. I was trying to keep up with you. It went in my face and I lost my balance."

She'd been trying to keep up with him! She sounded as if she was blaming *him* – as if she'd forgotten that she had whipped his horse on in the first place.

"Can you get up?" Alex asked.

"I don't think so."

Alex sighed. Keeping a tight hold on the reins, he slid off his horse. Fiona couldn't have timed it better. She had fallen right in the middle of the tunnel. He forced himself not to panic. According to her calculations, the next train must still be at least ten minutes away. He reached down to help her up. His foot came to rest on one of the rails ... and he felt something. Under his foot. Shivering up his leg. The track was vibrating.

The train was on its way.

"You've got to stand up," he said, trying to keep the fear out of his voice. He could already see the train in his imagination, thundering along the line. When it plunged into the tunnel, it would be a five hundred tonne torpedo that would smash them to pieces. He could hear the grinding of the wheels, the roar of the engine. Blood and darkness. It would be a horrible way to die.

But he still had time. "Can you move your toes?" he asked.

"I think so." Fiona was clutching onto him.

"Then your ankle's probably sprained, not broken. Come on."

He dragged her up, wondering if it would be possible to stay inside the tunnel, at the edge of the track. If they hugged the wall, the train might simply go past them. But Alex knew there wouldn't be enough space. And even if the train missed them, it would still hit the horse. Suppose it derailed? Dozens of people could be killed.

"What train comes this way?" he asked. "Does it carry passengers?"

"Yes." Fiona was sounding tearful. "It's a Virgin train. Heading up to Glasgow."

Alex sighed. It was just his luck to get a Virgin train that arrived on time.

Fiona froze. "What's that?" she asked.

She had heard the clanging of a bell. What was it? Of course – the level-crossing! It was signalling the approach of the train, the barrier lowering itself over the road.

And then Alex heard a second sound that made his blood run cold. For a moment he couldn't breathe. It was extraordinary. His breath had got stuck in his lungs and refused to get up to his mouth. His whole body was paralysed as if some switch had been thrown in his brain. He was simply terrified.

The screech of a train whistle. It was still a mile or more away but the tunnel was acting as a sound conductor and he could feel it almost cutting into him. And now there was another noise. The rolling thunder of the diesel engine. It was moving fast towards them. Underneath his foot, the rail was vibrating more violently.

Alex gulped for air and forced his legs to obey him. "Get on the horse," he shouted. "I'll help you."

Not caring how much pain he caused her, he dragged Fiona next to the horse and forced her up towards the saddle. The noise was getting louder with every second that passed. The rail was humming softly, like a giant tuning-fork. The very air inside the tunnel seemed to be in motion, spinning left and right as if trying to get out of the way.

Fiona squealed and Alex felt her weight leave his arms as she fell onto the saddle. The horse whinnied and took a half-step sideways, and for a dreadful moment Alex thought she was going to ride off without him. There was just enough light to make out the shapes of both the animal and its rider. He saw Fiona grabbing the reins. She brought the horse back under control. Alex reached up and caught hold of its mane, using the thick hair to pull himself onto the saddle in front of Fiona. The noise of the approaching train was getting louder and louder. Soot and loose cement were trickling out of the curving walls. The wind currents were twisting faster, the rails singing. For a moment the two of them were tangled together, but then he had the reins and she was clinging onto him, her arms around his chest.

"Go!" he shouted, and kicked the horse.

The horse needed no encouragement. It raced for the light,

galloping up the railway line, throwing Alex and Fiona back and forth into each other.

Alex didn't dare look behind him, but he felt the train as it reached the mouth of the tunnel and plunged into it, travelling at one hundred and five miles per hour. A shock wave hammered into them. The train was punching the air out of its way, filling the space with solid steel. The horse understood the danger and burst forward with new speed, its hooves flying over the sleepers in great strides. Ahead of them the tunnel mouth opened up but Alex knew, with a sickening sense of despair, that they weren't going to make it. Even when they got out of the tunnel, they would still be hemmed in by the sides of the bridge. The second level-crossing was a hundred metres further down the line. They might get out, but they would die in the open air.

The horse passed through the end of the tunnel. Alex felt the circle of darkness slip over his shoulders. Fiona was screaming, her arms wrapped around him so tightly that he could barely breathe. He could hardly hear her. The roar of the train was right behind him. As the horse began a desperate race over the bridge, he sneaked a glance round. He just had time to see the huge metallic beast roar out of the tunnel, towering over them, its body painted the brilliant red of the Virgin colours, the driver staring in horror from behind his window. There was a second blast from the train whistle, this one all-consuming, exploding all around them. Alex knew what he had to do. He pulled on one rein, kicking with the opposite foot at the same time. He just hoped the horse would understand what he wanted.

And somehow it worked. The horse veered round. Now it was facing the side of the bridge. There was a final, deafening blast from the train. Diesel fumes smothered them.

The horse jumped.

The train roared past, barely missing them. But now they were in the air, over the side of the bridge. The carriages were still thundering past; a red blur. Fiona screamed again. Everything seemed to be happening in slow motion as they fell. One moment they were next to the bridge, a moment later underneath it and still falling. The green river rose up to receive them.

The horse with its two riders plummeted through the air and crashed into the river. Alex just had time to snatch a breath. He was afraid the water wouldn't be deep enough, that all three of them would end up with broken bones. But then they had hit the surface and passed through, down into a freezing, dark green whirlpool that sucked at them greedily, threatening to keep them there for ever. Fiona was torn away from him. He felt the horse kick itself free. Bubbles exploded out of his mouth and he realized he was yelling.

Finally, Alex rose to the surface again. The water was rushing past and, dragged back by his clothes and shoes, he clumsily swam for the nearest bank.

The train driver hadn't stopped. Perhaps he had been too frightened by what had happened. Perhaps he wanted to pretend it hadn't happened at all. The train had gone.

Alex reached the bank and pulled himself, shivering, onto the grass. There was a splutter and a cough from behind him and Fiona appeared. She had lost her riding hat and her long black hair was hanging over her face. Alex looked past her. The horse had also managed to reach dry land. It trotted forward and shook itself, seemingly unharmed. Alex was glad about that. At the end of the day, the horse had saved both their lives.

He stood up. Water dripped out of his clothes. There was no feeling anywhere in his body. He wondered if it was because of the cold water or the shock of what he had just been through. He went over to Fiona and helped her to her feet.

"Are you all right?" he asked.

"Yes." She was looking at him strangely. She wobbled and he put out a hand to steady her. "Thank you," she said.

"That's all right."

"No." She held onto his hand. Her shirt had fallen open and she threw back her head, shaking the hair out of her eyes. "What you did back there ... it was fantastic. Alex, I'm sorry I've been such a beast to you all week. I thought – because you were only here for charity and all the rest of it – I thought you were just an oik. But I was wrong about you. You're really great. And I know we're going to be friends now." She half closed her eyes and moved towards him, her lips slightly parted. "You can kiss me if you like," she said.

Alex let go of her and turned away. "Thanks, Fiona," he said. "But frankly I'd prefer to kiss the horse."

SPECIAL EDITION

The helicopter circled twice over Haverstock Hall before beginning its descent. It was a Robinson R44 four-seater aircraft, American-built. There was only one person – the pilot – inside. Sir David Friend had returned from London and he and his wife came outside to watch it land in front of the house. The engine noise died down and the rotors began to slow. The cabin door slid open and the pilot got out, dressed in a one-piece leather flying suit, helmet and goggles.

The pilot walked up to them, extending a hand. "Good morning," she said. "I'm Mrs Stellenbosch from the academy."

If Sir David and Lady Caroline had been thrown by their first sight of Alex, the appearance of this assistant director, as she called herself, left them frozen to the spot. Sir David was the first to recover. "You flew the helicopter yourself?"

"Yes, I'm qualified." Mrs Stellenbosch had to shout over the noise of the rotors, which were still turning.

"Would you like to come in?" Lady Caroline asked. "Perhaps you'd like some tea?"

She led them into the house and through to the living room, where Mrs Stellenbosch sat, her legs apart, her helmet on the sofa beside her. Sir David and Lady Caroline sat opposite her. Tea was brought in on a tray.

"Do you mind if I smoke?" Mrs Stellenbosch asked. She reached into a pocket and took out a small packet of cigars without waiting for an answer. She lit one and blew smoke. "What a very beautiful house you have, Sir David. Georgian, I would say, but decorated with such taste! And where, may I ask, is Alex?"

"He went for a walk," Sir David said.

"Perhaps he's a little nervous." She smiled again and took the teacup Lady Caroline had proffered. "I understand that Alex has been a great source of concern to you."

Sir David Friend nodded. His eyes gave nothing away. For the next few minutes, he told Mrs Stellenbosch about Alex, how he had been expelled from Eton, how out of control he had become. Lady Caroline listened to all this in silence, occasionally holding her husband's arm.

"I'm at my wit's end," Sir David concluded. "We have an older daughter and she's perfect. But Alex? He hangs around the house. He doesn't read. He doesn't show any interest in anything. His appearance ... well, you'll see for yourself. Point Blanc Academy is our last resort, Mrs Stellenbosch. We're desperately hoping you can sort him out."

The assistant director poked at the air with her cigar, leaving a grey trail. "I'm sure you've been a marvellous father, Sir David," she purred. "But these modern children! It's heartbreaking the way some of them behave. You've done the right thing in coming to us.

As I'm sure you know, the academy has had a remarkable success rate over the past eleven years."

"What exactly do you do?" Lady Caroline asked.

"We have our methods." The woman's eyes twinkled. She tapped ash into her saucer. "But I can promise you, we'll sort out all Alex's problems. Don't you worry! When he comes home, he'll be a completely different boy!"

Meanwhile, Alex was crossing a field about a kilometre away from the house. He had seen the helicopter land and knew that his time had come. But he wasn't ready to leave yet. Mrs Jones had telephoned him the night before. Once again, MI6 weren't going to send him into what might be enemy territory empty-handed.

He watched as a combine harvester rumbled slowly towards him, cutting a swathe through the grass. It jerked to a halt a short distance away and the door of the cabin opened. A man got out – with difficulty. He was so fat that he had to squeeze himself out, first one buttock, then the next, finally his stomach, shoulders and head. The man was wearing a checked shirt and blue overalls – a farmer's outfit. But even if he'd had a straw hat and a blade of corn between his teeth, Alex could never have imagined him actually farming anything.

The man grinned at him. "Hello, old chap!" he said.

"Hello, Mr Smithers," Alex replied.

Smithers worked for MI6. He had supplied the various devices Alex had used on his last mission.

"Very nice to see you again!" he exclaimed. He winked. "What do you think of the cover? I was told to blend in with the countryside."

"The combine harvester's a great idea," Alex said. "Except this is April. There isn't anything to harvest."

"I hadn't thought of that!" Smithers beamed. "The trouble is, I'm not really a field agent. *Field* agent!" He looked around him and laughed. "Anyway, I'm jolly glad to have the chance to work with you again, Alex. To think up a few bits and pieces for you. It's not often I get a teenager. Much more fun than the adults!"

He reached into the cabin and pulled out a suitcase. "Actually, it's been a bit tricky this time," he went on.

"Have you got another Nintendo Game Boy?" Alex asked.

"No. That's just it. The school doesn't allow Game Boys – or any computers at all, for that matter. They supply their own laptops. I could have hidden a dozen gadgets inside a laptop, but there you are! Now, let's see..." He opened the case. "I'm told there's still a lot of snow up at Point Blanc, so you'll need this."

"A ski suit," Alex said. That was what Smithers was holding.

"Yes. But it's highly insulated and also bulletproof." He pulled out a pair of green-tinted goggles. "These are ski goggles. But in case you have to go anywhere at night, they're actually infrared. There's a battery concealed in the frame. Just press the switch and you'll be able to see for about twenty metres, even if there's no moon."

Smithers reached into the case a third time. "Now, what else would a boy of your age have with him? Fortunately, you're allowed to take a Sony Discman – provided all the CDs are classical." He handed Alex the machine.

"So while people are shooting at me in the middle of the night, I get to listen to music," Alex said.

"Absolutely. Only don't play the Beethoven!" Smithers held up the disc. "The Discman converts into an electric saw. The CD is diamond-edged. It'll cut through just about anything. Useful if you need to get out in a hurry. There's also a panic button I've built in. If the balloon goes up and you need help, just press fast forward three times. It'll send out a signal which our satellite will pick up. And then we can fast forward you out!"

"Thank you, Mr Smithers," Alex said. But he was disappointed and it showed.

Smithers understood. "I know what you want," he said, "but you know you can't have it. No guns! Mr Blunt is adamant. He thinks you're too young."

"Not too young to get killed though."

"Yes, well. I've given it a bit of thought and rustled up a couple of ... defensive measures, so to speak. This is just between you and me, you understand. I'm not sure Mr Blunt would approve."

He held out a hand. There was a gold ear-stud lying in two pieces in the middle of his palm; a diamond shape for the front and a catch to hold it at the back. The stud looked tiny surrounded by so much flesh. "They told me you'd had your ear pierced," he said. "So I made you this. Be very careful after you've put it in. Bringing the two pieces together will activate it."

"Activate what?" Alex looked doubtful.

"The ear-stud is a small but very powerful explosive device. Separating the two pieces again will set it off. Count to ten and it'll blow a hole in just about anything – or anyone, I should add."

"Just so long as it doesn't blow my ear off," Alex muttered.

"No, no. It's perfectly safe so long as the pieces remain attached." Smithers smiled. "And finally – I'm *very* pleased with this. It's exactly what you'd expect any young boy leaving for school to be given, and I bought it specially for you." He had produced a book.

Alex took it. It was a hardback edition of *Harry Potter and the Chamber of Secrets*. "Thanks," he said, "but I've already read it."

"This is a special edition. There's a gun built into the spine and the chamber is loaded with a stun dart. Just point it and press the author's name on the spine. It'll knock out an adult in less than five seconds."

Alex smiled. Smithers climbed back into the combine harvester. For a moment he seemed to have wedged himself permanently in the doorway, but then, with a grunt, he managed to go the whole way. "Good luck, old chap," he said. "Come back in one piece! I really do quite enjoy having you around!"

It was time to go.

Alex's luggage was being loaded into the helicopter and he was standing next to his "parents" clutching the Harry Potter book. Eva Stellenbosch was waiting for him beneath the rotors. He had been shocked by her appearance and at first he'd tried to hide it. But then he'd relaxed. He didn't have to be polite. Alex Rider might be well-mannered but Alex Friend wouldn't give a damn what she thought. He glanced at her scornfully now and noticed that she was watching him carefully as he said goodbye to the Friends.

Once again, Sir David Friend acted his part perfectly. "Goodbye, Alex," he said. "You will write to us and let us know you're OK?"

"If you want," Alex said.

Lady Caroline moved forward and kissed him. Alex backed away from her as if embarrassed. He had to admit that she looked genuinely sad.

"Come, Alex." Mrs Stellenbosch was in a hurry to get away. She told him that they would need to stop in Paris to refuel.

And then Fiona appeared, crossing the lawn towards them. Alex hadn't spoken to her since the business at the tunnel. Nor had she spoken to him. He had rejected her and he knew she would never forgive him. She hadn't come down to breakfast this morning and he'd assumed she wouldn't show herself again until he'd gone. So what was she doing here now?

Suddenly Alex knew. She'd come to cause trouble – one last jab below the belt. He could see it in her eyes and in the way she flounced across the lawn with her hands rolled into fists.

Fiona didn't know he was a spy. But she must know that he was here for a reason and she had probably guessed it had something to do with the woman from Point Blanc. So she had decided to come out and spoil things for him. Maybe she was going to ask questions. Maybe she was going to tell Mrs Stellenbosch that he wasn't really her brother. Either way, Alex knew that his mission would be over before it had even begun. All his work memorizing the files and all the time he had spent with the family would have been for nothing.

"Fiona!" Sir David muttered. His eyes were grave. He had come to the same conclusion as Alex.

She ignored him. "Are you here for Alex?" she asked, speaking directly to Mrs Stellenbosch.

"Yes, my dear."

"Well, I think there's something you should know."

There was only one thing Alex could do. He lifted the book and pointed it at Fiona, then pressed the spine once, hard. There was no noise, but he felt the book shudder in his hand. Fiona put her hand to the side of her leg. All the colour drained out of her face. She crumpled to the grass.

Lady Caroline ran over to her. Mrs Stellenbosch looked puzzled. Alex turned to her, his face blank. "That's my sister," he said. "She gets very emotional."

Two minutes later the helicopter took off. Alex watched through the window as Haverstock Hall got smaller and smaller and then disappeared behind them. He looked at Mrs Stellenbosch hunched over the controls, her eyes hidden by her goggles. He eased himself into his seat and let himself be carried away into the darkening sky. Then the clouds rolled in. The countryside was gone. So was his only weapon. Alex was on his own.

ROOM 13

It was raining in Paris. The city was looking tired and disappointed, the Eiffel Tower fighting against a mass of heavy cloud. There was nobody sitting at the tables spread outside the cafés and for once the little kiosks selling paintings and postcards were being ignored by the tourists hurrying back to their hotels. It was five o'clock in the afternoon and the evening was drawing in. The shops and offices were emptying, but the city didn't care. It just wanted to be left alone.

The helicopter had landed in a private area of Charles de Gaulle Airport and a car had been waiting to drive them in. Alex had said nothing during the flight and now he sat on his own in the back, watching the buildings flash by. They were following the Seine, moving surprisingly fast along a wide dual carriageway that dipped above and below the water level. Their route took them past Notre-Dame. Then they turned off, weaving their way through a series of back streets with small restaurants and boutiques fighting for space on the pavements.

"The Marais," Mrs Stellenbosch said.

Alex pretended to show no interest. In fact, he had stayed in the Marais district once before and knew it as one of the smartest and most expensive quarters of Paris.

The car turned into a large square and stopped. Alex glanced out of the window. He was surrounded on four sides by the tall, classical houses for which Paris is famous. But the square had been disfigured by a single modern hotel. It was a white rectangular block, the windows fitted with dark glass that allowed no view to the inside. It rose up four floors, with a flat roof and the name HÔTEL DU MONDE in gold letters above the main door. If a spaceship had landed in the square, crushing a couple of buildings to make room for itself, it couldn't have looked more out of place.

"This is where we're staying," Mrs Stellenbosch said. "The hotel is owned by the academy."

The driver had taken their cases out of the boot. Alex followed the assistant director towards the entrance, the door sliding open automatically to allow them in. The reception was cold and faceless, white marble and mirrors, with a single potted plant tucked into a corner as an afterthought. There was a small reception desk with an unsmiling male receptionist in a dark suit and glasses, a computer and a row of pigeon holes. Alex counted them. There were fifteen. Presumably the hotel had fifteen rooms.

"*Bonsoir,* Madame Stellenbosch." The receptionist nodded his head slightly. He ignored Alex. "I hope you had a good journey from England," he continued, still speaking in French. Alex gazed blankly, as if he hadn't understood a word. Alex Friend wouldn't speak French. He wouldn't have bothered to learn. But Ian Rider had made certain that his nephew spoke French almost as soon as he spoke English. Not to mention German and Spanish as well.

The receptionist took down two keys. He didn't ask either of them to sign in. He didn't ask for a credit card. The school owned the hotel, so there would be no bill when they left. He gave Alex one of the keys.

"I hope you are not superstitious," he said, speaking in English now.

"No," Alex replied.

"It is room thirteen. On the first floor. I am sure you will find it most agreeable." The receptionist smiled.

Mrs Stellenbosch took her key. "The hotel has its own restaurant," she said. "We might as well eat here tonight. We don't want to go out in the rain. Anyway, the food here is excellent. Do you like French food, Alex?"

"Not much," Alex said.

"Well, I'm sure we'll find something that you like. Why don't you freshen up after the journey?" She looked at her watch. "We'll eat at seven. An hour and a half from now. It will give us an opportunity to talk together. Might I suggest, perhaps, some smarter clothes for dinner? The French are informal, but – if you'll forgive me saying so, my dear – you take informality a little far. I'll call you at five to seven. I hope the room is all right."

Room thirteen was at the end of a long, narrow corridor. The door opened into a surprisingly large space, with views over the square. There was a double bed with a black and white cover, a television and mini-bar, a desk and, on the wall, a couple of framed pictures of Paris. A porter had carried up Alex's cases and, as soon as he was gone, Alex kicked off his shoes and sat down on the bed. He wondered why they had come here. He knew the helicopter had needed refuelling, but that shouldn't have necessitated an overnight stop. Why not fly straight on to the school?

He had more than an hour to kill. First he went into the bathroom – more glass and white marble – and took a long shower. Then, wrapped in a towel, he went back into the room and put the television on. Alex Friend would watch a lot of television. There were about thirty channels to choose from. Alex skipped past the French ones and stopped on MTV. He wondered if he was being monitored. There was a large mirror next to the desk and it would have been easy enough to conceal a camera behind it. Well, why not give them something to think about? He opened the mini-bar and poured himself a glass of gin. Then he went into the bathroom, refilled the bottle with water and put it back in the fridge. Drinking alcohol and stealing! If she was watching, Mrs Stellenbosch would know that she had her hands full with him.

He spent the next forty minutes watching television and pretending to drink the gin. Then he took the glass into the bathroom and dumped it in the sink, allowing the liquid to run out. It was time to get dressed. Should he do what he was told and put on smart clothes? In the end, he compromised. He put on a shirt, but kept the same jeans. A moment later, the telephone rang. His call to dinner.

Mrs Stellenbosch was waiting for him in the restaurant, an airless room in the basement. Soft lighting and mirrors had been used to make it feel more spacious, but it was still the last place Alex would have chosen. The restaurant could have been anywhere, in any part of the world. There were two other diners – businessmen by the look of them – but otherwise they were alone. Mrs Stellenbosch had changed into a black evening dress with feathers at the collar and she wore an antique-looking necklace of black and silver beads. The smarter her clothes, Alex thought, the uglier she looked. She was smoking another cigar.

"Ah, Alex!" She blew smoke. "Did you have a rest? Or did you watch TV?"

Alex didn't say anything. He sat down and opened the menu, then closed it again when he saw that it was all in French.

"You must let me order for you. Some soup to start, perhaps? And then a steak. I've never yet met a boy who doesn't like steak."

"My cousin Oliver is a vegetarian," Alex said. It was something he had read in one of the files.

The assistant director nodded as if she already knew this. "Then he doesn't know what he is missing," she said. A pale-faced waiter came over and she placed the order in French. "What will you drink?" she asked.

"I'll have a Coke."

"A repulsive drink, I always think. I have never understood the taste. But, of course, you shall have what you want."

The waiter brought Alex a Coke and a glass of champagne for Mrs Stellenbosch. Alex watched the bubbles rising in the two glasses, his black, hers a pale gold.

"*Santé*," she said.

"I'm sorry?"

"It's French for 'good health'."

"Oh. Cheers."

There was a moment's silence. The woman's eyes were fixed on him – as if she could see right through him. "So, you were at Eton," she said casually.

"That's right." Alex was suddenly on his guard.

"What house were you in?"

"The Hopgarden." It was the name of a real house at the school. Alex had read the file carefully.

"I visited Eton once. I remember a statue. I think it was a king. It was just through the main gate..."

She was testing him. Alex was sure of it. Did she suspect him, or was it simply a precaution, something she always did? "You're talking about Henry the Sixth," he said. "His statue's in College Yard. He founded Eton."

"But you didn't like it there."

"No."

"Why not?"

"I didn't like the uniform and I didn't like the beaks." Alex was careful not to use the word "teachers". At Eton, they're known as beaks. He half smiled to himself. If she wanted a bit of Eton-speak, he'd give it to her. "And I didn't like the rules. Getting fined by the pop. Or being put in the tardy book. I was always getting rips and infoes or being put on the bill. The divs were boring—"

"I'm afraid I don't really understand a word you're saying."

"Divs are lessons," Alex explained. "Rips are when your work is no good—"

"All right!" She drew a line with her cigar. "Is that why you set fire to the library?"

"No," Alex said. "That was just because I don't like books."

The first course arrived. Alex's soup was yellow and had something floating in it. He picked up his spoon and poked at it suspiciously. "What's this?" he demanded.

"*Soupe de moules*."

He looked at her blankly.

"Mussel soup. I hope you enjoy it."

"I'd have preferred Heinz tomato," Alex said.

The steaks, when they came, were typically French; barely cooked at all. Alex took a couple of mouthfuls of the bloody meat, then threw down his knife and fork and used his fingers to eat the chips. Mrs Stellenbosch talked to him about the French Alps, about skiing and about her visits to various European cities. It was easy to look bored. He *was* bored. And he was beginning to feel tired. He took a sip of Coke, hoping the cold drink would wake him up. The meal seemed to be dragging on all night.

But at last the puddings – ice cream with white chocolate sauce – had come and gone. Alex declined coffee.

"You look tired," Stellenbosch said. She had lit another cigar. The smoke curled around her head and made him feel dizzy. "Would you like to go to bed?"

"Yes."

"We don't need to leave until midday tomorrow. You'll have time for a visit to the Louvre, if you'd like that."

Alex shook his head. "Actually, paintings bore me."

"Really? What a shame!"

Alex stood up. Somehow his hand knocked into his glass, spilling the rest of the Coke over the pristine white tablecloth. What was the matter with him? Suddenly he was exhausted.

"Would you like me to come up with you, Alex?" the woman asked. She was looking carefully at him, a tiny glimmer of interest in her otherwise dead eyes.

"No. I'll be all right." Alex stepped away. "Good night."

Getting upstairs was an ordeal. He was tempted to take the lift but he didn't want to lock himself into that small, windowless cubicle. He would have felt suffocated. He climbed the stairs, his shoulder resting heavily against the wall, stumbled down the corridor and somehow got the key into the lock. When he finally got inside, the room was spinning. What was going on? Had he drunk more of the gin than he had intended or was he...?

Alex swallowed. He had been drugged. There had been something in the Coke. It was still on his tongue, a sort of bitterness. There were only three steps between him and his bed, but it could have been a mile away. His legs wouldn't obey him any more. Just lifting one foot took all his strength. He fell forward, reaching out with his arms. Somehow he managed to propel himself far enough. His chest and shoulders hit the bed, sinking into the mattress. The room was spinning round him, faster and faster. He tried to stand up, tried to speak – but nothing came. His eyes closed. Gratefully, he allowed the darkness to take him.

Thirty minutes later, there was a soft click and the room began to change.

If Alex had been able to open his eyes, he would have seen the desk, the mini-bar and the framed pictures of Paris begin to rise up the wall. Or so it might have seemed to him. But in fact the walls weren't moving. The floor was sinking on hidden hydraulics, taking the bed – with Alex on it – into the depths of the hotel. The entire room was nothing more than a huge lift which was carrying him, one centimetre at a time, into the basement and beyond. Now the walls were metal sheets. He had left the wallpaper, the lights and the pictures high above him. He was dropping through what might have been a ventilation shaft with four steel rods guiding him to the bottom. Brilliant light suddenly flooded over him. There was another soft click. He had arrived.

The bed had come to rest in the centre of a gleaming underground clinic. Scientific equipment crowded in on him from all sides. There were a number of cameras – digital, video, infrared and X-ray. There were instruments of all shapes and sizes, many of them unrecognizable.

A tangle of wires spiralled out from each machine to a bank of computers that hummed and blinked on a long worktable against one of the walls. A window had been cut into the wall on the other side. The room was air-conditioned. Had Alex been awake, he might have shivered in the cold. His breath appeared as a faint white cloud hovering around his mouth.

A plump man wearing a white coat was waiting to receive him. The man was about forty, with yellow hair slicked back and a face that was rapidly sinking into middle-age, with puffy cheeks and a thick, fatty neck. The man had glasses and a small moustache. He had two assistants with him. They were also wearing white coats. Their faces were blank.

The three of them set to work at once. Handling Alex as if he were a sack of vegetables – or a corpse – they picked him up and stripped off all his clothes. Then they began to photograph him, using a conventional camera to begin with. Starting at his toes, they moved upwards, clicking off at least a hundred pictures, the flash igniting and the film automatically spooling forward. Not one inch of his body escaped their examination. A lock of his hair was snipped off and slid into a plastic envelope. An opthalmoscope was used to produce a perfect image of the back of his eye. They made a moulding of his teeth, slipping a piece of putty into his mouth and manipulating his chin to make him bite down. They made a careful note of the birthmark on his left shoulder, the scar on his arm and even his fingerprints. Alex bit his nails. That was recorded too.

Finally, they weighed him on a large, flat scale and then measured him – his height, chest, waist, inside leg, hand size and so on – making a note of every measurement on clipboards.

And all the time, Mrs Stellenbosch watched from the other side of the window. She never moved. The only sign of life anywhere in her face was the cigar, clamped between her lips. It glowed red and the smoke trickled up.

The three men had finished. The one with the yellow hair spoke into a microphone. "We're all done," he said.

"Give me your opinion, Mr Baxter." The woman's voice echoed out of a concealed speaker.

"It's a cinch." The man called Baxter was English. He spoke with an upper-class accent. And he was obviously pleased with himself. "He's got a good bone structure. Very fit. Interesting face. You notice the pierced ear? He's had that done recently. Nothing else to say, really."

"When will you operate?"

"Whenever you say, old girl. Just let me know."

Mrs Stellenbosch turned to the other two men. *"Rhabillez-le!"* She snapped the two words.

The two assistants put Alex's clothes back on him again. This took longer than taking them off. As they worked, they made a careful note of all the brand names. The Quiksilver shirt. The Gap socks. By the time they had dressed him, they knew as much about him as a doctor knows about a newborn baby. It had all been noted down. And the information would be passed on.

Mr Baxter walked over to the worktable and pressed a button. At once, the carpet, bed and hotel furniture began to rise up. They disappeared through the ceiling and kept going. Alex slept on as he was carried back up the shaft, finally arriving in the space that he knew as room thirteen.

There was nothing to show what had happened. The whole experience had evaporated, as quickly as a dream.

"MY NAME IS GRIEF"

The academy at Point Blanc had been built by a lunatic. For a time it had been used as an asylum. Alex remembered what Alan Blunt had told him as the helicopter began its final descent, the red and white helipad looming up to receive it. The photograph in the brochure had been artfully taken. Now that he could see the building for himself, he could only describe it as ... mad.

It was a jumble of towers and battlements, green sloping roofs and windows of every shape and size. Nothing fitted together properly. The overall design should have been simple enough; a circular central area with two wings. But one wing was longer than the other. The two sides didn't match. The academy was four floors high but the windows were spaced in such a way that it was hard to tell where one floor ended and the next began. There was an internal courtyard that wasn't quite square, with a fountain that had frozen solid. Even the helipad, jutting out of the roof, was ugly and awkward, as if a spaceship had smashed into the brickwork and lodged in place.

Mrs Stellenbosch flicked off the controls. "I will take you down to meet the director," she shouted over the noise of the blades. "Your luggage will be brought down later."

It was cold on the roof, the snow covering the mountain still hadn't melted and everything was white for as far as the eye could see.

The academy was built into the side of a steep slope. A little further down, Alex saw a great iron tongue that started at ground level but then curved outwards as the mountainside dropped away. It was a ski-jump – the sort of thing he had seen at the Winter Olympics. The end of the curve was at least fifty metres above the ground and, far below, Alex could make out a flat area shaped like a horseshoe where the jumpers were meant to land.

He was staring at it, imagining what it would be like to propel yourself into space with only two skis to break your fall, when the woman grabbed his arm. "We don't use it," she said. "It is forbidden. Come now. Let's get out of the cold."

They went through a door in the side of one of the towers and down a narrow spiral staircase – each step a different distance apart – that took them all the way to the ground floor. Now they were in a long, narrow corridor with plenty of doors but no windows.

"Classrooms," Mrs Stellenbosch explained. "You will see them later."

Alex followed her through the strangely silent building. The central heating had been turned up high inside the academy and the atmosphere was warm and heavy. They stopped at a pair of modern glass doors which opened into the courtyard that Alex had seen from above. From the heat back into the cold again, Mrs

Stellenbosch led him through the doors and past the frozen fountain. A movement caught his eye and Alex glanced up. This was something he hadn't noticed earlier. A sentry stood on one of the towers. He had a pair of binoculars round his neck and a submachine-gun slung across one arm.

Armed guards? In a school? Alex had only been here a few minutes and already he was unnerved.

"Through here." Mrs Stellenbosch opened another door for him and he found himself in the main reception hall of the academy. A log fire was burning in a massive fireplace with two stone dragons guarding the flames. A grand staircase led upwards. The hall was lit by a chandelier with at least a hundred bulbs. The walls were wood panelled. The carpet was thick, dark red. A dozen pairs of eyes pursued Alex as he followed Mrs Stellenbosch towards the next corridor. The hall was decorated with animal heads. A rhino, an antelope, a water buffalo and, saddest of all, a lion. Alex wondered who had shot them.

They came to a single door, which suggested they had come to the end of their journey. So far Alex hadn't encountered any boys but, glancing out of the window, he saw two more guards marching slowly past, both of them cradling machine guns.

Mrs Stellenbosch knocked on the door.

"Come in!" Even with just two words, Alex caught the South African accent.

The door opened and they went into a huge room that made no sense. Like the rest of the building, its shape was irregular, none of the walls running parallel. The ceiling was about seven metres high, with windows running the whole way and giving an impressive view of the slopes. The room was modern, with soft lighting coming from units concealed in the walls. The furniture was ugly, but not as ugly as the further animal heads on the walls and the zebra skin on the wooden floor. There were three chairs next to a small fireplace. One of them was gold and antique. A man was sitting in it. His head turned as Alex came in.

"Good afternoon, Alex," he said. "Please come and sit down."

Alex sauntered into the room and took one of the chairs. Mrs Stellenbosch sat in the other.

"My name is Grief," the man continued. "Dr Grief. I am very pleased to meet you and to have you here."

Alex stared at the man who was the director of Point Blanc, at the white-paper skin and the eyes burning behind the red spectacles. It was like meeting a skeleton and for a moment he was lost for words. Then he recovered. "Nice place," he said.

"Do you think so?" There was no emotion whatsoever in Grief's voice. So far he had moved only his neck. "This building was designed in 1857 by a Frenchman who was certainly the world's worst architect. This was his only commission. When the first owners moved in, they had him shot."

"There are still quite a few people here with guns." Alex glanced out of the window as another pair of guards walked past.

"Point Blanc is unique," Dr Grief explained. "As you will soon discover, all the boys who have been sent here come from families of great wealth and importance. We have had the sons of emperors and industrialists. Boys like yourself. It follows that we could very easily become a target for terrorists. The guards are therefore here for your protection."

"That's very kind of you." Alex felt he was being too polite. It was time to show this man what sort of person he was meant to be. "But to be honest, I don't really want to be here myself. So if you'll just tell me how I get down into town, maybe I can get the next train home."

"There is no way down into town." Dr Grief lifted a hand to stop

Alex interrupting. Alex looked at his long, skeletal fingers and at the eyes glinting red behind the spectacles. The man moved as if every bone in his body had been broken and then put back together again; he seemed both old and young at the same time and somehow not completely human. "The skiing season is over ... it's too dangerous now. There is only the helicopter and that will take you from here only when I say so." The hand lowered itself again. "You are here, Alex, because you have disappointed your parents. You were expelled from school. You have had difficulties with the police—"

"That wasn't my bloody fault!" Alex protested.

"Don't interrupt the doctor!" Mrs Stellenbosch said.

Alex glanced at her balefully.

"Your appearance is displeasing," Dr Grief went on. "Your language also. It is our job to turn you into a boy of whom your parents can be proud."

"I'm happy as I am," Alex said.

"That is of no relevance." Dr Grief fell silent.

Alex shivered. There was something about this room; so big, so empty, so twisted out of shape. "So what are you going to do with me?" Alex asked.

"There will be no lessons to begin with," Mrs Stellenbosch said. "For the first couple of weeks we want you to assimilate."

"What does that mean?"

"To assimilate. To conform ... to adapt ... to become like." It was as if she were reading out of a dictionary. "There are six boys at the academy at the moment. You will meet them and you will spend time with them. There will be opportunities for sport and for being social. There is a good library here and you will read. Soon, you will learn our methods."

"I want to call my mum and dad," Alex said.

"The use of telephones is forbidden," Mrs Stellenbosch explained. She tried to smile sympathetically, but with *her* face it wasn't quite possible. "We find it makes our students homesick," she went on. "Of course, you may write letters if you wish."

"I prefer e-mails," Alex said.

"For the same reason, personal computers are not permitted."

Alex shrugged, and swore under his breath.

Dr Grief had seen him. "You will be polite to the assistant director!" he snapped. He hadn't raised his voice but the words came out acid. "You should be aware, Alex, that Mrs Stellenbosch has worked with me now for twenty-six years and that when I met her she had been voted Miss South Africa five years in a row."

Alex looked at the apelike face. "A beauty contest?" he asked.

"The weightlifting championships." Dr Grief glanced at the fireplace. "Show him," he said.

Mrs Stellenbosch got up and went over to the fireplace. There was a poker lying in the grate. She took it with both hands. For a moment she seemed to concentrate. Alex gasped. The solid metal poker, at least two centimetres thick, was slowly bending. Now it was u-shaped. Mrs Stellenbosch wasn't even sweating. She brought the two ends together and dropped it back into the grate. It clanged against the stone.

"We enforce strict discipline here at the academy," Dr Grief said. "Bedtime is at ten o'clock – not a minute past. We do not tolerate bad language. You will have no contact with the outside world without our permission. You will not attempt to leave. And you will do as you are told instantly, without hesitation. And finally" – he leant towards Alex – "you are permitted only in certain parts of this building." He gestured with a hand and for the first time Alex noticed a second door at the far end of the room. "My private quarters are through there. You will remain on the ground floor and the first floor only. That is where the bedrooms and classrooms are located. The second and third floors are out of bounds. The basement also. This is again for your safety."

"You're afraid I'll trip on the stairs?" Alex asked.

Dr Grief ignored him. "You may leave," he said.

"Wait outside the office, Alex," Mrs Stellenbosch said. "Someone will be along to collect you."

Alex stood up.

"We will make you into what your parents want," Dr Grief said.

"Maybe they don't want me at all."

"We can arrange that too."

Alex went.

"An unpleasant boy ... a few days ... faster than usual ... the Gemini Project ... closing down..."

If the door hadn't been so thick, Alex would have been able to hear more. The moment he had left the room he'd cupped his ear against the keyhole, hoping to pick up something that might be useful to MI6. Sure enough, Dr Grief and Mrs Stellenbosch were busily talking on the other side, but Alex heard little and understood less.

A hand clamped down on his shoulder and he twisted round, annoyed with himself. A so-called spy caught listening at the keyhole! But it wasn't one of the guards. Alex found himself looking up at a round-faced boy with long dark hair, dark eyes and pale skin. He was wearing a very old *Star Wars* T-shirt, torn jeans and a baseball cap. Recently he had been in a fight, and it looked like he'd got the worst of it. There was a bruise around one of his eyes and a gash on his lip.

"They'll shoot you if they catch you listening at doors," the boy said. He looked at Alex with hostile eyes. Alex guessed he was the sort of boy who wouldn't trust anyone easily. "I'm James Sprintz," he said. "They told me to show you round."

"Alex Friend."

"So what did you do to get sent to this dump?" James asked as they walked back down the corridor.

"I got expelled from Eton."

"I got thrown out of a school in Düsseldorf." James sighed. "I thought it was the best thing that ever happened to me. Until my dad sent me here."

"What does your dad do?" Alex asked.

"He's a banker. He plays the money markets. He loves money and has lots of it." James's voice was flat, unemotional.

"Dieter Sprintz?" Alex remembered the name. He'd made the front page of every newspaper in England a few years before. The One Hundred Million Dollar Man. That was how much he had made in just twenty-four hours. At the same time the pound had crashed and the British government had almost collapsed.

"Yeah. Don't ask me to show you a photograph because I don't have one. This way."

They had reached the main hall with the dragon fireplace. From here, James showed him to the dining-room, a long, high-ceilinged room with six tables and a hatch leading into the kitchen. After that, they visited two living-rooms, a games room and a library. The academy reminded Alex of an expensive hotel in a ski resort – and not just because of its setting. There was a sort of heaviness about the place, a sense of being cut off from the real world. The air was warm and silent and, despite the size of the rooms, Alex couldn't help feeling claustrophobic. If the place *had* been a hotel, it would have been an unpopular one. Grief had said there were only six boys living there. The building could have housed sixty. Empty space was everywhere.

There was nobody in either of the living-rooms – just a collection of armchairs, desks and tables – but they found a couple of boys in the library. This was a long, narrow room with old-fashioned oak shelves lined with books in a variety of languages. A suit of medieval Swiss armour stood in an alcove at the far end.

"This is Tom. And Hugo," James said. "They're probably doing extra maths or something, so we'd better not disturb them."

The two boys looked up and nodded briefly. One of them was reading a textbook. The other was writing. They were both much more smartly dressed than James and didn't look very friendly.

"Creeps," James said as soon as they had left the room.

"In what way?"

"When I was told about this place, they said *all* the kids had problems. I thought it was going to be wild. Do you have a cigarette?"

"I don't smoke."

"Great. I get here and it's like a museum or a monastery or ... I don't know what. It looks like Dr Grief's been busy. Everyone's quiet, hard-working, boring. God knows how he did it. Sucked their brains out with a straw or something. A couple of days ago I got into a fight with a couple of them, just for the hell of it." He pointed to his face. "They beat the crap out of me and then went back to their studies. Really creepy!"

They went into the games room, which contained table tennis, darts, a widescreen TV and a snooker table. "Don't try playing snooker," James said. "The room's on a slant and all the balls roll to the side."

Then they went upstairs. This was where the boys had their study bedrooms. Each one contained a bed, an armchair, a television ("It only shows the programmes Dr Grief wants you to see," James said), a wardrobe and a desk, with a second door leading into a small bathroom with a toilet and shower. None of the rooms were locked.

"We're not allowed to lock them," James explained. "We're all stuck here with nowhere to go, so nobody bothers to steal anything. Hugo Vries – the boy in the library – used to nick anything he could get his hands on. He was arrested for shoplifting in Amsterdam."

"But not any more?"

"He's another success story. He's flying home next week. His father owns diamond mines. Why bother shoplifting when you can afford to buy the whole shop?"

Alex's study was at the end of the corridor, with views over the ski-jump. His suitcases had already been carried up and were waiting for him on the bed. Everything felt very bare but, according to James, the study bedrooms were the only part of the school which the boys were allowed to decorate themselves. They could choose their own duvets and cover the walls with their own posters.

"They say it's important that you express yourself," James said. "If you haven't brought anything with you, Miss Stomach-bag will take you into Grenoble."

"Miss Stomach-bag?"

"Mrs Stellenbosch. That's my name for her."

"What do the other boys call her?"

"They call her Mrs Stellenbosch." James paused by the door. "This is a deeply weird place, Alex. I've been to a lot of schools because I've been thrown out of a lot of schools. But this one is the pits. I've been here for six weeks now and I've hardly had any lessons. They have music evenings and discussion evenings and they try to get me to read. But otherwise I've been left on my own."

"They want you to assimilate," Alex said, remembering what Dr Grief had said.

"That's *their* word for it. But this place ... they may call it a school, but it's more like being in prison. You've seen the guards."

"I thought they were here to protect us."

"If you think that, you're a bigger idiot than I thought. Think about it! There are about thirty of them. Thirty armed guards for seven kids. That's not protection. That's intimidation." James examined Alex for a second time. "It would be nice to think that someone has finally arrived who I can relate to," he said.

"Maybe you can," Alex said.

"Yeah. But for how long?"

James left, closing the door behind him.

Alex began to unpack. The bulletproof ski suit and infrared goggles were at the top of the first case. It didn't look as if he would be needing them. It wasn't as if he even had any skis. Then came the Discman. He remembered the instructions Smithers had given him. "If the balloon goes up, just press fast forward three times." He was almost tempted to do it now. There was something unsettling about the academy. He could feel it even now, in his room. He was like a goldfish in a bowl. Looking up, he almost expected to see a pair of huge eyes looming over him and he knew that they would be wearing red-tinted glasses. He weighed the Discman in his hand. He couldn't hit the panic button – yet. He had nothing to report back to MI6. There was nothing to connect the school with the deaths of the two men in New York and the Black Sea.

But if there was anything, he knew where he would find it. Why were two whole floors of the building out of bounds? Presumably the guards slept up there but, even though Dr Grief seemed to employ a small army, that would still leave a lot of empty rooms.

The second and third floors. If something was going on at the academy, it had to be going on there.

A bell sounded downstairs. Alex swung his case shut, left his room and walked down the corridor. He saw another couple of boys walking ahead of him, talking quietly together. Like the boys he had seen in the library, they were both clean and well-dressed, with hair cut short and smartly groomed. Majorly creepy, James had said. Even on first sight, Alex had to agree.

He reached the main staircase. The two boys had gone down. Alex glanced in their direction, then went up. The staircase turned a corner and stopped. Ahead of him was a sheet of metal that rose up from the floor to the ceiling and all the way across, blocking off the view. The wall had been added recently, like the helipad. Someone had carefully and deliberately cut the building in two.

There was a door set in the metal wall and beside it a keypad with nine buttons demanding a code. Alex reached for the door handle, his hand closing around it. He didn't expect the door to open – but nor did he expect what happened next. The moment his fingers came into contact with the handle, an alarm went off, a shrieking siren that echoed throughout the building. A few seconds later he became aware of footsteps on the stairs and turned to find two guards facing him, their guns raised.

Neither of them spoke to him. One of them pushed past him and punched a code into the keypad. The alarm stopped. And then Mrs Stellenbosch was there, hurrying forward on her short, stubby legs.

"Alex!" she exclaimed. Her eyes were filled with suspicion. "What are you doing here? The director told you that the upper floors are forbidden."

"Yeah ... well I forgot." Alex looked straight at her. "I heard the bell go and I was on my way to the dining-room."

"The dining-room is downstairs."

"Right."

Alex walked past the two guards, who stepped aside to let him pass. He felt Mrs Stellenbosch watching him as he went. Metal doors, alarms and guards with machine guns. What were they hiding? And then he remembered something else. The Gemini Project. Those were the words he had heard when he was listening at Dr Grief's door.

Gemini. The twins. One of the twelve star signs.

But what did it mean?

Turning the question over in his mind, Alex went down to meet the rest of the school.

THINGS THAT GO CLICK IN THE NIGHT

At the end of his first week at Point Blanc, Alex drew up a list of the six boys with whom he shared the school. It was mid-afternoon and he was alone in his room. There was a notepad open in front of him. It had taken him about half an hour to put together the names and the few details that he had. He only wished he had more.

HUGO VRIES (14) Dutch, lives in Amsterdam. Brown hair, green eyes. Father's name: Rudi, owns diamond mines. Speaks little English. Reads and plays guitar. Very solitary. Sent to PB for shoplifting and arson.

TOM McMORIN (14) Canadian, from Vancouver. Parents divorced. Mother runs media empire (newspapers, TV). Reddish hair, blue eyes. Well-built, chess player. Car thefts and drunken driving.

NICOLAS MARC (14) French, from Bordeaux? Expelled from private School in Paris, cause unknown – drinking? Brown hair, brown eyes, very fit all-rounder. Good at sport but hates losing. Tattoo of devil on left shoulder. Father: Anthony Marc - airlines, pop music, hotels. Never mentions his mother.

CASSIAN JAMES (14) American.
Fair hair, brown eyes. Mother: Jill,
studio chief in Hollywood. Parents
divorced. Loud voice. Swears a lot.
Plays jazz piano. Expelled from
three schools. Various drug offences
- sent to PB after smuggling
arrest but won't talk about it
now. One of the kids who beat
up James. Stronger than he looks.

JOE CANTERBURY (14) American.
Spends a lot of time with Cassian.
(helped him with James). Brown hair,
blue eyes. Mother (name unknown) New
York senator. Father something big
at the Pentagon. Vandalism, truancy,
Shoplifting. Sent to PB after stealing
and smashing up car. Vegetarian.
Permanently chewing gum. Has he
given up smoking?

JAMES SPRINTZ (14) German, lives in Düsseldorf. Brown hair, brown eyes, pale. Father: Dieter Sprintz, banker, well-known financier (the One Hundred Million Dollar Man). Mother living in England. Expelled for wounding a teacher with an air-pistol. My only friend at PB! And the only one who really hates it here.

Lying on his bed, Alex studied the list. What did it tell him? Not a great deal.

First, all the boys were the same age – fourteen. The same age as him. At least three of them, and possibly four, had parents who were either divorced or separated. They all came from hugely wealthy backgrounds. Blunt had already told him that was the case, but Alex was surprised by just how diverse the parents were. Airlines, diamonds, politics and movies. France, Germany, Holland, Canada and America. All of the parents were at the top of his or her field and those fields covered just about every human activity. He himself was supposed to be the son of a supermarket king. Food. That was another world industry he could tick off.

At least two of the boys had been arrested for shoplifting. Two of them had been involved with drugs. But Alex knew that the list somehow hid more than it revealed. With the exception of James, it was hard to pin down what made the boys at Point Blanc different. In a strange way, they all looked the same.

Their eyes and hair were different colours. They wore different clothes. All the faces were different: Tom handsome and confident, Joe quiet and watchful. And of course they spoke not only with different voices but in several languages. James had talked about brains being sucked out with straws and he had a point. It was as if the same consciousness had somehow invaded them all. They had become puppets dancing on the same string.

The bell rang downstairs. Alex looked at his watch. It was exactly one o'clock – lunch-time. That was another thing about the school. Everything was done to the exact minute. Lessons from nine until twelve. Lunch from one to two. And so on. James made a point of being late for everything and Alex had taken to joining him. It was a tiny rebellion, but a satisfying one. It showed they still had a little control over their lives. The other boys, of course, turned up like clockwork. They would be in the dining-room now, waiting quietly for the food to be served.

Alex rolled over on the bed and reached for a pen. He wrote a single word on the pad, underneath the names.

Brainwashing?

Maybe that was the answer. According to James, the other boys had arrived at the academy two months before him. He had been there for six weeks. That added up to just fourteen weeks in total and Alex knew that you didn't take a bunch of delinquents and turn them into perfect students just by giving them good books. Dr Grief had to be doing something else. Drugs? Hypnosis? Something.

He waited five more minutes, then hid the notepad under his mattress and left the room. He wished he could lock the door. There was no privacy at Point Blanc. Even the bathrooms had no locks. And Alex still couldn't shake off the feeling that everything he did, even everything he thought, was somehow being monitored, noted down. Evidence to be used against him.

It was ten past one when he reached the dining-room and, sure enough, the other boys were already there, eating their lunch and talking quietly amongst themselves. Nicolas and Cassian were at one table. Hugo, Tom and Joe were at another. Nobody was flicking peas. Nobody even had their elbows on the table. Tom was talking about a visit he had made to some museum in Grenoble. Alex had only been in the room for a few seconds but already his appetite had gone.

James had arrived just ahead of him and was standing at the hatch, helping himself to food. Most of the food arrived precooked and one of the guards heated it up. Today it was stew. Alex got his lunch and sat next to James. The two of them had their own table. They had become friends quite effortlessly. Everyone else ignored them.

"You want to go out after lunch?" James asked.

"Sure. Why not?"

"There's something I want to talk to you about."

Alex looked past James at the other boys. There was Tom, at the head of the table, reaching out for a jug of water. He was dressed in a polo jersey and jeans. Next to him was Joe Canterbury, the American. He was talking to Hugo now, waving a finger to emphasize a point. Where had Alex seen that movement before? Cassian was just behind them, round-faced, with fine, light brown hair, laughing at a joke.

Different but the same. Watching them closely, Alex tried to work out what that meant.

It was all in the details, the things you wouldn't notice unless you saw them all together like they were now. The way they were all sitting with their backs straight and their elbows close to their sides. The way they held their knives and forks. Hugo laughed and Alex realized that for a moment he had become a mirror image of Cassian. It was the same laugh. He watched Joe eat a mouthful of food. Then he watched Nicolas. They were two different boys. There was no doubting that. But they ate in the same way, as if they were mimicking each other.

There was a movement at the door and suddenly Mrs Stellenbosch appeared. "Good afternoon, boys," she said.

"Good afternoon, Mrs Stellenbosch." Five people answered, but Alex heard only one voice. He and James remained silent.

"Lessons this afternoon will begin at three o'clock. The subjects will be Latin and French."

The lessons would be taught by Dr Grief or Mrs Stellenbosch. There were no other teachers at the school. Alex hadn't yet been taught anything. James dipped in and out of class, depending on his mood.

"There will be a discussion this evening in the library," Mrs Stellenbosch went on. "The subject is 'violence in television and film'. Mr McMorin will be opening the debate. Afterwards there will be hot chocolate and Dr Grief will be giving a lecture on the works of Mozart. Everyone is welcome to attend."

James jabbed a finger into his open mouth and stuck out his tongue. Alex smiled. The other boys were listening quietly.

"Dr Grief would also like to congratulate Cassian James on winning the poetry competition. His poem is pinned to the notice-board in the main hall. That is all."

She turned and left the room. James rolled his eyes. "Let's go out and get some fresh air," he said. "I'm feeling sick."

The two of them went upstairs and put on their coats. James had the room next door to Alex and had done his best to make it more homely. There were posters of old sci-fi movies on the walls and a mobile of the solar system dangling above the bed. A lava lamp bubbled and swirled on the bedside table, casting an orange glow. There were clothes everywhere. James obviously didn't believe in hanging them up. Somehow he managed to find a scarf and a single glove. He shoved one hand into a pocket. "Let's go!" he said.

They went back down and along the corridor, passing the games room. Nicolas and Cassian were playing table tennis and Alex stopped at the door to watch them. The ball was bouncing back and forth and Alex found himself mesmerized. He stood there for about sixty seconds, watching. Kerplink, kerplunk, kerplink, kerplunk – neither of the boys were scoring. There it was again. Different but the same. Obviously there were two boys there. But the way they played, the style of their game, was identical. If it had been one boy, knocking a ball up against a mirror, the result would have looked much the same. Alex shivered. James was standing at his shoulder. The two of them moved away.

Hugo was sitting in the library. The boy who had been sent to Point Blanc for shoplifting was reading a Dutch edition of *National Geographic* magazine. They reached the hall and there was Cassian's poem, prominently pinned to the notice-board. He had been sent to Point Blanc for smuggling drugs. Now he was writing about daffodils.

Alex pushed open the main door and felt the cold wind hit his face. He was grateful for it. He needed to be reminded that there was a real world outside.

It had begun to snow again. The two boys walked slowly round the building. A couple of guards walked towards them, speaking softly in German. Alex had counted thirty guards at Point Blanc, all of them young German men, dressed in uniform black roll-neck sweaters and black padded waistcoats. The guards never spoke to the boys. They had pale, unhealthy faces and close-cropped hair. Dr Grief had said they were there for his protection, but Alex still wondered. Were they there to keep intruders out – or the boys in?

"This way," James said.

James walked ahead, his feet sinking into the thick snow. Alex followed, looking back at the windows on the second and third floors. It was maddening. Half of the castle – perhaps more – was closed off to him and he still couldn't think of a way of getting up there. He couldn't climb. The brickwork was too smooth and there was no convenient ivy to provide handholds. The drainpipes looked too fragile to take his weight.

Something moved. Alex stopped in his tracks.

"What is it?" James asked.

"There!" Alex pointed at the third floor. He thought he'd seen a figure watching them from a window two floors above his room. It was only there for a moment. The face seemed to be covered – a white mask with narrow slits for the eyes. But even as he pointed, the figure stepped back, out of sight.

"I don't see anything," James said.

"It's gone."

They walked on, heading for the abandoned ski-jump. According to James, the jump had been built just before Grief had bought the academy. There had been plans to turn the building into a winter sports training centre. The jump had never been used. They reached the wooden barriers that lay across the entrance and stopped.

"Let me ask you something," James said. His breath was misting in the cold air. "What do you think of this place?"

"Why do we have to talk out here?" Alex asked. Despite his coat, he was beginning to shiver.

"Because when I'm inside the building, I get the feeling that someone is listening to every word I say."

Alex nodded. "I know what you mean." He considered the question James had put to him. "I think you were right the first day we met," he said. "This place is creepy."

"So how would you feel about getting out of here?"

"You know how to fly the helicopter?"

"No. But I'm going." James paused and looked around. The two guards had gone into the school. There was nobody else in sight. "I can trust you, Alex, because you've only just got here. He hasn't got to you yet." *He* was Dr Grief. James didn't need to say the name. "But believe me," he went on, "it won't be long. If you stay here, you're going to end up like the others. Model students – that's exactly the term for them. It's like they're all made out of Plasticene! Well, I've had enough. I'm not going to let him do that to me!"

"Are you going to run away?" Alex asked.

"Who needs to run?" James looked down the slope. "I'm going to ski."

Alex looked at the slope. It plunged steeply down, stretching on for ever. "Is that possible?" he asked. "I thought—"

"I know Grief says it's too dangerous. But he would, wouldn't he. It's true it's black runs all the way down and there'll be tons of moguls—"

"Won't the snow have melted?"

"Only further down." James pointed. "I've been right down to the bottom," he said. "I did it the first week I was here. All the slopes run into a single valley. It's called La Vallée de Fer. You can't actually make it as far as the town because there's a train track that cuts across. But if I can get to the track, I reckon I can walk the rest of the way."

"And then?"

"A train back to Düsseldorf. If my dad tries to send me back here, I'll go to my mum in England. If she doesn't want me, I'll disappear. I've got friends in Paris and Berlin. I don't care. All I know is, I've got to split and if you know what's good for you, you'll come too."

Alex considered. He was tempted to join the other boy, if only to help him on his way. But he had a job to do. "I don't have any skis," he said.

"Nor do I." James spat into the snow. "Grief took all the skis when the season ended. He's got them locked up somewhere."

"On the third floor?"

"Maybe. But I'll find them. And then I'm out of here." He reached out to Alex with his ungloved hand. "Come with me."

Alex shook his head. "I'm sorry, James. You go, and good luck to you. But I'll stick it out a bit longer. I don't want to break my neck."

"OK. That's your lookout. I'll send you a postcard."

The two of them walked back towards the school. Alex gestured at the window where he had seen the masked face. "Have you ever wondered what goes on up there?" he asked.

"No." James shrugged. "I suppose that's where the guards live."

"Two whole floors?"

"There's a basement as well. And Dr Grief's rooms. Do you think he sleeps with Miss Stomach-bag?" James made a face. "That's a pretty gross thought, the two of them together. Darth Vader and King Kong. Well, I'm going to find my skis and get out of here, Alex. And if you've got any sense, you'll come too."

* * *

Alex and James were skiing together down the slope, the blades cutting smoothly through the surface snow. It was a perfect night. Everything frozen and still. They had left the academy behind them. But then Alex saw a figure ahead of them. Dr Grief was there! He was standing motionless, wearing his dark suit, his eyes quite hidden by his red-lensed spectacles. Alex veered away from him. He lost control. He was moving faster and faster down the slope, his poles flailing at the air, his skis refusing to turn. He could see the ski-jump ahead of him. Someone had removed the barriers. He felt his skis leave the snow and shoot forward onto solid ice. And then it was a screaming drop down, tearing ever further into the night, knowing there was no way back. Dr Grief laughed and at the same moment there was a click and Alex shot into space, spinning a mile above the ground and then falling, falling, falling...

He woke up.

He was lying in bed, the moonlight spilling onto the covers. He looked at his watch. Two-fifteen. He played back the dream he had just had. Trying to escape with James. Dr Grief waiting for them. He had to admit, the academy was beginning to get to him. He didn't usually have bad dreams. But the school and the people in it were slipping under his skin, working their way into his mind.

He thought about what he had heard. Dr Grief laughing – and something else ... a clicking sound. That was strange. What had gone "click"? Had it actually been part of the dream? Suddenly Alex was completely awake. He got out of bed, went to the door and turned the handle. He was right. He hadn't imagined the sound. While he was asleep, the door had been locked from outside.

Something had to be happening – and Alex was determined to see what it was. He got dressed as quickly as possible, then knelt down and examined the lock. He could make out two bolts, at least a centimetre in diameter, one at the top and one at the bottom. They must have been activated automatically. One thing was sure. He wasn't going to get out through the door.

That left the window. All the bedroom windows were fastened with a steel rod that allowed them to open ten centimetres but no more. Alex picked up his Discman, put in the Beethoven CD and turned it on. The CD spun round – moving at a fantastic speed – then slowly edged forward, still spinning, until it protruded from the casing. Alex pressed the edge of the CD against the steel rod. It took just a few seconds. The CD cut through the steel like scissors through paper. The rod fell away, allowing the window to swing fully open.

It was snowing. Alex turned the CD player off and threw it back on his bed. Then he put on his coat and climbed out of the window. He was one floor up. Normally a fall from that height would have broken an ankle or a leg. But it had been snowing for the best part of ten hours and a white bank had built up against the wall right beneath him. Alex lowered himself as far as he could, then let go. He fell through the air and hit the snow, disappearing as far as his waist. He was freezing and damp before he had even started. But he was unhurt.

He climbed out of the snow and began to move round the side of the building, making for the front. He would just have to hope that the main entrance wasn't locked too. But somehow he was sure it wouldn't be. His door had been locked automatically. Presumably a switch had been thrown and all the others had been locked too. Most of the boys would be asleep. Even the ones who were awake wouldn't be going anywhere, leaving Dr Grief free to do whatever he wanted, coming and going as he pleased.

Alex had just made it to the side of the building when he heard the guards approach, boots crunching. There was nowhere to hide so he threw himself face-down into the snow, hugging the shadows. There were two of them. He could hear them talking softly in German but he didn't dare look up. If he made any movement, they would see him. If they came too close, they would probably see him anyway. He held his breath, his heart pounding.

The guards walked past and round the corner. Their path would take them under his room. Would they see the open window? Alex had left the light off. Hopefully there would be no reason for them to look up. But he was still aware that he might not have much time. He had to move – now.

He lifted himself up and ran forward. His clothes were covered in snow and more flakes were falling, drifting into his eyes. It was the coldest part of the night and Alex was shivering by the time he reached the main door. What would he do if it was locked after all? He certainly wouldn't be able to stay out in the open until morning.

But the door was unlocked. Alex pushed it open and slipped into the warmth and darkness of the main hall. The dragon fireplace was in front of him. There had been a fire earlier in the evening and the burnt-out logs were still smouldering in the hearth. Alex held his hands against the glow, trying to draw a little warmth into himself. Everything was silent. The empty corridors stretched into the distance, illuminated by a few low-watt bulbs that had been left on at intervals. Only now did it occur to Alex that he could have been mistaken from the start. Perhaps the doors were locked every night as part of the security. Perhaps he had jumped too quickly to the wrong conclusion and there was nothing going on after all.

"No...!"

It was a boy's voice. A long, quavering shout that echoed through the school. A moment later, Alex heard feet stamping along a wooden corridor somewhere above. He looked for somewhere to hide and found it inside the fireplace, right next to the logs. The actual fire was contained in a metal basket. There was a wide space on each side between the basket and the brickwork that swept up to become the chimney. Alex crouched low, feeling the heat on the side of his face and legs. He looked out, past the two dragons, waiting to see what would happen.

Three people were coming down the stairs. Mrs Stellenbosch was the first. She was followed by two of the guards, dragging something between them. It was a boy! He was face-down, dressed only in his pyjamas, his bare feet sliding down the stone steps. Mrs Stellenbosch opened the library door and went in. The two guards followed. The door crashed shut. The silence returned.

It had all happened very quickly. Alex had been unable to see the boy's face. But he was sure he knew who it was. He had known just from the sound of his voice.

James Sprintz.

Alex eased himself out of the fireplace and crossed the hall, making for the library door. There was no sound coming from the other side. He knelt down and looked through the keyhole. No lights were on inside the room. He could see nothing. What should he do? If he went back upstairs, he could make it back to his room without being seen. He could wait until the doors were unlocked and then slip into bed. Nobody would know he had been out.

But the only person in the school who had shown him any kindness was on the other side of the library door. He had been dragged down here. Perhaps he was being brainwashed ... beaten, even. Alex couldn't just turn round and leave him.

Alex had made his decision. He threw open the door and walked in.

The library was empty.

He stood in the doorway, blinking. The library only had one

door. All the windows were closed. There was no sign that anyone had been there. The suit of armour stood in its alcove at the end, watching him as he moved forward. Could he have been mistaken? Could Mrs Stellenbosch and the guards have gone into a different room?

Alex went over to the alcove and looked behind the armour, wondering if it might conceal a second exit. There was nothing. He tapped a knuckle against the wall. Curiously, it seemed to be made of metal, but unlike the wall across the stairs there was no handle, nothing to suggest a way through.

There was nothing more he could do here. Alex decided to go back to his room before he was discovered.

But he had only just made it to the first floor when he heard voices once again ... more guards, walking slowly down the corridor. Alex saw a door and slipped inside, once again ducking out of sight. He was in the laundry room. There was a washing-machine, a tumble-drier and two ironing-boards. At least it was warm in here. He felt himself surrounded by soap fumes.

The guards had gone. There was a metallic click that seemed to stretch the length of the corridor and Alex realized that all the doors had been unlocked at the same time. He could go back to bed.

He crept out and hurried forward. His footsteps took him past James Sprintz's room, next to his own. He noticed that James's door was open. And then a voice called out from inside.

"Alex?" It was James.

No. That wasn't possible. But there was someone in his room.

Alex looked inside. The light went on.

It *was* James. He was sitting up in bed, bleary-eyed, as if he had just woken up. Alex stared at him. He was wearing the same pyjamas as the boy he had just seen dragged into the library ...

but that *couldn't* have been him. It must have been someone else.

"What are you doing?" James asked.

"I thought I heard something," Alex said.

"But you're dressed. And you're soaking wet!" James looked at his watch. "It's almost three..."

Alex was surprised that so much time had passed. It had only been two-fifteen when he'd woken up. "Are you all right?" he asked.

"Yeah."

"You haven't...?"

"What?"

"Nothing. I'll see you later."

Alex crept back to his own room. He closed the door, then stripped off his wet clothes, dried himself with a towel and got back into bed. If it wasn't James he had seen being taken into the library, who was it? And yet it *had* been James. He had heard the cry, seen the limp form on the stairs. So why was James lying now?

Alex closed his eyes and tried to get back to sleep. The movements of the night had created more puzzles and had solved nothing. But at least he'd got something out of it all.

He now knew how to get up to the second floor.

SEEING DOUBLE

James was already eating his breakfast when Alex came down: eggs, bacon, toast and tea. He had the same breakfast every day. He raised a hand in greeting as Alex came in. But the moment he saw him, Alex got the feeling that something was wrong. James was smiling but he seemed somehow distant, as if his thoughts were on other things.

"So what was all that about last night?" James asked.

"I don't know..." Alex was tempted to tell James everything – even the fact that he was here under a false name and had been sent to spy on the school. But he couldn't do it. Not here, so close to the other boys. "I think I had some sort of bad dream."

"Did you go sleepwalking in the snow?"

"No. I thought I saw something, but I couldn't have. I just had a weird night." He changed the subject, lowering his voice. "Have you thought any more about your plan?" he asked.

"What plan?"

"Skiing."

"We're not allowed to ski."

"I mean ... escaping."

James smiled as if he'd only just remembered what Alex was talking about. "Oh – I've changed my mind," he said.

"What d'you mean?"

"If I ran away, my dad would only send me back again. There's no point. I might as well grin and bear it. Anyway, I'd never get all the way down the mountain. The snow's too thin."

Alex stared at James. Everything he was saying was the exact opposite of what he had said the day before. He almost wondered if this was the same boy. But of course it was. He was as untidy as ever. The bruises – fading now – were still there on his face. Dark hair, dark brown eyes, pale skin – it was James. And yet at the same time, something had happened. He was sure of it.

Then James twisted round and Alex saw that Mrs Stellenbosch had come into the room, wearing a particularly nasty lime-green dress that just came down to her knees. "Good morning, boys!" she announced. "We're starting today's lessons in ten minutes. The first lesson is history in the tower room." She walked over to Alex's table. "James, I hope you're going to join us today?"

James shrugged. "All right, Mrs Stellenbosch."

"Excellent. We're looking at the life of Adolf Hitler. Such an interesting man. I'm sure you'll find it most valuable." She walked away.

Alex turned to James. "You're going to lessons?"

"Why not?" James had finished eating. "I'm stuck here and there isn't much else to do. Maybe I should have gone to lessons before. You shouldn't be so negative, Alex." He waved a finger to underline what he was saying. "You're wasting your time."

Alex froze. He had seen that movement before – the way he had waved his finger. Joe Canterbury, the American boy, had done exactly the same thing yesterday.

Puppets dancing on the same string.

What had happened the night before?

Alex watched James leave with the others. He felt he had lost his only friend at Point Blanc and suddenly he wanted to be away from this place, off the mountain and back in the safe world of Brookland School. There might have been a time when he had wanted this adventure. Now he just wanted out of it. Press fast forward three times on his Discman and MI6 would come for him. But he couldn't do that until he had something to report.

Alex knew what he had to do. He got up and left the room.

He had seen the way the night before when he was hiding in the fireplace. The chimney bent and twisted its way to the open air – he had been able to see a chink of light from the bottom. Moonlight. The bricks outside the academy might be too smooth to climb, but inside the chimney they were broken and uneven, with plenty of hand and footholds. Maybe there would be a fireplace on the second or third floor. But even if there wasn't, the chimney would still lead him to the roof and – assuming there weren't any guards waiting for him there – he might then be able to find a way down.

Alex reached the fireplace with the two stone dragons. He looked at his watch. Nine o'clock. Lessons would continue until lunch and nobody would wonder where he was. The fire had finally gone out, although the ashes were still warm. Would one of the guards come to clean it? He would just have to hope they would leave it until the afternoon. He looked up the chimney. He could see a narrow slit of bright blue. The sky seemed a very long way away and the chimney was narrower than he had thought. What if he got stuck? He forced the thought out of his head, reached for a crack in the brickwork and pulled himself up.

The inside of the chimney smelled of a thousand fires. Soot hung in the air and Alex couldn't breathe without taking it in. He managed to find some purchase for his feet and pushed, sliding himself about one metre up. Now he was wedged inside, forced into a sitting position with his feet against one wall, his back against the other and his legs and bottom hanging in the air. He wouldn't need to use his hands at all. He only had to straighten his legs to push himself up, using the pressure of his feet against the wall to keep himself in place. Push and slide. He had to be careful. Every movement brought more soot trickling down. He could feel it in his hair. He didn't dare look up. If it went into his eyes he would be blinded. Push and slide again, then again. Not too fast. If his feet slipped he would fall all the way back down. He was already a long way above the fireplace. How far had he come? At least one floor ... meaning that he had to be on his way to the second. If he fell from this height he would break both his legs.

The chimney was getting darker and tighter. The light at the top didn't seem to be getting any nearer. Alex found it difficult to manoeuvre himself. He could barely breathe. His entire throat seemed to be coated in soot. He pushed again and this time his knees banged into brickwork, sending a spasm of pain down to his feet. Pinning himself in place, Alex reached up and tried to feel where he was going. There was an L-shaped wall jutting out above his head. His knees had hit the bottom part of it. But his head was behind the upright section. Whatever the obstruction was, it effectively cut the passageway in half, leaving only the narrowest of gaps for Alex's shoulders and body to pass through.

Once again, the nightmare prospect of getting stuck flashed

into his mind. Nobody would ever find him. He would suffocate in the dark.

He gasped for breath and swallowed soot. One last try! He pushed again, his arms stretching out over his head. He felt his back slide up the wall, the rough brickwork tearing at his shirt. Then his hands hooked over what he realized must be the top of the L. He pulled himself up and found himself looking into a second fireplace, sharing the main chimney. That was the obstruction he had just climbed round. Alex levered himself over the top and dived clumsily forward. More logs and ashes broke his fall. He had made it to the second floor!

He crawled out of the fireplace. Only a few weeks before, at Brookland, he'd been reading about Victorian chimney-sweeps; how boys as young as six had been forced into virtual slave labour. He'd never thought he would learn how they had felt. He coughed and spat into the palm of his hand. His saliva was black. He wondered what he must look like. He would need to take a shower before he was seen.

He stood up. The second floor was as silent as the ground and the first. Soot trickled out of his hair and for a moment he was blinded. He propped himself against a statue while he wiped his eyes. Then he looked again. He was leaning on a stone dragon, identical to the one on the ground floor. He looked at the fireplace. That too was identical. In fact...

Alex wondered if he hadn't somehow made a terrible mistake. He was standing in a hall that was the same in every detail as the hall on the ground floor. There were the same corridors, the same staircase, the same fireplace – even the same animal heads staring miserably from the walls. It was as if he had climbed in a circle, arriving back where he had begun. He turned round. No. Here was one difference. There was no main door. He could look down on the front courtyard from the window; there was a guard leaning against a wall, smoking a cigarette. This *was* the second floor. But it had been constructed as a perfect replica of the ground.

Alex tiptoed forward, worried that somebody might have heard him climb out of the fireplace. But there was no one around. He followed the corridor as far as the first door. On the ground floor, this would be the library. Gently, a centimetre at a time, he opened the door. It led into a second library – again the spitting image of the first. It had the same tables and chairs, the same suit of armour guarding the same alcove. He ran an eye along one of the shelves. It even had the same books.

But there was one difference – at least, one difference that Alex could see. He felt as if he had strayed into one of those puzzles they sometimes print in comics or magazines. Two identical pictures. But ten deliberate mistakes. Can you spot them? The mistake here was that there was a large television set on a bracket built into the wall. The television was on. Alex found himself looking at an image of yet another library. He was beginning to feel dizzy. What was the library on the television screen? It couldn't be this one because Alex himself was not being shown. So it had to be the library on the ground floor.

Two identical libraries. You could sit in one and watch the other. But why? What was the point?

It took Alex about ten minutes to discover that the entire second floor was a carbon copy of the ground floor, with the same dining-room, living-room and games room. Alex went over to the snooker table and placed a ball in the middle. It rolled into the corner pocket. The room was on the same slant. A television screen showed the games room downstairs. It was the same as the library; one room spying on another.

He retraced his steps and climbed the stairs to the third floor.

He wanted to find his own room, but first he went into James's. It was another perfect copy; the same sci-fi posters, the same mobile hanging over the bed, the same lava lamp on the same table. Even the same clothes strewn over the floor. So these rooms weren't just built to be the same. They were carefully maintained. Whatever happened downstairs, happened upstairs. But did that mean there had been somebody living here, watching every movement that James Sprintz made, doing everything he did? And if so, had somebody else been doing the same for him?

Alex went next door. It was like stepping into his own room. Again there was the same bed, the same furnishings – and the same television. He turned it on. The picture showed his room on the first floor. There was the Discman, lying on the bed. There were his wet clothes from the night before. Had somebody been watching when he cut through the window and climbed out into the night? Alex felt a jolt of alarm, then forced himself to relax. This room – the copy of his room – was different. Nobody had moved in here yet. He could tell, just by looking around him. The bed hadn't been slept in. And the smaller details hadn't been copied. There was no Discman in the duplicate room. No wet clothes. He had left the wardrobe door open downstairs. In here it was closed.

The whole thing was like some sort of mind-bending puzzle. Alex forced himself to think it through. Every single boy who arrived at the academy was watched. All his actions were duplicated. If he hung a poster on the wall of his room, an identical poster was hung in an identical room. There would be someone living in this room doing everything that Alex did. He remembered the figure he had glimpsed the day before ... someone wearing what looked like a white mask. Perhaps that person had been about to move in. But all the evidence suggested that for some reason he wasn't here yet.

And that still left the biggest question of all. What was the point? To spy on the boys was one thing. But to copy everything they did?

A door swung shut and he heard voices, two men walking down the corridor outside. Alex crept over to the door and looked out. He just had time to see Dr Grief walk through a door with another man, a short, plump figure in a white coat. They had gone into the laundry room. Alex slipped out of the duplicate bedroom and followed them.

"...you have completed the work. I am grateful to you, Mr Baxter."

"Thank you, Dr Grief."

They had left the door open. Alex crouched down and looked through. Here at last was a section of the third floor that didn't mirror the first. There were no washing-machines or ironing-boards here. Instead, Alex found himself looking into a room with a row of sinks and through a second set of doors leading into a fully equipped operating theatre at least twice as big as the laundry room on the first floor. At the centre of the room was an operating table. The walls were lined with shelves containing surgical equipment, chemicals and – scattered across the surface – what looked like black and white photographs.

An operating theatre! What was its role in this bizarre, devilish jigsaw puzzle? The two men had walked into it and were talking together, Grief standing with one hand in his pocket. Alex chose his moment, then slipped into the outer room, crouching down beside one of the sinks. From here he could watch and listen as the two of them talked.

"So, I hope you're pleased with the last operation." It was Mr Baxter who was speaking. He had half-turned towards the doors and Alex could see a round, flabby face with yellow hair and a thin moustache. Baxter was wearing a bow tie and a checked suit underneath his white coat. Alex had never seen the man before. He was certain of it. And yet at the same time, he thought he knew him. Another puzzle!

"Entirely," Dr Grief replied. "I saw him as soon as the bandages came off. You have done extremely well."

"I always *was* the best. But that's what you paid for." Baxter chuckled. His voice was oily. "And while we're on that subject, maybe we should talk about my final payment?"

"You have already been paid the sum of one million American dollars."

"Yes, Dr Grief." Baxter smiled. "But I was wondering if you might not like to think about a little ... bonus?"

"I thought we had an agreement." Dr Grief turned his head very slowly. The red spectacles homed in on the other man like searchlights.

"We had an agreement for my work, yes. But my silence is another matter. I was thinking of another quarter of a million. Given the size and the scope of your Gemini Project, it's not so much to ask. Then I'll retire to my little house in Spain and you'll never hear from me again."

"I will never hear from you again?"

"I promise."

Dr Grief nodded. "Yes. I think that is a good idea."

His hand came out of his pocket. Alex saw that it was holding an automatic pistol with a thick silencer protruding from the barrel. Baxter was still smiling as Grief shot him once, through the middle of the forehead. He was thrown off his feet and onto the operating table. He lay still.

Dr Grief lowered the gun. He went over to a telephone, picked it up and dialled a number. There was a pause while his call was answered.

"This is Grief. I have some garbage in the operating theatre that needs to be removed. Could you please inform the disposal team?"

He put down the phone and, glancing one last time at the still figure on the operating table, walked to the other side of the room. Alex saw him press a button. A section of the wall slid open to reveal a lift on the other side. Dr Grief got in. The lift doors closed.

Alex straightened up, too shocked to think straight. He staggered forward and went into the operating theatre. He knew he had to move fast. The disposal team that Dr Grief had called for would be on their way. But he wanted to know what sort of operations took place here. Mr Baxter had presumably been the surgeon. But for what sort of work had he been paid a million dollars?

Trying not to look at the body, Alex looked around. On one shelf was a collection of surgical knives, as horrible as anything he had ever seen, the blades so sharp that he could almost feel their touch just looking at them. There were rolls of gauze, syringes, bottles containing various liquids. But nothing to say why Baxter had been employed. Alex realized it was hopeless. He knew nothing about medicine. This room could have been used for anything from ingrown toenails to full-blown heart surgery.

And then he saw the photographs. He recognized himself, lying on a bed that he thought he knew too. It was Paris! Room thirteen at the Hôtel du Monde. He remembered the black and white bedspread, as well as the clothes he had been wearing that night. The clothes had been removed in most of the photographs. Every inch of him had been photographed, sometimes close up, sometimes wider. In every picture, his eyes were closed. Looking at himself, Alex knew that he had been drugged and remembered how the dinner with Mrs Stellenbosch had ended.

The photographs disgusted him. He had been manipulated by people who thought he was worth nothing at all. From the moment he had met them, he had disliked Dr Grief and his assistant director. Now he felt pure loathing. He still didn't know what they were doing. But they were evil. They had to be stopped.

He was shaken out of his thoughts by the sound of footsteps coming up the stairs. The disposal team! He looked around him and cursed. He didn't have time to get out and there was nowhere in the room to hide. Then he remembered the lift. He went over to it and urgently stabbed at the button. The footsteps were getting nearer. He heard voices. Then the panels slid open. Alex stepped into a small silver box. There were five buttons: S, R, 1, 2, 3. He pressed R. He had remembered enough French to know that the R must stand for *rez-de-chaussée*, or ground floor. Hopefully, the lift would take him back where he had begun.

The doors slid shut a few seconds before the guards entered the theatre. Alex felt his stomach lurch as he was carried down. The lift slowed. He realized that the doors could open anywhere. He might find himself surrounded by guards – or by the other boys in the school. Well, it was too late now. He had made his choice. He would just have to cope with whatever he found.

But he was lucky. The doors slid open to reveal the library. Alex assumed this was the real library and not another copy. The room was empty. He stepped out of the lift, then turned round. He was facing the alcove. The lift doors formed the alcove wall. They were brilliantly camouflaged, with the suit of armour now sliced exactly in two, one half on each side. As the doors closed automatically, the armour slid back together again, completing the disguise. Despite himself, Alex had to admire the simplicity of it. The entire building was a fantastic box of tricks.

Alex looked at his hands. They were still filthy. He had forgotten that he was completely covered in soot. He crept out of the library, trying not to leave black footprints on the carpet. Then he hurried back to his room. When he got there, he had to remind himself that it was indeed his room and not the copy two floors above. But the Discman was there – and that was what he most needed.

He knew enough. It was time to call for the cavalry. He pressed the fast forward button three times, then went to have a shower.

DELAYING TACTICS

It was raining in London, the sort of rain that seems never to stop. The early evening traffic was huddled together, going nowhere. Alan Blunt was standing at the window looking out over the street when there was a knock at the door. He turned away reluctantly, as if the city at its most damp and dismal held some attraction for him. Mrs Jones came in. She was carrying a sheet of paper. As Blunt sat down behind his desk he noticed the words *Most Urgent* printed in red across the top.

"We've heard from Alex," Mrs Jones said.

"Oh yes?"

"Smithers gave him a Euro-satellite transmitter built into a portable CD player. Alex sent a signal to us this morning ... at ten twenty-seven hours, his time."

"Meaning?"

"Either he's in trouble or he's found out enough for us to go in.

Either way, we have to pull him out."

"I wonder..." Blunt leant back in his chair, deep in thought. As a young man, he had gained a first class honours degree in mathematics at Cambridge University. Thirty years later, he still saw life as a series of complicated calculations. "Alex has been at Point Blanc for how long?" he asked.

"A week."

"As I recall, he didn't want to go. According to Sir David Friend, his behaviour at Haverstock Hall was, to say the least, antisocial. Did you know that he knocked out Friend's daughter with a stun dart? Apparently he also nearly got her killed in an incident in a railway tunnel."

"He was playing a part," she said. "Exactly what you told him to do."

"Playing it too well, perhaps," Blunt murmured. "Alex may no longer be one hundred per cent reliable."

"He sent the message." Mrs Jones couldn't keep the exasperation out of her voice. "For all we know, he could be in serious trouble. We gave him the device as an alarm signal. To let us know if he needed help. He's used it. We can't just sit back and do nothing."

"I wasn't suggesting that." Alan Blunt looked curiously at her. "You're not forming some sort of attachment to Alex Rider, are you?" he asked.

Mrs Jones looked away. "Don't be ridiculous."

"You seem worried about him."

"He's fourteen years old, Alan! He's a child, for heaven's sake!"

"You used to have children."

"Yes." Mrs Jones turned to face him again. "Perhaps that does make a difference. But even you must admit that he's special. We don't have another agent like him. A fourteen-year-old boy! The perfect secret weapon. My feelings about him have nothing to do with it. We can't afford to lose him."

"I just don't want to go blundering into Point Blanc without any firm information," Blunt said. "First of all, this is France we're talking about – and you know what the French are like. If we're seen to be invading their territory they'll kick up one hell of a fuss. Secondly, Grief has got hold of boys from some of the wealthiest families in the world. If we go storming in with the SAS or whatever, the whole thing could blow up into a major international incident."

"You wanted proof that the school was connected to the deaths of Roscoe and Ivanov," Mrs Jones said. "Alex may have it."

"He may have it and he may not. A twenty-four hour delay shouldn't make a great deal of difference."

"Twenty-four hours?"

"We'll put a unit on standby. They can keep an eye on things. If Alex is in trouble, we'll find out soon enough. It could play to our favour if he's managed to stir things up. It's exactly what we want. Force Grief to show us his hand."

"And if Alex contacts us again?"

"Then we'll go in."

"We may be too late."

"For Alex?" Blunt showed no emotion. "I'm sure you don't need to worry about him, Mrs Jones. He can look after himself."

The telephone rang and Blunt answered it. The interview was over. Mrs Jones got up and left to make the arrangements for an SAS unit to fly into Geneva. Blunt was right, of course. Delaying tactics might work in their favour. Clear it with the French. Find out what was going on. And it was only twenty-four hours.

She would just have to hope Alex could survive that long.

* * *

Alex found himself eating his breakfast on his own. For the first time, James Sprintz had decided to join the other boys. There they were – the six of them, suddenly the best of friends. Alex looked carefully at the boy who had once been his friend, trying to see what it was that had changed about him. He knew the answer. It was everything and nothing. James was exactly the same and completely different at the same time.

Alex finished his food and got up. James called out to him. "Why don't you come to class this morning, Alex? It's Latin."

Alex shook his head. "Latin's a waste of time."

"Is that what you think?" James couldn't keep the sneer out of his voice and for a moment Alex was startled. For just one second it hadn't been James talking at all. It had been James who had moved his mouth. But it had been Dr Grief speaking the words.

"You enjoy it," Alex said. He hurried out of the room.

Almost twenty-four hours had passed since he had pressed the fast forward on the Discman. Alex wasn't sure what he had been expecting. A fleet of helicopters flying the Union Jack would have been reassuring. But so far nothing had happened. He even wondered if the alarm signal had worked. At the same time, he was annoyed with himself. He had seen Grief shoot the man called Baxter in the operating theatre and he had panicked. He knew that Grief was a killer. He knew that the academy was far more than the finishing school it pretended to be. But he still didn't have all the answers. What exactly was Dr Grief doing? Was he responsible for the deaths of Michael J. Roscoe and Viktor Ivanov? And if so, why?

The fact was, he didn't know enough. And by the time MI6 arrived, Baxter's body would be buried somewhere in the mountains and there would be nothing to prove there was anything wrong. Alex would look like a fool. He could almost imagine Dr Grief telling his side of the story...

"Yes. There is an operating theatre here. It was built years ago. We never use the second and third floors. There is a lift, yes. It was built before we came. We explained to Alex about the armed guards. They're here for his protection. But as you can see, gentlemen, there is nothing unpleasant happening here. The other boys are fine. Baxter? No, I don't know anyone by that name. Obviously Alex has been having bad dreams. I'm amazed that he was sent here to spy on us. I would ask you to take him with you when you leave..."

He had to find out more – and that meant going back up to the second floor. Or perhaps down. Alex remembered the letters in the secret lift. R for *rez-de-chaussée*. S had to stand for *sous-sol*. The French for basement.

He went over to the Latin classroom and looked in through the half-open door. Dr Grief was out of sight, but Alex could hear his voice.

"Felix qui potuit rerum cognoscere causas..."

There was the sound of scratching; chalk on a blackboard. And there were the six boys, sitting at their desks, listening intently. James was sitting between Hugo and Tom, taking notes. Alex looked at his watch. They would be there for another hour. He was on his own.

He walked back down the corridor and slipped into the library. He had woken up still smelling faintly of soot and had no intention of making his way back up the chimney. Instead he crossed over to the suit of armour. He knew now that the alcove disguised a pair of elevator doors. They could be opened from inside. Presumably there was some sort of control on the outside too.

It took him just a few minutes to find it. There were three buttons built into the breastplate of the armour. Even close to, the buttons looked like part of the suit – something the medieval knight would have used to strap the thing on. But when Alex pressed the middle button, the armour moved. A moment later, it split in half again and he found himself looking into the waiting lift.

This time he pressed the bottom button. The lift seemed to travel a long way, as if the basement of the building had been built far underground. Finally the doors slid open again. Alex looked out into a curving passageway with tiled walls that reminded him a little of a London tube station. The air was cold down here. The passage was lit by naked bulbs, screwed into the ceiling at intervals.

He looked out, then ducked back. There was a guard at the end of the corridor, sitting at a table reading a newspaper. Would he have heard the lift doors open? Alex leant forward again. The guard was absorbed in the sports pages. He hadn't moved. Alex slipped out of the lift and crept down the passage, moving away from him. He reached the corner and turned into a second passageway lined with steel doors. There was nobody else in sight.

Where was he? There had to be something down here or there wouldn't be any need for a guard. Alex went over to the nearest of the doors. There was a spyhole set in the front and he looked through into a bare white cell with two bunk beds, a toilet and a sink. There were two boys in the cell. One he had never seen before, but he recognized the other. It was the red-haired boy called Tom McMorin. But he had seen Tom in Latin just a few minutes ago! What was he doing here?

Alex moved on to the next cell. This one also held two boys. One was a fair-haired, fit-looking boy with blue eyes and freckles. Once again, he recognized the other. It was James Sprintz. Alex examined the door. There were two bolts but, as far as he could see, no key. He drew back the bolts and jerked the door handle down. The door opened. He went in.

James stood up, astonished to see him. "Alex! What are you doing here?"

Alex closed the door. "We haven't got much time," he said. He was speaking in a whisper even though there was little chance of being overheard. "What happened to you?"

"They came for me the night before last," James said. "They dragged me out of bed and into the library. There was some sort of lift—"

"Behind the armour."

"Yes. I didn't know what they were doing. I thought they were going to kill me. But then they threw me in here."

"You've been here for two days?"

"Yes."

Alex shook his head. "I saw you having breakfast upstairs fifteen minutes ago."

"They've made duplicates of us." The other boy had spoken for the first time. He had an American accent. "All of us! I don't know how they've done it or why. But that's what they've done." He glanced at the door with anger in his eyes. "I've been here for months. My name's Paul Roscoe."

"Roscoe? Your dad's—"

"Michael Roscoe."

Alex fell silent. He couldn't tell this boy what had happened to his father and he looked away, afraid that Paul would read it in his eyes.

"How did you get down here?" James asked.

"Listen," Alex said. He was speaking rapidly now. "I was sent here by MI6. My name isn't Alex Friend. It's Alex Rider. Everything's going to be OK. They'll send people in and get you all freed."

"You're ... a *spy*?" James was obviously startled.

Alex nodded. "I'm a sort of spy, I suppose," he said.

"You've opened the door. We can get out of here!" Paul Roscoe stood up, ready to move.

"No!" Alex held up his hands. "You've got to wait. There's no way down the mountain. Stay here for now and I'll come back with help. I promise you. It's the only way."

"I can't—"

"You have to. Trust me, Paul. I'm going to have to lock you back in so that nobody will know I've been here. But it won't be for long. I'll come back!"

Alex couldn't wait for any more argument. He went back to the door and opened it.

Mrs Stellenbosch was standing outside.

He only just had time to register the shock of seeing her. He tried to bring up a hand to protect himself, to twist his body into position for a karate kick. But it was already too late. Her arm shot out, the heel of her hand driving into his face. It was like being hit by a brick wall. Alex felt every bone in his body rattle. White light exploded behind his eyes. Then he was out.

HOW TO RULE THE WORLD

"Open your eyes, Alex. Dr Grief wishes to speak to you."

The words came from across an ocean. Alex groaned and tried to lift his head. He was sitting down, his arms pinned behind his back. The whole side of his face felt bruised and swollen and there was the taste of blood in his mouth. He opened his eyes and waited for the room to come into focus. Mrs Stellenbosch was standing in front of him, her fist curled loosely in her other hand. Alex remembered the force of the blow that had knocked him out. His whole head was throbbing and he ran his tongue over his teeth to see if there were any missing. It was fortunate he had rolled with the punch. Otherwise she might have broken his neck.

Dr Grief was sitting in his golden chair, watching Alex with what might have been curiosity or distaste or perhaps a little of both. There was nobody else in the room. It was still snowing outside and there was a small fire burning in the hearth, but the flames weren't as red as Dr Grief's eyes.

"You have put us to a great deal of inconvenience," he said.

Alex straightened his head. He tried to move his hands, but they had been chained together behind the chair.

"Your name is not Alex Friend. You are not the son of Sir David Friend. Your name is Alex Rider and you are employed by the British Secret Service." Dr Grief was simply stating facts. There was no emotion in his voice.

"We have microphones concealed in the cells," Mrs Stellenbosch explained. "Sometimes it is useful for us to hear the conversations between our young guests. Everything you said was overheard by the guard who summoned me."

"You have wasted our time and our money," Dr Grief continued. "For that you will now be punished. It is not a punishment you will survive."

The words were cold and absolute and Alex felt the fear that they triggered. It coursed through his bloodstream, closing in on his heart. He took a deep breath, forcing himself back under control. He had signalled MI6. They would be on their way to Point Blanc. They might appear any minute now. He just had to play for time.

"You can't do anything to me," he said.

Mrs Stellenbosch lashed out and he was thrown backwards as the back of her hand sliced into the side of his head. Only the chair kept him upright. "When you speak to the director, you refer to him as 'Dr Grief'," she said.

Alex looked round again, his eyes watering. "You can't do anything to me, Dr Grief," he said. "I know everything. I know about the Gemini Project. And I've already told London what I know. If you do anything to me, they'll kill you. They're on their way here now."

Dr Grief smiled and in that single moment Alex knew that nothing he said would make any difference to what was about to happen to him. The man was too confident. He was like a poker player who had not only managed to see all the cards but had stolen the four aces for himself.

"It may well be that your friends are on their way," he said. "But I do not think you have told them anything. We have been through your luggage and found the transmitting device concealed in the Discman. I noted also that it is an ingenious electric saw. But as for the transmitter, it can send out a signal but not a message. Quite how you have learnt about the Gemini Project is of no interest to me. I assume you overheard the name whilst eavesdropping at a door. We should have been more careful – but for British intelligence to send in a child ... that was something we could not expect.

"Let us assume then that your friends do come calling. They will find nothing wrong. You yourself will have disappeared. I shall tell them that you ran away. I will say that my men are looking for you even now, but I very much fear you will have died a cold and lingering death on the mountainside. Nobody will guess what I have done here. The Gemini Project will succeed. It has *already* succeeded. And even if your friends do take it upon themselves to kill me, that will make no difference. I cannot be killed, Alex. The world is already mine."

"You mean it belongs to the kids you've hired to act as doubles," Alex said.

"Hired?" Dr Grief muttered a few words to Mrs Stellenbosch in a harsh, guttural language. Alex assumed it must be Afrikaans. Her thick lips parted and she laughed, showing heavy, discoloured teeth. "Is that what you think?" Dr Grief asked. "Is that what you believe?"

"I've seen them."

"You don't know what you've seen. You have no understanding of my genius! Your little mind couldn't begin to encompass what I have achieved." Dr Grief was breathing heavily. He seemed to come to a decision. "It is rare enough for me to come face to face with the enemy," he said. "It has always been my frustration that I will never be able to communicate to the world the brilliance of what I have done. Well, since I have you here – a captive audience, so to speak – I shall allow myself the luxury of describing the Gemini Project. And when you go, screaming, to your death, you will understand that there was never any hope for you. That you could not hope to come up against a man like me and win. Perhaps that will make it easier for you."

"I will smoke, if you don't mind, Doctor," Mrs Stellenbosch said. She took out her cigars and lit one. Smoke danced in front of her eyes.

"I am, as I am sure you are aware, South African," Dr Grief began. "The animals in the hall and in this room are all souvenirs of my time there; shot on safari. I still miss my country. It is the most beautiful place on this planet.

"What you may not know, however, is that for many years I was one of South Africa's foremost biochemists. I was head of the biology department at the University of Johannesburg. I later ran the Cyclops Institute for Genetic Research in Pretoria. But the height of my career came in the 1960s when, although I was still in my twenties, John Vorster, the prime minister of South Africa, appointed me Minister for Science—"

"You've already said you're going to kill me," Alex said, "but I didn't think that meant you were going to bore me to death."

Mrs Stellenbosch coughed on her cigar and advanced on Alex, her fist clenched. But Dr Grief stopped her. "Let the boy have his little joke," he said. "There will be pain enough for him later."

The assistant director glowered at Alex.

Dr Grief went on. "I am telling you this, Alex, only because it will help you understand. You perhaps know nothing about South Africa. English schoolchildren are, I have found, the laziest and most ignorant in the world. All that will soon change! But let me tell you a little bit about my country, as it was when I was young.

"The white people of South Africa ruled everything. Under the laws that came to be known to the world as apartheid, black people were not allowed to live near white people. They could not marry white people. They could not share white toilets, restaurants, sports halls or bars. They had to carry passes. They were treated like animals."

"It was disgusting," Alex said.

"It was wonderful!" Mrs Stellenbosch murmured.

"It was indeed perfect," Dr Grief agreed. "But as the years passed, I became aware that it would also be short-lived. The uprising at Soweto, the growing resistance and the way the entire world – including your own, stinking country – ganged up on us, I knew that white South Africa was doomed and I even foresaw the day when power would be handed over to a man like Nelson Mandela."

"A criminal!" Mrs Stellenbosch added. Smoke was dribbling out of her nostrils.

Alex said nothing. It was clear enough that both Dr Grief and his assistant were mad. Just how mad they were was becoming clearer with every word they spoke.

"I looked at the world," Dr Grief said, "and I began to see just how weak and pathetic it was becoming. How could it happen that a country like mine could be given away to people who would have no idea how to run it? And why was the rest of the world so determined for it to be so? I looked around me and I saw that the people of America and Europe had become stupid and weak. The fall of the Berlin Wall only made things worse. I had always admired the Russians, but they quickly became infected with the same disease. And I thought to myself, if I ruled the world, how much stronger it would be. How much better—"

"For you, perhaps, Dr Grief," Alex said. "But not for anyone else."

Grief ignored him. His eyes, behind the red glasses, were brilliant. "It has been the dream of very few men to rule the entire world," he said. "Hitler was one. Napoleon another. Stalin, perhaps, a third. Great men! Remarkable men! But to rule the world in the twenty-first century requires something more than military strength. The world is a more complicated place now. Where does real power lie? In politics. Prime ministers and presidents. But you will also find power in industry, in science, in the media, in oil, in the Internet... Modern life is a great tapestry and if you wish to take control of it all, you must seize hold of every strand.

"This is what I decided to do, Alex. And it was because of my unique position in the unique place that was South Africa that I was able to attempt it." Grief took a deep breath. "What do you know about nuclear transplantation?" he asked.

"I don't know anything," Alex said. "But as you said, I'm an English schoolboy. Lazy and ignorant."

"There is another word for it. Have you heard of cloning?"

Alex almost burst out laughing. "You mean ... like Dolly the sheep?"

"To you it may be a joke, Alex. Something out of science fiction. But scientists have been searching for a way to create exact replicas of themselves for more than a hundred years. The word itself is Greek for 'twig'. Think how a twig starts as one branch but then splits into two. This is exactly what has been achieved with lizards, with sea urchins, with tadpoles and frogs, with mice and, yes, on the fifth of July 1996, with a sheep. The theory is simple enough. Nuclear transplantation. To take the nucleus out of an egg and replace it with a cell taken from an adult. I won't tire you with the details, Alex. But it is not a joke. Dolly was the perfect copy of a sheep that had died six years before Dolly was born. She was the end result of no less than one hundred years of experimentation. And in all that time, the scientists shared a single dream. To clone an adult human. I have achieved that dream!"

He paused.

"If you want a round of applause, you'll have to take off the handcuffs," Alex said.

"I don't want applause," Grief snarled. "Not from you. What I want from you is your life ... and that I will take."

"So who did you clone?" Alex asked. "Not Mrs Stellenbosch, I hope. I'd have thought one of her was more than enough."

"Who do you *think*? I cloned myself!" Dr Grief grabbed hold of the arms of his chair, a king on the throne of his own imagination. "Twenty years ago I began my work," he explained. "I told you – I was Minister for Science. I had all the equipment and money that I needed. Also – this was South Africa! The rules that hampered other scientists around the world did not apply to me. I was able to use human beings – political prisoners – for my experiments. Everything was done in secret. I worked without stopping for twenty years. And then, when I was ready, I stole a very large amount of money from the South African government and moved here.

"This was in 1981. And six years later, almost a whole decade before an English scientist astonished the world by cloning a sheep, I did something far, far more extraordinary – here, at Point Blanc. I cloned myself. Not just once! Sixteen times. Sixteen exact copies of me. With my looks. My brains. My ambition. And my determination."

"Were they all as mad as you too?" Alex asked, and flinched as Mrs Stellenbosch hit him again, this time in the stomach. But he wanted to make them angry. If they were angry, they might make mistakes.

"To begin with they were babies," Dr Grief said. "Sixteen babies from sixteen mothers – who were themselves biologically irrelevant. They would grow up to become replicas of myself. I have had to wait fourteen years for the babies to become boys and the boys to become teenagers. Eva here has looked after all of them. You have met them – some of them."

"Tom, Cassian, Nicolas, Hugo, Joe. And James..." Now Alex understood why they had somehow all looked the same.

"Do you see, Alex? Do you have any idea what I have done? I will never die because, even when this body is finished with, I will live on in them. I am them and they are me. We are one and the same."

He smiled again. "I was helped in all this by Eva Stellenbosch, who had also worked with me in the South African government. She had worked in the SASS – our own secret service. She was one of their principal interrogators."

"Happy days!" Mrs Stellenbosch smiled.

"Together we set up the academy. Because, you see, that was the second part of my plan. I was creating sixteen copies of myself. But that wasn't enough. You remember what I said about the strands of the tapestry? I had to bring them here, to draw them together—"

"To replace them with copies of yourself!" Suddenly Alex saw it all. It was totally insane. But it was the only way to make sense of everything he had seen.

Dr Grief nodded. "It was my observation that families with wealth and power frequently had children who were ... troubled. Parents with no time for their sons. Sons with no love for their parents. These children became my targets, Alex. Because, you see, I wanted what these children had.

"Take a boy like Hugo Vries. One day his father will leave him with a fifty per cent stake in the world's diamond market. Or Tom McMorin; his mother has newspapers all over the world. Or Joe Canterbury; his father at the Pentagon, his mother a senator. What better start for a life in politics? What better start for a future president of the United States, even? Fifteen of the most promising children who have been sent here to Point Blanc, I have replaced with copies of myself. Surgically altered, of course, to look exactly like the originals."

"Baxter, the man you shot—"

"You have been busy, Alex." For the first time, Dr Grief looked surprised. "The late Mr Baxter was a plastic surgeon. I found him working in Harley Street, London. He had gambling debts. It was easy to bring him under my control and it was his job to operate on my family, to change their faces, their skin colour – and where necessary their bodies – so that they would exactly resemble the teenagers they replaced. From the moment the real teenagers arrived here at Point Blanc, they were kept under observation—"

"With identical rooms on the second and third floors."

"Yes. My doubles were able to watch their targets on television monitors. To copy their every movement. To learn their mannerisms. To eat like them. To speak like them. In short, to become them."

"It would never have worked!" Alex twisted in his chair, trying to find some leverage in the handcuffs. But the metal was too tight. He couldn't move. "Parents would know that the children you sent back were fakes!" he insisted. "Any mother would know it wasn't her son, even if he looked the same."

Mrs Stellenbosch giggled. She had finished her cigar. Now she lit another.

"You are quite wrong, Alex," Dr Grief said. "In the first place, you are talking about busy, hard-working parents who had little or no time for their children in the first place. And you forget that the very reason why these people sent their sons here was because they *wanted* them to change. It is the reason why all parents send their sons to private schools. Oh yes – they think the schools will make their children better, more clever, more confident. They would actually be disappointed if those children came back the same.

"And nature, too, is on our side. A boy of fourteen leaves home for six or seven weeks. By the time he gets back, nature will have made its mark. The boy will be taller. He will be fatter or thinner. Even his voice will have changed. It's all part of puberty and the parents when they see him will say, 'Oh Tom, you've got so big – and you're so grown up!' And they will suspect nothing. In fact, they would be worried if the boy had *not* changed."

"But Roscoe guessed, didn't he?" Alex knew he had arrived at the truth, the reason why he had been sent here in the first place. He knew why Roscoe and Ivanov had died.

"There have been two occasions when the parents did not believe what they saw," Dr Grief admitted. "Michael J. Roscoe in New York. And General Viktor Ivanov in Moscow. Neither man completely guessed what had happened. But they were unhappy. They argued with their sons. They asked too many questions."

"And the sons told you what had happened."

"You might say that I told myself. The sons, after all, are me.

But yes. Michael Roscoe knew something was wrong and called MI6 in London. I presume that is how you were unlucky enough to become involved. I had to pay to have Roscoe killed just as I paid for the death of Ivanov. But it was to be expected that there would be problems. Two out of sixteen is not so catastrophic, and of course it makes no difference to my plans. In many ways, it even helps me. Michael J. Roscoe left his entire fortune to his son. And I understand that the Russian president is taking a personal interest in Dimitry Ivanov following the loss of his father.

"In short, the Gemini Project has been an outstanding success. In a few days' time, the last of the children will leave Point Blanc to take their places in the heart of their families. Once I am satisfied that they have all been accepted, I will, I fear, have to dispose of the originals. They will die painlessly.

"The same cannot be said for you, Alex Rider. You have caused me a great deal of annoyance. I propose, therefore, to make an example of you." Dr Grief reached into his pocket and took out a device that looked like a pager. It had a single button, which he pressed. "What is the first lesson tomorrow morning, Eva?" he asked.

"Double biology," Mrs Stellenbosch replied.

"As I thought. You have perhaps been to biology lessons where a frog or a rat has been dissected, Alex," he said. "For some time now, my children have been asking to see a human dissection. This is no surprise to me. At the age of fourteen, I first attended a human dissection myself. Tomorrow morning, at nine-thirty, their wish will be granted. You will be brought into the laboratory and we will open you up and have a look at you. We will not be using anaesthetic and it will be interesting to see how long you survive before your heart gives out. And then, of course, we shall dissect your heart."

"You're sick!" Alex yelled. Now he was thrashing about in the chair, trying to break the wood, trying to get the handcuffs to come apart. But it was hopeless. The metal cut into him. The chair rocked but stayed in one piece. "You're a madman!"

"I am a scientist!" Dr Grief spat the words. "And that is why I am giving you a scientific death. At least in your last minutes you will have been some use to me." He looked past Alex. "Take him away and search him thoroughly. Then lock him up for the night. I'll see him again first thing tomorrow morning."

Alex had seen Dr Grief summon the guards but he hadn't heard them come in. He was seized from behind, the handcuffs were unlocked and he was jerked backwards out of the room. His last sight of Dr Grief was of the man stretching out his hands to warm them at the fire, the twisting flames reflected in his glasses. Mrs Stellenbosch smiled and blew out smoke.

Then the door slammed shut and Alex was dragged down the corridor knowing that Blunt and the secret service had to be on their way – but wondering if they would arrive before it was too late.

BLACK RUN

The cell measured two metres by four metres and contained a bunk bed with no mattress and a chair. The door was solid steel. Alex had heard a key turn in the lock after it was closed. He had not been given anything to eat or drink. The cell was cold but there were no blankets on the bed.

At least the guards had left the handcuffs off. They had searched Alex expertly, removing everything they had found in his pockets. They had also removed his belt and the laces of his shoes. Perhaps Dr Grief had thought he would hang himself. He needed Alex fresh and alive for the biology lesson.

It was about two o'clock in the morning but Alex hadn't slept. He had tried to put out of his mind everything Grief had told him. That wasn't important now. He knew that he had to escape before nine-thirty because – like it or not – it seemed he was on his own.

More than thirty-six hours had passed since he had pressed the panic button that Smithers had given him – and nothing had happened. Either the machine hadn't worked or for some reason MI6 had decided not to come. Of course, it was possible that something might happen before breakfast the next day. But Alex wasn't prepared to risk it. He had to get out. Tonight.

For the twentieth time he went over to the door and knelt down, listening carefully. The guards had dragged him back down to the basement. He was in a corridor separate from the other prisoners. Although everything had happened very quickly, Alex had tried to remember where he was being taken. Out of the lift and turn left. Round the corner and then down a second passageway to a door at the end. He was on his own. And listening through the door, he was fairly sure that they hadn't posted a guard outside.

It had to be now – the middle of the night. When they had searched him, the guards hadn't quite taken everything. Neither of them had even noticed the gold stud in his ear. What had Smithers said? "It's a small but very powerful explosive. Separating the two pieces activates it. Count to ten and it'll blow a hole in just about anything..."

Now was the time to put it to the test.

Alex reached up and unscrewed the ear-stud. He pulled it out of his ear, slipped the two pieces into the keyhole of the door, stepped back and counted to ten.

Nothing happened. Was the stud broken, like the Discman transmitter? Alex was about to give up when there was a sudden flash, an intense sheet of orange flame. Fortunately there was no noise. The flare continued for about five seconds, then went out. Alex went back to the door. The stud had burned a hole in it, the size of a two pound coin. The melted metal was still glowing. Alex reached out and pushed. The door swung open.

Alex felt a momentary surge of excitement, but he forced himself to remain calm. He might be out of the cell but he was still in the basement of the academy. There were guards everywhere. He was on top of a mountain with no skis and no obvious way down. He wasn't safe yet. Not by a long way.

He slipped out of the room and followed the corridor back round to the lift. He was tempted to find the other boys and release them but he knew that they couldn't help. Taking them out of their cells would only put them in danger. Somehow, he found his way back to the lift. He noticed that the guard-post he had seen that morning was empty. Either the man had gone to make himself a coffee or Grief had relaxed security in the academy. With Alex and all the other boys locked up, there was nobody left to guard. Or so they thought. Alex hurried forward. It seemed that luck was on his side.

He took the lift back to the first floor. He knew that his only way off the mountain lay in his bedroom. Grief would certainly have examined everything he had brought with him. But what would he have done with it? Alex crept down the dimly lit corridor and into his room. And there it all was, lying in a heap on his bed. The ski suit. The goggles. Even the Discman with the Beethoven CD. Alex heaved a sigh of relief. He was going to need all of it.

He had already worked out what he was going to do. He couldn't ski off the mountain. He still had no idea where the skis were kept. But there was more than one way to take to the snow. Alex froze as a guard walked along the corridor outside the room. So not everyone at the academy was asleep! He would have to move fast. As soon as the broken cell door was discovered, the alarm would be raised.

He waited until the guard had gone, then stole into the laundry room a few doors down. When he came out, he was carrying a long flat object made of lightweight aluminium. He carried it into his bedroom, closed the door and turned on one small lamp. He was afraid that the guard would see the light if he returned. But he couldn't work in the dark. It was a risk he had to take.

He had stolen an ironing-board.

Alex had only been snowboarding three times in his life. The first time, he had spent most of the day falling or sitting on his bottom. Snowboarding is a lot harder to learn than skiing – but as soon as you get the hang of it, you can advance fast. By the third day, Alex had learned how to ride, edging and cutting his way down the beginner slopes. He needed a snowboard now. The ironing-board would have to do.

He picked up the Discman and turned it on. The Beethoven CD spun, then slid forward, its diamond edge jutting out. Alex made a mental calculation, and began to cut. The ironing-board was wider than he would have liked. He knew that the longer the board, the faster he could go, but if he left it too long he would have no control. The ironing-board was flat. Without any curve at the front – or the nose, as it was called – he would be at the mercy of every bump or upturned root. But there was nothing he could do about that. He pressed down and watched as the spinning disc sliced through the metal. Carefully Alex drew it round, forming a curve. About half the ironing-board fell away. He picked up the other half. It almost reached his chest, with a point at one end and a curve at the back. Perfect.

Now he sliced off the supports, leaving about six centimetres sticking up. He knew that the rider and the board can only work together if the bindings are right and he had nothing; no boots, no straps, no highback to support his heel. He was just going to have to improvise. He tore two strips of sheet from the bed, then slipped into his ski suit. He would have to tie one of his trainers to what was left of the ironing-board supports. It was horribly dangerous. If he fell, he would dislocate his foot.

But he was almost ready. Quickly Alex zipped up the ski suit. Smithers had said it was bulletproof and it occurred to him that he was probably going to need it. He put the goggles around his neck. The window still hadn't been repaired. He dropped the ironing-board out, then climbed out after it.

There was no moon now. Alex found the switch concealed in the goggles and turned it. He heard a soft hum as the hidden battery activated, and suddenly the side of the mountain glowed an eerie green and Alex was able to see the trees and the deserted ski-run falling away.

He carried the ironing-board over to the edge of the snow and used the sheet to tie it to his foot. Carefully he took up his position, his right foot at forty degrees, his left foot at twenty. He was goofy-footed. That was what the instructor had told him. His feet should have been the other way round. But this was no time to worry about technique. Alex stood where he was, contemplating what he was about to do. He had only ever done green and blue runs – the colours given to the beginner and intermediate slopes. He knew from James that this mountain was an expert black all the way down. His breath rose up in green clouds in front of his eyes. Could he do it? Could he trust himself?

An alarm bell exploded behind him. Lights came on throughout the academy. Alex pushed forward and set off, picking up speed with every second. The decision had been made for him. Now, whatever happened, there could be no going back.

Dr Grief, wearing a long silver dressing gown, stood beside the open window in Alex's room. Mrs Stellenbosch was also in a robe – hers was pink silk and looked strangely hideous, hanging off her lumpy body. Three guards stood watching them, waiting for instructions.

"Who searched the boy?" Dr Grief asked. He had already been shown the cell door with the circular hole burnt into the lock.

None of the guards answered, but their faces had gone pale.

"This is a question to be answered in the morning," Dr Grief continued. "For now, all that matters is that we find him and kill him."

"He must be walking down the mountainside!" Mrs Stellenbosch said. "He has no skis. He won't make it. We can wait until morning and pick him up in the helicopter."

"I think the boy may be more inventive than we believe." Dr Grief picked up the remains of the ironing-board. "You see? He has improvised some sort of sleigh or toboggan. All right..." He had come to a decision. Mrs Stellenbosch was glad to see the certainty return to his eyes. "I want two men on snowmobiles, following him down. Now!" One of the guards hurried out of the room.

"What about the unit at the foot of the mountain?" Mrs Stellenbosch said.

"Indeed." Dr Grief smiled. He had always kept a guard and a driver at the end of the last valley in case anybody ever tried to leave the academy on skis. It was a precaution that was about to pay off. "Alex Rider will have to arrive in la Vallée de Fer. Whatever he's using to get down, he'll be unable to cross the railway line. We can have a machine gun set up waiting for him. Assuming he does manage to get that far, he'll be a sitting duck."

"Excellent," Mrs Stellenbosch purred.

"I would have liked to watch him die. But, yes. The Rider boy has no hope at all. And we can return to bed."

* * *

Alex was on the edge of space, seemingly falling to certain death. In snowboarding language, he was catching air – meaning that he had shot away from the ground. Every ten metres he went forward, the mountainside disappeared another five metres downward. He felt the world spin around him. The wind whipped into his face. Then somehow he brought himself in line with the next section of the slope and shot down, steering the ironing-board ever further from Point Blanc. He was moving at a terrifying speed, trees and rock formations passing in a luminous green blur across his night-vision goggles. In some ways the steeper slopes made it easier. At one point he had tried to make a landing on a flat part of the mountain – a tabletop – to slow himself down. He had hit the ground with such a bone-shattering crash that he had nearly blacked out and had taken the next twenty metres almost totally blind.

The ironing-board was shuddering and shaking crazily and it took all his strength to make the turns. He was trying to follow the natural fall-line of the mountain but there were too many obstacles in the way. What he most dreaded was melted snow. If the board landed on a patch of mud at this speed, he would be thrown and killed. And he knew that the further down he went, the greater the danger would become.

But he had been travelling for five minutes and so far he had only fallen twice – both times into thick banks of snow that had protected him. How far down could it be? He tried to remember what James Sprintz had told him, but thinking was impossible at this speed. He was having to use every ounce of his conscious thought simply to stay upright.

He reached a small lip where the surface was level and drove the edge of the board into the snow, bringing himself to a skidding halt. Ahead of him the ground fell away alarmingly. He hardly dared look down. There were thick clumps of trees to the left and to the right. In the distance there was just a green blur. The goggles could only see so far.

And then he heard the noise coming up behind him. The scream of at least two – maybe more – engines. Alex looked back over his shoulder. For a moment there was nothing. But then he saw them – black flies swimming into his field of vision. There were two of them, heading his way.

Grief's men were riding specially adapted Yamaha Mountain Max snowmobiles equipped with 700cc triple-cylinder engines. The bikes were flying over the snow on their 141-inch tracks, effortlessly moving five times faster than Alex. The 300-watt headlights had already picked him out. Now the men sped towards him, cutting the distance between them with every second that passed.

Alex leapt forward, diving into the next slope. At the same moment, there was a sudden chatter, a series of distant cracks, and the snow leapt up all around him. Grief's men had machine guns built into their snowmobiles! Alex yelled as he swooped down the mountainside, barely able to control the sheet of metal under his feet. The makeshift binding was tearing at his ankle. The whole thing was vibrating crazily. He couldn't see. He could only keep going, trying to keep his balance, hoping that the way ahead was clear.

The headlights of the nearest Yamaha shot out and Alex saw his own shadow stretching ahead of him on the snow. There was another chatter from the machine gun and Alex ducked down, almost feeling the fan of bullets spray over his head. The second bike screamed up, coming parallel with him. He *had* to get off the mountainside. Otherwise he would be shot or run over. Or both.

He forced the board onto its edge, making a turn. He had seen a gap in the trees and he made for it. Now he was racing through the forest, with branches and trunks whipping past like crazy animations in a computer game. Could the snowmobiles follow him through here? The question was answered by another burst from the machine guns, ripping through the leaves and branches. Alex searched for a narrower path. The board shuddered and he was almost thrown forward head-first. The snow was getting thinner! He edged and turned, heading for two of the thickest trees. He passed between them with millimetres to spare. Now – follow that!

The Yamaha snowmobile had no choice. The rider had run out of paths. He was travelling too fast to stop. He tried to follow Alex between the trees, but the snowmobile was too wide. Alex heard the collision. There was a terrible crunch, then a scream, then an explosion. A ball of orange flame leapt over the trees, sending black shadows in a crazy dance. Ahead of him Alex saw another hillock and, beyond it, a gap in the trees. It was time to leave the forest.

He swooped up the hillock and out, once again catching air. As he left the trees behind him, two metres above the ground, he saw the second snowmobile. It had caught up with him. For a moment the two of them were side by side. Alex doubled forward and grabbed the nose of his board. Still in mid-air, he twisted the tip of the board, bringing the tail swinging round. He had timed it perfectly. The tail slammed into the second rider's head, almost throwing him out of his seat. The rider yelled and lost control. His snowmobile jerked sideways as if trying to make an impossibly tight turn. Then it left the ground, cartwheeling over and over again. The rider was thrown off, then screamed as the snowmobile completed its final turn and landed on top of him. Man and machine were bounced across the surface of the snow and then lay still. Alex slammed into the snow and skidded to a halt, his breath clouding green in front of his eyes.

A second later he pushed off again. Ahead of him he could see that all the pistes were leading into a single valley. This must be the bottleneck called la Vallée de Fer. So he'd actually done it! He'd reached the bottom of the mountain. But now he was trapped. There was no other way round. He could see lights in the distance. A city. Safety. But he could also see the railway line stretching right across the valley, from left to right, protected on both sides by an embankment and a barbed-wire fence. The glow from the city illuminated everything. On one side the track came out of the mouth of a tunnel. It ran for about a hundred metres in a straight line before a sharp bend carried it round the other side of the valley and it disappeared from sight.

The two men in the grey van saw Alex snowboarding towards them. They were parked on a road on the other side of the railway line and had been waiting for only a few minutes. They hadn't seen the explosion and wondered what had happened to the two guards on their snowmobiles. But that wasn't their concern. Their orders were to kill the boy. And there he was, right out in the open, expertly managing the last black run through the valley. Every second brought him closer to them. There was nowhere for him to hide. The machine gun was a Belgian FN MAG and would cut him in half.

Alex saw the van. He saw the machine gun aiming at him. He couldn't stop. It was too late to change direction. He had come this far, but now he was finished. He felt the strength draining out of him. Where were MI6? Why did he have to die, out here, on his own?

And then there was a sudden blast as a train thundered out of the tunnel. It was a goods train, travelling at about twenty miles an hour. It had at least thirty carriages, pulled by a diesel engine, and it formed a moving wall between Alex and the gun, protecting him. But it would only be there for a few seconds. He had to move fast.

Barely knowing what he was doing, Alex found a last mound of snow and, using it as a launch pad, swept up into the air. Now he was level with the train ... now above it. He shifted his weight and came down onto the roof of one of the carriages. The surface was covered in ice and for a moment he thought he would fall off the other side, but he managed to swing round so that he was snowboarding along the carriage tops, jumping from one to another, at the same time being swept along the track – away from the gun – in a blast of freezing air.

He had done it! He had got away! He was still sliding forward, the train adding its speed to his own. No snowboarder had ever moved so fast. But then the train reached the bend in the track. The board had no purchase on the icy surface. As the train sped round to the left, the centrifugal force threw Alex to the right. Once again he soared into the air. But he had finally run out of snow.

Alex hit the ground like a rag doll. The snowboard was torn off his feet. He bounced twice, then hit a wire fence and came to rest with blood spreading around a deep gash in his head. His eyes were closed.

The train ploughed on through the night.

Alex lay still.

AFTER THE FUNERAL

The ambulance raced down the Avenue Maquis de Gresivaudan in the north of Grenoble, heading towards the river. It was five o'clock in the morning and there was no traffic yet, no need for the siren. Just before the river it turned off into a compound of ugly modern buildings. This was the second biggest hospital in the city. The ambulance pulled up outside the *Service des Urgences*. Paramedics ran towards it as the back doors flew open.

Mrs Jones got out of her hired car and watched as the limp, unmoving body was lowered on a stretcher, transferred to a trolley and rushed in through the double doors. There was already a saline drip attached to his arm. An oxygen mask covered his face. It had been snowing up in the mountains but down here there was only a dull drizzle, sweeping across the pavements. A doctor in a white coat was bending over the stretcher. He sighed and shook his head. Mrs Jones saw this. She crossed the road and followed the stretcher in.

A thin man with close-cropped hair, wearing a black jersey and padded waistcoat, had also been watching the hospital. He saw Mrs Jones without knowing who she was. He had also seen Alex. He took out a mobile telephone and made a call. Dr Grief would want to know...

Three hours later the sun had risen over the city. Grenoble is largely modern and even with its perfect mountain setting it struggles to be attractive. On this damp, cloudy day it was clearly failing.

Outside the hospital, a car drew up and Eva Stellenbosch got out. She was wearing a silver and white chessboard suit, with a hat perched on her ginger hair. She carried a leather handbag and for once she had put on make-up. She wanted to look elegant. She looked like a man in drag.

She walked into the hospital and found the main reception desk. There was a young nurse sitting behind a bank of telephones and computer screens. Mrs Stellenbosch addressed her in fluent French.

"Excuse me," she said. "I understand that a young boy was brought here this morning. His name is Alex Friend."

"One moment, please." The nurse entered the name into her computer. She read the information on the screen and her face became serious. "May I ask who you are?"

"I am the assistant director of the academy at Point Blanc. He is one of our students."

"Are you aware of the extent of his injuries, madame?"

"I was told that he was involved in a snowboarding accident." Mrs Stellenbosch took out a small handkerchief and dabbed at her eyes.

"He tried to snowboard down the mountains at night. He was involved in a collision with a train. His injuries are very serious, madame. The doctors are operating on him now."

Mrs Stellenbosch nodded, swallowing her tears. "My name is Eva Stellenbosch," she said. "May I wait for any news?"

"Of course, madame."

Mrs Stellenbosch took a seat in the reception area. For the next hour she watched as people came and went, some walking, some in wheelchairs. There were other people waiting for news of other patients. One of them, she noticed, was a serious-looking woman with black hair, badly cut, and very black eyes. She was from England – glancing occasionally at a copy of the London *Times*.

Then a door opened and a doctor came out. Doctors have a certain face when they come to give bad news. This doctor had it now. "Madame Stellenbosch?" he asked.

"Yes?"

"You are the director of the school...?"

"The assistant director, yes."

The doctor sat next to her. "I am very sorry, madame. Alex Friend died a few minutes ago." He waited while she absorbed the news. "He had multiple fractures. His arms, his collar bone, his leg. He had also fractured his skull. We operated, but unfortunately there had been massive internal bleeding. He went into shock and we were unable to bring him round."

Mrs Stellenbosch nodded, struggling for words. "I must notify his family," she whispered.

"Is he from this country?"

"No. He is English. His father ... Sir David Friend ... I'll have to tell him." Mrs Stellenbosch got to her feet. "Thank you, doctor. I'm sure you did everything you could."

Out of the corner of her eye, Mrs Stellenbosch noticed that the woman with the black hair had also stood up, letting her newspaper fall to the floor. She had overheard the conversation. She was looking shocked.

Both women left the hospital at the same time. Neither of them spoke.

The aircraft waiting on the runway was a Lockheed Martin C-130 Hercules. It had landed just after midday. Now it waited beneath the clouds while three vehicles drove towards it. One was a police car, one a Jeep and one an ambulance.

The Saint-Geoirs airport at Grenoble does not see many international flights, but the plane had flown out from England that morning. From the other side of the perimeter fence, Mrs Stellenbosch watched through a pair of high-powered binoculars. A small military escort had been formed. Four men in French uniforms. They had lifted up a coffin which seemed pathetically small when balanced on their broad shoulders. The coffin was simple. Pinewood with silver handles. A Union Jack was folded in a square in the middle.

Marching in time, they carried the coffin towards the waiting plane. Mrs Stellenbosch focused the binoculars and saw the woman from the hospital. She had been travelling in the police car. She stood watching as the coffin was loaded into the plane, then got back into the car and was driven away. By now, Mrs Stellenbosch knew who she was. Dr Grief kept extensive files and had quickly identified her as Mrs Jones; deputy to Alan Blunt, head of Special Operations for MI6.

Mrs Stellenbosch stayed until the end. The doors of the plane were closed. The Jeep and the ambulance left. The plane's propellers began to turn and it lumbered forward onto the runway. A few minutes later it took off. As it thundered into the air, the clouds opened as if to receive it and for a moment its silver wings were bathed in brilliant sunlight. Then the clouds rolled back and the plane disappeared.

Mrs Stellenbosch took out her mobile. She dialled a number and waited until she was connected. "The little swine has gone," she said.

She got back into her car and drove away.

After Mrs Jones had left the airport, she returned to the hospital and took the stairs to the second floor. She came to a pair of doors guarded by a policeman who nodded and let her pass through. On the other side was a corridor leading to a private wing. She walked down to a door, this one also guarded. She didn't knock. She went straight in.

Alex Rider was standing by the window, looking out at the view of Grenoble on the other side of the River Isère. Outside, high above him, five steel and glass bubbles moved slowly along a cable, ferrying tourists up to the Fort de la Bastille. He turned round as Mrs Jones came in. There was a bandage around his head but otherwise he seemed unhurt.

"You're lucky to be alive," she said.

"I thought I was dead," Alex replied.

"Let's hope Dr Grief believes as much." Despite herself, Mrs Jones couldn't keep the worry out of her eyes. "It really was a miracle," she said. "You should have at least broken something."

"The ski suit protected me," Alex said. He tried to think back to the whirling, desperate moment when he had been thrown off the train. "There was undergrowth. And the fence sort of caught me." He rubbed his leg and winced. "Even if it was barbed wire."

He walked back to the bed and sat down. After they had finished examining him, the French doctors had brought him fresh clothes. Military clothes, he noticed. Combat jacket and trousers.

He hoped they weren't trying to tell him something.

"I've got three questions," he said. "But let's start with the big one. I called for help two days ago. Where were you?"

"I'm very sorry, Alex," Mrs Jones said. "There were ... logistical problems."

"Yes? Well, while you were having your logistical problems, Dr Grief was getting ready to cut me up!"

"We couldn't just storm the academy. That could have got you killed. It could have got you all killed. We had to move in slowly. Try and work out what was going on. How do you think we found you so quickly?"

"That was my second question."

Mrs Jones shrugged. "We've had people in the mountains ever since we got your signal. They've been closing in on the academy. They heard the machine-gun fire when the snowmobiles were chasing you and followed you down on skis. They saw what happened with the train and radioed for help."

"All right. So why all the business with the funeral? Why do you want Dr Grief to think I'm dead?"

"That's simple, Alex. From what you've told us, he's keeping fifteen boys prisoner in the academy. These are the boys that he plans to replace." She shook her head. "I have to say, it's the most incredible thing I've ever heard. And I wouldn't have believed it if I'd heard it from anyone else except you."

"You're too kind," Alex muttered.

"If Dr Grief thought you'd survived last night, the first thing he would do is kill every one of those boys. Or perhaps he'd use them as hostages. We only had one hope if we were going to take him by surprise. He had to believe you were dead."

"You're going to take him by surprise?"

"We're going in tonight. I told you, we've assembled an attack squad here in Grenoble. They were up in the mountains last night. They plan to set off as soon as it's dark. They're armed and they're experienced." Mrs Jones hesitated. "There's just one thing they don't have."

"And what's that?" Alex asked, feeling a sudden sense of unease.

"They need someone who knows the building," Mrs Jones said. "The library, the secret lift, the placement of the guards, the passage with the cells—"

"No way!" Alex exclaimed. Now he understood the military clothes. "Forget it! I'm not going back up there! I almost got killed trying to get away! Do you think I'm mad?"

"Alex, you'll be looked after. You'll be completely safe—"

"No!"

Mrs Jones nodded. "All right. I can understand your feelings. But there's someone I want you to meet."

As if on cue, there was a knock on the door and it opened to reveal a young man, also in combat dress. The man was well-built with black hair, square shoulders and a dark, watchful face. He was in his late twenties. He saw Alex and shook his head. "Well, well, well. There's a turn up for the books," he said. "How's it going, Cub?"

Alex recognized him at once. It was the soldier he had known as Wolf. When MI6 had sent him for eleven days' SAS training in Wales, Wolf had been in charge of his unit. If training had been hell, Wolf had only made it worse, picking on Alex from the start and almost getting him thrown out. In the end though, it had been Wolf who had nearly lost his place with the SAS and Alex who had saved him. But Alex still wasn't sure where that left him, and the other man was giving nothing away.

"Wolf!" Alex said.

"I heard you got busted up." Wolf shrugged. "I'm sorry. I forgot the flowers and the bunch of grapes."

"What are you doing here?" Alex asked.

"They called me in to clear up the mess you left behind you."

"So where were you when I was being chased down the mountain?"

"It seems you were doing fine on your own."

Mrs Jones took over. "Alex has done a very good job up to now," she said. "But the fact is that there are fifteen young prisoners up at Point Blanc and our first priority must be to save them. From what Alex has told us, we know there are about thirty guards in and around the school. The only chance those boys have is for an SAS unit to break in. It's happening tonight." She turned to Alex. "The unit will be commanded by Wolf."

The SAS never use rank when they are on active service. Mrs Jones was careful only to use Wolf's code-name.

"Where does the boy come into this?" Wolf demanded.

"He knows the school. He knows the position of the guards and the location of the prison cells. He can lead you to the lift—"

"He can tell us everything we need to know here and now," Wolf interrupted. He turned to Mrs Jones. "We don't need a kid," he said. "He's just going to be baggage. We're going in on skis. Maybe there'll be blood. I can't waste one of my men holding his hand—"

"I don't need to have my hand held," Alex retorted angrily. "She's right. I know more about Point Blanc than any of you. I've been there – and got out of there, no thanks to you. Also, I've met some of those boys. One of them is a friend of mine. I promised I'd help him and I will."

"Not if you get killed."

"I can look after myself."

"Then it's agreed," Mrs Jones said. "Alex will lead you in there but then will take no further part in the operation. And as for his safety, Wolf, I hold you personally responsible."

"Personally responsible. Right," Wolf growled.

Alex couldn't resist a smile. He'd held his ground and he'd be going back in with the SAS. Then he realized. A few moments ago, he'd been arguing violently against doing just that. He glanced at Mrs Jones. She'd manipulated him, of course, bringing Wolf into the room. And she knew it.

Wolf nodded. "All right, Cub," he said. "Looks like you're in. Let's go play."

"Sure, Wolf," Alex sighed. "Let's go play."

NIGHT RAID

They came skiing down from the mountain. There were seven of them. Wolf was the leader. Alex was at his side. The other five men followed. They had changed into white trousers, jackets and hoods – camouflage that would help them blend into the snow. A helicopter had dropped them two kilometres north of and two hundred metres above Point Blanc and, equipped with night vision goggles, they had quickly made their way down. The weather had settled again. The moon was out. Despite himself, Alex enjoyed the journey, the whisper of the skis cutting through the ice, the empty mountainside bathed in white light. And he was part of a crack SAS unit. He felt safe.

But then the academy loomed up below him, and once again he shivered. Before they had left, he had asked for a gun – but Wolf had shaken his head.

"I'm sorry, Cub. It's orders. You get us in, then you get out of sight."

* * *

There were no lights showing in the building. The helicopter crouched on the helipad like a glittering insect. The ski-jump stood to one side, dark and forgotten. There was nobody in sight. Wolf held up a hand and they slid to a halt.

"Guards?" he whispered.

"Two patrolling. One on the roof."

"Let's take him out first."

Mrs Jones had made her instructions clear. There was to be no bloodshed unless absolutely necessary. The mission was to get the boys out. The SAS could take care of Dr Grief, Mrs Stellenbosch and the guards at a later date.

Now Wolf held out a hand and one of the other men passed him something. It was a crossbow – not the medieval sort but a sophisticated, hi-tech weapon with a microflite aluminium barrel and laser scope. He loaded it with an anaesthetic dart, lifted it up and took aim. Alex saw him smile to himself. Then his finger curled and the dart flashed across the night, travelling at one hundred metres a second. There was a faint sound from the roof of the academy. It was as if someone had coughed. Wolf lowered the crossbow.

"One down," he said.

"Sure," Alex muttered. "And about twenty-nine to go."

Wolf signalled and they continued down, more slowly now. They were about twenty metres from the school when they saw the main door open. Two men walked out, machine guns hanging from their shoulders. As one, the SAS men veered to the right, disappearing round the side of the school. They stopped within reach of the wall, dropping down to lie flat on their stomachs. Two of the men had moved slightly ahead. Alex noticed that they had kicked off their skis at the very same moment they had come to a halt.

The two guards approached. One of them was talking quietly in German. Alex's face was half buried in the snow. He knew that the combat clothes would make them invisible. He half-lifted his head just in time to see two figures rise out of the ground like ghosts from the grave. Two coshes swung in the moonlight. The guards crumpled. In seconds they were tied up and gagged. They wouldn't be going anywhere that night.

Wolf signalled again. The men got up and ran forward, making for the main door. Alex hastily pulled his own skis off and followed. They reached the door in a line, their backs against the wall. Wolf looked inside to check that it was safe. He nodded. They went in.

They were in the hall with the stone dragons and the animal heads. Alex found himself next to Wolf and quickly gave him his bearings, pointing out the different rooms.

"The library?" Wolf whispered. He was totally serious now. Alex could see the tension in his eyes.

"Through here."

Wolf took a step forward, then crouched down, his hand whipping into one of the pouches of his jacket. Another guard had appeared, patrolling the lower corridor. Dr Grief was taking no more chances. Wolf waited until the man had gone past, then nodded. One of the other SAS men went after him. Alex heard a thud and the clatter of a gun dropping.

"So far, so good," Wolf whispered.

They went into the library. Alex showed Wolf how to summon the lift and Wolf whistled softly as the suit of armour smoothly divided into two parts. "This is quite a place," he muttered.

"Are you going up or down?"

"Down. Let's make sure the kids are all right."

There was just room for all seven of them in the lift. Alex had warned Wolf about the guard at the table, within sight of the lift, and Wolf took no chances – he came out firing. In fact, there were two guards there. One of them was holding a mug of coffee, the other lighting a cigarette. Wolf fired twice. Two more anaesthetic darts travelled the short distance along the corridor and found their targets. Again, it had all happened in almost total silence. The two guards collapsed and lay still. The SAS men stepped out into the corridor.

Suddenly Alex remembered. He was angry with himself for not mentioning it before. "You can't go into the cells," he whispered. "They're wired up for sound."

Wolf nodded. "Show me!"

Alex showed Wolf the passage with the steel doors. Wolf pointed to one of the men. "I want you to stay here. If we're found, this is the first place Grief will come."

The man nodded. He understood. The rest of them went back to the lift, up to the library and out into the hall.

Wolf turned to Alex. "We're going to have to deactivate the alarm," he explained. "Do you have any idea—?"

"This way. Grief's private rooms are on the other side..."

But before he could finish, three more guards appeared, walking down the passageway. Wolf shot one of them – another anaesthetic dart – and one of his men took out the other two. But this time they were a fraction of a second too slow. Alex saw one of the guards bring his gun round. He was probably unconscious before he managed to fire. But at the last moment, his finger tightened on the trigger. Bullets sprayed upwards, smashing into the ceiling, bringing plaster and wood splinters showering down. Nobody had been hit, but the damage had been done. The lights flashed on. An alarm began to ring.

Twenty metres away, a door opened and more guards poured through.

"Down!" Wolf shouted.

He had produced a grenade. He tugged the pin out and threw it. Alex hit the ground and a second later there was a soft explosion as a great cloud of tear gas filled the far end of the passage. The guards staggered, blind and helpless. The SAS men quickly took them out.

Wolf grabbed hold of Alex and dragged him close. "Find somewhere to hide!" he shouted. "You've got us in. We'll do the rest now."

"Give me a gun!" Alex shouted back. Some of the gas had reached him and he could feel his eyes burning.

"No. I've got orders. At the first sign of trouble, you're to get out of the way. Find somewhere safe. We'll come for you later."

"Wolf...!"

But Wolf was already up and running. Alex heard machine-gun fire coming from somewhere below. So Wolf had been right. One of the guards had been sent to take care of the prisoners – but there had been an SAS man waiting for him. And now the rules had changed. The SAS couldn't afford to risk the lives of the prisoners. There was going to be bloodshed. Alex could only imagine the battle that must be taking place. But he was to be no part of it. His job was to hide.

More explosions. More gunfire. There was a bitter taste in Alex's mouth as he made his way back to the stairs. It was typical of MI6. Half the time they would happily get him killed. The other half they treated him like a child.

Suddenly a guard appeared, running towards the sound of the fighting. Alex's eyes were still smarting from the gas and now he made use of it. He brought his hand up to his face, pretending to cry. The guard saw a fourteen-year-old boy in tears. He stopped. At that moment Alex twisted round on his left foot, driving the upper part of his right foot sideways into the man's stomach – the roundhouse kick or *mawashi geri* he had learned in karate. The guard didn't even have time to cry out. His eyes rolled and he went limp. Alex felt a little better after that.

But there was still nothing more for him to do. There was another round of gunfire, then the quiet blast of a second gas grenade. Alex went into the dining-room. From here he could look out through the windows at the side of the building and the helipad above. He noticed that the blades of the helicopter were turning. Somebody was inside it. He moved closer to the window. It was Dr Grief! He had to let Wolf know.

He turned round.

Mrs Stellenbosch was standing in front of him.

He had never seen her look less human. Her entire face was contorted with anger, her lips rolled outwards, her eyes ablaze.

"You didn't die!" she exclaimed. "You're still alive!" Her voice was almost a whine, as if somehow none of it had been fair. "You brought them here. You ruined everything!"

"That's my job," Alex said.

"What was it that made me look in here?" Mrs Stellenbosch giggled to herself. Alex could see what little sanity she had left was slipping away. "Well, at least this is one bit of business I'm finally going to be able to finish."

Alex tensed himself, feet apart, centre of gravity low. Just like he had been taught. But it was useless. Mrs Stellenbosch lurched into him, moving with frightening speed. It was like being run over by a bus. Alex felt the full impact of her body weight, then cried out as two massive hands seized hold of him and threw him head-first across the room. He crashed into a table, knocking it over, then rolled out of the way as Mrs Stellenbosch followed up her first attack, lashing out with a kick that would have taken his head off his shoulders if it hadn't missed by less than a centimetre.

He scrambled to his feet and stood there, panting for breath. For a moment his vision was blurred. Blood trickled out of the corner of his mouth. Mrs Stellenbosch charged again. Alex threw himself forward, using another of the tables for leverage. His feet swung round, scything through the air, both his heels catching her on the back of the head. Anyone else would have been knocked out by the blow. But although Alex felt the jolt of it running all the way up his body, Mrs Stellenbosch hardly faltered. As Alex left the table, her hands swung down, smashing through the thick wood. The table fell apart and she walked through it, grabbing him again, this time by the neck. Alex felt his feet leave the floor. With a grunt she hurled him against the wall. Alex yelled, wondering if his back had been broken. He slid to the floor. He couldn't move.

Mrs Stellenbosch stopped, breathing heavily. She glanced out of the window. The helicopter's blades were at full speed now. The helicopter rocked forward then rose into the air. It was time to go.

She reached down and picked up her handbag. She took out a gun and aimed at Alex. Alex stared at her. There was nothing he could do.

Mrs Stellenbosch smiled. "And this is *my* job," she said.

The dining-room door swung open.

"Alex!" It was Wolf. He was holding a machine gun.

Mrs Stellenbosch lifted the gun up and fired three shots. Each one of them found its target. Wolf was hit in the shoulder, the arm and the chest. But even as he fell back, he opened fire himself. The heavy bullets slammed into Mrs Stellenbosch. She was hurled backwards into the window, which smashed behind her. With a scream she disappeared out into the night and the snow, head-first, her heavy stockinged legs trailing behind her.

The shock of what had happened gave Alex new strength. He got to his feet and ran over to Wolf. The SAS man wasn't dead but he was badly hurt, his breath rattling.

"I'm OK," he managed to say. "Came looking for you. Glad I found you."

"Wolf..."

"OK." He tapped at his chest and Alex saw that he was wearing body armour under his jacket. There was blood coming from his arm but the other two bullets hadn't reached him. "Grief..." he said.

Wolf gestured and Alex looked round. The helicopter had left its launch pad. It was flying low outside the academy. Alex saw Dr Grief in the pilot's seat. He had a gun. He fired. There was a yell and a body fell from somewhere above. One of the SAS men.

Suddenly Alex was angry. Grief was a freak, a monster. He was responsible for all this – and he was going to get away. Not knowing what he was doing, he snatched up Wolf's gun and ran through the broken window, past the dead body of Mrs Stellenbosch and into the night. He tried to aim. The blades of the helicopter were whipping up the surface snow, blinding him, but he pointed the gun up and fired. Nothing happened. He pulled the trigger again. Still nothing. Either Wolf had used all his ammunition or the gun had jammed.

Dr Grief pulled at the controls and the helicopter banked away, following the slope of the mountain. It was too late. Nothing could stop him.

Unless...

Alex threw down the gun and ran forward. There was a snowmobile lying idle a few metres away, its engine still running. The man who had been riding it was lying face down in the snow.

Alex leapt onto the seat and turned the throttle full on. The snowmobile roared away, skimming over the ice, following the path of the helicopter.

Dr Grief saw him. The helicopter slowed and turned. Grief raised a hand – waving goodbye.

Alex caught sight of the red spectacles, the slender fingers raised in one last gesture of defiance. With his hands gripping the handlebars Alex stood up on the foot-grips, tensing himself for what he knew he had to do. The helicopter moved away again, gaining altitude. In front of Alex, the ski-jump loomed up. He was travelling at seventy, eighty kilometres an hour, snow and wind rushing past him. Ahead of him there was a wooden barrier shaped like a cross.

Alex smashed through it, then threw himself off.

The snowmobile plunged down, its engine screaming.

Alex rolled over and over in the snow, ice and wood splinters in his eyes and mouth. He managed to get to his knees.

The snowmobile reached the end of the ski-jump.

Alex watched it rocket into the air, propelled by the huge metal slide.

In the helicopter Dr Grief just had time to see 225 kilograms of solid steel come hurtling towards him out of the night, its head-lights blazing, its engine still screaming. His eyes, bright red, opened wide in shock.

The explosion lit up the entire mountain. The snowmobile had become a torpedo and it hit its target with perfect accuracy. The helicopter disappeared in a huge fireball, then plunged down. It was still burning when it hit the ground.

Behind him, Alex became aware that the shooting had stopped. The battle was over. He walked slowly back to the academy, shivering suddenly in the cold night air. As he approached, a man appeared at the broken window and waved. It was Wolf, propping himself against the wall but still very much alive. Alex went over to him.

"What happened to Grief?" he asked.

"It looks like I sleighed him," Alex replied.

On the slopes, the wreckage of the helicopter flickered and burnt as the morning sun began to rise.

DEAD RINGER

A few days later, Alex found himself sitting opposite Alan Blunt in the faceless office in Liverpool Street, with Mrs Jones twisting another sweet between her fingers. It was 1 May, a bank holiday in England – but somehow he knew that holidays never came to the building that called itself the Royal & General bank. Even the spring seemed to have stopped at the window. Outside, the sun was shining. Inside, there were only shadows.

"It seems that once again we owe you a debt of thanks," Blunt was saying.

"You don't owe me anything," Alex said.

Blunt looked genuinely puzzled. "You have quite possibly changed the future of this planet," he said. "Of course, Grief's plan was monstrous, crazy. But the fact remains that his..." He searched for a word to describe the test-tube creations that had been sent out of Point Blanc. "...his *offspring* could have caused a great many problems. At the very least they would have had money. God knows what they would have got up to had they remained undiscovered."

"What's happened to them?" Alex asked.

"We've traced all fifteen of them and we have them under lock and key," Mrs Jones answered. "They were quietly arrested by the intelligence services of each country where they lived. We'll take care of them."

Alex shivered. He had a feeling he knew what Mrs Jones meant by those last words. And he was certain that nobody would ever see the fifteen Grief replicas again.

"Once again, we've had to hush this up," Blunt continued. "This whole business of ... cloning. It causes a great deal of public disquiet. Sheep are one thing – but human beings!" He coughed. "The families involved in this business have no desire for publicity, so they won't be talking. They're just glad to have their real sons returned to them. The same, of course, goes for you, Alex. You've already signed the Official Secrets Act. I'm sure we can trust you to be discreet."

There was a moment's pause. Mrs Jones looked carefully at Alex. She had to admit that she was worried about him. She knew everything that had happened at Point Blanc – how close he had come to a horrible death, only to be sent back into the academy for a second time. The boy who had come back from the French Alps was different to the boy who had left. There was a coldness about him, as tangible as the mountain snow.

"You did very well, Alex," she said.

"How is Wolf?" Alex asked.

"He's fine. He's still in hospital but the doctors say he'll make a complete recovery. We hope to have him back on operations in a few weeks."

"That's good."

"We only had one fatality in the raid on Point Blanc. That was the man you saw falling from the roof. Wolf and another man were injured. Otherwise, it was a complete success." She paused. "Is there anything else you want to know?"

"No." Alex shook his head. He stood up. "You left me in there," he said. "I called for help and you didn't come. Grief was going to kill me, but you didn't care."

"That's not true, Alex!" Mrs Jones looked at Blunt for support but he didn't meet her eyes. "There were difficulties..."

"It doesn't matter. I just want you to know that I've had enough. I don't want to be a spy any more and if you ask me again, I'll refuse. I know you think you can blackmail me. But I know too much about you now, so that won't work any more." He walked over to the door. "I used to think that being a spy would be exciting and special ... like in the films. But you just used me. In a way, the two of you are as bad as Grief. You'll do anything to get what you want. Well, I want to go back to school. Next time, you can do it without me."

There was a long silence after Alex had left. At last, Blunt spoke. "He'll be back," he said.

Mrs Jones raised an eyebrow. "You really think so?"

"He's too good at what he does ... too good at the job. And it's in his blood." He stood up. "It's rather odd," he said. "Most schoolboys dream of being spies. With Alex, we have a spy who dreams of being a schoolboy."

"Will you really use him again?" Mrs Jones asked.

"Of course. There was a file that came in only this morning. An interesting situation in the Zagros Mountains of Iraq. Alex may be the only answer." He smiled at his number two. "We'll give him a while to settle down and then we'll call him."

"He won't answer."

"We'll see," Blunt said.

* * *

Alex walked home from the bus stop and let himself into the elegant Chelsea house that he shared with his housekeeper and closest friend, Jack Starbright. Alex had already told Jack where he had been and what he had been doing, but the two of them had made an agreement never to discuss his involvement with MI6. She didn't like it and she worried about him. But at the end of the day they both knew there was nothing more to be said.

She seemed surprised to see him. "I thought you'd just gone out," she said.

"No."

"Did you get the message by the phone?"

"What message?"

"Mr Bray wants to see you this afternoon. Three o'clock at the school."

Henry Bray was the head teacher at Brookland. Alex wasn't surprised by the summons. Bray was the sort of head who managed to run a busy comprehensive and still find time to take a personal interest in every pupil who went there. He had been worried by Alex's long absences. So he had called a meeting.

"Do you want lunch?" Jack asked.

"No thanks." Alex knew that he would have to pretend he had been ill again. Doubtless MI6 would produce another doctor's note in due course. But the thought of lying to his head teacher spoiled his appetite.

He set off an hour later, taking his bicycle, which had been returned to the house by the Putney police. He cycled slowly. It was good to be back in London, to be surrounded by normal life. He turned off the King's Road and pedalled down the side road where – it felt like a month ago – he had followed the man in the white Skoda. The school loomed up ahead of him. It was empty now and would remain so until the summer term.

But as Alex arrived, he saw a figure walking across the yard to the school gates and recognized Mr Lee, the elderly school caretaker.

"You again!"

"Hello, Bernie," Alex said. That was what everyone called him.

"On your way to see Mr Bray?"

"Yeah."

The caretaker shook his head. "He never told me he was going to be here today. But he never tells me anything! I'm just going down to the shops. I'll be back at five to lock up – so make sure you're out by then."

"Right, Bernie."

There was nobody in the playground. It felt strange, walking across the tarmac on his own. The school seemed bigger with nobody there, the yard stretching out too far between the red-brick buildings, with the sun beating down, reflecting off the windows. Alex was dazzled. He had never seen the place so empty and so quiet. The grass on the playing-fields looked almost too green. Any school without schoolchildren has its own peculiar atmosphere and Brookland was no exception.

Mr Bray had an office in D block, which was next to the science building. Alex reached the swing-doors and opened them. The walls here would normally be covered in posters but they had all been taken down at the end of term. Everything was blank, off-white. There was another door open to one side. Bernie had been cleaning the main laboratory. He had rested his mop and bucket to one side when he'd gone to the shops – to pick up twenty cigarettes, Alex presumed. The man had been a chain-smoker all his life and Alex knew he'd die with a cigarette between his lips.

Alex climbed up the stairs, his heels rapping against the stone surface. He reached a corridor – left for biology, right for physics – and continued straight ahead. A second corridor, with full-length windows on both sides, led into D block. Bray's study was directly ahead of him. He stopped at the door, vaguely wondering if he should have smartened up for the meeting. Bray was always snapping at boys with their shirts hanging out or ties crooked. Alex was wearing a denim jacket, T-shirt, jeans and Nike trainers – the same clothes he had worn that morning at MI6. His hair was still too short for his liking, although it had begun to grow back. All in all, he still looked like a juvenile delinquent – but it was too late now. And anyway, Bray didn't want to see him to discuss his appearance. His non-appearance at school was more to the point.

He knocked on the door.

"Come in!" a voice called.

Alex opened the door and walked into the head teacher's study, a cluttered room with views over the playground. There was a desk, piled high with papers, and a black leather chair with its back towards the door. A cabinet full of trophies stood against one wall. The others were mainly lined with books.

"You wanted to see me," Alex said.

The chair turned slowly round.

Alex froze.

It wasn't Henry Bray sitting behind the desk.

It was himself.

He was looking at a fourteen-year-old boy with fair hair cut very short, brown eyes and a slim, pale face. The boy was even dressed identically to him. It took Alex what felt like an eternity to accept what he was seeing. He was standing in a room looking at himself sitting in a chair. The boy *was* him.

With just one difference. The boy was holding a gun.

"Sit down," he said.

Alex didn't move. He knew what he was facing and he was angry with himself for not having expected it. When he had been handcuffed at the academy, Dr Grief had boasted to him that he had cloned himself sixteen times. But that morning Mrs Jones had traced "all fifteen of them". That left one spare – one boy waiting to take his place in the family of Sir David Friend. Alex had glimpsed him while he was at the academy. Now he remembered the figure with the white mask, watching him from a window as he walked over to the ski-jump. The white mask had been bandages. The new Alex had been spying on him as he recovered from the plastic surgery that had made the two of them identical.

And even today there had been clues. Perhaps it had been the heat of the sun – or the fall-out from his visit to MI6. But he had been too wrapped up in his own thoughts to see them: Jack, when he got home – "I thought you'd just gone out"; Bernie, at the gate – "You again!"

They had both thought they'd just seen him. And in a sense, they had. They had seen the boy sitting opposite him now. The boy who was aiming a gun at his heart.

"I've been looking forward to this," the other boy said. Despite the hatred in his voice, Alex couldn't help marvelling. The voice wasn't the same as his. The boy hadn't had enough time to get it right. But otherwise he was a dead ringer.

"What are you doing here?" Alex said. "It's all over. The Gemini Project is finished. You might as well turn yourself in. You need help."

"I need just one thing," the second Alex sneered. "I need to see you dead. I'm going to shoot you. I'm going to do it now. You killed my father!"

"Your father was a test tube," Alex said. "You never had a mother or a father. You're a freak. Handmade in the Alps ... like a cuckoo clock. What are you going to do when you've killed me? Take my place? You wouldn't last a week. You may look like me, but too many people know what Grief was trying to do. And I'm sorry, but you've got *fake* written all over you."

"We would have had everything! We would have had the whole world!" The replica Alex almost screamed the words and for a moment Alex thought he heard Dr Grief somewhere in there, blaming him from beyond the grave. But then the creature in front of him *was* Dr Grief ... or part of him. "I don't care what happens to me," he went on, "just so long as you're dead."

The hand with the gun stretched out. The barrel was pointing at him. Alex looked the boy straight in the eye.

And he saw the hesitation.

The fake Alex couldn't quite bring himself to do it. They were too similar. The same height, the same build – the same *face*. For the other boy, it would be like shooting himself. Alex still hadn't closed the door. He threw himself backwards, out into the corridor. At the same time, the gun went off, the bullet exploding millimetres above his head and crashing into the far wall. Alex hit the ground on his back and rolled out of the doorway as a second bullet slammed into the floor. And then he was running, putting as much space between himself and his double as he could.

There was a third shot as he sprinted down the corridor and the window next to him shattered, glass showering down. Alex reached the stairs and took them three at a time, afraid that he would trip and break an ankle. But then he was at the bottom, heading for the main door, swerving only when he realized that he would make too easy a target as he crossed the playground. Instead he dived into the laboratory, almost falling head-first over Bernie's bucket and mop.

The laboratory was long and rectangular, divided into work stations with Bunsen burners, flasks and dozens of bottles of chemicals spread out on shelves that stretched the full length of the room. There was another door at the far end. Alex dived behind the furthest desk. Would his double have seen him come in? Might he be looking for him, even now, out in the yard?

Cautiously Alex poked his head over the surface, then ducked down as four bullets ricocheted around him, splintering the wood and smashing one of the gas pipes. Alex heard the hiss of escaping gas, then there was another gunshot and an explosion that hurled him backwards, sprawling onto the floor. The last bullet had ignited the gas. Flames leapt up, licking at the ceiling. Then the sprinkler system went off, spraying the entire room. Alex tracked back on his hands and feet, searching for shelter behind fire and water, hoping that the other Alex would be blinded. His shoulders hit the far door. He scrambled to his feet. There was another shot. But then he was through – with another corridor and a second flight of stairs straight ahead.

The stairs led nowhere. He was halfway up before he remembered. There was a single classroom at the top, used for biology. It had a spiral staircase leading to the roof. The school had so little land that they'd planned to build a roof garden. Then they'd run out of money. There were a couple of greenhouses. Nothing more.

There was no way down! Alex looked over his shoulder and saw the other Alex reloading his gun, already on his way up. He had no choice. He had to continue even though he knew that he was soon going to be trapped.

He reached the biology classroom and slammed the door shut behind him. There was no lock and the tables were all bolted into the floor, otherwise he might have been able to make a barricade. The spiral staircase was ahead of him. He ran up it without stopping, through another door and out onto the roof. Alex stopped to catch his breath and see what he could do next.

He was standing on a wide, flat area with a fence running all the way round. There were half a dozen terracotta pots filled with earth. A few plants sprouted out, looking more dead than alive. Alex sniffed the air. Smoke was curling up from the windows two floors below and he realized that the sprinkler system had failed to put out the fire. He thought of the gas pouring into the room and the chemicals stacked up on the shelves. He could be standing on a time bomb! He had to find a way down.

But then he heard feet on metal and realized that his double had reached the top of the spiral staircase. Alex ducked behind one of the greenhouses. The door crashed open.

Smoke followed the fake Alex out onto the roof. He took a step forward. Now Alex was behind him.

"Where are you?" shouted the double. His hair was soaked and his face contorted with anger.

Alex knew his moment had come. He would never have a better chance. He ran forward. The other Alex twisted round and fired. The bullet creased his shoulder, a molten sword drawn across his flesh. But then he had reached his replica, grabbing him around the neck with one hand and seizing hold of his wrist with the other, forcing the gun away. There was a huge explosion in the laboratory below and the entire building shook, but neither of the boys seemed to notice it. They were locked in an embrace, two reflections that had become tangled up in the mirror, the gun over their heads, fighting for control.

The flames were tearing through the building. Fed by a variety of chemicals, they burst through the roof, melting the asphalt. In the far distance the scream of fire engines penetrated the sun-filled air. Alex pulled with all his strength, trying to bring the gun down. The other Alex clawed at him, swearing – not in English but in Afrikaans.

The end came very suddenly.

The gun twisted and fell to the ground.

One Alex lashed out, knocking the other down, then dived for the gun.

There was another explosion and a sheet of chemical flame leapt up. A crater had suddenly appeared in the roof, swallowing up the gun. The boy saw it too late and fell through. With a yell, he disappeared into the smoke and fire.

One Alex Rider walked over to the hole and looked down.

The other Alex Rider lay on his back, two floors below. He wasn't moving. The flames were closing in.

The first fire engines had arrived at the school. A ladder slanted up towards the roof.

A boy with short fair hair and brown eyes, wearing a denim jacket, T-shirt and jeans, walked to the edge of the roof and began to climb down.

SKELETON KEY

IN THE DARK

Night came quickly to Skeleton Key.

The sun hovered briefly on the horizon, then dipped below. At once, the clouds rolled in – first red, then mauve, silver, green and black as if all the colours in the world were being sucked into a vast melting pot. A single frigate bird soared over the mangroves, its own colours lost in the chaos behind it. The air was close. Rain hung waiting. There was going to be a storm.

The single engine Cessna Skyhawk SP circled twice before coming in to land. It was the sort of plane that would barely have been noticed, flying in this part of the world. That was why it had been chosen. If anyone had been curious enough to check the registration number printed under the wing, they would have learnt that this plane belonged to a photographic company based in Jamaica. This was not true. There was no company and it was already too dark to take photographs.

There were three men in the aircraft. They were all dark-skinned, wearing faded jeans and loose, open-neck shirts. The pilot had long black hair, deep brown eyes and a thin scar running down the side of his face. He had met his two passengers only that afternoon. They had introduced themselves as Carlo and Marc but he doubted these were their real names. He knew that their journey had begun a long time ago, somewhere in Eastern Europe. He knew that this short flight was the last leg. He knew what they were carrying. Already, he knew too much.

The pilot glanced down at the multifunction display in the control panel. The illuminated computer screen was warning him of the storm that was closing in. That didn't worry him. Low clouds and rain gave him cover. The authorities were less vigilant during a storm. Even so, he was nervous. He had flown into Cuba many times, but never here. And tonight he would have preferred to have been going almost anywhere else.

Cayo Esqueleto. Skeleton Key.

There it was, stretching out before him, thirty-eight kilometres long and nine kilometres across at its widest point. The sea around it, which had been an extraordinary, brilliant blue until a few minutes ago, had suddenly darkened, as if someone had thrown a switch. Over to the west, he could make out the twinkling lights of Puerto Madre, the island's second biggest town. The main airport was further north, outside the capital of Santiago. But that wasn't where he was heading. He pressed on the joystick and the plane veered to the right, circling over the forests and mangrove swamps that surrounded the old, abandoned airport at the bottom end of the island.

The Cessna had been equipped with a thermal intensifier, similar to the sort used in American spy satellites. He flicked a switch and glanced at the display. A few birds appeared as tiny pinpricks of red. There were more dots pulsating in the swamp. Crocodiles or perhaps manatees. And a single dot about twenty metres from the runway. He turned to speak to the man called Carlo but there was no need. Carlo was already leaning over his shoulder, staring at the screen.

Carlo nodded. There was only one man waiting for them, as agreed. Anyone hiding within a few hundred metres of the airstrip would have shown up. It was safe to land.

The pilot looked out of the window and there was the runway. It was a rough strip of land on the edge of the coast, hacked out of the jungle and running parallel with the sea. The pilot would have missed it altogether in the dying light but for the two lines of electric bulbs burning at ground level, outlining the path for the plane.

The Cessna swooped out of the sky. At the last minute it was buffeted about by a sudden, damp squall that had been sent to try the pilot's nerve. The pilot didn't blink and a moment later the wheels hit the ground and the plane was bouncing and shuddering along, dead centre between the two rows of lights. He was grateful they were there. The mangroves – thick bushes, half floating on pools of stagnant water – came almost to the edge of the runway. Go even a couple of metres in the wrong direction and a wheel might snag. It would be enough to destroy the plane.

The pilot flicked switches. The engine died and the twin-bladed propellers slowed down and came to a halt. He looked out of the window. There was a jeep parked next to one of the buildings and it was here that the single man – the red dot on his screen – was waiting. He turned to his passengers.

"He's there."

The older of the two men nodded. Carlo was about thirty years old with black, curly hair. He hadn't shaved. Stubble the colour of cigarette ash clung to his jaw. He turned to the other passenger. "Marc? Are you ready?"

The man who called himself Marc could have been Carlo's younger brother. He was barely twenty-five and, although he was trying not to show it, he was scared. There was sweat on the side of his face, glowing green as it caught the light from the control panel. He reached behind him and took out a gun, a German-built 10mm Glock automatic. He checked it was loaded, then slipped it into the waistband at the back of his trousers, under his shirt.

"I'm ready," he said.

"There is only him. There are two of us." Carlo tried to reassure Marc. Or perhaps he was trying to reassure himself. "We're both armed. There is nothing he can do."

"Then let's go."

Carlo turned to the pilot. "Have the plane ready," he commanded. "When we walk back, I will give you a sign." He raised a hand, one finger and thumb forming an O. "That is the signal that our business has been successfully concluded. Start the engine at that time. We don't want to stay here one second longer than we have to."

They got out of the plane. There was a thin layer of gravel on the runway which crunched beneath their combat boots as they walked round the side to the cargo door. They could feel the sullen heat in the air, the heaviness of the night sky. The island seemed to be holding its breath. Carlo reached up and opened a door. In the back of the plane was a black container, about one metre by two. With difficulty, he and Marc lowered it to the ground.

The younger man looked up. The lights on the landing-strip dazzled him but he could just make out a figure standing still as a statue beside the jeep, waiting for them to approach. He hadn't moved since the plane had landed. "Why doesn't he come to us?" he asked.

Carlo spat and said nothing.

There were two handles, one on either side of the container. The two men carried it between them, walking awkwardly, bending over their load. It took them a long time to reach the jeep. But at last they were there. For a second time, they set the box down.

Carlo straightened up, rubbing his palms on the side of his jeans. "Good evening, General," he said. He was speaking in English. This was not his native language. Nor was it the general's. But it was the only language they had in common.

"Good evening." The general did not bother with names that he knew would be false anyway. "You had no trouble getting here?"

"No trouble at all, General."

"You have it?"

"One kilogram of weapons grade uranium. Sufficient to build a bomb powerful enough to destroy a city. I would be interested to know which city you have in mind."

General Alexei Sarov took a step forward and the lights from the runway illuminated him. He was not a big man, yet there was something about him that radiated power and control. He still carried with him his years in the army. They could be seen in his close-cut, iron-grey hair, his watchful pale blue eyes, his almost emotionless face. They were there in the very way he carried himself. He was perfectly poised; relaxed and wary at the same time. General Sarov was sixty-two years old but looked twenty years younger. He was dressed in a dark suit, a white shirt and a narrow dark blue tie. In the damp heat of the evening, his clothes should have been creased. He should have been sweating. But to look at him, he could have just stepped out of an air-conditioned room.

He crouched down beside the container, at the same time producing a small device from his pocket. It looked like a car cigarette lighter with a dial attached. He found a socket in the side of the box and plugged the device in. Briefly, he examined the dial. He nodded. It was satisfactory.

"You have the rest of the money?" Carlo asked.

"Of course." The general straightened up and walked over to the Jeep. Carlo and Marc tensed themselves – this was the moment when he might produce a gun. But when he turned round he was holding a black leather attaché-case. He flicked the locks and opened it. The case was filled with banknotes: one hundred dollar bills neatly banded together in packets of fifty. One hundred packets in all. A total of half a million dollars. More money than Carlo had ever seen in his life.

But still not enough.

"We've had a problem," Carlo said.

"Yes?" Sarov did not sound surprised.

Marc could feel the sweat as it drew a comma down the side of his neck. A mosquito was whining in his ear but he resisted the urge to slap it. This was what he had been waiting for. He was standing a few steps away, his hands hanging limply by his side. Slowly, he allowed them to creep behind him, closer to the concealed gun. He glanced at the ruined buildings. One might once have been a control tower. The other looked like a customs shed. Both of them were broken and empty, the brickwork crumbling, the windows smashed. Could there be someone hiding there? No. The thermal intensifier would have shown them. They were alone.

"The cost of the uranium." Carlo shrugged. "Our friend in Miami sends his apologies. But there are new security systems all over the world. Smuggling – particularly this sort of thing – has become much more difficult. And that's meant extra expense."

"How much extra expense?"

"A quarter of a million dollars."

"That's unfortunate."

"Unfortunate for you, General. You're the one who has to pay."

Sarov considered. "We had an agreement," he said.

"Our friend in Miami hoped you'd understand."

There was a long silence. Marc's fingers reached out behind his back, closing around the Glock automatic. But then Sarov nodded. "I will have to raise the money," he said.

"You can have it transferred to the same account that we used before," Carlo said. "But I have to warn you, General. If the money hasn't arrived in three days, the American intelligence services will be told what has happened here tonight ... what you've just received. You may think you are safe here on this island. I can assure you, you won't be safe any more."

"You're threatening me," Sarov muttered. There was something at once calm and deadly in the way he spoke.

"It's nothing personal," Carlo said.

Marc produced a cloth bag. He unfolded it, then tipped the money out of the case and into the bag. The case might contain a radio transmitter. It might contain a small bomb. He left it behind.

"Good night, General," Carlo said.

"Good night." Sarov smiled. "I hope you enjoy the flight."

The two men walked away. Marc could feel the money, the bundles pressing through the cloth against the side of his leg. "The man's a fool," he whispered, returning to his own language. "An old man. Why were we afraid?"

"Let's just get out of here," Carlo said. He was thinking about what the general had said: *I hope you enjoy the flight*. Had he been smiling when he said that?

He made the agreed signal, pressing his finger and thumb together. At once the Cessna's engine started up.

General Sarov was still watching them. He hadn't moved, but

now his hand reached once again into his jacket pocket. His fingers closed around the radio transmitter waiting there. He had wondered if it would be necessary to kill the two men and their pilot. Personally, he would have preferred not to, even as an insurance policy. But their demands had made it necessary. He should have known they would be greedy. Given the sort of people they were, it was almost inevitable.

Back in the plane, the two men were strapping themselves into their seats while the pilot prepared for take-off. Carlo heard the engine rev up as the plane slowly began to turn. Far away, there was a low rumble of thunder. Now he wished that they had turned the plane round immediately after they had landed. It would have saved some precious seconds and he was eager to be away, back in the air.

I hope you enjoy the flight.

There had been no emotion whatsoever in the general's voice. He could have meant what he was saying. But Carlo guessed he would have spoken exactly the same way if he had been passing a sentence of death.

Next to him, Marc was already counting the money, running his hands through the piles of notes. He looked back at the ruined buildings, at the waiting Jeep. Would Sarov try something? What sort of resources did he have on the island? But as the plane turned in a tight circle, nothing moved. The general stayed where he was. There was nobody else in sight.

The runway lights went out.

"What the...?" The pilot swore viciously.

Marc stopped his counting. Carlo understood at once what was happening. "He's turned the lights off," he said. "He wants to keep us here. Can you take off without them?"

The plane had turned a half-circle so that it was facing the way it had come. The pilot stared out through the cockpit window, straining to see into the night. It was very dark now, but there was an ugly, unnatural light pulsating in the sky. He nodded. "It won't be easy, but..."

The lights came back on again.

There they were, stretching into the distance, an arrow that pointed to freedom and an extra profit of a quarter of a million dollars. The pilot relaxed. "It must have been the storm," he said. "It disrupted the electricity supply."

"Just get us out of here," Carlo muttered. "The sooner we're in the air, the happier I'll be."

The pilot nodded. "Whatever you say." He pressed down on the controls and the Cessna lumbered forward, picking up speed quickly. The runway lights blurred, guiding him forward. Carlo settled back into his seat. Marc was watching out of the window.

And then, seconds before the wheels left the ground, the plane suddenly lurched. The whole world twisted as a giant, invisible hand seized hold of it and wrenched it sideways. The Cessna had been travelling at one hundred and fifty kilometres per hour. It came to a grinding halt in a matter of seconds, the deceleration throwing all three men forward in their seats. If they hadn't been belted in, they would have been hurled out of the front window – or what was left of the shattered glass. At the same time there was a series of ear-shattering crashes as something whipped into the fuselage. One of the wings had dipped down and the propeller was torn off, spinning into the night. Suddenly the plane was still, resting tilted on one side.

For a moment, nobody moved inside the cabin. The plane's engines rattled and stopped. Then Marc pulled himself up in his seat. "What happened?" he screamed. "What happened?" He had bitten his tongue. Blood trickled down his chin. The bag was still open and money had spilled into his lap.

"I don't understand..." The pilot was too dazed to speak.

"You left the runway!" Carlo's face was twisted with shock and anger.

"I didn't!"

"There!" Marc was pointing at something and Carlo followed his quivering finger. The door on the underside of the plane had buckled. Black water was seeping in underneath, forming a pool around their feet.

There was another rumble of thunder, closer this time.

"He did this!" the pilot said.

"What did he do?" Carlo demanded.

"He moved the runway!"

It had been a simple trick. As the plane had turned, Sarov had switched off the lights on the runway using the radio transmitter in his pocket. For a moment, the pilot had been disoriented, lost in the darkness. Then the plane had finished its turn and the lights had come back on. But what he hadn't known, what he wouldn't have been able to see, was that it was a second set of lights that had been activated – and that these ran off at an angle, leaving the safety of the runway and continuing over the surface of the swamp.

"He led us into the mangroves," the pilot said.

Now Carlo understood what had happened to the plane. The moment its wheels touched the water, its fate had been sealed. Without solid ground beneath it, the plane had become bogged down and toppled over. Swamp water was even now pouring in as they slowly sank beneath the surface. The branches of the mangrove trees that had almost torn the plane apart surrounded them, bars of a living prison.

"What are we going to do?" Marc demanded, and suddenly he was sounding like a child. "We're going to drown!"

"We can get out!" Carlo had suffered whiplash injuries in the collision. He moved one arm painfully, unfastening his seat belt.

"We shouldn't have tried to cheat him!" Marc cried. "You knew what he was. You were told—"

"Shut up!" Carlo had a gun of his own. He pulled it out of the holster underneath his shirt and balanced it on his knee. "We'll get out of here and we'll deal with him. And then somehow we'll find a way off this damn island."

"There's something..." the pilot began.

Something had moved outside.

"What is it?" Marc whispered.

"Shhh!" Carlo half stood up, his body filling the cramped space of the cabin. The plane tilted again, settling further into the swamp. He lost his balance then steadied himself. He reached out, past the pilot, as if he was going to climb out of the broken front window.

Something huge and horrible lunged towards him, blocking out what little light there was in the night sky. Carlo screamed as it threw itself head-first into the plane and onto him. There was a glint of white and a dreadful grunting sound. The other men were screaming too.

General Sarov stood watching. It wasn't raining yet but the water was heavy in the air. There was a flash of lightning that seemed to cross the sky almost in slow motion, relishing its journey. In that moment, he saw the Cessna on its side, half buried in the swamp. There were now half a dozen crocodiles swarming all over it. The largest of them had dived head-first into the cockpit. Only its tail was visible, thrashing about as it gorged itself.

He reached down and lifted up the black container. Although it had taken two men to carry it to him, it seemed to weigh nothing in his hands. He placed it in the Jeep, then stood back. He allowed himself the rare privilege of a smile and felt it, briefly, on his lips. Tomorrow, when the crocodiles had finished their meal, he would send in his field workers – the *macheteros* – to recover the banknotes. Not that the money was important. He was the owner of one kilogram of weapons grade uranium. As Carlo had said, he now had the power to destroy a small city.

But Sarov had no intention of destroying a city.

His target was the entire world.

MATC

Alex caught the ball on the top of his chest, bounced it forward and kicked it into the back of the net. It was then that he noticed the man with the large white dog. It was a warm, bright Friday afternoon, the weather caught between late spring and early summer. This was only a practice match but Alex took the game seriously. Mr Wiseman, who taught PE, had selected him for the first team and he was looking forward to playing against other schools in west London. Unfortunately, his school, Brookland, didn't have its own playing fields. This was a public field and anyone could walk past. And they could bring their dogs.

Alex recognized the man at once and his heart sank. At the same time he was angry. How could he have the nerve to come here, into the school arena, in the middle of a game? Weren't these people ever going to leave him alone?

The man's name was Crawley. With his thinning hair, blotchy

...ioned clothes, he looked like a junior army officer ...ps a teacher in a second-rate private school. But Alex ...w the truth. Crawley belonged to MI6. Not exactly a spy, but someone who was very much a part of that world. Crawley was an office manager in one of the country's most secret offices. He did the paperwork, made the arrangements, set up the meetings. When someone died with a knife in their back or a bullet in their chest, it would be Crawley who had signed on the dotted line.

As Alex ran back to the centre line, Crawley walked over to a bench, dragging the dog behind. The animal didn't seem to want to walk. It didn't want to be there at all. Crawley sat down. He was still sitting there ten minutes later when the final whistle blew and the game came to an end. Alex considered for a moment. Then he picked up his jersey and went over to him.

Crawley seemed surprised to see him. "Alex!" he exclaimed. "What a surprise! I haven't seen you since ... well, since you got back from France."

It had only been four weeks since MI6 had forced Alex to investigate a school for the super-rich in south-east France. Using a false name, he had become a student at the Point Blanc Academy only to find himself taken prisoner by the mad headmaster, Dr Grief. He had been chased down a mountain, shot at and almost dissected alive in a biology class. Alex had never wanted to be a spy and the whole business had convinced him he was right. Crawley was the last person he wanted to see.

But the MI6 man was beaming. "Are you on the school team? Is this where you play? I'm surprised I haven't noticed you before. Barker and I often walk here."

"Barker?"

"The dog." Crawley reached out and patted it. "He's a Dalmatian."

"I thought Dalmatians had spots."

"Not this one." Crawley hesitated. "Actually, Alex, it's a bit of luck running into you. I wonder if I could have a word with you?"

Alex shook his head. "Forget it, Mr Crawley. I told you the last time. I'm not interested in MI6. I'm a schoolboy. I'm not a spy."

"Absolutely!" Crawley agreed. "This has got nothing to do with the ... um ... company. No, no, no." He looked almost embarrassed. "The thing is, what I wanted to ask you was ... how would you like a front row seat at Wimbledon?"

The question took Alex completely by surprise. "Wimbledon? You mean ... the tennis?"

"That's right." Crawley smiled. "The All England Tennis Club. I'm on the committee."

"And you're offering me a ticket?"

"Yes."

"What's the catch?"

"There is no catch, Alex. Not really. But ... let me explain." Alex was aware that the other players were getting ready to leave. The school day was almost over. He listened as Crawley went on. "The thing is, you see, a week ago we had a break-in. Security at the club is always tight but someone managed to climb over the wall and get into the Millennium Building through a forced window."

"What's the Millennium Building?"

"It's where the players have their changing rooms. It's also got a gym, a restaurant, a couple of lounges and so on. We have closed-circuit television cameras but the intruder disabled the system – along with the main alarm. It was a thoroughly professional job. We'd never have known anyone had been there except for a stroke of luck. One of our night guards saw the man leaving. He was Chinese, in his early twenties—"

"The guard?"

"The intruder. Dressed from head to foot in black with some sort of rucksack on his back. The guard alerted the police and we had the whole place searched. The Millennium Building, the courts, the cafés ... everywhere. It took three days. There are no terrorist cells active in London at the moment, thank goodness, but there was always a chance that some lunatic might have planted a bomb. We had the anti-terrorist squad in. Sniffer dogs. Nothing! Whoever it was had vanished into thin air and it seemed he'd left nothing behind.

"Now, here's the strange thing, Alex. He didn't leave anything, but nor did he *take* anything. In fact, nothing seems to have been touched. As I say, if the guard hadn't seen this chap, we'd never have known he had been there. What do you make of that?"

Alex shrugged. "Maybe the guard disturbed him before he could get his hands on whatever it was he wanted."

"No. He was already leaving when he was seen."

"Could the guard have imagined it?"

"We examined the cameras. The film is timecoded and we discovered that they had definitely been out of action for two hours. From midnight until two in the morning."

"Then what do you think, Mr Crawley? Why are you telling me this?"

Crawley sighed and stretched his legs. He was wearing suede shoes, shabby and down at heel. The dog had fallen asleep. "My belief is that somebody is intending to sabotage Wimbledon this year," he said. Alex was about to interrupt but Crawley held up a hand. "I know it sounds ridiculous and I have to admit, the other committee members don't believe me. On the other hand, they don't have my instincts. They don't work in the same business as me. But think about it, Alex. There had to be a reason for such a carefully planned and executed break-in. But there *is* no reason. Something's wrong."

"Why would anyone want to sabotage Wimbledon?"

"I don't know. But you have to remember, the Wimbledon tennis fortnight is a huge business. There are millions of pounds at stake. Prize money alone adds up to eight and a half million. And then there are television rights, merchandising rights, corporate sponsorship... We get VIPs flying in from all over the planet – everyone from film stars to presidents – and tickets for the men's final have been known to change hands for literally thousands of pounds. It's not just a game. It's a world event, and if anything happened ... well, it doesn't bear thinking about."

Crawley obviously had been thinking about it. He looked tired. The worry was deep in his eyes.

Alex thought for a moment. "You want me to look around." He smiled. "I've never been to Wimbledon. I've only ever seen it on TV. I'd love a ticket for Centre Court. But I don't see how a one-day visit would actually help."

"Exactly, Alex. But a one-day visit isn't quite what I had in mind."

"Go on."

"Well, you see, I was wondering if you would consider becoming a ballboy."

"You're not serious?"

"Why not? You can stay there for the whole fortnight. You'll have a wonderful time and you'll be right in the middle of things. You'll see some great matches. And I'll be able to relax a little, knowing you're there. If anything is going on, there's a good chance you might spot it. Then you can call me and I'll take care of it." He nodded. It was obvious that he had managed to persuade himself, if not Alex. "It's not as if this is dangerous or anything. I mean ... it's Wimbledon. There'll be plenty of other boys and girls there. What d'you think?"

"Don't you have enough security people already?"

"Of course we have a security company. They're easy to see – which makes them easy to avoid. But you'd be invisible, Alex. That's the whole point."

"Alex...?"

It was Mr Wiseman who had called out to him. The teacher was waiting for him. All the other players had left now, apart from two or three boys kicking the ball amongst themselves.

"I'll just be a minute, sir," Alex called back.

The teacher hesitated. It was rather strange, one of the boys talking to this man in his old-fashioned blazer and striped tie. But on the other hand, this was Alex Rider and the whole school knew there was something odd about him. He had been away from school twice recently, both times without any proper explanation, and the last time he had turned up again, the whole science block had been destroyed in a mysterious fire. Mr Wiseman decided to ignore the situation. Alex could look after himself and he would doubtless turn up later. He hoped.

"Don't be too long!" he said.

He walked off and Alex found himself left on his own with Crawley.

He considered what he had just been told. Part of him mistrusted Crawley. Was it just a coincidence, his coming upon Alex on a playing field in the middle of a game? Unlikely. In the world of MI6, where everything was planned and calculated, there were no coincidences. It was one of the reasons why Alex hated it. They had used him twice now, and both times they hadn't really cared if he had lived or died, as long as he was useful to them. Crawley was part of that world and in his heart Alex disliked him as much as the rest of it.

But at the same time, he told himself, he might be reading too much into this. Crawley wasn't asking him to infiltrate a foreign embassy or parachute into Iraq or anything remotely dangerous. He was being offered two weeks at Wimbledon. It was as simple as that. A chance to watch some tennis and – if he was unlucky – spot someone trying to get their hands on the club silver. What could possibly go wrong?

"All right, Mr Crawley," he said. "I don't see why not."

"That's wonderful, Alex. I'll make the arrangements. Come on, Barker!"

Alex glanced at the dog and noticed that it had just woken up. It was staring at him with pink, bloodshot eyes. Warning him? Did the dog know something he didn't?

But then Crawley jerked on the leash and, before the dog could give away any of its master's secrets, it was quickly pulled away.

Six weeks later, Alex found himself on Centre Court, dressed in the dark green and mauve colours of the All England Tennis Club. What must surely be the final game in this qualifying round was about to begin. One of the two players sitting just centimetres away from him would go forward to the next round with a chance of winning the half a million pounds prize money that went with the winner's trophy. The other would be on the next bus home. It was only now, as he knelt beside the net and waited for the serve, that Alex really understood the power of Wimbledon and why it had won its place on the world calendar. There was simply no competition like it.

He was surrounded by the great bulk of the stadium, with thousands and thousands of spectators rising ever higher until they disappeared into the shadows at the very top. It was hard to make out any of the faces. There were too many of them and they seemed too far away. But he felt the thrill of the crowd as the players walked to their ends of the court, the perfectly striped grass seeming to glow beneath their feet. There was a clatter of applause, echoing upwards, and then a sudden stillness. Photographers hung, vulture-like, over huge telephoto lenses while beneath them, in green-covered bunkers, television cameras swung round to take in the first serve. The players faced each other: two men whose whole lives had led up to this moment and whose future in the game would be decided in the next few minutes. It was all so very English – the grass, the strawberries, the straw hats. And yet it was still bloody, a gladiatorial contest like no other.

"Quiet please, ladies and gentlemen..."

The umpire's voice rang out through the various speakers and then the first player served. Jacques Lefevre was French, twenty-two years old and new to the tournament. Nobody had expected him to get this far. He was playing a German, Jamie Blitz, one of the favourites in this year's competition. But it was Blitz who was losing – two sets down, five games to two. Alex watched him as he waited, balancing on the balls of his feet. Lefevre served. The ball thundered close to the centre line. An ace.

"Fifteen love."

Alex was close enough to see defeat in the German's eyes. This was the cruelty of the game; the psychology of it. Lose your mental edge and you could lose everything. That was what had happened to Blitz now. Alex could almost smell it in his sweat. As he walked to the other side of the court to face the next serve, his whole body looked heavy, as if it was taking all his strength just to keep himself there. He lost the next point and the one after. Alex sprinted across the court, snatched up a ball and just had time to roll it up to the ballboy at left base one. Not that it would be needed. It looked as if there would be only one more serve in the game.

And sure enough, Lefevre managed a final ace, falling to his knees, fists clenched in triumph. It was a pose seen hundreds of times before on the courts of Wimbledon and the audience duly rose to its feet, applauding. But it hadn't been a good match. Blitz should have won. Certainly the game shouldn't have ended in three straight sets. He had been terribly off form and the young Frenchman had walked all over him.

Alex collected the last of the balls and sent them rolling up to the far corner. He stood to attention while the players shook hands, first with each other, then with the umpire. Blitz walked towards him and started packing up his sports bag. Alex studied his face. The German looked dazed, as if he couldn't quite believe he had lost. Then he picked up his things and walked away. He gave one last salute to the audience and walked off the court. Lefevre was still signing autographs for the front row. Blitz had already been forgotten.

"It was a really bad game," Alex said. "I don't know what was wrong with Blitz. He seemed to be sleepwalking half the time."

It was an hour later and Alex was sitting at a table in the Complex, the set of rooms underneath the umpire's office at the corner of Number One Court where the two hundred boys and girls who work throughout the tournament have their meals, get changed and relax. He was having a drink with two other ballboys and a ballgirl. He had become good friends with the girl in the last couple of weeks – so much so that she'd invited him to join her and her family when they went down to Cornwall after Wimbledon finished. She was dark-haired, with bright blue eyes and freckles. She was also a fast runner and very fit. She went to a convent school in Wimbledon and her father was a journalist working in business and current affairs, but there was nothing remotely serious about her. She loved jokes, the ruder the better, and Alex was sure that her laughter could be heard as far away as Court Nineteen. Her name was Sabina Pleasure.

"It's too bad," Sabina said. "But I like Lefevre. He's cute. And he's only a bit older than me."

"Seven years," Alex reminded her.

"That's nothing these days. Anyway, I'll be back on Centre Court tomorrow. It's going to be hard to keep my eye on the game."

Alex smiled. He really liked Sabina, even if she did seem to have a fixation with older men. He was glad now that he had accepted Crawley's offer. "Just make sure you keep your hands on the right balls," he said.

"Rider!" The voice cut through the general chat in the cafeteria and a small, tough-looking man came striding out of a side office. This was Wally Walfor, the ex-RAF sergeant responsible for the ballboys and girls.

"Yes, sir?" Alex had spent four weeks training with Walfor and he had decided that the man was less of a monster than he pretended to be.

"I need someone for standby. Do you mind?"

"No, sir. That's fine." Alex drained his drink and stood up. He was glad that Sabina looked sorry to see him go.

Standby involved waiting outside the umpire's office in case he was needed on one of the courts or anywhere inside the grounds. In fact, Alex would enjoy sitting outside in the sun, watching the crowds. He took his tray back to the counter and was about to leave when he noticed something that made him stop and think.

There was a security guard talking on a public telephone in the corner of the room. There was nothing strange about that. There were always guards posted on the entrance to the Complex and they occasionally slipped down for a glass of water, or perhaps to use the toilet. The guard was talking quickly and excitedly, his eyes shining, as if he was passing on important news. It was impossible to hear what he was saying in the general hubbub of the cafeteria, but even so Alex sidled a little closer in the hope of picking up a few words. And that was when he noticed the tattoo. With so many ballboys and girls in the room and with the cooks busy behind the counter, the temperature had risen. The guard had taken off his jacket. He was wearing a short-sleeved shirt. And there, on his arm, just where the material ended, was a large red circle. Alex had never seen anything quite like it. A plain, undecorated circle with no writing, no sign of a picture. What could it mean?

The guard suddenly turned and saw Alex looking at him. It had happened very quickly and Alex was annoyed with himself for not taking more care. The guard didn't stop talking but he shifted his body so that the arm with the tattoo was away from Alex's view. At the same time, he covered the tattoo with his free hand. Alex smiled at him and gestured, as if he was waiting for the phone. The guard muttered a few more words and hung up. Then he put his jacket back on and moved away. Alex waited until he had gone back upstairs, then followed him. The guard had disappeared. Alex took his place on the bench outside the umpire's office and considered.

A telephone conversation in a crowded cafeteria. It shouldn't have meant anything. But the strange thing was, Alex had seen the guard a short while before, about an hour before the Blitz–Lefevre game had begun. Alex had been sent over to the Millennium Building to deliver a racquet to one of the other competitors and had been directed to the players' lounge. Climbing the staircase that swept up from the main reception, he had found himself in a large, open area with television monitors on one side and computer terminals on the other, and bright red and blue sofas in between. He knew he was privileged to be there. This was a private place. Venus Williams was sitting on one of the sofas. Tim Henman was watching a game on TV. And there was Jamie Blitz himself, getting a plastic cup of iced mineral water from the dispenser against the far wall.

The guard had also been there. Alex had noticed him standing rather awkwardly near the stairs. He was watching Blitz, but at the same time he was using a mobile phone. At least, that was what it looked like. But Alex had thought at the time that there was something strange about him. Although the mobile was at his ear, he wasn't actually talking. All his attention was on Blitz. Alex had watched as Blitz drank his water and walked away. The guard had walked off a few seconds later.

What had he been doing inside the Millennium Building? That was the first question Alex asked himself now as he sat in the sunshine, listening to the thwack of distant tennis balls and the applause of an unseen crowd. And there was something else, more puzzling. If the guard had a mobile phone, and if that phone had been working just a few hours ago, why had he needed to make a call from the public telephone in the corner of the Complex? Of course, his battery could have gone down. But even so, why use that particular phone? There were telephones all over the club, up on the surface. Could it be that he didn't want to be seen?

And why did he have a red circle tattooed on his arm? He hadn't wanted that to be seen. Alex was certain he had tried to cover it up.

And there was something else. Maybe it was just coincidence, but the guard, just like the man who had broken into the All England Tennis Club to begin with, was Chinese.

BLOOD AND STRAWBERRIES

Alex didn't make a conscious decision to follow the guard, but over the next few days he seemed drawn to him almost as if by accident. He spotted him twice more; once searching handbags at gate five and again giving directions to a couple of spectators.

Unfortunately, it was impossible to keep track of him all the time. That was the one flaw in Crawley's plan. Alex's job as a ballboy kept him on Centre Court throughout much of the day. The ballboys and girls worked a rotation system, two hours on, two hours off. At best, he could only be a part-time spy. And when he was actually on court, he quickly forgot the guard, the telephone and the entire business of the break-in as he found himself absorbed by the drama of the game.

But two days after Blitz had left Wimbledon, Alex found himself once again shadowing the guard. It was about half an hour before afternoon play was due to begin and Alex was about to report into the Complex when he saw him entering the Millennium Building again. That was strange in itself. The building had its own security staff. The public couldn't get past the reception desk without a pass. So what was he doing inside? Alex glanced at his watch. If he was late, Walfor would yell at him and possibly even move him to one of the less interesting perimeter courts. But there was still time. And he had to admit, his curiosity was aroused.

He went into the Millennium Building. As usual, nobody questioned him. His ballboy uniform was enough. He climbed the stairs, passed through the players' lounge and into the restaurant at the other side. The guard was there, ahead of him. Once again he had his mobile phone in his hand. But he wasn't making a call. He was simply standing, watching the players and the journalists as they finished their lunch.

The dining room was large and modern, with a long buffet for hot food and a central area with salads, cold drinks and fruit. There must have been about a hundred people eating at the tables and Alex recognized one or two famous faces among them. He glanced at the guard. He was standing in a corner, trying not to be noticed. At the same time, his attention seemed to be fixed on a table next to one of the windows. Alex followed the direction of his gaze. There were two men sitting at the table. One was wearing a jacket and tie. The other was in a tracksuit. Alex didn't know the first man but the second was Owen Bryant, another world-class player, an American. He would be playing later that afternoon.

The other man could have been his manager, or perhaps his agent. The two of them were talking, quietly, intensely. The manager spoke and Bryant laughed. Alex moved further into the restaurant, keeping close to the wall. He wanted to see what the guard was going to do, but he didn't want to be seen. He was glad that the restaurant was fairly crowded. There were enough people moving about to screen him.

Bryant stood up. Alex saw the guard's eyes narrow. Now the mobile phone was on its way to his ear. But he hadn't dialled a number. Bryant went over to a water dispenser and pulled a cup out of the plastic cylinder. The guard pressed a button on his phone. Bryant helped himself to some water. Alex watched as a bubble of air mushroomed up to the surface inside the plastic tank. The tennis player carried the water back to the table and sat down. The manager said something. Bryant drank his water. And that was it. Alex had seen the whole thing.

But what *had* he seen?

He had no time to answer the question. The guard was already moving, heading for the exit. Alex came to a decision. The main door was between himself and the guard and now he made for it too, keeping his head low as if he wasn't looking where he was going. He timed it perfectly. Just as the guard reached the door, Alex crashed into him. At the same moment, he swung an arm carelessly, knocking the guard's hand. The mobile phone fell to the floor.

"Oh – I'm sorry," Alex said. Before the guard could stop him, he had leant down and picked up the phone. He weighed it in his hand for a moment before passing it back. "Here you are," he said.

The guard said nothing. For a moment his eyes were locked into Alex's and Alex found himself being inspected by two very black pupils that had no life at all. The man's skin was pale and pockmarked, with a sheen of sweat across his upper lip. There was no expression anywhere on his face. Alex felt the telephone being wrenched out of his hand and then the guard had gone, the door swinging shut behind him.

Alex's hand was still in mid-air. He looked down at his palm. He was worried that he had given himself away, but at least he had learned something from the exchange. The mobile phone was a fake. It was too light. There was nothing on the screen. And it had no recognizable logo: Nokia, Panasonic, Virgin ... nothing.

He turned back to the two men at the table. Bryant had finished his water and crumpled the plastic cup in his hand. He was shaking hands with his friend, about to leave.

The water...

Alex had had an idea that was completely absurd and yet made some sort of sense out of what he had seen. He walked back across the restaurant and crouched down beside the dispenser. He had seen the same machines all over the tennis club. He took a cup and used its rim to press the tap underneath the tank. Water, filtered and chilled, ran into the cup. He could feel it, ice-cold against his palm.

"What the hell do you think you're doing?"

Alex looked up to see a red-faced man in a Wimbledon blazer towering over him. It was the first unfriendly face he'd seen since he had arrived. "I was just getting some water," he explained.

"I can see that! That's obvious. I mean, what are you doing in this restaurant? This is reserved for players, officials and press."

"I know that," Alex said. He forced himself not to lose his temper. He had no right to be here and if the official – whoever he was – complained, he might well lose his place as a ballboy. "I'm sorry, sir," he said. "I brought a racquet over for Mr Bryant. I delivered it just now. But I was thirsty, so I stopped to get a drink."

The official softened. Alex's story sounded perfectly reasonable. And he had enjoyed being addressed as "sir". He nodded. "All right. But I don't want to see you in here again." He reached out a hand and took the plastic cup. "Now on your way."

Alex arrived back at the Complex about ten minutes before play began. Walfor glowered at him but said nothing.

That afternoon, Owen Bryant lost his match against Jacques Lefevre, the same unknown Frenchman who had so unexpectedly beaten Jamie Blitz two days before. The final score was 6–4, 6–7, 4–6, 2–6. Although Bryant had won the first set, his play had steadily deteriorated throughout the afternoon. It was another surprising result. Like Blitz, Bryant had been a favourite to win.

Twenty minutes later, Alex was back in the basement restaurant, sitting with Sabina, who was drinking a Coke Lite.

"My mum and dad are here today," she was saying. "I managed to get them tickets and in return they've promised to get me a new surfboard. Have you ever surfed, Alex?"

"What?" Alex was miles away.

"I was talking about Cornwall. Surfing..."

"Yes, I've surfed." Alex had learnt with his uncle, Ian Rider. The spy whose death had so abruptly changed Alex's life. The two of them had spent a week together in San Diego, California. That had been years ago. Years that sometimes felt like centuries.

"Is there something wrong with your drink?" Sabina asked.

Alex realized he was holding his Coke in front of him, balancing it in his hand, staring at it. But he was thinking about water.

"No, it's fine..." he began.

And then, out of the corner of his eye, he saw the guard. He had come back downstairs into the Complex. Once again he was using the telephone in the corner. Alex saw him put in a coin and dial a number.

"I'll be right back," he said.

He got up and made his way over to the phone. The guard was standing with his back to him. This time he might be able to get close enough to hear what was being said.

"...will be completely successful." The guard was talking in English but with a thick accent. He still had his back to Alex. There was a pause. Then: "I'm going to meet him now. Yes ... straight away. He'll give it to me and I'll bring it to you." Another pause. Alex got the feeling that the conversation was coming to an end. He took a few steps back. "I have to go," the guard said. "Bye." He put the receiver down and walked away.

"Alex...?" Sabina called to him. She was on her own, sitting where he had left her. He realized she must have been watching what he did. He raised a hand and waved to her. He would have to find some way to explain all this later.

The guard didn't climb back up to the surface. Instead he took a door which led to a long corridor, stretching into the distance. Alex opened the door and followed.

The All England Tennis Club covers a huge area. On the surface it looks a bit like a theme park, though one whose only theme is tennis. Thousands of people stream along paths and covered walkways, an uninterrupted flow of brilliant white shirts, sunglasses and straw hats. As well as the courts, there are tearooms and cafés, restaurants, shops, hospitality tents, ticket booths and security points.

But there is a second, less well-known world underneath all this. The entire club is connected by an underground maze of corridors, tunnels and roads, some big enough to drive a car through. If it's easy to get lost above ground, it's even easier to lose yourself below. There are very few signs and there's nobody standing at the corner to offer you information. This is the world of the cooks and the waiters, the refuse collectors and the delivery men. Somehow they find their way around, coming up in the daylight exactly where they are needed before disappearing again.

The corridor in which Alex found himself was called the Royal Route and connected the Millennium Building with Court Number One, allowing the players to make their way to the game without being seen. It was clean and empty, with a bright blue carpet. The guard was about twenty metres ahead of him and it felt eerie to be so suddenly alone. There were just the two of them there. Above them, on the surface, there would be people everywhere, milling about in the sunlight. Alex was grateful for the carpet, which muffled the sound of his feet. It seemed that the guard was in a hurry. So far he hadn't stopped or turned round.

The guard reached a wooden door marked RESTRICTED. Without stopping, he went through. Alex paused for a moment, then followed. Now he found himself in an altogether grimier environment, a cement corridor with yellow industrial markings and fat ventilation pipes overhead. The air smelt of oil and garbage, and Alex knew that he had arrived at the so-called Buggy Route, a supply lane that forms a great circle underneath the club. A couple of teenagers in green aprons and jeans walked past him, pushing two plastic bins. A waitress went the other way, carrying a tray of dirty plates. There was no sign of the guard and for a moment Alex thought he'd lost him. But then he saw a figure disappearing behind a series of translucent plastic strips that hung from the ceiling to the floor. He could just make out the man's uniform on the other side of the barrier. He hurried forward and went through.

Alex realized two things at the same moment. He no longer had any idea where he was – and he was there on his own.

He was in an underground chamber, banana-shaped, curving round, with concrete pillars supporting the roof. It looked like an underground carpark and there were indeed three or four cars parked in bays next to the raised walkway where he was standing now. But most of the space was taken up by trash. There were empty cardboard boxes, wooden pallets, a rusting cement mixer, bits of old fencing and broken down coffee vending machines, thrown out and left to rot on the damp cement floor. The air smelled bad and Alex could hear a constant whine, like an electric saw, coming from a garbage compactor just out of his sight. And yet the area was also used for the storage of food and drink. There were beer barrels, hundreds of bottles of fizzy drinks, gas cylinders and, clustered together, eight or nine massive white boxes – refrigerators, each one carrying the label RAWLINGS REFRIGERATION.

Alex looked up at the roof. It was slanting upwards and the shape reminded him of something. Of course! The raked seating around Court Number One! That was where he was – in the loading bay beneath the tennis court. This was the underbelly of Wimbledon all right. This was where all the supplies arrived and where all the trash left. And right now, ten thousand people were sitting just a few metres above his head, enjoying the game, unaware that everything they consumed throughout the day began and ended here.

But where was the guard? Why had he come here and who was he going to meet? Alex crept forward carefully, once again feeling very alone. He was on a raised platform with the single word DANGER repeated in yellow letters along its edge. He didn't need to be told. He came to a flight of steps and went down, moving into the main body of the chamber, on the same level as the refrigerators. He walked past a stack of gas cylinders, pressurized carbon dioxide. He had no idea what they were for. Half the things down here seemed to have been dumped for no good reason.

He was fairly sure now that the guard had gone. Why would he want to meet anyone down here? For the first time since he had left the Complex, Alex played back the telephone conversation in his mind.

I'm going to meet him now. Yes ... straight away. He'll give it to me...

It sounded ridiculous, fake, like something out of a bad film. Even as Alex realized this and knew that he had been tricked, he heard the screaming sound, saw the dark shape rushing out of the shadows. He was in the middle of the concrete floor, out in the open. The guard was behind the wheel of a fork-lift truck, the metal prongs jutting out towards him like the horns of an enormous bull. Powered by its forty-eight volt electric engine, the truck was speeding towards him on pneumatic tyres. Alex glanced up and saw the heavy wooden pallets, a dozen of them, balanced high above the cabin. He saw the guard's smile, a gleam of ugly teeth in an uglier face. The truck covered the distance between them with astonishing speed then came to a sudden halt as the guard slammed on the brake. Alex yelled and threw himself to one side. The wooden pallets, carried forward by the truck's momentum, slid off the forks and came clattering down. Alex should have been crushed, would have been, but for the beer barrels. A line of them had taken the weight of the pallets, leaving a tiny triangle of space. Alex heard the wood smashing centimetres above his head. Splinters rained down on his neck and back. Dust and dirt smothered him. But he was still alive. Choking and half blinded, he crawled forward as the fork-lift truck reversed and prepared to come after him again.

How could he have been so stupid? The guard had seen him that first time in the Complex, when he had made his telephone call. Alex had stood there, gaping at the tattoo on the man's arm and had thought that his ballboy uniform would be enough to protect him. And then, in the Millennium Building, Alex had clumsily knocked into him to get his hands on the mobile phone. Of course the guard had known who he was and what he was doing. It didn't matter that he was a teenager. He was dangerous. He had to be taken out.

And so he had laid a trap so obvious that it wouldn't have fooled ... well, a schoolboy. Alex might want to think of himself as some sort of superspy who had twice saved the whole world, but that was nonsense. The guard had made a fake phone call and tricked Alex into following him into this desolate area. And now he was going to kill him. It wouldn't matter who he was or how much he had found out once he was dead.

Choking and sick, Alex staggered to his feet just as the fork-lift truck bore down on him a second time. He turned and ran. The guard looked almost ridiculous, hunched up in the tiny cabin. But the machine he was driving was fast, powerful and incredibly flexible, spinning a full circle on a ten pence piece. Alex tried changing direction, sprinting to one side. The truck spun round and followed. Could he make it back to the raised platform? No. Alex knew it was too far away.

Now the guard reached out and pressed a button. The metal forks shuddered and dropped down so that they were less like horns, more like the twin swords of some nightmare medieval knight. Which way should he dive? Left or right? Alex just had time to make up his mind before the truck was on him. He dived to the right, rolling over and over on the concrete. The guard pulled the joystick and the machine spun round again. Alex twisted and the heavy wheels missed him by barely a centimetre, then crashed into one of the pillars.

There was a pause. Alex got up, his head spinning. For a brief second, he hoped that the collision might have knocked the guard out, but with a sick feeling in his stomach he saw the man step out of the cabin, brushing a little dust off the arm of his jacket. He was moving with the slow confidence of a man who knew that he was in total command. And Alex could already see why. Automatically, the guard had taken the stance of a martial arts expert; feet slightly apart, centre of gravity low. His hands were curving in the air, waiting to strike. He was still smiling. All he could see was a defenceless boy – and one already weakened by two encounters with the fork-lift truck.

With a sudden cry, he lashed out, his right hand slicing towards Alex's throat. If the blow had made contact, Alex would have been killed. But at the last second he brought up both his fists, crossing his arms to form a block. The guard was taken by surprise and Alex took advantage of the moment to kick out with his right foot, aiming for the groin. But the guard was no longer there, having swivelled to one side, and in that moment Alex knew he was up against a fighter who was stronger, faster and more experienced than him and that he really didn't have a chance.

The guard swung round, and this time the back of his hand caught Alex on the side of his head. Alex heard the crack. For a moment he was blinded. He reeled backwards, crashing into a metal surface. It was the door of one of the fridges. Somehow he caught hold of the handle and as he stumbled forward, the door opened. He felt a blast of cold across the back of his neck and perhaps that was what revived him and gave him the strength to throw himself forward, ducking underneath another vicious kick that had been aimed at his throat.

Alex was in a bad way and he knew it. His nose was bleeding. He could feel the warm blood trickling down over the corner of his mouth. His head was spinning and the electric light bulbs seemed to be flashing in front of his eyes. But the guard wasn't even breathing heavily. For the first time, Alex wondered what it was that he had stumbled onto. What could be so important to the guard that he would be ready to murder a fourteen-year-old boy in cold blood, without even asking questions? Alex wiped the blood away from his mouth and cursed Crawley for coming to him on the football pitch, cursed himself for listening. A front row seat at Wimbledon? At Wimbledon cemetery, perhaps.

The guard started walking towards him. Alex tensed himself, then dived out of the way, avoiding a lethal double strike of foot and fist. He landed next to a dustbin, overflowing with rubbish. Using all his strength, he picked it up and threw it, grinning through gritted teeth as the bin crashed into his attacker, spilling rotting food all over him. The guard swore and stumbled backwards. Alex ran round the back of the fridge, trying to catch his breath, searching for a way out.

He had only seconds to spare. He knew that the guard would be coming after him and next time he would finish it. He'd had enough. Alex looked left and right. He saw the cylinders of compressed gas and dragged one out of its wire frame. The cylinder seemed to weigh a ton but Alex was desperate. He wrenched the tap on and heard the gas jetting out. Then, holding the cylinder in front of him with both hands, he stepped forward. At that moment, the guard appeared round the side of the fridge. Alex jerked forward, his muscles screaming, shoving the cylinder into the man's face. The gas exploded into the man's eyes, temporarily blinding him. Alex brought the cylinder down, then up again. The metal rim clanged into the guard's head, just above his nose. Alex felt the jolt of solid steel against bone. The guard reeled back. Alex took another step forward. This time he swung the cylinder like a cricket bat, hitting the man with incredible force in the shoulders and neck. The guard never had a chance. He didn't even cry out as he was thrown off his feet and sent hurtling forward into the open fridge.

Alex dropped the cylinder and groaned. It felt as if his arms had been wrenched out of their sockets. His head was still spinning and he wondered if his nose had been broken. He limped forward and looked into the fridge.

There was a curtain of plastic sheets and behind it a mountain of cardboard boxes, each and every one of them filled to the brim with strawberries. Alex couldn't help smiling. Strawberries and cream was one of Wimbledon's greatest traditions, served at crazy prices in the kiosks and restaurants above ground. This was where they were stored. The guard had landed in the middle of the boxes, crushing many of them. He was unconscious, half buried in a blanket of strawberries, his head resting on a bright red pillow of them. Alex stood in the doorway, leaning on the frame for support, allowing the cold air to wash over him. There was a thermostat next to him. Outside, the weather was hot. The strawberries had to be kept chilled.

He took one last look at the man who had tried to kill him.

"Out cold," he said.

Then he reached out and twisted the thermostat control, sending the temperature down below zero.

Out colder.

He closed the fridge door and limped painfully away.

THE CRIBBER

It had taken the engineer just a few minutes to take the water dispenser apart. Now he reached inside and carefully disengaged a slim glass phial from a tangle of wires and circuit boards.

"Built into the filter," he said. "There's a valve system. Very ingenious."

He passed the phial to a stern-looking woman who held it up to the light, examining its contents. The phial was half filled with a transparent liquid. She swilled it round, applied a little to her index finger and sniffed it. Her eyes narrowed. "Librium," she announced. She had a clipped, matter-of-fact way of speaking. "Nasty little drug. A spoonful will put you out cold. A couple of drops, though ... they'll just confuse you. Basically knock you off balance."

The restaurant, and indeed the entire Millennium Building, had been closed for the night. There were three other men there. John

Crawley was one. Next to him stood a uniformed policeman, obviously senior. The third man was white-haired and serious, wearing a Wimbledon tie. Alex was sitting to one side, feeling suddenly tired and out of place. Nobody apart from Crawley knew that he worked for MI6. As far as they were concerned, he was just a ballboy who had somehow stumbled on the truth.

Alex was dressed in his own clothes now. He had phoned Crawley, then taken a shower and changed, leaving his ballboy uniform back in his locker. Somehow he knew that he had worn it for the last time. He wondered if he would be allowed to keep the shorts, shirt and Hi-Tec trainers with the crossed racquets logo embroidered on the tongue. The uniform is the only payment Wimbledon ballboys and girls receive.

"It's pretty clear what was going on," Crawley was saying now. "You remember, I was worried about that break-in we had, Sir Norman." This to the man in the club tie. "Well, it seems I was right. They didn't want to steal anything. They came here to fix up the water dispensers. In the restaurant, in the lounge and probably all over the building. Remote control ... is that right, Henderson?"

Henderson was the man who had taken the water dispenser apart. Another MI6 operative. "That's right, sir," he replied. "The dispenser functioned perfectly normally, giving out iced water. But when it received a radio signal – and that's what our friend was doing with the fake mobile phone – it injected a few millilitres of this drug, Librium. Not enough to show up in a random blood test if anybody happened to be tested. But enough to destroy their game."

Alex remembered the German player, Blitz, leaving the court after he'd lost his match. He had looked dazed and out of focus. But he had been more than that. He had been drugged.

"It's transparent," the woman added. "And it has virtually no taste. In a cup of iced water it wouldn't have been noticed."

"But I don't understand!" Sir Norman cut in. "What was the point?"

"I think I can answer that," the policeman said. "As you know, the guard isn't talking, but the tattoo on his arm would indicate that he is – or was – a member of the Big Circle."

"And what exactly would that be?" Sir Norman spluttered.

"It's a triad, sir. A Chinese gang. The triads, of course, are involved in a range of criminal activities. Drugs. Vice. Illegal immigration. And gambling. I would guess this operation was related to the latter. Like any other sporting event, Wimbledon attracts millions of pounds' worth of bets. Now, as I understand it, the young Frenchman – Lefevre – began the tournament with odds of three hundred to one against his actually winning."

"But then he beat Blitz and Bryant," Crawley said.

"Exactly. I'm sure Lefevre had no idea, personally, what was going on. But if all his opponents were drugged before they went onto the court... Well, it happened twice. It could have gone on right up to the final. Big Circle would have made a killing! A hundred thousand pounds bet on the Frenchman would have brought them thirty million."

Sir Norman stood up. "The important thing now is that nobody finds out about this," he said. "It would be a national scandal and disastrous for our reputation. In fact we'd probably have to begin the whole tournament again!" He glanced at Alex but spoke to Crawley. "Can this boy be trusted not to talk?" he asked.

"I won't tell anyone what happened," Alex said.

"Good. Good."

The policeman nodded. "You did a very good job," he added. "Spotting this chap in the first place and then following him and all the rest of it. Although, I have to say, I think it was rather irresponsible to lock him in the deep freeze."

"He tried to kill me," Alex said.

"Even so! He could have frozen to death. As it is, he may well have lost a couple of fingers from frostbite."

"I hope that won't spoil his tennis playing."

"Well, I don't know..." The policeman coughed. He was clearly unable to make Alex out. "Anyway, well done. But next time, do try to think what you're doing. I'm sure you wouldn't want anyone to get hurt!"

To hell with the lot of them!

Alex stood watching the waves, black and silver in the moonlight as they rolled into the sweeping curve of Fistral Beach. He was trying to put the policeman, Sir Norman and the whole of Wimbledon out of his mind. He had more or less saved the entire All England Tennis Tournament and although he hadn't been expecting a season ticket in the royal box and tea with the Duchess of Kent, nor had he thought he would be bundled out quite so hastily. He had watched the finals, on his own, on TV. At least they'd let him keep his ballboy uniform.

And there was one other good thing that had come out of it all. Sabina hadn't forgotten her invitation.

He was standing on the veranda of the house her parents had rented, a house that would have been ugly anywhere else in the world but which seemed perfectly suited to its position on the edge of a cliff overlooking the Cornish coast. It was old-fashioned, square, part brick, part white-painted wood. It had five bedrooms, three staircases and too many doors. Its garden was more dead than alive, blasted by salt and sea spray. The house was called Brook's Leap, although nobody knew who Brook was, why he had leapt, or even if he had survived. Alex had been there for three days. He had been invited to stay the week.

There was a movement behind him. A door had opened and Sabina Pleasure stepped out, wrapped in a thick towelling robe, carrying two glasses. It was warm outside. Although it had been raining when Alex arrived – it nearly always seemed to be raining in Cornwall – the weather had cleared and this was suddenly a summer's night. Sabina had left him outside while she went in to have a bath. Her hair was still wet. The robe fell loosely down to her bare feet. Alex thought she looked much older than her fifteen years.

"I brought you a Coke," she said.

"Thanks."

The veranda was wide, with a low balcony, a swing-chair and a table. Sabina set the glasses down then sat down herself. Alex joined her. The wooden frame of the swing chair creaked and they swung together, looking out at the view. For a long time neither of them said anything. Then, suddenly...

"Why don't you tell me the truth?" Sabina asked.

"What d'you mean?"

"I was just thinking about Wimbledon. Why did you leave straight after the quarter-finals? You were there one minute. Court Number One! And then—"

"I told you," Alex cut in, feeling uncomfortable. "I wasn't well."

"That's not what I heard. There was a rumour that you were involved in some sort of fight. And that's another thing. I've noticed you in your swimming shorts. I've never seen anyone with so many cuts and bruises."

"I'm bullied at school."

"I don't think so. I've got a friend who goes to Brookland. She says you're never there. You keep disappearing. You were away twice last term and the day you got back, half the school burnt down."

Alex leant forward and picked up his Coke, rolling the cold glass between his hands. An aeroplane was crossing the sky, tiny in the great darkness, its lights blinking on and off.

"All right, Sab," he said. "I'm not really a schoolboy. I'm a spy, a teenage James Bond. I have to take time off from school to save the world. I've done it twice so far. The first time was here in Cornwall. The second time was in France. What else do you want to know?"

Sabina smiled. "All right, Alex. Ask a stupid question..." She drew her legs up, snuggling into the warmth of the towelling robe. "But there *is* something different about you. You're like no boy I've ever met."

"Kids?" Sabina's mother was calling out from the kitchen. "Shouldn't you be thinking about bed?"

It was ten o'clock. The two of them would be getting up at five to catch the surf.

"Five minutes!" Sabina called back.

"I'm counting."

Sabina sighed. "Mothers!"

But Alex had never known his mother.

Twenty minutes later, getting into bed, he thought about Sabina Pleasure and her parents; her father a slightly bookish man with long grey hair and spectacles, her mother round and cheerful, more like Sabina herself. There were only the three of them. Maybe that was what made them so close. They lived in west London and rented this house for four weeks every summer.

He turned off the light and lay back in the darkness. His room, set high up in the roof of the house, had only one small window and he could see the moon, glowing white, as perfectly round as a one penny piece. From the moment he had arrived, they'd treated him as if they'd known him all his life. Every family has its own routine and Alex had been surprised how quickly he had fallen in with theirs, joining them on long walks along the cliffs, helping with the shopping and the cooking, or simply sharing the silence – reading and watching the sea.

Why couldn't he have had a family like this? Alex felt an old, familiar sadness creep up on him. His parents had died before he was even a few weeks old. The uncle who had brought him up and who had taught him so much had still been, in many ways, a stranger to him. He had no brothers or sisters. Sometimes he felt as isolated as the plane he had seen from the veranda, making its long journey across the night sky, unnoticed and alone.

Alex pulled the pillows up around his head, annoyed with himself. He had friends. He enjoyed his life. He'd managed to catch up with his work at school and he was having a great holiday. And with a bit of luck, with the Wimbledon business behind him, MI6 would leave him alone. So why was he letting himself slip into this mood?

The door opened. Somebody had come into his room. It was Sabina. She was leaning over him. He felt her hair fall against his cheek and smelled her faint perfume; flowers and white musk. Her lips brushed gently against his.

"You're much cuter than James Bond," she said.

And then she was gone. The door closed behind her.

Five-fifteen the next morning.

If this had been a schoolday, Alex wouldn't have woken up for another two hours, and even then he would have dragged himself out of bed unwillingly. But this morning he had been awake in an instant. He had felt the energy and tension coursing through him. And walking down to Fistral Beach with the dawn light pink in the sky, he could feel it still. The sea was calling to him, daring him to come in.

"Look at the waves!" Sabina said.

"They're big," Alex muttered.

"They're huge. This is amazing!"

It was true. Alex had been surfing twice before – once in Norfolk, once with his uncle in California – but he had never seen anything like this. There was no wind. The local radio station had warned of deep water squalls and an exceptionally high tide. Together these had produced waves that took his breath away. They were at least ten feet high, rolling slowly inland as if they carried the weight of the whole ocean on their shoulders. The crash as they broke was huge, terrifying. Alex could feel his heart pounding. He looked at the moving walls of water, the dark blue, the foaming white. Was he really going to ride one of these monsters on a flimsy board made of nothing more than a strip of fibreglass?

Sabina had seen him hesitate. "What d'you think?" she asked.

"I don't know..." Alex replied and realized he was shouting to make himself heard above the roar of the waves.

"The sea's too strong!" Sabina was a good surfer. The morning before, Alex had watched her skilfully manoeuvring some nasty reefbreaks close to the shore. But now she looked uncertain. "Maybe we should go back to bed!" she yelled.

Alex took in the whole scene. There were another half-dozen surfers on the beach and, in the far distance, a man steadying a jet ski in the shallow water. He knew that he and Sabina would be the youngest people there. Like her, he was wearing a three millimetre neoprene wetsuit and boots which would protect him from the cold. So why was he shivering? Alex didn't have his own board but had rented an Ocean Magic thruster. Sabina's was a wider, thicker board, going for stability rather than speed, but Alex preferred the thruster for its grip and the feeling of control provided by its three fins. He was glad also that he had chosen an eight-foot-four. If he was going to catch waves as big as these, he was going to need the extra length.

If...

Alex wasn't sure he was going into the water. The waves looked about twice as tall as him and he knew that if he made a mistake he could all too easily get killed. Sabina's parents had forbidden her to go in if the sea looked too rough and he had to admit, it had never looked rougher. He watched another wave come crashing down and might have turned back if he hadn't heard one surfer calling to another, the words whipping across the empty sands.

"The Cribber!"

It couldn't be true. The Cribber had come to Fistral Beach. Alex had heard the name many times. The Cribber had become a legend not just in Cornwall but throughout the surfing world. Its first recorded visit had been in September 1966, more than twenty feet high, the most powerful wave ever to hit the English coast. Since then there had been occasional sightings, but few had seen it and fewer still had managed to take the ride.

"The Cribber! The Cribber!" The other surfers were calling its name, whooping and shouting. He watched them dance across the sand, their boards over their heads. Suddenly he knew that he had to go into the water. He was too young. The waves were too big. But he would never forgive himself if he missed the chance.

"I'm going!" he shouted and ran forward, carrying his board in front of him, the tail connected to his ankle by a tough urethane leash. Out of the corner of his eye he saw Sabina raise a hand in a gesture of good luck, but by then he had reached the edge of the sea and felt the cold water grip his ankles. He threw the board down and dived on top of it, the momentum carrying him forward. And then he was lying flat on his stomach, his legs stretched out behind him, his hands paddling furiously over the top of the board. This was the most exhausting part of the journey. Alex concentrated on his arms and shoulders, keeping the rest of his body still. He had a long way to go. He needed to conserve energy.

He heard a sound above the pounding of the sea and noticed the jet ski pulling away from the shore. That puzzled him. PWCs – personal water craft – were rare in Cornwall and he certainly hadn't seen this one before. Normally they were used to tow surfers out to the bigger waves, but this jet ski was striking out on its own. He could see the rider, hooded, in a black wetsuit. Was he – or she – planning to ride the Cribber on a machine?

He forgot about it. His arms were getting tired now and he hadn't even made it halfway. His cupped hands scooped the water and he felt himself shoot forward. The other surfers were well ahead of him. He could see the point where the waves crested, about twenty metres away. A mountain of water rose up in front of him and he duck-dived through it. For a moment he was blind. He tasted salt and the chill of the water hammered into his skull. But then he was out the other side. He fixed his eyes on the horizon and redoubled his efforts. The thruster carried him forward as if it had somehow been filled with a life of its own.

Alex stopped and drew breath. Suddenly everything seemed very silent. He was still lying on his stomach, rising and falling as he was swept over the waves. He looked back at the shoreline and was surprised to see how far he had come. Sabina was sitting watching him, a tiny speck in the distance. The nearest surfer was about thirty metres away; too far to help if anything went wrong. There was a knot of fear in his stomach and he wondered if he hadn't been a bit hasty, coming out here on his own. But it was too late now.

He sensed it before he saw it. It was as if the world had chosen that moment to come to an end and all nature was taking one final breath. He turned and there it was. The Cribber was coming. It was hurtling towards him. Now it was too late to change his mind.

For a few seconds Alex stared in astonishment at the rolling, curving, thundering water. It was like watching a four-storey building wrench itself out of the ground and hurl itself onto the street. It was built entirely out of water, but the water was alive. Alex could feel its incredible strength. Suddenly, awesomely, it rose up in front of him. And went on rising until it had blotted out the sky.

Techniques that he had learnt a long time ago took over automatically. Alex grabbed the edge of the board and turned round so that he was once again facing the shore. He forced himself to wait until the last second. Move too late and he would miss everything. But too early and he would simply be crushed. His muscles tensed. His teeth were chattering. His whole body seemed to have become electrified.

Now!

This was the most difficult part, the movement that was hardest to learn but impossible to forget. The pop-up. Alex could feel the board travelling with the pulse of the wave. His speed and the speed of the water had become one. He brought his hands down, flat on the board, arched his back and pushed. At the same time, he brought his right leg forward. Goofy-footed. When he was snowboarding, he was exactly the same. But he didn't care, as long as he could actually stand up without losing his balance, and already he was doing just that, balancing the two main forces, speed and gravity, as the thruster sliced diagonally across the wave.

He stood straight, his arms out, his teeth bared, perfectly centred on the board. He had done it! He was riding the Cribber. Sheer exhilaration coursed through him. He could feel the power of the wave. He was part of it. He was plugged into the world and although he must be travelling at sixty, seventy kilometres per hour, time seemed to have slowed down almost to a halt and he was frozen in this one, perfect moment that would be with him for the rest of his life. He yelled out loud, an animal cry that he couldn't even hear. Spray rushed into his face, exploding around him. He could barely feel the thruster under his feet. He was flying. He had never been more alive.

And then he heard it over the roar of the waves. It was coming up fast to one side of him, the whine of a petrol engine. To hear anything mechanical here, at this time, was so unlikely that he thought he must have imagined it. Then he remembered the jet ski. It must have gone out to sea and then circled round, behind the waves. Now it was coming in fast.

His first thought was that the rider was "dropping in". It was one of the unwritten laws of surfing. Alex was up and riding. This was his wave. The rider had no right to cut into his space. But at the same time, he knew that was crazy. Fistral Beach was practically deserted. There was no need to fight for space. And anyway, a jet ski coming after a surfer ... it was unheard of.

The engine was louder now. Alex couldn't see the jet ski. His entire concentration was fixed on the Cribber, on keeping his balance, and he didn't dare turn round. He was suddenly aware of the rushing water, thousands of gallons of it, thundering under his feet. If he fell he would die, ripped apart before he could drown. What was the jet ski doing? Why was it coming so close?

Alex knew he was in danger quite suddenly and with total certainty. What was happening had nothing to do with Cornwall and his surfing holiday. His other life, his life with MI6, had caught up with him. He remembered being chased down the mountainside at Point Blanc and knew that the same thing was happening again. Who or why didn't matter. He had just seconds to do something before the jet ski ran him down.

He flicked his head and saw it for just a second. A black nose like a torpedo. Gleaming chrome and glass. A man squatting low over the controls, his eyes fixed on Alex. The eyes were filled with hatred. They were less than a metre away.

There was only one thing Alex could do and he did it instantly, without thinking. The aerial is a move that demands split-second timing and total confidence. Alex twisted round and projected himself off the top of the wave and out into the air. At the same time, he crouched down and seized hold of the thruster, one hand on each side. Now he really was flying, suspended in mid-air as the wave rolled away beneath him. He saw the jet ski race past, covering the area where he had been only seconds before. He spun round, drawing an almost complete circle in the air. At the last moment, he remembered to place his foot right in the centre of the board. This would take all his weight when he landed.

The water rushed up to meet him. Alex finished his circle and plunged once again onto the face of the wave. It was a perfect landing. Water exploded around him but he remained upright and now he was just behind the jet ski. The rider turned back and Alex saw the look of astonishment on his face. The man was Chinese. Impossibly, incredibly, he was holding a gun. Alex saw it come up, water dripping off the barrel. This time there was nowhere he could go. He didn't have the strength to try another aerial. With a shout, he threw himself off the board and forward, onto the jet ski. He felt a jolt, his leg almost being pulled off as his board was torn away by the suddenly malevolent water.

There was an explosion. The man had fired. But the bullet missed. Alex thought he felt it pass over his shoulder. At the same moment, his hands grabbed the man's throat. His knees crashed into the side of the jet ski. And then the entire world was whipped away as man and machine lost control and tumbled into a spinning vortex of water. Alex's leg jerked a second time and he felt the leash snap. He heard a shout. Suddenly the man wasn't there any more. Alex was on his own. He couldn't breathe. Water pounded down on him. He felt himself being sucked helplessly into it. He couldn't struggle. His arms and legs were useless. He had no strength left. He opened his mouth to scream and the water rushed in.

Then his shoulder hit something hard and he knew he had reached the bottom of the sea and that this would have to be his grave. He had dared to play with the Cribber and the Cribber had taken its revenge. Somewhere, far above, another wave broke over him, but Alex didn't see it. He lay where he was, finally at peace.

TWO WEEKS IN THE SUN

Alex wasn't sure what was more surprising. To be still alive, or to find himself back in the London headquarters of the Special Operations division of MI6.

The fact that he was still breathing was, he knew, entirely down to Sabina. She had been sitting on the beach, watching in awe as he rode the Cribber towards her. She had seen the jet ski coming up behind him even before he did and had known instinctively that something was wrong. She had started running the moment Alex had leapt into the air and was already in the water by the time he crashed down next to the jet ski and then disappeared below the surface. Later on, she would say that there had been a collision ... a terrible accident. From that distance, it was impossible to see what had really taken place.

Sabina was a strong swimmer and luck was on her side. Although the water was murky and the waves still huge, she knew where Alex had gone down and she was there in less than a minute. She found him on her third dive, dragged his unconscious body to the surface and then pulled him ashore. She had learnt mouth-to-mouth resuscitation at school and she used that knowledge now, pressing her lips against his, forcing the air into his lungs. Even then, she was sure that Alex was dead. He wasn't breathing. His eyes were closed. Sabina pounded on his chest – once, twice – and was finally rewarded with a sudden spasm and a fit of coughing as Alex came to. By then, some of the other surfers had arrived. One of them had a mobile phone and called for an ambulance. There was no sign of the man on the jet ski.

Alex had been lucky too. As it turned out, he had ridden the Cribber just far enough to be near the end of its journey, when the wave had been at its weakest. A ton of water had fallen onto him, but five seconds earlier and it might have been ten tons. Also, he hadn't been too far from the shore when Sabina found him. Any further out and she might never have found him at all.

Five days had passed since then.

It was Monday morning, the start of a new week. Alex was sitting in room 1605, on the sixteenth floor of the anonymous building in Liverpool Street. He had sworn that he would never return here. The man and the woman with him in the room were the last two people he wanted to see. And yet here he was. He had been drawn in as easily as a fish in a net.

As usual, Alan Blunt didn't seem particularly pleased to see him, preferring to study the file on the desk in front of him rather than the boy himself. It was the fifth or sixth time Alex had met the man in overall command of this section of MI6 and he still knew almost nothing about him. Blunt was about fifty, a man in a suit in an office. He didn't seem to smoke and Alex couldn't imagine him drinking either. Was he married? Did he have children? Did he spend his weekends walking in the park or fishing or watching football matches? Somehow Alex doubted it. He wondered if Blunt had any existence at all outside these four walls. He was a man defined by his work. His whole life was devoted to secrets, and in the end his own life had become a secret itself.

He looked up from the neatly printed report. "Crawley had no right to involve you in this business," he said.

Alex said nothing. For once, he wasn't sure that he disagreed.

"The Wimbledon tennis championships. You nearly got yourself killed." He glanced quizzically at Alex. "And this business in Cornwall. I don't like my agents getting involved in dangerous sports."

"I'm not one of your agents," Alex said.

"There's enough danger in the job without adding to it," Blunt went on, ignoring him. "What happened to the man on the jet ski?" he asked.

"We're interrogating him now," Mrs Jones replied.

The deputy head of Special Operations was wearing a grey trouser suit, with a black leather handbag that matched her eyes. There was a silver brooch on her lapel, shaped like a miniature dagger. It seemed appropriate.

She had been the first to visit Alex as he'd recovered in hospital in Newquay and she at least had been concerned about what had happened. Of course, she had shown little or no emotion. If anyone had asked, she would have said that she didn't want to lose someone who had been useful to her and who might be useful again. But Alex suspected this was only half the story. She was a woman and he was fourteen years old. If Mrs Jones had a son, he could well be the same age as Alex. That made a difference – one that she wasn't quite able to ignore.

"We found a tattoo on the man's arm," she continued. "It seems that he was also a member of the Big Circle gang." She turned to Alex. "The Big Circle is a relatively new triad," she explained. "It's also, unfortunately, one of the most violent."

"I think I'd noticed," Alex said.

"The man you knocked out and refrigerated at Wimbledon was a *Sai-lo*. That means 'little brother'. You have to understand how these people work. You smashed their operation and made them lose face. That's the last thing they can afford. So they sent someone after you. He hasn't said anything yet but we believe he's a *Dai-lo*, or a 'big brother'. He'll have a rank of 438 ... that's one under the Dragon Head, the leader of the triad. And now he's failed too. It's a little unfortunate, Alex, that as well as half-drowning him, you also broke his nose. The triad will take that as another humiliation."

"I didn't do anything," Alex said. It was true. He remembered how the thruster had finally been torn away from his ankle. It wasn't his fault that it had hit the man in the face.

"That's not how they'll see it," Mrs Jones went on. She sounded like a schoolteacher. "What we're dealing with here is *Guan-shi*."

Alex waited for her to explain.

"*Guan-shi* is what gives Big Circle its power," she said. "It's a system of mutual respect. It ties all the members together. It essentially means that if you hurt one of them, you hurt them all. And if one of them becomes your enemy, they all do."

"You attack one of their people at Wimbledon," Blunt rasped, "they send another down to Cornwall."

"You take out their man in Cornwall, the order goes out to the other members of the triad to kill you," Mrs Jones said.

"How many other members are there?" Alex asked.

"About nineteen thousand at the last count," Blunt replied.

There was a long silence, punctured only by the distant traffic sixteen floors below.

"Every minute you stay in this country, you're in danger," Mrs Jones said. "And there's not a great deal we can do. Of course, we have some influence with the triads. If we let the right people know that you're protected by us, it may be possible to call them off. But that's going to take time and the fact of the matter is, they're probably working on the next plan of attack right now."

"You can't go home," Blunt said. "You can't go back to school. You can't go anywhere on your own. That woman who looks after you, the housekeeper, we've already arranged for her to be sent out of London. We can't take any chances."

"So what am I meant to do?" Alex asked.

Mrs Jones glanced at Blunt, who nodded. Neither of them looked particularly concerned and he suddenly realized that things had worked out exactly as they wanted. Somehow, without knowing it, he had played right into their hands.

"By coincidence, Alex," Mrs Jones began, "a few days ago we had a request for your services. It came from an American intelligence service. The Central Intelligence Agency – or CIA as you probably know them. They need a young person for an operation they happen to be mounting and they wondered if you might be available."

Alex was surprised. MI6 had used him twice and both times they had stressed that nobody was to know. Now, it seemed, they had been boasting about their teenage spy. Worse than that, they had even been preparing to lend him out, like a library book.

As if reading his mind, Mrs Jones raised a hand. "We had told them, of course, that you had no wish to continue in this line of work," she said. "That was, after all, what you had told us. A schoolboy, not a spy. That's what you said. But it does seem now that everything has changed. I'm sorry, Alex, but for whatever reason, you've chosen to go back into the field and unfortunately you're in danger. You have to disappear. This might be the best way."

"You want me to go to America?" Alex asked.

"Not exactly America," Blunt cut in. "We want you to go to Cuba ... or, at least, to an island just a few miles south of Cuba. It's called Cayo Esqueleto. That's Spanish. It means—"

"Skeleton Key," Alex said.

"That's right. Of course, there are plenty of keys off the coast of America. You'll have heard of Key Largo and Key West. This one was discovered by Sir Francis Drake. The story goes that when he landed there, the place was uninhabited. But he found a single skeleton, a conquistador in full armour, sitting on the beach. That was how the island got its name. Anyway, no matter what it's called, it's actually a very beautiful place. A tourist resort. Luxury hotels, diving, sailing... We're not asking you to do anything dangerous, Alex. Quite the contrary. You can think of this as a paid holiday. Two weeks in the sun."

"Go on," Alex said. He couldn't help sounding doubtful.

"The CIA is interested in Cayo Esqueleto because of a man who lives there. He's a Russian. He has a huge house – some might even call it a palace – on a sort of isthmus, that is to say, a narrow strip of land at the very northern tip of the island. His name is General Alexei Sarov."

Blunt pulled a photograph out of the file and turned it round so that Alex could see. It showed a fit-looking man in military uniform. The picture had been taken in Red Square, Moscow. Alex could see the onion-shaped towers of the Kremlin behind him.

"Sarov belongs to a different age," Mrs Jones said, taking over. "He was a commander in the Russian army at a time when the Russians were our enemies and still part of the Soviet Union. This wasn't very long ago, Alex. The collapse of communism. It was only in 1989 that the Berlin Wall came down." She stopped. "I suppose none of this means very much to you."

"Well, it wouldn't," Alex said. "I was only two years old."

"Yes, of course. But you have to understand, Sarov was a hero of the old Russia. He was made a general when he was only thirty-eight – the same year that his country invaded Afghanistan. He fought there for ten years, rising to be second in command of the Red Army. He had a son who was killed there. Sarov didn't even go to the funeral. It would have meant abandoning his men and he wouldn't do that – not even for one day."

Alex looked at the photograph again. He could see the hardness in the man's eyes. It was a face without a shred of warmth.

"The war in Afghanistan ended when the Soviets withdrew in 1989," Mrs Jones continued. "At the same time, the whole country was falling apart. Communism came to an end and Sarov left. He made no secret of the fact that he didn't like the new Russia with its jeans and Nike trainers and McDonald's on every street corner. He left the army, although he still calls himself General, and went to live—"

"In Skeleton Key." Alex finished the sentence.

"Yes. He's been there for ten years now – and this is the point, Alex. In two weeks' time, the Russian president is planning to meet him there. There's nothing surprising in that. The two men are old friends. They even grew up in the same part of Moscow. But the CIA are worried. They want to know what Sarov is up to. Why are the two men meeting? Old Russia and new Russia. What's going on?"

"The CIA want to spy on Sarov."

"Yes. It's a simple surveillance operation. They want to send in an undercover team to take a look around before the president arrives."

"Fine." Alex shrugged. "But why do they need me?"

"Because Skeleton Key is a communist island," Blunt explained. "It belongs to Cuba, one of the last places in the Western world where communism still exists. Getting in and out of the place is extremely difficult. There's an airport at Santiago. But every plane is watched. Every passenger is checked. They're always on the lookout for American spies and anyone who is even slightly suspect is stopped and turned away."

"And that's why the CIA have come to us," Mrs Jones continued. "A single man might be suspicious. A man and a woman might be a team. But a man and a woman travelling with a child...? That has to be a family!"

"That's all they want from you, Alex," Blunt said. "You go in with them. You stay at their hotel. You swim, snorkel and enjoy the sun. They do all the work. You're only there as part of their cover."

"Couldn't they use an American boy?" Alex asked.

Blunt coughed, obviously embarrassed. "The Americans would never use one of their own young people in an exercise like this," he said. "They have a different set of rules to us."

"You mean they'd be worried about getting him killed."

"We wouldn't have asked you, Alex," Mrs Jones broke the awkward silence. "But you have to leave London. In fact, you have to leave England. We're not trying to get you killed. We're trying to protect you and this is the best way. Mr Blunt is right. Cayo Esqueleto is a beautiful island and you're really very lucky to be going there. You can look on the whole thing as a free holiday."

Alex thought it over. He looked from Alan Blunt to Mrs Jones, but of course they were giving nothing away. How many agents had sat in this room with the two of them, listening to their honeyed words?

It's a simple job. Nothing to it. You'll be back in two weeks...

His own uncle had been one of them, sent to check on security in a computer factory on the south coast. But Ian Rider had never made it back.

Alex wanted none of it. There were still a few weeks of the summer holidays left and he wanted to see Sabina again. The two of them had talked about northern France and the Loire Valley, youth hostels and hiking. He had friends in London. Jack Starbright, his housekeeper and closest friend, had offered to take him with her when she visited her parents in Chicago. Seven weeks of normality. Was it too much to ask?

And yet, he remembered what had happened on the Cribber when the man on the jet ski had caught up with him. Alex had seen his eyes for just a few seconds but there had been no mistaking their cruelty and fanaticism. This was a man who had been prepared to chase him across the top of a twenty-foot wave in order to mow him down from behind – and he had come perilously close to succeeding. Alex knew, with a sick certainty, that the triad would try again. He had offended them ... not once now, but twice. Blunt was right about that. Any hope of an ordinary summer had gone out the window.

"If I help your friends in the CIA, you can get the triad to leave me alone?" he asked.

Mrs Jones nodded. "We have contacts in the Chinese underworld. But it will take time, Alex. Whatever happens, you're going to have to go into hiding – at least for the next couple of weeks."

So why not do it in the sun?

Alex nodded wearily. "All right," he said. "It seems I don't really have a lot of choice. When do you want me to leave?"

Blunt took an envelope out of the file. "I have your air ticket here," he said. "There's a flight this afternoon."

Of course, they had known he would accept.

"We will want to keep in touch with you while you're away," Mrs Jones muttered.

"I'll send you a postcard," Alex said.

"No, Alex, that's not quite what I had in mind. Why don't you go and have a word with Smithers?"

Smithers had an office on the eleventh floor of the building and at first Alex had to admit he was disappointed.

It was Smithers who had designed the various gadgets Alex had used on his previous missions and Alex had expected to find him somewhere in the basement, surrounded by cars and motorbikes, hi-tech weapons and men and women in white coats. But this room was boring: large, square and anonymous. It could have belonged to the chief executive of almost anything; an insurance company, perhaps, or a bank. There was a steel and glass desk with a telephone, a computer, "in" and "out" trays and an angle-poise lamp. A leather sofa stood against one wall, and on the other side of the room was a silver filing cabinet with six drawers. A picture hung on the wall behind the desk; a view of the sea. But disappointingly, there were no gadgets anywhere. Not so much as an electric pencil sharpener.

Smithers himself was behind the desk, tapping at the computer with fingers almost too big for the keys. He was one of the fattest people Alex had ever met. Today he was wearing a black three-piece suit with what looked like an old school tie perched limply on the great bulge of his stomach. Seeing Alex, he stopped typing and swivelled round in a leather chair that must have been reinforced to take his weight.

"My dear boy!" he exclaimed. "How delightful to see you. Come in, come in! How have you been keeping? I hear you had a bit of trouble, that business in France. You really must look after yourself, Alex. I'd be mortified if anything happened to you. Door!"

Alex was surprised when the door swung shut behind him.

"Voice activated," Smithers explained. "Do, please, sit down."

Alex sat on a second leather chair on the other side of the desk. As he did so, there was a low hum and the anglepoise lamp swivelled round and bent towards him like some sort of metallic bird taking a closer look. At the same time, the computer screen flickered and a human skeleton appeared. Alex moved a hand. The skeleton's hand moved. With a shudder, he realized he was looking at – or rather, through – himself.

"You're looking well," Smithers said. "Good bone structure!"

"What...?" Alex began.

"It's just something I've been working on. A simple X-ray device. Useful if anyone is wearing a gun." Smithers pressed a button and the screen went blank. "Now, Mr Blunt tells me that you're off to join our friends in the CIA. They're fine operators. Very, very good – except, of course, you can never trust them and they have no sense of humour. Cayo Esqueleto, I understand...?"

He leant forward and pressed another button on the desk. Alex glanced at the painting on the wall. The waves had begun to move! At the same time, the image shifted, pulling back, and he realized that he was looking at a plasma television screen with a picture beamed by satellite from somewhere above the Atlantic Ocean. Alex found himself looking down on an irregularly shaped island surrounded by turquoise water. The image was time coded and he realized that it was being broadcast into the room live.

"Tropical climate," Smithers muttered. "There'll be quite a lot of rainfall at this time of year. I've been developing a poncho that doubles as a parachute, but I don't think you'll need that. And I've got a marvellous mosquito coil. As a matter of fact, mosquitoes are about the only thing it *won't* knock out. But you won't need that either! In fact, I'm told the only thing you actually do need is something to help you keep in touch."

"A secret transmitter," Alex said.

"Why does it have to be secret?" Smithers pulled open a drawer and took out an object which he placed in front of Alex.

It was a mobile phone.

"I've already got one, thanks," Alex muttered.

"Not one like this," Smithers retorted. "It gives you a direct link with this office, even when you're in America. It works underwater – and in space. The pads are fingerprint sensitive so only you can use it. This is the model five. We also have a model seven. You hold it upside down when you dial or it blows up in your hand—"

"Why can't I have that model?" Alex asked.

"Mr Blunt has forbidden it." Smithers leant forward conspiratorially. "But I have put in a little extra for you. You see the aerial just here? Dial 999 and it'll shoot out like a needle. Drugged, of course. It'll knock out anyone in a twenty-metre range."

"Right." Alex picked up the phone. "Have you got anything else?"

"I was told you weren't to have any weapons..." Smithers sighed, then leant forward and spoke into a potted plant. "Could you bring them up, please, Miss Pickering?"

Alex was beginning to have serious doubts about this office – and these were confirmed a moment later when the leather sofa suddenly split in half, the two ends moving away from each other. At the same time, part of the floor slid aside to allow another piece of sofa to shoot silently into place, turning the two-seater into a three-seater. A young woman had been carried up with the new piece. She was sitting with her legs crossed and her hands on her knee. She stood up and walked over to Smithers.

"These are the items you requested," she said, handing over a package. She produced a sheet of paper and placed it in front of him. "And this report just came in from Cairo."

"Thank you, Miss Pickering."

Smithers waited until the woman had left – using the door this time – then glanced quickly at the report. "Not good news," he muttered. "Not good news at all. Oh well..." He slid the report into the "out" tray. There was a flash of electricity as the paper self-destructed. A second later, there were only ashes left. "I'm bending the rules doing this," he went on. "But there were a couple of things I'd been developing for you and I don't see why you shouldn't take them with you. Better safe than sorry."

He turned the package upside down and a bright pink packet of bubblegum slid out. "The fun of working with you, Alex," Smithers said, "is adapting the things you'd expect to find in the pockets of a boy your age. And I'm extremely pleased with this one."

"Bubblegum?"

"It blows rather special bubbles. Chew it for thirty seconds and the chemicals in your saliva react with the compound, making it expand. And as it expands, it'll shatter just about anything. Put it in a gun, for example, and it'll crack it open. Or the lock on a door."

Alex turned the packet over. Written in yellow letters on the side was the word BUBBLE 0-7. "What flavour did you make it?" he asked.

"Strawberry. Now, this other device is even more dangerous and I'm sure you won't need it. I call it the Striker and I'd be very happy to have it back."

Smithers shook the package and a keyring slid out to join the bubblegum on the desk. It had a plastic figurine attached, a footballer wearing white shorts and a red shirt. Alex leant forward and turned it over. He found himself looking at a three centimetre high model of Michael Owen.

"Thanks, Mr Smithers," he said. "But personally I've never supported Liverpool."

"This is the prototype. We can always do another footballer next time. The important thing is the head. Remember this, Alex. Twist it round twice clockwise and once anticlockwise and you'll arm the device."

"It'll explode?"

"It's a stun grenade. Flash and a bang. A ten second fuse. Not powerful enough to kill – but in a confined space it will incapacitate the opposition for a couple of minutes, which might give you a chance to get away."

Alex pocketed the Michael Owen figure and the bubblegum along with the mobile telephone. He stood up, feeling more confident. This might be a simple surveillance operation, a paid holiday as Blunt had put it, but he still didn't want to go empty-handed.

"Good luck, Alex," Smithers said. "I hope you get on all right with the CIA. They're not really like us, you know. And heaven knows what they'll make of you."

"I'll see you, Mr Smithers."

"I've got a private lift if you're going downstairs." As Smithers spoke, the six drawers of the filing cabinet slid open, three going one way, three going the other, to reveal a brightly lit cubicle behind.

Alex shook his head. "Thanks, Mr Smithers," he said. "I'll take the stairs."

"Whatever you say, old boy. Just look after yourself. And whatever you do, don't swallow the gum!"

NOT SO SPECIAL AGENTS

Alex stood at the window, trying to make sense of the world in which he now found himself. Seven hours on a plane had drained something out of him which even the surprise of a seat in first class had been unable to put back. He felt disengaged, as if his body had managed to arrive but had left half his brain somewhere behind.

He was looking at the Atlantic Ocean. It was on the other side of a strip of dazzling white sand that stretched into the distance with loungers and umbrellas laid out like measurements on a ruler. Miami was at the southernmost tip of the United States of America and it seemed that half the people who came to the city had simply followed the sun. He could see hundreds of them, lying on their backs in the tiniest of bikinis and swimming trunks, thighs and biceps pounded to perfection in the gym and then brought out to roast. Sun worshippers? No. These people were here because they worshipped themselves.

It was late afternoon and the heat was still intense. But in England, eight thousand kilometres away, it was night – and Alex was struggling to stay awake. He was also cold. The air-conditioning in the building had been turned up to maximum. The sun might be shining on the other side of the glass but in this neat, expensive office, he was chilled. Miami Ice, he thought.

It hadn't been the welcome he had expected. There had been a driver waiting for him when he arrived at the airport, a heavy-set man in a suit with Alex's name on a card. The man was wearing sunglasses that obliterated his eyes, offering Alex two reflections of himself.

"You Rider?"

"Yes."

"The car's this way."

The car turned out to be a stretch limousine. Alex felt ridiculous sitting alone in a long, narrow compartment with two leather seats facing each other, a drinks cabinet and a TV screen. It was nothing like a car at all, and he was glad that the windows, like the driver's glasses, were darkened. Nobody would be able to see in. He watched as the shops and boatyards on the airport perimeter slipped past and then they were suddenly crossing the water on a wide causeway that skimmed across the bay towards Miami Beach. Now the buildings were low-rise, barely taller than the palm trees that surrounded them, and painted astonishing shades of pink and pale blue. The roads were wide, but more people seemed to be sweeping half naked down the centre line on roller blades than driving.

The limousine stopped outside a ten-storey white building with lines so sharp it could have been cut out of a giant sheet of paper. There was a coffee bar on the ground floor, with offices up above.

Leaving Alex's cases in the car, they went in through the lobby and took the lift (elevator, Alex reminded himself) up to the tenth. It opened directly onto the reception area of what looked like an ordinary office, with two efficient girls behind a curving mahogany desk. A sign read: CENTURION INTERNATIONAL ADVERTISING. CIA, Alex thought. Great!

"Alex Rider for Mr Byrne," the driver said.

"This way." One of the girls gestured at a door to one side. Alex wouldn't even have noticed it otherwise.

Everything was different on the other side of the reception area.

Alex was confronted by two glass tubes with two sliding doors – one in, one out. The driver gestured and he stepped inside. The door closed automatically and there was a hum as he was scanned – for both conventional and biological weapons, he guessed. Then the door opened on the other side and he followed the driver down a blank, empty corridor and into an office.

"I hope you don't feel homesick, so far away from England."

The driver had gone and Alex was alone with another man, this one aged about sixty, with grizzled white hair and a moustache. He looked fit, but he moved slowly, as if he had just got out of bed or needed to get into it. He was wearing a dark suit that looked out of place in Miami, a white shirt and a knitted tie. His name was Joe Byrne and he was the deputy director for operations in the Covert Action section of the CIA.

"No," Alex said, "I feel fine." This wasn't true. He was already wishing he hadn't come. He would have liked to be back in London, even if it had meant hiding from the triads somehow. But he wasn't going to tell Byrne that.

"You have quite a reputation," Byrne said.

"Do I?"

"You bet." Byrne smiled. "Dr Grief and that guy in England –

Herod Sayle. Don't worry, Alex! We're not meant to know about these things but these days ... nothing happens in the world without someone hearing about it. You can't cough in Kabul without someone recording it in Washington." He smiled to himself. "I have to hand it to you Brits. Here at the CIA, we've used cats and dogs – we tried to put a cat into the Korean embassy with a bug in its collar. It was a neat operation and it would have worked, but unfortunately they ate it. But we've never used a kid before. Certainly not a kid like you..."

Alex shrugged. He knew Byrne was trying to be friendly, but at the same time the old man was uneasy and it showed.

"You've done some great work for your country," Byrne concluded.

"I'm not sure I did it for my country," Alex said. "It's just that my country didn't give me a lot of choice."

"Well, we're really grateful you've agreed to help us now. You know, the United States and Great Britain have always had a special relationship. We like to help each other." There was an awkward silence. "I met your uncle once," Byrne said. "Ian Rider."

"He was here in Miami?"

"No. It was in Washington. He was a good man, Alex. A good agent. I was sorry to hear—"

"Thanks," Alex said.

Byrne coughed. "You must be tired. We've booked you a hotel just a few blocks from here. But first I want you to meet special agents Turner and Troy. They should be here any moment."

Turner and Troy. They were going to be Alex's mother and father. He wondered which one was which.

"Anyway, the three of you will be leaving for Cayo Esqueleto the day after tomorrow," Byrne said. He sat down on the arm of a chair. His eyes had never left Alex. "You need a bit of time to get over your jet-lag and, more importantly, you need to get to know your new mum and dad." He hesitated. "I should mention to you, Alex, that they weren't too crazy about your part in this operation. Don't get me wrong. They know you're a pretty smart operator. But you *are* fourteen."

"Fourteen and three months," Alex said.

"Yeah. Sure." Byrne wasn't sure if Alex was serious. "Obviously, they're not used to having young people like you around when they're in the field. It bugs them. But they'll get used to it. And the main thing is, once you've helped get them onto the island, you'll be able to keep out of their way. I'm sure Alan Blunt told you – just stay in the hotel and enjoy yourself. The whole thing should only take a week. Two weeks, tops."

"What exactly are they hoping to achieve?" Alex asked.

"Well, they need to get into the Casa de Oro. That's Spanish. It means 'golden house'. It's an old plantation house that General Sarov has at one end of the island. But it's not going to be easy, Alex. The island narrows and there's a single track road with water on either side leading up to the outer wall. The place itself is more like a castle than a house. Anyway, that's not your problem. We have people on the island who can help us find a way in. And once we get in we can bug the place. We have cameras the size of a pin!"

"You want to know what General Sarov is doing."

"Exactly." Byrne glanced down at his brightly polished shoes and suddenly Alex wondered if the CIA man was keeping something from him. It all sounded too straightforward – and what had Smithers said? *You can never trust them*. Byrne seemed pleasant enough, but now he wondered.

There was a knock on the door. Without waiting for an answer, a man and woman walked in. Byrne stood up. "Alex," he said, "I'd like you to meet Tom Turner and Belinda Troy. People ... this is Alex Rider."

The atmosphere in the room became icy in an instant. Alex had never met two people less pleased to see him.

Tom Turner was about forty, a handsome man, with fair, close-cropped hair, blue eyes and a face that managed to be both tough and boyish. He was dressed – strangely – in jeans, a white open-necked shirt and a loose, soft leather jacket. There was nothing wrong with the clothes. They just didn't seem to suit him. This was a man who had been moulded by the work he did. With his clean-shaven, rather plastic looks, he reminded Alex of a dummy in a shop window. Turn him over, Alex thought, and you'd find CIA stamped on the soles of his feet.

Belinda Troy was a couple of years older than him, slim, with brown frizzy hair tumbling down to her shoulders. She was also casually dressed in a loose-fitting skirt and T-shirt, with a brightly coloured bag dangling from her shoulder and a loose string of beads around her neck. She didn't seem to be wearing any make-up. Her lips were pressed tightly together. Not quite scowling, but still a hundred miles away from a smile. She reminded Alex of a schoolteacher ... maybe one in a nursery school. Troy closed the door and sat down. Somehow she had managed to avoid looking at Alex from the moment she had entered the room. It was as if she was trying to pretend he wasn't there.

Alex looked from one to the other. The strange thing was that, despite their appearances, there was something identical about Tom Turner and Belinda Troy. It was as if they had both survived the same bad accident. They were hard-bitten, emotionless, empty. Now he knew why the CIA needed him. If they'd tried to get these two into Skeleton Key on their own, they'd have been identified as spies before they'd even got off the plane.

"It's nice to meet you, Alex," Turner said in a way that made it sound quite the opposite.

"How was the flight?" Troy asked. And then, before Alex could answer, "I guess it must have been scary. Travelling on your own."

"I had to close my eyes during take-off," Alex said. "But I stopped trembling when we got to thirty-five thousand feet."

"You're scared of flying?" Turner was astonished.

"That's crazy!" Troy turned to Byrne. "You're putting this kid into a CIA operation and already we find out he's scared of flying!"

"No, no, Belinda! Tom!" Byrne was embarrassed. "I think Alex was joking."

"Joking?"

"That's right. He's just got a different sense of humour."

Troy was tight-lipped. "Well, I don't find it funny," she said. "In fact, I think this whole idea is crazy. I'm sorry, sir..." she went on quickly, before Byrne could interrupt her. "You tell me this boy has a reputation. But he's still a minor! Suppose he makes a dumb-ass joke when we're in the field? He could blow our cover! And what about that accent of his? You're not going to tell me he's American?"

"He doesn't sound American," Turner agreed.

"Alex won't need to talk," Byrne said. "And if he does, I'm sure he can put on an accent."

Turner coughed. "Permission to speak, sir?"

"Go ahead, Turner."

"I agree one hundred per cent with special agent Troy, sir. I've got nothing against Alex. But he's not trained. He's not tested. He's not American!"

"Goddammit!" Suddenly Byrne was angry. "We've been through all this. You know how tough security is on the island – and with the Russian president on the way, it's going to be worse than ever. You go into Santiago Airport on your own and you won't make it out the other side. Remember what happened to Johnson! He went in on his own, dressed up as a birdwatcher. That was three months ago and we haven't heard from him since!"

"Well find us an American kid!"

"That's enough, Turner. Alex has flown thousands of miles to help us and I think you could at least show a little appreciation. Both of you. Alex..." Byrne gestured at Alex to sit down. "Can I get you anything? You want a drink? A Coke?"

"I'm fine," Alex said, and sat down.

Byrne opened a drawer in his desk and took out a bundle of papers and official documents. Alex recognized the green cover of an American passport. "Now this is how we're going to work it," he began. "The first thing is, all three of you are going to need fake IDs when you go into Cayo Esqueleto. I thought it would be easier to keep your first names – so it's Alex Gardiner who's going to be travelling with his mum and dad, Tom and Belinda Gardiner. Look after these documents, by the way. The agency is prohibited from manufacturing false passports and I had to pull strings to get hold of them. When this is over, I want them back."

Alex opened the passport. He was amazed to find his own photograph already in place. His age was the same, but according to the passport he had been born in California. He wondered how it had been done. And when.

"You live in Los Angeles," Byrne explained. "You're at high school in west Hollywood. Your dad's in the movie business and this is a week's vacation to do some diving and see the sights. I'll give you some stuff to read tonight, and of course everything's been backstopped."

"What does that mean?" Alex asked.

"It means that if anyone asks anything about the Gardiner family living in LA, it'll all check out. The school, the neighbourhood, everything. There are people out there who'll say they've known you all your life." Byrne paused. "Listen, Alex. You have to understand. The United States of America is not at war with Cuba. Sure, we've had our differences, but for the most part we've managed to live side by side. But they do things their way. Cuba – and that means Cayo Esqueleto – is a country in its own right. They find you're a spy, they're going to put you in jail. They're going to interrogate you. Maybe they'll kill you – and there's nothing we can do to stop them. It's been three months since we heard from Johnson and my gut feeling is we're never going to hear from him again."

There was a long silence.

Byrne realized he'd gone too far. "But nothing's going to happen to you," he said. "You're not part of this operation. You're just watching from the sideline." He turned to the two agents. "The important thing is to start acting like a unit. You only have two days until you leave. That means spending time together. I guess Alex will be too tired for dinner tonight but you can start by having breakfast together tomorrow. Spend the day together. Start thinking like a family. That's what you've got to be."

It was strange. Lying in bed in Cornwall, Alex had wished he could belong to a family. And now the wish had come true – though not in the way he had intended.

"Any questions?" Byrne asked.

"Yes, sir. I have a question," Turner said. He was sulking. His mouth had become little more than a straight line quickly drawn across his handsome face. "You want us to play happy families tomorrow. OK, sir, if that's an order, I'll do my best. But I think you're forgetting that tomorrow I'm meant to be seeing the Salesman. I don't think he'll be expecting me to turn up with my wife and child."

"The Salesman?" Byrne was annoyed.

"I'm seeing him at midday."

"What about Troy?"

"I'll be there as back-up," Troy said. "This is standard procedure—"

"All right!" Byrne thought for a moment. "The Salesman is on the water, right? Turner – you'll go onto the boat. So Alex can stay with Troy, on land. Safely out of the way."

Byrne stood up. The meeting was over. Alex felt another wave of tiredness surge through him and had to fight off a yawn. Byrne must have noticed. "You get some rest, Alex," he said. "I'm sure you and I will meet again. And I really am grateful you've agreed to help." He held out a hand. Alex shook it.

But special agent Troy was still sullen. "We'll have breakfast at ten-thirty," she said. "That'll give you time to read all the paper-work. Not that you'll probably sleep that much anyway. Where are you staying?"

Alex shrugged.

"I've put him up at the Delano," Byrne said.

"OK. We'll pick you up there."

Turner and Troy turned round and left the room. Neither of them bothered to say goodbye.

"Don't mind them," Byrne said. "This is a new situation for them. But they're good agents. Turner entered the military straight after college and Troy has worked with him many times before. They'll look after you when you're out in the field. I'm sure every-thing will work out fine."

But somehow Alex doubted it. And he was still puzzled. A lot of work, a lot of thought had gone into this operation. False papers – with his photograph – had been prepared before he had even known he was coming. A whole identity had been set up for him in

Los Angeles. And another agent, Johnson, had possibly died.

A simple surveillance operation? Byrne was nervous. Alex was sure of it. Maybe Turner and Troy were too.

Whatever was happening on Skeleton Key, they weren't telling him the full truth. Somehow, he'd have to find that out for himself.

It was a room that didn't really look like a room at all. It was too big. It had too many doors – and not just doors but archways, alcoves and a wide terrace open to the sun. The floor was marble, a chessboard of green and white squares that seemed somehow to exaggerate its size. The furniture was ornate, antique – and it was everywhere. Highly polished tables and chairs. Pedestals with vases and statuettes. Huge, gold-framed mirrors. Spectacular chandeliers. A giant stuffed crocodile lay in front of a massive fireplace. The man who had killed it sat opposite.

General Sarov was sipping black coffee out of a tiny porcelain cup. Caffeine is addictive and Sarov allowed himself only one thimbleful of coffee once a day. It was his single vice and he savoured it. Today he was dressed in a casual linen suit, but on this man it looked almost formal, with not a crease in it. His shirt was open at the collar revealing a neck that could have been carved out of grey stone. A ceiling fan turned slowly, a few metres above the desk where he was sitting. Sarov savoured the last mouthful of coffee, then lowered the cup and saucer back onto his desk. The porcelain made no sound as it came to rest on the polished surface.

There was a knock at the door – one of the doors – and a man walked into the room. *Walked*, however, was the wrong word. There was no word to describe exactly how this man moved.

Everything about him was wrong. His head sat at an angle on

shoulders which were themselves crooked and hunched. His right arm was shorter than his left arm. His right leg, however, was several centimetres longer than his left. His feet were encased in black leather shoes, one heavier and larger than the other. He was wearing a black leather jacket and jeans, and as he approached Sarov his muscles rippled beneath the cloth as if with a life of their own. Nothing in his body was co-ordinated, so although he was moving forwards, he seemed to be trying to go backwards or sideways. His face was the worst part of him. It was as if it had been taken to pieces and put back together again by a child with only a vague knowledge of the human form. There were about a dozen scars on his neck and around his cheeks. One of his eyes was red, permanently bloodshot. He had long, colourless hair on one half of his head. On the other, he was completely bald.

Although it would have been impossible to tell from looking at him, this man was only twenty-eight years old and, until a few years ago, had been the most feared terrorist in Europe. His name was Conrad. Very little was known about him, although it was said that he was Turkish, that he had been born in Istanbul, the son of a butcher, and that when he was nine he had blown up his school with a bomb made in chemistry class when he was given a detention for being late.

Again, nobody knew who had trained Conrad or, for that matter, who had employed him. He was a chameleon. He had no political beliefs and operated simply for money. It was believed that he had been responsible for outrages in Paris, Madrid, Athens and London. One thing was certain. The security services of nine different countries were after him, he was number four on the CIA's most wanted list, and there was an official bounty of two million dollars on his head.

His career had come to a sudden and unexpected end in the

winter of 1998 when a bomb that he had been carrying – intended for an army base – had detonated early. The bomb had quite literally blown him apart, but it hadn't quite managed to kill him. He had been stitched back together by a team of Albanian doctors in a research centre near Elbasan. It was their handiwork that was so visible now.

He was working as Sarov's personal assistant and secretary. He had done so for two years. Such work would once have been beneath him but Conrad had little choice now. And anyway, he understood the scope of Sarov's vision. In the new world that the Russian intended to create, Conrad would have his rewards.

"Good morning, comrade," Sarov said. He spoke in fluent English. "I hope we've managed to recover the rest of the banknotes from the swamp."

Conrad nodded. He preferred not to speak.

"Excellent. The money will, of course, have to be laundered. Then it can be paid back into my account." Sarov reached out and opened a leather-bound diary. There were a number of entries, each one in perfect handwriting. "Everything is proceeding according to schedule," he went on. "The construction of the bomb...?"

"Complete." Conrad seemed to have difficulty getting the word out of his mouth. He had to twist his face to make it happen at all.

"I knew I could rely on you. The Russian president will be arriving here in just five days' time. I had an email from him confirming it today. Boris tells me how much he's looking forward to his holiday." Sarov smiled very briefly. "It will, of course, be a holiday that he is unlikely to forget. You have the rooms prepared?"

Conrad nodded.

"The cameras?"

"Yes, General."

"Good." Sarov ran a finger down the diary pages. He stopped at a single word that had been underlined with a question mark. "There still remains the question of the uranium," he said. "I always knew that the purchase and delivery of nuclear material would be dangerous and delicate. The men in the aircraft threatened me and they have paid the price. But they were, of course, working for a third party."

"The Salesman," Conrad said.

"Indeed. By now, the Salesman will have heard what happened to his messenger boys. When no further payment arrives from me, he may decide to go ahead with his threat and alert the authorities. It's unlikely, but it's still a risk I am not prepared to take. We have less than two weeks until the bomb is detonated and the world takes on the shape that I have decided to give it. We cannot take any chances. And so, my dear Conrad, you must go to Miami and remove the Salesman from our lives – which will, I fear, involve removing him from his."

"Where is he?"

"He operates out of a boat, a cruise liner called *Mayfair Lady*. It's usually moored at the Bayside Marketplace. The Salesman feels safer on the water. Speaking personally, I will feel safer when he is underneath it." Sarov closed the diary. The meeting was over. "You can leave straight away. Report to me when it is done."

Conrad nodded a third time. The metal pins in his neck rippled briefly as his head moved up and down. Then he turned round and walked, limped, *dragged* himself out of the room.

DEATH OF A SALESMAN

They had a late breakfast at a café in Bayside Marketplace, right on the quayside, with boats moored all around them and bright yellow and green water taxies nipping back and forth. Tom Turner and Belinda Troy had knocked on Alex's door at ten o'clock that morning. In fact, Alex had been awake for several hours. He had fallen asleep fast, slept heavily and woken too early – the classic pattern of trans-Atlantic jet-lag. But at least he'd had plenty of time to read through the papers that Joe Byrne had given him. He now knew everything about his new identity – the best friends he had never met, the pet dog he had never seen, even the high school grades he had never achieved.

And now he was sitting with his new mother and father watching the tourists on the boardwalk, strolling in and out of the pretty white-fronted boutiques that cluttered the area. The sun was already high, the glare coming off the water almost blinding.

Alex slipped on a pair of Oakley Eye Jackets and the world on the other side of the black iridium lenses became softer and more manageable. The glasses had been a present from Jack. He hadn't expected to need them so soon.

There was a book of matches on the table with the words THE SNACKYARD printed on the cover. Alex picked it up and turned it over in his fingers. The matches were warm. He was surprised the sun hadn't set them alight. A waiter in black and white, complete with bow tie, came over to take the order. Alex glanced at the menu. He had never thought it possible to have so much choice for breakfast. At the next table a man was eating his way through a stack of pancakes with bacon, hash browns and scrambled eggs. Alex was hungry but the sight took away his own appetite.

"I'll just have some orange juice and toast," he said.

"Wholemeal or granary?"

"Granary. With butter and jam—"

"You mean *jelly*!" Troy paused until the waiter had gone. "No American kid asks for jam." She scowled. "You ask for that at Santiago Airport and we'll be in jail – or worse – before you can blink."

"I wasn't thinking," Alex began.

"You don't think, you get killed. Worse, you get us killed." She shook her head. "I still say this is a bad idea."

"How's Lucky?" Turner asked.

Alex's head spun. What was he talking about? Then he remembered. Lucky was the Labrador dog that the Gardiner family was supposed to have back in Los Angeles. "He's fine," Alex said. "He's being looked after by Mrs Beach." She was the woman who lived next door.

But Turner wasn't impressed. "Not fast enough," he said. "If you have to stop to think about it, the enemy will know you're telling a lie. You have to talk about your dog and your neighbours as if you've known them all your life."

It wasn't fair, of course. Turner and Troy hadn't prepared him. He hadn't realized the test had already begun. In fact, this was the third time Alex had gone undercover with a new identity. He had been Felix Lester when he had been sent to Cornwall, and Alex Friend, the son of a multimillionaire, in the French Alps. Both times he had managed to play the part successfully and he knew that he could do it again now as Alex Gardiner.

"So how long have you been with the CIA?" Alex asked.

"That's classified information," Turner replied. He saw the look on Alex's face and softened. "All my life," he said. "I was in the marines. It's what I always wanted to do, even when I was a kid ... younger than you. I want to die for my country. That's my dream."

"We shouldn't be talking about ourselves," Belinda said angrily. "We're meant to be a family. So let's talk about the family!"

"All right, Mom," Alex muttered.

They asked him a few more questions about Los Angeles while they waited for the food to arrive. Alex answered on autopilot. He watched a couple of teenagers go past on skateboards and wished he could join them. That was what a fourteen-year-old should be doing in the Miami sunshine. Not playing spy games with two sour-faced adults who had already decided they weren't going to give him a chance.

The food came. Turner and Troy had both ordered fruit salad and cappuccino – decaffeinated with skimmed milk. Alex guessed they were watching their weight. His own toast came – with grape jelly. The butter was whipped and white and seemed to disappear when it was spread.

"So who is the Salesman?" Alex asked.

"You don't need to know that," Turner replied.

Alex decided he'd had enough. He put down his knife. "All right," he said. "You've made it pretty clear that you don't want to work with me. Well, that's fine, because I don't want to work with you either. And for what it's worth, nobody would ever believe you were my parents because no parents would ever behave like you two!"

"Alex—" Troy began.

"Forget it! I'm going back to London. And if your Mr Byrne asks why, you can tell him I didn't like the jelly so I went home to get some jam."

He stood up. Troy was on her feet at the same time. Alex glanced at Turner. He was looking uncertain too. He guessed that they would have been glad to see the back of him. But at the same time, they were afraid of their boss.

"Sit down, Alex," Troy said. She shrugged. "OK. We were out of line. We didn't mean to give you a hard time."

Alex met her eyes. He slowly sat down again.

"It's just gonna take us a bit of time to get used to the situation," Troy went on. "Turner and me ... we've worked together before ... but we don't know you."

Turner nodded. "You get killed, how's that gonna make us feel?"

"I was told there wasn't going to be any danger," Alex said. "Anyway, I can look after myself."

"I don't believe that."

Alex opened his mouth to speak, then stopped himself. There was no point arguing with these people. They'd already made up their minds, and anyway, they were the sort who were always right. He'd met teachers just like them. But at least he'd achieved something now. The two special agents had decided to loosen up.

"You want to know about the Salesman?" Troy began. "He's a

crook. He's based here in Miami. He's a nasty piece of work."

"He's Mexican," Turner added. "From Mexico City."

"So what does he do?"

"He does just what his name says. He sells things. Drugs. Weapons. False identities. Information." Troy ticked off the list on her fingers. "If you need something and it's against the law, the Salesman will supply it. At a price, of course."

"I thought you were investigating Sarov."

"We are." Turner hesitated. "The Salesman may have sold something to Sarov. That's the connection."

"What did he sell?"

"We don't know for sure." Turner was looking increasingly nervous. "We just know that two of the Salesman's agents flew into Skeleton Key recently. They flew in but they didn't fly out again. We've been trying to find out what Sarov was buying."

"What's all this got to do with the Russian president?" Alex still wasn't sure he was being told the truth.

"We won't know that until we know what it was that Sarov bought," Troy said, as if explaining something to a six-year-old.

"I've been working undercover with the Salesman for a while now," Turner went on. "I'm buying drugs. Half a million dollars' worth of cocaine, being flown in from Colombia. At least, that's what he thinks." Turner smiled. "We have a pretty good relationship. He trusts me. And today just happens to be the Salesman's birthday, so he invited me to go for a drink on his boat."

Alex looked across to the sea. "Which one is it?"

"That one." Turner pointed at a boat moored at the end of a jetty about fifty metres away. Alex drew a breath.

It was one of the most beautiful boats he had ever seen. Not sleek, white and fibreglass like so many of the cruisers he had seen moored around Miami. Not even modern. She was called

Mayfair Lady and was an Edwardian classic motor yacht, eighty years old, like something out of a black and white film. The boat was one hundred and twenty feet long with a single funnel rising over its centre. The main saloon was at deck level, just behind the bridge. A sweeping line of fifteen or more portholes suggested cabins and dining-rooms below. The boat was cream with natural wood trimmings, a wooden deck and brass lamps under the canopies. A tall, slender mast rose up at the front with a radar, the boat's one visible connection with the twenty-first century. *Mayfair Lady* didn't belong in Miami. She belonged in a museum. And every boat that came near her was somehow ugly by comparison.

"It's a nice boat," Alex said. "The Salesman must be doing well."

"The Salesman should be in jail," Troy muttered. She had seen the admiring look in Alex's eyes and didn't approve. "And one day that's where we're going to put him."

"Thirty years to life," Turner agreed.

Troy dug her spoon into her fruit salad. "All right, Alex," she said, "let's start again. Your maths teacher. What's her name?"

Alex looked round. "Her name is Mrs Hazeldene. And – nice try – but we learn *maths* in England. Americans learn *math*."

Troy nodded but didn't smile. "You're getting there," she said.

They finished their breakfast. The CIA agents tested Alex on a few more details, then lapsed into silence. They didn't ask him about his life in England, his friends, or how he had stumbled into the world of MI6. They didn't seem to want to know anything about him.

The skateboarders had stopped playing and were slumped on the boardwalk, drinking Cokes. Turner looked at his watch. "Time to go," he muttered.

"I'll stay with the kid," Troy said.

"I shouldn't be more than twenty minutes." Turner stood up, then slapped his hand against his head. "Hell! I didn't get the Salesman a birthday present!"

"He won't mind," Troy said. "Tell him you forgot."

"You don't think he'll be upset?"

"It's OK, Turner. Invite him out for lunch another time. He'll like that."

Turner smiled. "Good idea."

"Good luck," Alex said.

Turner got up and left. As he walked away, Alex noticed a man in a bright Hawaiian shirt and white trousers coming from the opposite direction. It was impossible to see the man's face because he was wearing sunglasses and a straw hat. But he must have been involved in some sort of terrible accident – his legs were dragging awkwardly and there seemed to be no life in his arms. For a moment he was right next to Turner on the boardwalk. Turner didn't notice him. Then, moving surprisingly quickly, he had gone.

Alex and Troy watched as Turner walked all the way along to *Mayfair Lady*. There was a ramp at the end of the jetty, leading up to deck level. It allowed the crew to wheel supplies on board. A couple of men were just finishing as Turner arrived. He spoke to them. One of them pointed in the direction of the saloon cabin. Turner went up the ramp and disappeared on board.

"What happens now?" Alex asked.

"We wait."

For about fifteen minutes nothing happened. Alex tried to talk to Troy but her attention was fixed on the boat and she said nothing. He wondered about the relationship between the two agents. They obviously knew each other well and Byrne had told him they'd worked together before. Neither of them showed their emotions, but he wondered if their friendship might be more than professional.

Then Alex saw Troy sit up in her seat. He followed her eyes back to the boat. Smoke was coming out of the funnel. The engines had started up. The two crewmen Turner had spoken to were on the jetty. One of them untied the boat, then climbed onboard. The other one walked off. Slowly, *Mayfair Lady* began to move away from her mooring.

"Something's gone wrong," Troy whispered. She wasn't talking to Alex. She was talking to herself.

"What d'you mean?"

Her head snapped round as she remembered he was there. "It was a ten minute meeting. Tom wasn't meant to be going anywhere."

Tom. It was the first time she had used his first name.

"Maybe he changed his mind," Alex suggested. "Maybe the Salesman invited him on a cruise."

"He wouldn't have gone. Not without me. Not without cover. It's against company procedure."

"Then..."

"His cover's been blown." Troy's face was suddenly pale. "They must have found out he's an agent. They're taking him out to sea with them..."

She was standing up now but not moving, paralysed with indecision. The boat was still moving gracefully. Already a full half of its length was projecting out beyond the jetty. Even if she ran forward, she would never reach it in time.

"What are you going to do?" Alex asked.

"I don't know."

"Are they going to...?"

"If they know who he is, they'll kill him." She snapped the

words as if this was somehow Alex's fault, as if it was a stupid question that he should never have asked. And maybe it was this that decided him. Suddenly, before he even knew what he was doing, he was on his feet and running. He was angry. He was going to show them that he was more than the dumb English kid they obviously thought he was.

"Alex!" Troy called out.

He ignored her. He had already reached the boardwalk. The two teenagers he had seen earlier were sitting in the sun, finishing their drinks, and they didn't see him snatch one of their skateboards and jump onto it. It was only as he pushed off, propelling himself over the wooden surface towards the departing boat, that one of them shouted in his direction, but by then it was too late.

Alex was balanced perfectly. Snowboards, skateboards, surfboards, they were all the same to him. And this skateboard was a beauty, a Flexdex downhill racer with ABEC5 racing bearings and kryptonic wheels. How typical of Miami kids to buy only the best. He shifted his weight, suddenly aware that he had neither helmet nor knee-pads. If he came off now, it was going to hurt. But that was the least of his worries. The boat was pulling away. Even as Alex watched, the stern with its churning propellers slid past the end of the jetty. Now the boat was at sea. He could see the name, *Mayfair Lady*, dwindling as it moved into the distance. In seconds it would be too far away to reach.

Alex hit the ramp that the men had been using to load and unload the boat. He soared upwards and suddenly he was in mid-air, flying. He felt the skateboard fall away from his feet, heard it splash into the sea. But his own momentum carried him forward. He wasn't going to make it! The boat was moving too fast. Alex was plunging down now, following an arc that was going to miss the stern by centimetres. It would bring him crashing down into the water – and then what? The propellers! They would slice him to pieces. Alex stretched out his arms and somehow his scrabbling fingers made contact with the rail that curved round the back of the boat. His body smashed into the metal stern, his feet dipping into the water above the propellers.

He felt the breath punched out of him. Somebody on the boat must have heard. But he couldn't worry about that now. He would just have to hope that the noise of the engines had covered the collision. Using all his strength, he pulled himself up and over the rail. And then, finally, he was on the deck, soaked to the knees, his entire body aching from the impact. But he was onboard. And miraculously, he hadn't been seen.

He crouched down, taking stock of his surroundings. The stern deck was a small, semi-enclosed area, shaped like a horseshoe. In front of him was the saloon cabin with a single window facing back and the door a little further down the side. There was a stack of supplies underneath a tarpaulin and also two large cans. Alex unscrewed one of the lids and sniffed. It was full of petrol. The Salesman obviously planned to be away for some time.

The entire deck, both port and starboard, was overshadowed by a canopy hanging down on either side of the main saloon and there was a wooden lifeboat suspended on two pulleys above his head. Resting briefly against the stern rail, Alex knew he was safe provided nobody actually walked to the back of the boat. How many crew members would there be? Presumably there was a captain at the wheel. He might have someone with him. Looking up, Alex glimpsed a pair of feet crossing the upper deck on the roof of the saloon. That made three. There could be two or three more inside. Six perhaps in total?

He looked back. The port of Miami was already slipping away behind him. Alex got up and slipped off his shoes and socks. Then he crept forward, moving absolutely silently, still nervous about being spotted from the upper deck. The first two windows of the saloon were closed but the third was open and crouching below it he heard a voice. A man was talking. He had a thick Mexican accent and every time he spoke the letter S, he whistled softly.

"You are a foolish man. Your name is Tom Turner. You work for the CIA. And I am going to kill you."

Another man spoke briefly. "You're wrong. I don't know what you're talking about." Alex recognized Turner's voice. He glanced left and right. Then, with his shoulders against the cabin wall, he levered himself upwards until his head reached the level of the window and he could look in.

The saloon cabin was rectangular, with a wooden floor partially covered by a carpet that had been rolled back – presumably to avoid bloodstains. Unlike the boat, the furniture was modern, office-like. There wasn't a great deal of it. Turner was sitting in a chair with his hands behind his back. Alex could see that some sort of parcel tape had been used to tie his arms and legs. He had already been beaten. His fair hair was damp and blood trickled out of the corner of his mouth.

There were two men in the cabin with him. One was a deckhand in jeans and black T-shirt, his stomach bulging out over his belt. The other had to be the Salesman. He was a round-faced man with very black hair and a small moustache. He was wearing a three-piece white suit, immaculately tailored, and brightly polished leather shoes. The deckhand was holding a gun, a large, heavy automatic. The Salesman was sitting in a cane chair, holding a glass of red wine. He rolled it in front of his nose, enjoying the aroma, then sipped.

"What a delicious wine!" he muttered. "This is Chilean. A Cabernet Sauvignon grown on my own estate. You see, my friend, I am successful. I have businesses all over the world. People want to drink wine? I sell wine. People want to take drugs? They are mad, but that is no concern of mine. I sell drugs. What is so wrong with that? I sell anything that anyone wishes to buy. But, you see, I am a careful man. I did not buy your story. I made certain enquiries. The Central Intelligence Agency is mentioned. And that is why you find yourself here."

"What do you want to know?" Turner rasped.

"I want to know when we are one hour out of Miami because that is when I intend to shoot you and dump you over the side." The Salesman smiled. "That is all."

Alex sank down again. There was no point listening to any more. He couldn't go into the cabin. There were two of them and only one of him. And although he had a weapon, it wouldn't be enough. Not against a gun. He needed a diversion.

Then he remembered the petrol. Glancing quickly at the upper deck he prepared to go back to the stern, then froze as the door of the bridge opened and a man came out. There was nothing Alex could do; nowhere he could hide. But he was lucky. The man, dressed in the faded uniform of a ship's captain, had been smoking a cigarette. He stopped long enough to throw the butt into the sea, then went back the way he had come without turning his head. It had been a close escape and Alex knew it could only be a matter of time before he was noticed. He had to move fast.

He ran on tiptoe to the petrol cans. He tried tilting one of them but it was too heavy. He looked around for a rag, couldn't find one and so took off his shirt, ripping it apart in his hands. Quickly he pushed the sleeve into the can, soaking it in petrol. Then he pulled it out, leaving only the end still dangling inside; a makeshift fuse. What would happen when he set fire to the petrol? Alex guessed that the explosion would be enough to attract the attention of everyone onboard but not strong enough to kill anyone or sink the boat. Since he was still going to be onboard, he would just have to hope he was right.

He reached into his pocket and took out the book of matches that he had been playing with in the restaurant. Cupping his hand to protect the flame from the breeze, he lit first one match, then the whole book. He touched the flame against the rag that had once been his shirt. The whole thing was alight in a second.

Running forward again, he returned to the saloon cabin. He could hear the Salesman still speaking inside.

"Another glass, I think. Yes. But then I'm afraid I must leave you. I have work to do."

Alex looked in. The Salesman was standing at a table, pouring himself a second glass of wine. Alex looked back over his shoulder. There was no one there. Nothing had happened. Why hadn't the petrol caught fire? Had the wind blown out his makeshift fuse?

And then it exploded. A great mushroom of flame and black smoke leapt into the air at the back of the boat, snatched away instantly by the wind. Somebody shouted. Alex saw that the petrol had splashed all over both decks. There was fire everywhere. The canopy right above his head was alight. Whatever had been packed underneath the tarpaulin was also blazing. More shouting. Footsteps thudded towards the stern deck. Now was the time to move.

"See what is happening!"

Alex heard the Salesman snap the command and a second later the deckhand came racing out. He disappeared round the other side of the cabin. That just left the Salesman himself, on his own with Turner. Alex waited a few seconds, then stepped into the doorway, once again reaching into his trouser pocket. Turner saw him before the Salesman. His eyes widened. The Salesman turned.

Alex saw that he had put down his glass and picked up a gun. For a moment neither of them moved. The Salesman was looking at a fourteen-year-old boy, barefoot and naked from the waist up. It obviously hadn't occurred to him that Alex could be any threat to him, that it was this boy who had set fire to his boat. And in that moment of hesitation, Alex made his move.

When he brought his hand up, he was holding a mobile phone. He had already dialled two nines before he'd gone in. He pressed the button for a third time as he aimed with the phone.

"It's for you!" he said.

He felt the phone shudder in his hand and, silently, the aerial spat out of the top, the plastic peeling back to reveal a shining needle. It travelled across the cabin and hit the Salesman square in the chest. The Salesman had reacted fast, already bringing his gun round. But a second later his eyes rolled and he slumped to the floor. Alex jumped over him, picked up a knife from the table and went over to Turner.

"What the hell...?" the CIA man began. Alex could see at once that he wasn't badly hurt. At the same time, his mood didn't seem to have improved. He looked from the phone to the unconscious figure of the Salesman. "What did you do to him?" he asked.

"He got the wrong number," Alex said. He cut through the adhesive tape.

Turner got to his feet and snatched up the gun that the Salesman had dropped. He checked the clip. The gun was fully loaded. "What happened?" he demanded. "I heard an explosion!"

"Yeah. That was me. I set the boat alight."

"What?"

"I set fire to the boat."

"But we're *on* the boat!"

"I know."

Before Alex could say any more, Turner moved, twisting round, snapping into combat position, arms up, legs apart. There was a stairwell at the far end of the cabin. Alex hadn't noticed it before. A figure had appeared, coming up from below. Turner fired twice. The figure crumpled back down. Turner stopped. Black smoke was seeping into the cabin. There was a second explosion and the entire boat rocked as if seized by a sudden squall. There was shouting outside on the deck. Looking out of the window, Alex could see flames.

"That must have been the second petrol tank," he said.

"How many tanks are there?"

"Just the two."

Turner seemed almost dazed. He forced himself to a decision. "The sea..." he said. "We're going to have to swim."

The CIA agent went first, edging sideways out of the cabin. Suddenly the deck was full of people. There were at least seven of them. Alex wondered where they had all come from. Two of them, young men in dirty white shirts and jeans, were fighting the flames with extinguishers. There were two on the roof, another on the deck. All of them were shouting.

Smoke was trailing into the sky behind the boat. The lifeboat was ablaze. Part of the canopy was on fire. At least nobody knew quite what had happened. Nobody had seen Alex come on board. The explosions had taken them all by surprise and all they cared about was getting the fire under control. However, as Turner came out of the cabin, one of the men on the upper deck saw him. He called out in Spanish.

"Move!" Turner shouted.

He ran for the edge of the boat. Alex followed. There was the deafening chatter of a machine gun and what was left of the canopy above his head was torn to shreds. Bullets smashed into the deck sending chips of wood flying. A glass bulb exploded. Alex wasn't even sure who was firing. All he knew was that he was trapped in the middle of smoke and flames and bullets and a lot of men who wanted him dead. He saw Turner dive over the side. There was another burst from the machine gun and Alex felt the deck rip itself apart centimetres from his bare feet. He yelled out. Splinters slammed into his ankle and heels. He spurted forward and threw himself over the handrail. For what felt like an eternity everything was chaos. He could feel the wind racing over his bare shoulders. There were more gunshots. Then he plunged head-first into the Atlantic and disappeared beneath the surface.

Alex allowed the ocean to embrace him. After the battlefield that *Mayfair Lady* had become, its water was warm and soothing. He swam down, a powerful breaststroke that took him ever deeper. Something whizzed past him and he realized that he was still being shot at. The further down he went, the safer he would be. He opened his eyes. The salt water stung but he needed to know how far he was going. He looked up. Light glimmered at the surface but there was no sign of the boat. His lungs were beginning to hurt. He needed to breathe. But still he waited. He would have been happy if he could have stayed underwater for an hour.

He couldn't. With his body crying out for oxygen, Alex kicked reluctantly for the surface. He came up gasping, with water streaming down his face. Turner was next to him. The CIA agent looked more dead than alive. Alex wondered if he had been hit, but there was no sign of any blood. Perhaps he was in shock.

"Are you all right?" Alex asked.

"Are you crazy?" Turner was so angry that he actually swallowed water as he spoke. He spluttered and fought to keep himself from going under. "You could have gotten us killed!"

"I just saved your life!" Alex was getting angry himself. He couldn't believe what he was hearing.

"You think so? Look!"

With a sense of dread, Alex swivelled round in the water. *Mayfair Lady* hadn't been destroyed. The fire was out. And the boat was coming back.

He had been underwater for perhaps ninety seconds. In that time, the ship had continued forward with all hands fighting the flames and nobody at the wheel. The engine had been at full throttle and it was now about five hundred metres away. But the captain had obviously returned to the bridge. The boat was wheeling round. Alex could make out four or five men standing at the bow. All of them were armed. They had seen him. One of them pointed and shouted. He and Turner were helpless, floating in the water with perhaps one weapon between them. Soon the boat would reach them. They were sitting targets, to be picked off like ducks in a fair.

What could he do? He looked at Turner, hoping the older man would produce something, some rabbit out of the hat. Didn't the CIA have gadgets? Where was the inflatable speedboat or the concealed aqualung? But Turner was helpless. He'd even managed to lose the gun.

Mayfair Lady completed her turn.

Turner swore.

The boat drew closer, slicing through the water.

And then it exploded. This time the explosions were huge, final. There were three of them, simultaneous, in the bow, the middle and the stern. *Mayfair Lady* was blown into three quite separate pieces, the funnel and main saloon heaving themselves out of the ocean as if trying to escape from the rest of the boat. Alex felt the shockwave travel through the water. The blast was deafening. A fist of water smashed into him, almost knocking him out. Pieces of wood, some of them on fire, rained down all around. He knew at once that nobody could have survived. And with that knowledge came a terrible thought.

Was it his fault? Had he killed them all?

Turner must have been thinking the same thing. He said nothing. The two of them watched as the three sections of what had once been a classic motor yacht sank and disappeared.

There was the sound of an outboard motor. Alex twisted round. A speedboat was racing towards them. He saw Belinda Troy at the wheel. She must have somehow commandeered it and come after them. She was on her own.

She helped Turner out of the water first, then Alex. For the first time, Alex realized that he couldn't see land. He felt that it had all happened so quickly. And yet *Mayfair Lady* had managed to put several kilometres between itself and the coast before it was destroyed.

"What happened?" Troy asked. The wind had caught her long hair and spread it all around her. She looked as if she was having hysterics. "I saw the boat blow. I thought you were—" She stopped and caught her breath. "What happened?" she repeated.

"It was the kid." Turner's voice was neutral. He was still trying to catch up with the events of the last few minutes. "He cut me free..."

"You were tied up?"

"Yes. The Salesman knew I was with the agency. He was going to kill me. Alex knocked him out. He had some sort of cell phone..." He was stating the facts, but there was no gratitude. The boat rocked gently. Nobody moved. "He blew up the boat. He killed them all."

"No." Alex shook his head. "The fire was out. You saw. They'd got the boat under control. They were turning round, about to come back—"

"For God's sake!" The CIA man was almost too tired to argue. "What do you think happened? You think one of the lights fused and *Mayfair Lady* just happened to blow up? You did it, Alex. You set the gas alight and that's what happened."

Gas. The American for petrol. It was one of the words they had tested him on at the Snackyard that morning. A century ago.

"I saved your life," Alex said.

"Yeah. Thanks, Alex." But Turner's voice was bleak.

Troy climbed behind the wheel and started the engine. The speedboat turned and they headed back towards the shore.

PASSPORT CONTROL

Alex had a window seat near the front of the plane. Troy was next to him with Turner on her other side, next to the aisle. A family on holiday (on *vacation*, he reminded himself). Troy was reading a magazine. Turner had a film script. He was meant to be a producer and had spent the journey making notes in the margin, just in case anyone happened to be looking. Alex was playing with a Game Boy Advance. He wondered about that. Turner had given it to him just before they'd left Miami. It had been very casual, standing in the departure lounge.

"Here, Alex. Something to keep you busy on the plane."

Alex was suspicious. He remembered that the last time he'd held a Game Boy, it had been filled with gadgets invented by Smithers at MI6. But as far as he could tell, this one was completely ordinary. At least, he'd got to level five of Rayman and so far it hadn't exploded in his hands.

He looked out the window. They had been in the air for about an hour. This had been their second flight of the day. They had gone from Miami to Kingston, Jamaica, and had caught the second plane there. They had been given the sort of snack that people expect, but never enjoy, on a plane. A sandwich, a small square of cake and a plastic tub of water. Now the stewardesses returned, hastily collecting the trays.

"This is your captain speaking. Please fasten your seat belts and return your seats to the upright position. We will shortly be coming in to land."

Alex looked out of the window again. The sea was an extraordinary shade of turquoise. It didn't look like water at all. Then the plane dipped and suddenly he saw the island. Both islands. Cuba itself was to the north. Cayo Esqueleto was below it. There wasn't a cloud in the sky and for a moment the land mass was perfectly clear, laid out as if on the surface of the world, two patches of emerald green with a coastline that seemed to shimmer an electric blue. The plane tilted. The islands disappeared and the next time Alex saw them the plane was coming in low, rushing towards a runway that seemed almost unreachable, hemmed in by offices and hotels and roads and palm trees. There was a control tower, ugly and misshapen. A low-rise terminal, prefabricated concrete and glass. Two more planes, already on the ground, surrounded by service trucks. There was a jolt as the back wheels came into contact with the tarmac. They were down.

Alex unclipped his seat belt.

"Wait a minute, Alex," Troy said. "The seat belt light is still on."

She was behaving like a mother. But the sort of mother she had chosen to be was bossy and demanding. Alex had to admit that it suited her. Anybody watching them might believe they were a family, but would have to add that they were an unhappy one.

Since the events in Miami, the two agents had practically ignored him. Alex found it hard to work them out. Turner would be dead if it hadn't been for him, but neither of them would admit it – as if, in some way, he had dented their professional pride. And they still insisted that he had blown up *Mayfair Lady*, killing everyone onboard. Even Alex was finding it hard to avoid a sense of responsibility. It was true that he had set fire to the petrol. What other reason could there have been for the explosion that had followed?

He tried to put it out of his mind. The plane had come to a halt and everyone had stood up, fighting for the overhead lockers in the cramped compartment. As Alex reached up to take his own bag, the Game Boy almost fell out of his grip. Turner's head snapped round. Alex saw a flash of alarm in his eyes. "Be careful with that!" he said.

So he was right. There was something hidden inside the Game Boy. It was typical of the CIA agents to keep him in the dark. But that hadn't stopped them asking him to carry it in.

It was midday, the worst time to arrive. As they came out of the plane, Alex felt the heat reflecting off the tarmac. It was hard to breathe. The air was heavy and smelt of diesel. He was sweating before he had even reached the bottom of the steps and the arrivals lounge offered no relief. The air-conditioning had broken down and Alex soon found himself trapped in a confined space with two or three hundred people and no windows. The terminal was more like a large shed than a modern airport building. The walls were a drab olive green, decorated by posters of the island that looked twenty years out of date. The passengers from Alex's flight caught up with passengers still being processed from the flight before and the result was a large, shapeless crowd of people and hand luggage, shuffling slowly forward towards three uniformed immigration officials in glass cabins. There were no queues. As each passport was stamped and one more person was allowed in, the crowd simply pressed forward, oozing through the security controls.

An hour later, Alex was still there. He was dirty and crumpled and he had a raging thirst. He looked to one side where a couple of old, splintered doors led into men's and women's toilets. There might be a tap inside but would the water even be drinkable? A guard in a brown shirt and trousers stood watching, leaning against the wall beside a floor-to-ceiling mirror, a machine gun cradled in his arms. Alex wanted to stretch his arms but he was too hemmed in. There was an old woman with grey hair and a sagging face standing right next to him. She smelt of cheap perfume. As he half-turned, he found himself almost embraced by her and recoiled, unable to hide his disgust. He glanced up and saw that there was a single security camera set in the ceiling. He remembered how worried Joe Byrne had been about security at Santiago Airport. But it seemed to him that just about anyone could have walked in and nobody would have noticed. The guard looked bored and half asleep. The camera was probably out of focus.

At last they reached passport control. The official behind the glass screen was young, with black greasy hair and glasses. Turner slid three passports and three completed immigration forms through. The official opened them.

"Don't fidget, Alex," Troy said. "We'll be through in a minute."

"Sure, Mom."

The passport man looked up at them. His eyes showed no welcome at all. "Mr Gardiner? What is the purpose of your visit?" he demanded.

"Vacation," Turner replied.

The man's eyes flickered briefly over the passports and then at the people to whom they belonged. He slid them under a scanner, yawning at the same time. The guard that Alex had noticed was nowhere near. He was gazing out of the window, watching the planes.

"Where do you live?" the official asked.

"Los Angeles." Turner's face was blank. "I'm in the movie business."

"And your wife?"

"I don't work," Troy said.

The official had come to Alex's passport. He opened it and checked the picture against the boy who stood in front of him. "Alex Gardiner," he said.

"How you doing?" Alex smiled at him.

"This is your first trip to Cayo Esqueleto?"

"Yeah. But I hope it won't be my last."

The passport official stared at him, his eyes magnified by the glasses. He seemed completely uninterested. "What hotel are you staying at?" he asked.

"The Valencia," Turner said quietly. He had already written the name on the three immigration forms.

Another pause. Then the official picked up a stamp and brought it crashing down three times – three gunshots in the confined space of the kiosk. He handed back the passports. "Enjoy your visit to Cayo Esqueleto."

Alex and the two CIA agents passed through the immigration room and into the luggage hall where their cases were already waiting, circling endlessly on an old, creaking conveyor-belt. And that was it, Alex thought. It couldn't have been easier! All that fuss and he hadn't even been needed in the first place.

He picked up his case.

At the same time, although he was unaware of it, his picture and passport details were already being transmitted to police headquarters in Havana, Cuba, along with those of Turner and Troy. The "family" had actually been photographed three times. Once by the overhead camera that Alex had seen in the arrivals lounge, but which was far more sophisticated than he would have believed. As old-fashioned as it looked, it could zoom in on the hole in a man's button or a single word written in a diary and blow it up fifty times if needed. They had been photographed a second time by a camera behind the mirror next to the toilets. And finally, a profile close-up shot had been taken by a camera concealed in a brooch worn by an old lady who smelled of cheap perfume and who had not, in fact, arrived on a plane but who was always there, mingling with the new arrivals, moving in on anyone who had aroused the suspicions of the people she worked for. The immigration forms that Turner had filled in were also on their way, sealed in a plastic bag. His answers to the standard questions mattered less to the authorities than the forms themselves. The paper had been specially formulated to record fingerprints, and in less than an hour these would be digitally scanned and checked against a huge database in the same police building.

The invisible machine that operated in the airport at Santiago had been focused on Turner and Troy before they had even arrived. They were American. They had said they were on vacation and their luggage (which had, of course, been searched as it came off the plane) contained the sunscreen, beach towels and basic medicines that you would expect an ordinary American family to pack. The labels on their clothes showed that they had all been bought in Los Angeles. But a single receipt tucked into the top pocket of one of Turner's shirts told another story. He had recently bought a book from a shop in Langley, Virginia. Langley is where the headquarters of the CIA are based. The little scrap of paper had been enough to set alarm bells ringing. This was the result.

The officer in charge of security at the airport was watching them carefully. He was sitting in a small, windowless office and their images were right in front of him, on a bank of television screens. He watched them as they continued out of baggage reclaim and into the arrivals hall. His finger hovered briefly beside a red button on his console. It still wasn't too late. He could pull them back in before they had reached the taxi stand. There were plenty of cells buried deep in the basement. And when normal questioning failed, there were always drugs.

And yet...

The head of security was called Rodriguez and he was good at his job. He had interrogated so many American spies that he sometimes said he could recognize one at a hundred metres. He had spotted "Mr and Mrs Gardiner" before they had even crossed the runway and had sent out his deputy to take a closer look. This was the bored-looking guard that Alex had seen.

But this time Rodriguez wasn't sure – and he couldn't afford to make mistakes. After all, Cayo Esqueleto needed its tourists. It needed the money that tourism brought. He might have his suspicions about the two adults, but they were two adults travelling with a child. He had overheard the brief conversation between Alex and the passport official. There were microphones concealed throughout the immigration hall. How old was the boy? Fourteen? Fifteen? Just another American kid being given two weeks on the beach.

Rodriguez made up his mind. He lifted his hand away from the alarm button. It was better to avoid the bad publicity. He watched the family disappear into the crowd.

Even so, the authorities would keep an eye on them. Later that day, just to be on the safe side, he would compile a report which would be sent along with the photographs and fingerprints to the local police in Cayo Esqueleto. A copy would also be forwarded to the very important gentleman who lived in the Casa de Oro. And perhaps someone would be sent to the Hotel Valencia to keep a close eye on the new arrivals.

Rodriguez settled in his chair and lit a cigarette. Another plane had landed. He leant forward and began to examine the arriving crowd.

The Valencia was one of those amazing hotels that Alex usually saw in dream holiday prizes on game shows. It was tucked away in a crescent-shaped cove with miniature villas spread out along the beach and a low-rise reception area almost lost in a miniature jungle of exotic shrubs and flowers. There was a doughnut-shaped swimming pool with a bar in the inner ring and stools poking up just above the level of the water. The whole place seemed to be asleep. This was certainly true of the few guests Alex could see, lying motionless on sunloungers.

Alex and his "parents" were sharing a villa with two bedrooms and a veranda sheltered from the sun by a sloping straw roof. There was a clump of palm trees, white sand, then the impossible blue of the Caribbean. Alex sat down briefly on his bed. It was covered with a single white sheet and a fan turned slowly in the ceiling. A brilliant green and yellow bird perched briefly on his windowsill then flew off towards the sea as if inviting him.

"Can I go for a swim?" he asked. He wouldn't normally have asked their permission but he figured it probably suited his role.

"Sure, honey!" Troy was unpacking. She had already warned Alex that he would have to stay in character whenever they were in the villa. The hotel might well be bugged. "But you be careful!"

Alex changed into his shorts and ran across the sand into the sea.

The water was perfect; warm and crystal clear. There was no shingle, only the softest carpet of sand. Tiny fish swam all around him, scattering instantly when he stretched out his hand. For the first time in his life, Alex was glad he had met Alan Blunt. This was certainly better than hanging out in west London. For once, things seemed to be going his way.

After he had swum, he climbed into a hammock stretched out between two trees and relaxed. It was about half past four and the afternoon felt as hot as it had been when they arrived. A waiter came up to him and he asked for a lemonade, charging it to his villa. His mum and dad could pay.

Mum and dad.

As he swung gently from side to side with the water trickling through his hair and drying on his chest, Alex wondered what his real parents would have been like if they hadn't both died in a plane crash soon after he was born. And what would it have been like for him, growing up in an ordinary home, with a mother to run to when he was hurt and a father to play with, to borrow money from or sometimes to avoid? Would it have made him any different? He would have been an ordinary schoolboy, worrying about exams – not spies and salesmen and exploding boats. He might have been a softer person. He'd probably have had more friends. And he certainly wouldn't have been lying in a hammock in the grounds of the Hotel Valencia.

He stayed there until his hair was dry and he knew it was time to get out of the sun. Turner and Troy hadn't come out to find him and he suspected they were busy with their own affairs. He was still sure there were a lot of things they weren't telling him. He remembered the Game Boy Advance. They had only mentioned it at the very last minute, just as they were about to get onto the plane. Could it be that they had wanted him to carry it onto the island, knowing that a fourteen-year-old would have less chance of being searched?

Alex rolled out of the hammock and dropped down onto the sand. A local man was walking past, selling strings of beads to the tourists out on the beach. He glanced at Alex and held up a necklace; a dozen different shells on a leather cord. Alex shook his head, then walked the short distance back to his villa. He still had the Game Boy in his hand luggage. Turner had forgotten to ask for it back. Alex slipped quietly into his room, took it out and examined it again. There seemed to be nothing out of the ordinary. It was bright blue with the single game, Rayman, lodged in the back. Alex weighed it in his hands. As far as he could tell it wasn't any heavier or lighter than it should have been.

Then he remembered. The Game Boy he had once been given by MI6 had been activated by pressing the PLAY button three times. Perhaps this model would work the same way. Alex turned it over and pressed the button. Once, twice ... a third time. Nothing happened. He gazed for a moment at the blank screen, annoyed with himself. He was wrong. It was just a game, given to him to keep him quiet on the plane. It was time to get dressed. He put the Game Boy on the bedside table and stood up.

The Game Boy squawked.

Alex snapped round, recognizing the sound without yet knowing what it was. The Game Boy was still squawking, a strange, metallic rattling sound. The screen had suddenly come to life. It was pulsating, green and white. What did it mean? He picked the machine up again. At once the noise died away and the lights on the screen faded out. He moved the Game Boy back towards the bedside table. It burst back into life.

Alex looked at the bedside table. There was nothing on it apart from an old-fashioned alarm clock, supplied by the hotel. He opened the drawer. There was a bible inside with the text printed in Spanish and English. Nothing else. So what was causing the Game Boy to act in this way? He swung it away. It became silent. He moved it back to the table. It started again.

The clock...

Alex looked more closely at the dial. The clock had a luminous face. He pressed the Game Boy right up against the glass and the squawking was suddenly louder than ever. Now Alex understood. The numbers on the clock face were faintly radioactive. That was what the Game Boy was picking up.

The Game Boy concealed a Geiger counter. Alex smiled grimly. Rayman was certainly the right game for this machine. Except that the rays it was looking for were radioactive ones.

What did it mean? Turner and Troy weren't on the island for a simple surveillance operation. He had been right. Both Blunt in London and Byrne in Miami had been lying to him from the very start. Alex knew that he was sitting only a few kilometres south of Cuba. Something he had learned in history came to his mind. Cuba. The 1960s. The Cuban missile crisis. Nuclear weapons trained on America...

He still couldn't be certain. He might be jumping to conclusions. But the fact was that the CIA had smuggled a Geiger counter into Skeleton Key and, as crazy as it sounded, there could only be one reason why they needed it.

They were looking for a nuclear bomb.

BROTHERHOOD SQUARE

Alex said little at dinner that night. Although the hotel had seemed empty earlier in the day, he was surprised how many guests had appeared for dinner in their loose skirts, shirts and suntans, and he knew it would be impossible to talk openly now.

They were sitting on the restaurant terrace which overlooked the sea, eating fish – as fresh as Alex had ever tasted – served with rice, salad and black beans. After the intense heat of the afternoon, the air was cool and welcoming. Two guitarists, lit by candles, were playing soft Latin music. Cicadas rasped and rattled in their thousands, hidden in the undergrowth.

The three of them talked like any family would. The towns they were going to visit, the beaches where they wanted to swim. Turner told a joke and Troy laughed loud enough to turn heads. But it was all fake. They weren't going anywhere and the joke hadn't been funny. Despite the food and the surroundings, Alex found himself hating every minute of the role he had been forced to play. The last time he had sat down with a family had been with Sabina and her parents in Cornwall. It seemed a very long time ago and this meal, with these people, somehow turned the memory sour.

But at last it was over and Alex was able to excuse himself and go to bed. He went back to his room, swinging the door shut behind him. For a moment he stood there with his shoulders resting against the wood. He looked around him. Something was wrong. He stepped forward carefully, his nerves jangling. Someone had been there. His case, which had been closed when he left, was now open. Had someone from the hotel been in and searched the room while he was at dinner? Were they still there now? He looked in the bathroom and behind the curtains. No one. Then he went over to the case. It took him a few moments to realize that only the Game Boy was missing. So that was what had happened! Turner or Troy must have somehow slipped into the room while he was out. The Game Boy with its hidden Geiger counter was central to their mission. They had taken it back.

Alex undressed quickly and got into bed, but suddenly he wasn't tired. He lay in the darkness, listening to the waves breaking against the sand. He could see thousands of stars through the open window. He had never realized there were so many of them, nor that they could shine so bright. Turner and Troy returned to their room about half an hour later. He heard them talking in low voices but couldn't make out what they said. He pulled the sheet over his head and forced himself to sleep.

The first thing he saw when he woke up the next morning was a note pushed under his door. He got out of bed and picked it up. It was written in block capitals.

GONE FOR A WALK. THOUGHT YOU NEEDED A REST.
WE'LL CATCH UP WITH YOU LATER. MOM XXX.

Alex tore the note in half, and then in half again. He scattered the pieces in the wastepaper basket and went out to breakfast. It occurred to him that it was a strange set of parents who would walk off, leaving their son behind, but he supposed there were probably plenty of families, with nannies and au pairs, who often did the same. He spent the morning on the beach, reading. There were some other boys of about his own age playing in the sea and he thought of joining them. But they didn't speak English and seemed too self-contained. At eleven o'clock, his "parents" still hadn't returned. Suddenly Alex was fed up, sitting there on his own in the grounds of the hotel. He was on an island on the other side of the world. He might as well see some of it! He got dressed and set off into town.

The heat struck him the moment he stepped outside the grounds of the hotel. The road curved inland, away from the sea, following a line of scrubland on one side and what looked like a tobacco plantation – a mass of fat, green leaves rising to chest height – on the other. The landscape was flat but there was no breeze coming in from the sea. The air was heavy and still. Alex was soon sweating and had to swat at the flies that seemed determined to follow him every step of the way. A few buildings, sun-bleached wood and corrugated iron, sprang up around him. A fly buzzed in his ear. He beat it away.

It took him twenty minutes to reach Puerto Madre, a fishing village that had grown into a dense and cluttered town. The buildings were an amazing jumble of different styles; rickety wooden shops, marble and brick houses, huge stone churches. Everything had been beaten down and baked by the sun – and sunlight was everywhere; in the dust, in the vivid colours, in the smells of spice and overripe fruit.

The noise was deafening. Radio music – jazz and salsa – blasted out of open windows. Extraordinary American cars, vintage Chevrolets and Studebakers like brilliantly coloured toys, jammed the streets, their horns blaring as they tried to make their way past horses and carts, motorized rickshaws, cigarette sellers and shoeshine boys. Old men in vests sat outside the cafés blinking in the sunlight. Women in tight-fitting dresses stood languidly in the doorways. Alex had never been anywhere louder or dirtier or more alive.

Somehow he found himself in the main square with a great statue at the centre; a revolutionary soldier with a rifle at his side and a grenade hanging from his belt. There must have been at least a hundred market stalls jammed into the square, selling fruit and vegetables, coffee beans, souvenirs, old books and T-shirts. And everywhere there were crowds, strolling in and out of the dollar shops and the ice-cream parlours, sitting at tables beneath sweeping colonnades, queuing up in the fast food restaurants and the *paladares* – tiny restaurants located inside private houses.

There was a street sign bolted to a wall. It read: PLAZA DE FRATERNIDAD. Alex had enough Spanish to translate that. Brotherhood Square. He somehow doubted that he would find much brotherhood here. A fat man in an old and dirty linen suit suddenly lurched up to him.

"You want cigars? The best Havana cigars. But at cheap, cheap price."

"Hey, *amigo*. I sell you a T-shirt..."

"*Muchacho!* You bring your parents to my bar..."

Before he knew it, he was surrounded. Alex realized how much he must stand out in this crowd of dark, tropical people milling about in their brightly coloured shirts and straw hats. He was hot and thirsty. He looked around him for somewhere to get a drink.

And that was when he saw Turner and Troy. The two special agents were sitting at a wrought iron table in front of one of the smarter restaurants, shaded by a great vine that sprawled and tumbled over the pockmarked wall. A neon sign hung over them, advertising Montecristo cigars. They were with a man, an islander, obviously deep in conversation. All three of them had drinks. Alex moved towards them, wondering if it would be possible to hear what they were saying.

The man they were talking to looked about seventy years old and was dressed in a dark shirt, loose trousers and a beret. He was smoking a cigarette which seemed to have been pushed through his lips dragging the skin with it. His face, arms and neck were sun-beaten and withered. But as he drew closer, Alex saw the light and the strength in his eyes. Troy said something and the man laughed, picked up his glass with a hand that was all bone and threw back the contents in one. He wiped the back of his hand across his mouth, said something and walked away. Alex had arrived just too late to eavesdrop on the conversation. He decided to make himself known.

"Alex!" As ever, Troy didn't look glad to see him.

"Hi, Mom." Alex sat down without being invited. "Any chance of a drink?"

"What are you doing here?" Turner asked. Once again his mouth was a straight line. His eyes were empty. "We told you to stay at the hotel."

"I thought this was meant to be a family holiday," Alex said. "And anyway, I finished searching the hotel this morning. There aren't any nuclear weapons there, in case you were wondering..."

Turner stared. Troy looked around nervously. "Keep your voice down!" she snapped, as if anyone could hear him in the din of the square.

"You lied to me," Alex said. "Whatever the reason you're here, you're not just spying on General Sarov. Why don't you tell me what this is really about?"

There was a long silence.

"What do you want to drink?" Troy asked.

Alex glanced down at Troy's glass. It contained a pale yellow liquid that looked good. "What have you got?" he asked.

"A *mojito*. It's a local speciality. A mixture of rum, fresh lemon juice, crushed ice, soda and mint leaves."

"That sounds fine. I'll have the same. Without the rum."

Turner called a waiter over and spoke briefly in Spanish. The waiter nodded and hurried away.

Meanwhile, Troy had come to a decision. "All right, Alex," she said. "We'll tell you what you want to know—"

"That's against orders!" Turner interrupted.

Troy looked angrily at him. "What choice do we have? Alex obviously knows about the Game Boy."

"The Geiger counter," Alex said.

Troy nodded. "Yes, Alex, that's what it is. And it's the reason why we're here." She lifted her own drink and took a sip. "We didn't want you to know this because we didn't want to frighten you."

"That's very kind of you."

"We were ordered not to!" She scowled. "But ... all right, since you know so much, you might as well know the rest of it. We believe there's a nuclear device hidden on this island."

"General Sarov...? You think he's got a nuclear bomb?"

"We shouldn't be doing this," Turner muttered.

But this time Troy ignored him. "Something is happening, here, on Skeleton Key," she went on. "We don't know what it is, but if you want the truth, it actually frightens us. In a few days' time, Boris Kiriyenko, the Russian president, is arriving for a two-week vacation. That's not such a big deal. He knew Sarov a long time ago. They were kids together. And it's not as if the Russians are our enemies any more."

Alex knew all this already. It was what Blunt had told him in London.

"But recently, and quite by coincidence, Sarov came to our attention. Turner and I were investigating the Salesman. And we discovered that among all the other things he'd been selling, he'd managed to get his hands on a kilogram of weapons grade uranium, smuggled out of Eastern Europe. For what it's worth, this is one of the biggest nightmares facing the security services today – the sale of uranium. But he'd done it – and if that wasn't bad enough, the person he'd sold it to—"

"—was Sarov." Alex finished the sentence.

"Yes. A plane flew into Skeleton Key and it didn't fly out again. Sarov was there to meet it." She paused. "And now, suddenly, we've got a meeting between these two men – the old general and the new president – and there may be a nuclear bomb in the picture. So you won't be surprised to hear that there are a whole lot of worried people in Washington. That's why we're here."

Alex absorbed what he was being told. Inside, he was seething. Blunt had promised him two weeks in the sun. But it looked like he'd been sent to the front line of World War Three.

"If it is a bomb, what's Sarov planning to do with it?" Alex asked.

"If we knew that, we wouldn't be here!" she snapped. Alex looked at her closely. He was amazed to see that she really was scared. She was trying not to show it but it was there, in her eyes and the tautness of her jaw.

"Our job is to find the nuclear material," Turner said.

"With the Geiger counter."

"Yes. We need to break into Casa de Oro and take a look around. That's what we were talking about just now."

"Who was he? The man you were with?"

Turner sighed. He had already said much more than he wanted to. "His name is Garcia. He's one of our assets."

"Assets?"

"That means he works for us," Troy explained. "We've been paying him over the years to keep us informed and to help us when we're here."

"He has a boat," Turner continued, "and we're going to need it because there's only one way into the Casa de Oro – and that's by sea. The house is built on a sort of plateau right at the tip of the island. It's an old sugar plantation. They used to grow sugar cane there and they've got an old mill that's still in full working order. Anyway, there's only one road that reaches it and it's narrow, with a steep drop down to the sea on both sides. There are security men and a gate. We'd never get in that way."

"But by boat—" Alex began.

"Not by boat..." Turner hesitated, wondering if he should go on. He looked at Troy, who nodded. "We're going to use scuba. You see, we know something that Sarov may not. There's a way into the grounds of the villa that goes past his defences. It's a natural fault line, a shaft inside the cliff that runs all the way from the top to the bottom."

"You're going to climb it?"

"There are metal rungs. Garcia's family has been on the island for centuries and they know every inch of the coastline. He swears the ladder is still there. Three hundred years ago it was used by smugglers to get from the villa to the beach without being seen.

There was a cave at the bottom. The shaft – they call it the Devil's Chimney – runs all the way up and comes out somewhere in the garden. That's our way in."

"Wait a minute." Alex was confused. "You said you were going to use scuba."

Troy nodded. "The water level has risen all around the island and the entrance to the cave is now submerged. It's about twenty metres underwater. But that's great for us. Most people have forgotten the cave is even there at all. Certainly, it won't be guarded. We swim down in scuba gear. We climb the ladder and get into the grounds. We search the villa."

"And if you find the bomb?"

"That's not our problem, Alex. Our work will be done."

The waiter arrived with Alex's drink. He picked up the glass. Even the feel of it, cold against his skin, came as a relief. He drank some. It was sweet and surprisingly refreshing. He set the glass down.

"I want to come with you," he said.

"Forget it. No way!" Troy sounded incredulous. "Why do you think I've told you all this? Only because you know too much already and I need you to understand that we mean business. You have to keep out of the way. This is not a child's game. We're not zapping the bad guy on a computer screen! This is the real thing, Alex. And you're going to stay in the hotel and wait for us to get back!"

"I'm coming with you," Alex insisted. "Maybe you've forgotten, but this is meant to be a family holiday. You dump me on my own in the hotel a second time, maybe somebody's going to notice. Maybe they're going to start wondering where you are."

Turner fiddled with the collar of his shirt. Troy looked away.

"I won't get in your way," Alex sighed. "I'm not asking to come scuba diving with you. Or climbing. I just want to be on the boat. Think about it. If the three of us go together, it'll look more like a family cruise."

Turner nodded slowly. "You know, Troy, the kid has a point."

Troy picked up her drink and gazed into it moodily, as if trying to find an answer inside the glass. "All right," she said at last. "You can come with us if that's what you really want. But you're not part of this, Alex. Your job was to help get us onto the island and if you ask me, we didn't even need you for that. You saw the security at the airport, it was a joke! But OK, since you're here, you might as well come along for the ride. But I don't want to hear you. I don't want to see you. I don't want to know you're there."

"Whatever you say." Alex sat back. He had got what he wanted, but he had to ask himself why he wanted it at all. Given the choice, he would have preferred to take the first plane off the island and put as much distance as possible between himself and the CIA and Sarov and the whole lot of them.

But that was a choice he didn't have. All Alex knew was that he didn't want to spend time in the hotel on his own, worrying. If there really was a bomb somewhere on the island, he wanted to be the first to hear about it. And there was something else. Turner and Troy seemed confident enough about this Devil's Chimney. They had assumed that it wasn't guarded and that it would take them all the way to the top. But they had been equally confident when they had gone to the Salesman's birthday party, and that had almost got Turner killed.

Alex finished his drink. "All right," he said. "So when do we go?"

Troy fell silent. Turner took out his wallet and paid for the drinks. "Straight away," he said. "We're doing it tonight."

THE DEVIL'S CHIMNEY

It was late afternoon when they set out from Puerto Madre, leaving the port with its fish markets and pleasure cruisers behind them. Turner and Troy were going to make the dive while it was still light. They would find the cave and wait there until sunset, then climb up into Casa de Oro under cover of darkness. That was the plan.

The man called Garcia had a boat that had known the sea too long. It wheezed and spluttered out of the harbour, trailing a cloud of evil-smelling black smoke. Rust had rippled and then burst through every surface like some bad skin disease. The boat had no visible name. A few flags fluttered from the mast, but they were little more than rags, with any trace of their original colours faded long ago. There were six air cylinders lashed to a bench underneath a canopy. They were the only new equipment in sight.

Garcia himself had greeted Alex with a mixture of hostility and suspicion. Then he had spoken at length, in Spanish, with Turner.

Alex had spent the best part of a year in Barcelona with his uncle and understood enough of the language to follow what they were saying.

"You never talked about a boy. What do you think this is? A tourist excursion? Who is he? Why did you bring him here?"

"It's none of your business, Garcia. Let's go."

"You paid for two passengers." Garcia held up two withered fingers, every bone and sinew showing through. "Two passengers ... that was what we agreed."

"You're being paid well enough. There's no point arguing. The boy's coming and that's the end of it!"

After that, Garcia fell into sullen silence. Not that there would have been any point talking anyway. The noise of the engine was too great.

Alex watched as the coastline of Cayo Esqueleto slipped past. He had to admit that Blunt had been right – the island was strangely beautiful with its extraordinary, deep colours; the palm trees packed together, separated from the sea by a brilliant ribbon of white sand. The sun was hovering, a perfect circle, over the horizon. A brown pelican, clumsy and comical on the ground, shot out of a pine tree and soared gracefully over their heads. Alex felt strangely at peace. Even the noise of the engine seemed to have drifted away.

After about half an hour, the land began to rise up and he realized they had reached the north point of the island. The vegetation fell back and suddenly he was looking at a sheer rock wall that dropped all the way, without interruption, to the sea. This must be the isthmus that he had been told about, with the road leading to the Casa de Oro somewhere at the top. There was no sign of the house itself but, craning his neck, he could just make out the top of a tower, white and elegant, with a pointed red slate roof. A watchtower. There was a single figure framed in an archway, barely more than a speck. Somehow Alex knew that it was an armed guard.

Garcia turned off the engine and moved to the back of the boat. For such an old man, he seemed very agile. He picked up an anchor and threw it over the side, then hoisted a flag – this one more identifiable than the othe rs. It showed a diagonal white stripe on a red background. Alex recognized the international scuba diving sign.

Troy came over to him. "We'll go down here and swim in to the coast," she said.

Alex looked up at the figure in the tower. There was a glint of sunlight reflecting off something. A pair of binoculars? "I think we're being watched," he said.

Troy nodded. "Yes. But it doesn't matter. Dive boats aren't allowed to come here but they sometimes do. They're used to it. The shore is strictly off-limits but there's a wreck somewhere ... people swim to that. We'll be fine, provided we don't draw attention to ourselves. Just don't do anything stupid, Alex."

Even now she couldn't resist lecturing him. Alex wondered what he would have to do to impress these people. He said nothing.

Turner had taken off his shirt, showing a hairless, muscular chest. Alex watched as he stripped down to his trunks, then pulled on a wetsuit which he had taken from a small cabin below. Quickly the two CIA agents got ready, attaching air cylinders to their buoyancy jackets – BCDs – then adding weight belts, masks and snorkels. Garcia was smoking, sitting to one side and watching all this with quiet amusement, as if it really had nothing to do with him.

At last they were ready. Turner had brought a waterproof bag with him and he unzipped it. Alex noticed the Game Boy sealed in a plastic bag inside. There were also maps, torches, knives and a harpoon gun.

"Leave it all, Turner," Troy said.

"The Game Boy...?"

"We'll come back for it." Troy turned to Alex. "Right, Alex," she said. "Listen up! We're going to make an exploratory dive to begin with. We'll be gone about twenty minutes. No longer. We need to find the cave entrance and check there are no security devices in operation." She glanced at her watch. It was only half past six. "The sun won't set for another hour," she continued. "We don't want to spend that long sitting in the cave, so we'll come back to the boat for the rest of our equipment, change tanks and make a second journey back. You don't have to worry about anything. As far as the people in the villa are concerned, we're just tourists doing a sunset dive."

"I'm a qualified diver," Alex said.

"The hell with that!" Turner cut in.

Troy agreed. "You talked your way onto the boat," she said. "Fine. Personally, I wish you'd stayed in the hotel. But maybe you were right about that, it might have raised suspicions."

"You're not coming with us," Turner said. He looked at Alex coldly. "We don't want any more people killed. You stay here with Garcia and leave the rest to us."

The two agents made their all-important buddy checks, each one looking over the other's equipment. No pipes twisted. Air in the tanks. Weights and releases. Finally, they went over to the side of the boat and sat with their backs facing the sea. They both put on their fins. Turner gave Troy the all-clear sign: second finger and thumb forming an O, with the other fingers raised. They lowered their masks and rolled over backwards, disappearing immediately into the depths of the sea.

That was the last time Alex saw them alive.

He sat with Garcia on the gently rocking boat. The sun was almost touching the horizon and a few clouds, deep red, had intruded into the sky. The air was warm and pleasant. Garcia sucked on his cigarette and the tip glowed.

"You American?" he asked suddenly, speaking in English.

"No. I'm English."

"Why you here?" Garcia smiled as if amused to find himself alone at sea with an English boy.

"I don't know." Alex shrugged. "How about you?"

"Money." The one word answer was enough.

Garcia came over and sat down next to Alex, examining him with two dark eyes that were suddenly very serious. "They don't like you," he said.

"I don't think so," Alex agreed.

"You know why?"

Alex said nothing.

"They are grown-ups. They think they are good at what they do. And then they find a child who is better. And not only that. He is an English child. Not an Americano!" Garcia chuckled and Alex wondered how much he had been told. "It makes them feel uncomfortable. It's the same all over the world."

"I didn't ask to be here," Alex said.

"But still you came. They would have been happier without you."

The boat creaked. A light breeze had sprung up, rippling the flags. The sun was sinking faster now and the whole sky was turning to blood. Alex looked at his watch. Ten to seven. The twenty minutes had passed quickly. He scanned the surface of the ocean but there was no sign of Turner or Troy.

Another five minutes passed. Alex was beginning to feel uneasy. He didn't know the two agents well, but guessed they were people who did everything by the book. They had their procedures, and if they said twenty minutes, they meant twenty minutes. They had been underwater now for twenty-five. Of course, they had enough oxygen for an hour. But even so, Alex wondered why they were taking so long.

A quarter of an hour later, they still hadn't come back. Alex couldn't disguise his fears. He was pacing the deck, looking left and right, searching for the tell-tale bubbles that would show them coming up, hoping to see their arms and heads breaking the surface of the water. Garcia hadn't moved. Alex wondered if the old man was even awake. A full forty minutes had passed since Turner and Troy had submerged.

"Something's wrong," Alex said. Garcia didn't answer. "What are we going to do?" Still Garcia refused to speak and Alex became angry. "Didn't they have a back-up plan? What did they tell you to do?"

"They tell me to wait for them." Garcia opened his eyes. "I wait an hour. I wait two hours. I wait all night..."

"But in another ten or fifteen minutes they're going to run out of air."

"Maybe they enter the Devil's Chimney. Maybe they climb up!"

"No. That wasn't their plan. And anyway, they've left all their equipment behind." Suddenly Alex had made up his mind. "Have you got any more scuba gear? Another BCD?"

Garcia stared at Alex, surprised. Then he slowly nodded.

Five minutes later, Alex stood on the deck dressed only in shorts and a T-shirt, with an oxygen cylinder strapped to his back and two respirators – one to breathe through, the other spare – dangling at his side. He would have liked to put on a wetsuit, but he hadn't been able to find one his size. He would just have to hope that the water wasn't too cold. The BCD he was wearing was old and it was too big for him, but he had quickly tested it and at least it worked. He looked at his instrument console; pressure gauge, depth gauge and compass. He had 3000psi in his air tank. More than he would need. Finally, he had a knife strapped to his leg. He probably wouldn't use it and would never normally have worn it. But he needed the reassurance. He went over to the side of the boat and sat down.

Garcia shook his head disapprovingly. Alex knew he was right. He was breaking the single most critical rule in the world of scuba diving. Nobody ever dives alone. He had been taught scuba by his uncle when he was eleven years old and if Ian Rider had been here now he would have been speechless with anger and disbelief. If you get into trouble – a snagged air hose or a valve failure – and you don't have a buddy, you're dead. It's as simple as that. But this was an emergency. Turner and Troy had been gone for forty-five minutes. Alex had to help.

"You take this," Garcia said suddenly. He was holding an out-of-date dive computer. It would show Alex how deep he was and how long he had been down.

"Thanks," Alex said. He took it.

Alex pulled his mask down, pushed the mouthpiece between his lips and breathed in. He could feel the oxygen and nitrogen mix rushing into the back of his throat. It had a slightly stale taste but he could tell it wasn't contaminated. He crossed his hands, holding his mask and respirator in place, then rolled over backwards. He felt his arm knock against something on the side as the world spun upside down. The water rushed up to greet him and then his vision was pulled apart like a curtain opening as he found himself plunging into the water.

He had left enough air in the BCD to keep him afloat and he made one last check, getting his bearings on the coastline so that he would know where to swim to and, more importantly, how to get back. At least the sea was still warm, although Alex knew that, with the sun rapidly setting, it wouldn't be for long. Cold is a dangerous enemy for the scuba diver, sapping the strength and concentration. The deeper he went, the colder it would get. He couldn't afford to hang around. He released the air from the BCD. At once the weights began to drag him down. The sea rose up and devoured him.

He swam down, squeezing his nose and blowing hard – equalizing – to stop the pain in his ears. For the first time he was able to look around him. There was still enough sunlight to illuminate the sea and Alex caught his breath, marvelling at the astonishing beauty of the underwater world. The water was dark blue and perfectly clear. There were a few coral heads dotted around him, the shapes and colours as alien as anything it's possible to find on the earth. He felt completely at peace, the sound of his own breathing echoing in his ears and each breath releasing a cascade of silver bubbles. With his arms loosely folded across his chest, Alex let his fins propel him towards the shore. He was fifteen metres down, about five metres above the sea bed. A family of brightly coloured groupers swam past him; fat lips, bulging eyes and strange, misshapen bodies. Hideous and beautiful at the same time. It had been a year since Alex had last gone diving and he wished he had time to enjoy this. He kicked forward. The groupers darted away, alarmed.

It didn't take him long to reach the edge of the cliff. The sea wall was of course much more than a wall; a seething mass of rock, coral, vegetation and fish life. A living thing. Huge gorgonian fans – leaves made of a thousand tiny bones – waved slowly from side to side. Clumps of coral exploded brilliantly all around him. A school of about a thousand tiny silver fish flickered past. There was a slither of movement as a moray eel disappeared behind a rock. He glanced at the dive computer. At least it seemed to be working. It told him he had been down for seven minutes.

He had to find the entrance to the cave. That was why he was here. He forced himself to ignore the colours and sights of the underwater kingdom and concentrate on the rock face. The time he had spent taking his bearings before the dive paid off now. He knew more or less where the tower at the Casa de Oro stood in relation to the boat and swam in that direction, keeping the rock wall on his left. Something long and dark flashed past high above him. Alex saw it out of the corner of his eye but by the time he had turned his head it was gone. Was there a boat on the surface? Alex went down another couple of metres, searching for the cave.

In the end, it wasn't hard to find. The entrance was circular, like a gaping mouth. This impression was heightened when Alex swam closer and looked inside. The cave hadn't always been underwater and over a period of time – millions of years – stalactites and stalagmites had grown, needle-sharp spears that hung down from the ceiling and protruded up from the floor. As always, Alex was unable to remember which was which. But even from a distance there was something menacing about the place. It was like looking into the open mouth of some giant, undersea monster. He could almost imagine the stalactites and stalagmites biting down, the whole thing swallowing him up.

But he had to go in. The cave wasn't very deep and apart from the rock formations it was empty, with a wide, sandy floor. He was thankful for that. Swimming too far into an underwater cave, at sunset, on his own, really would have been madness. He could see the back wall from the entrance – and there were the first of the metal rungs! They were dark red now and covered in green slime and coral, but they were clearly man-made, disappearing up the far wall and presumably continuing all the way to the top of the Devil's Chimney. There was no sign of Turner or Troy. Had the two agents decided to climb up after all? Should Alex try to climb after them?

Alex was about to swim forward when there was another movement just outside his field of vision. Whatever he had seen before had come back, swimming the other way. Puzzled, he looked up. And froze. He actually felt the air stop somewhere at the back of his throat. The last of the bubbles chased each other up to the surface. Alex just hung there, fighting for control. He wanted to scream. But underwater, it isn't possible to scream.

He was looking at a great white shark, at least three metres long, circling slowly above him. The sight was so unreal, so utterly shocking, that at first Alex quite literally didn't believe his eyes. It had to be an illusion, some sort of trick. The very fact that it was so close to him seemed impossible. He stared at the white underbelly, the two sets of fins, the downturned crescent mouth with its jagged, razor-sharp teeth. And there were the deadly, round eyes, as black and as evil as anything on the planet. Had they seen him yet?

Alex forced himself to breathe. His heart was pounding. Not just his heart – his whole body. He could hear his breath, as if amplified, in his head. His legs hung limp beneath him, refusing to move. He was terrified. That was the simple truth. He had never been so scared in his life.

What did he know about sharks? Was the great white going to attack him? What could he do? Desperately, Alex tried to draw on what little knowledge he had.

There were three hundred and fifty known species of shark but only very few of them were known to have attacked people. The great white – *carcharodon carcharias* – was definitely one of them. Not so good. But shark attacks were rare. Only about a hundred people were killed every year. More people died in car accidents. On the other hand, the waters around Cuba were notoriously dangerous. This was a single shark...

...still circling him, as if choosing its moment...

...and it might not have seen him. No. That wasn't possible. A shark's eyes are ten times more sensitive than a human being's.

Even in pitch darkness it can see eight metres away. And anyway, it doesn't need eyes. It has receptors built into its snout which can detect even the tiniest electrical current. A beating heart, for example.

Alex tried to force himself to calm down. His own heart was generating minute amounts of electricity. His terror would guide the creature towards him. He had to relax!

What else? Don't splash. Don't make any sudden movements. Advice given to him by Ian Rider came echoing back across the years. A shark will be attracted to shiny metal objects, to brightly coloured clothes, and to fresh blood. Alex slowly turned his head. His oxygen cylinder had been painted black. His T-shirt was white. There was no blood. Was there?

He turned his hands over, examining himself. And then he saw it. Just above the wrist on his left arm. There was a small gash. He hadn't even noticed it, but now he remembered catching his wrist on the side of the boat as he fell backwards. A tiny amount of blood, brown rather than red, twisted upwards out of the wound.

Tiny, but enough. A shark can smell one drop of blood in twenty-five gallons of water. Who had taught him that? He had forgotten, but he knew it was true. The shark had smelt him...

...and was still smelling him, slowly closing in...

The circles were getting smaller. The shark's fins were down. Its back was arched. And it was moving in a strange, jerky pattern. The three textbook signs of an imminent attack. Alex knew that he had only seconds between life and death. Slowly, trying not to make any disturbance in the water, he reached down. The knife was still there, strapped to his leg, and he carefully unfastened it. The weapon would be tiny against the bulk of the great white and the blade would seem pathetic compared to those vicious teeth. But Alex felt better having it in his hand. It was something.

He looked around him. Apart from the cave itself, there was nowhere to hide – and the cave was useless. The mouth was too wide. If he went inside, the shark would simply follow him. And yet, if he made it to the ladder, he might be able to climb it. That would take him out of the water – up the Devil's Chimney and onto dry land. True, he would surface in the middle of the Casa de Oro. But no matter how bad General Sarov might be, he couldn't be worse than the shark.

He had made his decision. Slowly, keeping the shark in his sight, he began to move towards the cave's entrance. For a moment he thought the shark had lost interest in him. It seemed to be swimming away. But then he saw that he had been tricked. The creature turned and, as if fired from a gun, rushed through the water, heading straight for him. Alex dived down, air exploding from his lungs. There was a boulder to one side of the cave and he tried to wedge himself into a corner, putting it between himself and his attacker. It worked. The shark curved away. At that moment, Alex lunged forward with the knife. He felt his arm shudder as the blade cut into the thick hide just under the two front fins. As the shark flickered past, he saw that it was leaving a trail of what looked like brown smoke. Blood. But he knew that he had barely wounded it. He had managed a pinprick, nothing more. And he had probably angered it, making it all the more determined.

Worse, he was bleeding more himself. In his attempt to get out of the way, he had backed into the coral, which had cut his arms and legs. Alex felt no pain. That would come later. But now he really had done it. He had advertised himself: dinner, fresh and bleeding. It was a miracle that the great white hadn't been joined by a dozen friends.

He had to get into the cave. The shark was some distance away, out to sea. The cave entrance was just a few metres away to his left.

Two or three kicks and he would be in – then through the stalactites and stalagmites and onto the ladder. Could he do it in time?

Alex kicked with all his strength. At the same time he was thrashing with his hands and cursed noiselessly as he accidentally dropped the knife. Well, it would do him no good anyway. He kicked a second time. The entrance to the cave loomed up in front of him. He was in front of it now but not inside...

...And he was too late! The shark came hurtling towards him. The eyes seemed to have grown bigger. The mouth was stretched open in a snarl that contained all the hatred in the world. Its mouth was gaping, the dreadful teeth slicing through the water. Alex jerked backwards, twisting his spine. The shark missed him by centimetres. He felt the surge of water pushing him away. Now the shark was in the cave, but he wasn't. It was turning to attack again, and this time it wouldn't be confused by the rock wall and the boulders. This time Alex was right in its sights.

And then it happened. Alex heard a metallic buzz and, in front of his eyes, the stalagmites rose out of the floor and the stalactites dropped out of the ceiling, teeth that skewered the shark not once, but five or six times. Blood exploded into the water. Alex saw the dreadful eyes as its head whipped from side to side. He could almost imagine the creature howling in pain. It was completely trapped, as if in the jaws of a monster even more dreadful than itself. How had it happened? Alex hung in the water, shocked and uncomprehending. Slowly the blood cleared. And he understood.

Turner and Troy had been wrong a second time. Sarov had known about the Devil's Chimney and he had made sure that nobody could reach it by swimming through the cave. The stalagmites and stalactites were fake. They were made of metal, not stone, and were mounted on some sort of hydraulic spring. Swimming into the cave, the shark must have activated an infrared beam which in turn had triggered the ambush. Even as he watched, the deadly spears retracted, sliding back into the floor and ceiling. There was a hum and the body of the shark was sucked into the cave, disappearing into a trap. So the place even had its own disposal system! Alex was beginning to understand the nature of the man who lived in the Casa de Oro. Whatever else he might be, Sarov left nothing to chance.

And now he knew what had happened to the two CIA agents. Alex felt sick. All he wanted to do was get away. Not just out of the water but out of the country. He wished he had never come.

There was still a lot of blood in the water. Alex swam quickly, afraid that it would attract more sharks. But he paced himself, carefully measuring his ascent towards the surface. If a diver rises too quickly, nitrogen gets trapped in the bloodstream causing the painful and potentially lethal sickness known as the bends. That was the last thing Alex needed right now. He spent five minutes at three metres' depth – a final safety stop – then came up for air. The whole world had changed while he had been underwater. The sun had rolled behind the horizon and the sky, the sea, the land, the very air itself had become suffused with the deepest crimson. He could see Garcia's boat, a dark shadow, about twenty metres away and swam over to it. Suddenly he was cold. His teeth were chattering – although they had probably been chattering from the moment he had seen the shark.

Alex reached the side of the boat. Garcia was still sitting on the deck with a cigarette between his lips but didn't offer to help him out.

"Thanks a bunch," Alex muttered.

He slipped off his BCD – the oxygen tank came with it – and heaved it onto the boat, then pulled himself out of the water. He winced. Out of the water, he could feel the wounds that the coral had inflicted on his limbs. But there was no time to do anything about that now. As soon as he was standing on the deck, he unhooked his weight belt and dumped it to one side along with his mask and snorkel. There was a towel in Turner's bag. He took it out and used it to rub himself dry. Then he went over to Garcia.

"We have to go," he said. "Turner and Troy are dead. The cave is a trap. Do you understand? You have to take me back to the hotel."

Garcia still said nothing. For the first time, Alex noticed something about the cigarette in the man's mouth. It wasn't actually lit. Suddenly uneasy, Alex reached out. Garcia fell forward. There was a knife sticking out of his back.

Alex felt something hard touch him between his shoulder blades and a voice, which seemed to have trouble with the words it was saying, whispered from somewhere behind him.

"A little late to be out swimming, I think. I advise you now to keep very still."

A speedboat which had been lurking in the shadows on the other side of the diving boat roared to life, lights blazing. Alex stood where he was. Two more men climbed onboard, both of them speaking in Spanish. He just had time to glimpse the dark, grinning face of one of Sarov's *macheteros* before a sack was thrown over his head. Something touched his arm and he felt a sting and knew that he had just been injected with a hypodermic syringe. Almost at once, the strength went out of his legs and he would have collapsed but for the invisible hands that held him up.

And then he was lifted up and carried away. Alex began to wonder if it would have made any difference if the shark had reached him after all. The men who were carrying him off the boat were treating him like someone who was already dead.

THE CRUSHER

Alex couldn't move.

He was lying on his back on a hard, sticky surface. When he tried to raise his shoulders, he felt his T-shirt clinging to whatever it was underneath him. It was as if he had been glued into place. Whatever had been injected into him had removed all power of movement from his arms and legs. The bag still covered his head, keeping him in darkness. He knew that he had been loaded into the speedboat and taken back to the coast. Some sort of van had met him and brought him here. He had heard footsteps and rough hands had grabbed him, carrying him like a sack of vegetables. He guessed that three or four men had been involved in the journey, but they had barely spoken. Once he had heard the same man who had spoken to him on the boat. He had muttered a couple of words in Spanish. But his voice was so indistinct, the words so garbled, that Alex had found it hard to understand what he was saying.

Fingers brushed against the side of his neck and suddenly the bag was removed. Alex blinked. He was lying in a brightly lit warehouse or factory; the first thing he saw was the metal framework supporting the roof, with arc lamps hanging down. The walls were bare brick, whitewashed, the floor lined with terracotta tiles. There was machinery on both sides of him. Most of it looked agricultural and a hundred years out of date. There were chains and buckets and a complicated pulley system that fed into a series of metal wheels that could have come out of a giant antique watch, and next to them, a pair of earthenware cauldrons. Alex twisted round and saw more cauldrons on the other side and, in the distance, some sort of filtration system with pipes leading everywhere. He realized now that he was lying on a long conveyor-belt. He tried once again to get up or even roll off, but his body wouldn't obey him.

A man stepped into his line of vision.

Alex looked up into a pair of eyes that weren't actually quite a pair. They weren't positioned correctly in the man's face and one of them was bloodshot. Alex wondered if it could even see. The man had been horribly injured at some time. He was bald on one side of his head, but not on the other. His mouth was slanting. His skin was dead. In a beauty contest, he wouldn't even come a close second to the great white shark.

There were a couple of dark, unsmiling workers standing behind him. They were shabbily dressed, with moustaches and bandanas. Neither of them spoke. They seemed keenly interested in what was about to happen.

"Your name?" The movements of the man's mouth didn't quite match what he was saying, so seeing him speak was a bit like watching a badly dubbed film.

"Alex Gardiner," Alex said.

"Your real name?"

"I just told you."

"You lied. Your real name is Alex Rider."

"Why ask if you think you know?"

The man nodded as if Alex had asked a fair question. "My name is Conrad," he said. "We have met before."

"Have we?" Alex tried to think. Then he remembered. The man he had seen limping down the boardwalk in Miami wearing sunglasses and a straw hat! It was the same man.

Conrad leaned forward. "Why are you here?" he asked.

"I'm on vacation with my mom and dad." Alex decided it was time to pretend he was just an ordinary fourteen-year-old. "Where are they?" he demanded. "Why have you brought me here? What happened to the man on the boat? I want to go home!"

"Where is your home?" Conrad asked.

"I live in LA. De Flores Street, west Hollywood."

"No." There was no doubt at all in Conrad's voice. "Your accent is very convincing, but you are not American. You are English. The people you came with were called Tom Turner and Belinda Troy. They were agents of the CIA. They are now dead."

"I don't know what you're talking about. You've got the wrong guy."

Conrad smiled. At least, one side of his mouth smiled. The other could only manage a slight twitch. "Lying to me is stupid and a waste of time. I have to know why you are here," he said. "It is an unusual experience to interrogate a child, but it is one I shall enjoy. You are the only one left. So tell me, Alex Rider, why did you come to Cayo Esqueleto? What were you planning to do?"

"I wasn't planning to do anything!" Despite everything, Alex thought it was worth one last try. He was still speaking with an

American accent. "My dad's a film producer. He's got nothing to do with the CIA. Who are you? And why have you brought me here?"

"I am losing my patience!" Conrad took a break, as if the effort of talking was too much for him. "Tell me what I want to know."

"I'm on vacation!" Alex said. "I've already told you!"

"You have told me lies. Now you will tell me the truth."

Conrad leaned down and picked up a large metal box with two buttons – one red, one green – attached to a thick cable. He pressed the green button. At once, Alex felt a jolt underneath him. An alarm bell rang. Somewhere in the distance there was a loud whine as a machine started up. A few seconds later, the conveyor began to move.

Using all his strength, Alex fought against the drug that was in his system, forcing his head up so that he could look over his feet. What he saw sent a spasm of shock all the way through him. His head swam and he thought he was going to faint. The conveyor-belt was carrying him towards two huge, spinning grindstones about seven metres away. They were so close to each other they were almost touching. There was one underneath and one on top. The belt stopped just at the point where they met. Alex was slumped helplessly on the belt. There was nothing he could do. He was moving towards the grindstones at a rate of about ten centimetres a second. It would take him a little over a minute to reach them. When he did finally get there, he would be crushed. That was the death that this man had arranged for him.

"Do you know how sugar was produced?" Conrad asked. "This place, where you are now, is a sugar mill. The machinery used to be steam-powered but now it is electric. The sugar cane was delivered here by the *colonos* – the farmers. It was shredded and then placed on a belt to be crushed. After that it was filtered. Water was allowed to evaporate. Then the remaining syrup was placed in cauldrons and heated so that it formed crystals." Conrad paused to draw breath. "You, Alex, are at the beginning of that process. You are about to be fed into the crusher. I ask you to imagine the pain that lies ahead of you. Your toes will enter first. Then you will be sucked in one centimetre at a time. After your toes, your feet. Your legs and your knees. How much of you will pass through before you are allowed the comfort of death? Think about it! Whatever else it is, I can promise you that it will not be sweet."

Conrad raised the box with the two buttons. "Tell me what I want to know and I will press the red button. It stops the machine."

"You're wrong!" Alex shouted. "You can't do this!"

"I am doing this. And I am never wrong. Please, do not waste any more time. You have so little of it left..."

Alex lifted his head up again. The grindstones were getting closer with every second that passed. He could feel their vibration, transmitted down the conveyor-belt.

"How much did the agents know?" Conrad demanded. "Why were they here?"

Alex slumped back. The pounding of the two stones enveloped him. He looked past Conrad at the other two men. Would they let him do this? But their faces were impassive. "Please...!" he shouted. Then stopped himself. There was no mercy in this man. He had seen that at once. He gritted his teeth, biting back his fear. He wanted to cry. He could actually feel the tears in his eyes. This wasn't what he wanted. He had never asked to be a spy. Why should he be expected to die like one?

"You have perhaps fifty seconds more," Conrad said.

And that was when Alex made up his mind. There was no point in going silently to this bloody and unspeakable death. This wasn't a World War Two film with him as the hero. He was a schoolboy and everyone – Blunt, Mrs Jones, the CIA – had lied to him and played tricks on him to get him here. Anyway, Conrad already knew who he was. He had called him by his real name. Conrad knew that Troy and Turner had been American spies. There was only one piece of information he could add. The CIA were looking for a nuclear bomb. And why shouldn't he tell Conrad that? Maybe it would be enough to stop him using it.

"They were searching for a bomb!" he cried out. "A nuclear bomb. They know Sarov bought uranium from the Salesman. They came here with a Geiger counter. They were going to break into the villa and look for the bomb."

"How did they know?"

"I don't know..."

"Thirty seconds."

The rumbling and pounding was louder than ever. Alex looked up and saw the stones less than three metres away. Air was rushing between them and flowing over him. He could feel the breeze cold on his skin. The fact that he wasn't tied down, that his arms and legs were free, only made it all the worse. He couldn't move! The drug had turned him into a piece of living meat on its way to the mincer. Perspiration flowed down the side of his face then followed the line of his jaw and curved behind his neck.

"It was Turner!" Alex yelled. "He found out from the Salesman. He was working undercover. They found out that he'd sold you the uranium and they came here looking for the bomb."

"Did they know the purpose of the bomb?"

"No! I don't know. They didn't tell me. Now stop the machine and let me go."

Conrad considered for a moment. The box was still in his hand.

"No," he said. "I don't think so."

"What?" Alex screamed the single word. He could barely hear himself above the noise of the grindstones.

"You've been a bad boy," Conrad said. "And bad boys have to be punished."

"But you said—"

"I lied. Just like you. But of course I must kill you. You are of no further use..."

Alex went mad. He opened his mouth and screamed, trying to find the strength to separate himself from the conveyor-belt. His brain knew what it wanted. His body refused to obey. It was useless. He jerked upwards. His feet were moving ever closer to the spinning stones. Conrad took a step back. He was going to watch as Alex was fed through the crusher. The two workers behind him would clear up when it was over.

"No!" Alex howled.

"Goodbye, Alex," Conrad said.

And then – another voice. In another language. One that Alex didn't understand.

Conrad said something. Alex could no longer hear. The man's lips moved but any sound was snatched away by the roar of the machine.

Alex's bare toes were being battered by the wind that was forced through the stones. They were five centimetres away from being crushed. Four centimetres, three centimetres, two centimetres...

There was a gunshot.

Sparks. The smell of smoke.

The grindstones were still spinning. But the conveyor-belt had stopped. Alex's feet were jutting over the end of the belt. He could almost feel the spinning stone racing past his toes.

Then the voice came again, speaking now in English.

"My dear Alex. I'm so sorry. Are you all right?"

Alex tried to reply with the worst swear-word he knew. But it wouldn't come. He couldn't even breathe.

With a sense of gratitude, he passed out.

"You will have to forgive Conrad. He is an excellent assistant and useful in so many ways. But he can also be a little ... over-enthusiastic."

Alex had woken up in the most magnificent bedroom he had ever seen. He was lying on a four-poster bed opposite a floor-to-ceiling mirror in an ornate gold frame. All the furniture in the room was antique and wouldn't have been out of place in a museum. There was a painted chest at the foot of the bed, a massive wardrobe with elaborately carved doors, a chandelier with five curving arms. The shutters on the windows had been folded back to reveal a wrought iron balustrade looking out over a courtyard.

The man, who had introduced himself as General Alexei Sarov, was sitting on a chair next to the mirror, dressed in a dark suit. His legs were crossed. His back was completely straight. Alex examined the face with its grey hair and intelligent blue eyes. He recognized his voice from the sugar mill and knew – without knowing why – that it was the general who had saved him.

It was dark outside. Alex guessed it must be after midnight. Someone had dressed him in a white nightshirt that came down to his knees. He wondered how long he had been asleep. And how long the Russian had been waiting for him to wake up.

"Do you want something to eat?" That had been his first question.

"No, thank you. I'm not hungry."

"A drink then?"

"Some water..."

"I have some here."

The water came in a silver jug, served in a gleaming crystal glass. General Sarov poured it himself, then handed it to Alex. Alex reached out, grateful that the drug Conrad had pumped into him had worn off while he was asleep and that he could move his arms again. He sipped. The water was ice-cold. That was when Sarov began his apology, speaking in faultless English.

"Conrad had no orders to eliminate you. On the contrary, when I found out who you were, I very much wanted to meet you."

Alex wondered about that, but decided to ignore it for the moment. "How did you find out who I was?" he asked. There seemed no point in denying it now.

"We have a very sophisticated security system both here and in Havana." The general seemed uninterested in explaining more. "I'm afraid you've had a terrible ordeal."

"The people I came here with had a worse one."

Again the general raised a hand, brushing aside the details. "Your friends are dead. Were they your friends, Alex?" A brief pause. "I was of course perfectly well aware of the Devil's Chimney when I first moved into the Casa de Oro. I had a simple defence mechanism constructed. Diving is prohibited on this side of the island so when the occasional diver is foolish enough to enter the cave, he is only paying the price of his curiosity. They tell me that a shark was killed there..."

"It was a great white."

"You saw it?"

Alex said nothing. Sarov raised his hands, resting his chin on the tip of his fingers.

"You are as remarkable as I was told," he continued. "I have read your file, Alex. You have no parents. You were raised by an uncle who was himself a spy. You were trained by the Special Air

Service, the SAS, and sent on your first mission in the south of England. And then, just a few weeks later, to France… Some would say that you have had the luck of the devil, but I do not personally believe in the devil – or in God, for that matter. But I believe in you, Alex. You are quite unique."

Alex was getting tired of all this flattery. And he couldn't help but feel that there was something sinister in it. "Why am I here?" he asked. "What do you want with me?"

"Why you are here should be self-evident," Sarov answered. "Conrad wanted to kill you. I prevented him. But I cannot allow you to return to the hotel or, indeed, to leave the island. You will have to consider yourself my prisoner, although if the Casa de Oro is a prison, I hope you will find it a comfortable one. As to what I want with you…" Sarov smiled to himself, his eyes suddenly distant. "It is late," he announced suddenly. "We can talk about that tomorrow."

He stood up.

"Is it true that you have a nuclear bomb?" Alex asked.

"Yes."

Part of the puzzle fell into place. "You bought uranium from the Salesman. But then you ordered Conrad to kill him! You blew up his boat!"

"That is correct."

So Alex had been right all along. He had seen Conrad in Miami. Conrad had put some sort of explosive device on the *Mayfair Lady* – and it was that, not the fire, that had caused the destruction and loss of life. Turner and Troy had accused him unfairly.

"The nuclear bomb…" Alex said. "What are you going to do with it?"

"Are you afraid?"

"I want to know."

The general considered. "I will tell you only this for now," he said. "I do not imagine that you know a great deal about my country, Alex. The Union of Soviet Socialist Republics as it was once called. The USSR. Russia, as it is today. I do not suppose these things are taught to you in your Western schools."

"I know that communism is finished, if that's what you mean," Alex said. "And it's a bit late for a history lesson."

"My country was once a world power," Sarov continued, ignoring him. "It was one of the most powerful nations on the earth. Who put the first man into space? We did! Who made the greatest advances in science and technology? Who was feared by the rest of the world?" He paused. "You are right. Yes. Communism has been driven out. And what do you see in its place?" A flicker of anger appeared on his face – there only for a second and then it was gone. "Russia has become second-rate. There is no law and order. The prisons are empty and criminals control the streets. Millions of Russians are addicted to drugs. Millions more have AIDS. Women and children find work as prostitutes. And all this so that the people can eat McDonald's and buy Levi jeans and talk on their mobile telephones in Red Square!"

General Sarov walked over to the door.

"You ask me what I am going to do," he said. "I am going to turn back the page and undo the damage of the last thirty years. I am going to give my country back its pride and its position on the world stage. I am not an evil man, Alex. Whatever your superiors may have told you, my only wish is to stop the disease and to make the world a better place. I hope you can believe that. It matters very much to me that you should come to see things my way."

"You have a nuclear bomb," Alex said, speaking slowly. "I don't understand. How is that going to help you achieve what you want?"

"That will be revealed to you ... in time. Let us have breakfast together at nine o'clock. Then I will show you around the estate."

General Sarov nodded and left the room.

Alex waited a minute before slipping out of bed. He looked out into the courtyard, then went and tried the door. He wasn't surprised by what he found. Sarov had described the Casa de Oro as a prison and he was right. There was no way Alex could climb down into the courtyard. And the bedroom door was locked.

THE HOUSE OF SLAVES

A knock at the door woke Alex just after eight o'clock the next morning. As he sat up in bed, a woman dressed in black with a white apron came in, carrying a case which he recognized as his own. Sarov must have sent someone to the Hotel Valencia to collect it. Alex waited until the woman had gone, then got quickly out of bed and opened it. All his clothes were there. So were the Michael Owen figurine and the bubblegum that Smithers had given him. Only the mobile phone had gone. Clearly, Sarov didn't want him to phone home.

After what Sarov had said the night before, he decided to leave his Levi's in the case. Instead he chose a pair of baggy shorts, a plain T-shirt and the Reefer sandals he'd last used when he was surfing in Cornwall. He got dressed and went over to the window. The courtyard he had seen the night before was now bathed in sunlight. It was rectangular in shape, surrounded by a marble walkway and a series of arched colonnades. Two servants were sweeping the fine sand which covered the ground. Two more were watering the plants. He looked up and saw the watchtower that he had noticed from the boat. There was still a guard in place, his machine gun clearly visible.

At ten to nine, the door opened again. This time it was Conrad who came in, wearing a black shirt buttoned to the neck, black trousers and sandals that revealed four toes on one foot, only three on the other.

"*Desayuno!*" Alex recognized the Spanish word for breakfast. Conrad had spat the single word out as if it offended him to say it. He was clearly unhappy to see Alex again – but then of course, he'd had other plans.

"Good morning, Conrad!" Alex forced a smile to his face. After what had happened the night before, he was determined to show that the man didn't scare him. He pointed. "You seem to have forgotten some of your toes."

He walked over to the door. As he passed through into the corridor, Conrad was suddenly close to him. "It isn't over yet," he whispered. "The general may change his mind."

Alex continued forward. He found himself in a wide corridor above a second courtyard. He looked down at a stone fountain surrounded by white pillars. He could smell perfume in the air. The sound of water rippled through the house. Conrad pointed and Alex took a staircase down and into a room where breakfast had already been served.

General Sarov was sitting at a huge polished table, eating a plate of fruit. He was wearing a tracksuit. He smiled as Alex came in, and gestured towards an empty seat. There were a dozen to choose from.

"Good morning, Alex. You will have to forgive my clothes. I

always run before breakfast. Three times around the plantation. A distance of twenty-four miles. I'll change later. Did you sleep well?"

"Yes, thank you."

"Help yourself, please, to breakfast. There is fruit and cereal. Fresh bread. Eggs. Personally, I eat my eggs raw. This is a habit I have followed throughout my life. To cook food is to remove half its goodness. Up in smoke!" He raised a hand in the air. "Man is the only creature on the planet that needs to have his meat and vegetables burned or broiled before he can consume them. However, if you wish, I can have some eggs prepared the way you like."

"No thanks, General. I'll stick with the fruit and cereal."

Sarov noticed Conrad standing at the door. "I don't need you now, thank you, Conrad. We'll meet again at midday."

Conrad's one good eye narrowed. He nodded and left the room.

"I'm afraid Conrad doesn't like you," Sarov said.

"That's all right. I'm not crazy about Conrad." Alex glanced at the door. "What exactly is the matter with him?" he asked. "He doesn't look well."

"By any rights, he should be dead. He was involved in an explosion with a bomb which he happened to be carrying at the time. Conrad is something of a scientific miracle. There are more than thirty metal pins in his body. He has a metal plate in his skull. There are metal wires in his jaw and in most of his major joints."

"He must set off a lot of alarms in airports," Alex muttered.

"I would advise you not to make fun of him, Alex. He still very much hopes to kill you." Sarov touched his lips with a napkin. "I won't allow it to happen, but while we are discussing such unpleasant matters, perhaps I should lay down some house rules, so to speak. I have removed the mobile telephone which I found in your case and I should tell you that all the phones in the house require a code before they can be used. You are to make no contact with the outside world."

"My people may worry about me," Alex said.

"From what I know of Mr Blunt and his colleagues in London, that is unlikely. But it's unimportant. By the time they begin to ask questions, it will be too late."

Too late? Why? Alex realized he was still completely in the dark.

"The Casa de Oro is fenced all around. The fence is electrified. There is only one entrance and it is well guarded. Do not attempt to escape, Alex. If you do, you may be shot and that is not at all what I have planned. After today, I'm afraid I will be moving you to new quarters. As you may well be aware, I have important guests arriving and it would be better for you to 'have your own space' as I believe you say. You are still welcome to use the house, the pool, the grounds. But I would ask you to remain invisible. My guests speak very little English so there is no point approaching them. If you cause me any embarrassment, I will have you whipped."

General Sarov reached forward and pronged a slice of pineapple.

"But that's enough of this unpleasantness," he said. "We have the whole morning together. Do you ride?"

Alex hesitated. He didn't like horse-riding. "I have ridden," he said.

"Excellent."

Alex helped himself to some melon. "I asked you last night what you wanted with me," he said. "You still haven't given me a reply."

"All in good time, Alex. All in good time."

* * *

After breakfast, they walked out into the open air. Now Alex understood how the house had got its name. It was made of some sort of pale yellow brick that, with the sun beating down, really did look gold. Although the house was only two storeys high, it was spread over a vast area, with wide stone steps leading down to a formal garden. Blunt had described it as a palace, but it was more elegant than majestic with slender doors and windows, more archways and finely carved balustrades. Looking at the house, it was as if nothing had changed since the early nineteenth century when it had been built. But there were also armed guards on patrol. There were alarm bells and a series of spotlights mounted on metal brackets. Ugly reminders of the modern age.

They continued over to a stable block where a man was waiting with two magnificent horses; a white stallion for Sarov, a smaller grey for Alex. Riding was the one sport that Alex had never enjoyed. The last time he had got onto a horse it had almost killed him, and it was with reluctance that he took hold of the reins and swung himself into the saddle. Out of the corner of his eye he saw Sarov do the same and knew at once that the Russian was an expert, in total control of his steed.

They rode out together, Alex trying to keep his balance and not look too out of control. Fortunately, his horse seemed to know where they were going.

"This was a sugar farm once," Sarov explained, repeating what Troy had already told him. "Slaves worked here. There were almost a million slaves in Cuba and Cayo Esqueleto." He pointed at the tower. "That was the watchtower. They would ring a bell there at half past four in the morning for the slaves to start work. They were brought here from West Africa. They worked here. And they died here."

They passed close to a low, rectangular building some way from the main house. Alex noticed that the single door and all the windows were barred.

"That is the *barracón*," Sarov said. "The house of slaves. Two hundred of them slept in there, penned in like animals. If we have time, I will show you the punishment block. We still have the original stocks. Can you imagine, Alex, being fastened by your ankles for weeks, or even months at a time? Unable to move. Starving and thirsty..."

"I don't want to imagine it," Alex said.

"Of course not. The Western world prefers to forget the crimes that made it rich."

Alex was relieved when they broke into a canter. At least it meant there was no further need to talk. They followed a dirt track that brought them to the edge of the sea. Looking down, Alex could see where Garcia's boat had been moored the day before. It reminded him of the true nature of the man he was with. Sarov was being friendly. He evidently enjoyed having Alex as his guest. But he was a killer. And a killer with a nuclear bomb.

They came to the end of the track and continued more slowly now, with the sea on their right. The Casa de Oro had disappeared behind them.

"I wish to tell you something about myself," Sarov said suddenly. "In fact, I will tell you more than I have ever told anyone else."

He rode on for a few moments in silence.

"I was born in 1940," he began. "This was during the Second World War, the year before the Germans attacked my country. Perhaps that is why I have always been a patriot, why I have always thought my country should come first. I have spent much of my life serving it. In the army, fighting for what I believe in. I still believe I am serving it now."

He reined in his horse and turned to Alex, who had stopped beside him.

"I got married when I was thirty. A year later, my wife gave me something I had always wanted. A son. His name was Vladimir and from the moment he drew his first breath he was the best thing in my life. He grew into a handsome boy, and let me tell you, no father could have been prouder than I was of him. He did well at school, top in almost every class. He was a first-class athlete. I think he could one day have competed at Olympic level. But that was not to be..."

Alex already knew the end of this story. He remembered what Blunt had told him.

"I believed it was right for Vladimir to serve his country, just as I had," Sarov went on. "I wanted him to join the army. His mother disagreed. Unfortunately, that disagreement ended our marriage."

"You asked her to leave?"

"No. I didn't ask her to leave. I ordered her to. She departed from my house and I never saw her again. And Vladimir did join the army. This was in 1988 when he was sixteen years old. He was flown to Afghanistan where we were fighting a hard, difficult war. He had been there for just three weeks when he was sent to reconnoitre a village as part of a patrol. A sniper shot him and he died."

Sarov's voice cracked briefly and he stopped. But a moment later he continued in a careful, measured tone.

"The war ended a year later. Our government, weak and cowardly, had lost the spirit to fight. We withdrew. The whole thing had been for nothing. And this is what you must understand. This is the truth. There is nothing more terrible in this world than for a father to lose his son." He took a breath. "I believed I had lost Vladimir for ever. Until I met you."

"Me?" Alex was almost too startled to speak.

"You are just two years younger than Vladimir was when he died. But you have so much in common with him, Alex – even though you were brought up on the other side of the world! There is, first, a very slight resemblance. But it is not just your physical appearance. You too are serving your country. Fourteen years old and a spy! How rare it is to find any young person who is prepared to fight for his beliefs!"

"Well, I wouldn't go that far," Alex muttered.

"You have courage. That business at the sugar factory and in the cave would prove it even if your track record didn't speak volumes more. You speak many languages and one day, soon, you could learn Russian. You ride, you dive, you fight, and you aren't scared. I have never met a boy like you. Except one. You are like my Vladimir, Alex, and that is what I hope you will become."

"What are you getting at?" Alex asked. They still weren't moving and he was beginning to feel the heat of the sun. The horse was sweating and attracting flies. The sea was a long way beneath them and none of its breeze was reaching them.

"Isn't it obvious? I've read your file. You have grown up on your own. You had an uncle but you didn't even know what he was until he died. You have no parents. I have no son. We are both alone."

"We're a world apart, General."

"We don't need to be. I am planning something that will change the world for ever. When I am finished, the world will be a better, stronger, healthier place. You came here to prevent that happening. But when you understand what I'm doing, you will see that we do not need to be enemies. On the contrary! I want to adopt you!"

Alex stared. He didn't know what to say.

"You will be my son, Alex, and you will continue where Vladimir left off. I will be a father to you and we will share the new world I create. Don't speak now! Just consider. If I really believed you were my enemy, I would have allowed Conrad to kill you. But the moment I found out who you were, I knew that you couldn't be. We even have the same name, you and I. Alexei and Alex. I will adopt you, Alex. I will become the father you have lost."

"And what if I say no?"

"You will not say no!" Violence had slid into his eyes like smoke behind glass. His face was twisted as if in pain. Sarov took a deep breath and suddenly he was calm. "When you know the plan, you will join me."

"Then why don't you tell me the plan? Tell me what you're going to do!"

"Not yet, Alex. You're not ready yet. But you will be. And it will all happen very soon."

General Alexei Sarov pulled on his reins. The horse spun round and he galloped off, leaving the sea behind. Alex shook his head in wonderment. Then he kicked at the flanks of his own horse and followed.

That evening, Alex ate on his own. Sarov had excused himself, saying he had work to do. Alex didn't have much appetite. Conrad stood in the room watching his every mouthful and although he didn't speak, anger and hostility radiated out of him. The moment Alex finished, Conrad signalled, a single hand pointing to the door.

He followed Conrad out of the main house, down the steps and into the slave quarters, the *barracón* that Sarov had shown him earlier. It seemed that this was to be his new accommodation. The inside of the building was divided into a series of cells with bare brick walls and thick doors, each with a square grille in the centre.

But at least it had been modernized. There was electricity, fresh water and – mercifully in the heat of the night – air-conditioning. Alex knew he was a lot luckier than the hundreds of lost souls who had once been confined there.

There was a basin and a toilet hidden behind a screen in his cell. Alex's case had been carried over and placed on a bed which had a metal frame and a thin mattress but which was still comfortable enough. Sarov had also provided him with books to read. Alex glanced at the covers. They were English translations of Russian classics; Tolstoy and Dostoevsky. He guessed they must have been Vladimir's favourite authors.

Conrad closed and locked the door.

"Good night, Conrad," Alex called out. "I'll call you if I need anything."

He just managed to glimpse a bloodshot eye peering through the grille and knew that he had scored a point. Then Conrad was gone.

Alex lay on the bed for some time, thinking about what Sarov had said. Adoption! It was almost too much for him to take in. Only a week ago he had wondered what it would be like to have a father, and now two of them had turned up at once – first Tom Turner and now Sarov! Things were definitely going from bad to worse.

There was a burst of light outside the window. Night had been replaced by a hard, electric daylight. Alex rolled off the bed and went over to the barred window. It looked out onto the main square at the front of the house. The electric lights he had noticed earlier had all come on and the square was full of people. The guards – a dozen of them – had formed a line, machine guns resting against their chests. Servants and plantation workers had gathered around the door. Sarov himself was there, in a dark green uniform, several medals pinned to his chest. Conrad was behind him.

As Alex watched, four black limousines appeared, driving slowly along the lane that led up from the gatehouse. They were escorted by two motorcycles, the riders, like Sarov, in military dress. Dust spiralled behind the convoy, twisting up into the electric light.

They stopped. The car doors opened and about fifteen men got out. Alex could barely make out their faces against the blinding light. They were little more than silhouettes. But he saw one man – small, thin and bald, dressed in a suit. Sarov moved forward to meet him. The two men shook hands, then embraced. It was a signal for everyone to relax. Sarov gestured and the whole group began to move towards the house, leaving the motorcyclists behind.

Alex was certain he had seen the bald man before, in the newspapers. He knew now why he had been locked up in the slaves' quarters, out of harm's way. Whatever Sarov's plan was, the next phase had just begun.

The Russian president had arrived.

HEARTBEAT

Alex was let out of the slave house the following morning. It seemed he was going to be allowed to spend the day at liberty in the Casa de Oro ... although not on his own. An armed guard had been assigned to watch over him. The guard was in his twenties, roughly shaven. He spoke no English.

He led Alex first to breakfast, which he had on his own in the kitchen, not in the dining-room where he had eaten with Sarov. While Alex ate, he stood at the door, watching him nervously, as if he was a firework that had just failed to go off.

"*Como se llama usted*?" Alex asked. *What's your name?*

"Juan..." The guard was reluctant to part with even that piece of information and answered the rest of Alex's questions with monosyllables or silence.

It was another blazing hot day. The island seemed to be caught in the grip of an endless summer. Alex finished his breakfast and went out into the main hall, where a few of the servants were, as ever, sweeping the floor or carrying supplies into the kitchen. The guards were still in place, up in the tower and around the perimeter. Alex made his way to the stables. He wondered if he would be allowed to go riding again and was pleasantly surprised when the guard brought out his grey for him, already saddled and prepared.

He set off a second time, with Juan just a few paces behind him on a chestnut mare. Alex didn't particularly want to go riding. His thighs and backside were still sore from the day before. But he was interested in the perimeter fence that Sarov had mentioned. He had said that it was electrified. But even electric fences sometimes pass trees that can be climbed. And Alex had already decided that he had to find a way out.

He still had no idea what Sarov was planning. He had talked of changing the world. Making it better, stronger, healthier. He obviously thought of himself as some sort of hero – but he was a hero armed with a nuclear bomb. As he rode across the long grass, Alex wondered what Sarov intended to do. His first thought was that the Russian was going to blow up an American city. Hadn't America once been Russia's greatest enemy? But that made no sense. Millions of people would die but it wouldn't change the world. Certainly not for the better. Could his target be somewhere in Europe? Or was he perhaps going to use the bomb to blackmail world governments into giving him what he wanted? That seemed more likely. But at the same time, Alex doubted it. Whatever he was planning in some way involved the Russian president.

I am going to turn back the page and undo the damage of the last thirty years.

Suddenly Alex knew that despite their childhood friendship, Sarov hated the Russian president and wanted to take his place. That was what this was all about. A new Russia that would once again be a world power. With Sarov at its head.

And he was going to achieve it with a single nuclear blast.

Alex had to escape. He had to tell the CIA that Turner and Troy had been killed and that Sarov did have a bomb. Once they knew that, they would take over. And he wanted to put as many kilometres between himself and the Casa de Oro as he could. Sarov's feelings for him, his desire to adopt him, bothered him as much as anything else. The old man was slightly mad. True, Sarov had saved his life. But it was Sarov who had put his life in danger in the first place. Despite the heat of the morning, Alex shivered. This whole adventure had turned into something that was rapidly spinning out of control.

They had reached the edge of the plantation, this time on the side away from the sea. And there, sure enough, was the fence – about five metres high, solid steel, with a smaller fence coming up to chest level on either side. There were large red signs with the single word PELIGRO printed in white letters. Even without the warning, the fence reeked of danger. There was a low humming that seemed to be coming from the ground. Alex noticed the charred and broken skeleton of a bird hanging on the wire. It must have flown into the fence and been killed instantly. Well, one thing was certain. He wasn't going to climb over. The fence stretched through grassland with barely a single tree in sight.

Alex turned his horse towards the bottom end of the plantation and the entrance gate. Maybe he would be able to find a way through there. It took them about half an hour to reach it, riding at walking pace. The fence continued all the way. The entrance was marked by a crumbling stone guardhouse with no glass in the windows and a door hanging half off its hinges. There were two men inside and a third with a machine gun standing beside a barrier. As Alex reached them, a car passed through. One of the limousines that he had seen the night before was leaving the compound. That gave him an idea. There was only one way out of here and that was in a car. Presumably the president's men would be making several journeys. That might give him a chance...

They rode back to the stables and dismounted. With Juan a few steps behind him, Alex walked back into the house. Almost at once he heard voices coming from the other side, and the splash of water. He crossed the inner courtyard past the fountain and went through an archway. There was a swimming pool on the other side, long and rectangular, with palm trees growing on both sides, casting natural shadows over the tables and sunloungers. In the distance he saw a newly constructed tennis court. There were changing rooms, a sauna, an outside bar. From the back, the Casa de Oro looked like the playpen of a multimillionaire.

Sarov was sitting at a table with the president, both of them holding drinks; water for Sarov, a cocktail for his guest. The president had changed into red shorts and a flowery short-sleeved shirt that hung loosely off his slight frame. There were four men standing close to him. It was obvious that they were the presidential bodyguard. The men were huge, dressed in black, with uniform sunglasses and a coil of wire disappearing into their ears. There was something almost ludicrous about the scene. The little man in his holiday clothes. The giant bodyguards. Alex looked at the pool. There were three strikingly attractive women sitting on the side, their feet dangling in the water. They were all in their twenties, wearing bikinis. They looked local. Alex was surprised to see them. He had thought Sarov too cold-blooded to enjoy such company. Or had they been invited here for the president?

Alex wondered if he was meant to be in this part of the grounds and was about to leave when Sarov saw him and waved a hand, calling him over. With a sense of growing curiosity, Alex walked over. Sarov spoke quickly to the president, who nodded and smiled.

"Good morning, Alex!" Sarov seemed unusually cheerful. "I understand you went out riding again. Please let me introduce you to my old friend, Boris Kiriyenko, the president of Russia. Boris, this is the boy I was telling you about."

The Russian president reached out and took Alex's hand. Alex could smell the alcohol on his breath. Whatever he was drinking in the cocktail, he'd had too much of it. "It is a pleasure," he said, in heavily accented English. He pointed a finger at Alex's face and broke into Russian. Alex heard the name Vladimir mentioned twice.

Sarov answered briefly, then translated for Alex. "He says that you remind him of my son." He smiled. "Would you like to swim, Alex? You look as if you need it."

Alex glanced at the three girls. "Unusual lifeguards," he said.

Sarov laughed. "Some company for the president. He is, after all, on holiday, although unfortunately we do have a little work to do. Our local television station is naturally interested that we have such a distinguished visitor and Boris has agreed to give a brief interview. The crew will be here any minute now."

The president nodded but Alex wasn't sure if he'd understood.

"You can have the pool to yourself. We're going into Santiago after lunch, but I hope you'll join us for dinner, Alex. The chef has planned a special surprise for the main course."

There was a movement at the archway leading into the house. Conrad had appeared and with him was a short, serious-looking woman in a drab olive-green dress. There were two men behind her with cameras and lighting equipment.

"Ah! Here they are!" Sarov turned back to the president and suddenly Alex was forgotten.

He stripped to his swimming shorts and dived into the pool.

After the long horse ride the water was cool and refreshing. He noticed the three girls watching him as he swam past. One of them winked at him and another giggled. Meanwhile, the camera crew was setting up its equipment in the shade of the palm trees. The Russian president waved a hand and one of his bodyguards brought over another cocktail. Alex was surprised that such an insignificant-looking man could be the head of a huge country. But then, he thought, most politicians are small and shabby, the sort of people who have been bullied at school. That's why they become politicians.

Alex put him out of his thoughts and concentrated on his swimming. In his mind he went over what Sarov had just said. They were driving into the city after lunch. That meant the cars would be leaving the compound. It was his only chance. Alex knew that there was no way off the island. The moment he was found missing, the alarm would be raised. Every guard at the airport would be on the lookout for him and he doubted he would be able to get on a boat. But if he could at least find a telephone that worked without an access code, he would be able to get in touch with the American mainland and they would send someone to pull him out.

He finished his eighth length and twisted round for a ninth. The Russian president was sitting in a chair, being wired for sound. Juan, Alex's personal guard, was waiting for him at the other end of the pool. Alex sighed. He was going to have to do something about Juan.

The television interview began. Sarov was watching carefully and, again, Alex got the impression that there was more to all this than met the eye.

He pulled himself out of the pool and went back to his quarters to get changed.

* * *

Alex wore another pair of shorts and an Aertex shirt, both of them chosen because they were neutral colours, allowing him to blend in with the background. In his pocket he had a stick of the bubblegum that Smithers had given him. If everything went according to plan, he was going to need it.

Juan was standing outside the room. Alex was suddenly nervous about what he was going to do. After all, Sarov had already warned him what would happen if he tried to escape. He would be shot – or at the very least, whipped. But then he thought of the nuclear bomb. Sarov had to be stopped. His mind was made up.

He stopped suddenly and groaned. His whole face contorted with pain and he staggered to one side, putting out a hand to stop himself falling. Juan started forward, entering the room with a look of concern. At that moment, Alex straightened up. His foot shot out in a perfectly timed roundhouse kick that slammed into the soft flesh of the man's stomach. Juan didn't even cry out. With all the breath knocked out of him, he crumpled to the ground and lay still. Not for the first time, Alex thanked the five years' training that had given him a black belt – first grade *Dan* – in karate. Now he moved fast. He took the sheet off the bed and tore it into strips. He tied the man's hands and feet, then gagged him. Finally, he slipped out of the room, locking it behind him. It would be hours before the guard was found. By that time he would be away.

He came out of the *barracón*. The black limousines were still parked in front of the villa, waiting for the president and his men to leave. There was nobody in sight. Alex sprinted forward. Sarov had allowed him to wander around the grounds of the plantation, but only if he was accompanied. If anyone saw him without his guard, they might guess what had happened. He reached the edge of the house and stopped, breathless, his back against the wall. Even the short run had made him sweat in the intense heat of the afternoon. He examined the cars. There were three of them. The one that had left earlier that morning still hadn't come back. The question was, when the president went into Santiago, which one would he take? Or would all three accompany him?

Alex was about to dart forward when he heard footsteps approaching round the side of the house. It was either guards or workers – the moment they turned the corner, they would see him. There was a narrow door to one side. He hadn't noticed it before. He fumbled for the handle. Fortunately, it wasn't locked. Just as two men in military dress appeared a few metres away, both armed, he slipped inside, closing the door behind him.

The chill of an air-conditioning system brushed over him. He looked around. He was in a part of the house that looked completely different to the rest. Here, the wooden floors and antique furniture had given way to a hi-tech, modern look. Halogen lighting led the way down a short corridor with glass doors on either side. Intrigued, Alex crept forward. He came to the first door and looked inside.

There were two technicians sitting gazing at a bank of TV screens. The room wasn't large and looked like an editing suite in a television studio. Alex eased the door open. There was no chance that the technicians would hear him. They were both wearing headphones, plugged into the machinery in front of them. Alex looked at the screens.

Every room in the main house was under observation. He recognized at once the room in which he had woken up. There was the kitchen, the dining-room, the main courtyard with two of the president's men strolling across. He turned to another screen and stared. He was watching himself swimming lengths in the pool. That had been recorded too. And there was Sarov, sitting with his glass of water while, on the screen next to him, the president gave his interview to the crew that Alex had seen arrive.

It took Alex a moment to work out exactly what he was seeing. Everything was being recorded and edited. That was what the two technicians were doing now. The arrival of Boris Kiriyenko was playing on one screen. Next to it, the president emptied a glass of brandy, presumably the night before. On a third screen, the girls that Alex had seen at the swimming pool were introduced to him. They were simpering and smiling in low-cut dresses that left little to the imagination. Had he taken them to his room? If so, that would doubtless have been recorded too.

An image flickered. And there was the president giving his interview. One of the technicians must have been given the footage taken by the woman in the drab green dress. Kiriyenko was talking directly to the camera in the manner of a thousand politicians on *Newsnight* or *Panorama*. Totally serious – although he looked a little foolish in his flowery shirt. On the screen next to this one, the same Kiriyenko swam in the pool with one of the girls.

What did it all mean? Why did Sarov want this? Was the Casa de Oro nothing more than an elaborate, honeyed trap into which the president of Russia had unwittingly strayed?

Alex couldn't stay there any longer. Everything he saw made it more urgent for him to get out and warn the Americans. He was afraid he was going to miss the departure of the cars – and there wouldn't be a second chance.

He opened the door again and looked outside. The cars were still there but the guards had gone. He looked at his watch. It was two o'clock. If lunch hadn't finished already, it would do so shortly. It had to be now! He ran forward to the nearest car and felt for the boot release. Was it going to be locked? His thumb found the silver button and pressed and, to his relief, the boot opened. It was a big car with plenty of room. He threw himself inside, then reached up and pulled the lid back down, locking it.

At once he was trapped in pitch darkness and he had to force himself not to panic. It was like being buried alive. He tried to relax. This was going to work. Provided nobody opened the boot to put luggage in, he wouldn't be seen. The limousine would drive him out of the plantation and when they were parked in Santiago, he would make his escape.

Of course, the most difficult part was still to come. Alex couldn't see out of the car. He couldn't even see his own hand in front of his face. He was totally blind. He would simply have to guess when the driver and his passengers had gone and hope for the best. It was also impossible to open the boot from the inside. It was for this reason that Alex had brought along the gum. He would choose the moment and use the gum to blow his way out. With a bit of luck, he would slip away into the crowd before anyone realized what had happened.

But already he was wondering if this had been a good idea. It was hot inside the boot. He could imagine the sun beating down on the car, and realized that he had locked himself into an oven. Sweat was oozing out of every pore. His clothes were already sodden and he could hear it dripping onto the metal surface beneath him. How much air was there in the trunk? If Sarov didn't make a move soon, he'd have to blow the car open while it was still in the compound and face the consequences.

He fought down the panic and tried to breathe as shallowly as he could. His heart was thudding in his ears. He could feel the muscle hard at work in his chest as it pumped blood around his body. The veins in his neck and pulses were beating in rhythm. He wanted to stretch his legs but he didn't dare move in case he rocked the car. The minutes ticked by – and then he heard voices. There was the echoing clunk of a car door opening and the whole vehicle shifted from side to side as its passengers got in. Curled up in a foetal position, Alex waited for the boot to be thrown open, but it seemed that the president, or whoever was in the limousine, had decided not to bring any baggage. The car engine started up. Alex felt the vibrations and then, suddenly, they were moving, with Alex being jolted up and down as they started over the makeshift road.

After only about a minute they began to slow down again and Alex knew that they must be approaching the gate and checkpoint. That was another worry. Would the guards search the car? But he had already seen one limousine leave the villa that morning, and although the guards had been there he hadn't seen anyone open the boot. The car had stopped. Alex didn't move. Everything was black. He heard voices as if in the far distance. Somebody shouted something but he couldn't make out a word they said. The car seemed to have been there for ever. Why was it taking so long? Get on with it! Alex was finding it harder and harder to breathe. It felt as if the air was already running out.

And then the car started forward and he let out a sigh of relief. He could imagine the barrier rising to let them through. The Casa de Oro would be behind them now. How far was it to Santiago? How would he know for sure when they were there?

The car stopped again.

The boot opened.

Cruel sunlight came rushing in. Alex blinked, putting a hand up to protect himself.

"Get out!" a voice said, in English.

Alex climbed out, soaking wet with his own perspiration. Sarov was standing in front of him. Conrad was next to him, holding an automatic pistol, not even trying to hide the pleasure in his eyes. Alex looked around. The car hadn't even left the compound. It had simply rolled forward and turned round. That had been the movement he had felt. There were two guards watching him, their faces blank. One of them was holding a device that looked a little like a megaphone, the sort teachers used at sports days. It was connected by a long wire to a box just inside the building.

"If you had wanted to visit Santiago, you had only to ask," Sarov said. "But I don't think you wanted to visit the city. I think you were running away."

Alex said nothing.

"Where is Juan?" Sarov asked.

Alex still didn't speak.

Sarov gazed at the boy. He seemed pained, as if he didn't understand why Alex had disobeyed him and didn't know quite what to do. "You disappoint me, Alex," he said, at length. "You were down at the cave. You saw the extent of my security arrangements there. Did you really think for a single minute that I would allow a car to drive in or out of this compound without knowing exactly who or what was inside?"

He suddenly reached out and took the megaphone device from the guard. He pointed it at Alex's chest and pressed a button. At once, Alex heard a thumping sound that echoed through the air. It took him a second or two to realize that it was his own heart, amplified and transmitted out of a speaker system hidden somewhere inside the guardhouse.

"The car was scanned at the barrier," Sarov explained. "Every car is scanned at the barrier, using the machine I am holding now. A sophisticated sensor. This is what the guard heard. You can hear it now."

Thud ... thud ... thud...

Alex listened to his own heart.

Sarov was suddenly angry. Nothing in his face had changed, but his pale blue eyes had turned to ice and there was a dreadful deadness about him, as if his own life had suddenly been drained away. "Do you not remember what I told you?" he whispered. "If you tried to escape, you would be shot. Conrad very much wishes to shoot you. He believes I am a fool to have you here as my guest. He is right."

Conrad stepped forward, the gun raised.

Thud … thud … thud … thud…

Alex's heart was the animal inside him, beyond his control, responding to the fear he felt. There was nothing he could do to hide it. The heart was beating louder and faster, echoing out of the speakers.

"I don't understand you, Alex. Have you no idea what I'm offering you? Did you not hear a word that I said? I offer you my protection and you make an enemy of me! I want you to be my son, but you force me to destroy you instead."

Conrad touched the gun against Alex's heart.

Thudthudthudthudthudthudthud…

"Listen to the sound of your own terror. Do you hear it? And when you hear silence – it could be just a few seconds from now – that is when you will know you have died."

Conrad's finger tightened on the trigger.

Then Sarov turned off the sensor.

The heartbeat stopped.

Alex felt as if he had been shot. The sudden silence hit him like a hammer blow. Like a bullet from a gun. He fell to his knees, hollowed out, barely able to breathe. He knelt there in the dust, his hands at his sides. He no longer had the strength to stand up. Sarov looked at him and now there was only sadness in his face.

"He has learned his lesson," he said. "Take him back to his room."

He put down the sensor and, turning his back on the still kneeling boy, slowly climbed back into the car.

THE NUCLEAR DUSTBIN

At seven o'clock that evening, the door of Alex's cell opened and Conrad stood there, wearing a suit and tie. The smart clothes made his half-bald head, ruined face and red, twitching eye even uglier than usual. He reminded Alex of an expensive Guy Fawkes on bonfire night.

"You are invited to dinner," Conrad said.

"No thanks, Conrad," Alex replied. "I'm not hungry."

"The invitation is not one you may refuse." He tilted a hand to look at his watch. The hand had been inaccurately joined to the wrist. He had to move it a long way to see the watch face. "You have five minutes," he said. "You are expected to dress formally."

"I'm afraid I left my dinner jacket in England."

Conrad ignored him and closed the door.

Alex swung his legs off the bunk where he had been lying. He had been in the cell ever since his capture at the gate, vaguely wondering what was going to happen next. An invitation to dinner had been the last thing he'd expected. There had been no sign of Juan when he got back. Presumably the young guard had been reprimanded for his failure to watch over Alex and sent home. Or shot. Alex was beginning to realize that the people at the Casa de Oro meant business. He had no idea what Sarov had in mind for him this evening but he knew that the last time they had met, Alex had only just managed to escape with his life. He resembled the sixteen-year-old Vladimir, Sarov's lost son. Sarov must still have some fantasy about adopting him. Otherwise, he would now be dead.

He decided that, all in all, it would be wise to play along with this invitation to dinner. At the very least it might allow him to find out a little more about what was going on. Would the meal be filmed, he wondered? And if so, to what use would the film be put? Alex pulled a clean shirt and a pair of black Evisu trousers out of his case. He remembered that the mad headmaster, Dr Grief, had used hidden cameras at the Point Blanc academy to spy on the boys who were there. But this was different. The film that he had seen in the editing suite was being cut, pieced together, manipulated. It was going to be used for something. But what?

Conrad returned exactly five minutes later. Alex was ready for him. Once again he was escorted out of the slave house and up the steps to the main house. Inside, he heard the sound of classical music. He reached the courtyard and saw a trio – two elderly violinists and a plump lady with a cello – playing what sounded like Bach, the fountain tinkling softly behind them. There were about a dozen people gathered there, drinking champagne and eating canapés which were being carried round on silver trays by white-aproned waitresses. The four bodyguards were standing together in a tight, watchful circle. Another six men from the Russian delegation were chatting to the girls from the swimming pool, who glittered in sequins and jewellery.

The president himself was talking to Sarov, a glass in one hand and a huge cigar in the other. Sarov said something and he laughed out loud, smoke billowing from his lips. Sarov noticed Alex arrive and smiled.

"Ah, Alex! There you are! What will you have to drink?"

It seemed that the events of the afternoon had been forgotten. At least, they weren't to be mentioned again. Alex asked for a fresh orange juice and it was brought at once.

"I'm glad you're here, Alex," Sarov said. "I didn't want to start without you."

Alex remembered something Sarov had said at the swimming pool. Something about a surprise. He was beginning to have bad feelings about this dinner, but without knowing why.

The trio finished a piece of music and there was a light smattering of applause. Then a gong sounded and the guests moved into the dining-room. This was the same room where Alex and Sarov had eaten breakfast, but it had been transformed for the banquet. The glasses were crystal, the plates brilliant white porcelain, the knives and forks polished till they gleamed. The tablecloth, also white, looked brand new. There were thirteen places for dinner – six on each side and one at the head. Alex noted the number with a further sense of unease. Thirteen for dinner. Unlucky.

Everyone took their places at the table. Sarov had placed himself at the head, with Alex on one side of him, Kiriyenko on the other. The doors opened and the waitresses came back in, this time with bowls brimming over with tiny black eggs which Alex recognized as caviar. Presumably Sarov had it directly imported from the Black Sea – it must have been worth many thousands of pounds. Russians traditionally drink vodka with caviar and, as the bowls were positioned around the table, the guests were each given a small tumbler filled to the brim.

Then Sarov stood up.

"My friends," he began. "I hope you will forgive me if I address you in English. There is unfortunately one guest at this table who has yet to learn our glorious language."

There were smiles around the table and a few heads nodded in Alex's direction. Alex looked down at the tablecloth, unsure how to respond.

"This is for me a night of great significance. What can I tell you about Boris Nikita Kiriyenko? He has been my closest and dearest friend for more than fifty years! It is strange to think that I can still remember him as a child who teased animals, who cried when there was a fight, and who never told the truth." Alex glanced at Kiriyenko. The president was frowning. Sarov was presumably joking, but the joke had failed to amuse his guest. "It is even harder to believe this is the same man who has been entrusted with the privilege, the sacred honour, of leading our great country in these difficult times. Well, Boris has come here for a holiday. I'm sure he needs one after so much hard work. And that is the toast that I wish to make tonight. To his holiday! I hope that it will be longer and more memorable than he ever expected."

There was a brief silence. Alex could see that the guests were puzzled. Perhaps they'd had difficulty following Sarov's English. But he suspected it was what he had said that had thrown them, not how he had said it. They had come expecting a good dinner, but Sarov seemed to be insulting the president of Russia!

"Alexei, my old friend!" the president said. Boris had decided that it *was* a joke. He smiled and continued in his thickly accented English. "Why do you not join us?" he asked.

"You know that I never drink spirits," Sarov replied. "And I hope you will agree that at fourteen, my son is a little too young for vodka."

"I drank my first vodka aged twelve!" the president muttered.

Somehow, Alex wasn't surprised.

Kiriyenko lifted his glass. *"Na zdarovie!"* he said. They were about the only words of Russian that Alex understood. *Your health!*

"Na zdarovie!" Everyone round the table chorused the toast.

As one, they drank, throwing back the chilled vodka, as is traditional, in a single gulp.

Sarov turned to Alex. "Now it begins," he said quietly.

One of the bodyguards was the first to react. He had been reaching out to help himself to caviar when suddenly his hands jerked, dropping his fork and plate with a crash. Every head turned towards him. A second later, at the other end of the table, one of the other men threw himself forward, head-first, onto the table, his chair capsizing underneath him. As Alex watched, his eyes wide with horror, every person at the table began to react in the same way. One of them fell backwards, dragging the tablecloth with him, glasses and cutlery cascading into his lap. Several of them simply slumped where they sat. Another of the bodyguards managed to get to his feet and was scrabbling for a gun underneath his jacket, but then his eyes glazed and he collapsed. Boris Kiriyenko was the last to go. He was standing, swaying on his feet like a wounded bull. His fist was clenched as if he knew he had been betrayed and wanted to strike out at the man who had done it. Then he sat down heavily. His chair tilted and he was thrown onto the floor.

Sarov muttered a few words in Russian.

"What have you done?" Alex gasped. "Are they...?"

"They are unconscious, not dead," Sarov said. "They will, of course, have to be killed. But not yet."

"What are you planning?" Alex demanded. "What is it you're going to do?"

"We have a long journey," Sarov said. "I'll tell you on the way."

The entire compound was lit up. Men – guards and *macheteros* – were running everywhere. Alex was still dressed in the clothes he had worn for dinner. Sarov had changed into dark green military dress, this time without his medals. One of the black limousines was waiting. Conrad had driven up at the wheel of an army truck. As Alex watched, two more guards appeared at the main entrance of the Casa de Oro and began to walk down the wide steps. They were moving forward slowly, carrying something between them. The moment they appeared, everyone around them stopped.

It was a large silver chest about the size of a school trunk. Alex could just see that the top was flat metal, but that it had a number of switches and dials as well as some sort of slot device built into the side. Sarov watched while it was carried over and loaded into the truck. All the other men did the same, as if the two guards had just come out of a church and this was an effigy of a saint. Alex shuddered. He knew exactly what he was looking at and didn't need the Geiger counter to confirm it.

This was the nuclear bomb.

"Alex?" Sarov was holding the car door open for him. Dazed, Alex got in. He knew that he had reached the end. Sarov had shown his hand and put into action a series of events from which there could be no going back. And yet even now, at this late stage, he had no idea what the general intended to do.

Sarov sat next to him. A driver got in and they moved off, Conrad following behind in the truck. At the very last moment, as they passed through the barrier, Sarov glanced back, very briefly.

Alex saw the look in his eyes and knew that he had no intention ever to return. There were a hundred questions he wanted to ask, but he said nothing. This wasn't the time. Sarov was sitting quietly, his hands on his knees. But even he couldn't disguise the tension. Years of planning must have been building up to this.

They drove down darkened roads with just occasional flickers of light showing that the island was actually inhabited. No other cars came their way. After about ten minutes, they began to pass buildings. Looking out of the window, Alex saw men and women sitting in front of their houses, drinking rum, playing cards, smoking cigarettes or cigars beneath the night sky. They were on the outskirts of Santiago and suddenly they turned down a road that Alex recognized. He had taken it on the way in. They were going to the airport.

This time there was no security, no queues for passport control. Sarov didn't even have to enter the main terminal building. Two airport guards were waiting for him at a gate which was opened to allow him to drive straight onto the runway. The truck followed. Alex looked over the driver's shoulder and saw a plane, a Lear jet, parked on its own. They stopped.

"Out," Sarov said.

There was a breeze blowing across the airport runway, carrying with it the smell of aviation fuel. Alex stood on the tarmac, watching as the silver chest was loaded onto the plane, Conrad shouting instructions. He found it hard to believe that such an ordinary-looking thing could be capable of destruction on a massive scale. He remembered films he had seen. Flames and gale force winds rushing through whole cities, ripping them apart. Buildings crumbling. People turned to ashes in an instant. Cars and buses flicked like toys into oblivion. How could such a terrible bomb with so much power be so small? Conrad closed the cargo door himself. He turned to Sarov and nodded. Sarov gestured. Unwillingly, Alex walked forward and climbed the steps into the plane. Sarov was right behind him. Conrad and the two men who had been carrying the bomb followed. The door of the plane was closed and sealed.

Alex found himself in a luxurious compartment that was like no plane he had ever been in. There were only a dozen seats, each one upholstered in leather. The compartment was long and thickly carpeted, with a well stocked bar, a kitchen and, in front of the cockpit, a seventy-centimetre plasma television screen. Alex didn't ask what film they would be showing. He chose a window seat – but then they were all window seats. Sarov sat across the aisle from him. Conrad was one seat behind Sarov. The two guards sat at the far end of the compartment. Alex wondered why they were making the journey. To keep an eye on him?

And what journey, exactly, were they making? Were they crossing into America or travelling across the Atlantic?

Sarov must have been reading his mind. "I will explain to you in a moment," he said. "As soon as we are in the air."

In fact, it was about fifteen minutes before the Lear jet took off down the runway and lifted effortlessly off the ground. The cabin lights dimmed for take-off but as soon as they had reached thirty thousand feet, they came back on. The guards got up and began to serve hot tea which had been brewing in an urn in the kitchen. Sarov allowed himself a brief smile. He pressed a button in the arm of his chair and swung round so that he now faced Alex.

"You may be wondering why I decided not to kill you," he began. "This afternoon, when I found you in the car ... I came so close. Conrad is still annoyed with me. He believes I am making a mistake. He does not understand me. But I will tell you why you are still alive, Alex. You are working for British intelligence. You are a spy. And you were only doing your job. I admire that, and this is the reason why I have forgiven you. You are loyal to your country even as I am loyal to mine. My son Vladimir died for his country. I am proud that you were prepared to do the same for yours."

Alex took this in. "Where are we going?" he asked.

"We are going to Russia. To be precise, we are going to Murmansk, which is a port on the Kola Peninsula."

Murmansk! Alex tried to remember if he had heard the name before. It did seem familiar. Had he heard it in a news bulletin, or perhaps in a lesson at school? A port in Russia! But why would they be going there ... and carrying a nuclear bomb?

"You might like to know our flight path," Sarov continued. "We are crossing the Atlantic by the northern route. This involves flying over the Arctic Circle. In essence, we are taking a short cut, following the curvature of the earth. We will have to make two stops to refuel. One in Gander, in northern Canada. The other in the British Isles, in Edinburgh." Sarov must have seen the hopeful expression in Alex's eyes. He went on. "Yes. You will be home for an hour or two tomorrow. But please don't get any ideas. You will not be permitted to leave the plane."

"Will it really take so long to get there?" Alex asked.

"With the first stop and the time difference ... yes. We may also have to engage in some diplomatic pleasantries with both the Canadian and the British authorities. This is Kiriyenko's private plane. We have filed our flight plan with Euro Control and of course they recognized our serial number. They believe the president is onboard. I would imagine that the Canadian and the British governments might be keen to offer us hospitality."

"Who's flying the plane?"

"Kiriyenko's pilot. He is, however, loyal to me. A great many ordinary Russian people believe in me, Alex. They have seen the future ... my future. They prefer it to the version they have been offered by others."

"You still haven't told me what that future is. Why are we flying to Murmansk?"

"I will tell you now. And then we must both sleep. We have a long night ahead."

Sarov crossed his legs. There was a light directly above him and it beamed down, casting his eyes and mouth into shadow. He seemed at that moment both very old and very young. There was no expression in his face at all.

"Murmansk," he began, "is home to Russia's northern fleet of submarines. Or it was. It is now, quite simply, the world's biggest nuclear dustbin. The end of Russia as a world power has led to the rapid collapse of its army, air force and navy. I have already tried to explain to you what has happened to my country in the past thirty years. The way it has been allowed to fall apart, with poverty, crime and corruption sucking the people dry. Well, that process of decay can be seen most starkly in Murmansk.

"A fleet of nuclear submarines is moored there. I say 'moored' but I mean 'abandoned'. One of them, the *Lepse*, is more than forty years old and contains six hundred and forty-two bundles of fuel rods. These submarines have been left to rot and they are falling apart. Nobody cares. Nobody can find the money to do anything about them. It is a well documented fact, Alex, that these old submarines represent the single biggest threat to the world today. There are one hundred of them! I am talking about one fifth of the world's nuclear fuel. One hundred ticking time bombs, waiting to go off. An accident waiting to happen. An accident I have decided to arrange."

Alex opened his mouth to break in, but Sarov held up a hand for silence.

"Let me explain to you what would happen if just one of those submarines were to blow up," he continued. "First of all, a huge number of Russians in the Kola Peninsula and the north would be killed. Many more people would die in the neighbouring countries of Norway and Finland.

"Unusually for this time of year, the wind is blowing to the west, so the nuclear fallout would travel over Europe to your country. It is very possible that London would become uninhabitable. Over the years, thousands more people would fall ill and die slow, painful deaths."

"So why do it?" Alex shouted. "Why cause the explosion? What good will it do?"

"I am, if you like, giving the world a wake-up call," Sarov explained. "Tomorrow night I will land in Murmansk and I will place the bomb that you have seen amongst the submarines." He reached into his top pocket and took out a small plastic card. It had a magnetic stripe down one side like a credit card. "This is the key that will detonate the bomb," he said. "All the codes and information required are contained in the magnetic strip. All I have to do is insert the card into the bomb. At the time of the explosion itself, I will be on my way south to Moscow, out of harm's way.

"The explosion will be felt in every country in the world. You can imagine the shock and the outrage that it will create. And nobody will know that it was caused by a bomb that was deliberately carried to Murmansk. They will believe that it was one of the submarines. The *Lepse*, perhaps, or one of the others. I've already said – it was an accident waiting to happen. And when it does happen, nobody will begin to suspect the truth."

"Yes they will!" Alex said. "The CIA know you bought uranium. They'll find out their agents are dead—"

"Nobody will believe the CIA. Nobody ever believes the CIA. And anyway, by the time they have assembled their evidence against me, it will be too late."

"I don't understand!" Alex exclaimed. "You've already said you'll kill thousands of your own people. What's the point?"

"You are young. You know nothing of my people. But listen to me, Alex, and I will explain. When this disaster happens, the whole world will unite in its condemnation of Russia. We will be hated. And the Russian people will be ashamed. If only we had been less careless, less stupid, less poor, less corrupt. If only we were still the superpower we had once been. And it is at this moment that everyone – in Russia and in the world – will look to Boris Kiriyenko for leadership. The Russian president! And what will they see?"

"You made a film of him…" Alex muttered.

"We will release the film that shows him drunk beside the swimming pool. In his red shorts and flowered shirt. Playing with three half-naked women young enough to be his daughters! And we have interviewed him. We'll release that too."

"You've edited the interview!"

"Exactly." Sarov nodded, his eyes catching the light. "Our interviewer asked him about a train strike in Moscow and Kiriyenko, who was already half drunk, replied: 'This is my holiday. I'm too busy to deal with that.' We will change the question. 'What are you going to do about the accident in Murmansk?' And Kiriyenko will reply—"

"—'This is my holiday. I'm too busy to deal with that.'" Alex finished the sentence.

"The Russian people will see Kiriyenko for the weak, drunken imbecile that he is. They will very quickly blame him for the disaster at Murmansk – and with good reason. The northern fleet was once the pride of the whole nation. How could it have been allowed to become a rusting, leaking, lethal nuclear dump?"

The plane droned on. Conrad was listening intently to what Sarov was saying, his head balancing unevenly on his neck. The two guards at the back had gone to sleep.

"You said you would be in Moscow," Alex muttered.

"It will take less than twenty-four hours for the government to be swept out of power," Sarov replied. "There will be riots in the streets. Many Russians believe that life was better – much better – in the old days. They still believe in communism. Well, now their anger will be heard. It will be unstoppable. And I will be there to harness it, to use it to take power. I have followers who are waiting for it to happen. Before the nuclear cloud has settled, I will have total control of the country. And that is just the beginning, Alex. I will rebuild the Berlin Wall. There will be new wars. I will not rest until my kind of government, communist government, is the single dominant power in the world."

There was a long silence.

"You're prepared to kill millions of people to achieve this?" Alex asked.

Sarov shrugged. "Millions of people are dying in Russia right now. They can't afford food. They can't afford medicine—"

"And what happens to me?"

"I've already answered that question, Alex. I don't believe it was a coincidence that you turned up the way you did. I believe it was meant to happen. I was never meant to do this on my own. You will be with me tomorrow and when the bomb is primed and ready, we will leave together. First Murmansk, then Moscow. Don't you see what I'm offering you? You are not just going to be my son.

You are going to have power, Alex. You are going to be one of the most powerful people in the world."

The plane had already reached the coast of America and turned, beginning its journey north. Alex sank back in his seat, his head spinning. Absent-mindedly, he allowed his hand to slip into his trouser pocket. He had managed to bring one stick of the MI6 bubblegum with him. He also had the little figurine that was actually a stun grenade.

He closed his eyes and tried to work out what he was going to do.

SECURITY NIGHTMARE

Hours spent in a strange twilight that was neither night nor day. Trapped on the roof of the world, totally still yet hurtling ever further. Alex slept for the first part of the journey, knowing that he was tired and that he would need his strength. He had accepted what he had to do. Before, when they had been on Skeleton Key, a small part of him had been tempted to sit back and do nothing. After all, he had never asked to be there. All this had nothing to do with him.

But now everything had changed. He could see the nuclear blast in the Kola Peninsula. It was already there, in his imagination. Thousands of people would die instantly, tens of thousands later as the deadly radioactive particles spread over Europe. Britain would be one of the countries that would suffer. Alex had to stop it happening. He no longer had any choice.

It was going to be much more difficult this time. Sarov might have forgiven him for his failed escape attempt in the car but Alex knew he would no longer trust him. And he couldn't afford to make another mistake. If he was caught trying to escape a second time, there would be no reprieve, no mercy. In his heart, Alex seriously doubted that he would be able to slip past the Russian general or his twisted companion. Sarov was completely alert, as if he had been sitting there for ten minutes, not ten hours. Conrad was still watching him too. He was sitting quietly on the other side of the plane, a cat waiting for a mouse, his red eye blinking in the half-light.

And yet...

Alex had the two gadgets Smithers had given him. And they were going to be landing in Britain! Just the thought of being in his own country, surrounded by people who spoke his language, gave Alex new strength. He had a plan and it would work. It had to.

He must have slept through the refuelling stop at Gander and several hours of the flight because the next thing he knew, it was light outside and the two guards were clearing away a breakfast of raw fruit and yoghurt that had been prepared in the Lear jet's miniature kitchen. He looked out of the window. All he could see was cloud.

Sarov noticed that he had woken up. "Alex! Are you hungry?"

"No, thank you."

"Still, you must have something to drink. It's very easy to dehydrate on these long journeys." He spoke a few words of Russian to one of the guards, who disappeared and came back with a glass of grapefruit juice. Alex hesitated before bringing it to his lips, remembering what had happened to Kiriyenko. Sarov smiled. "You don't need to worry," he said. "It's just grapefruit juice. No added ingredients."

Alex drank. The juice was cold and refreshing after his long sleep.

"We will be landing in Edinburgh in about thirty minutes," Sarov told him. "We're already in British airspace. How does it feel to be home?"

"If you'd like to drop me, I can get a train to London."

Sarov shook his head. "I'm afraid not."

A few minutes later they began their descent. The pilot had been in radio communication with the airport and had confirmed that this was a routine refuelling stop. He would not be dropping or picking up any passengers and so needed no operating permit. Everything had been cleared with the airport authorities, making this touchdown as simple as a car pulling into a local garage. And despite Sarov's fears, the British government had not invited the supposed VIP passengers for a diplomatic breakfast in Edinburgh!

The plane broke through the cloud and, with his face pressed against the window, Alex suddenly saw countryside with miniature houses and cars dotted around it. The brilliant sunshine of the Caribbean had been replaced by the grey light and uncertain weather of a British summer's day. He felt a sense of relief. He was back! But at the same time, he knew Sarov would never allow him off the plane. In a way, it would have been less cruel if they had refuelled in Greenland or Norway. He was being given one last look at his own country. The next time he saw it, it would have been poisoned for generations to come. Alex reached into his pocket. His hand closed around the figurine of Michael Owen. The time was getting close...

The seat belt signs came on. A moment later, Alex felt the pressure in his ears as they dropped out of the sky. He saw a bridge, somehow delicate from this height, spanning a great stretch of water. The Forth Road Bridge ... it had to be. And there was Edinburgh, over in the west, its castle dominating the skyline. The airport came rushing up. He caught a glimpse of a bright, modern terminal, of waiting planes sitting on the apron surrounded by vans and trolleys. There was a bump as the wheels made contact with the runway and then the roar of the engines in reverse thrust. The plane slowed. They had landed.

Guided by the control tower, the Lear jet made its way to the end of the runway and into an area known as the fuel farm, far away from the main terminal. Alex gazed out of the window with a sinking feeling as the public buildings slid away behind him. For every second that they travelled, he would have further to run to raise the alarm – always assuming that he did even manage to get off the plane. The Michael Owen figure was in his hand now. What had Smithers told him? Twist the head twice one way and once the other to arm it. Wait ten seconds, then drop it and run. The confined space of an aircraft cabin seemed the perfect place to try it out. The only question was, how was Alex going to stop it knocking himself out too?

They came to a halt. Almost at once, a fuel truck began to drive towards them. Sarov had obviously prepared everything well in advance. There was a car following the truck and, looking out of the window, Alex saw that steps were being led up to the Lear jet's door. That was interesting. It seemed that somebody wanted to come onboard.

Sarov was watching him. "You will not speak, Alex," he said. "Not one single word. Before you even think of opening your mouth, I suggest you look behind you."

Conrad had moved into the seat directly behind Alex. He had a newspaper balanced on his lap. As Alex turned, he lifted it to reveal a large black pistol with a silencer, pointing directly at him.

"Nobody will hear anything," Sarov said. "If Conrad even thinks you are about to try something, he will fire. The bullet will pass through the seat and into your spine. Death will be instant but it will appear that you have simply fallen asleep."

Alex knew that it wouldn't be as easy as that. A person being shot in the back did not look like a person falling asleep. Sarov was taking huge risks. But this whole business was a huge risk. The stakes couldn't be higher. Alex had no doubt that if he tried to tell anyone what was happening he would be killed immediately.

The door of the plane opened and a ginger-haired man in blue overalls entered, carrying a sheaf of papers. Sarov rose to greet him. "Do you speak English?" the man asked in a Scottish accent.

"Yes."

"I have some papers here for you to sign."

Alex turned his head slightly. The man saw him and nodded. Alex nodded back. He could almost feel Conrad pressing the back of his seat with the gun. He said nothing. And then it was over. Sarov had signed the papers and returned the man's pen.

"Here's a receipt for you," the man said, handing Sarov a sheet. "And we'll have you back in the air in no time at all."

"Thank you." Sarov nodded.

"Are you going to come out and stretch your legs? It's a pleasant day here in Edinburgh. We can offer you some tea and shortbread if you want to come to the office."

"No, thank you. We're all a little tired. We'll stay where we are."

"OK. If you're absolutely sure, I'll get rid of the steps..."

They were going to take away the steps – and as soon as they were gone, Sarov would seal the door! Alex had only seconds in which to act. He waited until the man had left the cabin, then stood up. His hands were in front of him, the Michael Owen figure lying concealed in his palm.

"Sit down!" Conrad hissed.

"It's all right, Conrad," Alex said. "I'm not going anywhere. I'm just stretching my legs."

Sarov had sat down again. He was examining the paperwork the man had given him. Alex strolled past him. His mouth was dry and he was glad that the sensor that had been used at the gate of the Casa de Oro wasn't on the plane. If it had been turned on him now, his heartbeat would have been deafening. This was his last chance. Alex carefully measured out each step. If he had been walking towards his own scaffold, he couldn't have been more tense.

"Where are you going, Alex?" Sarov asked.

Alex turned Michael Owen's head twice.

"I'm not going anywhere."

"What's that you've got in your hands?"

Alex hesitated. But if he tried to pretend he had nothing, Sarov would become even more suspicious than he already was. He held up the figurine. "It's my lucky mascot," he said. "Michael Owen."

He took another step forward. He gave the player's head another turn back.

Ten ... nine ... eight ... seven...

"Sit down, Alex," Sarov said.

"I've got a headache," Alex said. "I just want some fresh air."

"You are not to leave the plane."

"I'm not going anywhere, General."

But Alex had already reached the door and felt the fresh Scottish breeze on his face. A tow truck was pulling the steps away. He watched as a gap opened up between them and the door.

Four ... three ... two...

"Alex! Return to your seat!"

Alex dropped the figurine and threw himself forward.

Conrad leapt up like an angry snake, the gun in his hand.

The figurine exploded.

Alex felt the blast behind him. There was a flash of light and a bang that sounded massively loud, although no windows broke and there was no fire or smoke. His ears rang and for a moment he couldn't see. But he was outside the plane. He had been outside the plane when the stun grenade went off. The steps were still moving away, disappearing in front of him. He was going to miss them! The asphalt surface of the fuel farm apron was five metres below. If he fell that distance, he would break a leg. He might even be killed. But he had made his move just in time. He landed flat on his stomach on the top of the staircase with his legs dangling in the air. Quickly he pulled himself to his feet. The man with the ginger hair was staring at him, astonished. Alex ran down the still-moving steps. As his feet came into contact with the ground, he felt a thrill of triumph. He was home. And it seemed that the stun grenade had done its job. There was no movement on the plane. Nobody was firing at him.

"What the hell do you think you're doing?" the man demanded.

Alex ignored him. This wasn't the right person to be talking to – and he needed to put as much distance as he could between himself and the plane. Smithers had said that the grenade would only incapacitate the enemy for a few minutes. Sarov and Conrad would wake up soon. And they would waste no time in coming after him.

He ran. Out of the corner of his eye, he saw the man snatch a radio out of his pocket and talk into it – but that didn't matter. There were other men around the plane, about to start refuelling. They must surely have heard the explosion. Even if Alex was recaptured, the plane wouldn't be allowed to leave.

But he had no intention of being recaptured. He had already noticed a row of administrative buildings on the perimeter of the airfield and he made for them, the breath rasping in his throat. He reached a door and pulled at it. It was locked! He looked through the window. There was a hallway on the other side and a public telephone, but for some reason the building was closed. For a moment he was tempted to smash the glass – but that would take too long. Cursing quietly, he left the door and ran the twenty metres to the next building.

This one was open. He found himself in a corridor with storerooms and offices on either side. There didn't seem to be anyone about. Now all he needed was a phone. He tried a door. It led into a room full of shelves with a photocopier and stationery supplies. The next door was locked. Alex was getting increasingly desperate. He tried another door and this time he was lucky. It was an office with a desk and, on the desk, a telephone. There was nobody inside. He ran in and snatched it up.

But it was only now he realized that he had no idea what number to ring. The mobile that Smithers had given him had been equipped with a hot key – a direct link to MI6. But nobody had ever given him a direct number. What was he to do? Dial the operator and ask for military intelligence? They would think he was mad.

He didn't have any time to waste. Sarov might already have recovered. Even now he might be on his way. The office had a window but it looked out the back, so there was no sign of the plane or the runway. Alex made a decision and dialled 999.

The line rang twice before it was answered.

It was a woman's voice. "You have rung the emergency services. Which service do you require?"

"Police," Alex said.

"Connecting you now..."

He heard the ring tone.

And then a hand came down onto the telephone, cutting him off. Alex swung round, breathless, expecting to see Sarov in front of him – or worse still, Conrad with the gun.

But it wasn't either of them. It was an airport security guard who had walked into the office while Alex was making his call. He was about fifty years old with greying hair and a chin that had sunk into his neck. His stomach bulged over his belt and his trousers stopped about two centimetres short of his ankles. The man had a radio attached to his jacket. His name – George Prescott – was written on a badge on his top pocket. He was looming over Alex with a stern look on his face and, with a sinking heart, Alex recognized a real security nightmare: a man with the self-important smugness of the traffic warden, the carpark attendant, any petty official.

"What are you doing here, laddie?" Prescott demanded.

"I need to make a telephone call," Alex said.

"I can see that. But this isn't a public telephone. This isn't even a public office. This is a secure complex. You shouldn't be in here."

"No, you don't understand. This is an emergency!"

"Oh yes? And what sort of emergency do you mean?" Prescott obviously didn't believe him.

"I can't explain. Just let me make the call."

The security guard smiled. He was enjoying himself. He spent five days a week plodding from one office to another, checking doors and turning off lights. It was good to have someone he could boss about. "You're not making any calls until you tell me what you're doing here!" he said. "This is a private office." His eyes narrowed. "Have you opened any drawers? Have you taken anything?"

Alex's nerves were screaming but he forced himself to remain calm. "I haven't taken anything, Mr Prescott," he said. "I just got off a plane that landed a few minutes ago—"

"What plane?"

"A private plane."

"Have you got a passport?"

"No."

"That's a very serious matter. You can't enter the country without a passport."

"My passport is on the plane!"

"Then I'll escort you back and we'll get it."

"No!" Alex could feel the seconds racing by. What could he say to this man that would persuade him to let him make the phone call? His mind was in a whirl and suddenly, for the first time in his life, he found himself blurting out the truth. "Listen," he said. "I know this is hard to believe, but I work for the government. The British government. If you let me call them, they'll prove it to you. I'm a spy—"

"A spy?" Prescott's face broke into a smile. But there was no humour in it at all. "How old are you?"

"Fourteen."

"A fourteen-year-old spy? I think you've been watching too much television, laddie."

"It's true!"

"I don't think so."

"Listen to me, please. A man has just tried to kill me. He's on a plane on the runway and unless you let me make this call, a lot of people are going to die."

"What?"

"He's got a nuclear bomb, for God's sake!"

That was a mistake. Prescott bristled. "I'll ask you not to take the name of the Lord in vain, if you don't mind." He came to a decision. "I don't know how you got here or what you're playing at, but you're coming with me to security and passport control in the main terminal." He reached out for Alex. "Come along now! I've had enough of your nonsense."

"It isn't nonsense. There's a man called Sarov. He's carrying a nuclear bomb. He's planning to detonate it in Murmansk. I'm the only one who can stop him. Please, Mr Prescott. Just let me phone the police. It'll only take me twenty seconds and you can stand here and watch me. Let me talk to them and afterwards you can take me wherever you like."

But the security guard wouldn't budge. "You're not making any calls and you're coming with me now," he said.

Alex made up his mind. He had tried pleading and he had tried telling the truth. Neither had succeeded, so he would just have to take the security guard out. Prescott moved round the desk, getting closer to him. Alex tensed himself, balancing on the balls of his feet, his fists ready. He knew that the man was only doing his job and he didn't want to hurt him but there was no other way.

And then the door opened.

"There you are, Alex! I was worried about you..."

It was Sarov.

Conrad was with him. Both of them looked ill – their skin white and eyes not quite focused. There was no expression on either man's face.

"Who are you?" Prescott demanded.

"I'm Alex's father," Sarov replied. "Isn't that right, Alex?"

Alex hesitated. He realized he was still in combat position, about to strike out. Slowly, he lowered his arms. He knew it was over and tasted the bitterness of defeat. There was nothing he could do. If he argued in front of Prescott, Sarov would simply kill both of them. If he tried to fight, the result would be just the same. Alex had just one hope left. If he walked out of here with Sarov and Conrad and the security guard was still alive, there was just a chance that he might tell his story to someone who would report it to MI6. It would certainly be too late for Alex. But the world might still be saved.

"Isn't that right, Alex?" Sarov was waiting for an answer.

"Yes," Alex said. "Hello, Dad."

"So what's all this business about bombs and spies?" Prescott asked.

Alex inwardly groaned. Why couldn't the man keep his mouth shut?

"Is that what Alex has been telling you?" Sarov asked.

"Aye. That and a whole lot more besides."

"Has he made a telephone call?"

"No." Prescott puffed himself up. "The wee rascal was helping himself to the phone when I came in. But I soon put a stop to that."

Sarov nodded slowly. He was pleased. "Well ... he does have a vivid imagination," he explained. "Alex has not been well lately. He has mental problems. Sometimes he finds it hard to distinguish between fantasy and reality."

"How did he get in here?" Prescott demanded.

"He must have slipped out of the plane when nobody was watching. He has, of course, no permission to be on British soil."

"Is he British?"

"No." Sarov took hold of Alex's arm. "And now we must return to the plane. We still have a long journey ahead of us."

"Wait a minute!" The guard wasn't going to let them off that easily. "I'm sorry, sir, but your son was strictly off-limits. And for that matter, so are you. You can't just go wandering around Edinburgh Airport like this! I'm going to have to report this."

"I quite understand." Sarov didn't seem at all perturbed. "I must get the boy back on the plane. But I will leave you with my assistant, who will give you all the details you require. If necessary, he will accompany you to your superior's office. And I have to thank you for preventing my son from making a telephone call, Mr

Prescott. That would have been most embarrassing for us all."

Without waiting for a reply, Sarov turned and, still holding Alex's arm, led him out of the room.

An hour later, the Lear jet took off on the last leg of its journey. Alex was sitting in the same seat as before but now he was handcuffed to it. Sarov hadn't hurt him and no longer seemed even aware that he was on the plane. In a way, that was the most frightening thing about him. Alex had expected anger, violence, perhaps even a sudden death at the hands of Conrad. But Sarov had done nothing. From the moment that Alex had been escorted back onto the plane, the Russian hadn't so much as looked at him. There had, of course, been problems. The explosion on the plane and Alex's leap out of it had raised all sorts of questions. The pilot had been in constant communication with the control tower. The sound of the explosion had been a faulty microwave oven, he'd explained. As for the boy? General Alexei Sarov, on the staff of the Russian president, was travelling with a nephew. The boy had high spirits. Very stupid, but everything was under control...

If this had been an ordinary private jet, the police would have been called. But it was registered to Boris Kiriyenko. It had diplomatic immunity. All in all, the authorities agreed, it would be easier to turn a blind eye and let it go.

George Prescott's body was discovered four hours later. He was sitting, slumped, in a stationery cupboard. There was a look of surprise on his face and a single, round bullet wound between his eyes.

By then, the Lear was in Russian airspace. Even as the alarm was raised and the police were finally called, the cabin lights were dimmed as the jet curved over the Kola Peninsula preparing for its final descent.

THE END OF THE WORLD

Airports are the same all over the world, but the one at Murmansk had managed to achieve a new level of ugliness. It had been built in the middle of nowhere so that, from the air, it looked like a mistake. At ground level, it offered just one low-rise terminal built out of glass and tired, grey cement, with eight white letters mounted on the roof.

МУРМАНСК

Alex recognized the Russian spelling. Murmansk. A city with thousands of people. He wondered how many of them would be alive in twelve hours' time.

Now handcuffed to one of the two guards who had flown with them all the way from Skeleton Key, he was led across an empty runway. It had rained recently. The asphalt was wet and greasy, with pools of dirty water all around. There were no other planes in sight. In fact, the airport didn't seem to be in use at all. A few lights burned, dull yellow, behind the glass. But there were no people. The single arrivals door was locked and chained as if the airport had given up all hope of anyone ever actually coming there.

They were expected. Three army trucks and a mud-streaked saloon car were waiting. A row of men stood to attention, dressed in khaki uniforms with black belts and boots almost like wellingtons rising to their calves. Each one of them carried a machine gun on a strap across his chest. Their commander, wearing the same uniform as Sarov, stepped forward and saluted. He and Sarov shook hands, then embraced. They spoke for a few minutes. Then the commander snapped an order. Two of his men ran to the plane and began to unload the silver chest that was Sarov's nuclear bomb. Alex watched as it was taken out of the back and loaded into one of the trucks. The soldiers were well disciplined. Here was enough power to destroy a continent, but not one head turned as it was carried past.

With the bomb in place, the soldiers swivelled round and, marching in time, approached the two remaining trucks and climbed in. His hands cuffed together now, Alex was bundled into the front seat of one, next to the driver. Nobody looked at him. Nobody seemed too curious about who he was. Sarov must have radioed ahead and warned them that he would be there. He examined the man driving the truck. He was tough and clean-shaven with clear blue eyes. There was no expression on his face. A professional soldier. Alex turned and looked out of the window in time to see Sarov and Conrad getting into the car.

They set off. There really was nothing outside the airport, just a flat, empty landscape where even the trees managed to be stunted and dull. Alex shivered and tried to cross his hands to rub warmth into his shoulders. There was a clink from the handcuffs and the driver glanced at him angrily.

They drove for about forty minutes down a road pitted with holes. A few buildings, modern and characterless, crept up on them and suddenly they were in Murmansk itself. Was it night or day? The sky was still light but the streetlamps were on. There were people on the pavements but they didn't seem to be going anywhere, just drifting along like sleepwalkers. Nobody looked at them as they followed a single road, four lanes wide. This was a boulevard in the centre of the city. It was absolutely straight and seemed to go nowhere, with blank, uninteresting buildings on either side. Murmansk was made up of row after row of almost identical apartment blocks like so many matchboxes. There didn't seem to be any cinemas, restaurants, shops – anything that would make life worth living.

There were no suburbs. The city just stopped and suddenly they were driving through empty tundra, heading for a horizon that had nothing at all to offer. They were fourteen hundred kilometres from the North Pole and there was nothing here. People with no life and a sun without a shred of warmth. Alex thought of the journey he had made. From Wimbledon to Cornwall. Then London, Miami and Skeleton Key. And finally here. Was it to be *finally*? What a horrible place to finish his life. He really had come to the end of the world.

There were no other cars on the road and no street signs. Alex stopped even trying to see where they were going. After another thirty minutes they began to slow down, then turned off. There was a crunching sound under the wheels as they left the asphalt surface and continued along gravel. Was this where the Russians kept their submarines? He could only see a chicken-wire fence and a dilapidated wooden kiosk trying to pass as a sentry box. They stopped in front of a red and white barrier. A man appeared, dressed in dark blue with a loose, flapping overcoat and, showing underneath it, a tunic and a striped T-shirt. He was a Russian sailor. He couldn't have been more than twenty years old and he looked confused. He ran over to the car and said something in Russian.

Conrad shot him. Alex saw the hand come out of the window and the flash of the gun, but it all happened so quickly that he could hardly believe it had happened at all. The young Russian was thrown backwards. Conrad fired a second time. There was another sailor in the sentry box – Alex hadn't even noticed him – and he shouted out, crumpling backwards. Nobody had spoken a word. Two soldiers climbed out of the front truck and went over to the barrier blocking the entrance. Was this really the entrance to a submarine base? Alex had seen more sophisticated security in a supermarket carpark. The soldiers simply lifted the barrier. The convoy moved on.

They followed a twisting, bumpy track down a hill and there, at last, was the sea. The first thing Alex saw was a fleet of ice-breakers, moored about eight hundred metres away, huge iron blocks sitting silently, impossibly on the sea. It seemed against the laws of nature that such monstrous things could float. There were no lights onboard, no movement at all. On the other side of the water, another grim stretch of coastline rose up, streaked with white; though whether this was salt or some sort of permanent snow, Alex couldn't say.

The trucks bounced down and suddenly they were in a harbour, surrounded by cranes, gantries, warehouses and sheds. It was a devil's playground of twisted steel and cement, of hooks and chains, pulleys and cables, drums, wooden pallets and huge steel containers. Rusting ships sat in the water or stood on dry land, suspended on a network of stilts. Cars, lorries and tractors, some obviously derelict, stood idle at the water's edge. There was a row of long wooden cabins to one side, each one numbered in yellow and grey paint. They reminded Alex of buildings he'd seen in old World War Two movies, in prisoner of war camps. Could this be where the other sailors slept? If so, they must all be in bed. The harbour was deserted. Nothing moved.

They stopped and Alex felt the truck rock as the soldiers poured out behind him. A moment later he saw them, their machine guns raised, and wondered if he was meant to follow them. But the driver shook his head, gesturing at him to stay where he was. Alex watched the men fan out across the compound, moving quickly as they made for the cabins. There was no sign of Sarov. He must still be in the car, which was parked round the other side.

A long pause. Then someone gave a signal. There was the smash of wood, a door being forced open, then the concentrated chatter of machine-gun fire. Somebody shouted. An electric bell began to ring, the sound all too small and ineffective. Three half-dressed men appeared round the side of the cabins and sprinted forward, trying to find shelter among the containers. More gunfire. Alex saw two of them go down, followed by the third, his hands scrabbling at the air as he was hit in the back. There was a single shot from a window. One man was trying to fight back. A grenade curved through the air and onto the roof of the building. There was an explosion and half the wall blew out, turned into matchsticks. The next time Alex looked, the window and presumably the man behind it had been destroyed.

The attack had come without any warning at all. Sarov's men had been well armed and prepared. There had only been a handful of sailors at the yard and they had all been asleep. It was over very quickly. The ringing stopped. Smoke curled out of the damaged building. A figure floated past, face-down in the water. The harbour had been taken. Sarov was in total command.

The driver got out of the truck, went quickly round the front and opened the door for Alex. He climbed down awkwardly, his hands still chained together. Sarov's men had moved into the second phase of the operation. Alex saw bodies being carried out of sight. One of the other trucks reversed, moving closer to the water's edge. The commander from the airport called out an order and the soldiers scattered, taking up positions that they must have worked out months before. It seemed unlikely that anybody would have had time to raise the alarm, but if anyone approached the yard from Murmansk, they would find it defended. Sarov was standing to one side with Conrad beside him. He was looking at something. Alex followed his eyes.

And there were the submarines!

Alex gasped. Here was what this whole thing had been about! There were just four of them, bloated metal beasts that lay half submerged in the sea, secured by ropes as thick as a man's arm. Each one was the size of an office building turned on its side. The submarines had no markings whatsoever and no flags. They seemed to be coated in black oil or tar. Their conning towers, set well back, were closed and solid. Alex shivered. He'd never thought that a machine could actually emanate evil, but these did. They were as dark and as cold as the water that lapped about them. They looked just like the bombs that they had become.

Three of the submarines were in a line, moored against the side of the harbour. The fourth was in a bay of its own, a little way out. Alex noticed a crane at the end of a quay, right next to the water. Years ago it might have been painted yellow but most of the colour had flaked off. The control cabin was only about ten metres above the ground with a ladder reaching up to it. The arm of the crane slanted up, then bent down, mimicking the neck and head of a bird. This was a crane with no hook. Instead there was a metal disc like an oversized bath plug dangling underneath the arm, connected to it by a chain and a series of electric cables.

Conrad shouted something and the driver led Alex over to a solid handrail on the edge of the quay. It had obviously been placed there to stop anyone falling in and it was securely bolted to the ground. The driver unlocked one of Alex's hands then pulled with the chain, leading him like a dog. He walked him over to the handrail and cuffed him to it. Alex was left standing on his own in the middle of everything. He jerked at the chain but it was useless. He wasn't going anywhere.

Alex could only stand and watch as two of the soldiers lifted the bomb out of the truck as carefully as they could. He saw the strain in their faces as they set it on the ground right next to the edge of the quay and only a few metres from the crane. Sarov walked over, Conrad limping along next to him. Conrad looked at Alex and one corner of his mouth twitched into a smile.

Sarov reached into his jacket pocket and took out the plastic card he had shown Alex on the plane. He held it for a moment, then fed it into the slot on the side of the nuclear bomb. At once, the silver chest came to life. A series of red lights began to blink on a panel. Alex saw a line of digits on a liquid crystal display. Hours, minutes and seconds. They were already counting down. The magnetic stripe on the card had activated the bomb. Somewhere inside the chest, electronic wheels were turning. The detonation sequence had begun.

Then Sarov came over to Alex.

He stood there, examining him as if for the first and last time. As ever, his face gave nothing away, but Alex detected something in the man's eyes. Sarov would have denied it. He would have been angered if anyone had suggested it. But the sadness was there. It was plain to see.

"And so we come to the end," he said. "You are standing in the Nuclear Submarine Repair Shipyard of Murmansk. You may be interested to know that the soldiers we met at the airport have all served with me in the past and are loyal to me still. The entire compound is now under my control and as you have seen, the nuclear bomb is primed. I'm afraid I cannot stay with you any longer. I have to return to the airport to ensure that everything is ready for our flight to Moscow. I will leave Conrad to place the bomb in position on the submarine, directly over the nuclear reactor that is still there inside. It is possible that the detonator in the bomb will also trigger the reactor, doubling or trebling the force of the explosion. This will mean very little to you, as you will be vaporized instantly – before your brain has time even to work out what has happened. Conrad is very disappointed. He had hoped I would allow him to kill you himself."

Alex said nothing.

"I am so sorry, Alex, that in the end you were so much more stupid than I had thought, although perhaps I should have expected it. A Western child, brought up and educated in Britain ... a country that is itself only a shadow of what it once was. Why couldn't you see what I was offering you? Why couldn't you accept your place in the new world? You could have been my son. You chose to be my enemy. And this is where it has brought you."

There was another, long silence. Sarov reached out and gently stroked Alex's cheek. He looked into the boy's eyes one last time. Then he turned on his heel and walked away. Alex watched him get into his car and drive off.

The other soldiers were a distance away, still in their places around the site. But here at the centre, with the crane, the submarines and the nuclear bomb, Alex and Conrad were on their own. It was as if they had the whole harbour to themselves.

Conrad stepped forward and stopped very close to Alex. "I have a job to do," he rasped. "But then we will have a little time together. Strange though it is, Sarov still cares about you. He told me to leave you alone. But I think, this time, I must disobey the general. You are mine! And I intend to make you suffer..."

"Just talking to you makes me suffer," Alex said.

Conrad ignored him. He went over to the crane and climbed the short ladder into the cabin. Alex saw him start up the controls and a moment later the metal disc swung round so that it was over the bomb, then began to descend. Conrad handled the crane expertly. The disc fell quickly, stopped, then gently came into contact with the surface of the chest. Alex heard a loud click and a moment later the chest suddenly swayed and left the ground. Now he understood. The metal disc was a powerful electromagnet. Conrad was operating a magnetic hoist, using it to carry the bomb across the water and deposit it on the submarine. The whole operation would take him about three minutes. Then he would come for Alex.

Alex had run out of time. He had to act now.

The stick of bubblegum that Smithers had given him was in his right pocket. Only his left hand was free and it took him a few precious seconds to get it out, unwrap it and shove it into his mouth. He wondered what Conrad would think if he had seen him. Certainly Sarov wouldn't have been amused. A Western boy about to face death and all he could think about was gum!

Alex chewed. Smithers had managed to get one part of the formula right. The gum did indeed taste of strawberries. He wondered how long he should leave it in his mouth. His saliva was meant to activate it, but how much saliva did it need? He chewed until the gum felt soft and manageable and the strawberry taste had faded away. Then he spat it into his hand and quickly pressed it into the handcuff, forcing it into the lock.

The silver chest had travelled all the way across the water. Alex saw it swinging gently over the submarine. Inside the control cabin, Conrad leant forward. Slowly he lowered the chest until it landed on the metal surface. The wires and chains attached to the hoist sagged, then straightened again. The hoist began to move back towards the quay. But it had left the bomb behind.

Something was definitely happening inside the handcuffs. Alex heard a very faint hissing. The pink gum was expanding. It was oozing back out of the lock and there was much more gum coming out than he had put in. There was a sudden crack. The metal had shattered. Alex felt a painful sting as a piece of broken metal cut into his wrist. But then the handcuffs fell open. He was free!

Conrad had seen what had happened. He was already climbing out of the crane. He hadn't turned off the controls and the magnet was still coming back on its own, just a few metres above the water. The bomb was out of reach on the other side. Even as Alex looked around for a weapon, Conrad reached the bottom of the ladder and rushed towards him. Suddenly they were face to face.

Conrad smiled. The smile tugged at the one side of his face that could move. The other side, with the bald scalp above it, remained still. Alex could see at once that, despite all his terrible injuries, Conrad was utterly confident. A moment later, he knew why. Fired by hatred, Conrad moved with surprising speed. He was standing in combat stance one moment, a blur the next. Alex felt a foot kick him in the chest. The world spun and he was thrown to the ground, winded and bruised. Meanwhile, Conrad had landed lightly on his feet. He wasn't even out of breath.

Painfully, Alex picked himself up. Conrad walked towards him and lashed out a second time. His foot missed by a centimetre as

Alex dived back to the ground, rolling over and over to the water's edge. A hand reached out and grabbed hold of his shirt. Alex saw the dreadful stitch-marks where the hand had been sewn back onto the wrist. He was dragged to his feet. Conrad slapped him with tremendous force. Alex tasted blood. The hand released him. He stood, swaying, trying to find some sort of defence.

But he had none. For all his strength and skill, Conrad had beaten him. And now he was coming in for the kill. Alex saw it in his face...

And then, out of nowhere, came a sudden clanging. The alarm bell had started up again. There was a burst of gunfire and, seconds later, an explosion. Someone had thrown another grenade. Conrad stopped dead in his tracks, his head twisting round. There was more gunfire. Impossible though it was, it seemed that the harbour was under attack.

With new strength, Alex ran forward. He had seen a metal rod lying on the ground amongst all the other debris. His hands closed around it and he swept it up, grateful to have something that felt like a weapon in his hands. Conrad turned to face him. The shooting had intensified. Now it seemed to be coming from two directions as Sarov's men defended themselves against an enemy that had come from nowhere. There was a screech of tyres, and in the far distance Alex saw a jeep come smashing through one of the chicken-wire fences. It skidded to a halt and three men jumped out and took cover. They were all dressed in blue. What was going on here? The Russian navy against the Russian army? And who, exactly, had raised the alarm?

But even if Sarov's plans had been revealed, even if a rescue operation had somehow been put in place, Alex was still in grave danger. Conrad was on the balls of his feet, looking to find a way past the metal rod. And what about the nuclear bomb? Alex didn't know if Sarov had primed it to go off in five hours or five minutes. Knowing how mad he was, it could have been either.

Conrad leapt forward. Alex lunged with the metal pole and felt it ram into the man's shoulder. But his smile of satisfaction vanished as Conrad grabbed hold of the rod with both hands. He had allowed Alex to hit him simply because that would bring the rod within his reach. Alex pulled back, but Conrad was much too strong for him. He felt the metal being torn out of his hands, cutting into his palms. Alex let go of the rod, then cried out as Conrad swung it viciously like a scythe. The metal slammed into the side of Alex's leg and he was down again, on his back, unable to move.

More gunfire. Although his vision was dimmed, Alex saw two more grenades arc through the air. They landed next to one of the ships and exploded, a huge fireball of flame. Two of Sarov's men were lifted into the air. Two or even three machine guns began to chatter simultaneously. There were screams. More flames.

Conrad stood over him.

He seemed to have forgotten what was happening in the shipyard. Or perhaps he didn't care. He pulled up one sleeve, then the other. Finally he dropped down so that he was sitting on Alex's chest, one knee on either side. His hands closed around Alex's throat.

Gently, enjoying what he was doing, he began to squeeze.

Alex felt himself being slowly strangled. He couldn't breathe. There were already black spots in front of his eyes. But he had seen something that Conrad hadn't. It was slowly making its way back towards them, crossing the water. The magnetic disc.

Conrad had left the controls on in the cabin in his haste to get over to Alex. Was it possible...? Alex remembered what Sarov had told him about his assistant. He had metal pins all over his body.

There were metal wires in his jaw and a metal plate in his head...

The magnet was almost over them, blotting out the sky. Alex couldn't breathe. Conrad's hands were tight around his throat. He had only seconds left.

With the last of his strength, he suddenly lashed out with both his fists, at the same time jerking his body up. Conrad was taken by surprise. He started back, his hands loosening. The magnet was right above him. Alex saw the shock in his face as all the metal plates, pins and wires in his body entered the magnetic field. Conrad yelled and disappeared, plucked into the air by invisible hands. His back smashed into the disc with a terrible snapping sound. At once he went still, attached to the disc by his shoulders, his arms and legs hanging down. The crane continued moving, carrying the limp body in a gentle curve over the quay.

Alex gasped for breath. The world swam back into focus. "What an attractive man," he muttered.

Slowly, he pulled himself to his feet, then staggered over to the handrail where he had been chained. He propped himself against it, no longer able to stand without its support. There was a burst of gunfire, longer and more powerful than any that had gone before. A helicopter had appeared, flying in low over the sea. He saw an airman sitting in the open doorway, his legs dangling, a huge gun cradled in his lap. One of Sarov's trucks was blown off its wheels, twisted over twice and exploded in flames.

The bomb...

Alex could work out what was happening here later. Nobody would be safe until the bomb was defused. His throat was still burning. It took all his strength to draw breath. But now he ran forward and climbed into the crane. He had operated a crane before. He knew it couldn't be too difficult. He reached out and took the controls. At the same moment, one of Sarov's men fired at him. The bullet clanged against the metal casing of the cabin. Alex ducked instinctively and pulled a lever.

The magnetic disc stopped and swung in the air with Conrad stuck beneath it like a broken doll. Alex pushed forward and it began to drop down into the sea. No! That wasn't what he wanted. He pulled the lever back and it stopped abruptly. How did you turn off the magnet? Alex looked around him and saw a switch. He pressed it. A light came on over his head. Wrong switch! There was a button set in the control stick he was holding and he tried that. At once, Conrad fell free. He plunged into the grey, freezing water and sank immediately. With all the metal inside him, Alex thought, it was hardly surprising.

He pulled the control stick towards him and the magnet rose again. A soldier ran across the quay towards him. There was a burst of fire from the helicopter and the man fell down and lay still. Now ... concentrate! Alex tried a second lever and this time the magnet began its return journey over to the submarine. It seemed to take for ever. Alex was only partly aware of the battle still raging all around him. It seemed that the Russian authorities had arrived in force. Sarov's men were heavily outnumbered but were still fighting back. They knew they had nothing to lose.

The magnet reached the submarine. Alex dropped it towards the silver chest, remembering how delicately it had been done by Conrad. He was less skilled – and winced as the heavy disc smashed into the top. Damn! He would set the thing off himself if he wasn't careful. He pressed the button in the control stick a second time and actually felt the magnet come alive and knew that the nuclear bomb was in its grip. He pulled back, lifting the magnetic hoist. The silver chest came clear of the submarine.

Now, a centimetre at a time, he swung the arm of the crane over the water, bringing the nuclear bomb back towards the harbour.

A second bullet slammed into the crane and the window shattered right next to his head. Alex cried out. Glass fragments showered over him. He thought he was going to be blinded. But when he next looked up, the nuclear bomb was over the quay and he knew that he was nearly finished.

He lowered it. At the very moment it touched the ground, there was another explosion, louder and closer than any that had gone before. But it wasn't nuclear. One of the warehouses had shattered. Another was on fire. A second helicopter had arrived and it was strafing the ground, whipping dust and debris into the air. It was hard to be sure, but Alex thought that Sarov's men were losing ground. There seemed to be less return fire. Well, in a few more seconds, it wouldn't matter. All he had to do was retrieve the plastic card.

He pulled the magnet clear, jumped from the crane, then ran over to the chest. He could see the card, half protruding from the slot where Sarov had inserted it. The lights were still blinking, the numbers spinning. There was less gunfire around him now. Looking over his shoulder, he saw more men in blue edging slowly into the compound, coming in from all sides. He reached down and pulled out the card. The lights on the nuclear bomb went out. The numbers disappeared. He had done it!

"Put it back."

The words were softly spoken but each one dripped menace. Alex looked up and saw Sarov in front of him. Somehow he must have learnt that the compound was under attack and had made his way back. How much time had passed since the two of them had last faced each other? Thirty minutes? An hour? However long it had been, Sarov had changed. He was smaller, shrunken. The light in his eyes had gone out and what little colour there had been in his skin seemed to have become muddied. He had been wounded fighting his way back into the harbour. There was a rip in his jacket and a slowly spreading red stain. His left hand hung useless.

But his right hand was holding a gun.

"It's over, General," Alex said. "Conrad is dead. The Russian army is here. Someone must have tipped them off."

Sarov shook his head. "I can still detonate the bomb. There is an override. You and I will die. But the end result will be the same."

"A better world?"

"That's all I ever wanted, Alex. All of this...! I was only ever doing what I believed in."

Alex felt an enormous tiredness creeping up on him. He weighed the card in his hand. It was strange really. From one Skeleton Key to another. It all came down to this.

Sarov raised the gun. The blood was spreading more rapidly now. He swayed on his feet. "Give me the card or I will shoot you," he said.

Alex lifted the card then suddenly flicked it. It spun twice in the air, then disappeared into the water. "Go ahead then, if that's what you want," he said. "Shoot me!"

Sarov's eyes flickered over to the lost card, then back to Alex. "Why...?" he whispered.

"I'd rather be dead than have a father like you," Alex said.

There were voices shouting. Footsteps coming nearer.

"Goodbye, Alex," Sarov said.

He raised the gun and fired a single shot.

AFTER ALEX

"We've lost Alex Rider," Mrs Jones said. "I'm sorry, Alan. I know it's not what you wanted to hear. But that's the end of it."

The head of MI6 Special Operations and his number two were having lunch together in a restaurant near Liverpool Street Station. They ate there frequently, although not often together. The restaurant was in a basement with low, vaulted ceilings, soft lighting and bare brick walls. Blunt liked the starched white tablecloths and the old-fashioned service. Also, the food was poor so few people came there. That was useful when he wanted to have a conversation such as this.

"Alex did very well," he muttered.

"Oh yes. I had an e-mail from Joe Byrne in Virginia. Of course, he was upset about the loss of his own two agents in the underwater cave, but he was full of praise for Alex. He definitely owes us a favour ... which will at least be useful in the future." She took a bread roll and broke it in half. "It wouldn't surprise me if the CIA didn't start training their own teenage spy now. The Americans are always copying our ideas."

"When we're not copying theirs," Blunt remarked.

"That's true."

They paused as the waiter came over with the first course. Grilled sardines for Mrs Jones, soup for Blunt. Neither dish looked particularly appetizing but that didn't matter. Neither of them had much of an appetite.

"I've looked through the files and I think I have the general picture," Blunt said. "But perhaps you can fill me in on some of the details. In particular, I'd like to know how the Russian authorities found out about Sarov in time."

"That was because of what happened at Edinburgh Airport," Mrs Jones explained. She looked down at her plate. There were four sardines lying side by side, complete with heads and tails. If it was possible for a fish to look unhappy, these had managed it. She squeezed lemon over them. The juice formed tears beneath the unblinking eyes.

"Alex ran into a security guard called George Prescott," she went on. "He'd managed to escape from Sarov's plane using a gadget Smithers had given him."

"I don't recall authorizing Smithers—" Blunt began.

"Alex wanted to use a telephone," Mrs Jones cut in. "Obviously, he was going to warn us about Murmansk, what Sarov was planning. This man, Prescott, stopped him."

"Unfortunate."

"Yes. It must have been very frustrating. Alex actually told him that he was a spy and that he was working for us, but then Sarov caught up with him. Prescott was killed – and that was the end of it. Or it would have been ... but we were extremely fortunate.

Prescott had a radio transmitter clipped to his jacket. It was turned on throughout his conversation with Alex and his office heard every word that was said. Of course, they didn't believe Alex either, but when Prescott was found with a bullet in his head they put two and two together and got on to us as fast as they could. I was the one who alerted the authorities at Murmansk and I must say that the Russians acted very promptly. They pulled a naval force together, plus two helicopter gunships, and stormed the yard."

"What happened to the bomb?"

"They have it. According to their people, it would have been big enough to blow a sizeable hole in the Kola Peninsula. The fallout would have contaminated Norway, Finland and, for that matter, most of Great Britain. And I really do think the backlash would have been enough to force Kiriyenko out of power. Nobody likes him very much anyway."

"Where is Kiriyenko?" Blunt's soup was almost cold. He had forgotten what was meant to be in it.

"The Cuban authorities found him locked up on Skeleton Key. Shouting his head off and blaming everyone except himself." Mrs Jones shook her head. "He's back in Moscow now. Sarov gave him a bad scare, but then he gave us all a bad scare. If it hadn't been for Alex, who knows what might have happened."

"What do the Cubans have to say about all this?"

"They've disowned Sarov. Nothing to do with them. They had no idea what he was planning. What's so terrifying is that he nearly got away with it!"

"If it hadn't been for Alex Rider..."

The two of them finished their first course in silence.

"Where is Alex now?" Blunt asked eventually.

"He's home."

"How is he?"

Mrs Jones sighed. "It would seem that Sarov shot himself," she said. "Alex was standing right in front of him. The trouble with you, Alan, is that you've never had children and you refuse to accept the fact that, at the end of the day, Alex is only a child. He's already been through far more than any fourteen-year-old could possibly be expected to ... and this last mission! I would say it was his toughest yet. And at the very end he actually saw what Sarov did!"

"I suppose Sarov didn't want to be taken alive," Blunt muttered.

"I wish it was as simple as that. It seems that Sarov had some sort of ... attachment to Alex. He saw him as the son he had lost. Alex rejected him and it pushed him over the edge. *That's* why he did it. He couldn't live with himself any more."

Blunt signalled and a waiter came over and poured the wine. It was unusual for the two spymasters to drink at lunchtime but Blunt had selected a half bottle of Chablis, which had been sitting in an ice bucket beside their table. Another waiter served the main courses. The food sat on the table untouched.

"What happened with that business with the triads?" Blunt asked.

"Oh – I've sorted all that out. We had a couple of their people in jail and I arranged for them to be released. Flown back to Hong Kong. It was enough. They'll leave Alex alone."

"So why do you say we've lost him?"

"The truth is, we shouldn't have used him in the first place."

"We didn't use him. It was the CIA."

"You know that doesn't make any difference." Mrs Jones tasted the wine. "The point is, I was the one who debriefed him and all I can say is ... he's not the same. I know, I've said this all before. But I was seriously worried about him, Alan. He was so silent and withdrawn. He'd been badly hurt."

"Any broken bones?"

"For heaven's sake! Children can be hurt in other ways! I'm sorry, but I do feel very strongly about this. We can't use him again. It isn't fair."

"Life isn't fair." Blunt picked up his own glass. "I think you're forgetting that Alex has just saved the world. That boy is fast becoming one of our most effective operatives. He's the best secret weapon we have. We can't afford to be sentimental about him. We'll let him rest. I dare say he needs to catch up at school, and then there's the summer holidays. But you know as well as I do, if the need arises, there's nothing to discuss. We'll use him again. And again..."

Mrs Jones put down her knife and fork. "I'm suddenly not very hungry," she said.

Blunt glanced at her. "I hope you're not getting a conscience," he said. "If you're really worried about Alex, bring him in and we'll have a little heart to heart."

Mrs Jones looked her boss straight in the eye. "He may have trouble finding yours," she said.

The next day was a Saturday. Alex got up late, showered, dressed and went down to a breakfast that his housekeeper, Jack Starbright, had prepared for him. She had cooked all his favourite things but he ate little of it, sitting at the table in silence. Jack was desperately worried about him. The day before she had tried to get him to see a doctor and for the first time in his life he had snapped at her. Now she wasn't sure what to do. If things didn't get better she would talk to that woman – Mrs Jones. Jack wasn't supposed to know what was going on, but she had a good idea. She would make them do something. Things couldn't go on like this.

"What you going to do today?" she asked.

Alex shrugged. There was a bandage round his hand where the metal pole had cut him and a number of grazes on his face. Worst of all though were the bruises around his neck. Conrad had certainly left his mark.

"D'you want to see a film?"

"No. I thought I'd go for a walk."

"I'll come with you, if you like."

"No. Thanks, Jack, but I'm OK on my own."

Ten minutes later, Alex left the house. The weather forecast had said it would be a bright day but in fact it was close and cloudy. He started walking towards the King's Road, wanting to lose himself in the crowds. He had no real idea where he was going. He just needed to think.

Sarov was dead. Alex had turned away as the man had raised the gun towards his own heart, not bearing to see any more. Minutes later it had all been over. The Repair Yard had been secured, the bomb removed. Alex himself had been whisked away by helicopter, first to a hospital in Moscow and then back to London. Someone had told him that Kiriyenko wanted to see him. There was talk of a medal. Alex had declined. He just wanted to go home.

And that's where he was. Everything had worked out all right. He was a hero!

So why did he feel like this? And how exactly *was* it that he felt? Depressed? Exhausted? He was both of those things – but worse still, he felt empty. It was almost as if he had died in the Submarine Repair Shipyard of Murmansk and had somehow returned to London as a ghost. Life was all around him but he wasn't a part of it. Even lying in his own bed, in his own house, he felt he no longer belonged.

So much had happened to him but he wasn't allowed to talk about it with anyone. He couldn't even tell Jack. She would be horrified and upset – and there was nothing she could do anyway. He had missed more weeks of school and knew that it wasn't just the work he would have to catch up with. Friendships move on too. People already thought he was weird. It wouldn't be long before nobody was talking to him at all.

He would never have a father. He knew this now. He would never have an ordinary life. Somehow, he had got himself trapped. A ghost. That was what he had become.

Alex hadn't heard the car stop behind him. He hadn't heard the door open and close. But there were suddenly footsteps running up behind him and before he could move, a hand had been thrown around his chest.

"Alex!"

He spun round. "Sabina!"

Sabina Pleasure was standing in front of him, panting after the short run, wearing a Robbie Williams T-shirt and jeans, a brightly coloured straw bag over her shoulder. Her face was lit up with pleasure. "Thank goodness I found you. I've been after you for weeks. You never gave me your phone number but it's lucky I knew your address. Mum and Dad drove me over..." She gestured at her parents, sitting in the car. They both raised a hand, waving at Alex through the windscreen. "I was going to look in just in case you were at home. And here you are!" She looked at his neck, examining his bruises. "You look terrible! Have you been involved in a car smash?"

"Not exactly."

"Anyway, Alex," she interrupted. "I'm really pissed off with you. I saved your life in Cornwall, in case you don't remember – although I have to say that giving you the kiss of life on the beach *was* the high point of the holiday – and the next thing I knew, you'd simply vanished. I didn't even get so much as a thank-you card."

"Well, I was, sort of ... busy."

"Being James Bond, I suppose?"

"Well..." Alex didn't know what to say.

Sabina took his arm. "You can tell me all about it later. Mum and Dad have invited you to lunch and we want to talk about the South of France."

"What about it?"

"That's where we're going this summer. And you're coming too. We've got some friends who've lent us a house and a pool and it's going to be great." She looked closely at his face. "Don't tell me you had other plans?"

Alex smiled. "No, Sabina, I haven't got any plans."

"That's settled then. Now, what do you want for lunch? I fancy an Italian – but he's been ignoring me so you'll have to do!" She laughed.

Alex and Sabina walked down the street together. Alex glanced up. The clouds had parted and the sun was out.

It looked as if it was going to be a bright day after all.

EAGLE STRIKE

PROLOGUE

The Amazon jungle. Fifteen years ago.

It had taken them five days to make the journey, cutting their way through the dense, suffocating undergrowth, fighting through the very air, which hung heavy, moist and still. Trees as tall as cathedrals surrounded them, and a strange, green light – almost holy – shimmered through the vast canopy of leaves. The rainforest seemed to have an intelligence of its own. Its voice was the sudden screech of a parrot, the flicker of a monkey swinging through the branches overhead. It knew they were there.

But so far they had been lucky. They had been attacked, of course, by leeches and mosquitoes and stinging ants. But the snakes and scorpions had left them alone. The rivers they had crossed had been free of piranhas. They had been allowed to go on.

They were travelling light. They carried with them only their basic rations: map, compass, water bottles, iodine tablets, mosquito nets and machetes. Their single heaviest item was the 88 Winchester rifle with Sniperscope that they were going to use to kill the man who lived here in this impenetrable place, one hundred miles south of Iquitos in Peru.

The two men knew each other's names but never used them. It was part of their training. The older of the two called himself Hunter. He was English, although he spoke seven languages so fluently that he could pass himself off as a native of many of the countries he found himself in. He was about thirty, handsome, with the close-cut hair and watchful eyes of a trained soldier. The other man was slim, fair-haired and twitching with nervous energy. He had chosen the name of Cossack. He was just nineteen years old. This was his first kill.

Both men were dressed in khaki – standard jungle camouflage. Their faces were also painted green, with dark brown stripes across their cheeks. They had reached their destination just as the sun had begun to rise, and were standing there now, utterly still, ignoring the insects that buzzed around their faces, tasting their sweat.

In front of them was a clearing, man-made, separated from the jungle by a ten metre high fence. An elegant colonial house with wooden verandas and shutters, white curtains and slowly rotating fans stood at the heart of it, with two more low brick buildings about twenty metres behind. Accommodation for the guards. There must have been about a dozen of them patrolling the perimeter and watching from rusting metal towers. Perhaps there were more inside. But they were lazy. They were shuffling around, not concentrating on what they were supposed to be doing. They were in the middle of the jungle. They thought they were safe.

A four-seater helicopter stood waiting on a square of asphalt. It would take the owner of the house just twenty steps to walk from the front door to the helicopter. That was the only time he would be visible. That was when he would have to die.

The two men knew the name of the man they had come to kill, but they didn't use that either. Cossack had spoken it once but Hunter had corrected him.

"Never call a target by his real name. It personalizes him. It opens a door into his life and, when the time comes, it may remind you what you are doing and make you hesitate."

Just one of the many lessons Cossack had learnt from Hunter. They referred to the target only as the Commander. He was a military man – or he had been. He still liked to wear military-style clothes. With so many bodyguards he was in command of a small army. The name suited him.

The Commander was not a good man. He was a drug dealer, exporting cocaine on a massive scale. He also controlled one of the most vicious gangs in Peru, torturing and killing anyone who got in his way. But all this meant nothing to Hunter and Cossack. They were here because they had been paid twenty thousand pounds to take him out – and if the Commander had been a doctor or a priest it would have made no difference to them.

Hunter glanced at his watch. It was two minutes to eight in the morning and he had been told the Commander would be leaving for Lima on the hour. He also knew that the Commander was a punctual man. He loaded a single .308 cartridge into the Winchester and adjusted the Sniperscope. One shot was all he would need.

Meanwhile Cossack had taken out his field glasses and was scanning the compound for any sign of movement. The younger man was not afraid, but he was tense and excited. A trickle of perspiration curved behind his ear and ran down his neck. His mouth was dry. Something tapped gently against his back and he wondered if Hunter had touched him, warning him to stay calm. But Hunter was some distance away, concentrating on the gun.

Something moved.

Cossack only knew for certain it was there when it climbed over his shoulder and onto his neck – and by then it was too late. Very slowly, he turned his head. And there it was, at the very edge of his field of vision. A spider, clinging to the side of his neck, just underneath the line of his chin. He swallowed. From the weight of it he had thought it was a tarantula – but this was worse, much worse. It was very black with a small head and an obscene, swollen body, like a fruit about to burst. He knew that if he could have turned it over, he would have found a red hourglass marking on its abdomen.

It was a black widow. Latrodectus curacaviensis. *One of the deadliest spiders in the world.*

The spider moved, its front legs reaching out so that one was almost touching the corner of Cossack's mouth. The other legs were still attached to his neck, with the main body of the spider now hanging under his jaw. He wanted to swallow again but he didn't dare. Any movement might alarm the creature, which anyway needed no excuse to attack. Cossack guessed that this was the female of the species: a thousand times worse than the male. If it decided to bite him, its hollow fangs would inject him with a neurotoxic venom which would paralyse his entire nervous system. He would feel nothing at first. There would just be two tiny red pricks on his skin. The pain – waves of it – would come in about an hour. His eyelids would swell. He would be unable to breathe. He would go into convulsions. Almost certainly he would die.

Cossack considered raising a hand and trying to flick the hideous thing off. If it had been anywhere else on his body he might have taken the chance. But it had settled on his throat, as if fascinated by the pulse it had found there. He wanted to call to Hunter, but he couldn't risk moving the muscles in his neck. He was barely breathing. Hunter was still making the final adjustments, unaware of what was going on. What could he do?

In the end he whistled. It was the only sound he dared make. He was horribly aware of the creature hanging off him. He felt the prick of another leg, this time touching his lip. Was it about to climb onto his face?

Hunter looked round and saw at once that something was wrong. Cossack was standing unnaturally still, his head contorted, his face, underneath the paint, completely white. Hunter took a step so that Cossack now stood between him and the compound. He had lowered the rifle, the muzzle pointing towards the ground.

Hunter saw the spider.

At the same moment, the door of the house opened and the Commander came out: a short, plump man dressed in a dark tunic hanging open at the collar. Unshaven, he was carrying a briefcase and smoking a cigarette.

Twenty steps to the helicopter – and he was already moving briskly, talking to the two bodyguards who accompanied him. Cossack's eyes flickered over to Hunter. He knew the organization that had employed them would not forgive failure, and this was the only chance they would get. The spider moved again and, looking down, Cossack saw its head: a cluster of tiny, gleaming eyes – half a dozen of them – gazing up at him, uglier than anything in the world. His skin was itching. The whole side of his face wanted to peel itself away. But he knew that there was nothing Hunter could do. He had to fire now. The Commander was only ten steps away from the helicopter. The blades were already turning. Cossack wanted to scream at him. Do it! The sound of the gunshot would frighten the spider and it would bite. But that wasn't important. The mission had to succeed.

It took Hunter less than two seconds to make a decision. He could use the tip of the gun to brush away the black widow. He might succeed in getting rid of it before it bit Cossack. But by then the Commander would be in his helicopter, behind bulletproof glass. Or he could shoot the Commander. But once he had fired the gun, he would have to turn and run immediately, disappear into the jungle. There would be no time to help Cossack; there would be nothing he could do.

He made his decision, swept up the gun, aimed and fired.

The bullet, white-hot, flashed past, cutting a line in Cossack's neck. The black widow disintegrated instantly, blown apart by the force of the shot. The bullet continued across the clearing and through the fence and – still carrying tiny fragments of the black widow with it – buried itself in the Commander's chest. The Commander had been about to climb into the helicopter. He stopped as if surprised, put a hand to his heart, and crumpled. The bodyguards twisted round, shouting, staring into the jungle, trying to see the enemy.

But Hunter and Cossack had already gone. The jungle swallowed them in seconds, although it was more than an hour before they stopped to catch their breath.

Cossack was bleeding. There was a red line that could have been drawn with a ruler across the side of his neck, and the blood had seeped down, soaking into his shirt. But the black widow hadn't bitten him. He held out a hand, accepting a water bottle from Hunter, and drank.

"You saved my life," he said.

Hunter considered. "To take a life and save a life with one bullet ... that's not bad going."

Cossack would have the scar for the rest of his life. But that would not be a very long time. The life of the professional assassin is often short. Hunter would die first, in another country, on another mission. Later it would be his turn.

Right now he said nothing. They had done their job. That was all that mattered. He gave back the water bottle, and as the sun beat down and the jungle watched and reflected upon what had happened, the two men set off together, cutting and hacking their way through the mid-morning heat of another day.

NOT MY BUSINESS

Alex Rider lay on his back, drying out in the midday sun.

He could feel the salt water from his last swim trickling through his hair and evaporating off his chest. His shorts, still wet, clung to him. He was, at that moment, as happy as it is possible to be; one week into a holiday that had been perfect from the moment the plane had touched down in Montpellier and he had stepped out into the brilliance of his first Mediterranean day. He loved the South of France – the intense colours, the smells, the pace of life that hung onto every minute and refused to let go. He hadn't any idea what time it was, except that he was getting hungry and guessed it must soon be lunch. There was a brief burst of music as a girl with a radio walked past, and Alex turned his head to follow her. And that was when the sun went in, the sea froze, and the whole world seemed to catch its breath.

He wasn't looking at the girl with the radio. He was looking past her, down to the sea wall that divided the beach from the jetty, where a yacht was just pulling in. The yacht was enormous, almost the size of one of the passenger boats that carried tourists up and down the coast. But no tourists would ever set foot on this craft. It was completely uninviting, cruising silently through the water, with tinted glass in the windows and a massive bow that rose up like a solid white wall. A man stood at the very front, staring straight ahead, his face blank. It was a face that Alex recognized instantly.

Yassen Gregorovich. It had to be.

Alex sat perfectly still, supporting himself on one arm, his hand half buried in the sand. As he watched, a man in his twenties appeared from the cabin and busied himself mooring the boat. He was short and apelike, wearing a string vest that showed off the tattoos which completely covered his arms and shoulders. A deckhand? Yassen made no offer to help him with his work. A third man hurried along the jetty. He was fat and bald, dressed in a cheap white suit. The top of his head had been burnt by the sun and the skin had turned an ugly, cancerous red.

Yassen saw him and climbed down, moving like spilt oil. He was wearing blue jeans and a white shirt open at the neck. Other men might have had to struggle to keep their balance walking down the swaying gangplank, but he didn't even hesitate. There was something inhuman about him. With his close-cropped hair, his hard blue eyes and pale, expressionless face, he was obviously no holidaymaker. But only Alex knew the truth about him. Yassen Gregorovich was a contract killer, the man who had murdered his uncle and changed his own life. He was wanted all over the world.

So what was he doing here in a little seaside town on the edge of the marshes and lagoons that made up the Camargue? There was nothing in Saint-Pierre apart from beaches, campsites, too many restaurants and an oversized church that looked more like a fortress. It had taken Alex a week to get used to the quiet charm of the place. And now this!

"Alex? What are you looking at?" Sabina murmured, and Alex had to force himself to turn round, to remember that she was there.

"I'm..." The words wouldn't come. He didn't know what to say.

"Do you think you could rub a little more suncream into my back? I'm overheating..."

That was Sabina. Slim, dark-haired, and sometimes much older than her fifteen years. But then she was the sort of girl who had probably swapped toys for boys before she hit eleven. Although she was using factor 25, she seemed to need more suncream rubbed in every fifteen minutes, and somehow it was always Alex who had to do it for her. He glanced quickly at her back, which was in fact perfectly bronzed. She was wearing a bikini made out of so little material that it hadn't bothered with a pattern. Her eyes were covered by a pair of fake Dior sunglasses (which she had bought for a tenth of the price of the real thing) and she had her head buried in *The Lord of the Rings*, at the same time waving the suncream.

Alex looked back at the yacht. Yassen was shaking hands with the bald man. The deckhand was standing near by, waiting. Even at this distance Alex could see that Yassen was very much in charge; that when he spoke, the two men listened. Alex had once seen Yassen shoot a man dead just for dropping a package. There was still an extraordinary coldness about him that seemed to neutralize even the Mediterranean sun. The strange thing was that there were very few people in the world who would have been able to recognize the Russian. Alex was one of them. Could Yassen's being here have something to do with him?

"Alex...?" Sabina said.

The three men moved away from the boat, heading into the town. Suddenly Alex was on his feet.

"I'll be right back," he said.

"Where are you going?"

"I need a drink."

"I've got water."

"No, I want a Coke."

Even as he swept up his T-shirt and pulled it over his head, Alex knew that this was not a good idea. Yassen Gregorovich might have come to the Camargue because he wanted a holiday. He might have come to murder the local mayor. Either way, it had nothing to do with Alex and it would be crazy to get involved with Yassen again. Alex remembered the promise he had made the last time they had met, on a rooftop in central London.

You killed Ian Rider. One day I'll kill you.

At the time he had meant it – but that had been then. Right now he didn't want anything to do with Yassen or the world he represented.

And yet...

Yassen was here. He had to know why.

The three men were walking along the main road, following the line of the sea. Alex doubled back across the sand, passing the white concrete bullring that had struck him as bizarre when he'd first come here – until he had remembered that he was only about a hundred miles from Spain. There was to be a bullfight tonight. People were already queuing at the tiny windows to buy tickets, but he and Sabina had decided they would keep well clear. "I hope the bull wins," had been Sabina's only comment.

Yassen and the two men turned left, disappearing into the town centre. Alex quickened his pace, knowing how easy it would be to lose them in the tangle of lanes and alleyways that surrounded the church. He didn't have to be too careful about being seen. Yassen thought he was safe. It was unlikely that, in a crowded holiday resort, he would notice anyone following him. But with Yassen you never knew. Alex felt his heart thumping with every step he took. His mouth was dry, and for once it wasn't the sun that was to blame.

Yassen had gone. Alex looked left and right. There were people crowding in on him from all sides, pouring out of the shops and into the open-air restaurants that were already serving lunch. The smell of paella filled the air. He cursed himself for hanging back, for not daring to get any closer. The three men could have disappeared inside any of the buildings. Could it be, even, that he had imagined seeing them in the first place? It was a pleasant thought, but it was dashed a moment later when he caught sight of them sitting on a terrace in front of one of the smarter restaurants in the square, the bald man already calling for menus.

Alex walked in front of a shop selling postcards, using the racks as a screen between himself and the restaurant. Next came a café serving snacks and drinks beneath wide, multicoloured umbrellas. He edged into it. Yassen and the other two men were now less than ten metres away and Alex could make out more details. The deckhand was pushing bread into his mouth as if he hadn't eaten for a week. The bald man was talking quietly, urgently, waving his fist in the air to emphasize a point. Yassen was listening patiently. With the noise of the crowd all around, Alex couldn't make out a word any of them were saying. He peered round one of the umbrellas and a waiter almost collided with him, letting loose a torrent of angry French. Yassen glanced in his direction and Alex ducked away, afraid that he had drawn attention to himself.

A line of plants in wooden tubs divided the café from the restaurant terrace where the men were eating. Alex slipped between two of the tubs and moved quickly into the shadows of the restaurant interior. He felt safer here, less exposed. The kitchens were right behind him. To one side was a bar and in front of it about a dozen tables, all of them empty. Waiters were coming in and out with plates of food, but all the customers had chosen to eat outside.

Alex looked out through the door. And caught his breath. Yassen had got up and was walking purposefully towards him. Had he been spotted? But then he saw that Yassen was holding something: a mobile phone. He must have received a call and was coming into the restaurant to take it privately. Another few steps and he would reach the door. Alex looked around him and saw an alcove screened by a bead curtain. He pushed through it and found himself in a storage area just big enough to conceal him. Mops, buckets, cardboard boxes and empty wine bottles crowded around him. The beads shivered and became still.

Yassen was suddenly there.

"I arrived twenty minutes ago," he was saying. He was speaking English with only a very slight trace of a Russian accent. "Franco was waiting for me. The address is confirmed and everything has been arranged."

There was a pause. Alex tried not to breathe. He was centimetres away from Yassen, separated only by the fragile barrier of brightly coloured beads. But for the fact that it was so dark inside after the glare of the sun, Yassen would surely have seen him.

"We'll do it this afternoon. You have nothing to worry about. It is better for us not to communicate. I will report to you on my return to England."

Yassen Gregorovich clicked off the phone and suddenly became quite still. Alex actually saw the moment, the sudden alertness as some animal instinct told Yassen that he had been overheard. The phone was still cradled inside the man's hand, but it could have been a knife that he was about to throw. His head was still but his eyes glanced from side to side, searching for the enemy. Alex stayed where he was behind the beads, not daring to move. What should he do? He was tempted to make a break for it, to run out into the open air. No. He would be dead before he had taken two steps. Yassen would kill him before he even knew who he was or why he had been there. Very slowly, Alex looked around for a weapon, for anything to defend himself with.

And then the kitchen door swung open and a waiter came out, swerving round Yassen and calling to someone at the same time. The stillness of the moment was shattered. Yassen slipped the phone into his trouser pocket and went out to rejoin the other men.

Alex let out a huge sigh of relief.

What had he learnt?

Yassen Gregorovich had come here to kill someone. He was sure of that much. *The address is confirmed and everything has been arranged.* But at least Alex hadn't heard his own name mentioned. So he was right. The target was probably some Frenchman, living here in Saint-Pierre. It would happen sometime this afternoon. A gunshot or perhaps a knife flashing in the sun. A fleeting moment of violence and someone somewhere would sit back, knowing they had one enemy less.

What could he do?

Alex pushed through the bead curtain and made his way out of the back of the restaurant. He was relieved to find himself in the street, away from the square. Only now did he try to collect his thoughts. He could go to the police, of course. He could tell them that he was a spy who had worked, three times now, for MI6 – British military intelligence. He could say that he had recognized Yassen, knew him for what he was, and that a killing would almost certainly take place that afternoon unless he was stopped.

But what good would it do? The French police might understand him, but they would never believe him. He was a fourteen-year-old English schoolboy with sand in his hair and a suntan. They would take one look at him and laugh.

He could go to Sabina and her parents. But Alex didn't want to do that either. He was only here because they had invited him, and why should he bring murder into their holiday? Not that they would believe him any more than the police. Once, when he had been staying with her in Cornwall, Alex had tried to tell Sabina the truth. She had thought he was joking.

Alex looked around at the tourist shops, the ice-cream parlours, the crowds strolling happily along the street. It was a typical picture-postcard view. The real world. So what the hell was he doing getting mixed up again with spies and assassins? He was on holiday. This was none of his business. Let Yassen do whatever he wanted. Alex wouldn't be able to stop him even if he tried. Better to forget that he had ever seen him.

Alex took a deep breath and walked back down the road towards the beach to find Sabina and her parents. As he went he tried to work out what he would tell them: why he had left so suddenly and why he was no longer smiling now that he was back.

That afternoon, Alex and Sabina hitched a lift with a local farmer to Aigues-Mortes, a fortified town on the edge of the salt marshes. Sabina wanted to escape from her parents and hang out in a French café, where they could watch the locals and tourists rub shoulders in the street. She had devised a system for marking French teenagers for good looks – with points lost for weedy legs, crooked teeth or bad dress sense. Nobody had yet scored more than seven out of twenty and Alex would normally have been happy sitting with her, listening to her as she laughed out loud.

But not this afternoon.

Everything was out of focus. The great walls and towers that surrounded him were miles away, and the sightseers seemed to be moving too slowly, like a film that had run down. Alex wanted to enjoy being here. He wanted to feel part of the holiday again. But seeing Yassen had spoilt it all.

Alex had met Sabina only a month before, when the two of them had been helping at the Wimbledon tennis tournament, but they had struck up an immediate friendship. Sabina was an only child. Her mother, Liz, worked as a fashion designer; her father, Edward, was a journalist. Alex hadn't seen very much of him. He had started the holiday late, coming down on the train from Paris, and had been working on some story ever since.

The family had rented a house just outside Saint-Pierre, right on the edge of a river, the Petit Rhône. It was a simple place, typical of the area: bright white with blue shutters and a roof of sun-baked terracotta tiles. There were three bedrooms and, on the ground floor, an airy, old-fashioned kitchen that opened onto an overgrown garden with a swimming pool and a tennis court with weeds pushing through the asphalt. Alex had loved it from the start. His bedroom overlooked the river, and every evening he and Sabina had spent hours sprawled over an old wicker sofa, talking quietly and watching the water ripple past.

The first week of the holiday had disappeared in a flash. They had swum in the pool and in the sea, which was less than a mile away. They had gone walking, climbing, canoeing and, once (it wasn't Alex's favourite sport), horse-riding. Alex really liked Sabina's parents. They were the sort of adults who hadn't forgotten that they had once been teenagers themselves, and more or less left him and Sabina to do whatever they wanted on their own. And for the last seven days everything had been fine.

Until Yassen.

The address is confirmed and everything has been arranged. We'll do it this afternoon...

What was the Russian planning to do in Saint-Pierre? What bad luck was it that had brought him here, casting his shadow once again over Alex's life? Despite the heat of the afternoon sun, Alex shivered.

"Alex?"

He realized that Sabina had been talking to him, and looked round. She was gazing across the table with a look of concern. "What are you thinking about?" she asked. "You were miles away."

"Nothing."

"You haven't been yourself all afternoon. Did something happen this morning? Where did you disappear to on the beach?"

"I told you. I just needed a drink." He hated having to lie to her but he couldn't tell her the truth.

"I was just saying we ought to get going. I promised we'd be home by five. Oh my God! Look at that one!" She pointed at another teenager walking past. "Four out of twenty. Aren't there *any* good-looking boys in France?" She glanced at Alex. "Apart from you, I mean."

"So how many do I get out of twenty?" Alex asked.

Sabina considered. "Twelve and a half," she said at last. "But don't worry, Alex. Another ten years and you'll be perfect."

Sometimes horror announces itself in the smallest of ways.

On this day it was a single police car, racing along the wide, empty road that twisted down to Saint-Pierre. Alex and Sabina were sitting in the back of the same truck that had brought them. They were looking at a herd of cows grazing in one of the fields when the police car – blue and white with a light flashing on the roof – overtook them and tore off into the distance. Alex still had Yassen on his mind and the sight of it tightened the knot in the pit of his stomach. But it was only a police car. It didn't have to mean anything.

But then there was a helicopter, taking off from somewhere not so far away and arcing into the brilliant sky. Sabina saw it and pointed at it.

"Something's happened," she said. "That's just come from the town."

Had the helicopter come from the town? Alex wasn't so sure. He watched it sweep over them and disappear in the direction of Aigues-Mortes, and all the time his breaths were getting shorter and he felt the heavy weight of some nameless dread.

And then they turned a corner and Alex knew that his worst fears had come true – but in a way that he could never have foreseen.

Rubble, jagged brickwork and twisted steel. Thick black smoke curling into the sky. Their house had been blown apart. Just one wall remained intact, giving the cruel illusion that not too much damage had been done. But the rest of it was gone. Alex saw a brass bed hanging at a crazy angle, somehow suspended in mid-air. A pair of blue shutters lay in the grass about fifty metres away. The water in the swimming pool was brown and scummy. The blast must have been immense.

A fleet of cars and vans was parked around the building. They belonged to the police, the hospital, the fire department and the anti-terrorist squad. To Alex they didn't look real: more like brightly coloured toys. In a foreign country, nothing looks more foreign than its emergency services.

"Mum! Dad!"

Alex heard Sabina shout the words and saw her leap out of the truck before they had stopped moving. Then she was running across the gravel drive, forcing her way between the officials in their different uniforms. The truck stopped and Alex climbed down, unsure whether his feet would come into contact with the ground or if he would simply go on, right through it. His head was spinning; he thought he was going to faint.

Nobody spoke to him as he continued forward. It was as if he wasn't there at all. Ahead of him he saw Sabina's mother appear from nowhere, her face streaked with ashes and tears, and he thought to himself that if she was all right, if she had been out of the house when the explosion happened, then maybe Edward Pleasure had escaped too. But then he saw Sabina begin to shake and fall into her mother's arms, and he knew the worst.

He drew nearer, in time to hear Liz's words as she clutched hold of her daughter.

"We still don't know what happened. Dad's been taken by helicopter to Montpellier. He's alive, Sabina, but he's badly injured. We're going to him now. You know your dad's a fighter. But the doctors aren't sure if he's going to make it or not. We just don't know..."

The smell of burning reached out to Alex and engulfed him. The smoke had blotted out the sun. His eyes began to water and he fought for breath.

This was his fault.

He didn't know why it had happened but he was utterly certain who was responsible.

Yassen Gregorovich.

None of my business. That was what Alex had thought. This was the result.

THE FINGER ON THE TRIGGER

The policeman facing Alex was young, inexperienced, and struggling to find the right words. It wasn't just that he was having difficulty with the English language, Alex realized. Down here in this odd, quiet corner of France, the worst he would usually have to deal with would be the occasional drunk driver or maybe a tourist losing his wallet on the beach. This was a new situation and he was completely out of his depth.

"It is the most terrible affair," he was saying. "You have known Monsieur Pleasure very long time?"

"No. Not very long time," Alex said.

"He will receive the best treatment." The policeman smiled encouragingly. "Madame Pleasure and her daughter are going now to hospital but they have requested us to occupy us with you."

Alex was sitting on a folding chair in the shadow of a tree. It was just after five o'clock but the sun was still hot. The river flowed past a few metres away and he would have given anything to dive into the water and swim, and keep swimming, until he had put this whole business behind him.

Sabina and her mother had left about ten minutes ago and now he was on his own with this young policeman. He had been given a chair in the shade and a bottle of water, but it was obvious that nobody knew what to do with him. This wasn't his family. He had no right to be here. More officials had turned up: senior policemen, senior firemen. They were moving slowly through the wreckage, occasionally turning over a plank of wood or moving a piece of broken furniture as if they might uncover the one simple clue that would tell them why this had taken place.

"We have telephoned to your consul," the policeman was saying. "They will come to take you home. But they must send a representative from Lyon. It is a long way. So tonight you must wait here in Saint-Pierre."

"I know who did this," Alex said.

"Comment?"

"I know who was responsible." Alex glanced in the direction of the house. "You have to go into the town. There is a yacht tied to the jetty. I didn't see the name but you can't miss it. It's huge ... white. There's a man on the yacht; his name is Yassen Gregorovich. You have to arrest him before he can get away."

The policeman stared at Alex, astonished. Alex wondered how much he had understood.

"I am sorry? What is it that you say? This man, Yassen..."

"Yassen Gregorovich."

"You know him?"

"Yes."

"Who is he?"

"He's a killer. He is paid to kill people. I saw him this morning."

"Please!" The policeman held up a hand. He didn't want to listen to any more. "Wait here."

Alex watched him walk away towards the parked cars, presumably to find a senior officer. He took a sip of water, then stood up himself. He didn't want to sit here watching the events from a folding chair like a picnicker. He walked towards the house. There was an evening breeze but the smell of burnt wood still hung heavily all around. A scrap of paper, scorched and blackened, blew across the gravel. On an impulse, Alex reached down and picked it up.

He read:

caviar for breakfast, and the swimming pool at his Wiltshire mansion is rumoured to have been built in the shape of Elvis Presley. But Damian Cray is more than the world's richest and most successful pop star. His business ventures – including hotels, TV stations and computer games – have added millions more to his personal fortune.

The questions remain. Why was Cray in Paris earlier this week and why did he arrange a secret meeting with

That was all there was. The paper turned black and the words disappeared.

Alex realized what he was looking at. It must be a page from the article that Edward Pleasure had been working on ever since he had arrived at the house. Something to do with the mega-celebrity Damian Cray...

"Excusez-moi, jeune homme..."

He looked up and saw that the policeman had returned with a second man, this one a few years older, with a downturned mouth and a small moustache. Alex's heart sank. He recognized the type before the man had even spoken. Oily and self-important, and wearing a uniform that was too neat, there was disbelief etched all over his face.

"You have something to tell us?" he asked. He spoke better English than his colleague.

Alex repeated what he had said.

"How do you know about this man? The man on the boat."

"He killed my uncle."

"Who was your uncle?"

"He was a spy. He worked for MI6." Alex took a deep breath. "I think *I* may have been the target of the bomb. I think he was trying to kill *me*..."

The two policemen spoke briefly together, then turned back to Alex. Alex knew what was coming. The senior policeman had rearranged his features so that he now looked down at Alex with a mixture of kindness and concern. But there was arrogance there too: *I am right. You are wrong. And nothing will persuade me otherwise.* He was like a bad teacher in a bad school, putting a cross beside a right answer.

"You have had a terrible shock," the policeman said. "The explosion ... we already know that it was caused by a leak in the gas pipe."

"No..." Alex shook his head.

The policeman held up a hand. "There is no reason why an assassin would wish to harm a family on holiday. But I understand. You are upset; it is quite possible that you are in shock. You do not know what it is you are saying."

"Please—"

"We have sent for someone from your consulate and he will arrive soon. Until then it would be better if you did not interfere."

Alex hung his head. "Do you mind if I go for a walk?" he said. The words came out low and muffled.

"A walk?"

"Just five minutes. I want to be on my own."

"Of course. Do not go too far. Would you like someone to accompany you?"

"No. I'll be all right."

He turned and walked away. He had avoided meeting the policemen's eyes and they doubtless thought he was ashamed of himself. That was all right. Alex didn't want them to see his fury, the black anger that coursed through him like an arctic river. They hadn't believed him! They had treated him like a stupid child!

With every step he took, images stamped themselves on his mind. Sabina's eyes widening as she took in the wreck of the house. Edward Pleasure being flown to some city hospital. Yassen Gregorovich on the deck of his yacht, gliding off into the sunset, another job done. And it was Alex's fault! That was the worst of it. That was the unforgivable part. Well, he wasn't going to sit there and take it. Alex allowed his rage to carry him forward. It was time to take control.

When he reached the main road, he glanced back. The policemen had forgotten him. He took one last look at the burnt-out shell that had been his holiday home, and the darkness rose up in him again. He turned away and began to run.

Saint-Pierre was just under a mile away. It was early evening by the time he arrived there and the streets were packed with people in a festive mood. In fact, the town seemed busier than ever. Then he remembered. There was a bullfight tonight and people had driven in from all around to watch it.

The sun was already dipping behind the horizon but daylight still lingered in the air as if accidentally left behind. The street lamps were lit, throwing garish pools of orange onto the sandy pavements. An old carousel turned round and round, a spinning blur of electric bulbs and jangling music. Alex made his way through it all without stopping. Suddenly he was on the other side of the town and the streets were quiet again. The night had advanced and everything was a little more grey.

He hadn't expected to see the yacht. At the back of his mind he had thought that Yassen would have left long ago. But there it still was, moored where he had seen it earlier that day, a lifetime ago. There was nobody in sight. It seemed that the whole town had gone to the bullfight. Then a figure stepped out of the darkness and Alex saw the bald man with the sunburn. He was still dressed in the white suit. He was smoking a cigar, the smouldering tip casting a red glow across his face.

There were lights glinting behind the portholes of the boat. Would he find Yassen behind one of them? Alex had no real idea what he was doing. Anger was still driving him blindly on. All he knew was that he had to get onto the yacht and that nothing was going to stop him.

The man's name was Franco. He had stepped down onto the jetty because Yassen hated the smell of cigar smoke. He didn't like Yassen. More than that; he was afraid of him. When the Russian had heard that Edward Pleasure had been injured, not killed, he had said nothing, but there had been something intense and ugly in his eyes. For a moment he had looked at Raoul, the deckhand. It had been Raoul who had actually placed the bomb ... too far from the journalist's room, as it turned out. The mistake was his. And Franco knew that Yassen had very nearly killed him there and then. Perhaps he still would. God – what a mess!

Franco heard a shoe scraping against loose rubble and saw a boy walking towards him. He was slim and suntanned, wearing shorts and a faded Stone Age T-shirt, with a string of wooden beads around his neck. He had fair hair which hung in strands over his forehead. He must be a tourist – he looked English. But what was he doing here?

Alex had wondered how close he could get to the man before his suspicions were aroused. If it had been an adult approaching the boat, it would have been a different matter; the fact that he was only fourteen was the main reason he had been so useful to MI6. People didn't notice him until it was too late.

That was what happened now. As the boy came closer, Franco was struck by the dark brown eyes set in a face that was somehow too serious for a boy of that age. They were eyes that had seen too much.

Alex drew level with Franco. At that moment, he lashed out, spinning round on the ball of his left foot, kicking with the right. Franco was taken completely by surprise. Alex's heel struck him hard in the stomach – but straight away Alex knew that he had underestimated his opponent. He had expected to feel soft fat beneath the flapping suit. But his foot had slammed into a ring of muscle, and although Franco was hurt and winded, he hadn't been brought down.

Franco dropped the cigar and lunged, his hand already scrabbling in his jacket pocket. It came out holding something. There was a soft click and seven inches of glinting silver leapt out of nowhere. He had a flick knife. Moving much faster than Alex would have thought possible, he launched himself across the jetty. His hand swung in an arc. Alex heard the blade slicing the air. He swung again, and the knife flashed past Alex's face, missing him by a centimetre.

Alex was unarmed. Franco had obviously used the knife many

times before, and if he hadn't been weakened by the first kick, this fight would already have been over. Alex looked around, searching for anything he could defend himself with. There was almost nothing on the jetty – just a few old boxes, a bucket, a fisherman's net. Franco was moving more slowly now. He was fighting a kid – nothing more. The little brat might have surprised him with that first attack, but it would be easy enough to bring this to an end.

He muttered a few words in French: something low and ugly. Then, a second later, his fist swung through the air, this time carrying the knife in an upward arc that would have cut Alex's throat if he hadn't thrown himself backwards.

Alex cried out.

He had lost his footing, falling heavily onto his back, one arm outstretched. Franco grinned, showing two gold teeth, and stepped towards him, anxious to finish this off. Too late he saw that he had been tricked. Alex's hand had caught hold of the net. As Franco loomed over him, he sprang up, swinging his arm forward with all his strength. The net spread out, falling over Franco's head, shoulder and knife hand. He swore and twisted round, trying to free himself, but the movement only entangled him all the more.

Alex knew he had to finish this quickly. Franco was still struggling with the net but Alex saw him open his mouth to call for help. They were right next to the yacht. If Yassen heard anything, there would be nothing more Alex could do. He took aim and kicked a second time, his foot driving into the man's stomach. The breath was knocked out of him; Alex saw his face turn red. He was half out of the net, performing a bizarre dance on the edge of the jetty, when he lost his balance and fell. With his hands trapped he couldn't protect himself. His head hit the concrete with a loud crack and he lay still.

Alex stood, breathing heavily. In the distance he heard a trumpet blare and there was a scattered round of applause. The bullfight was due to begin in ten minutes. A small band had arrived and was about to play. Alex looked at the unconscious man, knowing he had had a close escape. There was no sign of the knife; maybe it had fallen into the water. Briefly he wondered if he should go on. Then he thought of Sabina and her father, and the next thing he knew he had climbed the gangplank and was standing on the deck.

The boat was called *Fer de Lance*. Alex noticed the name as he climbed up, and remembered seeing it somewhere else. That was it! It was on a school trip to London Zoo. It was some sort of snake. Poisonous, of course.

He was standing in a wide area with a steering wheel and controls next to a door on one side and leather sofas across the back. There was a low table. The bald man must have been sitting here before he went down for his smoke. Alex saw a crumpled magazine, a bottle of beer, a mobile phone and a gun.

He recognized the telephone. It was Yassen's. He had seen it in the Russian's hand back at the restaurant earlier that day. The phone was an odd colour – a shade of brown – otherwise Alex might have ignored it. But now he noticed that it was still turned on. He picked it up.

Alex quickly scrolled to the main menu and then to Call Register. He found what he was looking for: a record of all the calls Yassen had received that day. At 12.53 he had been talking to a number that began 44207. The 44 was England; the 207 meant it was somewhere in London. That was the call Alex had overheard in the restaurant. Quickly he memorized the number. It was the number of the person who had given Yassen his orders. It would tell him all he needed to know.

He picked up the gun.

He finally had it. Each time he had worked for MI6 he had asked them to give him a gun, and each time they had refused. They had supplied him with gadgets – but only tranquillizer darts, stun grenades, smoke bombs. Nothing that would kill. Alex felt the power of the weapon he was holding. He weighed it in his hand. The gun was a Grach MP-443, black, with a short muzzle and a ribbed stock. It was Russian, of course, new army issue. He allowed his finger to curl around the trigger and smiled grimly. Now he and Yassen were equals.

He padded forward, went through the door and climbed down a short flight of stairs that went below deck and into a corridor that seemed to run the length of the boat, with cabins on either side. He had seen a lounge above but he knew that it was empty. There had been no lights behind those windows. If Yassen was anywhere, he would be down here. Clutching the Grach more tightly, he crept along, his feet making no sound on the thickly carpeted floor.

He came to a door and saw a yellow strip of light seeping out of the crack below. Gritting his teeth, he reached for the handle, half hoping it would be locked. The handle turned and the door opened. Alex went in.

The cabin was surprisingly large, a long rectangle with a white carpet and modern wooden fittings along two of the walls. The third wall was taken up by a low double bed with a table and a lamp on each side. There was a man stretched out on the white cover, his eyes closed, as still as a corpse. Alex stepped forward. There was no sound in the room, but in the distance he could hear the band playing at the bullring: two or three trumpets, a tuba and a drum.

Yassen Gregorovich made no movement as Alex approached, the gun held out in front of him. Alex reached the side of the bed. This was the closest he had ever been to the Russian, the man who had killed his uncle. He could see every detail of his face: the chiselled lips, the almost feminine eyelashes. The gun was only a centimetre from Yassen's forehead. This was where it ended. All he had to do was pull the trigger and it would be over.

"Good evening, Alex."

It wasn't that Yassen had woken up. His eyes had been closed and now they weren't. It was as simple as that. His face hadn't changed. He knew who Alex was immediately, at the same time taking in the gun that was pointing at him. Taking it in and accepting it.

Alex said nothing. There was a slight tremble in the hand holding the gun and he brought his other hand up to steady it.

"You have my gun," Yassen said.

Alex took a breath.

"Do you intend to use it?"

Nothing.

Yassen continued calmly. "I think you should consider very carefully. Killing a man is not like you see on the television. If you pull that trigger, you will fire a real bullet into real flesh and blood. I will feel nothing; I will be dead instantly. But you will live with what you have done for the rest of your life. You will never forget it."

He paused, letting his words hang in the air.

"Do you really have it in you, Alex? Can you make your finger obey you? Can you kill me?"

Alex was rigid, a statue. All his concentration was focused on the finger curled around the trigger. It was simple. There was a spring mechanism. The trigger would pull back the hammer and release it. The hammer would strike the bullet, a piece of death just nineteen millimetres long, sending it on its short, fast journey into this man's head. He could do it.

"Maybe you have forgotten what I once told you. This isn't your life. This has nothing to do with you."

Yassen was totally relaxed. There was no emotion in his voice. He seemed to know Alex better than Alex knew himself. Alex tried to look away, to avoid the calm blue eyes that were watching him with something like pity.

"Why did you do it?" Alex demanded. "You blew up the house. Why?"

The eyes flickered briefly. "Because I was paid."

"Paid to kill me?"

"No, Alex." For a moment Yassen sounded almost amused. "It had nothing to do with you."

"Then who—"

But it was too late.

He saw it in Yassen's eyes first, knew that the Russian had been keeping him distracted as the cabin door opened quietly behind him. A pair of hands seized him and he was swung violently away from the bed. He saw Yassen whip aside as fast as a snake – as fast as a fer de lance. The gun went off, but Alex hadn't fired it intentionally and the bullet smashed into the floor. He hit a wall and felt the gun drop out of his hand. He could taste blood in his mouth. The yacht seemed to be swaying.

In the far distance a fanfare sounded, followed by an echoing roar from the crowd. The bullfight had begun.

MATADOR

Alex sat listening to the three men who would decide his fate, trying to understand what they were saying. They were speaking French, but with an almost impenetrable Marseilles accent – and they were using gutter language, not the sort he had learnt.

He had been dragged up to the main saloon and was slumped in a wide leather armchair. By now Alex had managed to work out what had happened. The deckhand, Raoul, had come back from the town with supplies and found Franco lying unconscious on the jetty. He had hurried on board to alert Yassen and had overheard him talking to Alex. It had been Raoul, of course, who had crept into the cabin and grabbed Alex from behind.

Franco was sitting in a corner, his face distorted with anger and hatred. There was a dark mauve bruise on his forehead where he had hit the ground. When he spoke, his words dripped poison.

"Give me the little brat. I will kill him personally and then drop him over the side for the fish."

"How did he find us, Yassen?" This was Raoul speaking. "How did he know who we are?"

"Why are we wasting our time with him? Let me finish him now."

Alex glanced at Yassen. So far the Russian had said nothing, although it was clear he was still in charge. There was something curious about the way he was looking at Alex. The empty blue eyes gave nothing away and yet Alex felt he was being appraised. It was as if Yassen had known him a long time and had expected to meet him again.

Yassen lifted a hand for silence, then went over to Alex. "How did you know you would find us here?" he asked.

Alex said nothing. A flicker of annoyance passed across the Russian's face. "You are only alive because I permit it. Please don't make me ask you a second time."

Alex shrugged. He had nothing to lose. They were probably going to kill him anyway. "I was on holiday," he said. "I was on the beach. I saw you on the yacht when it came in."

"You are not with MI6?"

"No."

"But you followed me to the restaurant."

"That's right." Alex nodded.

Yassen half smiled to himself. "I thought there was someone." Then he was serious again. "You were staying in the house."

"I was invited by a friend," Alex said. A thought suddenly occurred to him. "Her dad's a journalist. Was he the one you wanted to kill?"

"That is none of your business."

"It is now."

"It was bad luck you were staying with him, Alex. I've already told you. It was nothing personal."

"Sure." Alex looked Yassen straight in the eye. "With you it never is."

Yassen went back over to the two men and at once Franco began to jabber again, spitting out his words. He had poured himself a whisky which he downed in a single swallow, his eyes never leaving Alex.

"The boy knows nothing and he can't hurt us," Yassen said. He was speaking in English – for his benefit, Alex guessed.

"What you do with him?" Raoul asked, following in clumsy English too.

"Kill him!" This was Franco.

"I do not kill children," Yassen replied, and Alex knew that he was telling only half the truth. The bomb in the house could have killed anyone who happened to be there and Yassen wouldn't have cared.

"Have you gone mad?" Franco had slipped back into French. "You can't just let him walk away from here. He came to kill you. If it hadn't been for Raoul, he might have succeeded."

"Maybe." Yassen studied Alex one last time. Finally he came to a decision. "You were unwise to come here, little Alex," he said. "These people think I should silence you and they are right. If I thought it was anything but chance that brought you to me, if there was anything that you knew, you would already be dead. But I am a reasonable man. You did not kill me when you had the chance, so now I will give you a chance too."

He spoke rapidly to Franco in French. At first Franco seemed sullen, argumentative. But as Yassen continued, Alex saw a smile spread slowly across his face.

"How will we arrange this?" Franco asked.

"You know people. You have influence. You just have to pay the right people."

"The boy will be killed."

"Then you will have your wish."

"Good!" Franco spat. "I'll enjoy watching!"

Yassen came over to Alex and stopped just a short distance away. "You have courage, Alex," he said. "I admire that in you. Now I am going to give you the opportunity to display it." He nodded at Franco. "Take him!"

It was nine o'clock. The night had rolled in over Saint-Pierre, bringing with it the threat of a summer storm. The air was still and heavy and thick cloud had blotted out the stars.

Alex stood on sandy ground in the shadows of a concrete archway, unable to take in what was happening to him. He had been forced, at gunpoint, to change his holiday clothes for a uniform so bizarre that, but for his knowledge of the danger he was about to face, he would have felt simply ridiculous.

First there had been a white shirt and a black tie. Then came a jacket with shoulder pads hanging over his arms and a pair of trousers that fitted tight around his thighs and waist but stopped well short of his ankles. Both of these were covered in gold sequins and thousands of tiny pearls, so that as Alex moved in and out of the light he became a miniature fireworks display. Finally he had been given black shoes, an odd, curving black hat, and a bright red cape which was folded over his arm.

The uniform had a name. *Traje de luces*. The suit of lights worn by matadors in the bullring. This was the test of courage that Yassen had somehow arranged. He wanted Alex to fight a bull.

Now he stood next to Alex, listening to the noise of the crowd inside the arena. At a typical bullfight, he had explained, six bulls are killed. The third of these is sometimes taken by the least experienced matador, a *novillero*, a young man who might be in the ring for the first time. There had been no *novillero* on the programme tonight ... not until the Russian had suggested otherwise. Money had changed hands. And Alex had been prepared. It was insane – but the crowd would love him. Once he was inside the arena, nobody would know that he had never been trained. He would be a tiny figure in the middle of the floodlit ring. His clothes would disguise the truth. Nobody would see that he was only fourteen.

There was an eruption of shouting and cheering inside the arena. Alex guessed that the matador had just killed the second bull.

"Why are you doing this?" Alex asked.

Yassen shrugged. "I'm doing you a favour, Alex."

"I don't see it that way."

"Franco wanted to put a knife in you. It was hard to dissuade him. In the end I offered him a little entertainment. As it happens, he greatly admires this sport. This way he gets amused and you get a choice."

"A choice?"

"You might say it is a choice between the bull and the bullet."

"Either way I get killed."

"Yes. That is the most likely outcome, I'm afraid. But at least you will have a heroic death. A thousand people will be watching you. Their voices will be the last thing you hear."

"Better than hearing yours," Alex growled.

And suddenly it was time.

Two men in jeans and black shirts ran forward and opened a gate. It was like a wooden curtain being drawn across a stage and it revealed a fantastic scene behind. First there was the arena itself, an elongated circle of bright yellow sand. As Yassen had promised, it was surrounded by a thousand people, tightly packed in tiers. They were eating and drinking, many of them waving programmes in front of their faces, trying to shift the sluggish air, jostling and talking. Although all of them were seated, none of them were still. In the far corner a band played, five men in military uniforms, looking like antique toys. The glare from the spotlights was dazzling.

Empty, the arena was modern, ugly and dead. But filled to the brim on this hot Mediterranean night, Alex could feel the energy buzzing through it, and he realized that all the cruelty of the Romans with their gladiators and wild animals had survived the centuries and was fully alive here.

A tractor drove towards the gate where Alex was standing, dragging behind it a misshapen black lump that had until seconds ago been a proud and living thing. About a dozen brightly coloured spears dangled out of the creature's back. As it drew nearer, Alex saw that it was leaving a comma of glistening red in the sand. He felt sick, and wondered if it was fear of what was to come or disgust and hatred of what had been. He and Sabina had agreed that they would never in a million years go to a bullfight. He certainly hadn't expected to break that promise so soon.

Yassen nodded at him. "Remember," he said, "Raoul, Franco and I will be beside the *barrera* – that's right at the side of the ring. If you fail to perform, if you try to run, we will gun you down and disappear into the night." He raised his shirt to show Alex the Grach, tucked into his waistband. "But if you agree to fight, after ten minutes we will leave. If by some miracle you are still standing, you can do as you please. You see? I am giving you a chance."

The trumpets sounded again, announcing the next fight. Alex felt a hand press into the small of his back and he walked forward, giddy with disbelief. How had this been allowed to happen? Surely someone would see that underneath the fancy dress he was just an English schoolboy, not a matador or a *novillero* or whatever it was called. Someone would have to stop the fight.

But the spectators were already shouting their approval. A few flowers rained down in his direction. Nobody could see the truth and Franco had paid enough money to make sure they didn't find out until it was too late. He had to go through with this. His heart was thumping. The smell of blood and animal sweat rose in his nostrils. He was more afraid than he had ever been.

A man in an elaborate black silk suit with mother-of-pearl buttons and sweeping shoulders stood up in the crowd and raised a white handkerchief. This was the president of the bullring, giving the signal for the next fight. The trumpets sounded. Another gate opened and the bull that Alex was to fight thundered into the ring like a bullet fired from a gun. Alex stared. The creature was huge – a mass of black, shimmering muscle. It must have weighed seven or eight hundred kilograms. If it ran into him, it would be like being run over by a bus – except that he would be impaled first on the horns that corkscrewed out of its head, tapering to two lethal points. Right now it was ignoring Alex, running madly in a jagged circle, kicking out with its back legs, enraged by the lights and the shouting crowd.

Alex wondered why he hadn't been given a sword. Didn't matadors have anything to defend themselves with? There was a spear lying on the sand, left over from the last fight. This was a *banderilla*. It was about a metre long with a decorated, multi-coloured handle and a short, barbed hook. Dozens of these would be plunged into the bull's neck, destroying its muscles and weakening it before the final kill. Alex himself would be given a spear as the fight continued, but he had already made a decision. Whatever happened, he would try not to hurt the bull.

After all, it hadn't chosen to be here either.

He had to escape. The gates had been closed but the wooden wall enclosing the arena – the *barrera*, as Yassen had called it – was no taller than he was. He could run and jump over it. He glanced at the wall where he had just come in. Franco had taken his place in the front row. His hand was underneath his jacket and Alex had no doubt what it was holding. He could make out Yassen at the far end. Raoul was over to his right. Between them the three men had the whole ring covered.

He had to fight. Somehow he had to survive ten minutes. Maybe there were only nine minutes now. It felt as if an eternity had passed since he had entered the ring.

The crowd fell silent. A thousand faces waited for him to make his move.

Then the bull noticed him.

Suddenly it stopped its circling and lumbered towards him, coming to a halt about twenty metres away, its head low and its horns pointing at him. Alex knew with a sick certainty that it was about to charge. Reluctantly he allowed the red cape to drop so that it hung down to the sand. God – he must look an idiot in this costume, with no idea what he was meant to be doing. He was surprised the fight hadn't been stopped already. But Yassen and the two men would be watching his every move. Franco would need only the smallest excuse to draw his gun. Alex had to play his part.

Silence. The heat of the coming storm pressed down on him. Nothing moved.

The bull charged. Alex was shocked by the sudden transformation. The bull had been static and distant. Now it was bearing down on him as if a switch had been thrown, its massive shoulders heaving, its every muscle concentrated on the target that stood waiting, unarmed, alone. The animal was near enough now for Alex to be able to see its eyes: black, white and red, bloodshot and furious.

Everything happened very quickly. The bull was almost on top of him. The vicious horns were plunging towards his stomach. The stench of the animal smothered him. Alex leapt aside, at the same time lifting the cape, imitating moves he had seen ... perhaps on television or in the cinema. He actually felt the bull brush past, and in that tiny contact sensed its huge power and strength. There was a flash of red as the cape flew up. The whole arena seemed to spin, the crowd rising up and yelling. The bull had gone past. Alex was unhurt.

Although he didn't know it, Alex had executed a reasonable imitation of the *verónica*. This is the first and most simple movement in a bullfight, but it gives the matador vital information about his opponent: its speed, its strength, which horn it favours. But Alex had learnt only two things. Matadors were braver than he thought – insanely brave to do this out of choice! And he also knew he was going to be very lucky to survive a second attack.

The bull had stopped at the far end of the ring. It shook its head, and grey strings of saliva whipped from either side of its mouth. All around, the spectators were still clapping. Alex saw Yassen Gregorovich sitting among them. He alone was still, not joining in the applause. Grimly, Alex let the cape hang down a second time, wondering how many minutes had passed. He no longer had any sense of time.

He actually felt the crowd catch its breath as the bull began its second attack. It was moving even faster this time, its hooves pounding on the sand. The horns were once again levelled at him. If they hit him, they would cut him in half.

At the very last moment, Alex stepped aside, repeating the

movement he had made before. But this time the bull had been expecting it. Although it was advancing too fast to change direction, it flicked its head and Alex felt a searing pain along the side of his stomach. He was thrown off his feet, cartwheeling backwards and crashing down onto the sand. A roar exploded from the crowd. Alex waited for the bull to turn round and lay into him. But he had been lucky. The animal hadn't seen him go down. It had continued its run to the other side of the arena, leaving him alone.

Alex got to his feet. He put a hand down to his stomach. The jacket had been ripped open and when he took his hand away there was bright red blood on his palm. He was winded and shaken, and the side of his body felt as if it were on fire. But the cut wasn't too deep. In a way, Alex was disappointed. If he had been more badly hurt, they would have had to stop the fight.

Out of the corner of his eye he saw a movement. Yassen had stood up and was walking out. Had the ten minutes passed or had the Russian decided that the entertainment was over and that there was no point staying to watch the bloody end? Alex checked around the arena. Raoul was leaving too. But Franco was staying in his seat. The man was in the front row, only about ten metres away. And he was smiling. Yassen had tricked him. Franco was going to stay there. Even if Alex did manage to escape the bull, Franco would take out his gun and finish it himself.

Weakly Alex leant down and picked up the cape. The material had got torn in the last encounter and it gave Alex a sudden idea. Everything was in its right place: the cape, the bull, the single *banderilla*, Franco.

Ignoring the pain in his side, he started to run. The audience muttered and then roared in disbelief. It was the bull's job to attack the matador, but suddenly, in front of them, it seemed to be happening the other way round. Even the bull was taken unawares, regarding Alex as if he had forgotten the rules of the game or decided to cheat. Before it had a chance to move, Alex threw the cape. There was a short wooden handle sewn into the cloth and the weight of it carried the whole thing forward so that it landed perfectly – over the creature's eyes. The bull tried to shake the cloth free, but one of its horns had passed through the hole. It snorted angrily and stamped at the ground. But the cape stayed in place.

Everyone was shouting now. Half the spectators had risen to their feet and the president was looking around him helplessly. Alex ran and snatched up the *banderilla*, noticing the ugly hook, stained red with the blood of the last bull. In a single movement he swung it round and threw it.

His target wasn't the bull. Franco had started to rise out of his seat as soon as he'd realized what Alex was about to do; his hand was already scrabbling for his gun. But he was too late. Either Alex had been lucky or sheer desperation had perfected his aim. The *banderilla* turned once in the air, then buried itself in Franco's shoulder. Franco screamed. The point wasn't long enough to kill him, but the barbed hook kept the *banderilla* in place, making it impossible to pull out. Blood spread along the sleeve of his suit.

The whole arena was in an uproar. The crowd had never seen anything like this. Alex continued running. He saw the bull free itself from the red cape. It was already searching for him, determined to take its revenge.

Take your revenge another day, Alex thought. I have no quarrel with you.

He had reached the *barrera* and leapt up, grabbed the top and pulled himself over. Franco was too shocked and in too much pain to react; anyway, he had been surrounded by onlookers trying to help. He would never have been able to produce his gun and take aim. Everybody seemed to be on the edge of panic. The president signalled furiously and the band struck up again, but the musicians all began at different times and none of them played the same tune.

One of the men in jeans and black shirts sprinted towards Alex, shouting something in French. Alex ignored him. He hit the ground and ran.

At the very moment that Alex shot out into the night, the storm broke. The rain fell like an ocean thrown from the sky. It crashed into the town, splattered off the pavements and formed instant rivers that raced along the gutters and overwhelmed the drains. There was no thunder. Just this avalanche of water that threatened to drown the world.

Alex didn't stop. In seconds his hair was soaked. Water ran in rivulets down his face and he could barely see. As he ran he tore off the outer parts of the matador's costume, first the hat, then the jacket and tie, throwing each item away, leaving their memory behind.

The sea was on his left, the water black and boiling as it was hit by the rain. Alex twisted off the road and felt sand beneath his feet. He was on the beach – the same beach where he had been lying with Sabina when all this began. The sea wall and the jetty were beyond it.

He leapt onto the sea wall and climbed the heavy boulders. His shirt hung out of his trousers; it was already sodden, clinging to his chest.

Yassen's boat had left.

Alex couldn't be sure, but he thought he could see a vague shape disappearing into the darkness and the rain and he knew that he must have missed it by seconds. He stopped, panting. What had he been thinking of anyway? If the *Fer de Lance* had still been there, would he really have climbed aboard a second time? Of course not. He had been lucky to survive the first attempt. He had come here just in time to see it leave and he had learnt nothing.

No.

There was something.

Alex stood there for a few more moments with the rain streaming down his face, then turned and walked back into the town.

He found the phone box in a street just behind the main church. He had no money so was forced to make a reverse charge call and he wondered if it would be accepted. He dialled the operator and gave the number that he had found and memorized in Yassen's mobile phone.

"Who is speaking?" the operator asked.

Alex hesitated. Then... "My name is Yassen Gregorovich," he said.

There was a long silence as the connection was made. Would anyone even answer? England was an hour behind France but it was still late at night.

The rain was falling more lightly now, pattering on the glass roof of the phone box. Alex waited. Then the operator came back on.

"Your call has been accepted, monsieur. Please go ahead..."

More silence. Then a voice. It spoke just two words.

"Damian Cray."

Alex said nothing.

The voice spoke again. "Hello? Who is this?"

Alex was shivering. Maybe it was the rain; maybe it was a reaction to everything that had happened. He couldn't speak. He heard the man breathing at the end of the line.

Then there was a click and the phone went dead.

TRUTH AND CONSEQUENCE

London greeted Alex like an old and reliable friend. Red buses, black cabs, blue-uniformed policemen and grey clouds ... could he be anywhere else? Walking down the King's Road, he felt a million miles from the Camargue – not just home, but back in the real world. The side of his stomach was still sore and he could feel the pressure of the bandage against his skin, but otherwise Yassen and the bullfight were already slipping into the distant past.

He stopped outside a bookshop which, like so many of them, advertised itself with the wafting smell of coffee. He paused for a moment, then went in.

He quickly found what he was looking for. There were three books on Damian Cray in the biography section. Two of these were hardly books at all – more glossy brochures put out by record companies to promote the man who had made them so many millions. The first was called *Damian Cray – Live!* It was stacked next to a book called *Cray-zee! The Life and Times of Damian Cray*. The same face stared out from the covers. Jet-black hair cut short like a schoolboy's. A very round face with prominent cheeks and brilliant green eyes. A small nose, almost too exactly placed right in the middle. Thick lips and perfect white teeth.

The third book had been written quite a few years later. The face was a little older, the eyes hidden behind blue-tinted spectacles, and this Damian Cray was climbing out of a white Rolls-Royce, wearing a Versace suit and tie. The title of the book showed what else had changed: *Sir Damian Cray: The Man, The Music, The Millions*. Alex glanced at the first page, but the heavy, complicated prose soon put him off. It seemed to have been written by someone who probably read the *Financial Times* for laughs.

In the end he didn't buy any of the books. He wanted to know more about Cray, but he didn't think these books would tell him anything he didn't know already. And certainly not why Cray's private telephone number had been on the mobile phone of a hired assassin.

Alex walked back through Chelsea, turning off down the pretty, white-fronted street where his uncle, Ian Rider, had lived. He now shared the house with Jack Starbright, an American girl who had once been the housekeeper but had since become his legal guardian and closest friend. She was the reason Alex had first agreed to work for MI6. He had been sent undercover to spy on Herod Sayle and his Stormbreaker computers. In return she had been given a visa which allowed her to stay in London and look after him.

She was waiting for him in the kitchen when he got in. He had agreed to be back by one and she had thrown together a quick lunch. Jack was a good cook but refused to make anything that took longer than ten minutes. She was twenty-eight years old, slim, with tangled red hair and the sort of face that couldn't help being cheerful, even when she was in a bad mood.

"Had a good morning?" she asked as he came in.

"Yes." Alex sat down slowly, holding his side.

Jack noticed but said nothing. "I hope you're hungry," she went on.

"What's for lunch?"

"Stir-fry."

"It smells good."

"It's an old Chinese recipe. At least, that's what it said on the packet. Help yourself to some Coke and I'll serve up."

The food was good and Alex tried to eat, but the truth was that he had no appetite and he soon gave up. Jack said nothing as he carried his half-finished plate over to the sink, but then she suddenly turned round.

"Alex, you can't keep blaming yourself for what happened in France."

Alex had been about to leave the kitchen but now he returned to the table.

"It's about time you and I talked about this," Jack went on. "In fact, it's time we talked about everything!" She pushed her own plate of food away and waited until Alex had sat down. "All right. So it turns out that your uncle – Ian – wasn't a bank manager. He was a spy. Well, it would have been nice if he'd mentioned it to me, but it's too late now because he's gone and got himself killed, which leaves me stuck here, looking after you." She quickly held up a hand. "I didn't mean that. I love being here. I love London. I even love you.

"But *you're* not a spy, Alex. You know that. Even if Ian had some crazy idea about training you up. Three times now you've taken time off from school and each time you've come back a bit more bashed around. I don't even want to know what you've been up to, but personally I've been worried sick!"

"It wasn't my choice..." Alex said.

"That's my point exactly. Spies and bullets and madmen who want to take over the world – it's got nothing to do with you. So you were right to walk away in Saint-Pierre. You did the right thing."

Alex shook his head. "I should have done something. Anything. If I had, Sabina's dad would never—"

"You can't know that. Even if you'd called the cops, what could they have done? Remember – nobody knew there was a bomb. Nobody knew who the target was. I don't think it would have made any difference at all. And if you don't mind my saying so, Alex, going after this guy Yassen on your own was frankly ... well, it was very dangerous. You're lucky you weren't killed."

She was certainly right about that. Alex remembered the arena and saw again the horns and bloodshot eyes of the bull. He reached out for his glass and took a sip of Coke. "I still have to do something," he said. "Edward Pleasure was writing an article about Damian Cray. Something about a secret meeting in Paris. Maybe he was buying drugs or something."

But even as he spoke the words, Alex knew they couldn't be true. Cray hated drugs. There had been advertising campaigns – posters and TV – using his name and face. His last album, *White Lines*, had contained four anti-drugs songs. He had made it a personal issue. "Maybe he's into porn," he suggested weakly.

"Whatever it is, it's going to be hard to prove, Alex. The whole world loves Damian Cray." Jack sighed. "Maybe you should talk to Mrs Jones."

Alex felt his heart sink. He dreaded the thought of going back to MI6 and meeting the woman who was its deputy head of Special Operations. But he knew Jack was right. At least Mrs Jones would be able to investigate. "I suppose I could go and see her," he said.

"Good. But just make sure she doesn't get you involved. If Damian Cray *is* up to something, it's her business – not yours."

The telephone rang.

There was a cordless phone in the kitchen and Jack took the call. She listened for a moment, then handed the receiver to Alex. "It's Sabina," she said. "For you."

They met outside Tower Records in Piccadilly Circus and walked to a nearby Starbucks. Sabina was wearing grey trousers and a loose-fitting jersey. Alex had expected her to have changed in some way after all that had happened, and indeed she looked younger, less sure of herself. She was obviously tired. All traces of her South of France suntan had disappeared.

"Dad's going to live," she said as they sat down together with two bottles of juice. "The doctors are pretty sure about that. He's strong and he kept himself fit. But..." Her voice trembled. "It's going to take a long time, Alex. He's still unconscious – and he was badly burnt." She stopped and drank some of her juice. "The police said it was a gas leak. Can you believe that? Mum says she's going to sue."

"Who's she going to sue?"

"The people who rented us the house. The gas board. The whole country. She's furious..."

Alex said nothing. A gas leak. That was what the police had told him.

Sabina sighed. "Mum said I ought to see you. She said you'd want to know about Dad."

"Your dad had just come down from Paris, hadn't he?" Alex

wasn't sure this was the right time, but he had to know. "Did he say anything about the article he was writing?"

Sabina looked surprised. "No. He never talked about his work. Not to Mum. Not to anyone."

"Where had he been?"

"He'd been staying with a friend. A photographer."

"Do you know his name?"

"Marc Antonio. Why are you asking all these questions about my dad? Why do you want to know?"

Alex avoided the questions. "Where is he now?" he asked.

"In hospital in France. He's not strong enough to travel. Mum's still out there with him. I flew home on my own."

Alex thought for a moment. This wasn't a good idea. But he couldn't keep silent. Not knowing what he did. "I think he should have a police guard," he said.

"What?" Sabina stared at him. "Why? Are you saying ... it wasn't a gas leak?"

Alex didn't answer.

Sabina looked at him carefully, then came to a decision. "You've been asking a lot of questions," she said. "Now it's my turn. I don't know what's really going on, but Mum told me that after it happened, you ran away from the house."

"How did she know?"

"The police told her. They said you had this idea that someone had tried to kill Dad ... and that it was someone you knew. And then you disappeared. They were searching everywhere for you."

"I went to the police station at Saint-Pierre," Alex said.

"But that wasn't until midnight. You were completely soaked and you had a cut and you were dressed in weird clothes..."

Alex had been questioned for an hour when he had finally shown up at the gendarmerie. A doctor had given him three stitches and bandaged up the wound. Then a policeman had brought him a change of clothes. The questions had only stopped with the arrival of the man from the British consulate in Lyons. The man, who had been elderly and efficient, seemed to know all about Alex. He had driven Alex to Montpellier Airport to catch the first flight the next day. He had no interest in what had happened. His only desire seemed to be to get Alex out of the country.

"What were you doing?" Sabina asked. "You say Dad needs protection. Is there something you know?"

"I can't really tell you—" Alex began.

"Stuff that!" Sabina said. "Of course you can tell me!"

"I can't. You wouldn't believe me."

"If you don't tell me, Alex, I'm going to walk out of here and you'll never see me again. What is it that you know about my dad?"

In the end he told her. It was very simple. She hadn't given him any choice. And in a way he was glad. The secret had been with him too long and, carrying it alone, he had begun to feel it weighing him down.

He began with the death of his uncle, his introduction to MI6, his training and his first meeting with Yassen Gregorovich at the Stormbreaker computer plant in Cornwall. He described, as briefly as he could, how he had been forced, twice more, to work for MI6 – in the French Alps and off the coast of America. Then he told her what he had felt the moment he had seen Yassen on the beach at Saint-Pierre, how he had followed him to the restaurant, why in the end he had done nothing.

He thought he had skimmed over it all but in fact he talked for half an hour before arriving at his meeting with Yassen on the *Fer de Lance*. He had avoided looking directly at Sabina for much of the time as he talked, but when he reached the bullfight, describing how he had dressed up as a matador and walked out in front of a crowd of a thousand, he glanced up and met her eyes. She was looking at him as if seeing him for the first time. She almost seemed to hate him.

"I told you it wasn't easy to believe," he concluded lamely.

"Alex..."

"I know the whole thing sounds mad. But that's what happened. I am so sorry about your dad. I'm sorry I couldn't stop it from happening. But at least I know who was responsible."

"Who?"

"Damian Cray."

"The pop star?"

"Your dad was writing an article about him. I found a bit of it at the house. And his number was on Yassen's mobile phone."

"So Damian Cray wanted to kill my dad."

"Yes."

There was a long silence. Too long, Alex thought.

At last Sabina spoke again. "I'm sorry, Alex," she said. "I have never heard so much crap in all my life."

"Sab, I told you—"

"I know you said I wouldn't believe it. But just because you said that, it doesn't make it true!" She shook her head. "How can you expect anyone to believe a story like that? Why can't you tell me the truth?"

"It *is* the truth, Sab."

Suddenly he knew what he had to do.

"And I can prove it."

They took the tube across London to Liverpool Street Station and walked up the road to the building that Alex knew housed the Special Operations division of MI6. They found themselves standing in front of a tall, black-painted door, the sort that was designed to impress people coming in or leaving. Next to it, screwed into the brickwork, was a brass plaque with the words:

ROYAL & GENERAL
BANK PLC

LONDON

Sabina had seen it. She looked at Alex doubtfully.

"Don't worry," Alex said. "The Royal & General Bank doesn't exist. That's just the sign they put on the door."

They went in. The entrance hall was cold and businesslike, with high ceilings and a brown marble floor. To one side there was a leather sofa and Alex remembered sitting there the first time he had come, waiting to go up to his uncle's office on the fifteenth floor. He walked straight across to the glass reception desk where a young woman was sitting with a microphone curving across her mouth, taking calls and greeting visitors at the same time. There was an older security officer in uniform and peaked cap next to her.

"Can I help you?" the woman asked, smiling at Alex and Sabina.

"Yes," Alex said. "I'd like to see Mrs Jones."

"Mrs Jones?" The young woman frowned. "Do you know what department she works in?"

"She works with Mr Blunt."

"I'm sorry..." She turned to the security guard. "Do you know a Mrs Jones?"

"There's a Miss Johnson," the guard suggested. "She's a cashier."

Alex looked from one to the other. "You know who I mean," he said. "Just tell her that Alex Rider is here—"

"There is no Mrs Jones working at this bank," the receptionist interrupted.

"Alex..." Sabina began.

But Alex refused to give up. He leant forward so that he could speak confidentially. "I know this isn't a bank," he said. "This is MI6 Special Operations. Please could you—"

"Are you doing this as some sort of prank?" This time it was the security guard who was speaking. "What's all this nonsense about MI6?"

"Alex, let's get out of here," Sabina said.

"No!" Alex couldn't believe what was happening. He didn't even know exactly what it *was* that was happening. It had to be a mistake. These people were new. Or perhaps they needed some sort of password to allow him into the building. Of course. On his previous visits here, he had only ever come when he had been expected. Either that or he had been brought here against his will. This time he had come unannounced. That was why he wasn't being allowed in.

"Listen," Alex said. "I understand why you wouldn't want to let just anyone in, but I'm not just anyone. I'm Alex Rider. I work with Mr Blunt and Mrs Jones. Could you please let her know I'm here?"

"There *is* no Mrs Jones," the receptionist repeated helplessly.

"And I don't know any Mr Blunt either," the security guard added.

"Alex. Please..." Sabina was sounding more and more desperate. She really wanted to leave.

Alex turned to her. "They're lying, Sabina," he said. "I'll show you."

He grabbed her arm and pulled her over to the lift. He reached out and stabbed the call button.

"You stop right there!" The security guard stood up.

The receptionist reached out and pressed a button, presumably calling for help.

The lift didn't come.

Alex saw the guard moving towards him. Still no lift. He looked around and noticed a corridor leading away, with a set of swing doors at the end. Perhaps there would be a staircase or another set of lifts somewhere else in the building. Pulling Sabina behind him, Alex set off down the corridor. He heard the security guard getting closer. He quickened his pace, searching for a way up.

He slammed through the double doors.

And stopped.

He was in a banking hall. It was huge, with a domed ceiling and advertisements on the walls for mortgages, savings schemes and personal loans. There were seven or eight glass windows arranged along one side, with cashiers stamping documents and cashing cheques, while about a dozen customers – ordinary people off the street – waited in line. Two personal advisers, young men in smart suits, sat behind desks in the open-plan area. One of them was discussing pension schemes with an elderly couple. Alex heard the other answer his phone.

"Hello. This is the Royal & General Bank, Liverpool Street. Adam speaking. How may I help?"

A light flashed on above one of the windows. Number four. A man in a pinstripe suit went over to it and the queue shuffled forward.

Alex took all this in with one glance. He looked at Sabina. She was staring with a mixture of emotions on her face.

And then the security guard was there. "You're not meant to come into the bank this way," he said. "This is a staff entrance. Now, I want you to leave before you get yourself into real trouble. I mean it! I don't want to have to call the police, but that's my job."

"We're going." Sabina had stepped in and her voice was cold, definite.

"Sab—"

"We're going now."

"You ought to look after your friend," the security guard said. "He may think this sort of thing is funny, but it isn't."

Alex left – or rather allowed Sabina to lead him out. They went through a revolving door and out onto the street. Alex wondered what had happened. Why had he never seen the bank before? Then he realized. The building was actually sandwiched between two streets with a quite separate front and back. He had always entered from the other side.

"Listen—" he began.

"No. You listen! I don't know what's going on inside your head. Maybe it's because you don't have parents. You have to draw attention to yourself by creating this … fantasy! But just listen to yourself, Alex! I mean, it's pretty sick. Schoolboy spies and Russian assassins and all the rest of it…"

"It's got nothing to do with my parents," Alex said, feeling anger well up inside him.

"But it's got *everything* to do with mine. My dad gets hurt in an accident—"

"It wasn't an accident, Sab." He couldn't stop himself. "Are you really so stupid that you think I'd make all this up?"

"Stupid? Are you calling me stupid?"

"I'm just saying that I thought we were friends. I thought you knew me…"

"Yes! I thought I knew you. But now I see I was wrong. I'll tell you what's stupid. Listening to you in the first place was stupid. Coming to see you was stupid. Ever getting to know you … that was the most stupid thing of all."

She turned and walked away in the direction of the station. In seconds she had gone, disappearing into the crowd.

"Alex..." a voice said behind him. It was a voice that he knew.

Mrs Jones was standing on the pavement. She had seen and heard everything that had taken place.

"Let her go," she said. "I think we need to talk."

SAINT OR SINGER?

The office was the same as it had always been. The same ordinary, modern furniture, the same view, the same man behind the same desk. Not for the first time, Alex found himself wondering about Alan Blunt, head of MI6 Special Operations. What had his journey to work been like today? Was there a suburban house with a nice, smiling wife and two children waving goodbye as he left to catch the tube? Did his family know the truth about him? Had he ever told them that he wasn't working for a bank or an insurance company or anything like that, and that he carried with him – perhaps in a smart leather case, given to him for his birthday – files and documents full of death?

Alex tried to see the teenager in the man in the grey suit. Blunt must have been his own age once. He would have gone to school, sweated over exams, played football, tried his first cigarette and got bored at weekends like anybody else. But there was no sign of any child in the empty grey eyes, the colourless hair, the mottled, tightly drawn skin. So when had it happened? What had turned him into a civil servant, a spymaster, an adult with no obvious emotions and no remorse?

And then Alex wondered if the same thing would one day happen to him. Was that what MI6 were preparing him for? First they had turned him into a spy; next they would turn him into one of them. Perhaps they already had an office waiting with his name on the door. The windows were closed and it was warm in the room, but he shuddered. He had been wrong to come here with Sabina. The office on Liverpool Street was poisonous, and one way or another it would destroy him if he didn't stay away.

"We couldn't allow you to bring that girl here, Alex," Blunt was saying. "You know perfectly well that you can't just show off to your friends whenever—"

"I wasn't showing off," Alex cut in. "Her dad was almost killed by a bomb in the South of France."

"We know all about the business in Saint-Pierre," Blunt murmured.

"Do you know that it was Yassen Gregorovich who planted it?"

Blunt sighed irritably. "That doesn't make any difference. It's none of your business. And it's certainly nothing to do with us!"

Alex stared at him in disbelief. "Sabina's father is a journalist," he exclaimed. "He was writing about Damian Cray. If Cray wanted him dead, there must be a reason. Isn't it your job to find out?"

Blunt held up a hand for silence. His eyes, as always, showed nothing at all. Alex was struck by the thought that if this man were to die, sitting here at his desk, nobody would notice any difference.

"I have received a report from the police in Montpellier, and also from the British consulate," Blunt said. "This is standard practice when one of our people is involved."

"I'm not one of your people," Alex muttered.

"I am sorry that the father of your ... friend was hurt. But you might as well know that the French police have investigated – and you're right. It wasn't a gas leak."

"That's what I was trying to tell you."

"It turns out that a local terrorist organization – the CST – have claimed responsibility."

"The CST?" Alex's head spun. "Who are they?"

"They're very new," Mrs Jones explained. "CST stands for Camargue Sans Touristes. Essentially they're French nationalists who want to stop local houses in the Camargue being sold off for tourism and second homes."

"It's got nothing to do with the CST," Alex insisted. "It was Yassen Gregorovich. I saw him and he admitted it. And he told me that the real target was Edward Pleasure. Why won't you listen to what I'm saying? It was this article Edward was writing. Something about a meeting in Paris. It was Damian Cray who wanted him dead."

There was a brief pause. Mrs Jones glanced at her boss as if needing his permission to speak. He nodded almost imperceptibly.

"Did Yassen mention Damian Cray?" she asked.

"No. But I found his private telephone number in Yassen's phone. I rang it and I actually heard him speak."

"You can't know it was Damian Cray."

"Well, that was the name he gave."

"This is complete nonsense." It was Blunt who had spoken and Alex was amazed to see that he was angry. It was the first time Alex had ever seen him show any emotion at all and it occurred to him that not many people dared to disagree with the chief executive of Special Operations. Certainly not to his face.

"Why is it nonsense?"

"Because you're talking about one of the most admired and respected entertainers in the country. A man who has raised millions and millions of pounds for charity. Because you're talking about Damian Cray!" Blunt sank back into his chair. For a moment he seemed undecided. Then he nodded briefly. "All right," he said. "Since you have been of some use to us in the past, and since I want to clear this matter up once and for all, I will tell you everything we know about Cray."

"We have extensive files on him," Mrs Jones said.

"Why?"

"We keep extensive files on everyone who's famous."

"Go on."

Blunt nodded again and Mrs Jones took over. She seemed to know all the facts by heart. Either she had read the files recently or, more probably, she had the sort of mind that never forgot anything.

"Damian Cray was born in north London on the fifth of October 1950," she began. "That's not his real name, by the way. He was christened Harold Eric Lunt. His father was Sir Arthur Lunt, who made his fortune building multi-storey carparks. As a child, Harold had a remarkable singing voice, and aged eleven he was sent to the Royal Academy of Music in London. In fact, he used to sing regularly there with another boy who also became famous. That was Elton John.

"But when he was thirteen, there was a terrible disaster. His parents were killed in a bizarre car accident."

"What was bizarre about it?"

"The car fell on top of them. It rolled off the top floor of one of their carparks. As you can imagine, Harold was distraught. He left the Royal Academy and travelled the world. He changed his name and turned to Buddhism for a while. He also became a vegetarian. Even now, he never touches meat. The tickets for his concerts are made out of recycled paper. He has very strict values and he sticks to them.

"Anyway, he came back to England in the seventies and formed a band – Slam! They were an instant success. I'm sure the rest of this will be very familiar to you, Alex. At the end of the seventies the band split up, and Cray began a solo career which took him to new heights. His first solo album, *Firelight*, went platinum. After that he was seldom out of the UK or US top twenty. He won five Grammys and an Academy Award for Best Original Song. In 1986 he visited Africa and decided to do something to help the people there. He arranged a concert at Wembley Stadium, with all proceeds going to charity. Chart Attack – that was what it was called. It was a huge success and that Christmas he released a single: 'Something for the Children'. It sold four million copies and he gave every penny away.

"That was just the beginning. Since the success of Chart Attack, Cray has campaigned tirelessly on a range of world issues. Save the rainforests; protect the ozone layer; end world debt. He's built his own rehabilitation centres to help young people involved with drugs, and he spent two years fighting to have a laboratory closed down because it was experimenting on animals.

"In 1989 he performed in Belfast, and many people believe that this free concert was a step on the way towards peace in Northern Ireland. A year later he made two visits to Buckingham Palace. He was there on a Thursday to play a solo for Princess Diana's birthday; and on the Friday he was back again to receive a knighthood from the Queen.

"Only last year he was on the cover of *Time* magazine. 'Man of the Year. Saint or Singer?' That was the headline. And that's why your accusations are ridiculous, Alex. The whole world knows that Damian Cray is just about the closest thing we have to a living saint."

"It was still his voice on the telephone," Alex said.

"You heard someone give his name. You don't know it was him."

"I just don't understand it!" Now Alex was angry, confused. "All right, we all like Damian Cray. I know he's famous. But if there's a chance that he was involved with the bomb, why won't you at least investigate him?"

"Because we can't." It was Blunt who had spoken and the words came out flat and heavy. He cleared his throat. "Damian Cray is a multimillionaire. He's got a huge penthouse on the Thames and another place down in Wiltshire, just outside Bath."

"So what?"

"Rich people have connections and extremely rich people have very good connections indeed. Since the nineties, Cray has been putting his money into a number of commercial ventures. He bought his own television station and made a number of programmes that are now shown all around the world. Then he branched out into hotels – and finally into computer games. He's about to launch a new game system. He calls it the Gameslayer, and apparently it will put all the other systems – PlayStation 2, GameCube, whatever – into the shade."

"I still don't see—"

"He is a major employer, Alex. He is a man of enormous influence. And, for what it's worth, he donated a million pounds to the government just before the last election. Now do you understand? If it was discovered that we were investigating him, and merely on your say-so, there would be a tremendous scandal. The prime minister doesn't like us anyway. He hates anything he can't control. He might even use an attack on Damian Cray as an excuse to close us down."

"Cray was on television only today," Mrs Jones said. She picked up a remote control. "Have a look at this and then tell me what you think."

A TV monitor in the corner of the room flickered on, and Alex found himself looking at a recording of the mid-morning news. He guessed Mrs Jones probably recorded the news every day. She fast-forwarded, then ran the film at the correct speed.

And there was Damian Cray. His hair was neatly combed and he was wearing a dark, formal suit, white shirt and mauve silk tie. He was standing outside the American embassy in London's Grosvenor Square.

Mrs Jones turned up the sound.

"...the former pop singer, now tireless campaigner for a number of environmental and political issues, Damian Cray. He was in London to meet the president of the United States, who has just arrived in England as part of his summer vacation."

The picture switched to a jumbo jet landing at Heathrow Airport, then cut in closer to show the president standing at the open door, waving and smiling.

"The president arrived at Heathrow Airport in Air Force One, the presidential plane. He is due to have a formal lunch with the prime minister at number ten Downing Street today..."

Another cut. Now the president was standing next to Damian Cray and the two men were shaking hands, a long handshake for the benefit of the cameras which flashed all around them. Cray had sandwiched the president's hand between both his own hands and seemed unwilling to let him go. He said something and the president laughed.

"...but first he met Cray for an informal discussion at the American embassy in London. Cray is a spokesman for Greenpeace and has been leading the movement to prevent oil drilling in the wilds of Alaska, fearing the environmental damage this may cause. Although he made no promises, the president agreed to study the report which Greenpeace..."

Mrs Jones turned off the television.

"Do you see? The most powerful man in the world interrupts his holiday to meet Damian Cray. And he sees Cray before he even visits the prime minister! That should give you the measure of the man. So tell me! What earthly reason could he have to blow up a house and perhaps kill a whole family?"

"That's what I want you to find out."

Blunt sniffed. "I think we should wait for the French police to get back to us," he said. "They're investigating the CST. Let's see what they come up with."

"So you're going to do nothing!"

"I think we have explained, Alex."

"All right." Alex stood up. He didn't try to conceal his anger. "You've made me look a complete fool in front of Sabina; you've made me lose one of my best friends. It's really amazing. When you need me, you just pull me out of school and send me to the other side of the world. But when I need you, just this once, you pretend you don't even exist and you just dump me out on the street..."

"You're being over-emotional," Blunt said.

"No, I'm not. But I'll tell you this. If you won't go after Cray, I will. He may be Father Christmas, Joan of Arc and the Pope all rolled into one, but it was his voice on the phone and I know he was somehow involved in what happened in the South of France. I'm going to prove it to you."

Alex stood up and, without waiting to hear another word, left the room.

There was a long pause.

Blunt took out a pen and made a few notes on a sheet of paper. Then he looked at Mrs Jones. "Well?" he demanded.

"Maybe we should go over the files one more time," Mrs Jones suggested. "After all, Herod Sayle pretended to be a friend of the British people, and if it hadn't been for Alex..."

"You can do what you like," Blunt said. He drew a ring round the last sentence he had written. Mrs Jones could see the words *Yassen Gregorovich* upside down on the page. "Curious that he should have run into Yassen a second time," he muttered.

"And more curious still that Yassen didn't kill him when he had the chance."

"I wouldn't say that, all things considered."

Mrs Jones nodded. "Maybe we ought to tell Alex about Yassen," she suggested.

"Absolutely not." Blunt picked up the piece of paper and crumpled it. "The less Alex Rider knows about Yassen Gregorovich the better. I very much hope the two of them don't run into each other again." He dropped the paper ball into the bin underneath his desk. At the end of the day everything in the bin would be incinerated.

"And that," he said, "is that."

Jack was worried.

Alex had come back from Liverpool Street in a bleak mood and had barely spoken a word to her since. He had come into the sitting-room where she was reading a book and she had managed to learn that the meeting with Sabina hadn't gone well and that Alex wouldn't be seeing her again. But during the afternoon she managed to coax more and more of the story out of him until finally she had the whole picture.

"They're all idiots!" Alex exclaimed. "I know they're wrong but just because I'm younger than them, they won't listen to me."

"I've told you before, Alex. You shouldn't be mixed up with them."

"I won't be. Never again. They don't give a damn about me."

The doorbell rang.

"I'll go," Alex said.

There was a white van parked outside. Two men were opening the back and, as Alex watched, they unloaded a brand-new bicycle, wheeling it down and over to the house. Alex cast his eye over it. The bike was a Cannondale Bad Boy, a mountain bike that had been adapted for the city with a lightweight aluminium frame and one-inch wheels. It was silver and seemed to have come equipped with all the accessories he could have asked for: Digital Evolution lights, a Blackburn mini-pump ... everything top of the range. Only the silver bell on the handlebar seemed old-fashioned and out of place. Alex ran his hand over the leather saddle with its twisting Celtic design and then along the frame, admiring the workmanship. There was no sign of any welds. The bike was handmade and must have cost hundreds.

One of the men came over to him. "Alex Rider?" he asked.

"Yes. But I think there's been a mistake. I didn't order a bike."

"It's a gift. Here..."

The second man had left the bike propped up against the railings. Alex found himself holding a thick envelope. Jack appeared on the step behind him. "What is it?" she asked.

"Someone has given me a bike."

Alex opened the envelope. Inside was an instruction booklet and attached to it a letter.

Dear Alex,

I'm probably going to get a roasting for this, but I don't like the idea of you taking off on your own without any back-up. This is something I've been working on for you and you might as well have it now. I hope it comes in useful.

Look after yourself, dear boy. I'd hate to hear that anything lethal had happened to you.

All the best,

Smithers

PS This letter will self-destruct ten seconds after it comes into contact with the air so I hope you read it quickly!

Alex just had time to read the last sentence before the letters on the page faded and the paper itself crumpled and turned into white ash. He moved his hands apart and what was left of the letter blew away in the breeze. Meanwhile the two men had got back into the van and driven away. Alex was left with the bike. He flicked through the first pages of the instruction book.

BIKE PUMP – SMOKESCREEN
MAGNESIUM FLARE HEADLAMP
HANDLEBAR MISSILE EJECTION
TRAILRIDER JERSEY (BULLETPROOF)
MAGNETIC BICYCLE CLIPS

"Who is Smithers?" Jack asked. Alex had never told her about him.

"I was wrong," Alex said. "I thought I had no friends at MI6. But it looks like I've got one."

He wheeled the bicycle into the house. Smiling, Jack closed the door.

THE PLEASURE DOME

It was only in the cold light of morning that Alex began to see the impossibility of the task he had set himself. How was he supposed to investigate a man like Cray? Blunt had mentioned that he had homes in London and Wiltshire, but hadn't supplied addresses. Alex didn't even know if Cray was still in England.

But as it turned out, the morning news told Alex where he might begin.

When he came into the kitchen, Jack was reading the newspaper over her second cup of coffee. She took one look at him, then slid it across the table. "This'll put you off your cornflakes."

Alex turned the paper round – and there it was on the second page: Damian Cray looking out at him. A headline ran below the picture:

Cray Launches £100m Gameslayer

It's definitely the hottest ticket in London. Today game players get to see the eagerly anticipated Gameslayer, developed by Cray Software Technology, a company based in Amsterdam, at a cost rumoured to be in excess of one hundred million pounds. The state-of-the-art game system will be demonstrated by Sir Damian Cray himself in front of an invited audience of journalists, friends, celebrities and industry experts.

No expense has been spared on the launch, which kicks off at one o'clock and includes a lavish champagne buffet inside the Pleasure Dome that Cray has constructed inside Hyde Park. This is the first time that a royal park has been used for a purely commercial venture and there were some critics when permission was given earlier this year.

But Damian Cray is no ordinary businessman. He has already announced that twenty per cent of profits from the Gameslayer will be going to charity, this time helping disabled children throughout the UK. Yesterday Cray met with the United States president to discuss oil drilling in Alaska. It is said that the Queen herself approved the temporary construction of the Pleasure Dome, which uses aluminium and PTFE fabric (the same material used in the Millennium Dome). Its futuristic design has certainly proved an eye-opener for passing Londoners.

Alex stopped reading. "We have to go," he said.

"Do you want your eggs scrambled or boiled?"

"Jack..."

"Alex. It's a ticket-only event. What will we do?"

"I'll work something out."

Jack scowled. "Are you really sure about this?"

"I know, Jack. It's Damian Cray. Everyone loves him. But here's something they may not have noticed." He folded the paper and slid it back to her. "The terrorist group that claimed responsibility for the bomb in France was called Camargue Sans Touristes."

"I know."

"And this new computer game has been developed by Cray Software Technology."

"What about it, Alex?"

"Maybe it's just another coincidence. But CST... It's the same letters."

Jack nodded. "All right," she said. "So how do we get in?"

They took a bus up to Knightsbridge and crossed over into Hyde Park. Before he had even passed through the gates and into the park itself, Alex could see just how much had been invested in the launch. There were hundreds of people streaming along the pavements, getting out of taxies and limousines, milling around in a crowd that seemed to cover every centimetre of grass. Policemen on foot and on horseback stood at every corner, giving directions and trying to form people into orderly lines. Alex was amazed that the horses could remain so calm surrounded by so much chaos.

And then there was the Pleasure Dome itself. It was as if a fantastic spaceship had landed in the middle of the lake at the centre of Hyde Park. It seemed to float on the surface of the water, a black pod, surrounded by a gleaming aluminium frame, silver rods criss-crossing in a dazzling pattern. Blue and red spotlights swivelled and rocked, the beams flashing even in the daylight. A single metal bridge stretched across from the bank to the entrance but there were more than a dozen security men barring the way. Nobody was allowed to cross the water without showing their ticket. There was no other way in.

Music blared out of hidden speakers: Cray singing from his last album, *White Lines*. Alex walked down to the edge of the water. He could hear shouting and, even in the hazy afternoon sun, he was almost blinded by a hundred flashbulbs all exploding at the same time. The mayor of London had just arrived and was waving at the press pack, at least a hundred strong, herded together into a pen next to the bridge. Alex looked around and realized that he knew quite a few of the faces converging on the Pleasure Dome. There were actors, television presenters, models, DJs, politicians ... all waving their invitations and queuing up to be let in. This was more than the first appearance of a new game system. It was the most exclusive party London had ever seen.

And somehow he had to get in.

He ignored a policeman who was trying to move him out of the way and continued towards the bridge, walking confidently, as if he had been invited. Jack was a few steps away from him and he nodded at her.

It had been Ian Rider, of course, who had taught him the basics of pickpocketing. At the time it had just been a game, shortly after Alex's tenth birthday, when the two of them were together in Prague. They were talking about *Oliver Twist* and his uncle was explaining the techniques of the Artful Dodger, even providing his nephew with a quick demonstration. It was only much later that Alex had discovered that all this had been yet another aspect of his training; that all along his uncle had secretly been turning him into something he had never wanted to be.

But it would be useful now.

Alex was close to the bridge. He could see the invitations being checked by the burly men in their security uniforms: silver cards with the Gameslayer logo stamped in black. There was a natural crush here as the crowd arrived at the bottleneck and sorted itself into a single line to cross the bridge. He glanced one last time at Jack. She was ready.

Alex stopped.

"Somebody's stolen my ticket!" he shouted.

Even with the music pounding out, his voice was loud enough to carry to the crowd in the immediate area. It was a classic pickpocket's trick. Nobody cared about him, but suddenly they were worried about their own tickets. Alex saw one man pull open his jacket and glance into his inside pocket. Next to him a woman briefly opened and closed her handbag. Several people took their tickets out and clutched them tightly in their hands. A plump, bearded man reached round and tapped his back jeans pocket. Alex smiled. Now he knew where the tickets were.

He signalled to Jack. The plump man with the beard was going to be the mark – the one he had chosen. He was perfectly placed, just a few steps in front of Alex. And the corner of his ticket was actually visible, just poking out of the back pocket. Jack was going to play the part of the stall; Alex was in position to make the dip. Everything was set.

Jack walked ahead and seemed to recognize the man with the beard. "Harry!" she exclaimed, and threw her arms around him.

"I'm not..." the man began.

At that exact moment, Alex took two steps forward, swerved round a woman he vaguely recognized from a television drama series and slipped the ticket out of the man's pocket and placed it quickly under his own jacket, holding it in place with the side of his arm. It had taken less than three seconds and Alex hadn't even been particularly careful. This was the simple truth about pick-pocketing. It demanded organization as much as skill. The mark was distracted. All his attention was on Jack, who was still embracing him. Pinch someone on the arm and they won't notice if, at the same time, you're touching their leg. That was what Ian Rider had taught Alex all those years ago.

"Don't you remember me?" Jack was exclaiming. "We met at the Savoy!"

"No. I'm sorry. You've got the wrong person."

Alex was already brushing past, on his way to the bridge. In a few moments the mark would reach for his ticket and find it missing, but even if he grabbed hold of Jack and accused her, there would be no evidence. Alex and the ticket would have disappeared.

He showed the ticket to a security man and stepped onto the bridge. Part of him felt bad about what he had done and he hoped the man with the beard would still be able to talk his way in. Quietly he cursed Damian Cray for turning him into a thief. But he knew that, from the moment Cray had answered his call in the South of France, there could be no going back.

He crossed the bridge and gave the ticket up on the other side. Ahead of him was a triangular entrance. Alex stepped forward and went into the dome: a huge area fitted out with hi-tech lighting and a raised stage with a giant plasma screen displaying the letters CST. There were already about five hundred guests spread out in front of it, drinking champagne and eating canapés. Waiters were circulating with bottles and trays. A sense of excitement buzzed all around.

The music stopped. The lighting changed and the screen went blank. Then there was a low hum and clouds of dry ice began to pour onto the stage. A single word – GAMESLAYER – appeared on the screen; the hum grew louder. The Gameslayer letters broke up as an animated figure appeared, a ninja warrior, dressed in black from head to toe, clinging to the screen like a cut-down version of Spiderman. The hum was deafening now, a roaring desert wind with an orchestra somewhere behind. Hidden fans must have been turned on because real wind suddenly blasted through the dome, clearing away the smoke and revealing Damian Cray – in a white suit with a wide, pink and silver striped tie – standing alone on the stage, with his image, hugely magnified, on the screen behind.

The audience surged towards him, applauding. Cray raised a hand for silence.

"Welcome, welcome!" he said.

Alex found himself drawn towards the stage like everyone else. He wanted to get as close to Cray as he could. Already he was feeling that strange sensation of actually being in the same room as a man he had known all his life ... but a man he had never met. Damian Cray was smaller in real life than he seemed in his photographs. That was Alex's first thought. Nevertheless, Cray had been an A-list celebrity for thirty years. His presence was huge and he radiated confidence and control.

"Today is the day that I launch the Gameslayer, my new games console," Cray went on. He had a faint trace of an American accent. "I'd like to thank you all for coming. But if there's anyone here from Sony or Nintendo, I'm afraid I have bad news for you." He paused and smiled. "You're history."

There was laughter and applause from the audience. Even Alex found himself smiling. Cray had a way of including people, as if he personally knew everyone in the crowd.

"Gameslayer offers graphic quality and detail like no other system on the planet," Cray went on. "It can generate worlds, characters and totally complex physical simulations in real time thanks to the floating-point processing power of the system, which is, in a word, massive. Other systems give you plastic dolls fighting cardboard cut-outs. With Gameslayer, hair, eyes, skin tones, water, wood, metal and smoke all look like the real thing. We obey the rules of gravity and friction. More than that, we've built something into the system that we call pain synthesis. What does this mean? In a minute you'll find out."

He paused and the audience clapped again.

"Before I move on to the demonstration, I wonder if any of the journalists among you have any questions?"

A man near the front raised his hand. "How many games are you releasing this year?"

"Right now we only have the one game," Cray replied. "But there will be twelve more in the shops by Christmas."

"What is the first game called?" someone asked.

"Feathered Serpent."

"Is it a shoot-'em-up?" a woman asked.

"Well, yes. It is a stealth game," Cray admitted.

"So it involves shooting?"

"Yes."

The woman smiled, but not humorously. She was in her forties, with grey hair and a severe, schoolteacher face. "It's well known that you have a dislike of violence," she said. "So how can you justify selling children violent games?"

A ripple of unease ran through the audience. The woman might be a journalist, but somehow it seemed wrong to question Cray in this manner. Not when you were drinking his champagne and eating his food.

Cray, however, didn't seem offended. "That's a good question," he replied in his soft, lilting voice. "And I'll tell you, when we began with the Gameslayer, we did develop a game where the hero had to collect different-coloured flowers from a garden and then arrange them in vases. It had bunnies and egg sandwiches too. But do you know what? Our research team discovered that modern teenagers didn't want to play it. Can you imagine? They told me we wouldn't sell a single copy!"

Everyone broke into laughter. Now it was the female journalist who was looking uncomfortable.

Cray held up a hand again. "Actually, you've made a fair point," he went on. "It's true – I hate violence. Real violence ... war. But, you know, modern kids do have a lot of aggression in them. That's the truth of it. I suppose it's human nature. And I've come to think that it's better for them to get rid of that aggression playing harmless computer games, like mine, than out on the street."

"Your games still encourage violence!" the woman insisted.

Damian Cray frowned. "I think I've answered your question. So maybe you should stop questioning my answer," he said.

This was greeted by more applause, and Cray waited until it had died down. "But now, enough talk," he said. "I want you to see Gameslayer for yourself, and the best way to see it is to play it. I wonder if we have any teenagers in the audience, although now I come to think of it, I don't remember inviting any..."

"There's one here!" someone shouted, and Alex felt himself pushed forward. Suddenly everyone was looking at him and Cray himself was peering down from the stage.

"No..." Alex started to protest.

But the audience was already clapping, urging him on. A corridor opened up in front of him. Alex stumbled forward and before he knew it he was climbing up onto the stage. The room seemed to tilt. A spotlight spun round, dazzling him. And there it was.

He was standing on the stage with Damian Cray.

FEATHERED SERPENT

It was the last thing Alex could have expected.

He was face to face with the man who – if he was right – had ordered the death of Sabina's father. But *was* he right? For the first time, he was able to examine Cray at close quarters. It was a strangely unsettling experience.

Cray had one of the most famous faces in the world. Alex had seen it on CD covers, on posters, in newspapers and magazines, on television ... even on the back of cereal packets. And yet the face in front of him now was somehow disappointing. It was less real than all the images he had seen.

Cray was surprisingly young-looking, considering he was already in his fifties, but there was a taut, shiny quality to his skin that whispered of plastic surgery. And surely the neat, jet-black hair had to be dyed. Even the bright green eyes seemed somehow lifeless. Cray was a very small man. Alex found himself thinking of a doll in a toyshop. That was what Cray reminded him of. His superstardom and his millions of pounds had turned him into a plastic replica of himself.

And yet...

Cray had welcomed him onto the stage and was beaming at him as if he were an old friend. He was a singer. And, as he had made clear, he opposed violence. He wanted to save the world, not destroy it. MI6 had gathered files on him and found nothing. Alex was here because of a voice, a few words spoken at the end of a phone. He was beginning to wish he had never come.

It seemed that the two of them had been standing there for ages, up on the stage with hundreds of people waiting to see the demonstration. In fact, only a few seconds had passed. Then Cray held out a hand. "What's your name?" he asked.

"Alex Rider."

"Well, it's great to meet you, Alex Rider. I'm Damian Cray."

They shook hands. Alex couldn't help thinking that there were millions of people all around the world who would give anything to be where he was now.

"How old are you, Alex?" Cray asked.

"Fourteen."

"I'm very grateful to you for coming. Thanks for agreeing to help."

The words were being amplified around the dome. Out of the corner of his eye, Alex saw that his own image had joined Cray's on the giant screen. "We're very lucky that we do indeed have a teenager," Cray went on, addressing the audience. "So let's see how ... Alex ... gets on with the first level of Gameslayer One: Feathered Serpent."

As Cray spoke, three technicians came onto the stage, bringing with them a television monitor, a games console, a table and a chair. Alex realized that he was going to be asked to play the game in front of the audience – with his progress beamed up onto the plasma screen.

"Feathered Serpent is based on the Aztec civilization," Cray explained to the audience. "The Aztecs arrived in Mexico in 1195, but some claim that they had in fact come from another planet. It is on that planet that Alex is about to find himself. His mission is to find the four missing suns. But first he must enter the temple of Tlaloc, fight his way through five chambers and then throw himself into the pool of sacred flame. This will take him to the next level."

A fourth technician had come onto the stage, carrying a webcam. He stopped in front of Alex and quickly scanned him, pressed a button on the side of the camera and left. Cray waited until he had gone.

"You may have been wondering about the little black-suited figure that you saw on the screen," he said, once again taking the audience into his confidence. "His name is Omni, and he will be the hero of all the Gameslayer games. You may think him a little dull and unimaginative. But Omni is every boy and every girl in Britain. He is every child in the world ... and now I will show you why!"

The screen went blank, then burst into a digital whirl of colour. There was a deafening fanfare – not trumpets but some electronic equivalent – and the gates of a temple with a huge Aztec face cut into the wood appeared. Alex could tell at once that the graphic detail of the Gameslayer was better than anything he had ever seen, but a moment later the audience gasped with surprise and Alex perfectly understood why. A boy had walked onto the screen and was standing in front of the gates, awaiting his command. The boy was Omni. But he had changed. He was now wearing exactly the same clothes as Alex. He looked like Alex. More than that, he was Alex right down to the brown eyes and the hanging strands of fair hair.

Applause exploded around the room. Alex could see journalists scribbling in their notebooks or talking quickly into mobile phones, hoping to be the first with this incredible scoop. The food and the champagne had been forgotten. Cray's technology had created an avatar, an electronic double of him, making it possible for any player not just to play the game but to become part of it. Alex knew then that the Gameslayer would sell all over the world. Cray would make millions.

And twenty per cent of that would go to charity, he reminded himself.

Could this man really be his enemy?

Cray waited until everyone was quiet, and then he turned to Alex. "It's time to play," he said.

Alex sat down in front of the computer screen that the technicians had set up. He took hold of the controller and pressed with his left thumb. In front of him and on the giant plasma screen, his other self walked to the right. He stopped and turned himself the other way. The controller was incredibly sensitive. Alex almost felt like an Aztec god, in total control of his mortal self.

"Don't worry if you get killed on your first go," Cray said. "The console is faster than anything on the market and it may take you a while to get used to it. But we're all on your side, Alex. So – let's play Feathered Serpent! Let's see how far you can go!"

The temple gates opened.

Alex pressed down and on the screen his avatar walked forward and into a game environment that was alien and bizarre and brilliantly realized. The temple was a fusion of primitive art and science fiction, with towering columns, flaming beacons, complex hieroglyphics and crouching Aztec statues. But the floor was silver, not stone. Strange metal stairways and corridors twisted around the temple area. Electric light flickered behind heavily barred windows. Closed-circuit cameras followed his every move.

"You have to start by finding two weapons in the first chamber," Cray advised, leaning over Alex's shoulder. "You may need them later."

The first chamber was huge, with organ music throbbing and stained-glass windows showing cornfields, crop circles and hovering spaceships. Alex found the first weapon easily enough. There was a sword hanging high up on a wall. But he soon realized there were traps everywhere. Part of the wall crumbled as he climbed it and reaching out for the sword activated a missile which shot out of nowhere, aiming for the avatar. The missile was a double boomerang with razor-blade edges, rotating at lightning speed. Alex knew that if he was hit, he would be cut in half.

He stabbed down with his thumbs and his miniature self crouched. The boomerang spun past. But as it went, one of its blades caught the avatar on the arm. The audience gasped. A tiny flow of blood had appeared on the miniature figure's sleeve and its face – *Alex's* face – had distorted, showing pain. The experience was so realistic that Alex almost felt a need to check his own, real arm. He had to remind himself that it was only the avatar that had been wounded.

"Pain synthesis!" Cray repeated the words, his voice echoing across the Pleasure Dome. "In the Gameslayer world, we share all the hero's emotions. And should Alex die, the central processing unit will ensure that we feel his death."

Alex had climbed back down and was searching for the second weapon. The little wound was already healing, the blood flow slowing down. He dodged as another boomerang shot past his shoulder. But he still couldn't find the second weapon.

"Try looking behind the ivy," Cray suggested in a stage whisper, and the audience smiled, amused that Alex needed help so soon.

There was a crossbow concealed in an alcove. But what Cray hadn't told Alex was that the ivy covering the alcove contained a ten thousand volt charge. He found out soon enough. The moment his avatar touched the ivy, there was a blue flash and it was thrown backwards, screaming out loud, its eyes wide and staring. The avatar hadn't quite been killed, but it had been badly hurt.

Cray tapped Alex on the shoulder. "You'll have to be more careful than that," he said.

A buzz of excitement travelled through the audience. They had never seen anything like this before.

And that was when Alex decided. Suddenly MI6, Yassen, Saint-Pierre ... all of it was forgotten. Cray had tricked him into touching the ivy. He had deliberately injured him. Of course, it was just a game. It was only the avatar that had been hurt. But the humiliation had been his – and suddenly he was determined to get the better of Feathered Serpent. He wasn't going to be beaten. He wasn't going to share his death with anyone.

Grimly, he picked up the crossbow and sent the avatar forward, further into the Aztec world.

The second chamber consisted of a huge hole in the ground. It was actually a pit, fifty metres deep, with narrow pillars stretching all the way to the top. The only way to get from one side to the other was to jump from one pillar to the next. If he missed his step or overbalanced, he would fall to his death – and to make it more difficult it was pouring with rain inside the chamber, making the surfaces slippery. The rain itself was extraordinary. As Cray told the audience, the Gameslayer's image technology allowed every raindrop to be realized individually. The avatar was soaking wet, its clothes sodden and its hair plastered to its head.

There was a sudden electronic squawk. A creature with butterfly wings and the face and claws of a dragon swooped down, trying to knock the avatar off its perch. Alex brought the crossbow up and shot it, then took the last three leaps to the other side of the pit.

"You're doing very well," Damian Cray said. "But I wonder if you'll make it through the third chamber."

Alex was confident. Feathered Serpent was beautifully designed. Its texture maps and backgrounds were perfect. The Omni character was way ahead of the competition. But for all this, it was just another computer game, similar to ones that Alex had played on Xbox and PlayStation 2. He knew what he was doing. He could win.

He made easy work of the third section: a tall, narrow corridor with carved faces on either side. A hail of wooden spears and arrows fired out of the wooden mouths but not one of them came close as the avatar ducked and weaved, all the time running forward. A bubbling river of acid twisted along the corridor. The avatar jumped over it as if it were a harmless stream.

Now he came to an incredible indoor jungle where the greatest threat, among the trees and the creepers, was a huge robotic snake, covered in spikes. The creature looked horrific. Alex had never seen better graphics. But his avatar ran circles round it, leaving it behind so quickly that the audience barely had a chance to see it.

Cray's face hadn't changed, but now he was leaning over Alex, his eyes fixed on the screen, one hand resting on Alex's shoulder. His knuckles were almost white.

"You're making it look too easy," he murmured. Although the words were spoken light-heartedly, there was a rising tension in his voice.

Because the audience was now on Alex's side. Millions of pounds had been spent on the development of the Feathered Serpent software. But it was being beaten by the first teenager to play it. As Alex dodged a second robotic snake, someone laughed. The hand on his shoulder tightened.

He came to the fifth chamber. This was a mirror maze, filled with smoke and guarded by a dozen Aztec gods wrapped in feathers, jewellery and golden masks. Again, each and every one of the gods was a small masterpiece of graphic art. But although they lunged at the avatar, they kept on missing, and suddenly more of the people in the audience were laughing and applauding, urging Alex on.

One more god, this one with claws and an alligator tail, stood between Alex and the pool of fire that would lead him to the next level. All he had to do was get past it. That was when Cray made his move. He was careful. Nobody would see what happened and if they did it would simply look as if he was carried away by the excitement of the game. But he was quite deliberate. His hand suddenly moved to Alex's arm and closed tight, pulling it away from the controller. For a few brief seconds, Alex lost control. It was enough. The Aztec god reached out and its claws raked across the avatar's stomach. Alex actually heard his shirt being torn; he almost felt the pain as the blood poured out. His avatar fell to its knees, then pitched forward and lay still. The screen froze and the words GAME OVER appeared in red letters.

Silence fell inside the dome.

"Too bad, Alex," Cray said. "I'm afraid it wasn't quite as easy as you thought."

There was a scattering of applause from the audience. It was hard to tell if they were applauding the technology of the game or the way Alex had taken it on and almost beaten it. But there was also a sense of unease. Perhaps Feathered Serpent was too realistic. It really was as if a part of Alex had died there, on the screen.

Alex turned to Cray. He was angry. He alone knew that the man had cheated. But Cray was smiling again.

"You did great," he said. "I asked for a demonstration and you certainly gave us one. You make sure you leave your address with one of my assistants. I'll be sending you a free Gameslayer system and all the introductory games."

The audience heard this and applauded with more enthusiasm. For a second time, Cray held out a hand. Alex hesitated for a moment, then took it. In a way, he couldn't blame Cray. The man couldn't allow the Gameslayer to be turned into a laughing stock on its first outing. He had an investment to protect. But Alex still didn't like what had happened.

"Good to meet you, Alex. Well done..."

He climbed down from the stage. There were more demonstrations and more talks by members of Cray's staff. Then lunch was served. But Alex didn't eat. He had seen enough. He left the Pleasure Dome and crossed over the water, walking back through the park and all the way down to the King's Road.

Jack was waiting for him when he got home.

"So how did it go?" she asked.

Alex told her.

"What a cheater!" Jack scowled. "Mind you, Alex. A lot of rich men are bad losers and Cray is very rich indeed. Do you really think this proves anything?"

"I don't know, Jack." Alex was confused. He had to remind himself: a great chunk of the Gameslayer profits was going to charity. A huge amount. And he still had no proof. A few words on a phone. Was it enough to tie Cray in with what had happened in

Saint-Pierre? "Maybe we should go to Paris," he said. "That was where this all began. There was a meeting. Edward Pleasure was there. He was working with a photographer. Sabina told me his name. Marc Antonio."

"With a name like that, he should be easy enough to track down," Jack said. "And I love Paris."

"It still might be a waste of time." Alex sighed. "I didn't like Damian Cray. But now that I've met him..." His voice trailed off. "He's an entertainer. He makes computer games. He didn't look like the sort of man who'd want to hurt anyone."

"It's your call, Alex."

Alex shook his head. "I don't know, Jack. I just don't know..."

The launch of the Gameslayer was on the news that night. According to the reports, the entire industry had been knocked out by the graphic quality and the processing power of the new system. The part that Alex had played in the demonstration wasn't mentioned. However, something else was.

An event had taken place that had cast a cloud over what would otherwise have been a perfect day. It seemed that someone had died. A picture flashed up onto the screen, a woman's face, and Alex recognized her at once. It was the schoolteacherly woman who had put Cray on the spot, asking him awkward questions about violence. A policeman explained that she had been run over by a car as she left Hyde Park. The driver hadn't stopped.

The following morning Alex and Jack went to Waterloo and bought two tickets for Eurostar.

By lunchtime they were in Paris.

RUE BRITANNIA

"Do you realize, Alex," Jack said, "Picasso sat exactly where we're sitting now. And Chagall. And Salvador Dalí..."

"At this very table?"

"At this very café. All the big artists came here."

"What are you trying to say, Jack?"

"Well, I was just wondering if you'd like to forget this whole adventure thing and come with me to the Picasso Museum. Paris is such a fun place. And I've always found looking at pictures a lot more enjoyable than getting shot."

"Nobody's shooting at us."

"Yet."

A day had passed since they had arrived in Paris and booked into a little hotel that Jack knew, opposite Notre-Dame. Jack knew the city well. She had once spent a year at the Sorbonne, studying art. But for the death of Ian Rider and her involvement with Alex, she might well have gone to live there.

She had been right about one thing. Finding out where Marc Antonio lived had been easy enough. She had only telephoned three agencies before she found the one that represented the photographer, although it had taken all her charm – and rusty French – to cajole his telephone number out of the girl on the switchboard. Getting to meet him, however, was proving more difficult.

She had rung the number a dozen times during the course of the morning before it was answered. It was a man's voice. No, he wasn't Marc Antonio. Yes, this was Marc Antonio's house but he had no idea where he was. The voice was full of suspicion. Alex had been listening, sharing the receiver with Jack. In the end he took over.

"Listen," he said. His French was almost as good as Jack's, but then he had started learning when he was three years old. "My name is Alex Rider. I'm a friend of Edward Pleasure. He's an English journalist—"

"I know who he is."

"Do you know what happened to him?"

A pause. "Go on..."

"I have to speak to Marc Antonio. I have some important information." Alex considered for a moment. Should he tell this man what he knew? "It's about Damian Cray," he said.

The name seemed to have an effect. There was another pause, longer this time. Then...

"Come to la Palette. It's a café on the rue de Seine. I will meet you there at one o'clock."

There was a click as the man hung up.

It was now ten past one. La Palette was a small, bustling café on the corner of a square, surrounded by art galleries. Waiters with long white aprons were sweeping in and out, carrying trays laden with drinks high above their heads. The place was packed but Alex and Jack had managed to get a table right on the edge, where they would be most conspicuous. Jack was drinking a glass of beer; Alex had a bright red fruit juice – a *sirop de grenadine* – with ice. It was his favourite drink when he was in France.

He was beginning to wonder if the man he had spoken to on the telephone was going to show up. Or could he be here already? How were they going to find each other in this crowd? Then he noticed a motorcyclist sitting on a beaten-up Piaggio 125cc motorbike on the other side of the street; he was a young man in a leather jacket with black curly hair and stubble on his cheeks. He had pulled in a few minutes before but hadn't dismounted, as if he was waiting for someone. Alex met his eye; there was a flash of contact. The young man looked puzzled but then he got off his bike and came over, moving warily as if afraid of a trap.

"You are Alex Rider?" he asked. He spoke English with an attractive accent, like an actor in a film.

"Yes."

"I wasn't expecting a child."

"What difference does it make?" Jack demanded, coming to Alex's defence. "Are you Marc Antonio?" she asked.

"No. My name is Robert Guppy."

"Do you know where he is?"

"He asked me to take you to him." Guppy glanced back at the Piaggio. "But I have only room for one."

"Well, you can forget it. I'm not letting Alex go on his own."

"It's all right, Jack," Alex cut in. He smiled at her. "It looks like you get to visit the Picasso Museum after all."

Jack sighed. Then she nodded. "All right," she said. "But take care."

* * *

Robert Guppy drove through Paris like someone who knew the city well – or who wanted to die in it. He swerved in and out of the traffic, ignored red lights and spun across intersections with the blare of car horns echoing all around. Alex found himself clinging on for dear life. He had no idea where they were going but realized there was a reason for Guppy's dangerous driving. He was making sure they weren't being followed.

They slowed down on the other side of the Seine, on the edge of the Marais, close to the Forum des Halles. Alex recognized the area. The last time he had been here, he had called himself Alex Friend and had been accompanying the hideous Mrs Stellenbosch on the way to the Point Blanc Academy. Now they slowed down and stopped in a street of typically Parisian houses – six storeys high with solid-looking doorways and tall frosted windows. Alex noticed a street sign: rue Britannia. The street went nowhere and half the buildings looked empty and dilapidated. Indeed, the ones at the far end were shored up by scaffolding and surrounded by wheelbarrows and cement mixers, with a plastic chute for debris. But there were no workmen in sight.

Guppy got off the bike. He gestured at one of the doors. "This way," he said. He glanced up and down the street one last time, then led Alex in.

The door led to an inner courtyard with old furniture and a tangle of rusting bicycles in one corner. Alex followed Guppy up a short flight of steps and through another doorway. He found himself in a large, high-ceilinged room with whitewashed walls, windows on both sides and a dark wood floor. It was a photographer's studio. There were screens, complicated lamps on metal legs and silver umbrellas. But someone was also living here. To one side was a kitchen area with a pile of tins and dirty plates.

Robert Guppy closed the door and a man appeared from behind one of the screens. He was barefoot, wearing a string vest and shapeless jeans. Alex guessed he must be about fifty. He was thin, unshaven, with a tangle of hair that was black mixed with silver. Strangely, he only had one eye; the other was behind a patch. A one-eyed photographer? Alex couldn't see why not.

The man glanced at him curiously, then spoke to his friend.

"C'est lui qui a téléphoné?"

"Oui..."

"Are you Marc Antonio?" Alex asked.

"Yes. You say you are a friend of Edward Pleasure. I didn't know Edward hung out with kids."

"I know his daughter. I was staying with him in France when..." Alex hesitated. "You know what happened to him?"

"Of course I know what happened to him. Why do you think I am hiding here?" He gazed at Alex quizzically, his one good eye slowly evaluating him. "You said on the telephone that you could tell me something about Damian Cray. Do you know him?"

"I met him two days ago. In London..."

"Cray is no longer in London." It was Robert Guppy who spoke, leaning against the door. "He has a software plant just outside Amsterdam. In Sloterdijk. He arrived there this morning."

"How do you know?"

"We're keeping a close eye on Mr Cray."

Alex turned to Marc Antonio. "You have to tell me what you and Edward Pleasure found out about him," he said. "What story were you working on? What was the secret meeting he had here?"

The photographer thought for a moment, then smiled crookedly, showing nicotine-stained teeth. "Alex Rider," he muttered, "you're a strange kid. You say you have information to give me, but you come here and you ask only questions. You have a nerve. But I like that." He took out a cigarette – a Gauloise – and screwed it into his mouth. He lit it and blew blue smoke into the air. "All right. It is against my better judgement. But I will tell you what I know."

There were two bar stools next to the kitchen. He perched on one and invited Alex to do the same. Robert Guppy stayed by the door.

"The story that Ed was working on had nothing to do with Damian Cray," he began. "At least, not to start with. Ed was never interested in the entertainment business. No. He was working on something much more important ... a story about the NSA. You know what that is? It's the National Security Agency of America. It's an organization involved in counter-terrorism, espionage and the protection of information. Most of its work is top secret. Code makers. Code breakers. Spies...

"Ed became interested in a man called Charlie Roper, an extremely high-ranking officer in the NSA. He had information – I don't know how he got it – that this man, Roper, might have turned traitor. He was heavily in debt. An addict..."

"Drugs?" Alex asked.

Marc Antonio shook his head. "Gambling. It can be just as destructive. Ed heard that Roper was here in Paris and believed he had come to sell secrets – either to the Chinese or, more likely, the North Koreans. He met me just over a week ago. We'd worked together often, he and I. He got the stories; I got the pictures. We were a team. More than that – we were friends." Marc Antonio shrugged. "Anyway, we found out where Roper was staying and we followed him from his hotel. We had no idea who he was meeting, and if you had told me, I would never have believed it."

He paused and drew on his Gauloise. The tip glowed red. Smoke trickled up in front of his good eye.

"Roper went for lunch at a restaurant called la Tour d'Argent. It is one of the most expensive restaurants in Paris. And it was Damian

Cray who was paying the bill. We saw the two of them together. The restaurant is high up but it has wide glass windows with views of Paris. I took photographs of them with a telescopic lens. Cray gave Roper an envelope. I think it contained money, and, if so, it was a lot of money because the envelope was very thick."

"Wait a minute," Alex interrupted. "What would a pop singer want with someone from the NSA?"

"That is exactly what Ed wanted to know," the photographer replied. "He began to ask questions. He must have asked too many. Because the next thing I heard, someone had tried to kill him in Saint-Pierre and that same day they came for me. In my case the bomb was in my car. If I had turned the ignition, I wouldn't be speaking to you now."

"Why didn't you?"

"I am a careful man. I noticed a wire." He stubbed out the cigarette. "Someone also broke into my apartment. Much of my equipment was stolen, including my camera and all the photographs I had taken at la Tour d'Argent. It was no coincidence."

He paused.

"But why am I telling you all this, Alex Rider? Now it is your turn to tell me what you know."

"I was on holiday in Saint-Pierre—" Alex began.

That was as far as he got.

A car had stopped somewhere outside the building. Alex hadn't heard it approach. He only became aware of it when its engine stopped. Robert Guppy took a step forward, raising a hand. Marc Antonio's head snapped round. There was a moment's silence – and Alex knew that it was the wrong sort of silence. It was empty. Final.

And then there was an explosion of bullets and the windows shattered, one after another, the glass falling in great slabs to the floor. Robert Guppy was killed instantly, thrown off his feet with a series of red holes stitched across his chest. A light bulb was hit and exploded; chunks of plaster crumbled off the wall. The air rushed in, and with it came the sound of men shouting and footsteps stamping across the courtyard.

Marc Antonio was the first to recover. Sitting by the kitchen, he had been out of the line of fire and hadn't been hit. Alex too was shocked but uninjured.

"This way!" the photographer shouted and propelled Alex across the room even as the door burst open with a crash of splintering wood. Alex just had time to glimpse a man dressed in black with a machine gun cradled in his arms. Then he was pulled behind one of the screens he had noticed earlier. There was another exit here – not a door but a jagged hole in the wall. Marc Antonio had already climbed through. Alex followed.

"Up!" Marc Antonio pushed Alex ahead of him. "It's the only way!"

There was a wooden staircase, seemingly unused, old and covered in plaster dust. Alex started to climb ... three floors, four, with Marc Antonio just behind him. There was a single door on each floor but Marc Antonio urged him on. He could hear the man with the machine gun. He had been joined by someone else. The two killers were following them up.

He arrived at the top. Another door barred his way. He reached out and turned the handle and at that moment there was another burst of gunfire and Marc Antonio grunted and curved away, falling backwards. Alex knew he was dead. Mercifully, the door had opened in front of him. He tumbled through, expecting at any moment to feel the rake of bullets across his shoulders. But the photographer had saved him, falling between Alex and his pursuers. Alex had made it onto the roof of the building. He lashed out with his heel, slamming the door shut behind him.

He found himself in a landscape of skylights and chimney stacks, water tanks and TV aerials. The roofs ran the full length of the rue Britannia, with low walls and thick pipes dividing the different houses. What had Marc Antonio intended, coming up here? He was six floors above street level. Was there a fire escape? A staircase leading down?

Alex had no time to find out. The door flew open and the two men came through it, moving more slowly now, knowing he was trapped. Somewhere deep inside Alex a voice whispered – why couldn't they leave him alone? They had come for Marc Antonio, not for him. He was nothing to do with this. But he knew they would have their orders. Kill the photographer and anyone associated with him. It didn't matter who Alex was. He was just part of the package.

And then he remembered something he had seen when he entered the rue Britannia, and suddenly he was running, without even being sure that he was going in the right direction. He heard the clatter of machine-gun fire and black tiles disintegrated centimetres behind his feet. Another burst. He felt a spray of bullets passing close to him and part of a chimney stack shattered, showering him with dust. He jumped over a low partition. The edge of the roof was getting closer. The men behind him paused, thinking he had nowhere to go. Alex kept running. He reached the edge and launched himself into the air.

To the men with the guns it must have seemed that he had jumped to a certain death on the pavement six floors below. But Alex had seen building works: scaffolding, cement mixers – and an orange pipe designed to carry builders' debris from the different floors down to the street.

The pipe actually consisted of a series of buckets, each one bottomless, interlocking like a flume at a swimming pool. Alex couldn't judge his leap – but he was lucky. For a second or two he fell, arms and legs sprawling. Then he saw the entrance to the pipe and managed to steer himself towards it. First his outstretched legs, then his hips and shoulders, entered the tube perfectly. The tunnel was filled with cement dust and he was blinded. He could just make out the orange walls flashing past. The back of his head, his thighs and shoulders were battered mercilessly. He couldn't breathe and realized with a sick dread that if the exit was blocked he would break every bone in his body.

The tube was shaped like a stretched-out J. As Alex reached the bottom, he felt himself slowing down. Suddenly he was spat back out into daylight. There was a mound of sand next to one of the cement mixers and he thudded into it. All the breath was knocked out of him. Sand and cement filled his mouth. But he was alive.

Painfully he got to his feet and looked up. The two men were still on the roof, far above him. They had decided not to attempt his stunt. The orange tube had been just wide enough to take him; they would have got jammed before they were halfway. Alex looked up the street. There was a car parked outside the entrance to Marc Antonio's studio. But there was nobody in sight.

He spat and dragged the back of his hand across his lips; then he limped quickly away. Marc Antonio was dead, but he had given Alex another piece of the puzzle. And Alex knew where he had to go next. Sloterdijk. A software plant outside Amsterdam. Just a few hours on a train from Paris.

He reached the end of the rue Britannia and turned the corner, moving faster all the time. He was bruised, filthy and lucky to be alive. He just wondered how he was going to explain all this to Jack.

BLOOD MONEY

Alex lay on his stomach, watching the guards as they examined the waiting car. He was holding a pair of Bausch & Lomb prism system binoculars with 30x magnification, and although he was more than a hundred metres away from the main gate, he could see everything clearly ... right down to the car's number plate and the driver's moustache.

He had been here for more than an hour, lying motionless in front of a bank of pine trees, hidden from sight by a row of shrubs. He was wearing grey jeans, a dark T-shirt and a khaki jacket, which he had picked up in the same army supplies shop that had provided the binoculars. The weather had turned yet again, bringing with it an afternoon of constant drizzle, and Alex was soaked through. He wished now that he had brought the thermos of hot chocolate Jack had offered him. At the time, he'd thought she was treating him like a child – but even the SAS know the importance of keeping warm. They had taught him as much when he was training with them.

Jack had come with him to Amsterdam and once again it had been she who had checked them into a hotel, this time on the Herengracht, one of the three main canals. She was there now, waiting in their room. Of course, she had wanted to come with him. After what had happened in Paris, she was more worried about him than ever. But Alex had persuaded her that two people would have twice as much chance of being spotted as one, and her bright red hair would hardly help. Reluctantly she had agreed.

"Just make sure you get back to the hotel before dark," she said. "And if you pass a tulip shop, maybe you could bring me a bunch."

He smiled, remembering her words. He shifted his weight, feeling the damp grass beneath his elbows. He wondered what exactly he had learnt in the past hour.

He was in the middle of a strange industrial area on the outskirts of Amsterdam. Sloterdijk contained a sprawl of factories, warehouses and processing plants. Most of the compounds were low-rise, separated from each other by wide stretches of tarmac, but there were also clumps of trees and grassland as if someone had tried – and failed – to cheer the place up. Three windmills rose up behind the headquarters of Cray's technological empire. But they weren't the traditional Dutch models, the sort that would appear on picture postcards. These were modern, towering pillars of grey concrete with triple blades endlessly slicing the air. They were huge and menacing, like invaders from another planet.

The compound itself reminded Alex of an army barracks ... or maybe a prison. It was surrounded by a double fence, the outer one topped with razor wire. There were guard towers at fifty-metre intervals and guards on patrol all around the perimeter. In Holland, a country where the police carry guns, Alex wasn't surprised that the guards were armed. Inside, he could make out eight or nine buildings, low and rectangular, white-bricked with hi-tech plastic roofs. Various people were moving around, some of them transported in electric cars. Alex could hear the whine of the engines, like milk floats. The compound had its own communications centre, with five huge satellite dishes mounted outside. Otherwise, it seemed to consist of laboratories, offices and living quarters. One building stood out in the middle of it all: a glass and steel cube, aggressively modern in design. This might be the main headquarters, Alex thought. Perhaps he would find Damian Cray inside.

But how was he to get in? He had been studying the entrance for the last hour.

A single road led up to the gate, with a traffic light at each end. It was a complicated process. When a car or a truck arrived, it stopped at the bottom of the road and waited. Only when the first traffic light changed was it allowed to continue forward to the glass and brick guardhouse next to the gate. At this point, a uniformed man appeared and took the driver's ID, presumably to check it on a computer. Two more men examined the vehicle, checking that there were no passengers. And that wasn't all. There was a security camera mounted high up on the fence and Alex had noticed a length of what looked like toughened glass built into the road. When the vehicles stopped they were right on top of it, and Alex guessed that there must be a second camera underneath. There was no way he could sneak into the compound. Cray Software Technology had left nothing to chance.

Several trucks had entered the compound while he had been watching. Alex had recognized the black-clothed figure of Omni painted – life-sized – on the sides as part of the Gameslayer logo. He wondered if it might be possible to sneak inside one of the trucks, perhaps as it was waiting at the first set of lights. But the road was too open. At night it would be floodlit. Anyway, the doors would almost certainly be locked.

He couldn't climb the fences. The razor wire would see to that. He doubted he could tunnel his way in. Could he somehow disguise himself and mingle with the evening shift? No. For once his size and age were against him. Maybe Jack would have been able to attempt it, pretending to be a replacement cleaner or a technician. But there was no way he would be able to talk his way past the guards, particularly without speaking a word of Dutch. Security was too tight.

And then Alex saw it. Right in front of his eyes.

Another truck had stopped and the driver was being questioned while the cabin was searched. Could he do it? He remembered the bicycle that was chained to a lamppost just a couple of hundred metres down the road. Before he had left England he had gone through the manual that had come with it and had been amazed how many gadgets Smithers had been able to conceal in and around such an ordinary object. Even the bicycle clips were magnetic! Alex watched the gate slide open and the truck pass through.

Yes. It would work. He would have to wait until it was dark – but it was the last thing anyone would expect. Despite everything, Alex suddenly found himself smiling.

He just hoped he could find a fancy-dress shop in Amsterdam.

By nine o'clock it was dark but the searchlights around the compound had been activated long before, turning the area into a dazzling collision of black and white. The gates, the razor wire, the guards with their guns ... all could be seen a mile away. But now they were throwing vivid shadows, pools of darkness that might offer a hiding place to anyone brave enough to get close.

A single truck was approaching the main gate. The driver was Dutch and had driven up from the port of Rotterdam. He had no idea what he was carrying and he didn't care. From the first day he had started working for Cray Software Technology, he had known that it was better not to ask questions. The first of the two traffic lights was red and he slowed down, then came to a halt. There were no other vehicles in sight and he was annoyed to be kept waiting, but it was better not to complain. There was a sudden knocking sound and he glanced out of the window, looking in the side mirror. Was someone trying to get his attention? But there was no one there and a moment later the light changed, so he threw the gearstick into first and moved on again.

As usual he drove onto the glass panel and wound down his window. There was a guard standing outside and he passed across his ID, a plastic card with his photograph, name and employee number. The driver knew that other guards would inspect his truck. He sometimes wondered why they were so sensitive about security. After all, they were only making computer games. But he had heard about industrial sabotage ... companies stealing secrets from each other. He supposed it made sense.

Two guards were walking round the truck even as the driver sat there, thinking his private thoughts. A third was examining the pictures being transmitted by the camera underneath it. The truck had recently been cleaned. The word GAMESLAYER stood out on the side, with the Omni figure crouching next to it. One of the guards reached out and tried to open the door at the back. It was, as it should have been, locked. Meanwhile the other guard peered in through the front cabin window. But it was obvious that the driver was alone.

The security operation was smooth and well practised. The cameras had shown nobody hiding underneath the truck or on the roof. The rear door was locked. The driver had been cleared. One of the guards gave a signal and the gate opened electronically, sliding sideways to let the truck in. The driver knew where to go without being told. After about fifty metres he branched off the entrance road and followed a narrower track that brought him to the unloading bay. There were about a dozen other vehicles parked here, with warehouses on both sides. The driver turned off the engine, got out and locked the door. He had paperwork to deal with. He would hand over the keys and receive a stamped docket with his time of arrival. They would unload the vehicle the following day.

The driver left. Nothing moved. There was nobody else in the area.

But if anyone had walked past, they might have seen a remarkable thing. On the side of the truck, the black-clothed figure of Omni turned its head. At least, that was what it would have looked like. But if that person had looked more closely, they would have realized that there were two figures on the truck. One was painted; the other was a real person, clinging impossibly to the metal panelling in exactly the same position as the picture underneath.

Alex Rider dropped silently to the ground. The muscles in his arms and legs were screaming and he wondered how much longer he would have been able to hold on. Smithers had supplied four powerful magnetic clips with the bike and these were what Alex had used to keep himself in place: two for his hands, two for his feet. He quickly pulled off the black ninja suit he had bought that afternoon in Amsterdam, rolled it up and stuffed it into a bin. He had been in plain sight of the guards as the truck drove through the gate. But the guards hadn't looked too closely. They had expected to see a figure next to the Gameslayer logo and that was just what they had seen. For once they had been wrong to believe their eyes.

Alex took stock of his surroundings. He might be inside the compound, but his luck wouldn't last for ever. He didn't doubt that there would be other guards on patrol, and other cameras too. What exactly was he looking for? The strange thing was, he had no real idea. But something told him that if Damian Cray went in for all this security, then it must be because he had something to hide. Of course, it was still possible that Alex was wrong, that Cray was innocent. It was a comforting thought.

He made his way through the compound, heading for the great cube that stood at its heart. He heard a whining sound and ducked into the shadows next to a wall as an electronic car sped past with three passengers and a woman in blue overalls at the wheel. He became aware of activity somewhere ahead of him. An open area, brilliantly lit, stretched out behind one of the warehouses. A voice suddenly echoed in the air, amplified by a speaker system. It was a man speaking – but in Dutch. Alex couldn't understand a word. Moving more quickly, he hurried on, determined to see what was happening.

He found a narrow alleyway between two of the buildings and ran the full length, grateful for the shadows of the walls. At the end he came to a fire escape, a metal staircase spiralling upwards, and threw himself breathlessly behind it. He could hide here. But, looking between the steps, he had a clear view of what was happening ahead.

There was a square of black tarmac with glass and steel office blocks on all sides. The largest of these was the cube that Alex had seen from outside. Damian Cray was standing in front of it, talking animatedly to a man in a white coat, with three more men just behind him. Even from a distance Cray was unmistakable. He was the smallest person there, dressed in yet another designer suit. He had come out to watch some sort of demonstration. About half a dozen guards stood waiting, dotted around the square. Harsh white lights were being beamed down from two metal towers that Alex hadn't noticed before.

Watching through the fire escape, Alex saw that there was a cargo plane in the middle of the square. It took him a moment or two to accept what he was seeing. There was no way the plane could have landed there. The square was only just wide enough to contain it, and there wasn't a runway inside the compound, as far as he knew. It must have been carried here on a truck, possibly assembled on site. But what was it doing here? The plane was an old-fashioned one. It had propellers rather than jets, and wings high up, almost sitting on top of the main body. The words MILLENNIUM AIR were painted in red along the fuselage and on the tail.

Cray looked at his watch. A minute later the loudspeaker crackled again with another announcement in Dutch. Everyone stopped talking and gazed at the plane. Alex stared. A fire had started inside the main cabin. He could see the flames flickering behind the windows. Grey smoke began to seep out of the fuselage and suddenly one of the propellers caught alight. The fire seemed to spread out of control in seconds, consuming the engine and then spreading across the wing. Alex waited for someone to do something. If there was any fuel in the plane, it would surely explode at any moment. But nobody moved. Cray seemed to nod.

It was over as quickly as it had begun. The man in the white coat spoke into a radio transmitter and the fire went out. It was extinguished so quickly that if Alex hadn't seen it with his own eyes, he wouldn't have believed it had been there in the first place. They didn't use water or foam. There were no scorch marks and no smoke.

One moment the plane had been burning; the next it wasn't. It was as simple as that.

Cray and the three men with him spent a few seconds talking, before turning and strolling back into the cube. The guards in the square marched off. The plane was left where it was. Alex wondered what on earth he had got himself into. This had nothing to do with computer games. It made absolutely no sense at all.

But at least he had spotted Damian Cray.

Alex waited until the guards had gone, then twisted out from behind the fire escape. He made his way as quickly as he could around the square, keeping in the shadows. Cray had made a mistake. Breaking into the compound was virtually impossible, so he had worried less about security on the inside. Alex hadn't spotted any cameras, and the guards in the towers were looking out rather than in. For the moment he was safe.

He followed Cray into the building and found himself crossing the white marble floor of what was nothing more than a huge glass box. Above him he could see the night sky with the three windmills looming in the distance. The building contained nothing. But there was a single round hole in one corner of the floor and a staircase leading down.

Alex heard voices.

He crept down the stairs, which led directly into a large underground room. Crouching on the bottom step, concealed behind wide steel banisters, he watched.

The room was open-plan, with a white marble floor and corridors leading off in several directions. The architecture made him think of a vault in an ultra-modern bank. But the gorgeous rugs, the fireplace, the Italian furniture and the dazzling white Bechstein grand piano could have come out of a palace. To one side was a curving desk with a bank of telephones and computer screens. All the lighting was at floor level, giving the room a bizarre, unsettling atmosphere, with all the shadows going the wrong way. A portrait of Damian Cray holding a white poodle covered an entire wall.

The man himself was sitting on a sofa, sipping a bright yellow drink. He had a cherry on a cocktail stick and Alex watched him pick it off with his perfect white teeth and slowly eat it. The three men from the square were with him, and Alex knew at once that he had been right all along – that Cray was indeed at the centre of the web.

One of the men was Yassen Gregorovich. Wearing jeans and a polo neck, he was sitting on the piano stool, his legs crossed. The second man stood near him, leaning against the piano. He was older, with silver hair and a sagging, pockmarked face. He was wearing a blue blazer with a striped tie that made him look like a minor official in a bank or a cricket club. He had large spectacles that had sunk into his face as if it were damp clay. He looked nervous, the eyes behind the glass circles blinking frequently. The third man was darkly handsome, in his late forties, with black hair, grey eyes and a jawline that was square and serious. He was casually dressed in a leather jacket and an open-necked shirt and seemed to be enjoying himself.

Cray was talking to him. "I'm very grateful to you, Mr Roper. Thanks to you, Eagle Strike can now proceed on schedule."

Roper! This was the man Cray had met in Paris. Alex had a sense that everything had come full circle. He strained to hear what the two men were saying.

"Hey – please. Call me Charlie." The man spoke with an American accent. "And there's no need to thank me, Damian. I've enjoyed doing business with you."

"I do have a few questions," Cray murmured, and Alex saw him pick up an object from a coffee table next to the sofa. It was a metallic capsule, about the same shape and size as a mobile phone.

"As I understand it, the gold codes change daily. Presumably the flash drive is currently programmed with today's codes. But if Eagle Strike were to take place two days from now..."

"Just plug it in. The flash drive will update itself," Roper explained. He had an easy, lazy smile. "That's the beauty of it. First it will burrow through the security systems. Then it will pick up the new codes ... like taking candy from a baby. The moment you have the codes, you transmit them back through Milstar and you're set. The only problem you have, like I told you, is the little matter of the finger on the button."

"Well, we've already solved that," Cray said.

"Then I might as well move out of here."

"Just give me a couple more minutes of your valuable time, Mr Roper ... Charlie..." Cray said. He sipped his cocktail, licked his lips and set the glass down. "How can I be sure that the flash drive will actually work?"

"You have my word on it," Roper said. "And you're certainly paying me enough."

"Indeed so. Half a million dollars in advance. And two million dollars now. However..." Cray paused and pursed his lips. "I still have one small worry on my mind."

Alex's leg had gone to sleep as he crouched, watching the scene from the stairs. Slowly he straightened it out. He wished he understood more of what they were saying. He knew that a flash drive was a type of storage device used in computer technology. But who or what was Milstar? And what was Eagle Strike?

"What's the problem?" Roper asked casually.

"I'm afraid *you* are, Mr Roper." The green eyes in Cray's round, babyish face were suddenly hard. "You are not as reliable as I had hoped. When you came to Paris, you were followed."

"That's not true."

"An English journalist found out about your gambling habit. He and a photographer followed you to la Tour d'Argent." Cray held up a hand to stop Roper interrupting. "I have dealt with them both. But you have disappointed me, Mr Roper. I wonder if I can still trust you."

"Now you listen to me, Damian." Roper spoke angrily. "We had a deal. I worked here with your technical boys. I gave them the information they needed to load the flash drive, and that's my part of it over. How you're going to get to the VIP lounge and how you'll actually activate the system ... that's your business. But you owe me two million dollars, and this journalist – whoever he was – doesn't make any difference at all."

"Blood money," Cray said.

"What?"

"That's what they call money paid to traitors."

"I'm no traitor!" Roper growled. "I needed the money, that's all. I haven't betrayed my country. So quit talking like this, pay me what you owe me and let me walk out of here."

"Of course I'm going to pay you what I owe you." Cray smiled. "You'll have to forgive me, Charlie. I was just thinking aloud." He gestured, his hand falling limply back. The American glanced round and Alex saw that there was an alcove to one side of the room. It was shaped like a giant bottle, with a curved wall behind and a curving glass door in front. Inside was a table, and on the table a leather attaché-case.

"Your money is in there," Cray said.

"Thank you."

Neither Yassen Gregorovich nor the man with the spectacles had spoken throughout all this, but they watched intently as the American approached the alcove. There must have been some sort of sensor built into the door because it slid open automatically.

Roper went up to the table and opened the case. Alex heard the two locks click up.

Then Roper turned round. "I hope this isn't your idea of a joke," he said. "This is empty."

Cray smiled at him from the sofa. "Don't worry," he said. "I'll fill it." He reached out and pressed a button on the coffee table in front of him. There was a hiss and the door of the alcove slid shut.

"Hey!" Roper shouted.

Cray pressed the button a second time.

For an instant nothing happened. Alex realized he was no longer breathing. His heart was beating at twice its normal rate. Then something bright and silver dropped down from somewhere high up inside the closed-off room, landing inside the case. Roper reached in and held up a small coin. It was a quarter – a twenty-five cent piece.

"Cray! What are you playing at?" he demanded.

More coins began to fall into the case. Alex couldn't see exactly what was happening but he guessed that the room really was like a bottle, totally sealed apart from a hole somewhere above. The coins were falling through the hole, the trickle rapidly turning into a cascade. In seconds the attaché-case was full, and still the coins came, tumbling onto the pile, spreading out over the table and onto the floor.

Perhaps Charlie Roper had an inkling of what was about to happen. He forced his way through the shower of coins and pounded on the glass door. "Stop this!" he shouted. "Let me out of here!"

"But I haven't paid you all your money, Mr Roper," Cray replied. "I thought you said I owed you two million dollars."

Suddenly the cascade became a torrent. Thousands and thousands of coins poured into the room. Roper cried out, bending an arm over his head, trying to protect himself. Alex quickly worked out the mathematics. Two million dollars, twenty-five cents at a time. The payment was being made in just about the smallest of small change. How many coins would there be? Already they filled all the available floor space, rising up to the American's knees. The torrent intensified. Now the rush of coins was solid and Roper's screams were almost drowned out by the clatter of metal against metal. Alex wanted to look away but he found himself fixated, his eyes wide with horror.

He could barely see the man any more. The coins thundered down. Roper was trying to swat them away, as if they were a swarm of bees. His arms and hands were vaguely visible but his face and body had disappeared. He lashed out with a fist and Alex saw a smear of blood appear on the door – but the toughened glass wouldn't break. The coins oozed forward, filling every inch of space. They rose up higher and higher. Roper was invisible now, sealed into the glittering mass. If he was still screaming, nothing more could be heard.

And then, suddenly, it was over. The last coins fell. A grave of eight million quarters. Alex shuddered, trying to imagine what it must have been like to have been trapped inside. How had the American died? Had he been suffocated by the falling coins or crushed by their weight? Alex had no doubt that the man inside was dead. Blood money! Cray's sick joke couldn't have been more true.

Cray laughed.

"That was fun!" he said.

"Why did you kill him?" The man in the spectacles had spoken for the first time. He had a Dutch accent. His voice was trembling.

"Because he was careless, Henryk," Cray replied. "We can't make mistakes, not at this late stage. And it's not as if I broke any promises. I said I'd pay him two million dollars, and if you want to open the door and count it, two million dollars is exactly what you'll find."

"Don't open the door!" the man called Henryk gasped.

"No. I think it would be a bit messy." Cray smiled. "Well, we've taken care of Roper. We've got the flash drive. We're all set to go. So why don't we have another drink?"

Still crouching at the bottom of the stairs, Alex gritted his teeth, forcing himself not to panic. Every instinct told him to get up and run, but he knew he had to take care. What he had seen was almost beyond belief – but at least his mission was now clear. He had to get out of the compound, out of Sloterdijk, and back to England. Like it or not, he had to go back to MI6.

He knew now that he had been right all along and that Damian Cray was both mad and evil. All his posturing – his many charities and his speeches against violence – was precisely that; a facade. He was planning something that he called Eagle Strike, and whatever it was would take place in two days' time. It involved a security system and a VIP lounge. Was he going to break into an embassy? It didn't matter. Somehow he would make Alan Blunt and Mrs Jones believe him. There was a dead man called Charlie Roper. A connection with the National Security Agency of America. Surely Alex had enough information to persuade them to make an arrest.

But first he had to get out.

He turned just in time to see the figure looming above him. It was a guard, coming down the stairs. Alex started to react, but he was too late. The guard had seen him. He was carrying a gun. Slowly Alex raised his hands. The guard gestured and Alex stood up, rising above the stair rail. On the other side of the room, Damian Cray saw him. His face lit up with delight.

"Alex Rider!" he exclaimed. "I was hoping to see *you* again. What a lovely surprise! Come on over and have a drink – and let me tell you how you're going to die."

PAIN SYNTHESIS

"Yassen has told me all about you," Cray said. "Apparently you worked for MI6. I have to say, that's a very novel idea. Are you still working for them now? Did they send you after me?"

Alex said nothing.

"If you don't answer my questions, I may have to start thinking about doing nasty things to you. Or getting Yassen to do them. That's what I pay him for. Pins and needles ... that sort of thing."

"MI6 don't know anything," Yassen said.

He and Cray were alone in the room with Alex. The guard and the man called Henryk had gone. Alex was sitting on the sofa with a glass of chocolate milk that Cray had insisted on pouring for him. Cray was now perched on the piano stool. His legs were crossed and he seemed completely relaxed as he sipped another cocktail.

"There's no way the intelligence services could know anything about us," Yassen went on. "And if they did, they wouldn't have sent Alex."

"Then why was he at the Pleasure Dome? Why is he here?" Cray turned to Alex. "I don't suppose you've come all this way to get my autograph. As a matter of fact, Alex, I'm rather pleased to see you. I was planning to come and find you one day anyway. You completely spoilt the launch of my Gameslayer. Much too clever by half! I was very cross with you, and although I'm rather busy at the moment, I was going to arrange a little accident..."

"Like you did for that woman in Hyde Park?" Alex asked.

"She was a nuisance. She asked impertinent questions. I hate journalists, and I hate smart-arse kids too. As I say, I'm very glad you managed to find your way here. It makes my life a lot easier."

"You can't do anything to me," Alex said. "MI6 know I'm here. They know all about Eagle Strike. You may have the codes, but you'll never be able to use them. And if I don't report in this evening, this whole place will be surrounded before tomorrow and you'll be in jail..."

Cray glanced at Yassen. The Russian shook his head. "He's lying. He must have heard us talking from the stairs. He knows nothing."

Cray licked his lips. Alex realized that he was enjoying himself. He could see now just how crazy Cray was. The man didn't connect with the real world and Alex knew that whatever he was planning, it was going to be on a big scale – and probably lethal.

"It doesn't make any difference," Cray said. "Eagle Strike will have taken place in less than forty-eight hours from now. I agree with you, Yassen. This boy knows nothing. He's irrelevant. I can kill him and it won't make any difference at all."

"You don't have to kill him," Yassen said. Alex was surprised. The Russian had killed Ian Rider. He was Alex's worst enemy. But this was the second time Yassen had tried to protect him. "You can just lock him up until it's all over."

"You're right," Cray said. "I don't have to kill him. But I want to. It's something I want to do very much." He pushed himself off the piano stool and came over to Alex. "Do you remember I told you about pain synthesis?" he said. "In London. The demonstration... Pain synthesis allows game players to experience the hero's emotions – all his emotions, particularly those associated with pain and death. You may wonder how I programmed it into the software. The answer, my dear Alex, is by the use of volunteers such as yourself."

"I didn't volunteer," Alex muttered.

"Nor did the others. But they still helped me. Just as you will help me. And your reward will be an end to the pain. The comfort and the quiet of death..." Cray looked away. "You can take him," he said.

Two guards had come into the room. Alex hadn't heard them approach, but now they stepped out of the shadows and grabbed hold of him. He tried to fight back, but they were too strong for him. They pulled him off the sofa and away, down one of the passages leading from the room.

Alex managed to look back one last time. Cray had already forgotten him. He was holding the flash drive, admiring it. But Yassen was watching him and he looked worried. Then an automatic door shot down with a hiss of compressed air and Alex was dragged away, his feet sliding uselessly behind him, following the passageway to whatever it was that Damian Cray had arranged.

The cell was at the end of another underground corridor. The two guards threw Alex in, then waited as he turned round to face them. The one who had found him on the stairs spoke a few words with a heavy Dutch accent.

"The door closes and it stays closed. You find the way out. Or you starve."

That was it. The door slammed and Alex heard two bolts being drawn across. He heard the guards' footsteps fade into the distance. Suddenly everything was silent. He was on his own.

He looked around him. The cell was a bare metal box about five metres long and two metres wide with a single bunk, no water and no window. The door had closed flush to the wall. There was no crack round the side, not so much as a keyhole. He knew he had never been in worse trouble. Cray hadn't believed his story; he had barely even considered it. Whether Alex was with MI6 or not seemed to make no difference to him ... and the truth was that this time Alex really had got himself caught up in something without MI6 there to back him up. For once he had no gadgets to help him break out of the cell. He had brought the bicycle that Smithers had given him from London to Paris and then to Amsterdam. But right now it was parked outside Central Station in the city and would stay there until it was stolen or rusted away. Jack knew he had planned to break into the compound, but even if she did raise the alarm, how would anyone ever find him? Despair weighed down on him. He no longer had the strength to fight it.

And still he knew almost nothing. Why had Cray invested so much time and money in the game system he called Gameslayer? Why did he need the flash drive? What was the plane doing in the middle of the compound? Above all, what was Cray planning? Eagle Strike would take place in two days – but where, and what would it entail?

Alex forced himself to take control. He'd been locked up before. The important thing was to fight back – not to admit defeat. Cray had already made mistakes. Even speaking his own name on the phone when Alex called him from Saint-Pierre had been an error of judgement. He might have power, fame and enormous resources. He was certainly planning a huge operation. But he wasn't as clever as he thought. Alex could still beat him.

But how to begin? Cray had put him into this cell to experience what he called pain synthesis. Alex didn't like the sound of that. And what had the guard said? Find the way out – or starve. But there *was* no way out. Alex ran his hands across the walls. They were solid steel. He went over and examined the door a second time. Nothing. It was tightly sealed. He glanced at the ceiling, at the single bulb burning behind a thick pane of glass. That only left the bunk...

He found the trapdoor underneath, built into the wall. It was like a cat flap, just big enough to take a human body. Gingerly, wondering if it might be booby-trapped, Alex reached out and pushed it. The metal flap swung inwards. There was some sort of tunnel on the other side, but he couldn't see anything. If he crawled into it, he would be entering a narrow space with no light at all – and he couldn't even be sure that the tunnel actually went anywhere. Did he have the courage to go in?

There was no alternative. Alex examined the cell one last time, knelt down and pushed himself forward. The metal flap swung open in front of him, then travelled down his back as he crawled into the tunnel. He felt it hit the back of his heels and there was a soft click. What was that? He couldn't see anything. He lifted a hand and waved it in front of his face. It was as if it wasn't there. He reached out in front of him and felt a solid wall. God! He had walked – crawled rather – into a trap. This wasn't the way out after all.

He pushed himself back the way he had come, and that was when he discovered the flap was now locked. He kicked out with his feet but it wouldn't move. Panic, total and uncontrollable, overwhelmed him. He was buried alive, in total darkness, with no air. This was what Cray had meant by pain synthesis: a death too hideous to imagine.

Alex went mad.

Unable to control himself, he screamed out, his fists lashing against the walls of this metal coffin. He was suffocating.

His flailing hand hit a section of the wall and he felt it give way. There was a second flap! Gasping for air, he twisted round and into a second tunnel, as black and as chilling as the first. But at least there was some faint flicker of hope burning in his consciousness. There was a way through. If he could just keep a grip on himself, he might yet find his way back into the light.

The second tunnel was longer. Alex slithered forward, feeling the sheet metal under his hands. He forced himself to slow down. He was still completely blind. If there was a hole ahead of him, he would plunge into it before he knew what had happened. As he went, he tapped against the walls, searching for other passageways. His head knocked into something and he swore. The bad language helped him. It was good to direct his hatred against Damian Cray. And hearing his own voice reminded him he was still alive.

He had bumped into a ladder. He took hold of it with both hands and felt for the opening that must be above his shoulders. He was lying flat on his stomach, but slowly he manipulated himself round and began to climb up, feeling his way in case there was a ceiling overhead. His hand came into contact with something and he pushed. To his huge relief, light flooded in. He had opened some sort of trapdoor with a large, brightly lit room on the other side. Gratefully he climbed the last rungs and passed through.

The air was warm. Alex sucked it into his lungs, allowing his feelings of panic and claustrophobia to fade away. Then he looked up.

He was kneeling on a straw-covered floor in a room that was bathed in yellow light. Three of the walls seemed to have been built with huge blocks of stone. Blazing torches slanted in towards him, fixed to metal brackets. Gates at least ten metres high stood in front of him. They were made out of wood, with iron fastenings and a huge face carved into the surface. Some sort of Mexican god with saucer eyes and solid, blocklike teeth. Alex had seen the face before but it took him a few moments to work out where. And then he knew exactly what lay ahead of him. He knew how Cray had programmed pain synthesis into his game.

The gates had appeared at the start of Feathered Serpent, the game that Alex had played in the Pleasure Dome in Hyde Park. Then it had been a computerized image, projected onto a screen – and Alex had been represented by an avatar, a two-dimensional version of himself. But Cray had also built an actual physical version of the game. Alex reached out and touched one of the walls. Sure enough, they weren't really stone but some sort of toughened plastic. The whole thing was like one of those walk-throughs at Disneyland ... an ancient world reproduced with hi-tech modern construction. There had been a time when Alex wouldn't have believed it possible, but he knew with a sick certainty that once the gates opened, he would find himself in a perfect reconstruction of the game – and that meant he would be facing the same challenges. Only this time it would be for real: real flames, real acid, real spears and – if he made a mistake – real death.

Cray had told him that he had used other "volunteers". Presumably they had been filmed fighting their way through the various challenges; and all the time their emotions had been recorded and then somehow digitally transferred and programmed into the Gameslayer system. It was sick. Alex realized that the darkness of the underground passages hadn't even been part of the real challenge. That began now.

He didn't move. He needed time to think, to remember as much as he could about the game he had played at the Pleasure Dome. There had been five zones. First some sort of temple, with a crossbow and a sword concealed in the walls. Would Cray provide him with weapons in this reconstruction? He would have to wait and see. What came after the temple? There had been a pit with a flying creature: half butterfly, half dragon. After that Alex had run down a corridor – spears shooting out of the walls – and into a jungle, the home of the metallic snakes. Then there had been a mirror maze guarded by Aztec gods and finally a pool of fire, his exit to the next level.

A pool of fire. If that was reproduced here, it would kill him. Alex remembered what Cray had said. *The comfort and the quiet of death*. There was no way out of this madhouse. If he did manage to survive the five zones, he would be allowed to finish it by throwing himself into the flames.

Alex felt hatred well up inside him. He could actually taste it. Damian Cray was beyond evil.

What could he do? There would be no way back through the tunnels and Alex wasn't sure he had the nerve even to try. He had only one choice, and that was to continue. He had almost beaten the game once. That at least gave him a little hope. On the other hand, there was a world of difference between manipulating a controller and actually attempting the action himself. He couldn't move or react with the speed of an electronic figure. Nor would he be given extra lives. If he was killed once, he would stay dead.

He stood up. At once the gates swung silently open, and there ahead of him was the temple that he had last seen in the game. He wondered if his progress was being monitored. Could he at least rely on an element of surprise?

He walked through the gates. The temple was exactly how he remembered it from the screen at the Pleasure Dome: a vast space with stone walls covered in strange carvings and pillars, statues crouching at their base, stretching far above him. Even the stained-glass windows had been reproduced with images of UFOs hovering over fields of golden corn. And there too were the cameras, swivelling to follow him and, presumably, to record whatever progress he made. Organ music, modern rather than religious, throbbed all around him. Alex shivered, barely able to accept that this was really happening.

He walked further into the temple, every sense alert, waiting for an attack that he knew could come from any direction. He wished now that he had played Feathered Serpent more carefully. He had raced through the zones at such speed that he had probably missed half of the ambushes. His feet rang out on the silver floor. Ahead of him, rusting staircases that reminded him of a submarine or a submerged ship twisted upwards. He thought of trying one of them. But he hadn't gone that way when he was playing the game and preferred not to now. It was better to stick with what he knew.

The alcove that contained the crossbow was underneath a wooden pulpit, carved in the shape of a dragon. It was almost completely covered by what looked like green ivy – but Alex knew that the twisting vines carried an electrical charge. He could see the weapon resting against the stonework, and there was just enough of a gap. Was it worth the risk? Alex tensed himself, preparing to reach in, then threw himself full length on the floor. Half a second later and it would have been fatal. He had remembered the razor boomerang at the same instant that he had heard a whistling sound coming from nowhere. He had no time to prepare himself. He hit the ground so hard that the breath was driven out of him. There was a flash and a series of sparks. He felt a burning pain across his shoulders and knew that he hadn't been quite fast enough. The boomerang had sliced open his T-shirt, also cutting his skin. It had been a close thing. Any closer and he wouldn't even have made it into the second zone.

And silently the cameras watched. Everything was being recorded. One day it would be fed into Cray's software – presumably Feathered Serpent 2.

Alex sat up and tried to pull his torn shirt together. At least the boomerang had helped in one way. It had hit the ivy, cutting and short-circuiting the electric wires. Alex stretched an arm into the alcove and took out the crossbow. It was antique – wood and iron – but it seemed to be working. Even so, Cray had cheated him. There was an arrow in it, but it had no point. It was too blunt to damage anything.

He decided to take both the crossbow and the arrow with him anyway. He moved away from the alcove and over to the wall where he knew he would find the sword. It was about twenty metres above him but there were loose stones and handholds indicating a way up. Alex was about to start climbing but then he had second thoughts. He had already had one close escape. The wall would almost certainly be booby-trapped. He would be halfway up and a stone would come loose. If he fell, he would break a leg. Cray would enjoy that, watching him lie helpless on the silver floor until some other missile was fired into him to finish him off. And anyway, the sword would probably have no blade.

But thinking about it, Alex suddenly realized that he had the answer. He knew how to beat the simulated world that Cray had built.

Every computer game is a series of programmed events, with nothing random, nothing left to chance. When Alex had played the game in the Pleasure Dome, he had collected the crossbow and then used it to shoot the creature that had attacked him. In the same way, locked doors would have keys; poisons would have antidotes. No matter how much choice you might seem to have, you were always obeying a hidden set of rules.

But Alex had not been programmed. He was a human being and he could do what he wanted. It had cost him a torn shirt and a very narrow escape – but he had learnt his lesson. If he hadn't tried to get the crossbow, he wouldn't have made himself a target for the boomerang. Climbing up the wall to get the sword would put him in danger because he would be doing exactly what was expected.

To get out of the world that Cray had built for him, he had to do everything that *wasn't* expected.

In other words he had to cheat.

And he would start right now.

He went over to one of the blazing torches and tried to remove it from the wall. He wasn't surprised to find that the whole thing was bolted into place. Cray had thought of everything. But even if he controlled the holders, he couldn't control the flames themselves. Alex pulled off his shirt and wrapped it round the end of the wooden arrow. Then he set it on fire. He smiled to himself. Now he had a weapon that hadn't been programmed.

The exit door was at the far end of the temple. Alex was supposed to take a direct path to it. Instead, he went the long way round, staying close to the walls, avoiding any traps that might be lying in wait. Ahead of him he could see the second chamber – the rain-drenched pit with its pillars rising from the depths below and ending at floor level. He passed through the door and stopped on a narrow ledge; the tops of the pillars – barely bigger than soup plates – offered him a path of stepping stones across the void. Alex remembered the flying creature that had attacked him. He looked up. Yes, there it was, almost lost in the gloom: a nylon wire running from the opposite side to the door above his head. He thrust upwards with the burning arrow, holding the flame against the wire.

It worked. The wire caught fire and then snapped. Cray had built a robotic version of the creature that had attacked him in the game. Alex knew that it would have swooped down when he was halfway across, rushing into him and knocking him off his perch, causing him to plunge into whatever lay below. Now he watched with quiet satisfaction as the creature tumbled down from the ceiling and dangled in front of him, a jumble of metal and feathers that was more like a dead parrot than a mythical monster.

The way ahead was clear but the rain was still falling, splashing down from some hidden sprinkler system. The stepping stones would be slippery. Alex knew that his avatar would have been unable to remove its shoes for better grip. He quickly slipped off his trainers, tied them together and hung them round his neck. His socks went into his pocket. Then he jumped. The trick, he knew, was to do this quickly: not to stop, not to look down. He took a breath, then started. The rain blinded him. The tops of the pillars were only just big enough to contain his bare feet. On the very last one he lost his balance. But he didn't have to use his feet – he could move in a way that his avatar couldn't. He threw himself forward, stretching out his hands and allowing his own momentum to carry him towards safety. His chest hit the ground and he clung on, dragging his legs over the edge of the pit. He had made it to the other side.

A corridor ran off to the left, the walls close together and decorated with hideous Aztec faces. Alex remembered how his avatar had run through here, dodging between a hail of wooden spears. He glanced down and saw that there was what looked like a smoking stream in the floor.

Acid! What now?

He needed another weapon and he had an idea how to get one. He took out his socks, rolled them into a ball and threw them down the corridor. As he had hoped, the movement was enough to activate the sensors that controlled the hidden guns. Short wooden spears spat out of the lips of the Aztec gods at fantastic speed, striking the opposite walls. One of the spears broke in half. Alex picked it up and felt the needle-sharp point. It was exactly what he wanted. He tucked it into the belt of his trousers. He still had the crossbow; now he had a bolt that might fit it too.

The computer game had been programmed so that there was only one way forward. Alex had been able to dodge both the spears and the acid river easily enough when he was playing Feathered Serpent. But he knew he would be unable to do the same in this grotesque three-dimensional version. He would only have to take one false step and he would be finished. He could imagine splashing into the acid and then panicking. He would be driven straight into the path of the spears as he tried to reach the next zone. No. There had to be another way.

Alex forced himself to concentrate. Ignore the rules! He turned the three words over and over in his mind. Moving along the corridor wasn't an option. But how about up? He put on his shoes, then took a tentative step. The spears nearest the entrance had already been fired. He was safe so long as he didn't move too far down the corridor. He grabbed hold of the wall and, balancing the crossbow over his shoulder, began to climb. The Aztec heads made perfect footholds, and only when he was at the very top did he begin to make his way along, high above the floor and away from danger. One step at a time, he edged forward. He came to a camera mounted in the ceiling and, with a smile, wrenched out the wire. There was a lot of it and he decided to keep that too.

He reached the end of the corridor and climbed down into the fourth zone, the jungle. He was surprised to discover that the vegetation pressing in on him from all sides was real. He had expected plastic and paper. He could feel the heat in the air and the ground underfoot was soft and wet. What traps were waiting for him here? He remembered the robotic snakes that had barely managed to get close when he played the game, and searched warily for the tracks that would propel something similar his way.

There were no tracks. Alex took another step forward and stopped, paralysed by the horror of what he saw.

There was a snake, and, like the leaves and the creepers, it was real. It was as thick as a man's waist and at least five metres long, lying motionless in a patch of long grass. Its eyes were two black diamonds. For a brief second, Alex hoped it might be dead. But then its tongue flickered out and the whole body heaved, and he knew that he was facing a living thing – one that was beyond nightmares.

The snake had been encased in a fantastic body suit. Alex had no idea how long it could have survived wrapped up like this. As terrifying as the creature was, he still felt a spark of pity for it, seeing what had been done. The suit was made out of wire that had been twisted round and round the full length of the animal, with vicious spikes and razors welded on from the neck all the way to the tail. Looking past the tail, Alex could see dozens of lines cut into the soft ground. Whatever the snake touched, it sliced. It couldn't help itself. And it was slithering towards him.

He couldn't have moved if he had wanted to, but something told him that keeping still was the only chance he had. The snake had to be some sort of boa constrictor, part of the Boidae family. A useless piece of information he had picked up in biology class suddenly came back to him. The snake ate mainly birds and monkeys, finding its victims by smell, then coiling round and suffocating them. But Alex knew that if the snake attacked him, this wouldn't be how he would die. The razors and spikes would cut him to pieces.

And it was getting closer. Wave after wave of glinting silver rippled behind it as it dragged the razors along. Now it was just a metre away. Moving very slowly, Alex lowered the crossbow from his shoulder. He pulled the wire back to load it, then reached into the waistband of his trousers. The broken spear was still there. Trying not to give the snake any reason to attack him, Alex fixed the length of wood into the stock. He was lucky. The spear was exactly the right length.

He wasn't meant to have a weapon in this zone. That hadn't been part of the program. But despite everything Cray had thrown at him he still had the crossbow and now it was loaded.

Alex cried out. He couldn't help himself. The snake had suddenly jerked forward, dragging itself over his trainer. The razors cut into the soft material, only millimetres away from his foot. He instinctively kicked out. At once the snake reared back. Alex saw black flames ignite in its eyes. Its tongue flickered. It was about to launch itself at him. He brought the crossbow round and fired. There was nothing else he could do. The bolt entered the snake's mouth and continued out of the back of its head. Alex leapt back, avoiding the deadly convulsions of the creature's body. The snake thrashed and twisted, cutting the grass and the nearby bushes to shreds. Then it lay still. Alex knew that he had killed it, and he wasn't sorry. What had been done to the snake was revolting. He was glad he had put it out of its misery.

There was one more zone left – the mirror maze. Alex knew that there would be Aztec gods waiting for him. Probably guards in fancy dress. Even if he got past them, he would only find himself facing the pool of fire. But he'd had enough. To hell with Damian Cray. He looked up. He had disabled one of the security cameras and there weren't any others in view. He had found a blind spot in this insane playground. That suited him perfectly.

It was time to find his own way out.

THE TRUTH ABOUT ALEX

There are no gods crueller or more ferocious than those of the Aztecs. That was the reason why Damian Cray had chosen them to inhabit his computer game.

He had summoned three of them to patrol the mirror maze, the fifth and last zone in the huge arena he had built beneath the compound. Tlaloc, the god of rain, was half human, half alligator, with jagged teeth, clawlike hands and a thick scaly tail that dragged behind him. Xipe Totec, the lord of spring, had torn out his own eyes. They were still dangling in front of his gruesome, pain-distorted face. And Xolotl, bringer of fire, walked on feet that had been smashed and wrenched round to face backwards. Flames leapt out of his hands, reflected a hundred times in the mirrors and adding to the twisting clouds of smoke.

Of course, there was nothing supernatural about the three creatures waiting for Alex to appear. Beneath the grotesque masks, the plastic skin and make-up, they were nothing more than criminals, recently released from Bijlmer, the largest prison in the Netherlands. They now worked as guards for Cray Software Technology, but they had special duties too. This was one of them. The three men were armed with curved swords, javelins, steel claws and flame-throwers. They were looking forward to using them.

It was the one dressed as Xolotl who saw Alex first.

The camera in zone three had gone down, so there had been no way of knowing if Alex was on his way or if the snake had finished him. But suddenly there was a movement. The guard saw a figure lurch round a corner, naked to the waist. The boy was making no attempt to hide, and the guard saw why.

Alex Rider was soaked in blood. His entire chest was bright red. His mouth was opening and closing, but no sound came out. Then the guard saw the wooden spear sticking out of his chest. The boy had obviously tried to run down the corridor but hadn't quite made it. One of the spears had found its target.

Alex saw the guard and stopped. He dropped to his knees. One hand pointed limply at the spear, then fell. He looked upwards and tried to speak. More blood trickled out of his mouth. His eyes closed and he pitched to one side. He didn't move again.

The guard relaxed. The boy's death meant nothing to him. He reached into the pocket of his chain-mail shirt and took out a radio transmitter.

"It's over," he said, speaking in Dutch. "The boy's been killed by a spear."

Neon strips flickered on throughout the game zone. In the harsh white light the different zones seemed cruder, more like fairground attractions. The guards, too, looked ridiculous in their fancy dress. The dangling eyes were painted ping-pong balls. The alligator body was nothing more than a rubber suit. The backward-facing feet could have come out of a joke shop. The three of them formed a circle around Alex.

"He's still breathing," one of them said.

"Not for much longer." The second guard glanced at the point of the spear, covered in rapidly congealing blood.

"What shall we do with him?"

"Leave him here. It's not our job. Disposal can pick him up later."

They walked away. One of them stopped beside a wall, painted to look like crumbling stone, and pulled open a concealed panel to reveal a button. He pressed it and the wall slid open. There was a brightly lit corridor on the other side. The three men went off to change.

Alex opened his eyes.

The trick he had played was so old that he was almost ashamed. If it had been done on the stage, it wouldn't have fooled a six-year-old. But he supposed that circumstances were a little different here.

Left on his own in the miniature jungle, he had reclaimed the broken spear that he had used to kill the snake. He had tied it to his chest using the wire he had torn out of the security camera. Then he had covered himself with blood taken from the dead snake. That had been the worst part, but he'd had to make sure that the illusion would work. Steeling himself, he had scooped up some more of the blood and put it in his mouth. He could still taste it now and he was having to force himself not to swallow. But it had fooled the men completely. None of them had looked too closely. They had seen what they wanted to see.

Alex waited until he was certain he was alone, then sat up and untied the spear. He would just have to hope that the cameras had all been turned off when the game had ended. The exit was still open and Alex stole through, leaving the make-believe world behind him. He found himself in an ordinary corridor, stretching into the distance with tiled walls and plain wooden doors on either side. He knew that although the immediate danger was behind him, he could hardly afford to start relaxing yet. He was half naked and covered in blood. He was still trapped in the heart of the compound. And it could only be a matter of time before someone discovered that the body had disappeared and realized the trick that had been played.

He opened the first of the doors. It led into a storage cupboard. The second and third doors were locked, but halfway down the corridor he found a changing room with showers, lockers and a laundry basket. Alex knew that it would cost him precious minutes, but he had to get clean. He stripped and showered, then dried himself and got dressed again. Before he left the room he searched through the laundry basket and found a shirt to replace the one he had burnt. The shirt was dirty and two sizes too big, but he pulled it on gratefully.

Carefully he opened the door – and quickly closed it again as two men walked past, talking in Dutch. They seemed to be heading for the mirror maze, and Alex hoped they weren't part of the disposal team. If so, the alarm would be raised at any moment. He counted the seconds until they had gone, then crept out and hurried the other way.

He came to a staircase. He had no idea where it went, but he was certain he had to go up.

The stairs led to a circular area with several corridors leading off it. There were no windows. The only illumination came from industrial lights set at intervals in the ceiling. He looked at his watch. It was eleven-fifteen. Two and a quarter hours had passed since he had first broken into the compound; it felt much longer. He thought about Jack, waiting for him in the hotel in Amsterdam. She would be out of her mind with worry.

Everything was silent. Alex guessed that most of Cray's people would be asleep. He chose a corridor and followed it to another staircase. Again he went up, and found himself in a room that he knew. Cray's study. The room where he had seen the man called Charlie Roper die.

Alex was almost afraid to go in. But the room was deserted and, peering through the opening, he could see that the bottle-shaped chamber had been cleared, the money and the body taken away. It seemed strange to him that there should be no guard assigned to this room, at the very heart of Cray's network. But then again, why should there be? All the security was centred on the main gate. Alex was supposedly dead. Cray had nothing to fear.

Ahead of him was the staircase that he knew would lead up to the glass cube and out onto the square. But as tempted as he was to race over to it, Alex realized he would never have another opportunity like this. Somewhere in the back of his mind, he knew that even if he made it to MI6, he still had no real proof that Cray wasn't just the pop celebrity and businessman that everyone thought. Alan Blunt and Mrs Jones hadn't believed him the last time he'd seen them. They might not believe him again.

Ignoring his first instincts, Alex went over to the desk. There were about a dozen framed photographs on the surface, each and every one showing a picture of Damian Cray. Ignoring them, Alex turned his attention to the drawers. They were unlocked. The lower drawers contained dozens of different documents but most of them were nothing more than lists of figures and hardly looked promising. Then he came to the last drawer and let out a gasp of disbelief. The metallic capsule that Cray had been holding when he talked to the American was simply sitting there. Alex picked it up and weighed it in the palm of his hand. The flash drive. It contained computer codes. Its job was to break through some sort of security system. It had come with a price tag of two and a half million dollars. It had cost Roper his life.

And Alex had it! He wanted to examine it, but he could do that later. He slipped it into his trouser pocket and hurried over to the stairs.

Ten minutes later the alarms sounded throughout the compound. The two men that Alex had seen had indeed gone into the mirror maze to pick up the body and discovered that it wasn't there. They should have raised the alarm at once, but there had been a delay. The men had assumed that one of the other teams must have collected it and had gone to find them. It was only when they discovered the dead snake and the spear with the coil of wire that they put together what had taken place.

While this was happening, a van was driving out of the compound. Neither the tired guards at the gate nor the driver had noticed the figure lying flat, spreadeagled on the roof. But why should they? The van was leaving, not arriving. It didn't even stop in front of the security cameras. The guard merely checked the driver's ID and opened the gate. The alarm rang seconds after the van had passed through.

There was a system in place at Cray Software Technology. Nobody was allowed to enter or leave during a security alert. Every van was equipped with a two-way radio and the guard at the gate immediately signalled to the driver and told him to return. The driver stopped before he had even reached the traffic light and wearily obeyed. But it was already too late.

Alex slipped off the roof and dropped to the ground. Then he ran off into the night.

* * *

Damian Cray was back in his office, sitting on the sofa holding a glass of milk. He had been in bed when the alarm went off and now he was wearing a silver dressing gown, dark blue pyjamas and soft cotton slippers. Something bad had happened to his face. The life had drained out of it, leaving behind a cold, empty mask that could have been cut out of glass. A single vein throbbed above one of his glazed eyes.

Cray had just discovered that the flash drive had been taken from his desk. He had searched all the drawers, ripping them out, upturning them and scattering their contents across the floor. Then, with an inarticulate howl of rage, he had thrown himself onto the desktop, flailing about with his arms and sending telephones, files and photograph frames flying. He had smashed a paperweight into his computer screen, shattering the glass. And then he had sat down on the sofa and called for a glass of milk.

Yassen Gregorovich had watched all this without speaking. He too had been called from his room by the alarm bells, but, unlike Cray, he hadn't been asleep. Yassen never slept for more than four hours. The night was too valuable. He might go for a run or work out in the gym. He might listen to classical music. On this night he had been working with a tape recorder and a well-thumbed exercise book. He was teaching himself Japanese, one of the nine languages he had made it his business to learn.

Yassen had heard the alarms and known instinctively that Alex Rider had escaped. He had turned off the tape recorder. And he had smiled.

Now he waited for Cray to break the silence. It had been Yassen who had suggested quietly that Cray should look for the flash drive. He wondered if he would get the blame for the theft.

"He was meant to be dead!" Cray moaned. "They told me he was dead!" He glanced at Yassen, suddenly angry. "You knew he'd been in here."

"I suspected it," Yassen said.

"Why?"

Yassen considered. "Because he's Alex," he said simply.

"Then tell me about him!"

"There is only so much I can tell you." Yassen stared into the distance. His face gave nothing away. "The truth about Alex is that there is not a boy in the world like him," he began, speaking slowly and softly. "Consider for a moment. Tonight you tried to kill him – and not just simply with a bullet or a knife, but in a way that should have terrified him. He escaped and he found his way here. He must have seen the stairs. Any other boy – any man even – would have climbed them instantly. His only desire would have been to get out of here. But not Alex. He stopped; he searched. That is what makes him unique, and that is why he is so valuable to MI6."

"How did he find his way here?"

"I don't know. If you'd allowed me to question him before you sent him into that game of yours, I might have been able to find out."

"This is not my fault, Mr Gregorovich! You should have killed him in the South of France when you had the chance." Cray drank the milk and set the glass down. He had a white moustache on his upper lip. "Why didn't you?" he demanded.

"I tried..."

"That nonsense in the bullring! That was stupid. I think you knew he'd escape."

"I hoped he might," Yassen agreed. He was beginning to get bored with Cray. He didn't like being asked to explain himself, and when he spoke again it was almost as much for his own benefit as

Cray's. "I knew him..." he said.

"You mean ... before Saint-Pierre?"

"I met him once. But even then ... I knew him already. The moment I saw him, I knew who he was and what he was. The image of his father..." Yassen stopped himself. He had already said more than he had meant to. "He knows nothing of this," he muttered. "No one has ever told him the truth."

But Cray was no longer interested. "I can't do anything without the flash drive," he moaned, and suddenly there were tears brimming in his eyes. "It's all over! Eagle Strike! All the planning. Years and years of it. Millions of pounds. And it's all *your* fault!"

So there it was at last, the finger of blame.

For a few seconds, Yassen Gregorovich was seriously tempted to kill Damian Cray. It would be very quick: a three-finger strike into the pale, flabby throat. Yassen had worked for many evil people – not that he ever thought of them in terms of good and evil. All that mattered to him was how much they were prepared to pay. Some of them – Herod Sayle, for example – had planned to kill millions of people. The numbers were irrelevant to Yassen. People died all the time. He knew that every time he drew a breath, at that exact moment, somewhere in the world a hundred or a thousand people would be taking their last. Death was everywhere; it could not be measured.

But recently something inside him had changed. Perhaps it was meeting Alex again that had done it; perhaps it was his age. Although Yassen looked as if he was in his late twenties, he was in fact thirty-five. He was getting old. Too old, anyway, for his line of work. He was beginning to think it might be time to stop.

And that was why he now decided not to murder Damian Cray. Eagle Strike was only two days away. It would make him richer than he could have dreamt and it would allow him to return, at last, to his homeland, Russia. He would buy a house in St Petersburg and live comfortably, perhaps doing occasional business with the Russian mafia. The city was teeming with criminal activity and for a man with his wealth and experience, anything would be possible.

Yassen stretched out a hand, the same hand he would have used to strike his employer down. "You worry too much," he said. "For all we know, Alex may still be in the compound. But even if he has made it through the gate, he can't have gone far. He has to get out of Sloterdijk and back to Amsterdam. I have already instructed every man we have to get out there and find him. If he tries to get into the city, he will be intercepted."

"How do you know he's going into the city?" Cray demanded.

"It's the middle of the night. Where else could he go?" Yassen stood up and yawned. "Alex Rider will be back here before sunrise and you will have your flash drive."

"Good." Cray looked at the wreckage scattered across the floor. "And next time I get my hands on him I'll make sure he doesn't walk away. Next time I'll deal with him myself."

Yassen said nothing. Turning his back on Damian Cray, he walked slowly out of the room.

PEDAL POWER

The local train pulled into Amsterdam's Central Station and began to slow down. Alex was sitting on his own, his face resting against the window, barely conscious of the long, empty platforms or the great canopy stretching over his head. It was around midnight and he was exhausted. He knew Jack would be frantic, waiting for him at the hotel. He was eager to see her. He suddenly felt a need to be looked after. He just wanted a hot bath, a hot chocolate ... and bed.

The first time he had gone out to Sloterdijk, he had cycled both ways. But the second time, he had saved his energy and left the bike at the station. The journey back was short but he was enjoying it, knowing that every second put Cray and his compound a few more metres behind him. He also needed the time to think about what he had just been through, to try to understand what it all meant. A plane that burst into flames. A VIP lounge. Something called Milstar. The man with the pockmarked face...

And he still had no answer to the biggest question of all. Why was Cray doing all this? He was massively rich. He had fans all over the world. Only a few days ago he had been shaking hands with the president of the United States. His music was still played on the radio and his every appearance drew massive crowds. The Gameslayer system would make him another fortune. If ever there was a man who had no need to conspire and to kill, it was him.

Eagle Strike.

What did the two words mean?

The train came to a halt; the doors hissed open. Alex checked that the flash drive was still in his pocket and got out.

There was barely anyone around on the platform but the main ticket hall was more crowded. Students and other young travellers were arriving on the international lines. Some of them were slumped on the floor, leaning against oversized rucksacks. They all looked spaced out in the hard, artificial light. Alex guessed it would take him about ten minutes to cycle down to the hotel on the Herengracht. If he was awake enough to remember where it was.

He passed through the heavy glass doors and found his bike where he had left it, chained to some railings. He had just unlocked it when he stopped, sensing the danger before he even saw it. This was something he had never learnt. Even his uncle, who had spent years training him to be a spy, would have been unable to explain it; the instinct that now told him he had to move – and fast. He looked around him. There was a wide cobbled area leading down to an expanse of water, with the city beyond. A kiosk selling hot-dogs was still open. Sausages were turning over a burner but there was no sign of the vendor. A few couples were strolling across the bridges over the canals, enjoying a night that had become warm and dry. The sky wasn't black so much as a deep midnight blue.

Somewhere a clock struck the hour, the chimes echoing across the city.

Alex noticed a car, parked so that it faced the station. Its headlamps blinked on, throwing a beam of light across the square towards him. A moment later a second car did the same. Then a third. All three cars were the same: two-seater Smart cars. More lights came on. There were six vehicles parked in a semicircle around him, covering every angle of the station square. They were all black. With their short bodies and slightly bulbous driving compartments, they looked almost like toys. But Alex knew with a feeling of cold certainty that they weren't here for fun.

Doors swung open. Men stepped out, turned into black silhouettes by their own headlamps. For a split second nobody moved. They had him. There was nowhere for him to go.

Alex stretched out his left thumb, moving it towards the bell that still looked ridiculous, attached to the handlebar of his bike. There was a small silver lever sticking out. Pushing it would ring the bell. Alex pulled. The top of the bell sprang open to reveal five buttons inside, each one a different colour. Smithers had described them in the manual. They were colour-coded for ease of use. Now it was time to find out if they worked.

As if sensing that something was about to happen, the black shadows had begun to move across the square. Alex pressed the orange button and felt the shudder beneath his hands as two tiny heat-seeking missiles exploded out of the ends of the handlebars. Trailing orange flames, they shot across the square. Alex saw the men stop, uncertain. The missiles soared into the air, then curved back, their movement perfectly synchronized. As Alex had suspected, the hottest thing in the square was the grill in the hot-dog kiosk. The missiles fell on it, both striking at exactly the same time. There was a huge explosion, a fireball of flame that spread across the cobbles and was reflected in the water of the canal. Burning fragments of wood and pieces of sausage rained down. The blast hadn't been strong enough to kill anyone, but it had created the perfect diversion. Alex grabbed the bike and dragged it back into the station. The square was blocked. This was the only way.

But even as he re-entered the ticket hall, he saw other men running across the concourse towards him. At this time of night the crowds were moving slowly. Anyone running had to have a special reason, and Alex knew for certain that the reason was him. Cray's men must have been in radio contact with each other. Now that one group had spotted him, they would all know where he was.

He jumped on the bike and pedalled along the flat stone floor as fast as he could: past the ticket booths, the newspaper kiosks, the information boards and the ramps leading up to the platforms, trying to put as much space as he could between himself and his pursuers. A woman pushing a motorized cleaning machine stepped in front of him and he had to swerve, almost knocking over a bearded man with a vast rucksack. The man swore at him in German. Alex raced on.

There was a door at the very end of the main hall, but before he could reach it, it burst open and more men came running in, blocking his way. Pedalling furiously, Alex spun the bike round and headed for the one way out of this nightmare. An empty escalator, going down. Before he even knew what he was doing, he had launched himself onto the metal treads and was bouncing and shuddering head-first into the ground. He was thrown from side to side, his body slamming against the steel panels. He wondered if the front wheel would crumple with the strain or if the tyres would puncture against the sharp edges. But then he had reached the bottom and he was riding – bizarrely – through a subway station, with ticket windows on one side and automatic gates on the other.

He was glad it was so late. The station was almost empty. But still a few heads turned in astonishment as he entered a long passageway and disappeared from sight.

It was definitely the wrong time for this, but even so Alex found himself admiring the Bad Boy's handling ability. The aluminium frame was light and manageable but the solid down tube kept the bike stable. He came to a corner and automatically went into attack position. He pressed down on the outside pedal and put his weight on it, at the same time keeping his body low. His entire centre of gravity was focused on the point where the tyres came into contact with the ground, and the bike took the corner with total control. This was something Alex had learnt years ago, mountain biking in the Pennines. He had never expected to use the same techniques in a subway station under Amsterdam!

A second escalator brought him back up to street level and Alex found himself on the other side of the square, away from the station. The remains of the hot-dog kiosk were still burning. A police car had arrived and he could see the hysterical hot-dog salesman trying to explain what had happened to an officer. For a moment he hoped he would be able to slip away unnoticed. But then he heard the screech of tyres as one of the Smart cars skidded backwards in an arc and then shot forward in his direction. They had seen him! And they were after him again.

He began to pedal down the Damrak, one of the main streets in Amsterdam, quickly picking up speed. He glanced back. A second Smart car had joined the first, and with a sinking heart he knew that his legs would be no match for their engines. He had perhaps twenty seconds before they caught up with him.

Then a bell clanged and there was a loud metallic clattering. A tram was coming towards him, thundering along the tracks on its way to the station. Alex knew what he had to do. He could hear the Smart cars coming up behind him. The tram was a great metal box, filling his vision ahead. At the very last moment, he twisted the handlebars, throwing himself directly in front of the tram. He saw the driver's horrified face, felt the bicycle wheels shudder as they crossed the tracks. But then he was on the other side and the tram had become a wall that would – at least for a few seconds – separate him from the Smart cars.

Even so, one of them tried to follow. It was a terrible mistake. The car was halfway across the tracks when the tram hit it. There was a huge crash and the car spun away into the night. It was followed by a terrible grinding and metallic screaming as the tram derailed. The tram's second carriage whipped round and hit the other Smart car, batting it away like a fly. As Alex pedalled away from the Damrak, across a pretty, white-painted bridge, he left behind him a scene of total devastation, the first police sirens cutting through the air.

He found himself cycling through a series of narrow streets that were more crowded, with people drifting in and out of pornographic cinemas and striptease clubs. He had accidentally drifted into the famous red-light district of Amsterdam. He wondered what Jack would make of that. A woman standing in a doorway winked at him. Alex ignored her and rode on.

There were three black motorbikes at the end of the street.

Alex groaned. They were 400cc Suzuki Bandits and there could only be one reason why they were there, silent and unmoving. They were waiting for him. The moment their riders saw him, they kick-started their engines. Alex knew he had to get away – and fast. He looked around.

On one side of him dozens of people were streaming in and out of a parade of neon-lit shops. On the other a narrow canal stretched into the distance, with darkness and possible safety on the other side. But how was he going to get across? There wasn't a bridge in sight.

But perhaps there was a way. A boat was turning. It was one of the famous glass-topped cruisers, sitting low in the water and carrying tourists on a late-night dinner cruise. It had swung diagonally across the water so that it was almost touching both banks. The captain had misjudged the angle, and the boat seemed to be jammed.

Alex propelled himself forward. Simultaneously he pressed the green button under the bicycle bell. There was a water bottle suspended upside down under his saddle and out of the corner of his eye he saw a silver-grey liquid squirt out onto the road. He was hurtling towards the canal, leaving a snail-like trail behind him. He heard the roar of the Suzuki motorbikes and knew that they had caught up with him. Then everything happened at once.

Alex left the road, crossed the pavement and forced the bike up into the air. The first of the motorbikes reached the section of road that was covered with the ooze. At once the driver lost control, skidding so violently that he almost seemed to be throwing himself off on purpose. His bike smashed into a second bike, bringing that one down too. At the same time, Alex came hurtling down onto the reinforced glass roof of the tourist boat and began to pedal its full length. He could see diners gazing up at him in astonishment. A waiter with a tray of glasses spun round, dropping everything. There was the flash of a camera. Then he had reached the other side. Carried by his own momentum, he soared off the roof, over a line of bollards, and came to a skidding halt on the opposite bank of the canal.

He looked back – just in time to see that the third Bandit had managed to follow him. It was already in the air and the diners on the boat were gazing up in alarm as it descended towards them.

They were right to be scared. The motorbike was too heavy. It crashed onto the glass roof, which shattered beneath it. Bike and rider disappeared into the cabin as the tourists, screaming, threw themselves out of the way. Plates and tables exploded; the lights in the cabin fused and went out. Alex didn't have time to see more.

He wasn't going to be able to hide in the darkness after all. Another pair of Bandits had found him, roaring up the side of the canal towards him. Pedalling frantically, he tried to get out of sight, turning into one road, cutting down another, around a corner, across a square. His legs and thighs were on fire. He knew he couldn't go on much further.

And then he made his mistake.

It was an alleyway, dark and inviting. It would lead him somewhere he wouldn't be found. That was what he thought. But he was only halfway down it when a man suddenly stepped out in front of him, holding a machine gun. Behind him the two Bandits edged closer, cutting off the way back.

The man with the machine gun took aim. Alex's finger stabbed down, this time finding the yellow button. At once there was an explosion of brilliant white light as the magnesium flare concealed inside the Digital Evolution headlight ignited. Alex couldn't believe how much light was pouring out of the bike. The whole area was illuminated. The man with the machine gun was completely blinded.

Alex hit the blue button. There was a loud hiss. Somewhere under his legs a cloud of blue smoke poured out of the air pump connected to the bicycle frame. The two Bandits had been chasing up behind him, and they now plunged into the smoke and disappeared.

Everything was chaotic. Brilliant light and thick smoke. The man with the machine gun opened fire, sensing that Alex must be somewhere near. But Alex was already passing him and the bullets went wide, slicing into the first Bandit and killing the driver instantly. Somehow the second Bandit managed to get through, but then there was a thud, a scream and the sound of metal smashing into brick. The clatter of bullets stopped and Alex smiled grimly to himself, realizing what had happened. The man with the machine gun had just been run over by his friend on the bike.

His smile faded as yet another Smart car appeared from nowhere, still some distance away but already getting closer. How many of them were there? Surely Cray's people would decide they'd had enough and give it a rest. But then Alex remembered the flash drive in his pocket and knew that Cray would rip all Amsterdam apart to get it back.

There was a bridge ahead of him, an old-fashioned construction of wood and metal with thick cables and counterweights. It crossed a much wider canal and there was a single barge approaching it. Alex was puzzled. The bridge was far too low to allow the barge to pass. Then a red traffic light blinked on; the bridge began to lift.

Alex glanced back. The Smart car was about fifty metres behind him and this time there was nowhere to hide, nowhere else to go. He looked ahead of him. If he could just get to the other side of this canal, he really would be able to disappear. Nobody would be able to follow – at least not until the bridge had come down again. But it looked as if he was already too late. The bridge had split in half, both sections rising at the same speed, the gap over the water widening with every second.

The Smart car was accelerating.

Alex had no choice.

Feeling the pain, and knowing that he had reached the last reserves of his strength, Alex pushed down and the bike picked up speed. The car's engine was louder now, howling in his ears, but he didn't dare look back again. All his energy was focused on the rapidly rising bridge.

He hit the wooden surface when it was at a forty-five degree slant. Insanely he found himself thinking of some long-forgotten maths lesson at school. A right-angled triangle. He could see it clearly on the board. And he was cycling up its side!

He wasn't going to make it. Every time he pushed down on the pedals it was a little harder, and he was barely halfway up the slope. He could see the gap – huge now – and the dark, cold water below. The car was right behind him. It was so close he could hear nothing apart from its engine, and the smell of petrol filled his nostrils.

He pedalled one last time – and at the same moment pressed the red button in the bell: the ejector seat. There was a soft explosion right below him. The saddle had rocketed off the bike, propelled by compressed air or some sort of ingenious hydraulic system. Alex shot into the air, over his side of the bridge, over the gap and then down onto the other side, rolling over and over as he tumbled all the way down. As he spun round, he saw the Smart car. Incredibly, it had tried to follow him. It was suspended in mid-air between the two halves of the bridge. He could see the driver's face, the open eyes, the gritted teeth. Then the car plunged down. There was a great splash and it sank at once beneath the black surface of the canal.

Alex got painfully to his feet. The saddle was lying next to him and he picked it up. There was a message underneath. He wouldn't have been able to read it while the saddle was attached to the frame. *If you can read this, you owe me a new bike*.

Smithers had a warped sense of humour. Carrying the saddle, Alex began to limp back to the hotel. He was too tired to smile.

EMERGENCY MEASURES

The Saskia Hotel was an old building that had somehow managed to elbow its way between a converted warehouse and a block of flats. There were just five bedrooms, stacked on top of each other like a house of cards, each one with a view of the canal. The flower market was a short walk away and even at night the air smelt sweet. Jack had chosen it because it was small and out of the way. Somewhere, she hoped, where they wouldn't be noticed.

When Alex opened his eyes at eight the following morning, he found himself lying on a bed in a small, irregularly shaped room on the top floor, built into the roof. He hadn't folded the shutters and sunlight was streaming in through the open window. Slowly he sat up, his body already complaining about the treatment it had received the night before. His clothes were neatly folded on a chair but he couldn't remember putting them there. He looked over to the side and saw a note taped to the mirror.

Breakfast served until ten.
Hope you can make it downstairs! xxx

He smiled, recognizing Jack's handwriting.

There was a tiny bathroom, hardly bigger than a cupboard, leading off the main room and Alex went in and washed. He cleaned his teeth, thankful for the taste of the peppermint. Even nearly ten hours later he hadn't quite forgotten the taste of the snake's blood. As he got dressed, he thought back to the night before when he had finally limped into the reception area to discover Jack waiting for him in one of the antique chairs. He hadn't thought he had been too badly hurt but the look on her face had told him differently. She had ordered sandwiches and hot chocolate from the puzzled receptionist, then led him to the tiny lift that carried them up five floors. Jack hadn't asked any questions and Alex had been grateful. He was too tired to explain, too tired to do anything.

Jack had made him take a shower, and by the time he had come out she had somehow managed to get her hands on a pile of plasters, bandages and antiseptic cream. Alex was sure he needed none of them and he was relieved when they were interrupted by the arrival of room service. He had thought he would be too tired to eat, but suddenly he found that he was ravenously hungry and wolfed down the lot while Jack watched. At last he had stretched out on the bed.

He was asleep the moment he closed his eyes.

Now he finished dressing, checked his bruises in the mirror, and went out. He took the creaking lift all the way down to a vaulted, low-ceilinged cellar underneath the reception area. This was where breakfast was served. It was a Dutch breakfast of cold meats, cheeses and bread rolls, served with coffee. Alex saw Jack sitting at a table on her own in a corner. He went over and joined her.

"Hi, Alex," she said. She was obviously relieved to see him looking more like his old self. "How did you sleep?"

"Like a log." He sat down. "Do you want me to tell you what happened last night?"

"Not yet. I have a feeling it'll put me off my breakfast."

They ate, and then he told her everything that had happened from the moment he had entered Cray's compound on the side of the truck. When he finished, there was a long silence. Jack's last cup of coffee had gone cold.

"Damian Cray is a maniac!" she exclaimed. "I'll tell you one thing, Alex, I'm never going to buy another of his CDs!" She sipped her coffee, grimaced and put the cup down. "But I still don't get it," she said. "What do you think he's doing, for heaven's sake? I mean ... Cray is a national hero. He sang at Princess Diana's wedding!"

"It was her birthday," Alex corrected her.

"And he's given zillions to charity. I went to one of his concerts once. Every penny he made went to Save the Children. Or maybe I got the name wrong; maybe it was Beat Up and Try to Kill the Children! Just what the hell is going on?"

"I don't know. The more I think about it, the less sense it makes."

"I don't even want to think about it. I'm just relieved you managed to get out of there alive. And I hate myself for letting you go in alone." She thought for a moment. "It seems to me you've done your bit," she went on. "Now you have to go back to MI6 and tell them what you know. You can take them the flash drive. This time they'll have to believe you."

"I couldn't agree with you more," Alex said. "But first of all we have to get out of Amsterdam. And we're going to have to be careful. Cray is bound to have people at the station. And at the airport for that matter."

Jack nodded. "We'll take a bus," she said. "We can go to Rotterdam or Antwerp. Maybe we can get a plane from there."

They had finished their breakfast. Now they packed, paid and left the hotel. Jack used cash. She was afraid that with all his resources, Cray might be able to track a credit card. They picked up a taxi at the flower market and took it out to the suburbs, where they caught a local bus. Alex realized it was going to be a long journey home, and that worried him. Twelve hours had passed since he had heard Cray announce that Eagle Strike would take place in two days' time. It was already the middle of the morning.

Less than thirty-six hours remained.

Damian Cray had woken early and was sitting up in a four-poster bed with mauve silk sheets and at least a dozen pillows. There was a tray in front of him, brought in by his personal maid along with the morning newspapers, specially flown over from England. He was eating his usual breakfast of organic porridge, Mexican honey (made by his own bees), soya milk and cranberries. It was well known that Cray was a vegetarian. At different times he had campaigned against battery farming, the transportation of live animals and the importation of goose liver pâté. This morning he had no appetite but he ate anyway. He had a personal dietitian who never let him forget it when he missed breakfast.

He was still eating when there was a knock at the door and Yassen Gregorovich came into the room.

"Well?" Cray demanded. It never bothered him having people in his bedroom. He had composed some of his best songs in bed.

"I've done what you said. I have men at Amsterdam Central,

Amsterdam Zuid, Lelylaan, De Vlugtlaan ... all the local stations. There are also men at Schiphol Airport and I'm covering the ports. But I don't think Alex Rider will turn up at any of them."

"Then where is he?"

"If I were him, I'd head for Brussels or Paris. I have contacts in the police and I've got them looking out for him. If anybody sees him, we'll hear about it. But my guess is that we won't find him until he returns to England. He'll go straight to MI6 and the flash drive will go with him."

Cray threw down his spoon. "You seem very unconcerned about it all," he remarked.

Yassen said nothing.

"I have to say, I'm very disappointed in you, Mr Gregorovich. When I was setting up this operation, I was told you were the best. I was told you never made mistakes." There was still no answer. Cray scowled. "I was paying you a great deal of money. Well, you can forget that now. It's finished. It's all over. Eagle Strike isn't going to happen. And what about me? MI6 are bound to find out about all this and if they come after me..." His voice cracked. "This was meant to be my moment of glory. This was my life's work. Now it's been destroyed, and it's all thanks to you!"

"It's not finished," Yassen said. His voice hadn't changed, but there was an icy quality to it which might have warned Cray that once again he had come perilously close to a sudden and unexpected death. The Russian looked down at the little man, propped up on his pillows in the bed. "But we have to take emergency measures. I have people in England. I have given them instructions. You will have the flash drive returned to you in time."

"How are you going to manage that?" Cray asked. He didn't sound convinced.

"I have been considering the situation. All along I have

believed that Alex has been acting on his own. That it was chance that brought him to us."

"He was staying at that house in the South of France."

"Yes."

"So how do you explain it?"

"Ask yourself this question. Why was Alex so upset by what happened to the journalist? It was none of his business. But he was angry. He risked his life coming onto the boat, the *Fer de Lance*. The answer is obvious. The friend he was staying with was a girl."

"A girlfriend?" Cray smiled sarcastically.

"He must obviously have feelings for her. That is what set him on our trail."

"And do you think this girl...?" Cray could see what the Russian was thinking, and suddenly the future didn't seem so bleak after all. He sank back into the pillows. The breakfast tray rose and fell in front of him.

"What's her name?" Cray asked.

"Sabina Pleasure," Yassen said.

Sabina had always hated hospitals and everything about the Whitchurch reminded her why.

It was huge. You could imagine walking through the revolving doors and never coming out again. You might die; you might simply be swallowed up by the system. It would make no difference. Everything about the building was impersonal, as if it had been specially designed to make the patients feel like factory products. Doctors and nurses were coming in and out, looking exhausted and defeated. Even being close to the place filled Sabina with a sense of dread.

The Whitchurch was a brand-new hospital in south London.

Sabina's mother had brought her here. The two of them were in the carpark, sitting together in Liz Pleasure's VW Golf.

"Are you sure you don't want me to come with you?" her mother was saying.

"No. I'll be all right."

"He is the same, Sabina. You have to know that. He's been hurt. You may be shocked by how he looks. But underneath it all he's still the same."

"Does he want to see me?"

"Of course he does. He's been looking forward to it. Just don't stay too long. He gets tired..."

It was the first time Sabina had visited her father since he had been airlifted back from France. He hadn't been strong enough to see her until today and, she realized, the same was true of her. In a way, she had been dreading this. She had wondered what it would be like seeing him. He was badly burnt. He was still unable to walk. But in her dreams he was the same old dad. She had a photograph of him beside her bed and every night, before she went to sleep, she saw him as he had always been: shaggy and bookish but always healthy and smiling. She knew she would have to start facing reality the moment she walked into his room.

Sabina took a deep breath. She got out of the car and walked across the carpark, past Accident and Emergency and into the hospital. The doors revolved and she found herself sucked into a reception area that was at once too busy and too brightly lit. Sabina couldn't believe how crowded and noisy it was – more like the inside of a shopping mall than a hospital. There were indeed a couple of shops, one selling flowers, and next to it a café and delicatessen where people could buy sandwiches and snacks to carry up to the friends and relatives they were visiting. Signs pointed in every direction. Cardiology. Paediatrics. Renal.

Radiology. Even the names sounded somehow threatening.

Edward Pleasure was in Lister Ward, named after a nineteenth-century surgeon. Sabina knew that it was on the third floor but, looking around, she could see no sign of a lift. She was about to ask for directions when a man – a young doctor from the look of him – suddenly stepped into her path.

"Lost?" he asked. He was in his twenties, dark-haired, wearing a loose-fitting white coat and carrying a water cup. He looked as if he had stepped straight out of a television soap. He was smiling as if at some private joke and Sabina had to admit that maybe it was funny, her being lost when she was totally surrounded by signs.

"I'm looking for Lister Ward," Sabina said.

"That's on the third floor. I'm just going up there myself. But I'm afraid the lifts are out of order," the doctor added.

That was strange. Her mother hadn't mentioned it and she had been to the ward only the evening before. But Sabina imagined that in a hospital like this, things would break down all the time.

"There's a staircase you can take. Why don't you come along with me?"

The doctor crumpled his cup and dropped it in a bin. He walked through the reception area and Sabina followed.

"So who are you visiting?" the doctor asked.

"My dad."

"What's wrong with him?"

"He had an accident."

"That's too bad. How is he getting on?"

"This is the first time I've visited him. He's getting better ... I think."

They went through a set of double doors and down a corridor. Sabina noticed that they had left all the visitors behind them. The corridor was long and empty. It brought them to a hallway where five different passages converged. To one side was a staircase leading up, but the doctor ignored it. "Isn't that the way?" she asked.

"No." The doctor turned and smiled again. He seemed to smile a lot. "That goes up to Urology. You can get through to Lister Ward but this way's shorter." He gestured at a door and opened it. Sabina followed him through.

To her surprise she found herself back out in the open air. The door led into a partly covered area round the side of the hospital, where supply vehicles parked. There was a raised loading bay and a number of crates already stacked up. One wall was lined by a row of dustbins, each one a different colour according to what sort of refuse it was meant to take.

"Excuse me, I think you've—" Sabina began.

But then her eyes widened in shock. The doctor was lunging towards her, and before she knew what was happening he had grabbed her round the neck. Her first, and her only, thought was that he was some sort of madman, and her response was automatic. Sabina had been to self-defence classes; her parents had insisted. Without so much as hesitating, she whirled round, driving her knee between the man's legs. At the same time, she opened her mouth to scream. She had been taught that in a situation like this, noise was the one thing an attacker most feared.

But he was too fast for her. Even as the scream rose in her throat, his hand clamped tight over her mouth. He had seen what she was about to do and had twisted round behind her, one hand on her mouth, the other arm pinning her to him. Sabina knew now that she had assumed too much. The man had been wearing a white coat. He had been in the hospital. But of course he could have been anyone and she had been crazy to go with him. Never go anywhere with a stranger. How many times had her parents told her that?

An ambulance appeared, backing at speed into the service area. Sabina felt a surge of hope that gave her new strength. Whatever her attacker was planning to do, he had chosen the wrong place. The ambulance had arrived just in time. But then she realized that the man hadn't reacted. She had thought he would let her go and run away. On the contrary, he had been expecting the ambulance and began dragging her towards it. Sabina stared as the back of the ambulance burst open and two more men jumped out. This whole thing had been planned! The three of them were in it together. They had known she would be there, visiting her father, and had come to the hospital meaning to intercept her.

Somehow she managed to bite the hand that was clamped over her mouth. The fake doctor swore and let go. Sabina lashed out with her elbow and felt it crash into the man's nose; he reeled backwards and suddenly she was free. She tried again to scream, to raise the alarm, but the two men from the ambulance were on her. One of them was holding something silver and pointed but Sabina only knew that it was a hypodermic syringe when she felt it jab into her arm. She squirmed and kicked, but she felt the strength rush out of her like water falling through a trapdoor. Her legs buckled and she would have fallen if the two men hadn't caught hold of her. She wasn't unconscious. Her thoughts were clear. She knew that she was in terrible danger – more danger than she had ever known – but she had no idea why this was happening.

Helplessly, Sabina was dragged towards the ambulance and thrown in. There was a mattress on the floor and at least that broke her fall. Then the doors slammed shut and she heard a lock being turned from the outside. She was trapped, on her own in an empty metal box, unable to move as the drug took effect. Sabina felt total despair.

The two men walked off into the hospital grounds as if nothing had taken place. The fake doctor removed his white coat and stuffed it into one of the bins. He was wearing an ordinary suit underneath and he saw that there was blood on the front of his shirt. His nose was bleeding, but that was good. When he went back into the hospital, he would simply look like one of the patients.

The ambulance drove slowly away. If anyone had bothered to look, they would have seen that the driver was dressed in exactly the same clothes as the other crews. Liz Pleasure actually noticed it leave, sitting in her VW in the carpark. She was still there half an hour later, wondering what had happened to Sabina. But it would be a while yet before she realized that her daughter had disappeared.

UNFAIR EXCHANGE

It was five o'clock when Alex arrived at London's City Airport, the end of a long, frustrating day that had seen him travelling by road and by air across three countries. He and Jack had taken the bus from Amsterdam to Antwerp, arriving just too late for the lunchtime flight. They had killed three hours at the airport, finally boarding an old-fashioned Fokker 50 that seemed to take for ever crossing over to England. Alex wondered now if he had wasted too much time avoiding Damian Cray. A whole day had gone. But at least the airport was on the right side of London, not too far from Liverpool Street and the offices of MI6.

Alex intended to take the flash drive straight to Alan Blunt. He would have telephoned ahead but he couldn't be sure that Blunt would even take the call. One thing was certain. He wouldn't feel safe until he had handed over the device. Once MI6 had it in their hands, he would be able to relax.

That was his plan – but everything changed as he stepped into the arrivals hall. There was a woman sitting at a coffee bar reading the evening newspaper. The front page was open. It was almost as if it had been put there for Alex to see. A photograph of Sabina. And a headline:

SCHOOLGIRL DISAPPEARS FROM HOSPITAL

"This way," Jack was saying. "We can get a cab."

"Jack!"

Jack saw the look on his face and followed his eyes to the newspaper. Without saying another word, she hurried into the airport's only shop and bought a copy for herself.

There wasn't very much to the story – but at this stage there wasn't a lot to tell. A fifteen-year-old schoolgirl from south London had been visiting her father at Whitchurch Hospital that morning. He had recently been injured in a terrorist incident in the South of France. Inexplicably she had never reached the ward, but instead had vanished into thin air. The police were urging any witnesses to come forward. Her mother had already made a television appeal for Sabina to come home.

"It's Cray," Alex said. His voice was empty. "He's got her."

"Oh God, Alex." Jack sounded as wretched as he felt. "He's done this to get the flash drive. We should have thought..."

"There was no way we could have expected this. How did he even know she was my friend?" Alex thought for a moment. "Yassen." He answered his own question. "He must have told Cray."

"You have to go to MI6 straight away. It's the only thing you can do."

"No. I want to go home first."

"Alex – why?"

Alex looked down at the picture one last time, then crumpled the page in his hands. "Cray may have left a message for me," he said.

There was a message. But it came in a form that Alex hadn't quite expected.

Jack had gone into the house first, checking to make sure there was no one waiting for them. Then she called Alex. She looked grim as she stood at the front door.

"It's in the sitting-room," she said.

"It" was a brand-new widescreen television. Someone had been into the house. They had brought the television and left it in the middle of the room. There was a webcam perched on top; a brand-new red cable snaked into a junction box in the wall.

"A present from Cray," Jack murmured.

"I don't think it's a present," Alex said.

There was a remote control next to the webcam. Reluctantly Alex picked it up. He knew he wasn't going to like what he was about to see, but there was no way he could ignore it. He turned the television on.

The screen flickered and cleared and suddenly he found himself face to face with Damian Cray. Somehow he wasn't surprised. He wondered if Cray had returned to England or if he was transmitting from Amsterdam. He knew that this was a live image and that his own picture would be sent back via the webcam. Slowly he sat down in front of the screen. He showed no emotion at all.

"Alex!" Cray looked relaxed and cheerful. His voice was so clear he could have been in the room with them. "I'm so glad you got back safely. I've been waiting to speak to you."

"Where's Sabina?" Alex asked.

"Where's Sabina? Where's Sabina? How very sweet! Young love!"

The image changed. Alex heard Jack gasp. Sabina was lying on a bunk in a bare room. Her hair was dishevelled but otherwise she seemed unhurt. She looked up at the camera and Alex could see the fear and confusion in her eyes.

Then the picture switched back to Cray. "We haven't damaged her ... yet," he said. "But that could change at any time."

"I'm not giving you the flash drive," Alex said.

"Hear me out, Alex." Cray leant forward so that he seemed to come closer to the screen. "Young people these days are so hot-headed! I've gone to a great deal of trouble and expense on account of you. And the thing is, you *are* going to give me the flash drive because if you don't your girlfriend is going to die, and you are going to see it on video."

"Don't listen to him, Alex!" Jack exclaimed.

"He *is* listening to me and I'd ask you not to interrupt!" Cray smiled. He seemed totally confident, as if this were nothing more than another celebrity interview. "I can imagine what's going through your mind," he went on, speaking again to Alex. "You're thinking of going to your friends at MI6. I would seriously advise against it."

"How do you know we haven't been to them already?" Jack asked.

"I very much hope you haven't," Cray replied. "Because I am a very nervous man. If I think anyone is making enquiries about me, I will kill the girl. If I find myself being watched by people I don't know, I will kill the girl. If a policeman so much as glances at me in the street, I may well kill the girl. And this I promise you. If you do not bring me the flash drive, personally, before ten o'clock tomorrow morning, I will certainly kill the girl."

"No!" Alex was defiant.

"You can lie to me, Alex, but you can't lie to yourself. You don't work for MI6. They mean nothing to you. But the girl does. If you abandon her, you'll regret it for the rest of your life. And it won't end with her. I will hunt down the rest of your friends. Don't underestimate my power! I will destroy everything and everyone you know. And then I will come after you. So don't kid yourself. Get it over with now. Give me what I want."

There was a long silence.

"Where can I find you?" Alex asked. The words tasted sour in his mouth. They tasted of defeat.

"I am at my house in Wiltshire. You can get a taxi from Bath station. All the drivers know where I live."

"If I bring it to you..." Alex found himself struggling to find the right words. "How do I know that you'll let her go? How do I know you'll let either of us go?"

"Exactly!" Jack had chipped in again. "How do we know we can trust you?"

"I'm a knight of the realm!" Cray exclaimed. "The Queen trusts me; you can too!"

The screen went blank.

Alex turned to Jack. For once he was helpless. "What do I do?" he asked.

"Ignore him, Alex. Go to MI6."

"I can't, Jack. You heard what he said. Before ten o'clock tomorrow morning. MI6 won't be able to do anything before then, and if they try something, Cray will kill Sab." He rested his head in his hands. "I couldn't allow that to happen. She's only in this mess because of me. I couldn't live with myself afterwards."

"But, Alex... A lot more people could get hurt if Eagle Strike – whatever it is – goes ahead."

"We don't know that."

"You think Cray would do all this if he was just going to rob a bank or something?"

Alex said nothing.

"Cray is a killer, Alex. I'm sorry. I wish I could be more helpful. But I don't think you can just walk into his house."

Alex thought about it. He thought for a long time. As long as Cray had Sabina, he held all the cards. But perhaps there was a way he could get her out of there. It would mean giving himself up. Once again he would become Cray's prisoner. But with Sabina free, Jack would be able to contact MI6. And perhaps – just perhaps – Alex might come out of this alive.

Quickly he outlined his idea to Jack. She listened – but the more she heard, the unhappier she looked.

"It's terribly dangerous, Alex," she said.

"But it might work."

"You can't give him the flash drive."

"I won't give him the flash drive, Jack."

"And if it all goes wrong?"

Alex shrugged. "Then Cray wins. Eagle Strike happens." He tried to smile, but there was no humour in his voice. "But at least we'll finally find out what it is."

The house was on the edge of the Bath valley, a twenty-minute drive from the station. Cray had been right about one thing. The taxi driver knew where it was without needing a map or an address – and as the car rolled down the private lane towards the main entrance, Alex understood why.

Damian Cray lived in an Italian convent. According to the newspapers, he had seen it in Umbria, fallen in love with it and shipped it over, brick by brick. The building really was extraordinary. It seemed to have taken over much of the surrounding countryside, cut off from public view by a tall, honey-coloured brick wall with two carved wooden gates at least ten metres high.

Beyond the wall Alex could see a slanting roof of terracotta tiles, and beyond it an elaborate tower with pillars, arched windows and miniature battlements. Much of the garden had been imported from Italy too, with dark green, twisting cypresses and olive trees. Even the weather didn't seem quite English. The sun had come out and the sky was a radiant blue. It had to be the hottest day of the year.

Alex paid the driver and got out. He was wearing a pale grey, short-sleeved Trailrider cycling jersey without the elbow pads. As he walked down to the gates, he loosened the zip that ran up to the neck, allowing the breeze to play against his skin. There was a rope coming out of a hole in the wall and he pulled it. A bell rang out. Alex reflected that once this same bell might have called the nuns from their prayers. It seemed somehow wicked that a holy place should have been uprooted and brought here to be a madman's lair.

The gates opened electronically. Alex walked through and found himself in a cloister: a rectangle of perfectly mown grass surrounded by statues of saints. Ahead there was a fourteenth-century chapel with a villa attached, the two somehow existing in perfect harmony. He smelt lemons in the air. Pop music drifted from somewhere in the house. Alex recognized the song. *White Lines*: Cray was playing his own CD.

The front door of the house stood open. There was still nobody in sight, so Alex walked inside. The door led directly into a wide airy space with beautiful furniture arranged over a quarry-tiled floor. There was a grand piano made of rosewood, and a number of paintings, medieval altar pieces, were hanging on plain white walls. A row of six windows looked out onto a terrace with a garden beyond. White muslin curtains, hanging ceiling to floor, swayed gently in the breeze.

Damian Cray was sitting on an ornately carved wooden seat with a white poodle curled up in his lap. He glanced up as Alex came into the room. "Ah, there you are, Alex." He stroked the dog. "This is Bubbles. Isn't he beautiful?"

"Where's Sabina?" Alex asked.

Cray scowled. "I'm not going to be dictated to, if you don't mind," he said. "Especially not in my own home."

"Where is she?"

"All right!" The moment of anger had passed. Cray stood up and the dog jumped off his lap and ran out of the room. He crossed over to the desk and pressed a button. A few seconds later a door opened and Yassen Gregorovich came in. Sabina was with him. Her eyes widened when she saw Alex but she was unable to speak. Her hands were tied and there was a piece of tape across her mouth. Yassen forced her into a chair and stood over her. His eyes avoided Alex.

"You see, Alex, here she is," Cray said. "A little scared, perhaps, but otherwise unhurt."

"Why have you tied her up?" Alex demanded. "Why won't you let her talk?"

"Because she said some very hurtful things to me," Cray replied. "She also tried to assault me. In fact, frankly she has behaved in a very unladylike way." He scowled. "Now – you have something for me."

This was the moment that Alex had dreaded. He had a plan. Sitting on the train from London to Bath, in the taxi, and even walking into the house, he had been certain it would work. Now, facing Damian Cray, he suddenly wasn't so sure.

He reached into his pocket and took out the flash drive. The silver capsule had a lid, which Alex had opened, revealing a maze of circuitry inside. He had taped a brightly coloured tube in place, the nozzle pointing into the device. He held it up so that Cray could see.

"What is that?" Cray demanded.

"It's superglue," Alex replied. "I don't know what's inside your precious flash drive, but I doubt it'll work if it's gummed up with this stuff. I just have to squeeze my hand and you can forget Eagle Strike. You can forget the whole thing."

"How very ingenious!" Cray giggled. "But I don't actually see the point."

"It's simple," Alex said. "You let Sabina go; she walks out of here. She goes to a pub or a house and she telephones me here. You can give her the number. Once I know she's safe, I'll give you the flash drive."

Alex was lying.

As soon as Sabina had gone, he would squeeze the tube anyway. The flash drive would be filled with superglue, which would harden almost immediately. Alex was fairly sure it would make the device inoperable. He had no qualms about double-crossing Cray. It had been his plan all along. He didn't like to think what would happen to him, but that didn't matter. Sabina would be free. And as soon as Jack knew she was safe, she would be able to act. Jack would call MI6. Somehow Alex would have to stay alive until they arrived.

"Was this your idea?" Cray asked. Alex said nothing so he went on. "It's very clever. Very cute. But the question is..." He raised a finger on each hand. "Will it work?"

"I mean what I say." Alex held out the flash drive. "Let her go."

"But what if she goes straight to the police?"

"She won't."

Sabina tried to shout her disagreement from behind the gag. Alex took a breath.

"You'll still have me," he explained. "If Sabina goes to the police, you can do whatever you want to me. So that'll stop her.

Anyway, she doesn't know what you're planning. There's nothing she can do."

Cray shook his head. "I'm sorry," he said.

"What?"

"No deal!"

"Are you serious?" Alex closed his hand around the tube.

"Entirely."

"What about Eagle Strike?"

"What about your girlfriend?" There was a heavy pair of kitchen scissors on the desk. Before Alex could say anything, Cray picked them up and threw them to Yassen. Sabina began to struggle furiously, but the Russian held her down. "You've made a simple miscalculation, Alex," Cray continued. "You're very brave. You would do almost anything to have the girl released. But I will do anything to keep her. And I wonder how much you'll be prepared to watch, how far I'll have to go, before you decide that you might as well give me the flash drive anyway. A finger, maybe? Two fingers?"

Yassen opened the scissors. Sabina had suddenly gone very quiet and still. Her eyes pleaded with Alex.

"No!" Alex yelled. With a wave of despair he knew that Cray had won. He had gambled on at least getting Sabina out of here. But it wasn't to be.

Cray saw the defeat in his eyes. "Give it to me!" he demanded.

"No."

"Start with the little finger, Yassen. Then we'll work one at a time towards her thumb."

Tears formed in Sabina's eyes. She couldn't hide her terror.

Alex felt sick. Sweat trickled down the sides of his body under his shirt. There was nothing more he could do. He wished now that he had listened to Jack. He wished he had never come.

He threw the flash drive onto the desk.

Cray picked it up.

"Well, that's got that sorted," he said with a smile. "Now, why don't we forget all this unpleasantness and go and have a cup of tea?"

INSANITY AND BISCUITS

Tea was served outside on the lawn – but it was a lawn the size of a field in a garden like nothing Alex had ever seen before. Cray had built himself a fantasy land in the English countryside, with dozens of pools, fountains, miniature temples and grottoes. There was a rose garden and a statue garden, a garden filled entirely with white flowers, and another given over to herbs, which had been laid out like sections in a clock. And all around him he had constructed replicas of buildings that Alex recognized. The Eiffel Tower, the Colosseum in Rome, the Taj Mahal, the Tower of London: each one was exactly one-hundredth the scale of the original and all of them were jumbled together like picture postcards scattered on the floor. It was the garden of a man who wanted to rule the world but couldn't, and so had cut the world down to his own size.

"What do you think of it?" Cray asked as he joined Alex at the table.

"Some gardens have crazy paving," Alex replied quietly, "but I've never seen anything as crazy as this."

Cray smiled.

There were five of them sitting on the raised terrace outside the house: Cray, Alex, Yassen, the man called Henryk and Sabina. She had been untied and the gag taken off her mouth – and as soon as she had been freed, she had rushed over to Alex and thrown her arms around his neck.

"I'm so sorry," she had whispered. "I should have believed you."

That was all she had said. Apart from that she had been silent, her face pale. Alex knew that she was afraid. It was typical of Sabina not to want to show it.

"Well, here we all are. One happy family," Cray said. He pointed at the man with the silver hair and the pockmarked face. Now that he was closer to him, Alex could see that he was very ugly indeed. His eyes, magnified by the glasses, were slightly inflamed. He wore a denim shirt that was too tight and showed off his paunch.

"I don't think you've met Henryk," Cray added.

"I don't think I want to," Alex said.

"You mustn't be a bad loser, Alex. Henryk is very valuable to me. He flies jumbo jets."

Jumbo jets. Another piece of the puzzle.

"So where is he flying you?" Alex asked. "I hope it's somewhere far away."

Cray smiled to himself. "We'll come to that in a moment. In the meantime, shall I be mother? It's Earl Grey; I hope you don't mind. And do help yourself to a biscuit."

Cray poured five cups and set the pot down. Yassen hadn't spoken yet. Alex got the feeling that the Russian was uncomfortable being here. And that was another strange thing. He had always considered Yassen to be his worst enemy, but sitting here now he seemed almost irrelevant. This was all about Damian Cray.

"We have an hour before we have to leave," Cray said. "So I thought I might tell you a little about myself. I thought it might pass the time."

"I'm not really all that interested," Alex said.

Cray's smile grew a little thinner. "I can't believe that's true. You seem to have been interesting yourself in me for a considerable time."

"You tried to kill my father," Sabina said.

Cray turned round, surprised to hear her voice.

"Yes, that's right," he admitted. "And if you'll just shut up, I'm about to tell you why."

He paused. A pair of butterflies shimmered around a bed of lavender.

"I have had an extremely interesting and privileged life," Cray began. "My parents were rich. Super-rich, you might say. But not super. My father was a businessman and he was frankly rather boring. My mother didn't do anything very much; I didn't much like her either. I was an only child and naturally I was fabulously spoilt. I sometimes think that I was richer when I was eight years old than most people will be in their lifetime!"

"Do we have to listen to this?" Alex asked.

"If you interrupt me again, I'll ask Yassen to get the scissors," Cray replied. He went on. "I had my first serious row with my parents when I was thirteen. You see, they'd sent me to the Royal Academy in London. I was an extremely talented singer. But the trouble was, I hated it there. Bach and Beethoven and Mozart and Verdi. I was a teenager, for heaven's sake! I wanted to be Elvis Presley; I wanted to be in a pop group; I wanted to be famous!

"My father got very upset when I told him. He turned up his nose at anything popular. He really thought I'd failed him, and I'm afraid my mother agreed. They both had this idea that one day I'd be singing opera at Covent Garden or something ghastly like that. They didn't want me to leave. In fact, they wouldn't let me – and I don't know what would have happened if they hadn't had that extraordinary accident with the car. It fell on them, you know. I can't say I was terribly upset, although of course I had to pretend. But you know what I thought? I thought that God must be on my side. He wanted me to be a success and so He had decided to help me."

Alex glanced at Sabina to see how she was taking this. She was sitting rigidly in her chair, her cup of tea ignored. There was absolutely no colour in her face. But she was still in control. She wasn't giving anything away.

"Anyway," Cray continued, "the best thing was that my parents were out of the way and, even better, I had inherited all their money. When I was twenty-one, I bought myself a flat in London – actually it was more of a penthouse – and I set up my own band. We called ourselves Slam! As I'm sure you know, the rest is history. Five years later I went solo, and soon I was the greatest singer in the world. And that was when I started to think about the world I was in.

"I wanted to help people. All my life I've wanted to help people. The way you're looking at me, Alex, you'd think I'm some kind of monster. But I'm not. I've raised millions of pounds for charity. Millions and millions. And I should remind you, in case you've forgotten, that I have been knighted by the Queen. I am actually *Sir* Damian Cray, although I don't use the title because I'm no snob. A lovely lady, by the way, the Queen. Do you know how much money my Christmas single, 'Something for the Children', raised all on its own? Enough to feed a whole country!

"But the trouble is, sometimes being famous and being rich isn't enough. I *so* wanted to make a difference – but what was I to do when people wouldn't listen? I mean, take the case of the

Milburn Institute in Bristol. This was a laboratory working for a number of cosmetics companies, and I discovered that they were testing many of their products on animals. Now, I'm sure you and I would be on the same side about this, Alex. I tried to stop them. I campaigned for over a year. We had a petition with twenty thousand signatures and still they wouldn't listen. So in the end – I'd met people and of course I had plenty of money – I suddenly realized that the best thing to do would be to have Professor Milburn killed. And that's what I did. And six months later the institute closed down and that was that. No more animals harmed."

Cray rotated a hand over the biscuit plate and picked one out. He was obviously pleased with himself.

"I had quite a lot of people killed in the years that followed," he said. "For example, there were some extremely unpleasant people cutting down the rainforest in Brazil. They're still in the rainforest ... six feet underneath it. Then there was a whole boatload of Japanese fishermen who wouldn't listen to me. I had them deep-frozen in their own freezer. That will teach them not to hunt rare whales! And there was a company in Yorkshire that was selling landmines. I didn't like them *at all*. So I arranged for the entire board of directors to disappear on an Outward Bound course in the Lake District and that put a stop to that!

"I've had to do some terrible things in my time. Really, I have." He turned to Sabina. "I did hate having to blow up your father. If he hadn't spied on me, it wouldn't have been necessary. But you must see that I couldn't let him spoil my plans."

Every cell in Sabina's body had gone rigid and Alex knew she was having to force herself not to attack Cray. But Yassen was sitting right next to her and she wouldn't have got anywhere near.

Cray went on. "This is a terrible world, and if you want to make a difference, sometimes you have to be a bit extreme. And that's the point. I am extremely proud of the fact that I have helped so many people and so many different causes. Because helping people – *charity* – has been the work of my life."

He paused long enough to eat the biscuit he had chosen.

Alex forced himself to drink a little of the perfumed tea. He hated the taste but his mouth was completely dry. "I have a couple of questions," he said.

"Do, please, go ahead."

"My first one is for Yassen Gregorovich." He turned to the Russian. "Why are you working for this lunatic?" Alex wondered if Cray would hit him. But it would be worth it. All the signs indicated that the Russian didn't share Cray's world view. He seemed uncomfortable, out of place. It might be worth trying to sow a few seeds of discord between them.

Cray scowled, but did nothing. He signalled to Yassen to answer.

"He pays me," Yassen said simply.

"I hope your second question is more interesting," Cray snarled.

"Yes. You're trying to tell me that everything you've done is for a good cause. You think that all this killing is worth it because of the results. I'm not sure I agree. Lots of people work for charity; lots of people want to change the world. But they don't have to behave like you."

"I'm waiting..." Cray snapped.

"All right. This is my question. What is Eagle Strike? Are you really telling me it's a plan to make the world a better place?"

Cray laughed softly. For a moment he looked like the diabolical schoolboy he had once been, welcoming his own parents' death. "Yes," he said. "That's exactly what it is. Sometimes great people are misunderstood. You don't understand me and neither does your girlfriend. But I really do want to change the world. That's all I've ever wanted. And I've been very fortunate because my music has made it possible. In the twenty-first century, entertainers are much more influential than politicians or statesmen. I'm the only one who's actually noticed it."

Cray chose a second biscuit – a custard cream.

"Let me ask you a question, Alex. What do you think is the greatest evil on this planet today?"

"Is that including or not including you?" Alex asked.

Cray frowned. "Please don't irritate me," he warned.

"I don't know," Alex said. "You tell me."

"Drugs!" Cray spat out the single word as if it were obvious. "Drugs are causing more unhappiness and destruction than anything anywhere in the world. Drugs kill more people than war or terrorism. Did you know that drugs are the single biggest cause of crime in western society? We've got kids out on the street taking heroin and cocaine, and they're stealing to support their habits. But they're not criminals; they're victims. It's the drugs that are to blame."

"We've talked about this at school," Alex said. The last thing he needed right now was a lecture.

"All my life I've been fighting drugs," Cray went on. "I've done advertisements for the government. I've spent millions building treatment centres. And I've written songs. You must have listened to *White Lines...*"

He closed his eyes and hummed softly, then sang:

"The poison's there. The poison flows

It's everywhere – in heaven's name

Why is it that no one knows

How to end this deadly game?"

He stopped.

"But I know how to end it," he said simply. "I've worked it out. And that's what Eagle Strike is all about. A world without drugs.

Isn't that something to dream about, Alex? Isn't that worth a few sacrifices? Think about it! The end of the drug problem. And I can make it happen."

"How?" Alex was almost afraid of the answer.

"It's easy. Governments won't do anything. The police won't do anything. No one can stop the dealers. So you have to go back to the supplies. You have to think where these drugs come from. And where is that? I'll tell you...

"Every year, hundreds and hundreds of tons of heroin come from Afghanistan – in particular the provinces of Nangarhar and Helmand. Did you know production has increased by fourteen hundred per cent since the Taliban were defeated? So much for that particular war! Then, after Afghanistan, there's Burma and the golden triangle, with about one hundred thousand hectares of land used to produce opium and heroin. The government of Burma doesn't care. Nobody cares. And let's not forget Pakistan, manufacturing one hundred and fifty-five metric tons of opium a year, with refineries throughout the Khyber region and along the borders.

"On the other side of the world there's Colombia. It's the leading supplier and distributor of cocaine, but it also supplies heroin and marijuana. It's a business worth three billion dollars a year, Alex. Eighty tons of cocaine every twelve months. Seven tons of heroin. A lot of it ends up on the streets of American cities. In high schools. A tidal wave of misery and crime.

"But that's only a small part of the picture." Cray held up a hand and began to tick off other countries on his fingers. "There are refineries in Albania. Mule trains in Thailand. Coca crops in Peru. Opium plantations in Egypt. Ephedrine, the chemical used in heroin production, is manufactured in China. One of the biggest drugs markets in the world can be found in Tashkent, in Uzbekistan.

"These are the principal sources of the world's drug problem. This is where the trouble all starts. These are my targets."

"Targets..." Alex whispered the single word.

Damian Cray reached into his pocket and took out the flash drive. Yassen was suddenly alert. Alex knew he had a gun and would use it if he so much as moved.

"Although you weren't to know it," Cray explained, "this is actually a key to unlock one of the most complicated security systems ever devised. The original key was created by the National Security Agency and it is carried by the president of the United States. My friend, the late Charlie Roper, was a senior officer with the NSA, and it was his expertise, his knowledge of the codes, that allowed me to manufacture a duplicate. Even so, it has taken enormous effort. You have no idea how much computer processing power was required to create a second key."

"The Gameslayer..." Alex said.

"Yes. It was the perfect cover. So many people; so much technology. A plant with all the processing power I could ask for. And in reality it was all for this!"

He held up the little metal capsule.

"This key will give me access to two and a half thousand nuclear missiles. These are American missiles and they are on hair-trigger alert – meaning that they can be launched at a moment's notice. It is my intention to override the NSA's system and to fire twenty-five of those missiles at targets I have carefully chosen around the globe."

Cray smiled sadly.

"It is almost impossible to imagine the devastation that will be caused by twenty-five one-hundred-ton missiles exploding at the same time. South America, Central America, Asia, Africa ... almost every continent will feel the pain. And there will be pain, Alex. I am well aware of that.

"But I will have wiped out the poppy fields. The farms and the factories. The refineries, the trade routes, the markets. There will be no more drug suppliers because there will be no more drug supplies. Of course, millions will die. But millions more will be saved.

"That is what Eagle Strike is all about, Alex. The start of a new golden age. A day when all humanity will come together and rejoice.

"That day is now. My time has finally arrived."

EAGLE STRIKE

Alex and Sabina were taken to a room somewhere in the basement of the house and thrown inside. The door closed and suddenly they were alone.

Alex signalled to Sabina not to speak, then began a quick search. The door was a slab of solid oak, locked from the outside and probably bolted too. There was a single square window set high up in the wall, but it was barred and wouldn't have been big enough to crawl through anyway. There was no view. The room might once have been used to store wine; the walls were bare and undecorated, the floor concrete, and apart from a few shelves there was no furniture. A naked bulb hung on a wire from the ceiling. Alex was looking for hidden bugs. It was unlikely that Cray would want to eavesdrop on the two of them, but even so he wanted to be sure that they couldn't be overheard.

It was only when Alex had gone over every inch of the room

that he turned to Sabina. She seemed amazingly calm. He thought about all the things that had happened to her. She had been kidnapped and kept prisoner – bound and gagged. She had been brought face to face with the man who had ordered the execution of her father, and had listened as he outlined his mad idea to destroy half the world. And here she was locked up again with the near certainty that she and Alex wouldn't be allowed to leave here alive. Sabina should have been terrified. But she simply waited quietly while Alex completed his checks, watching him as if seeing him for the first time.

"Are you OK?" he asked at last.

"Alex..." It was only when she tried to speak that the emotion came. She took a breath and fought for control. "I don't believe this is happening," she said.

"I know. I wish it wasn't." Alex didn't know what to say. "When did they get you?" he asked.

"At the hospital. There were three of them."

"Did they hurt you?"

"They scared me. And they gave me some sort of injection." She scowled. "God – Damian Cray is such a creep! And I never realized he was so – *small*!"

That made Alex smile despite everything. Sabina hadn't changed.

But she was serious. "As soon as I saw him, I thought of you. I knew you'd been telling the truth all along and I felt so rotten for not believing you." She stopped. "You really are what you said. A spy!"

"Not exactly..."

"Do MI6 know you're here?"

"No."

"But you must have some sort of gadgets. You told me they

gave you gadgets. Haven't you got exploding shoelaces or something to get us out of here?"

"I haven't got anything. MI6 don't even know I'm here. After what happened at the bank – in Liverpool Street – I sort of went after Cray on my own. I was just so angry about the way they tricked you and lied about me. I was stupid. I mean, I had the flash drive in my hand ... and I gave it back to Cray!"

Sabina understood. "You came here to rescue me," she said.

"Some rescue!"

"After the way I treated you, you should have just dumped me."

"I don't know, Sab. I thought I had it all worked out. I thought they'd let you go and everything would turn out all right. I had no idea..." Alex kicked out at the door. It was as solid as a rock. "We have to stop him," he said. "We have to do something."

"Maybe he was making it up," Sabina suggested. "Think about it. He said he was going to fire twenty-five missiles all around the world. American missiles. But they're all controlled from the White House. Only the American president can set them off. Everyone knows that. So what's he going to do? Fly to Washington and try to break in?"

"I wish you were right." Alex shook his head. "But Cray's got a huge organization. He's put years of planning and millions of pounds into this. He's got Yassen Gregorovich working for him. He must know something we don't."

He went over to her. He wanted to put an arm round her but he ended up standing awkwardly in front of her instead. "Listen," he said. "This is going to sound really big-headed and you know I'd never normally tell you what to do. But the thing is, I have sort of been here before..."

"What? Locked up by a maniac who wants to destroy the world?"

"Well, yes. Actually I have." He sighed. "My uncle was trying to turn me into a spy when I was still in short trousers. I never even realized it. And it's true what I told you. They made me train with the SAS. Anyway, the truth is ... I know things. And it may be that we do get a chance to get back at Cray. But if that happens, you have to leave everything to me. You have to do what I say. Without arguing..."

"Forget it!" Sabina shook her head. "I'll do what you say. But it was my dad he tried to kill. And I can tell you, if Cray leaves a kitchen knife lying around, I'm going to shove it somewhere painful..."

"It may already be too late," Alex said gloomily. "Cray may just leave us here. He could have already left."

"I don't think so. I think he needs you; I don't know why. Maybe it's because you came closest to beating him."

"I'm glad you're here," Alex said.

Sabina looked at him. "I'm not."

Ten minutes later the door opened and Yassen Gregorovich appeared carrying two sets of what looked like white overalls with red markings – serial numbers – on the sleeves. "You are to put these on," he said.

"Why?" Alex asked.

"Cray wants you. You're coming with us. Do as you're told."

But Alex still hesitated. "What is this?" he demanded. There was something disturbingly familiar about what he was being asked to wear.

"It is a polyamide fabric," Yassen explained. The words meant nothing to Alex. "It is used in biochemical warfare," he added. "Now put it on."

With a growing sense of dread, Alex put the suit on over his own clothes. Sabina did the same. The overalls covered them completely, with hoods that would go over their heads. Alex realized that when they were fully suited up, they would be virtually shapeless. It would be impossible to tell that they were teenagers.

"Now come with me," Yassen said.

They were led back through the house and out into the cloister. There were now three vehicles parked on the grass: a Jeep and two covered trucks, both painted white with the same red markings as the suits. There were about twenty men, all in biochemical suits. Henryk, the Dutch pilot, was in the back of the jeep, nervously polishing his glasses. Damian Cray stood next to him talking, but seeing Alex he stopped and came over. He was bristling with excitement, walking jauntily, his eyes even brighter than normal.

"So you're here!" he exclaimed, as if welcoming Alex to a party. "Excellent! I've decided I want you to come along. Mr Gregorovich tried to talk me out of it, but that's the thing about Russians. No sense of humour. But you see, Alex, none of this would have happened without you. You brought me the flash drive; it's only fair you should see how I use it."

"I'd rather see you arrested and sent to Broadmoor," Alex said.

Cray simply laughed. "That's what I like about you!" he exclaimed. "You're so rude. But I do have to warn you, Yassen will be watching you like a hawk. Or maybe I should say like an eagle. If you do anything at all, if you so much as blink without permission, he'll shoot your girlfriend first. And then he'll shoot you. Do you understand?"

"Where are we going?" Alex asked.

"We're taking the motorway into London. It'll take us just a couple of hours. You and Sabina will be in the first truck with Yassen. Eagle Strike has begun, by the way. Everything is in place. I think you'll enjoy it."

He turned his back on them and went over to the Jeep. A few

minutes later the convoy left, rolling out of the gates and back up the lane to the main road. Alex and Sabina sat next to each other on a narrow wooden bench. There were six men with them, all armed with automatic rifles, slung over the white suits. Alex thought he recognized one of the faces from the compound outside Amsterdam. Certainly he knew the type. Pale skin, dead-looking hair, dark, empty eyes. Yassen sat opposite them. He too had put on a biochemical suit. He seemed to be staring at Alex, but he said nothing and his face was unreadable.

They travelled for two hours, taking the M4 towards London. Alex glanced occasionally at Sabina and she caught his eye once and smiled nervously. This wasn't her world. The men, the machine guns, the biochemical suits ... they were all part of a nightmare that had come out of nowhere and which still made no sense – with no sign of a way out. Alex was baffled too. But the suits suggested a dreadful possibility. Did Cray have biochemical weapons? Was he planning to use them?

At last they turned off the motorway. Looking out of the back flap, Alex saw a signpost to Heathrow Airport and suddenly he knew, without being told, that this was their true destination. He remembered the plane he had seen at the compound. And Cray, talking to him in the garden. *Henryk is very valuable to me. He flies jumbo jets*. The airport had to be part of it, but it still didn't explain so many things. The president of the United States. Nuclear missiles. The very name – Eagle Strike – itself. Alex was angry with himself. It was all there in front of him. Some sort of picture was taking shape. But it was still blurred, out of focus.

They stopped. Nobody moved. Then Yassen spoke for the first time. "Out!" A single word.

Alex went first, then helped Sabina down. He enjoyed feeling her hand in his. There was a sudden loud roar overhead and he looked up just in time to see an aircraft sweeping down out of the sky. He saw where they were. They had stopped on the top floor of an abandoned multi-storey carpark – a legacy of Sir Arthur Lunt, Cray's father. It was on the very edge of Heathrow Airport, near the main runway. The only car, apart from their own, was a burnt-out shell. The ground was strewn with rubble and old rusting oil drums. Alex couldn't imagine why they had come here. Cray was waiting for a signal. Something was going to happen. But what?

Alex looked at his watch. It was exactly half past two. Cray called them over. He had travelled in the Jeep with Henryk and now Alex saw that there was a radio transmitter on the back seat. Henryk turned a dial; there was a loud whine. Cray was certainly making a performance out of this. The radio had been connected to a loudspeaker so that they could all hear.

"It's about to begin," Cray said. He giggled. "Exactly on time!"

Alex looked up. A second plane was coming in. It was still too far away and too high up to be seen clearly, but even so, he thought he recognized something about its shape. Suddenly a voice crackled out of the loudspeaker in the Jeep.

"Attention, air traffic control. This is Millennium Air flight 118 from Amsterdam. We have a problem."

The voice had been speaking in English but with a heavy Dutch accent. There was a pause, an empty hissing, and then a woman's voice replied. "Roger, MA 118. What is your problem, over?"

"Mayday! Mayday!" The voice from the aircraft was suddenly louder. "This is flight MA 118. We have a fire on board. Request immediate clearance to land."

Another pause. Alex could imagine the panic in the control tower at Heathrow. But when the woman spoke again, her voice was professional, calm. "Roger your mayday. We have you on radar. Steer on 0-90. Descend three thousand feet."

"Air traffic control." The radio crackled again. "This is Captain Schroeder from flight MA 118. I have to advise you that I am carrying extremely hazardous biochemical products on behalf of the Ministry of Defence. We have an emergency situation here. Please advise."

The Heathrow woman replied immediately. "We need to know what is on board. Where is it and what are the quantities?"

"Air traffic control, we are carrying a nerve gas. We cannot be more specific. It is highly experimental and extremely dangerous. There are three canisters in the hold. We now have a fire in the main cabin. Mayday! Mayday!"

Alex looked again. The plane was much lower now and he knew exactly where he had seen it before. It was the cargo plane that he had seen in the compound outside Amsterdam. Smoke was streaming out of the side and even as Alex watched, flames suddenly exploded, spreading over the wings. To anyone watching, it would seem that the plane was in terrible danger. But Alex knew that the whole thing had been faked.

The control tower was monitoring the plane. "Flight MA 118, the emergency services have been alerted. We are beginning an immediate evacuation of the airport. Please proceed to twenty-seven left. You are cleared to land."

At once Alex heard the sound of alarms coming from all over the airport. The plane was still two or three thousand feet up, the flames trailing behind it. He had to admit that it looked totally convincing. Suddenly everything was starting to make sense. He was beginning to understand Cray's plan.

"Time to roll!" Cray announced.

Alex and Sabina were led back to the truck. Cray climbed into the Jeep next to Henryk, who was driving, and they set off. It was difficult for Alex to see what was happening now as he only had a view out of the back, but he guessed that they had left the carpark and were following the perimeter fence around the airport. The alarms seemed to have got louder; presumably they were getting nearer to them. A number of police sirens erupted in the distance and Alex noticed that the road had got busier as cars tore past, the drivers desperate to get away from the immediate area.

"What's he doing?" Sabina whispered.

"The plane isn't on fire," Alex said. "Cray's tricked them. He's evacuating the airport. That's how we're going to get in."

"But why?"

"Enough," Yassen said. "You don't speak now." He reached under his seat and produced two gas masks which he handed to Alex and Sabina. "Put these on."

"Why do I need it?" Sabina asked.

"Just do as I say."

"Well, it'll ruin my make-up." She put it on anyway.

Alex did the same. All the men in the truck, including Yassen, had gas masks. Suddenly they were completely anonymous. Alex had to admit that there was a certain genius to Cray's scheme. It was a perfect way to break into the airport. By now all the security personnel would know that a plane carrying a deadly nerve agent was about to crash-land. The airport was in the throes of a full-scale emergency evacuation. When Cray and his miniature army arrived at the main gate, it was unlikely that anyone would ask them for ID. In their biochemical suits they looked official. They were driving official-looking vehicles. The fact that they had arrived at the airport in record time wouldn't be seen as suspicious. It was more like a miracle.

It happened exactly as Alex suspected.

The Jeep stopped at a gate on the south side of the airport. The guards there were both young. One of them had only been in the job for a couple of weeks and was already panicking, faced with a red alert. The cargo plane hadn't landed yet but it was getting closer and closer, stumbling out of the air. The fire was worse, clearly out of control. And here were two trucks and an army vehicle filled with men in white suits, hoods and gas masks. He wasn't going to argue.

Cray leant out of the door. He was as anonymous as the rest of his men, his face concealed behind the gas mask. "Ministry of Defence," he snapped. "Biochemical Weapons division."

"Go ahead!" The guards couldn't hurry them through fast enough.

The plane touched down. Two fire engines and an assortment of emergency vehicles began to race towards it. Their truck overtook the Jeep and came to a halt. Looking out of the back, Alex saw everything.

It started with Damian Cray.

He was sitting in the passenger seat of the Jeep and had produced a radio transmitter. "It's time to raise the stakes," he said. "Let's make this a real emergency."

Somehow Alex knew what was about to happen. Cray pressed a button and at once the plane exploded, disappearing in a huge fireball that erupted out of it and at the same time consumed it. Fragments of wood and metal spun in all directions. Burning aviation fuel spilt over the runway, seeming to set it alight too. The emergency vehicles had fanned out as if to surround the wreckage, but then Alex realized that they had received new orders from the control tower. There was nothing more they could do. The pilot and his crew on the plane were certainly dead. Some unknown nerve gas could even now be leaking into the atmosphere. Turn round. Get out of there. Go!

Alex knew that Cray had cheated whoever had flown the plane, killing them with exactly the same cold-blooded ruthlessness with which he killed anyone who got in his way. The pilot would have been paid to send out the false alarm and then to fake a crash-landing. He wouldn't have known that there was a load of plastic explosive concealed on board. He might have expected a long stay in an English prison. He hadn't been told his job was to die.

Sabina wasn't watching. Alex couldn't see anything of her face – the gas mask had fogged up – but her head was turned away. For a moment he felt desperately sorry for her. What had she got into? And to think that this had all begun with a holiday in the South of France!

The truck jerked forward. They were inside the airport. Cray had managed to short-circuit the entire security system. Nobody would notice them – at least not for a while. But the questions still remained. What had they come for? Why here?

And then they slowed down one last time. Alex looked out. And at last everything made sense.

They had stopped in front of a plane, a Boeing 747-200B. But it was much more than that. Its body had been painted blue and white, with the words UNITED STATES OF AMERICA written across the main fuselage and the Stars and Stripes emblazoned on its tail. And there was the eagle, clutching a shield, just below the door, mocking Alex for not having guessed before. The eagle that had given Eagle Strike its name. It was the presidential seal and this was the presidential plane, Air Force One. This was the reason why Damian Cray was here.

Alex had seen it on the television in Blunt's office. The plane that had brought the American president to England. It flew him all over the world, travelling at just below the speed of sound. Alex knew very little about it, but then virtually all information about Air Force One was restricted. But one thing he did know.

Just about anything that could be done in the White House could be done on the plane, even while it was in the air.

Just about anything. Including starting a nuclear war.

There were two men standing guard on the steps that led up to the open door and the main cabin. They were soldiers, dressed in khaki combat gear and black berets. As Cray got out of the car, they brought up their guns, moving into a position of alert. They had heard the alarms. They knew something was happening at the airport but they weren't sure what it had to do with them.

"What's going on?" one of them asked.

Damian Cray said nothing. His hand came up and suddenly he was holding a pistol. He fired twice, the bullets making hardly any sound – or perhaps the noise of the gun was somehow dwarfed by the immensity of the plane. The soldiers twisted round and fell onto the tarmac. Nobody had seen what had happened. All eyes were on the runway and the still-burning debris of the cargo plane.

Alex felt a surge of hatred for Cray, for his cowardice. The American soldiers hadn't been expecting trouble. The president was nowhere near the airport. Air Force One wasn't due to take off for another day. Cray could have knocked them out; he could have taken them prisoner. But it had been easier to kill them; already he was putting the gun back into his pocket, two human lives simply brushed aside and forgotten. Sabina stood next to him, staring in disbelief.

"Wait here," Cray said. He had removed his gas mask. His face was flushed with excitement.

Yassen Gregorovich and half the men ran up the steps onto the plane. The other half stripped off their white suits to reveal American army uniforms underneath. Cray hadn't missed a trick. If anyone did chance to turn their attention away from the cargo plane, it would seem that Air Force One was under heavy guard and that everything was normal. In fact, nothing could have been further from the truth.

More gunfire came from inside the plane. Cray was taking no prisoners. Anyone in his way was being finished without hesitation, without mercy.

Cray stood next to Alex. "Welcome to the VIP lounge," he said. "You might like to know, that's what they call this whole section of the airport." He pointed at a glass and steel building on the other side of the plane. "That's where they all go. Presidents, prime ministers ... I've been in there once or twice as a matter of fact. Very comfortable, and no queues for passport control!"

"Let us go," Alex said. "You don't need us."

"Would you rather I killed you now, instead of later?"

Sabina glanced at Alex but said nothing.

Yassen appeared at the door of the plane and signalled. Air Force One had been taken. There was no one left to fight. Cray's men filed past him and made their way back down the stairs. One of them had been wounded; there was blood on the sleeve of his suit. So at least someone had tried to fight back!

"I think we can go on board," Cray said.

All his men were now dressed as American soldiers, forming a half circle round the steps leading up to the door of the plane, a defensive wall in the event of a counter-attack. Henryk had already climbed up; Alex and Sabina followed him. Cray was right behind them, holding his gun. So there were only going to be the five of them on the plane. Alex filed the information somewhere in his mind. At least the odds had been shortened.

Sabina was numb, walking as if hypnotized. Alex knew what she was feeling. His own legs almost refused to carry him, to take these steps, reserved for the most powerful man on the planet. As the door loomed up ahead, with another eagle mounted on its side, he saw Yassen appear from inside, dragging a body dressed in blue trousers and a blue waistcoat: one of the air stewards. Another innocent man sacrificed for Cray's mad dream.

Alex entered the plane.

Air Force One was like no other plane in the world. There were no seats cramped together, no economy class, nothing that looked even remotely like the inside of an ordinary jumbo jet. It had been modified for the president and his staff over three floors: offices and bedrooms, a conference room and kitchen ... four thousand square feet of cabin space in all. Somewhere inside, there was even an operating table, although it had never been used. Alex found himself in an open-plan living area. Everything had been designed for comfort, with a thick-pile carpet, low sofas and armchairs, and tables with old-fashioned electric lamps. The predominant colours were beige and brown, softly lit by dozens of lights recessed into the ceiling. A long corridor led down one side of the plane, with a series of smart offices and seating areas branching off. There were more sofas and occasional tables at intervals all the way down. The windows were covered with fawn-coloured blinds.

Yassen had cleared away the bodies but he had left a bloodstain on the carpet. It was horribly noticeable. The rest of the plane had been cleaned and vacuumed until it was spotless. There was a wheeled trolley against one of the walls and Alex noticed the gleaming crystal glasses, each one engraved with the words AIR FORCE ONE and a picture of the plane. A number of bottles stood on the lower shelf of the trolley: rare malt whiskies and vintage wines. It was service with a smile, all right. To fly on this plane was a privilege enjoyed by only a handful of people and they would be surrounded by total luxury.

Even Cray, who had his own private jet, looked impressed. He glanced at Yassen. "Is that it?" he asked. "Have we killed everyone who needs killing?"

Yassen nodded.

"Then let's get started. I'll take Alex. I want to show him... You wait here."

Cray nodded at Alex. Alex knew he had no choice. He took one last glance at Sabina and tried to tell her with his eyes: *I'll think of something. I'll get us out of here.* But somehow he doubted it. The enormity of Eagle Strike had finally hit him. Air Force One! The presidential plane. It had never been invaded in this way – and no wonder. Nobody else would have been mad enough to consider it.

Cray jabbed Alex with the gun, forcing him up a stairway. Half of him hoped they would meet someone. Just one soldier or one member of the cabin crew who had managed to escape and who might be lying in wait. But he knew that Yassen would have been thorough in his work. He had told Cray that the entire crew had been dealt with. Alex didn't like to think how many men and women there might have been on board.

They entered a room filled with electronic equipment from floor to ceiling. Hugely sophisticated computers stood next to elaborate telephone and radar systems with banks of buttons, switches and blinking lights. Even the ceiling was covered with machinery. Alex realized he was standing in the communications centre of Air Force One. Someone must have been working there when Cray took over the plane. The door wasn't locked.

"Nobody at home," Cray said. "I'm afraid they weren't expecting visitors. We have the place to ourselves." He took the flash drive out of his pocket. "This is the moment of truth, Alex," he said. "This is all thanks to you. But do, please, stay very still. I don't want to kill you until you've seen this, but if you so much as blink, I'm afraid I may have to shoot you."

Cray knew what he was doing. He laid the gun on the table next to him so that it would never be more than a few centimetres from his hand. Then he opened the flash drive and plugged it into a socket in the front of the computer. Finally he sat down and tapped out a series of commands on the keyboard.

"I can't explain exactly how this works," he said as he continued. "We don't have time, and anyway I've always found computers and all that stuff really dreary. But these computers here are just like the ones in the White House, and they're connected to Mount Cheyenne, which is where our American friends have their top-secret underground nuclear weapons control centre. Now, the first things you need to set off the nuclear missiles are the launch codes. They change every day and they're sent to the president, wherever he is, by the National Security Agency. I hope I am not boring you, Alex?"

Alex didn't reply. He was looking at the gun, measuring distances...

"The president carries them with him all the time. Did you know that President Carter actually lost the codes once? He sent them to the dry-cleaner's. But that's another story. The codes are transmitted by Milstar – the Military Strategic and Tactical Relay system. It's a satellite communications system. One set goes to the Pentagon and one set comes here. The codes are inside the computer and..."

There was a buzzing sound and a number of lights on the control panel suddenly went green. Cray let out a cry of pleasure. His face glowed green in the reflection.

"...and here they are now. Wasn't that quick! Strange though it may seem, I am now in control of just about all the nuclear missiles in the United States. Isn't that fun?"

He tapped more quickly on the keyboard and for a moment he

was transformed. As his fingers danced over the keys, Alex was reminded of the Damian Cray he had seen playing the piano at Earls Court and Wembley Stadium. There was a dreamy smile on his face and his eyes were far away.

"There is, of course, a fail-safe device built into it all," he continued. "The Americans wouldn't want just anyone firing off their missiles, would they! No. Only the president can do it, because of this..."

Cray took a small silver key out of his pocket. Alex guessed that it must be a duplicate, also provided by Charlie Roper. Cray inserted it into a complicated-looking silver lock built into the workstation and opened it. There were two red buttons underneath. One to launch the missiles. The other marked with two words which were of more interest to Alex. SELF-DESTRUCT.

Cray was only interested in the first of them.

"This is the button," he said. "The big button. The one you've read all about. The button that means the end of the world. But it's fingerprint sensitive. If it isn't the president's finger, then you might as well go home." He reached out and pressed the launch button. Nothing happened. "You see? It doesn't work!"

"Then all this has been a waste of time!" Alex said.

"Oh no, my dear Alex. Because, you see, you may remember that I recently had the privilege – the very great privilege – of shaking hands with the president. I insisted on it. It was that important to me. But I had a special latex coating on my own hand, and when we shook, I took a cast of his fingers. Isn't that clever?"

Cray removed what looked like a thin plastic glove from his pocket and slipped it onto his hand. Alex saw that the fingers of the glove were moulded. He understood. The president's fingerprints had been duplicated onto the latex surface.

Cray now had the power to launch his nuclear attack.

"Wait a minute," Alex said.

"Yes?"

"You're wrong. You're terribly wrong. You think you're making things better, but you're not!" He struggled to find the right words. "You'll kill thousands of people. Hundreds of thousands of people, and most of them will be innocent. They won't have anything to do with drugs..."

"There have to be sacrifices. But if a thousand people die to save a million, what's so wrong with that?"

"Everything is wrong with it! What about the fallout? Have you thought what it'll do to the rest of the planet? I thought you cared about the environment. But you're going to destroy it."

"It's a price worth paying, and one day the whole world will agree. You've got to be cruel to be kind."

"You only think that because you're insane."

Cray reached for the launch button.

Alex dived forward. He no longer cared about his own safety. He couldn't even protect Sabina. The two of them might be killed, but he had to stop this happening. He had to protect the millions who would die all over the world if Cray was allowed to continue. Twenty-five nuclear missiles falling simultaneously out of the sky! It was beyond imagination.

But Cray had been expecting the move. Suddenly the gun was in his hand and his arm was swinging through the air. Alex felt a savage blow on the side of his head as Cray struck him. He was thrown back, dazed. The room swam in front of his eyes, and he stumbled and fell.

"Too late," Cray muttered.

He reached out and drew a circle in the air with a single finger.

He paused.

Then he stabbed down.

"FASTEN YOUR SEAT BELTS"

The missiles had been activated.

All over America, in deserts and in mountains, on roads and railways, even out at sea, the launch sequences began automatically. Bases in North Dakota, Montana and Wyoming suddenly went onto red alert. Sirens howled. Computers went into frantic overdrive. It was the start of a panic that would spread in minutes all around the world.

And one by one the twenty-five rockets blasted into the air in a moment of terrible beauty.

Eight Minutemen, eight Peacekeepers, five Poseidons and four Trident D5s climbed into the upper atmosphere at exactly the same time, travelling at speeds of up to fifteen thousand miles per hour. Some were fired from silos buried deep under the ground. Some exploded out of specially adapted train carriages. Others came from submarines. And nobody knew who had given the order. It was a billion-dollar fireworks display that would change the world for ever.

And in ninety minutes it would all be over.

In the communications room the computer screens were flashing red. The entire operating board was ablaze with flashing lights. Cray stood up. There was a serene smile on his face.

"Well, that's it," he said. "There's nothing anyone can do now."

"They'll stop them!" Alex said. "As soon as they realize what's happened, they'll press a button and all your missiles will self-destruct."

"I'm afraid it's not quite as easy as that. You see, all the launch protocols have been obeyed. It was the Air Force One computer that set the missiles off; so only Air Force One can terminate them. I noticed you eyeing the little red button on the keyboard right here. SELF-DESTRUCT. But I'm afraid you're not going anywhere near it, Alex. We're leaving."

Cray gestured with the gun and Alex was forced out of the communications room and back down to the main cabin. His head was still hurting where Cray had hit him. He needed to recover his strength. But how much time did he have left?

Yassen and Sabina were waiting for them. As soon as Alex appeared, Sabina tried to go over to him but Yassen held her back. Cray sank into a sofa next to her.

"Time to go!" he said. He smiled at Alex. "You realize, of course, that once this plane is in the air, it's virtually indestructible. You could say it's the perfect getaway vehicle. That's the beauty of it. It has over two hundred and thirty miles of wiring inside the frame which is designed to withstand even the pulse of a thermonuclear blast. Not that it would make any difference anyway. If they did manage to shoot us down, the missiles would still find their target. The world would still be saved!"

Alex tried to clear his head. He had to think straight.

There were just the five of them on the plane. Sabina, Yassen, Damian Cray and himself – with Henryk in the cockpit. Alex looked out of the main door. The ring of fake American soldiers was still in place. Even if anyone at the airport glanced their way, they would see nothing wrong. Not that that was likely to happen. The authorities must still be concentrating on the cloud of deadly nerve gas that didn't in fact exist.

Alex knew that if he was going to do anything – if there was anything he could do – it would have to happen before the plane left the ground. Cray was right. Once the plane was in the air, he would have no chance at all.

"Close the door, Mr Gregorovich," Cray commanded. "I think we should be on our way."

"Wait a minute!" Alex started to get to his feet but Cray signalled to him to sit down. The gun was in his hand. It was a Smith and Wesson .40, small and powerful with its three and a half inch barrel and square handgrip. Alex knew that it was extremely dangerous to fire a gun on a normal plane. Breaking a window or penetrating the outer skin would depressurize the cabin and make flight impossible. But this, of course, was Air Force One. This was not a normal plane.

"Stay exactly where you are," Cray said.

"Where are you taking us?" Sabina demanded. Cray was still sitting on the sofa next to her. He obviously thought it would be better to keep her and Alex apart. He reached out and ran a finger across her cheek. Sabina shuddered. She found him revolting and didn't care if he knew it. "We're going to Russia," he said.

"Russia?" Alex looked puzzled.

"A new life for me. And a return home for Mr Gregorovich." Cray licked his lips. "As a matter of fact, Mr Gregorovich will be something of a hero."

"I rather doubt that." Alex couldn't keep the scorn out of his voice.

"Oh yes. Heroin is smuggled into the country – I am told – in lead-lined coffins, and the border guards simply look the other way. Of course, they're paid. Corruption is everywhere. Drugs are ten times less expensive in Russia than they are in Europe and there are at least three and a half million addicts in Moscow and St Petersburg. Mr Gregorovich will be ending a problem that has almost brought his country to its knees, and I know that the president will be grateful. So you see, it looks as if the two of us are going to live happily ever after – which, I'm afraid, is more than can be said for you."

Yassen had closed the door. Alex watched as he pulled the lever down, locking it. "Doors to automatic," said Yassen.

There was a speaker system active in the plane. Everything that was said in the main cabin could be heard in the cockpit. And, sitting at the flight deck, Henryk flicked a switch so that his voice too could be heard throughout the plane.

"This is your captain speaking," he said. "Please fasten your seat belts and prepare for take-off." He was joking: a grisly parody of a real departure. "Thank you for flying with Cray Airlines. I hope you have a pleasant flight."

The engines started up. Out of the window Alex saw the soldiers scatter and run back to the trucks. Their work was done. They would leave the airport and make their way home to Amsterdam. He glanced at Sabina. She was sitting very still and he remembered that she was waiting for him to do something. *I know things... You have to leave everything to me*. That was what he had told her. How very hollow the words sounded now.

Air Force One was equipped with four huge engines. Alex heard them as they began to turn. They were about to leave! Desperately he looked around him: at the closed door with its white lever slanting down, at the stairway leading up towards the cockpit, at the low tables and neatly arranged line of magazines, at the trolley with its bottles and glasses. Cray was sitting with his legs slightly apart, the gun resting on his thigh. Yassen was still standing by the door. He had a second gun. It was in one of his pockets but Alex knew that the Russian could draw, aim and fire before he had time to blink. There were no other weapons in sight, nothing he could get his hands on. Hopeless.

The plane jerked and began to pull back from its stand. Alex looked out of the window again and saw something extraordinary. There was a vehicle parked next to the VIP building, not far from the plane. It was like a miniature tractor, with three carriages attached, loaded with plastic boxes. As Alex watched, it was suddenly blown away as if it had been made of paper. The carriages spun round and broke free. The tractor itself crashed onto its side and skidded across the tarmac.

It was the engines! Normally a plane of this size would have been towed to an open area out of harm's way before it began to taxi. Cray, of course, wasn't going to wait. Air Force One had been put into reverse thrust and the engines – with a thrust rating of over two hundred thousand pounds – were so powerful that they would blow away anything or anyone who came near. Now it was the turn of the VIP building itself. Windows shattered, the glass exploding inwards. A security man had come out and Alex saw him thrown back like a plastic soldier fired from an elastic band. A voice came through on the speakers inside the cabin. Henryk must have connected up the radio so that they could hear.

"This is air traffic control to Air Force One." This time it was a man's voice. "You have no clearance to taxi. Please stop immediately."

The stairs that they had climbed to board the plane toppled to one side, crashing onto the tarmac. The plane was moving more quickly now, backing out onto the main apron.

"This is air traffic control to Air Force One. We repeat: you have no clearance to taxi. Can you please state your intentions..."

They were out in the open, away from the VIP lounge. The main runway was behind them. The rest of the airport must have been almost a mile away. Inside the cockpit Henryk put the plane into forward thrust, and Alex felt the jolt and heard the whine of the engines as once again they began to move. Cray was humming to himself, his eyes vacant, lost in his own world. But the Smith and Wesson was still in his hand and Alex knew that the slightest movement would bring an instant response. Yassen hadn't stirred. He also seemed wrapped up in his own thoughts, as if he was trying to forget that this was happening.

The plane began to pick up speed, heading for the runway. There was a computer in the cockpit and Henryk had already fed in all the necessary information: the weight of the plane, the outside air temperature, the wind speed, the pressure. He would take off into the breeze, now coming from the east. The main runway is nearly four thousand metres long and the computer had already calculated that the aircraft would only need two and a half thousand of them. It was almost empty. This was going to be an easy take-off.

"Air Force One. You have no clearance. Please abort immediately. Repeat: abort at once."

The voice from air traffic control was still buzzing in his headphones. Henryk reached up and turned the radio off. He knew that an emergency overdrive would have gone into operation and any other planes would be diverted out of his way. After all, this aircraft did belong to the president of the United States of America. Already the Heathrow authorities would be screaming at each other over the phone lines, fearing not just a crash but a major diplomatic incident. Downing Street would have been informed. All over London, officials and civil servants would be asking the same desperate question.

What the hell is going on?

A hundred kilometres above their heads, the eight Peacekeeper missiles were nearing the edge of space. Two of their rockets had already burnt out and separated, leaving only the last sections with their deployment modules and protective shrouds. The Minutemen and the other missiles that Cray had fired weren't far behind. All of them carried top-secret and highly advanced navigation systems. On-board computers were already calculating trajectories and making adjustments. Soon the missiles would turn and lock into their targets.

And in eighty minutes they would fall back to earth.

Air Force One was moving rapidly now, following the taxi paths to the main runway. Ahead was the holding point where it would make a sharp turn and begin pre-flight checks.

In the cabin Sabina examined Cray as if seeing him for the first time. Her face showed only contempt. "I wonder what they'll do with you when you get to Russia," she said.

"What do you mean?" Cray asked.

"I wonder if they'll get rid of you by sending you back to England or just shoot you and be done with it."

Cray stared at her. He looked as if he had been slapped across the face. Alex flinched, fearing the worst. And it came.

"I've had enough of these guttersnipes," Cray snapped. "They're not amusing me any more." He turned to Yassen. "Kill them."

Yassen seemed not to have heard. "What?" he asked.

"You heard me. I'm bored of them. Kill them now!"

The plane stopped. They had reached the holding point. Henryk had heard the instructions being given in the main cabin but he ignored what was happening as he went through the final procedures: lifting the elevators up and down, turning the ailerons. He was seconds away from take-off. As soon as he was satisfied that the plane was ready, he would push down the four thrust levers and they would rocket forward. He tested the rudder pedals and the nose wheel. Everything was ready.

"I do not kill children," Yassen said. Alex had heard him say exactly the same thing on the boat in the South of France. He hadn't believed him then, but he wondered now what was going on inside the Russian's mind.

Sabina watched Alex intently, waiting for him to do something. But trapped inside the plane, with the whine of the engines already beginning to rise, there was nothing he could do. Not yet...

"What are you saying?" Cray demanded.

"There is no need for this," Yassen said. "Take them with us. They can do no harm."

"Why should I want to take them all the way to Russia?"

"We can lock them in one of the cabins. You don't even need to see them."

"Mr Gregorovich..." Cray was breathing heavily. There was a bead of sweat on his forehead and his grip on the gun was tighter than ever. "If you don't kill them, I will."

Yassen didn't move.

"All right! All right!" Cray sighed. "I thought I was meant to be in charge, but it seems that I have to do everything myself."

Cray brought up his gun. Alex got to his feet.

"No!" Sabina cried.

Cray fired.

But he hadn't been aiming at Sabina or even at Alex. The bullet hit Yassen in the chest, spinning him away from the door. "I'm sorry, Mr Gregorovich," he said. "But you're fired."

Then he turned the gun on Alex.

"You're next," he said.

He fired a second time.

Sabina cried out in horror. Cray had aimed at Alex's heart, and in the confined space of the cabin there was little chance he could miss. The force of the bullet threw Alex off his feet and back across the cabin. He crashed to the ground and lay still.

Sabina threw herself at Cray. Alex was dead. The plane was taking off. Nothing mattered any more. Cray fired at her but the shot missed and suddenly she was right up against him, her hands clawing at his eyes, shouting all the time. But Cray was too strong for her. He brought an arm round, grabbed hold of her and threw her back against the door. She lay there, dazed and helpless. The gun came up.

"Goodbye, my dear," Cray said.

He aimed. But before he could fire, his arm was seized from behind. Sabina stared. Alex was up again and he was unhurt. It was impossible. But, like Cray, she had no way of knowing that he was wearing the bulletproof jersey that Smithers had given him with the bike. The bullet had hurt him; he thought it might have cracked a rib. But although it had knocked him down, it hadn't penetrated his skin.

Now Alex was on top of Cray. The man was small – only a little taller than Alex himself – but even so he was thickset and surprisingly strong. Alex managed to get one hand around Cray's wrist, keeping the gun away from him. But Cray's other hand grabbed Alex's neck, his fingers curling into the side of Alex's throat.

"Sabina! Get out of here!" Alex managed to shout the words before his air supply was cut off. The gun was out of control. He was using all his strength to stop Cray from aiming it at him and he wasn't sure how much longer he would be able to hold him off. Sabina ran over to the main door and pulled up the white handle to open it.

At that exact moment, in the cockpit, Henryk pushed the four thrust levers all the way down. From where he sat, the runway stretched out in front of him. The path was clear. Air Force One lurched forward and started to take off.

The main door flew open with a loud hiss. It had been set to automatic before the plane began to move, and as soon as Sabina had unlocked it, a pneumatic system had kicked in. An orange slide extended itself from the doorway like a giant tongue and began to inflate. The emergency slide.

Wind and dust rushed in, a miniature tornado that whirled madly through the cabin. Cray had brought the gun round, aiming at Alex's head, but the force of the wind surprised him. The magazines on the table flew into the air, flapping into his face like giant moths. The trolley of drinks broke loose and rattled across the carpet, bottles and glasses crashing down.

Cray's face was contorted, his perfect teeth in a twisted snarl, his eyes bulging. He swore, but no sound could be heard against the roar of the engines. Sabina was pressed against the wall, staring helplessly through the open doorway at the grass and concrete rushing past in a green and grey blur. Yassen wasn't moving; blood was spreading slowly across his shirt. Alex could feel the strength draining out of him. He relaxed his grip and the gun went off. Sabina screamed. The bullet had smashed a light fitting inches from her face. Alex jabbed down, trying to knock the gun out of Cray's hand. Cray slammed a knee into his stomach and Alex reeled back, gasping for breath. The plane continued, faster and faster, hurtling down the runway.

Behind the controls Henryk was suddenly sweating. The eyes behind the spectacles were confused. He had seen a light blink on, warning him that a door had opened and that the main cabin was depressurized. He was already travelling at a hundred and thirty miles an hour. Air traffic control must have realized what was happening and would have alerted the authorities. If he stopped now, he would be arrested. But did he dare take off?

And then the on-board computer spoke.

"V1..."

It was a machine voice. Utterly emotionless. Two syllables brought together by electronic circuitry. And they were the last two syllables Henryk wanted to hear.

Normally it would have been the first officer who called out the speeds, keeping an eye on the progress of the plane. But Henryk was on his own. He had to rely on the automated system. What the computer was telling him was that the plane was moving at one hundred and fifty miles per hour – V1 – decision speed. He was now going too fast to stop. If he tried to abort the take-off, if he put the engines into reverse, he would crash.

It is the moment every pilot dreads – and the single most dangerous moment in any flight. More plane crashes have been caused by a wrong decision at this time than by anything else. Every instinct in Henryk's body told him to stop. He was safe on the ground. A crash here would be better than a crash from fifteen hundred feet up in the air. But if he did try to stop, a crash would be the certain result.

He didn't know what to do.

*   *   *

The sun was setting in the town of Quetta in Pakistan, but life in the refugee camp was as busy as ever. Hundreds of people clutching blankets and stoves made their way through a miniature city of tents, while children, some of them in rags, queued for vaccinations. A row of women sat on benches, working on a quilt, beating and folding the cotton.

The air was cool and fresh in the Patkai Hills of Myanmar, the country that had once been Burma. Fourteen hundred metres above sea level, the breeze carried the scent of pine trees and flowers. It was half past nine at night and most people were asleep. A few shepherds sat alone with their flocks. Thousands of stars littered the night sky.

In Colombia, in the Urabá region, another day had dawned and the smell of chocolate wafted down the village street. The *campesinas* – the farmers' wives – had begun working at dawn, toasting the cacao beans, then splitting the shells. Children were drawn to their doors, taking in the rich, irresistible scent.

And in the highlands of Peru, north of Arequipa, families in colourful clothes made their way to the markets, some carrying the little bundles of fruit and vegetables that were all they had to sell. A woman in a bowler hat sat hunched up beside a row of sacks, each one filled with a different spice. Laughing teenagers kicked a football in the street.

These were the targets that the missiles had selected, far out in space. There were thousands – millions – more like them. And they were all innocent. They knew about the fields where the poppies were grown. They knew the men who worked there. But that was no concern of theirs. Life had to go on.

And none of them had any knowledge of the deadly missiles that were already closing in on them. None of them saw the horror that was coming their way.

*   *   *

The end came very quickly on Air Force One.

Cray was punching the side of Alex's head again and again. Alex still clung to the gun, but his grip was weakening. He finally fell back, bloody and exhausted. His face was bruised, his eyes half closed.

The emergency slide was jutting out now, horizontal with the plane. The rush of air was pushing it back, slanting it towards the wings. The plane was travelling at a hundred and eighty miles per hour. It would leave the ground in less than ten seconds' time.

Cray raised the gun one last time.

Then he cried out as something slammed into him. It was Sabina. She had grabbed hold of the trolley and used it as a battering ram. The trolley hit him behind the knees. His legs buckled and he lost his balance, toppling over backwards. He landed on top of the trolley, dropping the gun. Sabina dived for it, determined that he wouldn't fire another shot.

And that was when Alex rose up.

He had quickly gauged distances and angles. He knew what he had to do. With a cry he threw himself forward, his arms outstretched. His palms slammed into the side of the trolley. Cray yelled out. The trolley shot across the main area of the cabin and, with Cray still on top of it, out the door.

And it didn't stop there. The emergency slide slanted gently towards the ground that was shooting past far below. It was held in place by the rushing wind and by the compressed air inside it. The trolley bounced out onto the slide and began to roll down. Alex staggered over to the door just in time to see Cray begin his fairground ride to hell. The slide carried him halfway down, the force of the wind tilting him back towards the wings.

Damian Cray came into the general area of engine two.

The last thing he saw was the engine's gaping mouth. Then the wind rush took him. With a dreadful, inaudible scream he was pulled into the engine. The trolley went with him.

Cray was mincemeat. More than that, he was vaporized. In one second he had been turned into a cloud of red gas that disappeared into the atmosphere. There was simply nothing left. But the metal trolley offered more resistance. There was a bang like a cannon shot. A huge tongue of flame exploded out of the back as the engine was torn apart.

That was when the plane went out of control.

Henryk had decided to abort take-off and was trying to slow down, but now it was too late. An engine on one side had suddenly stopped. Both engines on the other side were still on full power. The imbalance sent the plane lurching violently to the left. Alex and Sabina were thrown to the floor. Lights fused and sparked all around them. Anything that wasn't securely fastened whirled through the air. Henryk fought for control but it was hopeless. The plane veered away and left the runway. That was the end of it. The soft ground was unable to support such a huge load. With a terrible shearing of metal, the undercarriage broke off and the whole thing toppled over onto one side.

The entire cabin twisted round and Alex felt the floor tilt beneath his feet. It was as if the plane was turning upside down. But finally it stopped. The engines cut out. The plane rested on its side and the scream of sirens filled the air as emergency vehicles raced across the tarmac.

Alex tried to move but his legs wouldn't obey him. He was lying on the floor and he could feel the darkness closing in. But he knew he had to stay conscious. His work wasn't finished yet.

"Sab?" He called out to her and was relieved when she got to her feet and came over.

"Alex?"

"You have to get to the communications room. There's a button. Self-destruct." For a moment she looked blank and he took hold of her arm. "The missiles..."

"Yes. Yes ... of course." She was in shock. Too much had happened. But she understood. She staggered up the stairs, balancing herself against the sloping walls. Alex lay where he was.

And then Yassen spoke.

"Alex..."

Alex didn't have enough strength left to be surprised. He turned his head slowly, expecting to see a gun in the Russian's hand. It didn't seem fair to him. After so much, was he really going to die now, just when help was on its way? But Yassen wasn't holding a gun. He had propped himself up against a table. He was covered in blood now and there was a strange quality to his eyes as the blue slowly drained out. Yassen's skin was even paler than usual and, as his head tilted back, Alex noticed for the first time that he had a long scar on his neck. It was dead straight, as if it had been drawn with a ruler.

"Please..." Yassen's voice was soft.

It was the last thing he wanted to do, but Alex crawled through the wreckage of the cabin and over to him. He remembered that Cray's death and the destruction of the plane had only happened because Yassen had refused to kill Sabina and him.

"What happened to Cray?" Yassen asked.

"He went off his trolley," Alex said.

"He's dead?"

"Very."

Yassen nodded, as if pleased. "I knew it was a mistake working for him," he said. "I knew." He fought for breath, narrowing his eyes for a moment. "There is something I have to tell you, Alex," he said. The strange thing was that he was speaking absolutely normally, as if this were a quiet conversation between friends. Despite himself, Alex found himself marvelling at the man's self-control. He must have only minutes to live.

Then Yassen spoke again and everything in Alex's life changed for ever.

"I couldn't kill you," he said. "I would never have killed you. Because, you see, Alex ... I knew your father."

"What?" Despite his exhaustion, despite all the pain from his injuries, Alex felt something shiver through him.

"Your father. He and I..." Yassen had to catch his breath. "We worked together."

"He worked with you?"

"Yes."

"You mean ... he was a spy?"

"Not a spy, no, Alex. He was a killer. Like me. He was the very best. The best in the world. I knew him when I was nineteen. He taught me many things..."

"No!" Alex refused to accept what he was hearing. He had never met his father, knew nothing about him. But what Yassen was saying couldn't be true. It was some sort of horrible trick.

The sirens were getting nearer. The first of the vehicles must have arrived. He could hear men shouting outside.

"I don't believe you," Alex cried. "My father wasn't a killer. He couldn't have been!"

"I'm telling you the truth. You have to know."

"Did he work for MI6?"

"No." The ghost of a smile flickered across Yassen's face. But it was filled with sadness. "MI6 hunted him down. They killed him. They tried to kill both of us. At the last minute I escaped, but he..." Yassen swallowed. "They killed your father, Alex."

"No!"

"Why would I lie to you?" Yassen reached out weakly and took hold of Alex's arm. It was the first physical contact the two had ever had. "Your father ... he did this." Yassen drew a finger along the scar on his neck, but his voice was failing him and he couldn't explain. "He saved my life. In a way, I loved him. I love you too, Alex. You are so very much like him. I'm glad that you're here with me now." There was a pause and a spasm of pain rippled across the dying man's face. There was one last thing he had to say. "If you don't believe me, go to Venice. Find Scorpia. And you will find your destiny..."

Yassen shut his eyes and Alex knew he would never open them again.

In the communications room Sabina found the button and pressed it. In space the first of the Minutemen blew itself into thousands of pieces, a brilliant, soundless explosion. Seconds later the other missiles did the same.

Air Force One was surrounded. A fleet of emergency vehicles had reached it and two trucks were spraying it down, covering it in torrents of white foam.

But Alex didn't know any of this. He was lying next to Yassen, his eyes closed. He had quietly and thankfully passed out.

RICHMOND BRIDGE

The swans really weren't going anywhere. They seemed happy just to circle slowly in the sunshine, occasionally dipping their beaks under the surface of the water, searching for insects, algae, whatever. Alex had been watching them for the last half-hour, almost hypnotized by them. He wondered what it was like to be a swan. He wondered how they managed to keep their feathers so white.

He was sitting on a bench beside the Thames, just outside Richmond. This was where the river seemed to abandon London, finally leaving the city behind it on the other side of Richmond Bridge. Looking upstream, Alex could see fields and woodland, absurdly green, sprawled out in the heat of the English summer.

An au pair, pushing a pram, walked past on the towpath. She noticed Alex and, although her expression didn't change, her hands tightened on the pram and she very slightly quickened her pace. Alex knew that he looked terrible, like something out of one of those posters put out by the local council. Alex Rider, fourteen, in need of fostering. His last fight with Damian Cray had left its marks. But this time it was more than cuts and bruises. They would fade like others had faded before. This time he had seen his whole life bend out of shape.

He couldn't stop thinking about Yassen Gregorovich. Two weeks had gone by but he was still waking up in the middle of the night, reliving the final moments on Air Force One. His father had been a contract killer, murdered by the very people who had now taken over his own life. It couldn't be true. Yassen must have been lying, trying to wound Alex in revenge for what had happened between them. Alex wanted to believe it. But he had looked into the dying man's eyes and had seen no deceit, only a strange sort of tenderness – and a desire for the truth to be known.

Go to Venice. Find Scorpia. Find your destiny...

It seemed to Alex that his only destiny was to be lied to and manipulated by adults who cared nothing about him. Should he go to Venice? How would he find Scorpia? For that matter, was Scorpia a person or a place? Alex watched the swans, wishing they could give him an answer. But they just drifted on the water, ignoring him.

A shadow fell across the bench. Alex looked up and felt a fist close tightly inside his stomach. Mrs Jones was standing over him. The MI6 agent was dressed in grey silk trousers with a matching jacket that hung down to her knees, almost like a coat. There was a silver pin in her lapel but no other jewellery. It seemed strange for her to be out here, in the sun. He didn't want to see her. Along with Alan Blunt, she was the last person Alex wanted to see.

"May I join you?" she asked.

"It seems you already have," Alex said.

She sat down next to him.

"Have you been following me?" Alex asked. He wondered how she had known he would be here and it occurred to him that he might have been under round-the-clock surveillance for the past fortnight. It wouldn't have surprised him.

"No. Your friend – Jack Starbright – told me you'd be here."

"I'm meeting someone."

"Not until twelve. Jack came in to see me, Alex. You should have reported to Liverpool Street by now. We need to debrief you."

"There's no point reporting to Liverpool Street," Alex said bitterly. "There's nothing there, is there? Just a bank."

Mrs Jones understood. "That was wrong of us," she said.

Alex turned away.

"I know you don't want to talk to me, Alex," Mrs Jones continued. "Well, you don't have to. But will you please just listen?"

She looked anxiously at him. He said nothing. She went on.

"It's true that we didn't believe you when you came to us – and of course we were wrong. We were stupid. But it just seemed so incredible that a man like Damian Cray could be a threat to national security. He was rich and he was eccentric; nevertheless, he was only a pop star with attitude. That was what we thought.

"But if you think we ignored you completely, Alex, you're wrong. Alan and I have different ideas about you. To be honest, if it had been my choice, we'd never have got you involved in the first place ... not even in that business with the Stormbreakers. But that's not the issue here." She took a deep breath. "After you had gone, I decided to take another look at Damian Cray. There wasn't a great deal I could do without the right authority, but I had him watched and all his movements were reported back to me.

"I heard you were at Hyde Park, in that dome when the

Gameslayer was launched. I also got a police report on the woman – the journalist – who was killed. It just seemed like an unfortunate coincidence. Then I was told there had been an incident in Paris: a photographer and his assistant killed. Meanwhile Damian Cray was in Holland, and the next thing I knew, the Dutch police were screaming about some sort of high-speed chase in Amsterdam: cars and motorbikes chasing a boy on a bicycle. Of course, I knew it was you. But I still had no idea what was going on.

"And then your friend, Sabina, disappeared at Whitchurch Hospital. That really got the alarm bells ringing. I know. You're probably thinking we were absurdly slow, and you're right. But every intelligence service in the world is the same. When they act, they're efficient. But often they get started too late.

"That was the case here. By the time we came to bring you in, you were already with Cray, in Wiltshire. We spoke to your housekeeper, Jack. Then we went straight to his house. But we missed you again and this time we had no idea where you'd gone. Now we know, of course. Air Force One! The CIA have been going crazy. Alan Blunt was called in to see the prime minister last week. It may well be that he is forced to resign."

"Well, that breaks my heart," Alex said.

Mrs Jones ignored this. "Alex ... what you've been through ... I know this has been very difficult for you. You were on your own, and that should never have happened. But the fact is, you have saved millions of lives. Whatever you're feeling now, you have to remember that. It might even be true to say that you saved the world. God knows what the consequences would have been if Cray had succeeded. Anyway, the president of the United States would very much like to meet you. So, for that matter, would the prime minister. And for what it's worth, you've even been invited to the

Palace, if you want to go. Of course, nobody else knows about you. You're still classified. But you should be proud of yourself. What you did was ... amazing."

"What happened to Henryk?" Alex asked. The question took Mrs Jones by surprise, but it was the only thing he didn't know. "I just wondered," he said.

"He's dead," Mrs Jones said. "He was killed when the plane crashed. He broke his neck."

"Well, that's that then." Alex turned to her. "Can you go now?"

"Jack is worried about you, Alex. So am I. It may be that you need help coming to terms with what happened. Maybe some sort of therapy."

"I don't want therapy. I just want to be left alone."

"All right."

Mrs Jones stood up. She made one last attempt to read him before she left. This was the fourth occasion she had met Alex at the end of an assignment. Each time she had known that he must have been, in some way, damaged. But this time something worse had happened. She knew there was something Alex wasn't telling her.

And then, on an impulse, she said, "You were on the plane with Yassen when he was shot. Did he say anything before he died?"

"What do you mean?"

"Did he talk to you?"

Alex looked her straight in the eye. "No. He never spoke."

Alex watched her leave. So it was true what Yassen had said. Her last question had proved it. He knew who he was.

The son of a contract killer.

Sabina was waiting for him under the bridge. He knew that this was going to be a brief meeting. There was nothing really left to say.

"How are you?" she asked.

"I'm OK. How's your dad?"

"He's a lot better." She shrugged. "I think he's going to be fine."

"And he's not going to change his mind?"

"No, Alex. We're leaving."

Sabina had told him on the phone the night before. She and her parents were leaving the country. They wanted to be on their own, to give her father time to recover fully. They had decided it would be easier for him to begin a new life and had chosen San Francisco. Edward had been offered a job by a big newspaper there. And there was more good news. He was writing a book: the truth about Damian Cray. It was going to make him a fortune.

"When do you go?" Alex asked.

"Tuesday." Sabina brushed something out of her eye and Alex wondered if it might have been a tear. But when she looked at him again, she was smiling. "Of course, we'll keep in touch," she said. "We can e-mail. And you know you can always come out if you want a holiday."

"As long as it's not like the last one," Alex said.

"It'll be weird going to an American school..." Sabina broke off. "You were fantastic on the plane, Alex," she said suddenly. "I couldn't believe how brave you were. When Cray was telling you all those crazy things, you didn't even seem scared of him." She stopped. "Will you work for MI6 again?" she asked.

"No."

"Do you think they'll leave you alone?"

"I don't know, Sabina. It was my uncle's fault, really. He started all this years ago and now I'm stuck with it."

"I still feel ashamed about not believing you." Sabina sighed. "And I understand now what you must have been going through.

They made me sign the Official Secrets Act. I'm not allowed to tell anyone about you." A pause. "I'll never forget you," she said.

"I'll miss you, Sabina."

"But we'll see each other again. You can come to California. And I'll let you know if I'm ever in London..."

"That's good."

She was lying. Somehow Alex knew that this was more than goodbye, that the two of them would never see each other again. There was no reason for it. That was just the way it was going to be.

She put her arms around him and kissed him.

"Goodbye, Alex," she said.

He watched her walk out of his life. Then he turned and followed the river, past the swans and off into the countryside. He didn't stop. Nor did he look back.

GROOSHAM GRANGE

Anthony Horowitz

New pupils are made to sign their names in blood...

The assistant headmaster has no reflection...

The French teacher disappears whenever there's a full moon...

Groosham Grange, David Eliot's new school, is a very weird place indeed!

"One of the funniest books of the year." *Young Telegraph*

"Hilarious ... speeds along at full tilt from page to page." *Books for Keeps*

RETURN TO GROOSHAM GRANGE

Anthony Horowitz

A year ago, David Eliot would have been happy to escape from his weird school and its ghoulish teachers. Now he's fighting for its survival. Someone is trying to get their hands on the Unholy Grail, the source of all power, and unless David can stop them, Groosham Grange will be history!

"A first-class children's novelist."
The Times Educational Supplement

"Horowitz has become a writer who converts boys to reading."
The Times

GRANNY

Anthony Horowitz

"He could see it in the wicked glimmer in her eyes, in the half-turned corner of her mouth. And it was so strong, so horrible that he shivered. She was ... *evil.*"

Joe Warden isn't happy. He has rich, uncaring parents, and he's virtually a prisoner in the huge family mansion, Thattlebee Hall. But his real problem is his granny. Not only is she physically repulsive and unbelievably mean, she seems to have some secret plan and that plan involves him! Can he thwart her evil scheme before he's turned into neoplasmic slime?

"Wickedly funny." *The Daily Telegraph*

"A hoot ... Anthony Horowitz has created a scary and unmissable old hag." *The Daily Mail*

"Hugely popular ... I can hear Horowitz fans drooling." *The Times*

THE DEVIL AND HIS BOY

Anthony Horowitz

London is dirty, distant and dangerous ... but that's where orphan Tom Falconer is heading. And he's got a whole assortment of vicious criminals hot on his heels.

Tom is helpless and alone until he meets Moll Cutpurse, a thirteen-year-old pickpocket. Together the two of them find themselves chased across the city by the murderous Ratsey. But it's only on the first night of a new play – *The Devil and His Boy* – that Tom realizes the fate of the Queen and indeed the entire country rests in his hands.

All the pace, excitement and last-minute escapes readers expect from an Anthony Horowitz novel are here, in a vivid and realistic Elizabethan setting.

THE SWITCH
Anthony Horowitz

"Tad opened his mouth to cry out. The boy did the same. And that was when he knew... He wasn't looking at a window. He was looking at a *mirror*."

Tad Spencer, only son of a fabulously rich businessman, has everything a boy could wish for. But one evening he makes the major mistake of wishing he was someone else. A switch takes place and when he wakes, he's Bob Snarby, trapped in a cruel and squalid funfair world inhabited by petty criminals, mysterious fortune-tellers and the murderous Finn. Worse is to follow, though, as Tad is subjected to monstrous experiments, uncovering home truths that put his very life in danger.

"A formidably well-written adventure story, every bit as exciting as anything by Dahl or Blyton." *The Independent*

THE FALCON'S MALTESER

Anthony Horowitz

"Johnny Naples opened his mouth and tried to speak. 'The falcon...' he said. Then a nasty, bubbling sound."

When vertically challenged Johnny Naples entrusts Tim Diamond with a package worth over three million pounds, he's making a big mistake. For Tim Diamond is probably the worst detective in the entire world. Next day, Johnny's dead. Tim gets the blame, his smart, wisecracking younger brother Nick gets the package – and every crook in town is out to get them!

"Any child with a quick sense of humour should love it... An abundance of jokes, most of them first-class."
The Times Literary Supplement

SOUTH BY SOUTH EAST

Anthony Horowitz

"McGuffin had finished talking. The telephone was dead and any minute now he'd be joining it. The stuff he had spilled down the coat was blood, his own blood..."

Tim Diamond, the world's worst private detective, is broke – as his much smarter younger brother Nick is quick to remind him. So, when a mysterious stranger offers Tim a wad of money for his overcoat, it seems like a stroke of good luck. But there are worse things in life than being broke. Being pumped full of lead for one – which is what happens to the stranger and could soon be the fate of the Diamond brothers too, unless they can outwit the unknown assassin on their tail!

PUBLIC ENEMY NUMBER TWO

Anthony Horowitz

"So there I was in a maximum-security prison outside London, accused of theft, trespass, criminal damage and cruelty to animals... Me ... public enemy number two!"

Framed for a jewel robbery, quick-thinking young Nick Diamond finds himself sharing a prison cell with Johnny Powers, Public Enemy Number One. His only chance of rescuing the situation is to nail the Fence, the country's master criminal. First, though, Nick has to get out of jail – which is where his older brother Tim, the world's worst private detective, comes in... But with Ma Powers and her gang waiting to greet the jailbirds, the heat is really on for the Diamond brothers in this explosive adventure!